Ember of Life

Ishtar Watson

Published 2023 by Dark Elves LLC, Virginia.
600 Princess Anne St. #7695
Fredericksburg, VA 22404

A previous edition of this book existed using the same title but was authored under my old name. This edition is the definitive edition and contains significant changes from the original.

eBook ISBN   978-1-960683-03-8

Paperback ISBN   978-1-960683-04-5

Hardcover ISBN   978-1-960683-05-2

I hereby dedicate this book to…

To the spirit of humanity, peace, and the freedom for all forms of human expression. May we learn a little humility and compassion.

To the LGBTQIA+ and Neurodivergent people of the world. We have always existed, and we always will.

To the archaeologists of the world. Without your dedication and skill, I would have been lost.

And to my spouse… thank you for being who you are.

Ishtar

DEAR ARCHAEOLOGISTS

I am professionally a computer scientist and an archaeology student. I have spent fifteen years studying the Neolithic and Late Mesolithic. At first, this was an effort to create the proper setting for my story, but it soon evolved into a full academic effort. I have a university background in archaeology, anthropology, and computer science, and I have engaged in experimental archaeology to understand and properly depict the ancient world as accurately as possible. For example, I grew flax, then harvested, processed, spun, and wove the flax into linen using only Neolithic tools and techniques, including wearing period clothing. The purpose of this six months of work was merely to write a few scenes involving flax farming accurately. Our understanding of the past is ever-evolving, and some details from my story may be incorrect, given time and research. You may disagree with my treatment of the Neolithic, from religion to clothing, but please know that any mistakes you find were made in good faith and not for lack of research. Additionally, some gaps in our understanding required a bit of conjecture to create a proper narrative.

~Ishtar

INTRODUCTION

Units of Measure

The modern era has established units of measure, such as the Le Système International d'Unités Meter or the English Foot. In ancient times, it is a reasonable assumption that measures were roughly standardized to the apparent mean lengths of arms, legs, the distance a person could walk given an average period, or by the seasons. The entire book is detailed in measures that correspond to this hypothesis. The choice to use these natural units, such as the length of a hand, is designed to bring the reader into the Neolithic world and help the reader appreciate the wonder that is standardized measure, one of our modern era's most overlooked achievements.

Nudity

Many of the characters are depicted in various degrees of nudity throughout the Ember series, from wearing no apparent upper garment to wholly nude. While this may come as a shock to many people, it is by no means out of place for the period in which the books are set. In our modern culture, nudity has become associated with sexuality, but the extreme nature of this relationship is a modern – recent – association. Social attitudes and the sexual relationship with nudity have arisen through historical, cultural, and religious means.

In the sixth millennium B.C.E., nudity was depicted in art in such a manner and frequency as to infer that it was not out of the ordinary nor taboo. At the dawn of the 21st century, several cultures still exist where little or no clothing is worn. Within these cultures, nudity and partial nudity are not considered sexualized elements, nor are they looked down upon as any form of depravity. It is important to cast aside our modern notions of modesty and sexuality when considering the social norms of an ancient society.

Misogyny

Misogyny has been a consistent component of humanity for much of recorded history. While certainly an attitude that needs to be eliminated, it would be dishonest not to portray it as it likely existed. To that end, many characters display varying degrees of misogyny, and some misandry, from all genders. It is important to remember that these individuals likely grew up in a society that shared these views. Be thankful that we have a society that is slowly progressing so that we can identify misogyny and be displeased by it. With luck, one-day misogyny may no longer exist other than as a conversational piece in a history class. May we live to be so fortunate.

Key Pronunciations

Kaelu	Kay-loo
Brig'dha	Brig-da
Aethen	A-thin
Aya'tar	Eye-ah-tar
Ianmu	Eye-on-Moo
Imkanar	Im-can-are
Isut'na	Eye-soot-na
Sar'Tawas	Sar-Tah-waz

An'an	An-An	Karut	Carrot
Anteanar	Ann-tee-nar	Kel	Kell
Asatar	Asa-tar	Kenis	Ken-ess
Caelwyn	Kale-win	Kuwar	Koo-wore
Eryi	Ear-ee	Kyra	K-eye-rah
Espe	Ess-pea	Mael	Male
Fanel	Fen-nel	Mear	Me-ear
Galar	Gah-lar	Meegin	Me-gin
Geb	Geb	Mohdan	Moe-dan
Gunar	Goo-nar	Nael	Nail
Hullamu	Hull-ah-moo	Nara'kit	Nara-kit
Idmasa	Id-mas-ah	Saranar	Sar-ah-nar
Inn'bry'th	Inn-br-eye-th	Tes	Tes
Isen'bryn	Eye-sin-brin	Ul'na'har	You'll-na-har
Isha'kau	E-sha-kah-oo	Ul'uer	You'll-ur
Ishayan	Eye-she-on	Utiakur	You-tick-ur
Isut	Eye-soot	Yan	Yan
Kam'ir	Kam-ear	Yari'aya	Yar-ee-eye-ah
Kamar	Kah-mar	Zah'namu	Zah-na-moo

RECAPITULATION

During the summer of 5500 BCE, a meteorite roughly the size of the 2013 Chelyabinsk Meteor slammed into the atmosphere – a prophetic red and green flame across the sky. A small Linear Pottery Culture village on the shore of the Rhine River situated roughly where the modern city of Mannheim was constructed was shaken by the event. A young non-binary woman with red hair and emerald green eyes, the colors of the meteor as it disintegrated, named Kaelu (which means ember from a fire) was given a quest by her people to travel west toward the end of the world.

Kaelu set off in a small boat which she quickly lost in a storm, forcing her to continue on foot. She was attacked by wolves, nearly becoming their food. Soon, she encountered men who she thought to befriend but who quickly captured her as a prize. She escaped after a time, but only after encountering a reluctant man named Pak. Free from captivity, she ran into a small Mesolithic resource gathering and trade group who befriended her and helped her build a new boat. While among the people, Kaelu learned proper archery skills and meets an old man, her paternal uncle, though she never realizes this.

Unfortunately, the men returned seeking revenge, though the reluctant man, Pak, killed his own leader as his loyalty and morality clashed with the ruthless orders he had been given. For her bravery, Kaelu's uncle declares her to be a warrior, a title that will define her.

Free once more, Kaelu traveled with the Mesolithic people far south to the Neolithic village of Nes, where Paris, France, now stands. There, they traded their wares, but unfortunately, a series of murders in their midst frightened the people of Nes. Even worse, a mysterious Mesolithic woman who lives among the Nes as an outsider becomes implicated, though she is innocent. The tribe chooses to sacrifice her to stop the murders, yet Kaelu and her friends cannot let this happen. The night before the sacrifice, they sneak into Nes and free the woman, coming face-to-face with the true murderer and defeating him. Afterward, Kaelu and Brig'dha leave their new friends and travel west to Brig'dha's homeland across the North Sea to what is now Cromer, England. After losing their way and nearly drowning, they finally make it, but not before considering their budding feelings, though they never express them for fear they are not shared.

PROLOGUE

The high priest knelt before the altar to the goddess An'an. It had been a troubling day, and he hoped for guidance. He adjusted his leather loincloth into a comfortable position, his old knees stiff upon the plastered floor of the dark, musty room. Before him sat a raised mudbrick altar with a female ceramic figurine reverently positioned at its center, wildflowers and wheat surrounding her. The figurine's body was extremely buxom to a point attainable only by the most powerful women of the proto-city. Large breasts, hips, and belly emphasized her fertility aspects, while the incised and painted lines forming stripes across her body portrayed her as a warrior – her two primary spheres of influence. An'an was a warrior goddess who demanded each person give their best, rewarding those who took risks and achieved great power. He sighed…

The rejection of such a promising priestess had certainly been risky, especially since her father was the city's ruler. She had performed every part of her initiation ritual flawlessly. Her body had been painted red with ochre stripes, just as An'an, and she had danced without err. Nevertheless, the high priest had seen the divine signs that told him in no uncertain terms that he must reject her. An'an had been extremely clear on this point, a voice in his head directly telling him, yet he wavered in the face of her will.

Of course, he still had his other lesser priestess Kit'tanu. She had birthed a healthy male child of her husband, a strong warrior of some repute. Yet, many rituals called for more than he and a lesser priestess could handle. He glanced toward the bull horns embedded into the plastered, mudbrick walls and sighed. An'an had another fate for the woman, though he knew not what. Only time would tell, though he hoped he lived long enough to learn that fate. That last part required convincing the rejected woman's mighty father that his reasons were just.

He began to pray to the Goddess for guidance. The ruler of the city was a violent man, and the act of rejecting the priestesshood of his only daughter might bring upon him a terrible wrath. His only hope was that he might find meaning to the signs he had seen, some additional piece of information that he could dangle in front of her father that might keep him from being beaten and impaled on a wooden pole. Luckily, it wasn't long before he felt a strange warmth glide across his body, a feeling he often had when communing with the divine – a feeling that stole his attention from the sounds of the wooden ladder to the roof entryway creaking behind him.

"Please provide me with a sign, An'an, daughter of the Moon, mighty warrioress of life and change," he pleaded to the goddess figurine before him. He rocked rhythmically as he chanted the words of invocation. If this failed, he would need to burn dried herbs and perhaps even ingest some magical plants to aid his perception. Unfortunately, that perception wasn't as it used to be when he was a younger man.

Behind the high priest, a young woman slowly approached, her bark fiber woven apron swishing with each step. Her bare feet strode without sound against the cold dirt floor. In her right hand, a leather cord dangled loosely, awaiting its deadly implementation. Slowly, she approached, her anger building as her distance waned. She had been robbed of her future, her destiny. Her mother had died at her birth, yet she lived. She had nearly died from sickness as a child, yet she lived through that, too. She was strong… yet she had been robbed. So many long harvests of prayer and preparation had been simply dismissed by the weak man who knelt before her. All of this because he saw some "sign." No, she wouldn't fight past all that, only to lose to this shriveled old husk of a man. In fact, she had another sign for him. She would show him a strong omen that he was bound for the next world.

Before her, the chanting high priest knelt before the altar, too busy with his pleading rogations to pay attention. The young woman stopped behind him, barely an arm's length from the man. She had never accepted mere fate. She had fought her brothers for autonomy, left a man who had tried to grope her unable to use his arm, and proven her skills with a blade at a young age. She was a woman who made her own fate… except in the case of An'an. The goddess was the source of her strength, the mother she had never known and the only will she bent to.

An'an, I do not know what you want of me, but I will have my vengeance upon this man. If you require my life in exchange, so be it, she thought as she gazed at the goddess figurine, about to perform high treason. An'an was a goddess of passion and strife, ruling over fertility, war, and the struggle for life. She rewarded those who did their best to achieve their ends and punished those too weak to take life by the horns. Behind the altar, the subjugated bull horns of An'an's mate, Gunmaer the Bull, sat as a visible reminder of her power.

The young woman crouched behind the older man and quietly looped the leather cord around both hands with a forearm's length stretched between them. With a smooth motion, she slipped the cord over the man's head and around his throat. She jerked the cord hard and pressed a knee into his back in one quick act. He reacted instantly, his surprise quickly igniting powerful self-preservation instincts. If the priest had been a younger man, she would have stood no chance against his strength as he writhed. Though he was old, the only thing keeping him from freeing himself was the strength of her legs as she pushed against his back, as her arm strength alone would not have been enough.

He twisted and pounded at her with his hands as he tried to free himself, his vision darkening as her muscles burned against the effort to kill him. Suddenly, the leather cord snapped under the strain, and the high priest was free and struggling to breathe against the damage she had already done to his throat. The woman fell backward from the force of her own leg pushing against the high priest. Wounded or not, he was still a man and twice her weight, a threat too dangerous to give even a moment to recover. She kicked out as hard as possible with her right leg catching his head with her foot and knocking him from his senses. In the brief moment her kick bought, she lifted her powerful legs, wrapping them around his neck. She lay back with her head and upper body out of his reach and squeezed her legs as tightly as she ever had.

For a short time, he struggled, digging into her legs with his fingernails as he fought to free himself from her vice-like grip. He was strong, yet she was a dancer and her muscles had greater endurance. Yet, if she ran out of strength before the reduced blood flow to his head stopped his struggle... The woman felt her burning legs might just give out as she forced them to squeeze beyond reason. Then, just as she neared exhaustion, the man stopped moving and lay motionless, other than an occasional twitch of his legs. She held her legs tightly around his throat for a little longer to make sure, though they were also in considerable pain and not easily unwrapped from the man.

With the deed done, the woman slowly stood on shaky legs and surveyed her work. On the floor lay the dead priest who had forever altered her life. His loosed fluids and vacant look confirmed his demise, as did the protruding tongue with burst blood vessels, an awful sight. She wasn't sure what she would do next, but one thing was for sure... her fate was now entirely in the hands of the Goddess.

"I am Ianmu'kimun, daughter of An'sankup'Anteanar, and I am yours to command," she spoke softly to the An'an figurine.

12

CHAPTER ONE

HUNTER, WE ARE HUNTED

The morality of taking a life has been long debated yet never fully resolved. Is it moral when a prehistoric hunter kills a deer to feed her family? What about when a wolf kills a deer? Can taking a life during a raid to obtain food to feed your starving family be justified? Many of these dilemmas may seem simple to answer, yet ask any group of two or more people, and you will likely get two or more answers. Ember and Brig'dha are both fervently against raiding, yet they hold no animosity toward the hungry wolf.

The war party slowly approached the village, weapons at the ready. Some men thirsted for action, adventure, and battle, while most feared what was to come. Earlier boasting and flamboyant words during their journey to the village were born more of their own fears than any real urge to do battle. Combat was dangerous, and even a small wound could leave a man crippled or bring him to a slow and painful death. There were no treatments for deep wounds, and anyone too injured to walk might have to lay where he fell, at the total mercy of his enemy. It was a grim task, but it was also a means to an end – starvation was an ever-present shadow.

There was also a touch of guilt at the prospect of raiding a tribe so close to their own. They might have even traded with these people in times past. With the poor gathering and the growth in the number of people in the region, their tribe would need the supplies they now moved to steal. If that meant that a few of them may not return or that several people in this tribe passed into the night, it was a sacrifice far better than watching their children starve. Each man had a spouse or a lover who waited for them, and several had children sleeping soundly waiting for father to return. Off to his right, the leader noticed an owl casually watching his men while feasting on a fallen pine marten, perhaps an omen? If it was, did he play the role of the owl or the pine marten?

Pushing introspection from his mind, lest he lose his nerve, the leader of the war party and his men, twenty in number, paused for a rest. The air was cold, and he watched a small fog form with each breath as he stood on a small hill surveying what lay before him. Not far below was the village they planned to attack. It was many days' walk from their village, providing a useful buffer against retaliation and reducing the chance that they might bump into members of this tribe on a later date.

His men prepared for what was to be done. The leader carefully braced his bow between his legs and bent the length of the weapon around the small of his back, gently pulling the nettle bowstring into place. As he prepared his weapon, he rhythmically chanted an appeal to the gods that his men would live and be victorious, though deep down, he hoped that few from the small village would die. The gods had not helped as his people ran low on food, so he wasn't quite sure if they would help now. Pulling the bowstring to ensure the weapon was ready, he concluded his prayer.

His men were not commonly raiders. In fact, they had been raided only this past gathering season. He had a regrettably clear idea of how to do this. Learning by example had proved painful and made the task at hand more troubling. As he remembered friends and family being wounded and killed in that raid, he felt the need to ask the gods for the safety of these he now sought to raid, not a typical request, yet one he felt must be made. He paused for a moment and looked up at the Moon to say a second prayer to the gods that not many people would die on either side.

Ember quietly approached the place where she had last spotted the small foraging roe deer. The forest was cold and growing slowly dark in the early evening, but, at least, the harsh cold season wind had not come. All around her, snow blanketed the ground, and an eerie quiet filled the trees. The gentle wind carried motes of pine and the fresh smell of fallen snow. The Moon was full, and its light would fill the forest with the aid of the soft snowy ground when it fully rose. The forest was quiet, and every sound echoed. As she stood in the quiet beauty of the forest, it felt to her as though the world extended in every direction for infinity and that she was the only one alive. She paused for a moment and closed her eyes to drink in the incredible beauty of the moonlit forest. Then, after a short break from reality, she opened her eyes and, with a deep breath of cool pine-scented air, blew a puff of visible breath before setting out on the gruesome task at hand.

She crouched low in the snow over a set of small deer tracks, easily spotted with the help of the Moon. The tracks were composed of pairs of hooves with the correct spacing to indicate an adult deer making its way slowly through the forest. Ember knew that she was closing in on her quarry. She again stood and brushed her waist-length red hair from her face. Though many in the tribe where she now lived, the people of Isen'bryn, wore their hair bound in many long thick braids, Ember always preferred her hair long and loose. It was the way of her people, and it helped keep her warm.

She noted a pair of light grey eyes along the edge of the eastern wood, briefly catching the dim moonlight. The animal was low to the ground, likely a red fox. She hoped it wouldn't make the screaming sound they were known for, as it might frighten her quarry. At least it wasn't a wolf, though she was far from the frightened woman who had first met a wolf in the forest with barely the clothes on her back. Now, she had a strong bow and the skills of a hunter – Ember was also a predator. With a whispered prayer to the spirits of the foxes for silence and luck, she adjusted her leggings and continued.

Foxes aside, one thing had been nagging her more recently, though it had started when she and Brig'dha had crossed the Greatest River nearly a full harvest before. It was a private thought, a wisp of love, something she had meant to bring up but could never find the right place or time to do. She had wished there had been a chance with Brig'dha, yet she knew there couldn't be. The wind blew gently, carrying the scent of deer and returning her to the moment. She would deal with these issues later.

Though the forest was cold, she was warmed by her thick fox fur coat and a pair of dark rabbit fur mittens, though not quite as nice as the pair given to her by her good friend Kis'tra of the Tornhemal, now lost beneath the waves of the Greatest River. She also wore heavy leggings made from red deer leather suspended by a woven leather belt tied around her waist. Under the coat, Ember wore her soft, doeskin shirt with freshly painted spots, though it was starting to wear, and a roe deer loincloth. Her feet were warmed by leather soled boots made from a frame of lime bark cordage, stuffed with dried grass and surrounded by an extra layer of warm rabbit fur. Under her eyes, she wore a long horizontal black line of pigment stretching from ear to ear. Below that line of paint were a series of black dots, the mark of her people. She wore two hawk feathers carefully bound with fiber strands in her hair, replacing her previous feathers which had worn out.

After removing her mittens, Ember reached over her shoulder and pulled free her bow from its place beside her quiver, her hands brushing against the soft fletchings of arrows. Across her back, she wore a leather quiver with six beautifully handcrafted arrows, each with an Isen'bryn-style composite arrowhead made from several tiny, razor-sharp flint pieces secured with pitch. Around her waist, an artfully crafted obsidian dagger hung with its exquisitely sharp double-edged blade and an old leather grip. The dagger had belonged to her father, Winterborn. He had fallen in battle defending her tribe against raiders when Ember was a baby. She never met him, but the weight of the dagger had continued to give her confidence long after his passing. She wondered what he would say if he could see her now as the woman she had become. *Woman...* she grimaced, the idea still sounding odd and uncomfortable as she thought it.

The time for the kill was quickly approaching as Ember emerged from the tree line and into a snow-covered field. The Moon had risen in the Northeast and hung low in the South. Before her, trees cast long shadows in the moonlight. She came to a stop and prepared for the kill. Ember carefully placed one of the limbs of her bow between her legs to hold it in place as she bent the bow over her back with as much force as she could muster. Then, with her muscles pulling as hard as they could, she carefully fit the bowstring into place over the horn of the bow. It was important not to leave a bow strung as it would lose its reflexive nature over time, but one also needed to be careful not to let the fragile limbs twist as the bow was carefully bent. Stringing a bow was an odd combination of fine dexterity and raw strength. Ember was sure her bow's next usage was likely very close at hand.

She slowly approached a thicket just over a small hill and set in the middle of a large field. She was sure that deer would be found around or within the dense cluster of trees forming the thicket. Ember emerged entirely from the woods stepping carefully on the soft packed snow and hoping the sound of her footfalls wouldn't travel too far. She found herself unconsciously pressing her hand against the front of her fox fur coat. She could feel the pressure of her hand pressing the small goddess pendant made from deer antler and given to her one and a half harvests before by her good friend Fire Blossom. Ember knew that she would return the pendant to Blossom one day, but in the meantime, the goddess pendant would bring her luck. It was a representation of the Moon Goddess from her lands. Gazing now at the Moon and felt the glow of the Goddess' light, and wondered if that light fell from the same goddess who watched her native lands.

As she felt the goddess pendant, thoughts of her friend Brig'dha came to mind. Not long after they arrived, Brig'dha took up the art of magic as a priestess. Typically, such roles took many harvests to learn, but Brig'dha picked up the art quickly. It seemed to many that she had a natural connection to the spirits and seemed touched by the Moon Goddess. Ember could not argue the point as Brig'dha had survived the death of her husband and many other people from an unknown sickness, as well as ritual sacrifice, and even a trip across the Greatest River. If anyone was touched by the gods, she suspected that Brig'dha was such a person.

As Ember approached the thicket, she carefully selected one of her handmade arrows from its quiver. The fletching was crafted from the beautiful white feathers of a winter goose and held in place by delicate deer sinew fibers. The long shaft was made from a straight piece of lightly oiled wood, skillfully smoothed with leather and grout to fly true. Each arrow had taken long nights to craft by hand. Ember slowly nocked the arrow against the bowstring and held the bow before her, ready to fire at a moment's notice. She knew she would only have one, perhaps two shots at best before the deer ran.

Her steps thundered in her mind as she tried desperately to move as quietly as a leaf in the wind. She knew that deer could hear much better than she, and now she stood wide open in a field approaching a thicket with nothing to hide her from the deer. Suddenly, a healthy deer stepped from the thicket. It wasn't a large deer, but it wasn't newborn either, which made it an acceptable target. Killing young or old deer was frowned upon, though It wasn't likely that she would find a newborn in the cold season, anyway. Its head was down in search of something in the snow to eat.

So, you're looking for something to eat? I'm very sorry, but so am I, Ember thought with sadness in her heart. She never liked taking any life, but the trading of one life for another was the way of the world. She approached the deer slowly at first but increased her speed as she felt that she was coming into range. The deer lifted its head suddenly, apparently aware of a sound approaching and ever on the alert. Ember held her course and kept calm as the moment of her attack came. The deer turned towards Ember and made ready to bolt in the opposite direction, but it was already too late. The huntress had stopped advancing and now took aim.

Ember's breathing slowed as she pulled the bowstring tautly until it touched her face. She let her final breath slowly escape her lips as a soft cloud of vapor and relaxed her fingers, letting loose the beautiful arrow to fly towards its deadly end. The deer turned away from Ember and sprang forward as its legs bit deeply into the snow, beginning to propel its powerful body away from the threat. The graceful creature was fast, but Ember's arrow was much faster. The arrow flew true, plunging suddenly behind the front leg and deep into the core of the animal. The deer continued to bolt for a distance, quickly disappearing into the woods. Ember slung her bow behind her back with the string crossing her chest. She pulled free the obsidian dagger and began the pursuit of the dying animal as fast as she could.

She would follow the droplets of blood through the snow and eventually find the deer. Ember hoped that the deer had not run very far, not only because it meant a shorter return journey for her but also because it meant that the deer had met with a swifter end. Allowing the creature to suffer unnecessarily was abhorrent to her, and might anger the spirits of the deer, though she accepted that a life must be traded for her to live. Nevertheless, the prospect of carrying a heavy deer all the way back to the village left Ember feeling tired before she had even started.

Ↄ Ↄ C
C Ↄ

The raiders slowly approached the village from the Southwest. There were plenty of supplies for the taking, and everyone seemed to be sleeping in the small round huts made of logs with mud and stick walls, their roofs thatched. The men slowly spread out, looking for the easiest materials to grab before they disappeared into the night. At the top of the list were foodstuffs that did not easily perish, such as salted meats, dried peas, and tubers. The leader cautiously entered the village and slowly approached a small lean-to that appeared to contain some kind of stored material. As he neared with his hand extended to push aside the thick leather flap covering the opening of the lean-to, the door to a hut next to him suddenly opened, spilling warm orange firelight into the night.

The leader ducked behind the small lean-to hoping that his presence had not been observed. Out came a tired-looking man wearing a long leather coat and an unbound pair of leather boots. The man walked a short distance away from the hut towards the edge of the village before stopping by a small bush and opening the front of his coat. An arc of steaming liquid appeared. The leader had performed this same action so many times, though many chose to relieve themselves within a hut rather than in the cold. He crouched low, hoping the man would finish and just return to his hut without ever noticing the danger that lurked in every direction.

The leader's thoughts seemed lost on several of his men, who slowly crept closer. Perhaps they only wished to silence the man if he became aware of them. The raiders surrounded the man, but he did not see them as their skin was painted black with soot, and they wore darkened leather. Slowly, one of the more battle-lusting raiders approached. The leader wanted to stop him, but there was no way to do so without alerting the entire village. All he could do was watch as the younger, more aggressive raider came to stand behind the man relieving himself. He sighed, knowing what would come next, yet powerless to stop it.

Grabbing the unsuspecting victim's mouth to keep him silent, the younger man slit his throat and slowly lowered his body to the ground. The snow before the man was blanketed by a spray of blood. The leader watched with mixed emotions. On the one hand, killing this poor villager would help prevent his men from being noticed as they collected the goods they needed. On the other, there was something wrong with killing a man while he was urinating that bothered the leader. There were just some things that you didn't do, and that was one of them. Shaking his head, the leader turned to discover what was in the lean-to.

ↄ ↄ ↄ

A weak orange light eerily radiated from cracks in a wooden door made from poles bound by sinew and leather, not far from where the man had been killed. Inside this round mud and log building, a ritual was about to begin. A middle-aged woman named Kelwyn and her two young children sat on fur mats awaiting a priestess as she completed her preparations for the blessing of the children. Placing a blessing from the Moon Goddess, one of many gods, upon each of the children was a paramount act that needed to be performed each full set of seasons to safeguard them in the coming seasons. One of the best times to perform the ritual was during the shortest day of the seasons when the power of the Goddess was strongest, and the veil between the living world and the world of the dead was thinnest.

What made this specific night better than any other in a long time was the simultaneous occurrence of a full Moon. After the longest night of the seasons, the first full moon was always an important time for blessings. The primary priestess to the gods and spirits for the people of Isen'bryn was old woman Glea. It was under her teaching that Brig'dha had quickly picked up the art of speaking with the gods. After her life-and-death struggles the previous seasons, it seemed easier for her to take up the role of priestess to the Goddess than would otherwise be the case. She supposed this had to do with how life and death struggles tended to put things into perspective, though it may also have been Brig'dha's need to ground herself and keep thoughts of what could not be from her mind. Ember was a friend, and that was the way it would remain.

Old woman Glea was actually quite pleased with the notion of a younger priestess to help ease her burden. On a night like tonight, Glea would be quite busy dealing with all the possessions and people who needed a blessing. Many would have to wait multiple days to have their turn. This was why Kelwyn had brought her two children to the younger priestess. While she wasn't skilled enough for the larger blessings, a simple blessing for children was well within Brig'dha's abilities. Besides, it would not require the Sun God, whom Brig'dha had rejected, and refused to commune with, a source of amusement among many.

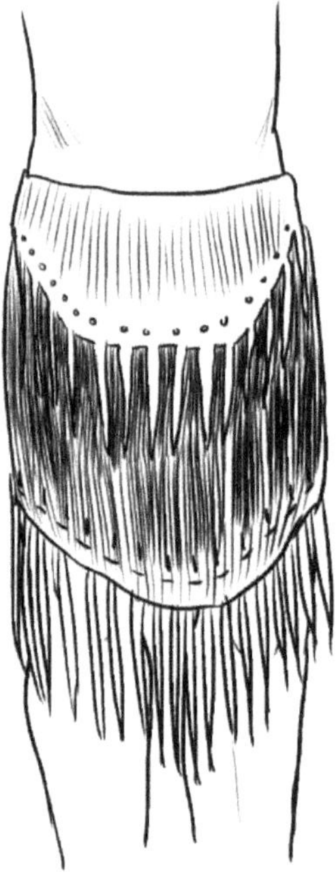

Leather wrap skirt

Brig'dha felt a strange anticipation, like an unknown scent on the air as she carefully sprinkled finely ground salt from a small, carved wooden pot over the head of the goddess figurine, which sat upon a sturdy wooden table. The well-made wood plank table provided an altar on which to pray and a convenient place to put important items, such as ceremonial salt. The salt would provide purification of the statuette to better please and invoke the Goddess. In truth, the statuette was not a goddess but simply an effigy that could be used to channel thoughts towards the Goddess as a focal point. A trained priestess or priest might use their imagination without needing such an object, but Brig'dha was still new to this, so the carved, wooden goddess statuette helped.

Behind her sat Kelwyn, the children, and a hot crackling fire that bathed the room in a warm, beautiful orange glow. Brig'dha had painted magical symbols over her entire body using paint made from black soot and oil. Her hair was left free and long in the same style as her friend, Ember, with several hawk feathers tied at various lengths. Covering her face was a ceremonial roe deer antler mask, while around her waist, Brig'dha wore a leather belt made from three braided leather cords. The leather belt firmly held a soft leather wrap skirt in place. She had removed her soft leather shirt for the ritual as it was of good quality, and she didn't want it to become soiled from soot.

The priestess snatched a small shell dish containing a rich ocher pigment from the altar. The ochre would be blessed, and symbols would be placed upon the two children's faces, providing them the protection they needed. The ritual was very short and quite simple to perform, making her current uneasy feelings even more out of place. Pushing those feelings aside, she chanted to the Goddess, hoping everything would be okay.

Goddess of the Moon, equal to the Sun, mother of the people, elder of the gods. I ask that you watch over young Kal and Ana, and guide their mother Kelwyn in their care. Please provide our people with enough food, warm shelter, clothes, and good weather. Mother of our people, please bless this ocher and the symbols created with it. Watch over our youngest.

Brig'dha finished her prayer with her eyes closed and the small pot of ocher held towards the goddess figurine. She felt a slight warm sensation rush through her body, a feeling that she often had when praying to the Goddess. The Moon Goddess was quite common, and many other people she had met had gods similar to hers. What was different about the people of Isen'bryn was that their gods had no names, only titles. It was said by the Elders that this was the way of many of the northern people, the "Greater People." Greater people was a term used to describe culturally similar people within the same region.

Brig'dha faced the children with a big smile and began applying the ocher paints to their faces. Her friend Ember never seemed interested in children, while Brig'dha was quite fond of them. She had a way of speaking to children which seemed to calm them. Ironically, though Ember would not be inclined to hold an infant, she was quite likely to behave like a child herself. Ember enjoyed hide and seek and other childish games even though she was a woman and not a girl… well, sort of. Now that she considered it, Ember was hardly like any women she had ever met. Brig'dha shook her head as she thought of Ember's antics. She was out there even now hunting some random deer in the middle of the night in the cold season, something no normal person would do. Brig'dha wished she were here with her so they could do something together to pass the time.

She sighed, glad to have anyone calling upon her this night. Many believed that she was cursed after explaining her story of having cheated death. People did not like that she had left with her husband and returned with Ember. It did not sit well with her people, and many wild stories had been conjectured by fellow tribe members. Brig'dha had ignored most of the tall tales, but she still felt ostracized by many in her tribe. This had caused her so much more pain, given the great risks she and Ember had endured just to return to her people. Her face remained neutral, but her thoughts continued to drift into the darkness of self-doubts and worry as she continued.

The children tried not to laugh and giggle as Brig'dha skillfully applied the paint to their faces. During the ritual, they had been so calm and had made not a sound, but sitting still for so long was wearing thin on their young patience. Brig'dha paused for a moment when she thought she heard a strange sound like someone walking outside of the hut. After all, it was a village, so she dismissed the sound when she heard it no more. She returned to painting the symbols, assuming that it was just someone from the village out to relieve themselves. She never understood why people left the warmth of a hut to do that when a quiet corner could be found. Most huts had an area away from the main hearth and sleeping areas just for such instances.

A gentle touch disrupted her thoughts as Kelwyn placed a hand upon her arm. Brig'dha hated most physical contact unless she initiated it, but she kept her emotions masked and neutral. She supposed it was best not to alienate one of the few people who had treated her well. *Ember's touch doesn't bother you…* she began to think, when Kelwyn spoke, breaking her unending introspection.

"Thank you…," Kelwyn said with a smile, then continued when Brig'dha said nothing, "I know some doubt your story, but I believe you." Brig'dha nodded her thanks, not having words to explain such a complex set of feelings. Some of her people had shown her respect due to her alleged travels with Ember, though the majority remained skeptical. Those had been terrifying days, but they had also been some of the most wonderful she had ever experienced. Of late, they had started to become the only thing she thought of other than the Goddess.

Both she and the redhead had taken to purposefully playing the part of friends. Ember had acted rather awkward several times, especially when they were alone or a bit close, which she suspected was due to the redhead picking up on her amorous signals. Staring a moment too long or otherwise acting flirty around a woman who didn't share her interests would either be ignored or make things awkward. At least the foxy warrior had been a delightful friend and Brig'dha's only close companion since returning. She was wandering back into introspection. Brig'dha suddenly snapped back into reality when she heard a strange, muffled sound not far from the hut. She eyed the door suspiciously. Could her friend already be back? Beside her, Kelwyn also seemed suddenly on edge.

☽ ☽ ☽

The leader thanked the spirits that this were going well, so far. His men had found several large leather sacks full of salted meats, wild grains, dried tubers, and other foods. Besides food, many weapons and tools had been found. His men were nearly loaded with supplies, and if they were lucky, they would leave without ever having been detected. He hoped that the one dead man would be the extent of their trouble this night. He would need to have a talk with the younger raider who had thought that a man needed to die simply because he had stepped outside to relieve himself. Such were the actions of the young and bold, but not the way of his people. Just as one didn't kill animals beyond what was necessary, the act of murder without purpose was a waste of the life the spirits had created.

His satisfaction in a successful raid was suddenly shattered by the shrill screams of a woman. Men could yell quite loudly, but only a woman could pierce the night with such a high-pitched sound that the leader wondered if the Moon itself might shatter. He turned to find a middle-aged woman from the tribe wrapped in furs. She had come from the same wooden hut as the man they had killed. Perhaps she was his wife or lover by her looks. Likely she had come to see what was taking him so long but had instead found him lying dead in a vast pool of blood and her tribe filled with silent raiders encumbered by stollen goods.

Before any of the raiders could do anything, she turned and ran screaming towards the central hut. It would be only a few moments before the entire tribe was awake and the fighting began. The leader turned to his men and signaled them to take what they could and leave. If they were lucky, they might still make it out without fighting. They were dressed for the cold weather and the snow, but these people would take a short while to get dressed to chase them. Pursuit during the cold season was out of the question unless you were fully prepared.

The entire village suddenly came alive with men rushing from huts with whatever tool or weapon they could find. The leader had not expected such a quick reaction. From each hut, villagers poured into the night while his men were slow to react, heavily laden as they were with stolen goods. He realized at that very moment that his people could either drop much of their loot and flee to avoid a fight or fight their way out with what they had taken. Regrettably, his people needed the food and tools, so a fight it would be. He reached for the hardened wooden club tied to his side, ignoring his bow. At this close range, the bow was not the best weapon. He could see several of his man nearby doing the same.

"Spirits, forgive me…" he mumbled.

ↄ ↄ   c

Brig'dha stared at the stretched hide door with foreboding as the strange sound suddenly faded. She glanced a confused look at Kelwyn when abruptly, the calm of night was startled by the shrill, horrified shriek of a woman. Brig'dha and Kelwyn exchanged alarmed glances as the sudden sounds of screaming and battle began to fill the night. Something horrible was happening outside, and only a thin door separated the women and children from whatever it was. If this was a raid, there was a chance men might come for them at any moment. Raids were hardly common, but stories were told, and both women knew what fate awaited them and the children.

Kelwyn pulled free a small flint cutting knife used for basic domestic work and began pushing her two children behind her and away from the door. Like any mother, she would die before letting someone harm her children. The problem was, armed only with a small utility knife, death would likely be the outcome if she were forced to fight.

"Come, children, come to mommy and away from the door. Whatever happens, stay calm and do exactly what mommy or the priestess tells you. Everything will be all right. It's probably just a bear. Besides, you have the protection of the Goddess, after all," she said with a glance toward Brig'dha, but with a little less confidence than she had hoped. The night was beginning to sound very alarming.

Brig'dha began to chant a prayer to the Goddess. The Horned God would be of more use in this situation, but he was a god for the warmer seasons, and the Moon was in the wrong phase, complicating things as the first full Moon following the longest night of the seasons was the Horned God's weakest moment. Worse, she did not have a knife to defend herself, and the only object she could find was a single antler from a small deer. The antler was used in some rituals, but it was hardly a weapon when no longer connected to a mighty deer.

Brig'dha was holding the antler and trying to determine how best to use it when the door to the small hut suddenly burst open. In stepped a man wearing dark fur, leather leggings, loincloth, and an extra-long winter coat studded with antler beads. His face was covered with soot to obscure him in the dark, and he held a look of desperation about him. His expression was chaotic at best, and his torn coat bore the marks of battle. To Brig'dha, he looked like a raider. A raider who had just lost the element of surprise and had turned to quick, opportunistic looting before he fled. Perhaps he hoped to snag something small but valuable from her hut on the edge of the village before running.

Very few raiding parties wished to hang around long enough to engage in a real fight and most tribes wouldn't even attempt to raid a tribe as big as hers. Large-scale combat in the northern lands was just not that common. Yet here stood an enigmatic raider, his eyes adjusting to the light as he towered over Brig'dha, who stood between him and Kelwyn and her children. She held the small antler though she knew it was only a token weapon compared to the skilled raider with his long dagger and war club.

The man quickly surveyed the situation and realized that he was in luck – the first of the night. A priestess, judging by her mask, a middle-aged woman, and two small children. With young children in their midst, he figured two women would likely not choose to fight him unless they absolutely had to. In his experience, women tended to act much more defensively when children were involved, even ignoring obvious chances to strike. Yet, he was quite sure both women would die before letting him harm the children. That made the presence of children either a benefit or a problem, depending on what he chose to do next.

Across the room sat a large flint nodule beckoning his grasp, perhaps the only material item in sight worth his time. Such a nodule could be traded for over a tenday's worth of deer meat from a neighboring tribe. The man pointed at the nodule and waved his war club, menacingly, indicating the price for not handing over the precious item. He would take the nodule, and he might even consider grabbing the priestess with long brown hair and hazel eyes peeking through her mask. Taking a woman might not be the best idea when his tribe had a food shortage, but he also needed a wife and perhaps someone to carry his loot. It was hard to ignore how similar the brown-haired woman looked to his elder sister, Kena. She had not approved of the raid, but her children needed to eat just as much as he did.

Brig'dha wanted so desperately for Ember to burst into the room and scare off the man, but she knew her friend was off somewhere in the woods hunting. She did not know what compelled Ember to hunt so late at night in the woods, but something about the full Moon seemed to attract her. *At least you're safe,* she thought. She recalled the night when she had sat bound to a wooden pole and waiting for her death by sacrifice when Ember had suddenly burst through the door and saved her. Tonight, she would have to save herself and others, it seemed. Behind her, Kelwyn made a fearful sound as her children began to cry. The man eyed her, suddenly more appraisingly, a look Brig'dha knew all too well.

Even if she acted, he would likely spot her movements and block them before she could do anything. He would expect her attack… yet, what if… Suddenly, an idea came to mind. She remembered Ember pretending to be shot to fool raiders into running right into her trap. As she slowly stepped back from the raider, a quick plan sprung into her mind. "Thank you, Ember," she mumbled as she dropped the antler, pretending to surrender to the man's demands, and moved to pick up the nodule. Her hands shook as though fear had engulfed her, though in truth, fear nearly had.

"Dou-beali Kaelu," the fearful priestess whispered in a muffled tone as she dropped the antler and moved to pick up the nodule. The raider was unsure what that meant though it sounded a little bit like his own words for 'give thanks,' followed by what sounded like a name, Kaelu. That sounded like a god or spirit, perhaps. The raider supposed the priestess was thanking some spirit that the man had not killed her. He felt a little sorry for having frightened her so badly, but his people could trade that flint nodule with a neighboring tribe for food. When the belly became empty, morality was the first to starve.

Brig'dha lifted the precious nodule and slowly approached the raider. She was afraid, but not so afraid that she shook. Despite that fact, she forced her arms to quiver as though she were on the edge of terror. She lifted the nodule towards the man, attempting to look as vulnerable as possible. If he did not expect what she was about to do and her movements were fast and clean, there was a chance that she could pull off her plan. Brig'dha whispered one more prayer to the Goddess as she held the nodule out for the man. Just as he reached for the item, she hurled the nodule straight down toward his foot. Then, without even waiting to see if it struck, she reached behind her and grabbed a handful of the ground salt from the wooden dish on the altar. The plan needed to flow without pause if it was to work.

After attaching his war club to his hip cord and switching to his flint dagger, the man reached forward to take the nodule from the woman, still not sure if he would try to take her as well. He had already decided to leave the older woman and children alone. He did not want their blood on his hands. As his fingers touched the nodule, the priestess suddenly hurled it straight down toward his foot, awkwardly. She was quick, but the man shifted his weight suddenly and pulled his foot out just in time to avoid the nodule. It was a clumsy move on both of their parts, leaving the raider in an unsteady position with his bodyweight suddenly shifted backward. He lifted his angry gaze towards the priestess, ready to retaliate for her feeble attempt at harming him when suddenly she raised an outstretched hand to the man's face, palm horizontal and open. His eyes quickly focused on a white powder in her palm and then her large, hazel eyes, just behind the salt. For a brief instant, their eyes met, and then she blew.

The gentle breath carried with it the instantaneous sting of powdered sea salt. The man stumbled backward, unable to see with burning eyes. It only took him a moment to realize that he had been "blinded" with salt and would soon be able to see. Still, for the next few moments, he was blinded. He slashed his dagger wildly, hoping to catch the flesh of the mischievous priestess. Gone from his mind was any notion of taking her with him. No one wanted a woman who was willing to fight back. Suddenly, he felt a strange punching sensation on his neck, followed by an odd and cool feeling mixed with horrible pain. The pain filled his shoulders and neck and kept growing. Was it magic? Had she cursed him? He stumbled backward, fumbling for the stretched-hide door.

Brig'dha stood before the man holding the bloody deer antler. The man had expected a weak and useless attack, and she had shown him exactly that. It had been a calculated move, but she suspected the man would easily dodge her slow attack, leaving him open for another. All she needed to do was blow a little salt in his eyes and then stab him in the small, exposed portion of his neck with the antler. The wound would not be immediately fatal, but it could be if it were not treated within a few days. The man crawled across the ground finding the door and climbing out. Brig'dha lifted his dagger but did not pursue him, pausing to lick the blood and salt from her hand. The idea of stabbing to death a wounded and blinded man went against her morals. She let loose a deep breath of air and thanked the Goddess that she had not faltered, as even the slightest hesitation or mistake would have been her downfall.

She turned to face Kelwyn with an exasperated expression. All she had hoped to do was prevent the raider from harming them. If all he had wanted was the flint and she could have been sure of that, she would have let him take it, but she simply couldn't take the risk that he would only ask for the flint and nothing more. Regardless of his intent, Brig'dha was glad that she had chosen not to kill the man. Anyone desperate enough to raid a village in the dead of the cold season probably had a starving family to take care of. Brig'dha whispered a prayer to the spirits of the cold and the Moon Goddess for the raiders' families, and for her people.

"It's... It's all true, isn't it? Everything that you and Kaelu said... All those things that you did?" Kelwyn whispered in shock, tears staining her face. When the man had first entered the room, she had been afraid for her children, but watching the moon priestess face down the enemy, and now standing victoriously before her, she felt a sense of control returning. It seemed that the blessings of the gods were indeed upon the children. Brig'dha quickly looked away, disliking eye contact, her mask of normality quickly returning.

CHAPTER TWO

A LIFE SPARED, A LIFE TAKEN

For every pleasure, possession, or purpose that can be named as a reason for any action or meaning, life must exist as the canvas upon which these are painted. Thus, the act of taking a life is perhaps the most severe action one sentient being can have upon another. When confronted with an enemy who endangers the lives of people we care about, it becomes difficult to separate the moralities of actions. The instinct to protect oneself and those one cares about overrides the niceties of the compassionate moral high ground. Should life be spared, should it be taken? These are questions we discuss at length and act upon in the heartbeat of the moment.

Something felt wrong to Ember as she approached the final hill, which separated her from the view of the village. For a moment, she thought that she heard the sound of screams in the distance, but perhaps it was the wind. Still, it was almost like she felt something she could not quite put her finger on. The forest at night could have this effect, and sounds had to be carefully judged before reacting. As she turned her head left and right, she thought she occasionally picked up strange noises from up ahead. Perhaps some men were having an argument or even a fight in the village. Those sorts of things did not happen very often, but they created quite a stir when they did. Ember adjusted the weight of her kill, which was already causing her shoulders to ache even though it was such a small deer. If there were a fight, she would arrive in just a few moments to see it. Maybe someone finally lost their patience with Yan, she mused.

As she crested the hill before the tribe, which acted as a natural sound barrier, the truth of what unfolded below took befell her. The sounds of terror and battle filled her ears with panic. Before her, people ran left and right, screaming. She was not sure exactly what was happening, but it looked like a raid. Ember dropped the deer and pulled free her bow, glad she hadn't properly unstrung it. She dashed down the hill with near reckless abandon, drawing an arrow from her quiver while trying to make sense of the commotion before her. She saw no raiders or, at least, anyone that she could identify as a raider. Even in the moonlit village, it was too dark to determine what was happening.

She approached the edge of the village quickly, making out the shape of a man lying on his back and clutching what looked like an arrow in his chest. She rushed over to the man and realized, to her horror, that she knew him. Vedhe lay on the ground in agony, his lifeblood covering the ground and his body shuddering in the throes of death. Someone had fired an arrow directly into his chest. The ribs could reflect an arrow making the chest a poor target, but this arrow had slipped in between his ribs and gotten into the vital parts deep inside. He looked up at her with a pleading expression, tears streaking from his eyes, as he tried to mumble something she could not understand.

She dropped to her knees before the man and grabbed his body, pressing it close to her. She held him that way and rocked slowly back and forth as she felt the shuddering calm and the last of his life leave him. Ember looked down at the man to see his pupils slowly dilating as his body twitched. She gently lay him down upon the ground as her tears fell upon his wounds, a rage began to build within her. In her mind's eye, Ember could see her mother East holding the body of her dying father Winterborn the same way she had just held this man. Is this how it was for her mother? She hardly knew Vedhe, yet she felt this much pain as she watched him die. How must it have been for her mother to watch her husband and lover pass in the same violent way? Without thinking, she reached for her bow and the loose arrow. She stood and began to search the village for any trace of the raiders. Ember had a personal problem with raiders, and this incident had done nothing but incite that problem.

Suddenly, a soot-covered raider stepped from behind a building with two large leather sacks of salted meat tied to his back and a war club in his hand. He looked as though he was about to flee into the woods. Ember knew that if she did nothing, he would harm nobody and leave, but for all she knew, this was the man who had killed Vedhe and perhaps others. It was important that raiders learned the cost of their deeds. Perhaps it would deter them from future raids... Or perhaps Ember just hated raiders more than anything. She carefully pushed her morals deep into the little hole in her mind where she hid them when they became too inconvenient.

Ember nocked an arrow against the bowstring and pulled the bowstring back, taut. She took aim at the man. Over and over, her fingers twitched on the verge of releasing the arrow. Part of her felt that it was wrong to shoot the man as she did not actually know that he had killed anyone, but another part told her this was the right thing to do. Just then, another raider burst forth from the village proper and turned towards Ember. She could not be sure if he was fleeing the village and had chosen a path that lay in Ember's direction by accident or if he was charging to attack her. With the man suddenly running straight at her, she could not take the chance. Ember acquired the new target and let loose her arrow.

The arrow flew true and plunged into the man just below his rib cage on his right side. He made a strange yelping sound and nearly fell, coming to a stop barely the length of a man from her and dropping to his knees in total shock. He held the arrow and began to roll around, screaming. Ember quickly nocked a second arrow and took aim at the other man who had not fled, stopping to observe the sounds behind him.

The first man turned to see a woman with long red hair, just discernible in the moonlight, leveling her arrow at him. He stepped backward, realizing that he was in the open and that the woman before him was a keen shot. On the ground not too far from him lay one of his companions with an arrow stuck in a very deadly place. The man rolled around in agony, but there was nothing much that he could do for him at this point. The dying man was the same young man who had drawn first blood that night. He supposed that it was the will of the gods in some way. He prayed under his breath that the gods would take greater mercy upon him as he had not actually harmed anyone. The man held his hand out with no alternative, hoping that the woman would not shoot. He carefully removed one bag and placed it on the ground, slowly backing away from the woman and heading toward the woods. With each step, he waited for the arrow to fly.

Ember approached the man looking him dead in the eyes. She expected to see the monster that was a vile raider, but instead, the man before her looked like any other. He stared back at her with a mixture of fear and shame. Ember supposed that he might just be taking the supplies for his family. The last season's gathering had been pretty devastating for many of the local tribes, and game had not been plentiful to the West. Still, the people of Isen'bryn had surprisingly fared well, likely owing to their small, but prosperous gardens and better-than-average hunting grounds.

The raider held his hands out, hoping that she would not fire. Ember cautiously observed him as he pulled one of the two sacks free and placed it on the ground. Was he handing back one of the bags in exchange for her mercy, she wondered? Something about his actions and the way he looked back at her struck Ember as a man desperate for food. That little place in her mind where her morality had hidden came open, and her humanity washed over her. She held her bow pointed at the man the entire time it took him to back away, then turn and run into the woods with a single bag. If he did have a family, she hoped that the food would help them.

"You just could have asked..." she whispered as she lowered her bow and turned to witness the end of the raid. By the sound of it, the raiders had fled into the woods, and the small skirmish was over. Ember slowly turned to the mortally wounded man rolling around in agony on the ground. Visions of the deer she had killed came back to her. In much the same way, this man was like that deer, wounded and dying. She pulled free her obsidian dagger and slowly approached to finish what she had started. Raider or deer, it was the only humane thing to be done.

ↄ ↄ ↄ

Brig'dha emerged from the hut with the raider's flint dagger in one hand and a wooden dish containing yarrow paste in the other. She had removed her deer-skull mask and wore her leather shirt and a heavy leather jacket as well as a pair of leather boots. It had been a short while since the sounds of battle had stopped, and she now felt safe leaving Kelwyn and her children in the hut while she assisted with the wounded. One of the many jobs of a priest or priestess was to do what she could to help those injured.

Most of the time, small wounds could be treated with yarrow paste. The problem was with deeper and deadlier punctures and lacerations where the blood ran dark. Wounds where the blood would not stop flowing or where objects were buried so deep within the body that they caused other problems, often led to death. At that point, the best that could be done for the person was to help them make the journey out of this world and into the next. This was something Brig'dha had trouble with, but looking up at the beautiful full Moon gave her strength.

Not far ahead of her was a man lying face down on the ground and not moving, a woman crying by his side. She rushed over to the man and rolled him over. Brig'dha was startled by what she saw. The man's name was Canael, a man skilled with tanning leather. His throat had been completely slit from side to side. The wide-eyed vacant look on his face told her that he had died a while ago. The ground before him was soaked with so much blood that he must have passed very quickly. Brig'dha turned to the woman. Her name was Saeve, and she was quite skilled at carving patterns into thick leather, as well as beadwork for clothing. Her skills showed as she wore a long leather shirt just visible under her furs with beads embedded all the way through it, exquisite work. She simply knelt by her now dead husband and wept while gently touching his hair as though she were neatening it. Brig'dha placed her hand on Saeve's shoulder and slowly brought her into an embrace. She hated touching others, but her empathy won over. She had left her hut to heal the wounds of the flesh, but now she found herself healing the wounds of the heart.

I'm so sorry, but you will make it past this. Trust me, I know, she thought, though she dared not speak when Saeve's pain was so fresh.

ᴐ ᴐ ᴐ

Ember entered the village with her obsidian dagger in hand, looking for anyone who might need help. There had been many with wounds but only a few significant injuries, as far as she could tell. Upon the ground in front of her was a dead raider with several men standing over him. One of the men, Aethen, was a friend to Ember. Aethen had long black hair set in many braids in the way of the people of Isen'bryn. He looked at Ember with his piercing gray eyes, a look of concern on his face. In his hand was a war club with a smear of wetness marring one side. The sickening wet club told Ember that he likely delivered the killing blow. She was impressed that he had fought a raider and defeated him in single combat by the looks of it. She had known that Aethen was a brave man with firm conviction, but she could not help but be impressed by his actions.

"Ember, I am glad to see that you are safe. Did you just arrive, or were you part of this fight?" Aethen asked, slowly turning to face her. The men standing with Aethen now turned to hear the woman's response. Ember had lived with the people of Isen'bryn for half of a harvest and had become quite adept at their language, but she still paused for a moment to make sure she understood his exact words. She strangely felt a mixture of exhilaration and sadness at what had happened. Battle could make a person feel excited one moment but horrified, shocked, depressed, and sick the next. She knew that soon her excitement would leave, and all the horror would return. Battle was an emotional storm that was hard to whether.

"I was returning with a deer when I saw this happening. I killed one of the raiders over there," she indicated with her finger, "but another one got away. He dropped a bag he was carrying, so not a total loss," she concluded. Thoughts of the dead man mixed with memories of her deer and slicing the throat of the wounded man. The scenes of death flashed in her eyes every time she closed them, so she simply kept them open.

Ember's emotions continued to swap between exhilaration and excitement, and terrible remorse. This is how it was when she killed those men a harvest before who had enslaved several young women. She knew that soon the emotions would overwhelm her.

"Aethen, will you cry for this man? He was your enemy, but will his death fill you with pain?" Ember asked, drawing confused looks from the men gathered around the body. He considered her for a few moments, guessing at what she meant. Ember had always puzzled him more than any other person. She was a woman of contradictions – a warrior who could take life, but also a woman who could create it. She was gentle and kind but as tough as any man. She often acted as young as a child, but suddenly she might become deadly serious and more adult than an elder. Studying her face, he wondered how women perceived the world. Was it different from men? Or did Ember even see things as other women did?

Part of Aethen wanted to tell Ember that he would be distraught over what he had done, but he knew that was not true. This man had been an enemy and had come to kill him and his people. He could find no reason to shed a tear over his death. This was the way men thought or, at least, every man that he had known. Perhaps she would understand, or perhaps she would not. By her own words, she had taken a life already this night. Aethen closed his eyes for a moment and banished all his thoughts. Sometimes he became overly introspective, but at least, Ember waited patiently.

"Do you cry over the body of the deer you kill? The deer had to die so that you could live... the same as this man. I feel even less sympathy for the man because he chose his fate... The deer did not," Aethen said firmly but with compassionate eyes. Ember did not know why most men seemed to be more insulated from their feelings than women, but sometimes she envied whatever it was they possessed. Perhaps men struggled with their emotions but buried them so deeply that they simply smoldered over time? Maybe they did not have the freedom to express them as she did, though she hoped that this was not true. Ember turned and walked away in thought, heading in the direction of Brig'dha's hut...

"By the gods, Brig'dha!" Ember suddenly said, having just remembered that she had not seen her beloved friend. She ran as fast as she could to the hut where Brig'dha, Ember, and a few others lived. The hut was on the outskirts of the village and was a place for people who did not have a large established family. Brig'dha had hoped to stay with the family of her now dead husband, but they had simply rejected her. They had done so subtly, but Brig'dha could tell that deep down, they either blamed her for his death or were unsure if she had a hand in it. Either way, Ember enjoyed living with Brig'dha, so it had worked out for the best.

ↄ ↄ ↄ

Brig'dha stepped a short distance from Saeve and her fallen husband. She needed time to be with him, alone. Staring off into the night, Brig'dha thought she noticed something moving in the bushes. She could not imagine an animal coming near her village with all that had just happened. She approached nervously with her weapon drawn, unsure of what she might find. To her surprise, it was a person crouched behind bushes. Brig'dha moved close enough to see who it was in the dim moonlight. Unexpectedly, it was the raider who had attacked her. The man lay on the ground clutching his wounded neck and trying desperately to rub the salt from his eyes. Brig'dha had only thought a little of the salt had gotten in, but it now seemed like much more had entered, and perhaps some sand. She stood back about the length of a man from him to try and decide what she might do.

Well, you didn't get far, did you? she thought. On the one hand, she could let the man go, but she was not sure that he could escape, at least until his eyes were cleared. On the other hand, she could bring him some water to help him clean his eyes, but should she help an enemy? She remembered how he had looked at her when he had broken into their hut. She was not sure, but it certainly looked to her at the time like he was thinking about taking more than the flint. She had been nearly helpless, yet now their roles were reversed. Brig'dha toyed with the idea of letting him free, but at the same time, if he were captured, he might provide some insight into the people who had attacked. His neck wound was pretty serious, and he did not seem to be running anywhere right now. She was unsure if he even realized that she was standing there.

"Brig'dha! Are you alright?" yelled Ember as she caught sight of the priestess and came rushing with her arms wide. Brig'dha turned and felt a rush of exhilaration as her friend came upon her and took her into deep embrace. For a moment, the two friends looked at one another, simply glad they had made it through this terrible event without losing each other. But, as their embrace continued, Brig'dha began to feel something more than just their simple joy. Hugging Ember just felt… right, much different than hugging her deceased husband had. She quickly released the radiant redhead before she held her too tightly, or too long.

That was when Brig'dha noticed that Ember's right hand was red with blood. The discovery took her breath for a brief moment, and she stood back frantically observing the hand, expecting to see some horrible wound. Somehow, the idea that both women could walk out of this battle unharmed didn't feel realistic. She almost expected tragedy, a terrible anticipation. Ember saw her looking and then indicated Brig'dha's own hand, which was also stained with the blood of another. They looked at each other and realized that they had both taken quite an active role in the skirmish. *Well, at least, we match,* Ember thought with dark mirth.

"Relax, it is not my blood. It belongs to one of the raiders… But I doubt that he will ask for it back," Ember said with a slightly humorous look. Brig'dha immediately scolded her for using humor with such a morbid subject and in such a grim moment, but she couldn't stay mad for more than a brief instant. Humor had always been Ember's mechanism for dealing with such situations. Ember stood before her like a rock, something solid in a world where everything else seemed fleeting. Brig'dha could not help but idolize her. She couldn't imagine the world without her friend.

"The Goddess won't let us be at peace," Brig'dha lamented, "She continues to test us and to force us to adapt. I… I think I'm growing tired of this place. I feel the spirits of my past haunting me each night..." *You are the only thing which brings me peace,* she added in her own mind. Ember pointed past Brig'dha to the man on the ground.

"It looks like one of your spirits is lying right over there. Did he do something to you?" she asked, changing the subject. Ember casually twirled her obsidian blade waiting to find out if this man had caused Brig'dha any trouble. In truth, Ember was not looking forward to killing another person, but some lines could not be crossed. One such line was causing harm to her friends. She had come to think of Brig'dha even more closely than a sister, much more than a mere friend, though sadly, no closer than that.

"He has caused me no harm. In fact, I am the one who caused him harm," Brig'dha said, placing her hand on Ember's shoulder to ease her tensions. She didn't put the dagger away, but she did lower it. Thoughts of Brig'dha's words continued to roll around in her head. Ember had quickly become bored with the people of Isen'bryn. They were not as welcoming as the people of Tornhemal nor as interesting as the people from the True South. Nevertheless, Brig'dha's words brought hope to Ember that perhaps it was time to leave.

This was not the first time that Brig'dha had expressed remorse for rejoining her people. She had expected to be taken in with open arms, but she had found only rejection. Many people simply did not believe the story of her travels with Ember or her explanation for how Mohdan, her husband, had died. The idea that two women had explored all that distance and fought so many dangers was simply too much for most people to believe. Among her people, a woman's role was significantly more domestic. A woman was simply not supposed to strap a bow across her back and journey into the unknown.

Brig'dha explained what had happened when the raider had attacked. What Ember had jokingly called "a spirit" was, in fact, a raider blinded by salt, and maybe some leftover sand, in his eyes. Even as Brig'dha explained, the man frantically rubbed at his eyes, trying to free them so he could run. He had not realized what she was doing when she blew, and so he had not reflexively closed his eyes in time. She supposed the sounds of two women speaking right beside his hiding place were probably more than a little unnerving to the raider. He knew that if he were discovered, his life was probably forfeit.

"I say that we tie him up and interrogate him," Ember said. Brig'dha agreed, not seeing any other options. Too many people from her own tribe were now wandering around, some approaching, for her to let the man leave. Besides, she could not help but wonder what he would have done to her if she had not defeated him. This way, he would get a chance to answer those questions. It would be up to the tribe to decide his fate, not hers. At this point, she was willing to let go of responsibility. Brig'dha turned to Ember and nodded her assent.

"All right there, buddy, you to stay nice and calm and let me tie you up. If you give me trouble, I'll thunk you over the head with a rock," Ember said to the man in her native tongue. Brig'dha held back a smile, having understood a little of what she had said. Ember dived into the bush knocking the man face-down. The man struggled to get her off him, but he seemed weaker than he should be. She suspected that the blood loss from his neck might have something to do with that. Geb, a tall and slightly older dark-haired woman, stepped from the corner of the hut holding a flint knife. She had been attracted by the sounds of struggle and had come to help. She halted her approach as she realized what was going on. Before her stood Brig'dha giving Ember advice as the reckless redhead attempted to hogtie a wounded raider.

"I guess you have this one under control," she said almost humorously. Geb, a fletcher by trade, was not known to say very much.

She was as tough as her husband, Nael. Unlike the tribes near Ember's birthplace, Isen'bryn women helped with the defense of their tribe just as the men, a common trait among tribes in more hostile areas.

"I poked him with an antler in the neck," Brig'dha said, though Geb suspected the "poke" was a little bit more intense, given the blood. A moment later, Nael stepped from behind the same hut carrying a war club and apparently ready to attack. Geb held her hand up, halting his advance. It took him only a moment to realize that the raider had been subdued.

"It is over. Brig'dha defeated the raider, and Ember is tying him up," she said. Geb smiled at the idea of a captive. Capturing an enemy might please their gods, especially if he could be made to talk.

The man continued to struggle face down as Ember straddled his back, but he stopped fighting the moment he felt the obsidian dagger pressed tightly against his throat. Ember had become annoyed with the struggling and decided to end it quickly. She motioned Brig'dha to come and help her tie the man. The priestess approached more cautiously than her feisty friend, pulling free a leather cord from Ember's quiver. Ember always carried supplies, like leather cord, when hunting. Sometimes she needed to tie deer legs or set some sort of trap.

It took only a few moments to bind the man's hands. He had stopped resisting with the prospect of having his throat slit by a dagger, the great equalizer. The two women pulled the man to his feet and checked him for weapons. He had a small war club attached to his side. Ember lifted the club and examined the end of it. She was shocked to find blood, though perhaps not too surprised. *This weapon has been used to hit somebody, but whom?* She lifted the club to allow Brig'dha to see the blood. She turned her head away in disgust. Brig'dha had wondered if this man had been capable of doing anything truly terrible to her... and now she knew. Would he have killed the children or perhaps taken her as a spoil? She found it less and less important to her if this man lived. Ember saw Brig'dha's expression and felt a touch of compassion for her. Evil men with cruel intentions were something Ember had some experience with.

"He may have been a bad one, but they are not all bad. I let a man go back there with one of our bags of food. You could tell by the look on his face that somewhere far from here, he had a hungry wife and children. Some men are good, and some are bad. My guess is this is one of the bad ones..." Ember said, turning her head to see several people coming, "and here come some of the better ones." Brig'dha looked less than convinced.

"Of course, women come in evil varieties as well... Remember Aya?" Ember said with a sarcastic smirk. Brig'dha gave Ember a confused frown at the notion. She remembered Aya all too well. She was a woman from the people of Tornhemal, a group of traders Ember had joined the previous harvest and who had helped Ember rescue Brig'dha from the village of Nes. The villagers had wanted to sacrifice Brig'dha to appease their gods, but Ember had saved her. Aya had plotted and schemed the entire time and had nearly gotten herself killed in the process. There were good men and bad men, but there were also good women and bad women. All humans came in all forms, and only a fool would condemn many people for the actions of one.

Behind them approached a group of villagers to see what they had found. First in the group was Galar, a tall brown-haired man with green eyes who had many times before actively opposed Brig'dha becoming a priestess. Galar did not like either woman, and believed their stories were likely false. Worse, he considered it possible that they had brought evil spirits from wherever they had traveled. A night like tonight would do nothing but strengthen his conviction. He was followed by an older, slightly balding man named Mael, an accomplished hunter. Even though he was much too young for the title, Mael was a good person and a respected elder. He was at least three times Ember's age, but his body had fared well in all those harvests. Behind Mael came Yan, a sly-looking man just a little older than Ember with long, honey-colored hair and gray-blue eyes.

Yan had an obvious interest in Ember, which he did little to hide. While Ember had to admit that Yan wasn't physically unattractive, physical attraction was only a tiny bit of the recipe for love. Ember had always considered personality more important than looks. The problem with Yan was how he eyed her. On many occasions, she had caught him staring lustfully at her in a sort of lewd fashion. Ember felt a strange, creepy sensation whenever she was near the man, and no matter how he looked, she could not escape that fact. Any man who came across as creepy had no chance, looks, or personality aside. Besides, while she found men attractive, she couldn't imagine living with one.

Brig'dha absolutely despised Yan and had suggested that Ember stay away from him on more than one occasion. She had grown up with the fool, though they had rarely ever interacted. Ember found it amusing how aggressive, and almost territorial, Brig'dha could be towards Yan, though she could never quite figure out why. It was important to find love as soon as possible, as life could be quite short.

Even though they were young, Ember wondered how she and Brig'dha would live if they left the Isen'bryn. Would they find husbands?

For some reason, Ember could not imagine Brig'dha with a second husband, besides, Ember had always enjoyed the company of women over men. She would be quite happy to remain by her friend's side. However, if Brig'dha did wish to find a man, she sadly knew it might add distance to their relationship, though they were extremely close friends. *Are we just friends,* she pondered as she continued to wonder where their futures would lead them, both as friends and in travel.

Where would they go, and for how long? She was hoping for at least another ten harvests of life, but one could never know. Around her lay people who thought they had many harvests left to love and be happy, and now they were dead. This was the way of life, a natural cycle. A person could become ill for no apparent reason or simply die from the pains of their teeth. If you were lucky enough to have a child, you could die before it was born or as it was birthed. That very child itself might die before it could even stand. This was why people had to love and enjoy life as much as possible, as it could be quick and cruel. There didn't seem to be an actual order to it. Life wasn't fair or unfair – it just was.

Besides the randomness of life and death, other aspects also seemed stochastic. No one knew why some people aged faster than others. A full harvest started at the end of the cold season and progressed through the thawing season, growing season, warm season, the harvest season, and finally into the next cold season. A person would be considered a child until they had physically developed, usually between 16 to 18 harvests, at which point they would be regarded as an adult, though most waited until at least 17 harvests to join with another. Both Ember and Brig'dha's people measured age by how many warm seasons had passed. Each warm season, everyone increased by one harvest age, though Brig'dha's people didn't call this a "harvest," not being proficient farmers. Most people had children by the time they reached 17 to 23 harvests age. The average life expectancy for most people was between 30 and 40 harvests, though occasionally, a person could live more than 60 harvests. It was assumed that the gods and the spirits played a part in this. Mael was at least 45 harvests of age, yet he still had most of his teeth and hair. More impressively, he could walk without any pain. Ember's thoughts were interrupted as the creature called "Galar" opened its mouth.

"So, did you two girls find one of the raiders that got away? Did he frighten you? I would have thought that the raiders would be too afraid to attack our village with the mighty Ember protecting us," Galar sardonically inquired, using the word "girls" rather than "women" as a sign of disrespect. Ember turned and stood tall before Galar, unwilling to back down. She was actually a hand length shorter than Galar though Ember was still pretty tall for a woman.

"Brig'dha defeated this man in single combat. She has taken him prisoner. We have done the hard work, so now you can interrogate him. Oh, and the raider I killed is back over that way," Ember said, motioning in the direction of the man she had killed, "but he won't be saying very much. Tell me, Galar, how many raiders did you defeat? Surely, we poor women, I mean 'girls,' could not have topped the number of raiders killed by the mighty Galar. I should run and make some children before I pee myself with fear…" she said with mirth. Galar reached for his war club, having just been heavily insulted by Ember. Mael stepped in between them and grabbed Galar's hand, stopping him. Mael wasn't sure whose life he was saving.

"Wait a moment, Galar, you had that coming for a while. You have said some pretty bad things about both of these women, and I think that they might have just proven their stories truer." Galar stood back with rage in his eyes and spit onto the ground. Mael chuckled, looking back and forth between the women and Galar. *Acting tough? You're not going to do anything you cowered,* Ember thought.

"Besides, if each of these women just defeated a raider, I don't think it would be the smartest thing for you to challenge them," Mael added with a smirk. It was true that Galar had said some pretty disparaging things about Ember and Brig'dha around the central fire during many nights. At first, Ember had simply not known what the man had been saying, and Brig'dha had been too shy to argue back. After Ember had learned enough of the language, she had simply ignored the man, deciding him not worth a fight. Now she stood victorious before him, a proud warrior in all her glory. As soon as those thoughts came to mind, the guilt and emotions hit their peak. She was done speaking to Galar.

Ember turned and slowly walked away from the village and towards the gentle slope that led to the Greatest River's shores without further acknowledgment. The village of Isen'bryn sat upon the edge of the Greatest River, and it was these very shores that Ember often stood upon gazing out into the never-ending expanse of water. The wind had become a gentle breeze, and the night had gone silent. It was not long before Ember found herself standing on that very sand. Her emotions were tumultuous as the exhilaration of battle faded like morning dew in the Sun. She stood before the world feeling shame at her actions and yet joy that people she cared about and knew had lived. Somewhere there was likely a woman, perhaps children, who waited for a man who would never come home. This was the reality of battle, unknown casualties, and conflicts of conscience that would never be resolved.

The Moon had gone below the horizon and set behind her just a short time ago. Ember looked up to see a never-ending expanse of stars with the Moon out of the way. The stars met the unusually still waters of the Greatest River and seemed to travel forever. They provided a welcome distraction from her thoughts. She did not know what made the stars slowly move and why some seemed brighter than others. To her left across the coastline and midway up was a single dot of light that never seemed to move. This was a star that she had heard that some of the men who traveled across the Greatest River were known to use. Ember had suspected that the Moon and some of the brighter stars could be used to navigate, but when she finally sat down and spent time observing them, they actually change their position over time.

"I still can't believe that we made it here alive," Brig'dha said as she came to stand behind Ember. Both women stood before two seas of eternity, one above and one below, and felt tiny by comparison. There was something peaceful to Ember about gazing at the stars. Right now, she needed their healing comfort, at least until the images of the dying raider faded. For a short while, they just stood with the gentle wind blowing in their hair. It had been a long night, and so much had happened. As Ember gazed at the stars, tears began to slowly drift down her face. She had killed a man, and though it was easy enough to reconcile that he was a raider, the thought that somewhere a child and a woman looked up at the same stars wondering if he would return filled Ember with despair. Every time she took a life, it cut her as deep as an obsidian blade.

"It's beautiful when you look at it," Ember said, gesturing toward the stars. More tears began to flow, and then suddenly, Ember felt the gentle embrace of Brig'dha from behind. The priestess held her tightly as she cried. Over time, the pain would numb, but the images in her mind of the man she had killed would never fully disappear.

I'm no good with a bow or words, but I can hold you, the priestess thought. For a short time, they just stood, Ember held tightly by her friend.

"You did it to make other people's lives better... To save people... To bring hope," Brig'dha said. "If you had not been the person that you are, I would have been sacrificed to some strange gods in a faraway land. What you did and who you are stopped that violent man who had killed so many people in Nes. Never stop being you." She referred to the death of the murderer Peerth. The crimes that Peerth the farmer had committed had been blamed upon Brig'dha, and it had been decided that she was to be put to death to appease the gods. Ember had taken it upon herself to save Brig'dha, soon aided by the help of her friends from the people of Tornhemal. It was that very spark of nobility and the will to do what was right at any cost which drew Brig'dha to her friend. The two women peered at the stars for a while longer. It had been a long night.

"I miss our travels. We should leave and return to the wilds," Brig'dha said. For a long moment, Ember thought upon the words she had just heard. She shared that sentiment and simply wanted to get away from it all. Perhaps a good place to go would be the True South, a land of warmth and lush greenery – a place far from bad memories. Most of all, she was glad that Brig'dha wanted to come.

"A life spared, a life taken... a balance," Ember said, more to the stars than anyone else.

ↄ ↄ ↄ

Early that morning, Brig'dha lay beneath a pile of furs in the small hut she and Ember shared on the outskirts of the village. Though some remained awake dealing with the aftermath, most of the tribe had returned asleep. Beside her, the resting redhead slept lightly, still a bit restless. She had initially experienced nightmares, or so it seemed as she rustled about under the furs, but she calmed after Brig'dha began stroking her hair. Nothing calmed Ember more than simply stroking her long hair, especially given Brig'dha's long fingernails.

She considered their time spent over the past ten moons since returning to her people. Brig'dha had become a priestess of the gods, though mostly the Moon Goddess, while Ember had worked to learn her language and hone her skills as a hunter. In that time, they had remained friends, yet never more. She had initially thought Ember had eyes only for men as she had caught Ember spending a bit too long eyeing several, yet she had also caught her doing the same to a few women, as well. Most people liked the opposite sex, and yet this wasn't universal. Homosexuality was common among animals and people, as were variations in between. Brig'dha had zero interest in men outside of friendship, yet perhaps Ember was a woman of many interests?

Yet if that were the case, why had the often-rapt redhead not stared at her? Why had she remained a friend and no more? They had been closer during the boat ride from the Great River to Inn'bry'th, coming close to what she had thought was flirting, and yet nothing had come of it in ten moons. Then again, Ember had remained by her side, even sharing the same dwelling, and sleeping beside her. She hadn't even once pursued a man in all that time. Perhaps, she… And that was when she felt the hand as acutely as if her entire body had been set alight. Glancing down, Brig'dha realized that the reposed redhead's hand had come to rest directly upon her breast. Beside her, Ember slept soundly, seeming to settle down the moment her hand came into contact with Brig'dha.

Waves of adrenalin danced through the bedazzled brunette's body as she felt the hand more acutely than she would have thought possible. She hated physical touch, likening it to brushing a flame when someone touched her. Yet, Ember's hand felt… right… the fire reduced to a warm ember. Besides, it seemed to calm the otherwise restless redhead, freeing the warrior of whatever demons had haunted her dreams until that moment. Neither woman had made a conscious choice to do this, and so Brig'dha remained still and let the hand be. She would need to watch more carefully for signs, any indicators that there was more to be had than friendship, but for now, she would merely watch and wait. She lay back, enjoying the connection until she eventually drifted to sleep.

CHAPTER THREE

SCHISM

Punishment may be defined as the consequence a society or authority levies against an entity due to a prohibited act. Justice may be defined as a measure of how appropriate a given punishment is for the prohibited act, and is based on the culture's concept of morality. An unlawful act and a punishment can both be just or unjust. In fact, the complex and usually gray concepts of law, justice, and morality make judging ancient societies' morals and legal actions dubious at best. To an ancient tribal society, the murder of its people and the theft of its precious resources were likely extremely high in severity. As a result, their punishments might entail what our modern society might consider harsh consequences, perhaps even cruel. Yet, losing loved ones from starvation in the winter is also cruel. It is essential to take a moment to consider the prehistoric viewpoint when evaluating the judgments of ancient peoples.

The meeting of the tribe was already in full swing when Brig'dha and Ember arrived. Unfortunately, both women had slept late and missed the beginning of the proceedings. Usually, tribal council was held with a small number of elders and those with issues to be discussed. However, given the nature of recent events, it had been decided that this meeting would be open to every single member of the tribe and be held outside in front of a large fire in the center of the village. With nearly 100 people in attendance and passions flaring over what had transpired the night before, this was sure to be an explosive event.

The meeting had started with four men wearing masks made from bark and feathers dancing around the central fire to purify the area. Rituals to remove the attackers' evil would have to be performed throughout the entire village, but at least, this meeting could occur safely once the dancers were complete. It was essential to take such precautions as a failure to remove an evil spirit could be deadly. Of special concern was any place where someone had died. Once the area was purified, the meeting began.

Ember and Brig'dha sat toward the back of the group, not wanting to draw too much attention to themselves. Aethen flashed them both a smile from his place closer to the front. Brig'dha glared back at Aethen, confused by his strange and out-of-place smile, while Ember waved back, understanding the gesture as welcoming. Brig'dha turned to Ember, confused, but she just returned a dismissive head nod, rolling her eyes. Ember had dealt recently with the advances of a slightly older and quite creepy man named Yan. By comparison, Aethen was nothing but cordial. She still wasn't sure why he had been so friendly of late. This hardly seemed like the event for anything flirtatious, so she assumed his gestures were a simple greeting. On the other hand, not far to her left sat Yan. Every now and then, she would catch him leering her direction. Ember had the strangest urge to provide him with some sort of obscene gesture in response, but she really could not think of any gesture that could be made which would have the proper effect.

The man currently speaking was Elder Aelraig, the village elder of at least 60 harvests and one of the oldest people in the entire village. Aelraig wore an unusual coat made from many different patches of fur and leather sewn together. Ember thought that the coat was possibly one of the strangest and ugliest pieces of clothing she had ever seen, but it apparently carried some significance to the elder, and he was often seen wearing it, even in the warm seasons. The man had a long white beard and almost no hair left on his head. One of his eyes was a milky gray color, and the other barely seemed to operate. Ember still could not imagine how anyone could live 60 harvests and still have any working parts. She wondered if, underneath all those furs, the rest of his parts still worked... She felt a little guilty even as she chuckled to herself. Her attention was interrupted as the elder switched to a new topic.

"Given what happened last night, I see no more reason for discussion. The only course of action is for us to return to the North. To return to our Greater People. Coming south was something our parents' parents chose. When I was a small child, it was said that I was one of the first born after having come South. It has been that long, but this land is no longer safe. The people of this land do not use their land wisely, and when a bad gathering occurs, they quickly resort to violence. That is the reason they attacked us last night... Simply for our food," he concluded.

He spoke of the Great Gathering, a significant increase in gathering which occurred just before the cold season came. Most tribes would gather, then travel from their warmer camps to hunting camps in choice areas. Brig'dha's people had found lands that were naturally good for both and had no need to travel. When migrations of animals, overpopulation of people, and drought or bad weather caused a scarcity of resources, places like the Isen'bryn's lands were often targets of hungry tribes. Ember's people grew enough crops to sustain them, yet most forest people chose not to do this. Instead, forest people tended to grow tiny gardens to supplement their hunting and gathering, but nothing more.

The people of the island of Inn'bry'th tended to grow crops loosely in flat, open areas or in slash and burn fields. They did not create large growing fields, use irrigation, or replant seeds. For them, agriculture was supplemental, yet over population and a drought had caused last harvest season's small crops and available game to dwindle. Most villages were spared, but a few of the tribes west of the Isen'bryn had fallen on hard times.

"Do not forget the other reason why we have more food and have fared better than the local tribes," interjected Elder Nuala, an older woman of at least 50 harvests, her rich, dark brown skin covered with tattoos of her past triumphs. With waist-length and loose flowing white hair, Nuala was a wise and respected elder who possessed incredible weaving skills. She was said to be a master at converting the bast fibers of nettle plants and tree bark into beautiful fabrics. Weaving was uncommon in the North, and most fiber was either imported or harvested from wild plants and trees. In the South, it was said that fabric was more common and was made at a faster rate, oddly. Nuala was known to support moving back North, which seemed to Ember at odds with her own profession.

"We hold a sacred power that the other tribes do not. Our magic items protect us and keep us in the good favor of the gods. I would not doubt if word of these magical items triggered this raid. Perhaps we should find out from the man that our own priestess Brig'dha captured. He could be made to talk, and I wonder what he would say," she spat with disgust.

Nuala had referred to the two items the tribe possessed, which were considered sacred and magical. The first item was a piece of amber made into a necklace. The amber piece was as long as a finger and half as wide. Amber was not very common to find, but what made this piece so special was not just its size but that it contained what appeared to be a small flower, forever frozen. It was said that the amber piece had the ability to grow crops and bring forth the spirits of nature. It was an object of fertility.

Ember was not sure if that was a true fact, but she had to admit that it was a thing of beauty and possibly only matched by her own large fist-sized lump of what appeared to be either frozen water or warm blue ice.

She had taken the blue ice object from the man who had tried to kill her over a harvest ago. Ember sometimes wondered if it had magical powers as well, but she had never detected any. On more than one occasion, she had placed the item in water to see if the water would cool. She even exposed one corner of it to fire and discovered no major effect other than some soot that she had to clean off.

The second magic item in the possession of the people of Isen'bryn was an extremely long bullhorn said to be from an ancient aurochs, a large form of wild cattle that could be found natively. What made the horn special was that it had carefully carved pictographs detailing the world's creation. If the story was followed all the way around the horn, the story of how the Moon Goddess gave birth to the world as a result of her mating with the Sun God unfolded. Ember had always been less impressed by this item than the amber. Every tribe she had encountered had a creation story. A female spirit or goddess mating with an aurochs was pervasive. Ember had wondered for the longest time if, in fact, all the various gods might just be different versions of the same story. Perhaps there was a moon goddess and a bull god, and every single tribe had just interpreted their stories differently?

Ember returned her attention to what was being said. While she had been lost in thought, as usual, several other speakers had come forward and presented their arguments for and against leaving. The consensus had been leaning towards the tribe heading north. The North was where they were from and where others like the Isen'bryn could be found. Brig'dha leaned over and gave Ember the look of dissatisfaction that she knew they both shared. Ember had no interest in heading to the North as she wasn't from these lands and the stories of the North sounded bleak. Ember's interest was in the South, a vast unexplored expanse of exotic people. She had heard tales of the amazing things to be had in the South, from purple dye to knives made of strange, slightly off-reddish stone that could slice through anything. Brig'dha had also made her thoughts plain to Ember. She had nearly lost all interest in remaining with her people, many of whom rejected her.

Perhaps the pair could simply leave and head back across the Greatest River and maybe even journey to where Ember was from. The problem was the dangers involved in such a trek. The prospect of braving the Greatest River again sent chills down Ember's spine. It would be nice to take more than just the two of them, though Ember was unsure who else would go. As if to underscore her thoughts, Mael stood before the group to propose a different plan.

"Everyone, I understand why you don't want to stay in this place. Returning to the North means returning to the people from which we came. If all of you wish to head to the North, that is what you must do. However, we have all heard the stories of our ancestors coming south and why they did. They wanted to trade with the mainland, and they wanted to meet new people. We can't do that if we return to where we came from. You can return north if you wish, but I will journey across the Greatest River and seek a new village and new lands. If anyone wants to come with me, this is where I am going. I will leave as soon as the snows begin to thaw," he said to a stunned crowd. Mael's plan had hit the tribe like a stone ax to wood. For once, Ember suddenly had all her attention focused on the meeting.

Mael had not just proposed a different plan which was the exact opposite of what most people were favoring, but he had just committed himself to execute the idea regardless of support. There was something about a person who had an idea and stood up to take on a challenge, which inspired others. Unfortunately, his act might very well cause a schism. Ember could see in the faces of many younger people an urge to follow him, but they were still held back, and she was unsure why. Elder Aelraig now stood with a dismissive look upon his face.

"Mael, your plan is a waste of people and time. I thought I had explained this to you a tenday ago when you discussed this with me. To journey across the Greatest River for trade is dangerous by itself, but to do that and then to journey until you find some land to settle is utterly foolish. You would be traveling through the wilds by yourself with any fools who would follow you. How do you think you would last at the mercy of the wilds? How long would it be until wolves surround you by the hundreds and tare your flesh from your bones?" he finished with a triumphant look. Many people turned to regard Mael, waiting for an answer to Aelraig's challenge. This pivotal moment was when Mael's suggestion would either gain supporters or be crushed. Instead, Ember stood up to answer that challenge.

"There are not hundreds of wolves. When they surround you, you can throw rocks at them, and they tend to leave you alone. I also found that fire works pretty well," she said, waiting for a moment for the weight of her words to sink in before she continued. "I, for one, will accept Mael's call to head south. I have met people from the far south, and I wish to meet others like them," she said. Ember's heart skipped a beat as she waited, hoping that Brig'dha would stand beside her. Her action had been impulsive, but that was how she lived... in the moment. Brig'dha stood and placed her hand on Ember's shoulder, showing her solidarity. Aelraig looked back at Ember with a frown.

"What do you know of wolves, woman? You may think rocks and fire work, but when they stare at you in the night, I bet you'll shake like a tree in the wind," he said, having obviously not listened to any of Ember's stories since her arrival. Ember glared back, deadly serious, the memories of the wolf attack which had nearly been her end returning as her eyes grew haunted. The place on her foot where the tree bark had dug into her flesh as she quickly climbed a tree with wolves at her heels still occasionally caused her slight discomfort. As she spoke in reply, Ember stared not at the people but off into the distance of her memories.

"I have been attacked by wolves... over a harvest ago, while sleeping by myself on the bank of the Great River. They came at night, at least four of them. They sneaked into my camp because I was a fool and let the fire die down. I awoke with one of those faces that you spoke of in mine. I ran to the river, where I held them back with rocks as I stood in the water. No matter how many times I hit them, they kept coming. When it finally seemed safe, I ran for a tree on the shore. Within moments, they were at my heels. I jumped in the air, grabbed hold of a branch, and quickly pulled myself into a tree. I came less than a hand's length from being their meal that night. That was the first time I encountered wolves. I have been there, and I have dealt with that. If you fear the journey, then do as you will but do not talk about things which you do not know of," Ember said.

Her tone and her expression spoke to the truth of her words. The fact that Ember had killed one of the raiders and that Brig'dha had taken the other prisoner the night before had passed around the village. This had confirmed in many people's minds the earlier stories Brig'dha had told of their travels. In truth, last night, only three raiders had been killed, and one had been captured. The hands which worked these deeds were small, but their actions lent strength to her words. For a short time, Ember and Aelraig glared at one another. This battle of eyes was only interrupted when Aethen stood, drawing the crowd's attention.

"I am with Mael, Brig'dha, and Ember," said Aethen standing to show his support. Ember was glad to see that her words had not been for nothing.

"We will also join them," announced Geb, as she and Nael stood to lend their support. Not far behind them, others began to stand in solidarity. Kes, Caelwyn, Eryi, Meegin, and others joined in. Slowly, more people arose to stand until 16 people stood, including Ember,

Brig'dha, and Mael. Most who stood were young and filled with wanderlust. Several people were couples, likely in search of a new future. Aelraig frowned at those standing, but he realized that there was not much that he could do to stop them. He was an elder, and the elders advised the people. They had no real control over anyone. Unfortunately, he knew that this meant the tribe would schism. There was not much that he could do about that.

"If it is your wish to throw your lives away on some foolish venture to the South, that is your right. I will pray to the gods for your safe journey though I suspect it will be of little use. The rest of us will return to the North as soon as the winds are warm." With that pronouncement, the entire tribe broke into a discussion about what had happened, and a short recess was called. Brig'dha turned to Ember with excited anticipation.

"I have always wanted to see the South, I mean the True South beyond the mountains," Brig'dha said. Ember smiled as well, pleased that the bashful brunette had agreed to go. If she had not, Ember wasn't sure what she would have done. They were friends, yet their relationship often felt like more than friendship. If Ember was being honest, she was starting to wonder if Brig'dha was as heterosexual as she had first thought, given how she spent just a little too long staring or holding hands. Luckily, she would have more time to learn the truth of this. *I'm just glad you stood beside me,* Ember thought.

"We will follow Mael and his group to see if they can start this new village. After that, who knows where we might go next. If I choose to go all the way to the True South, you will be with me, won't you?" Ember asked Brig'dha. The priestess looked back at the warrior with a confused smile.

"Does the Sun not rise every morning?" she purred with an uncharacteristic giggle. The women discussed the exciting prospect of the journey to the South for a short time while the rest of the village gossiped and argued over the dramatic events that had just occurred. An unprecedented change in the tribe would result in a fracture. Almost one in five of the tribe would leave to follow Mael across the mighty Greatest River to find a new homeland. Such changes were exceedingly rare in tribes and to be part of such a change was sure to be an incredible experience. As if to underscore this, Mael approached Ember during the break and stood before her, a proud smile on his face.

"I wish to thank you for your words. Aelraig hasn't been spoken to in that way since his wife died. Without your words, I fear that I would have journeyed to the South by myself." Ember smiled and nodded at the compliment. In reality, she suspected that the group would have been composed of Ember, Brig'dha, and Mael if she had not spoken. Strangely, Aethen had stood and counted himself among those who would leave. He had involved himself with Ember much more of late. She wondered just what kind of friend he wanted to be. Unfortunately, Yan had also stood among those who wanted to leave. *If we run out of rocks, perhaps we can throw Yan to the wolves,* she thought to herself with a laugh.

It wasn't long before the tribe reconvened, and order was restored to discuss more severe issues. Great Hunter Drost called upon everyone to be quiet so he could speak. This took a few moments, but the order was quickly restored as everyone knew what was to be discussed. This was a matter of vengeance.

"My people… last night was a night of pain and blood. We lost three people, and several others were wounded. Canael was killed by cowards from behind, men without the courage to even face him. Eark was killed while fighting off a raider who burst into his home and threatened his family. Vedhe was killed by a man too cowardly to even face him in combat. All these men were killed by savages, those food starved men of the West who do not have the common decency to simply ask," he said with contempt. Not far from him, the wives of the men softly cried.

"One of these men was captured and 'convinced' to speak of where he came from and of the reasons behind the raid," he continued. Ember was unsure how they had "convinced" the man during the short break during the meeting, but as two men dragged the raider out from the hut where he had stayed for the night, it became easy to guess. The man had been stripped and apparently beaten. Ember did not recall him looking quite so bruised when last she had seen him. His neck seemed to have stopped bleeding, but he was obviously in very poor shape. The man shivered against the cold, his dignity lost as well as any hope. Drost let the gathered people take in the sight of the raider before continuing.

"His people come from the Southwest; a village known as Catl'gort'nan. Their people suffered heavily from the late warm season's drought. They traveled this far in the hope that we would never meet again. While I feel for his need to feed his people, I cannot look past what he has done to mine. There is evidence that this man killed one of our men. The man who killed Eark fled from the house, but the weapon used was a club. This man carries a war club with the stain of blood," he said, holding the stained war club into the air as evidence that the man they had found had performed the deed.

"If he had stolen from us and had been caught, I would seek only his quick death. But this is a man who took the life of one of our own. This vile raider threatened Eark's family and then killed him simply for defending them. He threatened the life of our priestess, Brig'dha, along with Kelwyn and her children. I say we blind him, castrate him, and then break him with clubs. This is what must be done to such an enemy," he concluded with a great finality in his voice. All around him, the village erupted in cheers at the pronouncement. It was not really this one man the people hated, but the attack upon their village and very way of life which he represented. Ember was shocked by the sentence. Her own people would certainly kill a captured raider who may have killed one of their own, but not in such a painful and violent way. Ember wanted to stop these events before they could occur, but she knew there was no hope for this man. The fervor of the crowd was simply too great.

With the full agreement of the tribe, the sentence was to be carried out immediately. Ember and Brig'dha both stood and left. Neither woman had the will to see another person die, especially in such a violent manner. Several other members of the tribe who probably did not have the stomach for what was about to happen also left, but most people stayed behind to witness the gruesome execution. There was something about horrendous acts which seemed to attract people. This was how justice was handed out for most people, if it could be called justice. Brig'dha was starting to wish that she had simply killed the man when she had the chance.

This is not why I spared your life... I'm sorry, Brig'dha thought.

ᗡ ᗡ ᗡ

Far to the Southeast beyond the Greatest River, the Great River, and even beyond the mountains separating the True South from the Northern lands, lay a lush land filled with grassy rolling hills and marshes, ripe with game and fertile. In this distant landscape, the winds were always warmer and humid, and water rarely froze. There sat a vast city of mud-brick houses stacked upon one another like cubes, their layout complete disarray. Since time unknown, people of this city had built house upon house, cube upon cube. Upon the roofs of these cubic mud-brick houses and within their depths lived over 2000 people. The city of Nara'kit was one of two influential trade cities on the banks of the Brown River.

Nestled towards the center of the city was a large building of mud-brick in which an exhausted woman knelt praying to the idle of a bull's head and the small statuette of a goddess. The room was darker than most, illuminated by a single window. A fire had burned down in the central hearth, but it still filled the room with heat and a small amount of smoke. The floors were covered with rush matting, a form of basket-woven reed which made for a more comfortable surface to step upon than the otherwise cold mud-brick and dirt floor. The room had a musty smell, a mixture of cool humidity and wood smoke.

The tired woman was wrapped in a giant aurochs hide for warmth. Covering her shoulders was a shawl made of coarse linen. Around her waist, a leather cord suspended a large and quality made linen loincloth. Her feet were wrapped in thin leather boots as the weather was still too cool for sandals. Her arms and face had been carefully painted red, black, and white with the magical symbols required to receive a vision. She had been chanting since the previous evening, and now her voice was hoarse and her throat raw. She was not sure how much longer she could hold up, but her life had just been thrown upside down, and she was willing to try until she utterly fell unconscious from exhaustion.

Ianmu'kimun, or simply Ianmu to those who knew her, had stood the previous day before the high priest to be chosen to become a priestess of An'an, the goddess of fertility, life, and death. It had been assumed that she would be accepted, being the daughter of the city's leader, An'sankup'Anteanar, ruler of Nara'kit. It had been a shock to everyone involved, especially Ianmu, when the priest rejected her. He had said that her signs pointed to a different path. She should have known that she would be dismissed. She had always been rejected. Her mother had been a young priestess of An'an when her father had taken her during a fertility festival. It had not been long before Ianmu was born, but that birth had cost her mother her own precious life. One life spared, one life taken. This was the cycle of things, the way of life... The way of An'an.

The actions she had taken the day before might have been more out of anger than the actual will of the Goddess, but she did not regret having taken the life of the priest, and she would do it again if given a chance. Her only choice now was to pray for an answer, a direction in her life. It would not be long until someone noticed the dead priest though she wasn't sure how long it would take them to realize she was the killer. The marks around his neck had been red and too obviously the result of strangulation. It didn't matter anymore anyway. What was done was done, and she had only her future to look forward to, perhaps life or perhaps death.

Ianmu continued to chant until she felt a strange uneasiness and tunnel vision forming. She had been feeling faint for a while now, and finally, her body was giving in to lack of sleep. She had failed as a priestess, and now she was being rejected by the Goddess herself. Ianmu had thought several times of simply throwing herself off the tallest mud-brick building, but perhaps the city's warriors would find her and simply put her out of her misery. She was a woman who could see no future for herself. The darkness began to envelop her, and she welcomed it as an end. Ianmu had offered herself freely and fully to the Goddess, and if An'an would not have her, she would let death be her end.

She awoke lying on her back with tall grass surrounding her, a never-ending expanse of stars above. In front of her, a vulture flew, a vast and beautiful bird touched by the gods. The creature circled for a moment before coming lower and finally landing right on her chest. It was all in slow-motion, and somehow, she was not afraid as its powerful talons pressed against her soft skin without puncturing. Ianmu simply lay back and waited for the bird to do as it wished. Perhaps it would tear the flesh from her body and carry her off into the abyss of nothingness. Strangely enough, the bird seemed very interested in the woman. It looked her over, examining her body and making strange sounds as though it were approving. After a moment, the bird flapped its wings and flew off. The encounter was nearly a strange as the surreal grassy landscape on which she now lay.

Ianmu noticed someone approaching, someone who had been blocked from her sight by the large bird. As the bird flew, she could see that the figure approaching was a beautiful maiden with dark feathered bird wings sprouting from her arms. Her body was painted with the most intricate designs Ianmu had ever seen, using colors so rich that even the city leader could not have obtained them in such quantity. The scene was completely surreal. As the woman approached, she held a snake in one hand, and a bull stepped from behind her to rest her other hand upon. There was no mistaking it... She knew exactly who this was.

The goddess An'an gazed down upon the exhausted body of Ianmu. She smiled with a strange sort of nurturing expression that calmed as well as encouraged. Ianmu felt a strange mixture of helplessness and longing at the same time. All she ever wanted in life was a sense of direction, a purpose.

"You will change the fate of many people. You will be my messenger to the city of Isut'na. You will pluck the old plants from the ground and sow something new. You have always been misinterpreted, and this misinterpretation is your greatest tool, a cloak that protects you. I am the daughter of the Moon. I am the Maiden of the Sun. I will come to you again when your task is nearly complete. Go now, my secret priestess of change," An'an said as the bull made a loud sound and vultures flew overhead.

Ianmu awoke lying on the floor of the small room covered with sweat. Her own aurochs skin had fallen aside, but somehow she had not become cold. Rolling onto her side, she saw the Moon to the South through the small window in the white plastered mud-brick wall. It was full, and it would set before the night was long. She lay there with tears in her dark eyes. The Goddess had given her a second chance. She had not been rejected. Instead, she had been chosen for a special task that was secret to everyone, even to the high priest. She finally had a purpose to live, and she would carry out that purpose whether she lived or died. She was to be an instrument of change.

"Daughter of the Moon, goddess An'an, I am faithfully your priestess, and I will journey to Isut'na. I will conquer the city by your will, though I don't know how. Then, when you come again as the Maiden of the Sun, I will have victory or death upon my lips," she whispered upon trembling lips. Ianmu slowly stood, leaving her aurochs skin on the floor. She walked from the building towards an uncertain future.

CHAPTER FOUR
TO SOW THE SEEDS OF TREACHERY

Little is known about the details of sex and gender roles in the Neolithic. In fact, sex estimation can only provide a reasonable estimate of the most likely sex of an individual. We can interpret some details from the state of remains, such as the comparative health of male and female people and their grave goods. However, knowing the sex of a Neolithic person does not tell us their gender. Many cultures have more than two genders, making the assumption that Neolithic people followed a gender binary problematic. Luckily, the field of archaeology is undoing many of the sexist and problematic ideas of the past as we learn more.

Over the next five tendays, the tribe awaited the melting of the snows and the earliest point in the thawing season when travel might occur. Finally, on the morning of the 53rd day following the attack, Old Woman Glea, priestess of the Isen'bryn, stood on the small hills by the Greatest River and proclaimed that the time was now right for any who wished to journey to do so. The snows had mostly melted, and the rains had come, but the air was warmer than anticipated and the signs told of yet another warm harvest to come.

Meegin and Geb sat on old deerskins working antlers into beads using flint tools to scrape and score them, before breaking and smoothing them on stones. Meegin was the younger of the friends, and at the age of seventeen harvests, she would soon need to find a husband. She was a cheerful woman with long, honey-colored hair and green eyes, contrasting her extremely dark skin. Ever the dedicated worker, Meegin always seemed ready to smile, and never appeared to take anything too seriously. Her serious friend Geb, a woman with short, dark hair and blue eyes of twenty harvests, was her polar opposite. While Meegin was supremely feminine, Geb had always been, "one of the boys." Like her husband, she tended to wear leggings and a loincloth, the garb of most men, and was never seen in a leather or woven skirt. Geb often seemed mopey to Meegin, if not a little depressed, but she suspected that this was just her extra-serious attitude towards life.

Geb was considered to be the most expert fletcher of the tribe. Her arrows were said to be as accurate as a ray of light. Her husband Nael was well known for his cooking skills, but their claim to fame really came from her arrows. Though, no one would deny that her husband could roast an excellent deer leg. Normally, Meegin would help her search for feathers in the woods, but today Geb helped Meegin create beads for trade during their trip. Both women wondered what the morrow might bring, given the pronouncement that it was time to leave.

"I've listened so many times to Brig'dha's stories of the South, but I still can't imagine going there," Meegin said. "You suppose that I might find a good man in the South? Perhaps one of those traders Brig'dha spoke of. I wonder what kind of person he would be? Do you suppose that he will have a scar from some courageous fight? I do love scars. They make a man tough," she continued. Geb continued trying to score an antler before breaking it. She would have preferred to hunt for hawk feathers in the woods than breaking her fingers on such a tedious task, but unfortunately, they needed the beads. She vaguely wondered how a scar made a man, but suspected it was something known only to the flirty Meegin.

"I suppose we will learn soon. Glea is saying it's time to leave. I'm going to begin packing this very night," Geb said in her usual monotone voice. Meegin was never quite sure why Geb hung around her so much. Geb was older than her and had a husband. Stranger than that was her personality. She would listen to Meegin as she talked on and on, but Geb would rarely say anything in return. Many people would become annoyed with just how much she said, but Geb always seemed to merely listen. Meegin just assumed that she enjoyed the companionship. Fletching was a long and tiresome task, and listening to Meegin's never-ending discussions about the most random topics seemed to provide Geb with some sort of entertainment. Meegin sensed that Geb was less interested in the men of the South, already having a husband. Besides, she wasn't sure if Geb liked scars. She switched topics to something much more gossipy.

"I heard something really strange the other day. I heard Yan talking to Galar about something. They were standing behind the hut with those ugly old planks, you know the one by the woodpile? They should actually paint those planks. Maybe red? Red is a splendid color to paint wood..."

"Yes, the one by the woodpile. I know it," said Geb, always amazed by how many superfluous comments Meegin could produce. How could anyone speak so much but never say anything? Still, she found Meegin's voice relaxing as she worked. Sometimes, she even listened to what she was saying.

"Anyway, I just happened to be standing there trying to pick up several logs that I dropped when I heard them talking. I decided to sneak around the other side of the building and listen. So, Yan was telling Galar something about Ember. I don't know what it was, but he sounded really excited about it. They were talking for a short time, and then suddenly Galar got really angry and started yelling at Yan!" *Galar probably realized he was talking to Yan. That should make anyone angry,* Geb thought, sarcastically.

"People talk... People yell," Geb replied as she flexed the antler trying to force it to break where she had scored it.

"Yeah, but you know Galar hates Ember. So why would Yan talk to Galar about somebody he doesn't like?"

"Galar and Yan are friends, somehow. Besides, you don't like Galar, and you're talking to me about him," replied Geb absentmindedly. Meegin stared at her for a moment with a confused look before continuing with her endless ramblings.

"Here comes the juicy part. Galar said that Ember was cursed, and that Yan should find another woman." Geb snapped the antler, breathing a sigh of relief when it properly broke and realizing she was not very good with beads. All the while, Meegin stared wide-eyed, waiting for what she thought was the obvious conclusion to sink in. A bird flew overhead, and somewhere, a deer ate grass...

"Do you not get it? The only explanation is that Yan and Ember have a secret love affair! I bet that Ember is pregnant right now, and there will be twins! I bet that there's a secret love connection between Ember and Yan and that Galar only pretends to hate her when he really secretly wants her. Worse, if Yan gets ahold of Ember, then Brig'dha will also need a boyfriend," she finished with a worried expression.

"You have an entire imaginary tribe in your head, don't you?" Geb said. She looked up to find that Meegin was genuinely perplexed by her assumptions. How could anyone become so wrapped up in their own imagination? Geb shook her head and returned to her beading. If she were lucky, Meegin would start singing, something she regularly did. Her voice was simply beautiful and a simple tune would place Geb in a much better mood.

ꝏ ꝏ ꝏ

"I tried to talk him out of it, but he just won't listen," Galar spoke, quite exasperated. He simply thinks that she's just another pretty girl for

him to conquer. I don't think he realizes what kind of a snake she is."
Galar slowly paced around the inside of his hut. His brown hair hung
down his back in braids, and his green eyes pierced the darkness with
intensity. He had seen 23 harvests and had been set on the long path to
becoming an elder one day. He had the support of many people and was
well respected by most of the tribe. Everything had been moving along
fine until those two women had arrived with their wild stories of the
South. They had taken all the attention away from him at a time in his life
when he needed to do the most to prove himself at an early age to be
worthy of being a leader.

He tugged at the leather leggings fastened to a belt around his waist
as he paced. He wore a long leather shirt with bone beadwork and small
triangles cut into the bottom, which hung just past his waist. Protecting
the regions the leggings missed, he wore a loincloth made from soft
doeskin, which hung to his knees, and a pair of plain leather boots with
small bone beads sewn into their sides. Galar had always thought that his
life was more valuable than others. He was to become a leader, but those
two women had arrived and thrown the entire tribe into disarray. There
would have been no schism without them, and perhaps the tribe would
not even have chosen to move north.

How had Ember come to be in the fight when so many other hunters
had not even left their huts? He suspected the raiders would have just
stolen food and left without ever having fought had Ember not been there
to stir things up. Of course, he had no actual proof of these accusations,
but deep down, he was sure the woman had something to do with this. As
a result, his goals had been completely destroyed. If the tribe moved
north, they would likely join with another tribe. His position as an up-
and-coming leader would no longer be secure.

"If he doesn't listen to you, he will just have to find out the hard
way," Kyra said. A woman of 19 harvests with the same long brown hair
and green eyes as her husband, Kyra stood behind him as he ranted. Many
had joked that they had never produced a child because they were secretly
closely related, a taboo, of course. In reality, Galar and Kyra were not
related. Kyra's mother had come from a different tribe long before. Her
father had only been a second-generation member of the Isen'bryn. It was
just a random chance that both Kyra and Galar closely resembled each
other. Still, their lack of a child made Galar's quest to become a leader
even more difficult.

It wasn't as though Kyra had not tried. To her credit, she had danced
all the rituals, consumed many magical concoctions made by old woman

Glea, and even waited for a half Moon with the proper magical shapes drawn upon her abdomen. He simply could not understand what was preventing her from having a child. It was certainly not from lack of trying, and there was some fun in the act, but at this point, it was beginning to hurt his prospects. He tried to hide the resentment in his eyes, but several times he was sure she had seen it.

Given all that had suddenly turned against them, Galar and Kyra had decided that their best course of action was to head South and look for a new place to settle. Perhaps the spirits of this land conspired against them, though he could not be sure. Galar had finally chosen to be rid of the Isen'bryn, having failed at his long road towards becoming a leader. His only hold-up at this point came from Brig'dha and Ember, also heading south. However, Kyra had other interests, and unlike Galar, she had a complex plan that would see them in better standing.

"It will be a long trip to the South. Perhaps Ember and Brig'dha might have an accident along the way," Kyra suggested, playfully. Galar turned to regard her for a moment with a confused look. Had she just suggested a radical course of action, he wondered? He could never tell when she was only playing or being serious. She smiled and quickly stepped away from the firelight of the central hearth in a dismissive sort of manner. Galar assumed that she had just been either joking or speaking wishfully.

His wife could be manipulative, and she was not a woman who backed down, but he didn't suspect that she would kill anyone. He had to admit that she never really showed much care for the plight of others. She had a full range of emotions, but they didn't seem to be affected by other people. He suspected that she cared for him though it was hard to be entirely sure. In a society where marriage was often arranged and semi-compulsory, love was not always required.

Kyra adjusted her long one-piece sleeveless leather tunic. Most people wore multiple layers of clothing, which could be separated when the temperature changed. It was commonplace to wear nothing more than a loincloth inside a warm hut. Still, she had been stepping out of the hut periodically, so she had kept the tunic on for comfort. She would probably slip into something more comfortable later, but for right now, as she worked inside of the hut preparing for the long trip, the single long piece of leather clothing felt comfortable. It was well made and soft, made from many rabbit skins sewn together. Her feet were bare as she had just finished washing her boots and had placed them by the fire to dry. Kyra had been planning a secret way to deal with their many problems ever since the trip to the South had first been announced. Perhaps now was a good time to let Galar in on the plot.

"My love, which of the magic items did the elders say that we would take with us to the South? I can't seem to remember," she asked playfully. Kyra knew well which item was to be brought with the group heading south, but she had decided to draw Galar around to her idea rather than proposing it directly. Unfortunately, she had learned all too well that the best way to offer an idea to the headstrong and stubborn Galar was to help him discover the idea for himself.

"We are to take the Amber of Life. How could you have forgotten such an important fact?" he asked, confused. The bull's horn told the story of the creation of life and was more sacred to the Isen'bryn than the necklace. It was decided that those who would return to the greater people of the North would take the horn with them. Growing crops and cultivating a new land would be more important to the people heading to the South, so the Amber of Life would be taken. It would be carried with the group around the neck of Mael, the apparent group leader. Kyra pretended to suddenly remember this as she heard him say it. Coyly, she strode in front of Galar and turned to press her back to his chest in a spooning fashion. She grasped his hands from behind and placed them on her lower abdomen.

"The Amber of Life possesses the magic of fertility, does it not?" she asked, slowly rocking her hips back and forth. Galar was no fool, and her meaning quickly became apparent. He resented having been turned down when he had requested to borrow that very item to help bring fertility to Kyra.

"If we could possess the Amber of Life for even a single night, you would definitely have a child. The necklace is so powerful that you might even have several children at once!" he said with a beaming smile. Kyra looked back at him, unsure if he realized how dangerous and painful it was to have one child, let alone multiple.

"With a child, I could become a leader in our new tribe, and nobody would question my vitality," he said. She held back a frown at his self-centered answer, though she had not expected much more.

"Yes... But what if there were more to be had? What if that necklace were given to one of the large tribes of the South? Surely they would reward anyone who brought them such a prized item. Anyone who delivered such a thing would be immediately elevated to a high status within their tribe... An established tribe, with power. A place where our children can grow and where we would immediately be celebrated," she purred. Kyra slowly turned to face Galar. The look on his face told her that he was not entirely unaware that she was attempting manipulation, but the smile on his face suggested that he was open to such manipulation.

"You are suggesting that we take the necklace at some point in the South and trade it to a powerful village? You are much bolder than I give you credit for, my raven," he said as he carefully parted her hair to get a better look at her face. Raven was his pet name for Kyra and perhaps a much more apt choice than he had originally thought when he first used it.

"I don't really have to defeat Brig'dha or Ember. We should just cast this whole mess behind us and find a new tribe where we can live better lives," he said as he slowly pulled the leather cord at the top of ger dress, which fastened the front and back panels, watching the leather spill onto the floor. Kyra tilted her head to the ceiling with her eyes closed and laughed. Her proposal had been accepted, and with some luck, their lives might change for the better. Besides, if Galar could become dominant in a new tribe, and she could control him, then she would become ipso facto elder, without the risk. This is how their relationship worked, mutual manipulation. Then again, Galar's touch was its own subtle manipulation, she decided as she gasped.

ᴐ ᴐ ᴐ

The evening slowly approached as people began their final preparations to leave. It had been decided that the group would leave in the morning, at first light. There was to be a feast to honor and commemorate a people who would never be the same; a final goodbye to friends and family who may never see each other again. Emotions had run high the last few tendays, and there had been many levels of goodbye, but tonight was the last laugh, the last feast... a closing.

Brig'dha could smell the food cooking as she approached Mael, the group leader to head south. Mael was cleaning a rabbit to be cooked for the feast. Fresh game tended to be killed and dressed just before meals if possible. Aside from the coldest days of the cold season, meat did not last very long, cooked or otherwise. An animal could remain uncooked if properly dressed for a day or two and then kept for another day or two after being cooked. Sometimes pieces that had spoiled would have to be cut from the carcass, but anyone foolish enough to eat meat older than this ran the risk that the wandering spirit of the animal might return and kill them from the inside.

Mael stopped what he was doing as he heard someone approaching, turning to find Brig'dha. Memories of the bashful brunette playing as a child returned as he smiled, fondly. Mael was a good man and a well-respected hunter. His wife had died many harvests before from a mysterious illness that simply killed her within a few days. Not all illnesses had a source that could be found. In fact, often, a person would become ill with no known reason and slowly drift into death as their loved ones begged the spirits to save them in vain. This was part of the mystery of life and an ever-present fear in people's lives. Mael had carried on without his wife, but Brig'dha could not help but believe that her death may have helped spur him towards an interest in traveling to the distant lands. No loose ends. Of course, she also had no loose ends among her people. The only one she truly cared for was Ember... but she pushed that thought aside, focusing her mental storm of thoughts into coherent words.

"Brig'dha, always a pleasant surprise. Did you come to watch an old man gut a rabbit? I assure you that there are many more interesting things to see," he jested with a laugh as he scooped out more of the gore from the inside of the rabbit onto a piece of bark that could be taken and disposed of nearby. After a long, silent moment, she replied.

"I was wondering... um, I was wondering just how far we would travel? Ember and I traveled close to the True South, and I was wondering if we would also travel that far," she asked, softly. Mael stopped his cleaning for a moment and turned to regard Brig'dha, who promptly looked away. He had given some thought to a place he would like to go, but he was unsure if the group could make it. He supposed they would just keep traveling until they found a suitable land to settle. He had heard traders speak of a distant sea so vast that it was even larger than the Greatest River. Supposedly, this sea was directly south, all the way. The problem was that he did not know how far "all of the way" was.

"To tell you the truth, I am unsure of how far we will go. I had wondered if perhaps we might journey all the way to the Blue Sea if weather and provisions permit," he spoke, frankly.

"The Blue Sea? Is that a River?" Brig'dha asked. She had not remembered such a place in her journeys. The village where she had nearly been killed was called Nes, and it was situated deep inland, not near a major body of water.

"Aye, the Blue Sea. Think of it as a lake but so big that you cannot see the other shore. Larger than even the Greatest River. If you head south and ever so slightly to the East for many tendays, eventually you hit the water. You'll know that you are in the right place because you will pass mountains on your left after at least three tendays. That is the place that I wish that we could go." Brig'dha pondered this. Mael's plan was bold, but she had already committed to heading south, and she hated changing a plan. After a short silence, she replied softly, almost to herself.

"Ember and I will follow you to the Blue Sea if that's where you want to go. We are not afraid of travel, and we want to help as much as we can." She smiled a forced, nervous smile before turning to leave and heading to the feast. She paused when something wet brushed against her hand, an awful feeling. She looked down to find that Mael was holding the rabbit up to her. Its body was skinned, and it had been cleaned.

"Hey, do you mind taking this to get cooked? I have three more to clean, and it would save me some time. You did say you wanted to help, right?" he said with a smile. Brig'dha suppressed a shy chuckle, though the texture of the flesh touching her hand nearly made her cringe.

Ↄ Ↄ ↄ

The feast was the second largest Ember had ever attended, after the festival of Nes. The entire tribe had gathered around several large bonfires as the Sun sank beneath the sky to wherever it slumbered. The night would be dark with the Moon hiding from view. More and more, Ember had watched the sky with curiosity. She doubted that people would ever understand its mysteries, but that didn't stop her from watching and making her own guesses. Though she enjoyed the Moon, a night like this was extra dark and allowed her to see the great mysterious dots of light that filled the sky. Every now and then, she would see a tiny streak of light fly by. For some reason, the streaks of light never seemed to bump into the small dots of light. Ember wondered if she could ever deduce what these things were if she watched them long enough.

At the moment, her attention was taken by the feast. Before her lay deer hide and rush mats filled with reed dishes and reed bowls covered with various delights, such as the last of the cooked and salted tubers, fresh greens just sprouted from the woods, and roasted nuts from the previous harvest. More wonderful than these were the various meat dishes, from roasted deer to a pate of deer liver with salt and wild onions. On sticks, Ember saw fish roasted thoroughly, everything sprinkled with salt. Due to their proximity to the Greatest River, a salty river, salt was easily obtained and used in many dishes. Ember sometimes wondered if too much of the pleasant substance could be a problem, but how could anything taste so good and be bad?

Once, not long after they had joined the Isen'bryn, Ember had eaten part of a small handful of salt. It tasted so good to lick the salt, but when she was done, she felt strange. For a full day, she had felt sick and wasn't able to do much more than lie in her hut, drink water, and decide the best way to never do such a thing again. Ember still longed for salt, but she would never again overdo it.

Not far down from where she stood next to one of the larger fires knelt Brig'dha, along with Aethen and his friend Caelwyn. Caelwyn was a woodworker of 21 harvests of age, and a master at using an adze, a sharp stone-headed tool with a handle shaped similarly to an ax but specially designed for cutting deep into wood. Caelwyn had long black hair and deep brown eyes, similar to Aethen in many respects though his complexion was generally darker. Caelwyn was not much of a talker, and Ember was pretty sure that he would not keep anyone company on the long trip south. It did seem that most of the people preparing to go to the South were sitting near one another. The majority appeared to be people who did not have extended families or who were not close to their families. That made a lot of sense, considering they may never see one another again.

Ember paused for a moment as thoughts of her mother brought sudden emotions to her mind and a lump in her throat. It had been nearly two harvests since she had left her village and her mother behind. She had promised her mother that she would return one day though she was unsure when that promise would be kept. Life just kept getting in the way, and things were always so complicated. Perhaps she would one day come to peace with this and the many other demons from her past. Ember wondered if other people had regrets, and if they did, how did they deal with them? Her thoughts were interrupted when she heard her name called.

"Hey Ember, come sit with us. We saved you a seat!" yelled Tes, a younger lightly brunette woman with light blue eyes and perhaps the darkest complexion of anyone in the group. Her light-colored hair and eyes were a stark contrast to her dark, tanned skin. The people of Isen'bryn were generally darker than Ember, a mixture of tanned skin and natural darkness found in forest people. Tes and her friend Faenel, a woman with dark hair with heavy bangs, and blue eyes of eighteen harvests, sat side-by-side with an open place in between them and Brig'dha. Next to Faenel lay a small flute made from a bird's bone.

Tes was full of life and nearly as carefree as the talkative Meegin. Besides her contrasting looks, Tes was also known for her obsession with necklaces. There was never a time when at least five of them were not around her neck, and sometimes more. Many of her necklaces were made from basic clay beads, nothing too complicated. Unfortunately, the material to make a fine necklace could be quite costly in trade. As a result, Tes wore whatever she could find or borrow from her friends, such as Faenel.

Faenel was an artist in every respect – she decorated objects for people, played her flute, and even sang. Ember only wished that she could create such beauty, but she was glad that Faenel was along for the trip. Ember enjoyed listening to her sing, often accompanied by Tes dancing. It would be a shorter journey with somebody singing a beautiful song along the way. Of course, while Ember suspected that the long nights around a hot fire along the trip would be made more pleasant with their company, though nothing would make the trip more pleasant than her beautiful friend, Brig'dha… if only she could become more.

ɔ ɔ ɔ
ɔ ɔ ɔ

For the early part of the evening, the feast continued with much laughter, food, and merrymaking. The entire tribe joined in the celebration, and all tears and sorrow at the passing of loved ones or the impending loss of the group to head south had been banished for the night. This was the final time people could laugh together and say goodbye. It was also time for many rituals to be performed involving dance and elaborate costumes. Around fires, people painted from head to toe danced with feathers and masks, imploring the gods for a safe journey and good luck.

As with most feasts, the essential ingredient was food. Ember's people would sometimes celebrate with a magical drink which left a person feeling warm and inebriated, but the people of Isen'bryn did not acquire the magical brew often, and it was only used for the most important sacred rituals. Strangely, it seemed to Ember that the farther south one traveled, the more accessible the magical brew was. In the North, it was treated as a sacred liquid only to be possessed and consumed in small amounts during rituals, while in the South, it constituted a daily food. Ember hoped that the delicious and potent brew would become more accessible as the group traveled south, as she liked the strange out-of-body feeling it gave her.

Ember and Brig'dha sat together on deer hide mats near Mael, who had finally arrived after butchering more rabbits than he cared to remember. Not far down the table set Meegin, her reluctant friend Geb, Geb's husband Nael, Caelwyn, Eryi, Kel, and several others who would be traveling to the South. Ember knew all their faces and all their names, but she had not really learned a lot about some of the people who would be going with her. She did not expect too much trouble from most of the travelers, except perhaps Yan. Almost the moment she thought of him, the creepy man flashed a smile in her direction. Ember gave him a dirty expression and turned her attention to her friends. *You better not be talking about me you creepy son of a badger.*

ↄ ↄ ↄ

"So, do you think I can separate Ember from Brig'dha long enough to get her talking?" Aethen asked his friend Kel as they sat eating and watching the intricate dance moves of a woman named Gheryn. The woman gyrated around the festival area swaying her hips and singing in the mono-toned song of the northern people. Aethen repeated his question to Kel, who had been distracted by the sultry Gheryn.

"Kel, she's almost old enough to be your mother." Kel briefly turned his smile to Aethen, the smile of a wolf.

"She can be my mother anytime if she can dance like that," Kel said, uncharacteristically. While generally shy and not one to make inappropriate jokes, Kel had a soft spot for dancing, and the much older Gheryn was easily winning him over with her beautiful and well-practiced dance moves, uncommon among the Isen'bryn, who were not known for dancing. Aethen shook his head and asked his question a third time, this time finally receiving a response.

"The only time that Ember separates from Brig'dha is when she relieves herself, hunts, or goes swimming, which she hasn't done recently because of the cold. So, you can either become a tree in the woods and get urinated on, or a deer and get murdered, or a fish in the river and be lonely, but, either way, getting her attention will not come easy," Kel said with a smile. Athen considered his words, issuing an affirming grunt.

"Besides, I think they are both into women, so good luck," Kel laughed. Aethen frowned, quite sure that wasn't true. Brig'dha had married Mohdan and Ember was just... well, Ember. Sure, she gazed longingly at the befuddled brunette. Everyone saw and there had been speculation since Brig'dha was a child, but never had done anything in so long, which made no sense if they held any interest. No one was that dense, he laughed for reassurance. Aethen wondered if Kel had been drinking some of the sacred brew, given his uncharacteristically verbose responses, but perhaps the dancer was bringing it out of him.

Seeing that the younger man was completely enthralled, the older Gheryn maneuvered her way towards him, undulating even more than before and simply amusing herself at his apparent interest. Ember had been watching the dance as well when suddenly her eyes crossed paths with Aethen. Ember smiled back and then returned her eyes to the dancer, far to curious how she was able to make her back bend so far without breaking.

Aethen felt as though his heart had just stopped – the radiant redhead had just looked his way.

"Did you see that she looked right at me?!" he said excitedly to Kel.

"Why don't you go ask her if she can dance?" Kel suggested.

ꙅ ꙅ ꙅ

The dancing had ended, and many of the people had already left for bed as the feast wound down. Aethen sat on a makeshift wooden bench with his back against a hut eating a piece of deer meat from the stick on which it had been roasted. Many people had paired off to do what must be done after any celebration, but there were still plenty gathered around the central fires finishing off the rest of the food and trying to enjoy themselves as best as they could on a somber occasion, such as this.

Unlike the others, Aethen was not quite so downtrodden. At nineteen harvests of age, he was two harvests past the age where men began their quest for a wife, though this process often took multiple harvests with many men not finding a wife until their twenties. Aethen was not unattractive by his tribe's standards. His long black hair was tied in many braids, and his gray eyes held a mysterious attraction to many of the women of Isen'bryn. On many occasions, women had tried their best to attract his attention, but all of them had fallen short. It was only when he had met Ember that Aethen finally realized what he had been searching for.

Ember had an exotic flair about her. She was a long-haired redhead with green eyes, rare among forest people and uncommon among river dwellers. Besides her hair and eyes, nothing else was normal. Her face was slightly sharper defined than most women, with very high arching eyebrows and an intense stare, and her physique was reasonably muscular. Her native language also sounded different from what his people spoke, and he had heard her talking on several occasions, typically to herself. For some reason, he found this absolutely enticing. Her clothes were even different, having a different cut and shape. Instead of thick leather, Ember tended to wear many layers of lighter and thinner leather. Besides her clothes, she also wore much different body paints. She tended to wear lines and dotted patterns, while the Isen'bryn often used swirls. Unfortunately, his musings were interrupted by Kel.

"Hey, are you still alone? There are several women out there whose families would be quite happy to take you in. You just need to open up to them. Trust me, there's nothing quite so satisfying as women," he said as he came to find out why one of his friends was sitting by himself on such a liminal night. Kel was a dark-haired man with blue eyes of seventeen harvests age. Though adventurous and one of the best trackers Aethen had met, Kel was also quite shy among women. To hear him now boasting of a woman's touch as if he had much experience was enough to snap Aethen out of his thoughts of Ember.

"I know you're right, and before the attack, I was just about ready to give up and see if maybe Eryi or An were interested, but now we are headed south... Things have changed." Kel understood what he meant, but he really wished he could convince Aethen to choose a local woman. Normally, men traveled to new villages to find a wife, but there wasn't time for that now. Aethen had almost asked out An, but she was not headed south. Her family had several elders, so she would head north. Kel was looking forward to the trip to the South and to new faces. It had only been this previous warm season that he had broken up with Kesae, a slightly older woman he had been courting for some time, though there was a rumor that she had broken up with him, though neither would speak of it and Kasae's sister would merely give knowing looks when asked.

"Well, if you are going to sit back here and stare at the women from a distance, I guess I will let it pass this time. I mean, we are about to leave on a trip south, so... I suppose you have a point," he conceded. Aethen glanced up at Kel with a bemused smile. A childhood friend and cousin through his mother's line, Kel was the only man he had ever met who would try this hard to set him up with a woman. How could he possibly be angry at the man?

"Speaking of women, Gheryn seemed quite interested in showing off for you," Aethen teased as Kel turned to leave. Kel looked back with a catty smile, but said nothing, leaving his friend for an unspecified location. Aethen chose not to inquire as Kel hurried off.

CHAPTER FIVE

THE SOUTH

The Isen'bryn were a fictitious late Mesolithic people who originally came from what are now the lands around Edinburgh, Scotland. Several decades before Brig'dha was born, two smaller tribes merged and traveled south to lands now occupied by the town of Cromer, on the Eastern shore of England (known as East of England), to exploit the land expanse of Doggerland. Brig'dha's people who stayed behind, returning north, would one day become part of the many peoples who made up the Picts of Pictland (approximately present-day Scotland).

Spirits were high as the group headed out, waving their goodbyes to the village of Isen'bryn. There had been some sniffles here and there, and a few were somber, but most of the group maintained an aire of cheeriness, if not somewhat forced. This was their big adventure, and the small group had prepared itself over many tendays for the emotions they now faced. The big question was how this trip would turn out? Only a few of them had ever been greater than a few days distance from the tribe, aside from Brig'dha, Ember, and Mael. In a way, this made them ipso facto experts of the wilds. Ember and Brig'dha slowly trudged along toward the back of the group. Most of the others had never been on a long-distance trek and were eager to rush along as fast as they could go. Ember and Brig'dha knew better and walked more slowly in the back, waiting for the inexperienced to lose their excited attitudes.

Walking every day tended to cause pains in the shins and back of the legs, as well as in the feet. In fact, the group would probably walk for at least half of the day, each day, for as many as five days in a row before taking a day off to rest. It wasn't long before the travelers learned that the best course of action was not to achieve the greatest distance each day but to reach a reasonable pace with plenty of rest. Failure to set a comfortable pace and take plenty of rest would result in injury to the body and overall failure to reach one's goals. Extensive time spent walking would also require plenty of food, which a traveling group could not easily obtain. The average person might require double the usual amount of food due to exertion.

To pass the time, Ember had brought a smooth wooden branch half the length of her arm and a sharp piece of rock which was not good enough to become a real tool. Every time she saw an animal, she would make a notch in the stick. Ember figured that she would do this each day for a tenday and see if the number of animals changed. Maybe there were more animals in the North versus the South? It was one way to find out. The big trouble facing Ember was whether to count birds. The strange flying creatures would slowly return en masse, but they were hard to spot for right now. She suspected that she should stick solely to ground creatures.

Meanwhile, Brig'dha passed the time keeping her eyes open for any interesting rocks she might find. She doubted that she would find anything so amazing as a copper nugget, but a very small and high-quality pebble could be made into a good pendant for a necklace. Perhaps, by the time the trip ended, she would have just such a necklace, and might be able to trade it to Tes for something. The problem was that the mind had to remain somewhat occupied during long travel to ensure that people didn't become angry and start fighting. As a result, whenever a group of people walked for a long distance, they were encouraged to preoccupy themselves with such mundane tasks.

Aethen slowly shaped a knife blade of flint using pressure from a small piece of deer antler. Doing this while walking was extremely difficult and required significant concentration. Extended periods would pass between each fleck being removed, but this was a good technique given the considerable time he would be walking. The only thing that would have made this more perfect would have been if Ember had been walking in front of him. He would never tell her because it would make him sound strange, but he liked to look at her. She interested him in some way he could not quite describe, an interest that was not purely physical. It was as though her presence inspired him.

He still could not understand how Meegin and her friends Faenel and Geb could spend the entire time chatting, though Geb actually seemed to listen. Behind him, he could hear the women constantly chattering about various things. Over time, he realized that their chatting had a particular rhythm. He could not hear what they said most of the time, but he could hear the sounds of their words. One would start speaking slowly, then fast, then slowly again. In rhythmic waves, the speech would finally pick up towards a climax, and the other two women could be heard either giggling or saying something simultaneously. The strange pattern, up, down, up, then maximum, and finally giggles, continued day in and day out. He figured that they would eventually tire of this maddening rhythm, but he wasn't sure how long it might take.

As they walked, the scenery continued unchanged for the first few days. The skies were a dark blue with the infinite expanse of the Greatest River to the left and wide-open fields of shrubbery and rock to the right. Finding open paths to walk upon was complex, given the overgrowth of the terrain. Walking on the shore was even more treacherous, given that the beaches were often made from vast quantities of fist-sized or larger rocks. The air was crisp and cool with the salty taste and the smell of the Greatest River.

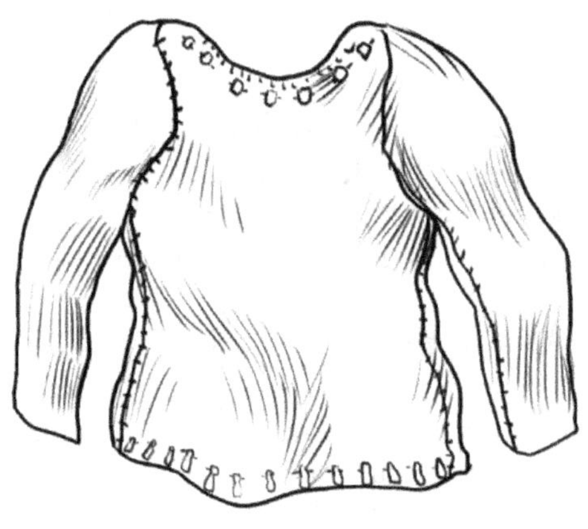

Leather shirt with beadwork

Most people wore thick leather leggings with extra-long and wide loincloths or leather wrap skirts, and boots made of leather hide and stuffed with dried grasses, leaves, or bast fibers. Ember wore her long doeskin leather shirt with black painted spots under her fox fur coat, along with a pair of leather leggings and a soft, roe deer loincloth. Her feet were clad in boots made from a lime bark fiber frame with leather soles, stuffed with grass. Beside her, Brig'dha strode wearing a soft leather shirt with a beaver fur coat, her legs protected by a leather wrap skirt, leather leggings, and a short loincloth beneath the skirt. Her feet were warmed by bast fiber frame shoes, similar to Ember's.

"It works, just like you said," Brig'dha abruptly said to Ember, pointing at her darkened skin. Ember had suggested that applying a small amount of nut oil mixed with three-times-burned animal bone char would produce a beautiful and rich pigment. The oily pigment would block the bitterness of the cold wind. Moreover, black always seemed to heat up faster in the Sun than any other color. If they had left at a much colder time, they would have worn even more, but they were caught in that terrible time between cold and warm when the temperature fluctuated quite often. Ember laughed at the overly dark areas on Brig'dha's face, but as the Greatest River's bitterly cold wind suddenly caught her face, and her laugh blew away with it.

"Do you have any more of that pigment?" Ember asked as Brig'dha began to smile.

Far ahead of the rest of the group, Mael walked with Yan blazing the trail. Mael continued to hold his stomach as he had been for at least a tenday of late. For the last harvest, he had felt a pain in his stomach that came and went with food and rest. He had dismissed it as just the result of growing older, but he had felt nauseated and vomited the previous day, and there had been blood. They had slept well the night before, and today he felt better, but he was beginning to worry that his sickness was an evil spirit.

Evil spirits could become trapped within the body and fester until they killed the host. Sometimes they would grow as large protrusions from the body. In the mainland, they could sometimes grow around the base of the neck, becoming large bulges, though he had never seen anything like that in the tribes living near the water. This was probably because certain types of spirits inhabited certain types of areas. He hoped that whatever was causing his stomach pain would soon leave. He had even considered asking the priestess Brig'dha for help, but he did not want to cause anyone worry. If he toughed it out, it would likely go away as everything always had. He just wished that it would not sap his strength as it did.

Five days of walking were followed by a day of rest. After this, five more days of walking would follow as the group trudged along, hoping to reach the most eastern shore of the island of Inn'bry'th at a good time for crossing the Greatest River. This easternmost point was known to be the best point to make any trip to the mainland. Conveniently, a large tribe was nestled right at this spot. Mael had brought with him several goods to trade for passage across the water. The way the system worked, there was a tribe on either side, and trade was performed between them. The tribes tended to wait until either enough trade goods waited for passage or until somebody provided a valuable enough trade before setting out.

The actual trip across the Greatest River was not always safe, and now and then, someone would die. This was the cost of trade.

Ɔ Ɔ Ɔ

It was upon a night of rest, six days after the group had left the Isen'bryn, when the Moon had finally descended to nearly below the horizon somewhere in the South. The night would be darker than most but a perfectly good time to relax. The following day would be a full day to recover and prepare for the next few days of walking. Most of the group sat around a large campfire with their feet fully uncovered even though the temperature was still cold. Those used to walking had tougher feet, but some of the travelers sported large blisters and sore patches. If not for the fact that they approached the village which would see them across the Greatest River, the group would have chosen to stay for several days and recover. Throughout many tendays, the walking routine would become easier as each member became more rugged.

As the group sat around the campfire, the oldest stories were told of a time when a human sacrifice was performed to ensure a safe journey across the water. Most group members found the idea offensive, but Mael explained that times were different. Mael waved his hands in the air over the crackling fire as he theatrically described all the terrible details of the sacrifice, a virgin woman, of course. Ember couldn't imagine what made a virgin so desirable, yet this strange feature was pervasive in many tales, regardless of how silly it really was. People were always interested in hearing scary stories, especially on a dark night by a hot fire. It was a joyful exchange of clichés. Ember nudged Geb with a smile and whispered a joke.

"Another good reason not to be a virgin, huh?" Geb turned an incredulous look upon Ember, a woman not known to have yet been with a man. Ember seemed pleased with her dirty little joke, and so the older married woman simply rolled her eyes and returned her attention to the story. A slight smile crept across her otherwise stern features. Geb always had a place in her heart for inappropriately funny jokes, though she wouldn't discuss it with anyone. Mael continued with his story, having missed the exchange.

"These days, we don't do such things. We have become civilized and no longer sacrifice for such reasons. We would only sacrifice to our gods if the signs show that there was no other way to avert some major disaster," he said.

"I don't see anything wrong with sacrificing an enemy warrior, like one of those raiders," offered Yan. He paused for a moment to see if anybody would disagree. Ember strongly disagreed, but she held her tongue, not wanting to get into the middle of an argument with Yan and, by extension, his friend Galar. Though Yan believed strongly in what he was saying, deep down, he was hoping he could engage Ember in an argument. He had always believed that the best strategy to pick up a woman was to engage with her. Even an argument was still engagement, and over time, he hoped that he might win Ember over.

Yan's biggest problem was separating her from the annoying brunette. Brig'dha never seemed to have an interest in any man, and she was always by Ember's side, preventing him from striking up a conversation. He had tried several times, but always Brig'dha would glare at him until he left. He just couldn't understand why he always had so much trouble with women, but sometimes a hunt required persistence. Seeing no disagreement, he continued.

"When you think about it, if the gods do favor the Isen'bryn, sacrificing our enemies to them is the only right thing to do. I'm sure this would please the Horned God, and maybe the Greatest River spirits. If you sacrifice one of the raiders and toss his body into the river, of course..." Ember turned her attention from Yan's explanation and muttered something to Brig'dha, which caught Galar's attention. Yan paused as he noticed Galar glaring at Ember.

"I'm sorry, Ember, what was that you said? You'll have to speak up. We didn't hear you," Galar said aloud in a condescending tone. Ember did not stand, but softly spoke, more to Yan than anyone else.

"It's easy to say that you will kill someone until you look them in the eyes and do it. No matter how much you hate your enemy, no matter how evil you think they are, you can't forget the pleading look in their eyes... The pain and the fear..." Ember dropped her head, and the group went silent. It was apparent to everyone who watched that Ember spoke from experience. Yan stood looking slightly embarrassed as Galar continued to glare at her.

Ember slowly stood and stepped away from the group with Brig'dha close behind, worried that she had just dampened the mood. Yan looked at everybody quite confused. He could not quite understand why she took the discussion so far, so fast. Somehow, he had triggered a very emotional and abrupt response. This was the death of enemies to his people that he spoke of, not the murder of innocent people. The thought of clubbing a raider in single combat and the glory such an act would bring did nothing but excite his imagination. Why couldn't she understand that need for glory? *You're just a fearful woman. You don't understand real power and glory,* he thought to himself. Deep down, he wondered why he had not dared to say that to her face.

ɔ ɔ ɔ

Eleven days had passed since the group had left the Isen'bryn with few signs of civilization. They had passed a few Geru'nas, wooden poles used to moor boats and used as signposts to lead people between villages. The group had often caught sight of small villages off in the distance or people fishing in a stretched hide boat. Overall, the landscape was quite beautiful and devoid of people. This wasn't a problem for Ember as she continued slicing notches in her sticks for each animal she saw. With 11 sticks notched, she had found that the number of animals seemed pretty consistent even as they traveled south. She supposed that a larger distance might be needed before noticing a change.

Ember had noticed that Meegin collecting feathers for Geb while Kel and Aethen tended to scout ahead, looking for food or anything which might prove a danger to the group. Yan had kept his distance from Ember following their heated exchange a few days before while Kyra and Galar kept to themselves. Overall, the group spread out with more and more distance between each person as time passed. This was expected as tensions between people always seemed to climb during the monotony of walking. Next to Ember, Brig'dha trudged along now and then bending over to examine a shiny pebble from the ground. For some reason, Ember found this habit quite amusing.

Brig'dha had not found many decent rocks, but she had found a multitude of beautiful feathers, a fact which had brought much chagrin from Meegin. A large collection of feathers, especially songbird feathers, could be worth a great deal in trade to the right people. Being of the giving sort, she had offered some of the prized feathers to Geb, the fletcher. Of course, Geb was quite used to being given free feathers, as many people liked her. She could never figure out why as she rarely said much and was never one to honey any words.

With all the feathers, she was glad she had brought her entire supply of long, straight shafts for making arrows, which she kept in a quiver over her back. As they camped each night, Geb would use a thin obsidian razor to slice the best feathers lengthwise, making two fins from each. As she walked the next day, she would tie three of these fins into place using a piece of bark fiber or deer sinew. Over time, she would apply pine tar to glue the feathers in place, then carefully wrap the fins tightly to the shaft using small sinew pieces. She would place a piece of sinew and her mouth and slowly chew on it for a few moments before removing it and carefully wrapping it around the feathers. The most important part was the twist – the slight twisting of a feather that made the arrow more accurate.

Creating tools, foods, and other goods was a nonstop effort, and even while walking, the work continued. The result was a functioning society that never ran out of the necessary tools it needed to keep going, even on the move. When Geb finished an arrow, she would hand it to Eryi, a natural artist, to paint. After each arrow was painted, it would be given to Brig'dha for blessing by the Goddess. Each blessed arrow was then distributed to anyone who needed it. The result was a juxtaposition of beauty and lethality. It only took the sight of a beautiful bird mauling a small insect to remind anyone of how commonplace nature arrived at this arrangement.

On her back Ember carried a quiver of twelve arrows and a few extra arrow shafts that did not have heads, and a couple of extra microlith, composite arrowheads, loose. Arrows were divided into an arrowhead with a small shaft protruding from its back which then connected to the full-length arrow shaft with feathered fletching at the end. When an arrow entered an animal, the shaft would often become detached but non-destructively because it merely slipped off. The arrowhead would be embedded deep within the animal and slowly wiggle its way around, causing more damage until the animal died. It was an effective way to kill animals and provide the group's food – a necessity.

Ɔ Ɔ Ɔ

The day had been long, and the night was soon to come when the group exited a copse of trees, and a small village came into sight. By the look of it, this was the village that Mael had been expecting to find slightly earlier that day. Of course, measuring time and distance was extremely difficult, and arrival expectations were at best an educated guess, but more likely just a hunch. Even so, the group was quite amazed that they had made it this far in such a short time. All that lay before them was the vast expanse of water known as the Greatest River.

The group halted upon a hill overlooking the small village set right on the water's edge. The village was surrounded by a small wooden palisade, something not found with the Isen'bryn. The huts were small wooden structures built from simple groups of long poles bound together with sinew and mud. The roofs of the buildings were made of thatch and rush. Some of the structures were built directly into the sides of low hills encircling portions of the village, while others were constructed on wooden stilts to prevent damage from flooding. This reminded Ember of Isen'bryn construction, ever so slightly. By her guess, she would suspect that as many as 100 people lived in this village, making it absolutely giant for the island.

The village was alive with people carrying out their daily lives. The scene was as domestic and commonplace as any village Ember had ever beheld. Men created stone tools or chopped wood into planks while women scraped-clean leather stretched over a wooden frame or chased about small children who ran freely in the village. Much of the village set upon a hillock elevated nearly two lengths of a man above the sandy beach. It was upon this sandy beach that Ember could see several large boats as well as a few smaller vessels, each moored to a geru'nas.

While the small boats were made of wooden frames with stretched hide creating their outer walls, the larger boats were made from massive fallen tree trunks. Each of the large tree trunk boats looked like it could hold as many as six or seven grown men and perhaps more women. The boats were reasonably wide with a deep keel and intrinsically strong. Each boat was made from a single tree trunk of exceptional size. Ember could only imagine how long it would have taken to fell each tree and construct a boat. With the help of the people from Tornhemal, Ember had created such a boat herself over a full harvest before, though on a much smaller scale.

The centers of the boats were dug out in a process that required hot coals from a fire being deposited in the center of the wood. This created small, controlled fires which could be used to char the inside wood until it was wide enough to fit a person. Such boats could not carry many people, but they were extremely rugged, made from a solid piece of wood. In all respects, the larger dugout boats resembled Ember's boat except for their vastly larger form. Ember could not even guess as to how heavy they must be.

As the group approached, several village men stepped forward with weapons, but they were not raised, nor did they seem hostile. It seemed that they were used to travelers, but nobody ever let their guard completely down. Mael stepped forward and raised his hand in greeting.

"We come to trade for passage across the Greatest River," he spoke slowly and clearly, but it appeared that the men before him understood his words as they smiled and nodded.

Entering the village, Ember could not help but notice how similar these people looked to the Isen'bryn. The weather was still quite chilly, and many people wore clothing somewhere between their winter and warm weather clothing. Ember saw a man standing over a pile of logs, cutting them in half with a stone ax. He wore leather leggings that attached to his waist belt. Looped through the belt was a long deer leather loincloth with dark patterns burned into it, though his warm, felt shirt hung so far below his waist that the loincloth could barely be seen. His feet were covered in thick but sturdy leather boots, and he wore what looked like a fox fur hat, every seem detailed with bone beads. The man glanced up from what he was doing and gave Ember a wink. She smiled back at him, not wanting to upset the locals, a friendly sort.

"All right, everyone, wait right here while I go find whoever is in charge and secure passage. We will probably stay here for the night and perhaps leave in the morning if the signs are right," Mael announced with a half-smile. Next, Brig'dha awkwardly stepped forward to address the group, a very uncharacteristic move for the shy priestess.

"I will be happy to read the signs and see if tomorrow is a good day to travel," she said, shyly. Though several of the group seemed to accept this offer as an obvious eventuality, Galar blatantly offered a different opinion.

"That will not be necessary. I'm not sure we can trust the signs the Goddess provides you, given your history, of course. We should ask a local priest," he said in a reasonably neutral tone. Brig'dha barely looked at him, her eyes rimmed with sadness and anger. How long were people going to judge her for that? All she had done was survive. What about not dying made her so suspicious? Brig'dha was about to say something when Ember placed a warm hand on her shoulder. Ember was no stranger to adversity or a judgmental audience – her only real friend.

"Don't worry about them. Let's step over to the water and read the signs. You can let Mael know what you find. Perhaps we will let Galar or his sister, err... I mean, wife, find a local priest," Ember said, trying to hold back a smirk. Galar glanced at the two women, his neutral expression still intact, unwilling to take the obvious bait. Anyone who knew him well knew that when he held that calm, neutral expression, it was about as far from his actual feelings as one could get. Kyra stepped forward with her large pack hoping that her husband Galar would help her remove it. When she looked up, she noticed that everyone was staring at Ember and Galar with apprehension. She had a feeling that she had just missed some exchange, but she hoped that Galar had everything under control.

"Stop messing around and help me get this pack off," she barked. Ember and Brig'dha chuckled as they walked off, taking that interruption as a cue to leave with their victory in hand. Barely perceptible to most, Kel was sure that he saw Galar's right eye twitch.

ɔ ɔ ɔ

Brig'dha removed her boots and carefully waded into the cold waters of the Greatest River, up to her shins. There was no way to read the signs of the gods without getting her feet wet though she hoped that she had cleared her mind enough to hear them. Ember sat on a driftwood log, just taking in the joy of not walking. There was something wonderful about not having to move, at least for a little while. The day had been long and exhausting. Suddenly, Ember caught sight of a tiny creature walking across the sand.

"A crab!" she exclaimed and began to pursue the tiny creature. The moon priestess turned to watch the fuss as the random redhead chased the curious crustacean across the sandy beach. She smiled, always adoring Ember's antics, though many found them annoying. The warrior was a friend, yet she wished so much that they could be more. Had she not caught Ember peering at her? Were the signs not there? Why wouldn't she just confess her feelings or ask her if she liked women? Why was she more afraid to take that risk than a voyage across the same water that had nearly killed her? As she watched Ember diving for the crab and ending up with a face full of sand, she realized the answer. If she never risked asking, she could never be let down. Yet if she never tried… She pushed such thoughts aside, needing mental clarity for her magic.

It was not long before Brig'dha felt the strange sensation of tingling traveling up her legs and down her spine. At first, she thought it was merely the cold, as she could barely feel her feet. However, it wasn't long before she realized that what she was feeling was quite possibly an omen. She glanced back at Ember to find her friend crawling around on the beach, apparently digging for small crabs that lived in the wet sand. Ignoring her eccentric friend, Brig'dha continued to wade farther into the water with her arms outstretched, pleading with the Goddess to provide more insight. The winds blew across her skin, and upon them, she could feel the danger that was to come – a subtle omen of danger to come.

Brig'dha was sure that the following day was not a good day to travel the waters, but how could she make anyone believe her? The poisonous words of Galar had already tainted the group. Brig'dha emerged from the water carrying her boots and full of ominous dismay. Ember looked up from the sands where she was digging for crabs. She had almost got ahold of one of the little creatures but quickly abandoned her crustacean quest at the sight of Brig'dha, forlorn.

"I guess that the Goddess doesn't look fondly upon our trip tomorrow?" she asked. Brig'dha shook her head no, but she had no words, only dismay. Brig'dha felt defeated until she looked up and saw Ember standing before her with a smile. Something about Ember always brought her strength. She had never felt that way with anyone else, not even her late husband.

"We will find Mael and tell him what you have seen. I'm sure he will listen as he isn't a fool like Galar. Now, stop moping and help me catch some crabs! If the birds can eat them, so can we! Enough salt makes anything taste good," Ember said with enthusiasm. In truth, she would have traded all the crabs she found for a bowl of salted cheese curds, a dish Forest People didn't seem to make as they didn't raise goats or sheep.

Brig'dha couldn't help but smile as she watched the redhead scurrying around the ground, chasing the curious crustacean. No matter how glum she was, the random redhead could always make her laugh. No one had made Brig'dha feel that way. The two friends spent a short time by the water hunting the small and elusive creatures, hoping to make some form of crab roast as Ember began to chat about some salted food made from goat's milk that left Brig'dha feeling slightly ill.

Ↄ Ↄ ↄ

That night the group sat cramped in a little hut waiting for the early morning to travel. Mael had just explained to everyone that tomorrow morning would be the best time for the trip. The local priest, a scrawny and balding man, named Grel, had exclaimed that the signs were good and favorable for a voyage. The group needed to leave just as the Sun rose. Each boat would carry eight people, two boats in total. The plan was to have three or four people rowing at a time, switching whenever they grew tired to the next group. If the rowing could be maintained at this pace, they might make landfall sometime late at night.

According to Grel, the Moon would not appear until a short time after sunset. It would remain for most of the night though it would only be halfway lit and quite low on the horizon. This was not the best Moon condition, but waiting for a full Moon that lasted most of the night would mean quite a lengthy stay. The big danger was to be trapped at night on the water in a storm or even simply without any moonlight. The Greatest River could become so dark that you could barely see an arm's length away.

Brig'dha and Ember listened to the pronouncement with dismay. They had tried to get spread privately to Mael for the entire evening, but he had been in the headman's hut for most of that time, and they had not had a single chance. Worse, it appeared that the local priest had an entirely different opinion of the situation. This did not bode well as the local priest would be more used to the weather patterns in this area than Brig'dha. Slightly emboldened, due more to frustration than lifted spirits, Brig'dha waited until Mael was finished and then stood to offer her suggestion. As she stood, all speech around the fire came to a halt as people waited to hear what she had to say, a common curtesy.

"The signs in the water say differently," Brig'dha all but whispered. "The spirits of the water speak of rough weather to come. I do not know if the rough weather will come tomorrow, but I urge caution. I have been in these waters before, and they are full of danger, vast monsters, and terrible storms." Yan made a snorting noise at her comments while Galar rolled his eyes. Kyra next spoke, her smile cool and calm.

"We thank you for your opinion, but I think that we should probably listen to the priest who knows what he is talking about. He has lived by the Greatest River for most of his life and is likely in good favor with the gods," she said with an aire of superiority. Brig'dha looked down after being chastised so directly. She was not a very confrontational person. She had met with this sort of reaction since she had returned to her people. She sometimes wondered why she and Ember had even stayed with them. The reality was that they had nowhere else to go after making it to the island. Hungry and tired, both women had needed a place to stay until they had recovered. Over a harvest had passed since that fateful day, and Brig'dha was glad to be free from her people. She no longer identified with the Isen'bryn and secretly wished that she and Ember might just leave once they reached the mainland.

In truth, Brig'dha did not know where they might go, but she had no interest in staying with her people. Perhaps they might live with Ember's Great River people, but Ember did not seem to have any interest in that, either. Brig'dha had brought this up many times before, and Ember had always changed the subject. She had never spoken of any falling out between herself and her people. In fact, Ember spoke highly of her mother and even wore a goddess pendant given to her by a friend who lived in her tribe. Ember's aversion to returning to her people was quite a mystery. She wondered if Ember felt the same way she did, or maybe it was wanderlust? Perhaps she would bring it up when, if, they made it to the mainland.

Ember watched Brig'dha slowly sink her head in thought. She assumed that Brig'dha was upset again at being shut down so quickly, but there was not much Ember could do. What she wanted to do was leave the people of Isen'bryn and take Brig'dha with her to some incredible place that they had never seen before. The idea of leaving for the great unknown was perhaps one of the most revolutionary ideas she had ever heard in her life, but she had done it before, and technically, it was what she was doing right now. The only difference would be that she and Brig'dha could do it alone and be free of the strife of these people.

She also had the burning desire to slap the smirk off Kyra's pretty face. She doubted the smug woman had any idea how close Ember had come just moments before to doing just that. Ember was not one for fighting, but she had been known to get into fights when she was a child. Ember hated bullies, and more than one of her peers had run back to their longhouse with a bloodied nose or blacked eye after Ember had caught them bullying others. Her mother would frown to know she remained proud of each bully she slapped. Unfortunately, the best strategy now would simply be to leave and find a new place once they reached the fabled True South.

Of all places that existed in the world, the one place that Ember wanted to visit was the True South. She heard stories of strange people with exotic ways who lived in massive villages. As it was told, the air was always warm, and the snow never came. Vast villages spanned large fields and could house more than 300 people. Perhaps when they reached the mainland, assuming they weren't eaten by some monster or drowned in a storm, Ember might bring the idea up to Brig'dha and see if she held any interest. She was utterly fed up with the likes of the bigot Galar, creepy Yan, and that daughter of an aurochs, Kyra.

CHAPTER SIX

LIVE!

Crossing large bodies of water was perhaps the most dangerous act of travel that could be found in the Neolithic world, mountain passes likely being second. Boats were not large nor designed for the extreme weather conditions that could be found on large bodies of water. A large wave or even a significant wind gust could topple a boat and deposit its occupants into the cold, dark water. Skilled or not, the North Sea was not a safe place for Neolithic travelers. Yet, evidence shows that Neolithic people were seafarers, developing and using many kinds of boats, including ocean-going craft.

The water was reasonably smooth when the two boats set out. Boat Master Vaerl was the man who would take them across the water, though the calm water did not seem to cheer him up even a little, evident as he perpetually grumbled. On the contrary, he seemed to frown about every part of the trip. Each boat now held eight people. Usually, one of the larger dugout boats might hold only five or six people, but several of the people in each boat were younger women who were typically lighter than most men. Additionally, very few supplies were taken, though Ember nearly had a tantrum until the water supplies were doubled. Worse, the boats sat lower in the water than Vaerl would have liked, but the trip had been well prayed for, and the weather did look calm.

As the navigator and veteran of several dozen crossings, Vaerl grumbled at the prow of the lead boat with Ember, Brig'dha, Aethen, Meegin, Geb, Nael, and Tes. The other boat was a short distance behind with Mael, Fanel, Galar, Kyra, Yan, Kel, Caelwyn, and Eryi. The entire experience would give Ember and Brig'dha an exciting chance to see how a more professional sailor made his way across the great expanse of water. Ember's first trip, technically Brig'dha's second, had been amateur at best, and they were lucky to have lived.

Ember was glad that Yan sat in a different boat from her. The night before, he had again made an advance on her. Each time he approached over the last few tendays, she had told him to leave her alone and had quietly stepped away. She knew that some men could be quite aggressive, and for that matter, some women too, but this was getting very annoying, if not a little creepy. If she had been forced to share a boat ride with the man, she was pretty sure that only one of them would make it to the next shore, and she was also pretty sure she would be the one.

The difference in seamanship was immediately apparent. Vaerl sat in the front of the boat, where he constantly kept an eye on the position of the rising Sun and the shifts in the winds, seemingly annoyed by each. He would hold a long piece of reed in his hand and see which direction the wind blew or toss a small bit of wood into the water to watch it float by to gauge their speed. Ember's interest in Vaerl's techniques ended pretty shortly when Aethen, Geb, and Tes tired and swapped rowing duties with Brig'dha, Nael, and Ember. Meegin stayed in reserve, ready to take over for anyone who became overly tired.

Not far astern, the other boat stayed close, always ensuring that they did not get too far behind. There had not been room for a second navigator in the already packed boats, making it critical that the boats remain together. Typically, Vaerl would never have attempted such a daring crossing with so many people, but his priest had assured him that the fair weather would remain, and the trade had been considerable. He still grumbled as he watched the horizon.

The day progressed with smooth waters, and only a few clouds in the western sky lazily blew their way. The morning's clouds had been slightly reddish with the light of dawn, but all in all, it was shaping up to be an uneventful day. Brig'dha was beginning to think the local priest, Grel, had been correct and that the signs she had seen had been false, or she had interpreted them incorrectly. The Sun was now low on the horizon, and the wind had picked up a little, the water becoming slightly choppy. Soon it would become dark... very dark. The group would stop rowing and take a break until the Moon rose a short time after sunset. Assuming Grel, Vaerl, and she were correct about the Moon, Brig'dha suspected that they would have illumination for the rest of the night. This would be significant if any headway were to be made.

At the very stern of the second boat, Mael sat holding his stomach and hoping for the best. His pains had been getting worse though he was unsure if he was merely suffering from the sickness which came from the water and affected some people. His racing heart did little to distract from the pain and waves of lightheadedness rolling through his body. Whatever the strange illness he had been feeling over the past few tendays was, it seemed to be worsening. It sapped his strength, leaving him weaker than he had ever been. If it got much worse, he would need to tell the party and perhaps even delay walking for maybe a tenday while he fought off whatever it was. With the night approaching and his turn at rowing concluded, he lay back in the dugout to nap and regain what strength he could. He felt the solid weight of the Amber of Life necklace around his neck, and it gave him some comfort.

As he lay back looking at the slowly appearing stars overhead, his thoughts drifted to his long-dead wife. He would like to have brought her along, but that was not to be. At least he could help his fellow tribesmen find a new life in the South. He might even convince them to let him be the leader so he could stop having to do so much. He laughed at the notion, but another sharp pain ended the laugh. Whatever this was, he hoped it wouldn't get worse.

Mael awoke from his short nap to find the Greatest River suddenly much more dangerous than when he had closed his eyes. Calm waters had been replaced with large swells lifting the boat greater than the length of a man and then slowly dropping them again. It only took him a moment to realize that a storm was soon to be upon them. Not far ahead, he could see the other boat with somebody waving at them to come closer, though he could not quite make out who it was in the rough water. At least, the Moon had not been completely blocked by clouds, though it only peaked through small holes in the canopy above. The pains in his stomach were agonizing from sitting on the boat for so long without proper rest, and the sudden stress was only amplifying the strange weakness in his body.

"Quickly, row so that we can hear what the people on the other boat are trying to say!" Mael yelled to his team, grabbing an oar and heeding his own words. It was only a short while before the second boat had pulled close to the first. Mael tried to signal with his hands and yell to the other boat but was having trouble due to spray and wind. The water was fast becoming frighteningly rough. He could make out boat master Vaerl yelling something on the other boat. Mael leaned forward and cupped his hand around his ears so he could hear what the other man was screaming.

"I saw fire… ahead! The shore is dead ahead! Row hard! Our lives depend on it!" Vaerl screamed, into the storm, waiting for Mael to acknowledge him. Mael wasted no time ordering his boat to row as hard as possible. Everyone groaned as they pulled as hard as they could against the rough waters. The icy spray of the Greatest River was monstrous and drenched everyone as the swells lifted the boat high into the air and dropped it suddenly. What frightened everyone most was the knowledge that even though the swells were nearly sinking them, they had all seen swells vastly larger than this from the shore, and violent those had been.

Things were beginning to pick up as the boats ploughed ahead at a much faster and less sustainable rate than they had been traveling. Mael was beginning to feel like they might make it. Off in the distance and through curtains of rain, he could see what looked like land. It was at that moment that the world went black. Clouds suddenly covered the Moon blanketing the world with an inky blackness so dark Mael could not even see his hands in front of his eyes. Fear overwhelmed him, and he pulled with his oar against the water, hoping to find strength in his exertion.

Ahead, he heard a scream, possibly from the first boat, but there was no way for him to see what was happening. Fear ran through his veins, and in his mind's eye, he could imagine their boat overturning and half of his party descending into the depths of the Greatest River. The only thing that helped keep his fear under control was the feel of the Amber of Life necklace. Its heavy presence against his chest was a fixed point he could hold on to.

Suddenly, the moonlight reappeared, revealing sudden horror. The first boat was nearly two lengths of a man higher than his boat, riding high on the crest of the largest swell he had seen this storm. Then, suddenly, the boat was gone. Worse, the vast swell was already beginning to lift the front of his boat. Mael screamed for everyone to hold on, but he could barely hear his own words, let alone anyone else. Then, holding onto the boat for dear life, he felt the entire wooden structure rise swiftly into the air faster than he had expected. The sheer violence of the water surprised him, leaving him feel as helpless as a child surrounded by wolves.

As the boat lurched into the air, Galar lost his grip on the slick side of the wooden hull.

His free hand reached blindly into the spray, finding purchase on Kyra's shoulder. She reacted in horror as her floundering husband's grasp threatened to break her own weak hold on the boat. Dropping her oar with her other hand, she grabbed his hand, pulling it free from her shoulder. Suddenly, the boat pitched higher as it came over the crest and then tumbled down the rogue swell. Kyra watched as her husband's shocked face faded into the spray, quickly grabbing the boat with her now free hand. Galar tumbled backward as the boat went down, slamming into Mael and sending both men over the edge and into the icy darkness.

Galar felt only cold and salty horror as he descended into the dark water. Down he went into the frigid abyss, all the while kicking frantically and trying to resurface. A merciful hand grasped Galar's arm and held him firmly against the pull of the water. A moment later, his head burst from the darkness to find Mael holding him above the water with one hand and holding the stern of the boat with the other. Blinking against the water in his eyes, Galar could see Kel and Yan reaching forward in a human chain to haul Mael in. Galar grabbed hold of Mael's arm and began to pull himself forward towards the boat. He assumed that as soon as he got on board, he could help pull Mael in, a post hoc rationalization at best as terror truly guided his movements.

Mael could feel himself being pulled free from the boat by the force of the water and Galar's frantic attempts to get himself back aboard. He wanted to yell at the young man to hold it together, to stop frantically pulling at him, or he might drown them both. He was too weak, and he could feel his body giving out. Whatever had been causing the pains in his body was being exaggerated tenfold by his present activities. All he could do was hold onto the boat and hope that Galar's desperate attempts to get aboard would quickly conclude.

Galar frantically climbed across Mael and into the arms of Kel, who pulled him into the boat. Kel reached back, ready to pull Mael aboard, but as soon as he caught Mael's wrist, he realized that the older man was in trouble. Too numb to even feel Kel's hand on his wrist, darkness filled the edges of Mael's vision. His hand slipped from the side of the boat, and he knew he was done for. He reached for the necklace, hoping that he could free it and hand it to Kel before he descended beneath the waves. His body grew numb as he froze and ran out of energy. The pain in his abdomen was excruciating, like being stabbed by a flint dagger. This was his final test as a man, and he would not fail. He must not.

ɔ ɔ C

Ember brushed the hair and salty water from her eyes. The vast swell that had just overtaken her boat was known as a rogue swell, a wave significantly larger than usual and very unpredictable. These sorts of waves did not exist in the small river where she had grown up, but they did exist in the Greatest River. There had been stories told by the Isen'bryn of such waves caring people from the shore completely at random, though Ember had never believed that they could be so deadly until this moment. Even the swells she had faced when she and Brig'dha had crossed the water not that many moons before had not been even half as large.

Looking ahead, she realized that everybody in her group had survived – most importantly, Brig'dha. She had kept her knees pressed against the buoyant brunette's back throughout the storm. She had initially worried for Meegin, who had screamed louder than she could have imagined, but the woman was still holding on. Satisfied that her team was soaking wet and frightened but otherwise alive, Ember turned her attention to see how the other boat had fared. To her surprise, the second boat was no more than two lengths of a man behind, much closer than she had expected. Suddenly, she realized that something was greatly wrong. At the stern of the boat, she could see what looked like Kel and Yan fighting hard to pull someone aboard the boat. But where was Mael? She realized in horror that Yan and Kel were attempting to rescue Mael, who had fallen out of the boat. For a moment, all she could do was watch barely able to process what she saw. Her shocked indecision ended when Yan fell backward, losing his grip, and Kel began screaming and waving his arms frantically. She realized at that moment that they had just let go of Mael.

Ember was bad at gathering, most work activities, and focusing on her tasks. Yet, Ember was by far the best swimmer, one of the few things she was actually good at. In fact, she was the best in her entire village and had swum her whole life. If ever there was a time to use that skill, this was certainly it. She couldn't let Mael drown. Though the large swell had passed, the water was still a black inky abyss with waves taller than a man stood and violence known only to such vast bodies of water. Could she even fight against water so cold and strong? She had done so once before and lived, though only by the grace of the water spirits.

Ember looked ahead to see that land was visible and not that far. At that moment, she again caught sight of Brig'dha. The priestess looked her in the eyes and knew exactly what she was thinking; that stoic look she had seen before rescuing the women from the raiding party clearly on her face. Brig'dha's mouth moved as she soundlessly screamed the Isen'bryn word for, no!

"Nea! Nae!" Brig'dha screamed into the abyss. She could see that Ember was planning to rescue their fallen leader. She understood her reasons and wished that something could be done, but she did not want to risk the life of her beloved friend. Brig'dha tried to reach for Ember, but the boat rocked back and forth, destabilizing her. Fear made her grip on the wood so hard that her hands might as well have been bound with sinew. As Ember clumsily stood on the pitching boat and tore off her heavy clothing, preparing to jump into the water, Brig'dha felt helpless panic overwhelm her. When Ember decided to help somebody, nothing could be done to stop her. It was a curse the redhead carried, something wonderful and yet, terrible. Brig'dha immediately dropped into a chant to the Goddess of the Moon to shine her light and to the spirits of the Greatest River to let Ember live. It was all that she could do.

Ember had removed her furs as soon as the water had become choppy with mist and had replaced them with a reed cloak and a rough leather hide shirt. She quickly ripped the reed cloak and leather shirt free and kicked her lime bark fiber boots from her feet. Using her dagger, she sliced her waist cord freeing herself from clothing. The clothing would provide no real warmth once in the icy water, and could potentially kill her as it became waterlogged and prevented her from swimming. She wouldn't have even known this if she hadn't fallen into the icy water with Brig'dha not so long ago. And now, she would take that same painful plunge once again. Ember took a deep breath and jumped into the black horror of the Greatest River.

She convulsed the moment she hit the water from the sheer cold. She had many times before swam in icy water as a child. Her tribe maintained strict rituals about cleanliness, and even on the coldest days, they were known to sit by the water's edge and clean themselves, though usually with large fires burning nearby. Ember thanked the spirits for those days, for without that experience of icy water from her youth, she was sure that she would have died from the sudden shock of the water. Instead, it was as cold as ice and sent pains through her body.

She surfaced and began to swim towards the stern of the second boat. Her body quickly became numb, but she continued to swim, more from muscle memory than from any actual feeling of the water. If the second boat had been more than just a few lengths of a man away, a rescue would not have been possible. It might still be impossible with the speed that her body was losing heat. Ember quickly passed the second boat, swimming as hard as she could not just for speed but also to keep her body moving. She was losing feeling at an alarming rate, and her body was beginning to shake uncontrollably. Within a short moment, she was at the stern of the boat where she could see Mael splashing in the water, his head just barely above the water. Their eyes met… then, suddenly, he was gone.

Ember reached forward and grabbed ahold of Mael's arm, fighting hard to pull him to the surface. Straining beyond reason, she got his head above the water, but his weight and the water's pull were so much stronger than she had imagined. She frantically reached for the boat, trying to pull the nearly spent Mael to safety, but she was not strong enough to swim for them both in such water. She suddenly felt something push into her chest, which was surprising since she could barely feel anything due to the water's cold embrace.

Just gasping for breath, his head barely above the fierce water, Mael breathed something using the last of his strength, a message he was literally dying to speak. She could not understand what he was saying, but he thrust the Amber of Life necklace into her chest. He spoke once more, his lungs nearly empty, but his lips just visible. She could barely make out his words over the sounds of the water.

"Take it… Emb… Live!" he breathed, when suddenly, a large wave crested over the top of the pair. The reckless redhead found herself pulled underwater. Above her, she could see the faint outline of the boat, but everything else was an eerie blackness. Below, she saw Mael holding the necklace as life disappeared from his eyes. She reached down and took ahold of it. Using his last motes of strength, Mael took hold of Ember's hand and broke her grasp upon him. Ember watched as Mael slowly sank beneath the waves. His expression had become calm with a sense of acceptance. He knew that she would live, and the necklace would not be lost. She wanted to cry out as she watched him die. She had no skill, trick, or luck to save him, just her tears quietly mixing with the Greatest River.

Ember's lungs cried out for air moments later, returning her to the present. She rotated her body to swim upward, but the waves had left her disoriented. That was when she realized she had no idea which direction was up or down in the cold darkness. Panic filled her as her lungs burned and death crept in. Not only had she failed to save Mael, but she was about to join him wherever the dead went. Her panic turned into terror-fueled horror as her lungs burned and darkness surrounded every direction in the inky abyss of the Greatest River. Suddenly, she caught sight of the Moon's glow just ahead. Ember's brain sent her numb body commands to swim, though she could no longer feel her limbs as she fought for air. Her head broke the surface as she gasped the icy wind.

Luckily, one of the boats was still in sight. She turned towards the boat, its low riding hull barely illuminated by the pale light of the Moon, a blessing of the Moon Goddess, for sure. She began to swim, wanting nothing more than to scream out in pain and frustration but needing every drop of her remaining strength to save her own life. Ember swam as hard as she could, but she wasn't sure if her arms were moving as she could not feel them. She had barely been able to place the necklace around her neck, so numb were her hands. Ember reached the side of the boat with her tunnel vision beginning to fade to black. She held her numb arm over the side as best as she could and hoped someone saw her as she was too weak to even speak. The night grew darker, and then there was nothing.

Ember awoke lying on a sandy beach, a vast fire burning right beside her and a second fire being lit. Brig'dha was at her side, gently stroking her damp hair and hovering over her in a motherly sort of way. Her side not facing the fire was covered by a fur blanket, while the side facing the fire was left exposed. She was still shaking, but she had lived. Ember slowly sat up and looked around, her body stiff with great pains radiating through her due to her sudden movement. Ironically, this was the second time she had awoken, having fallen unconscious in the water.

Memories of waking up beside Brig'dha on the shores of Inn'bry'th after dragging the unconscious woman ashore with the last of her strength returned. She had set a fire and tended to the buoyant brunette until she recovered. She hoped this would be the last time either would awaken from a water trip.

"We switched places," Brig'dha remarked, tears falling from puffy, red-rimmed eyes. For a moment, they stared at each other, the juxtaposition sinking in. Brig'dha's beautiful eyes filled her with the first warmth she had felt, more welcoming than even the fire. Ember felt something, a need building in her. Just a hand's length away leaned the beautiful brunette, her rich, dark skin framing large hazel eyes, like a beautiful forest spirit. All she wanted to do at that moment was…

"Well, we made it. umm, almost everyone did. Mael didn't make it," Aethen mumbled, suddenly appearing on her right, breaking her gaze upon the beautiful brunette. Ember felt dizzy, but she also felt calmer as she saw each person in the group one by one. It was not long before the memories of what had happened flooded back, and she was overwhelmed with sorrow. She felt devastated that she had not saved Mael, but what could she have done in such a violent storm? Between her breasts hung the Amber of Life, a necklace revered as magical. Mael used his last strength to make sure that she took the necklace and survived.

Ember was not sure if the necklace was magical or not, but a man that she respected had died believing that it was. She was sure the necklace and the people of the Isen'bryn would make it to a new home in the South. She would make sure that they did, in his honor.

ↄ ↄ ↄ

The day had started drearily but slowly cleared up as the storm passed towards the evening. For a long time, Ember lay in between the two fires, wrapped in a thick blanket of furs and recovering from her dramatic loss of body temperature. Brig'dha mostly remained by her side.

Ember felt guilty for letting Brig'dha baby her, but there was something nice about the extra attention, so Ember let herself sleep. Her mind was clouded with pain and regret over what had just happened, and sleep was a welcome grace. Many other tribe members sat around the fires near her for warmth. It wasn't so much that it was cold, but it was not warm either, and the rain made things worse. This was when everyone wished that they had a makeshift hut.

Boat Master Vaerl grumbled as he approached the fires where Galar, Aethen, Ember, and the rest sat warming themselves. He was not sure who was the leader at this point, given the loss of the only person he knew to be in charge, so he figured he would address everyone at once. The man was quite short with stubby arms and legs, and he wore an odd linen wrap around his head. Ember had not seen a man so grizzled looking as he, but she suspected it might have something to do with a life on the cold waters of the Greatest River.

"I know it's not much, but I am sorry about your loss. These things happen when you're on the water. You may think you're in control of the boat, but you are always at the mercy of the spirits," he spoke mournfully. Galar stood to address the man, almost as though he were asserting himself as a leader. In actuality, the death of Mael had provided an opportunity for Galar to take the lead. The only person who could rival him was Aethen, and Aethen was too kind-hearted to be aggressive after such a loss. Nevertheless, Galar would not let this kind of opportunity pass him by without taking the initiative.

"We thank you for your kind words. There was no way we could have known the storm was coming, and nothing could be done. But, as you said, these things just happen." Brig'dha looked up from a kneeling position beside a now sleeping Ember, scorn across her typically neutral face. She rarely spoke aloud, masking her feelings from her people lest she be judged for their rich and powerful nature, but this was too much.

"The Goddess and the spirits warned me, and I warned you. You should have listened... we all should have listened," she spat, ducking her head in shame. She was angry at the group and Galar, but especially with herself. She couldn't shake the thought that she could have tried harder. Worse, she had nearly lost Ember before she could even tell her how she felt. But how did she feel? Her mind descended into a discordant mixture of thoughts, regrets, emotions, and conflict. While her inner turmoil raged, her sudden rebuke had also publicly implicated Galar as being complicit in not heeding her warning. In the eyes of the group, Brig'dha had just cut the legs out from under Galar, once again. He wanted to respond to her; to tell everyone how foolish she was, but the fact that she had predicted the storm and that it had come was too much of a coincidence. He turned and stormed off before he made things worse in anger.

ɔ ɔ ɔ

Boat Master Vaerl decided that he would remain with the group until the next morning. Afterward, he would head North about a half day's travel to the village where he would find friends to help him return the boats with trade items. It was cumbersome, but this was the way trade was performed. He hoped the other village had a sizable supply of trade wares to make the trip doubly worth it. Luckily, one of the two large boats belonged to the other tribe and had been left on a previous trip. The boats were shared between both tribes and tended to move back and forth in this way. At least, he had gotten this strange band of people to help pull the boats ashore, as he was not strong enough to move them himself. Whatever strange social upheaval loomed over these people, he wanted nothing to do with it. At least, he was well traded for this trip, and he now had an amazing story to tell of a wild redhead who would jump headfirst into the Greatest River to save a drowning man. He grumbled, quite satisfied.

ɔ ɔ ɔ

That night, the entire group stood before a large fire on the beach by the Greatest River to attend a ritual for their fallen leader. Brig'dha was the only priestess in the group, so it fell upon her to perform the ritual. She had never performed a ritual like this in front of so many people, being so new to her role as a priestess. It was important to implore the Goddess and the spirits of the Greatest River to allow the spirit of Mael to leave this world and journey to the next.

The Isen'bryn believed that the world repeated itself. Each world would end, and a new one would be created. Only those whose spirits were rotten to the core would be destroyed when the world ended, but goodly spirits would travel to the next and be reborn. The most prized spirits, those of people of legendary feats and skill, had the option of being reborn as powerful spirits of rivers or mountains. This was not exactly what Ember believed, but it wasn't the worst creation story she had ever heard, and she hoped it was true so that Mael could return as a powerful spirit for good.

Before the ritual, Brig'dha had painted her entire body black with the ash from the fire, customary among her people during funerals. Ember had helped her get all the hard-to-reach places. The entire body painting was performed while Brig'dha chanted the magical words to empower the ash. Ember supposed that the symbolism had to do with the burning of wood and the destruction it caused, though she wasn't completely sure. Always one for fashion, she took the opportunity to apply horizontal lines across her arms and legs, though for decorative purposes only. Ember's people believed that the body should always be painted, as unpainted skin was indecent.

Brig'dha stood before everyone to implore the spirits to carry Mael into the next world. She wondered if the next world sat somewhere waiting to start, or perhaps it was already there, and people filtered into it slowly, much as people were born in this world. Ember had once suggested to Brig'dha that it was all circular with several worlds connected. If a person died in one world and were worthy, they would be born into the next, and so on. If your friend died in this world, was born in the next world, and then soon died there, and so on, they could potentially show back up again before you died. Brig'dha's head spun at the loops of logic that Ember wove, but it weirdly made sense to her.

As the ritual ended, Brig'dha cast sand from the beach into the water. Normally, the body would have been cremated, and only buried when away from a village. Without any of these things, or even a body, all she could do was perform the ritual on his behalf. Everyone stood for a short while in mournful silence, then slowly drifted off into the night without many words. Funerals were always such somber occasions.

A short time later, Ember found Brig'dha standing on the sandy beach gazing at the Greatest River. Ember had wanted to see it for so long, yet now, neither wished ever to see it again. As she approached, she heard the priestess softly weeping. Brig'dha sniffled, calming herself. Ember's closeness renewed her inner strength, something no one else had ever done. Brig'dha didn't grieve like others of her people, and some had even suggested she was numb to loss, but that wasn't true. Her emotions were a storm, just like the one that took Mael. She would process his loss and her part in it in time, but for now, having the redhead silently at her side was like moonlight in the darkest night.

"A life lost, but many lives spared. A balance," Brig'dha whispered.

CHAPTER SEVEN

PREY

The European wildcat existed throughout much of Europe, ranging from as north as Scotland to as far south as southern Greece, and even into Northern Africa. Resembling a Mackerel Tabby in color, these wildcats appeared as slightly larger variations of common household cats. It would be unlikely to find and domesticate such an animal in their natural environment, though individual instances may have occurred.

The thawing season was ending, and the growing season was at hand. It would not be long before the warm winds nurtured the vast fields of flowers and pollen. The world had become a young maiden about to bloom. Everything came in cycles: life, death, and then life once more. It saddened Ember when certain parts of the cycle occurred, but as the group strolled through the dense forests and beautiful thickets of the mainland, she could not help but be overwhelmed by the beauty such cycles wrought.

It had long been decided among the group that they would head south until they hit the water. Ember had some idea of how long that would be, having walked that distance herself nearly a full harvest before. By her reckoning, the trip south would take at least two moons, assuming the group stopped every few days for rest. A person simply could not walk for a tenday without at least a day or two of rest. If any group members had been old, very young, or wounded, this time estimate could be doubled or even tripled. Luckily, their group was now composed only of young, healthy individuals. As horrible as the thought was as it crossed her mind, Ember realized that with the death of Mael, the group would now move much faster. Ember would have gladly added a full harvest to the trip if she could have him back. Unconsciously she placed her hand on the necklace, in response.

To her right, a felled tree lay, its once majestic trunk stretched a dozen lengths of a man and height along the forest floor. Its vast root structure was torn from the very ground, likely from a storm, just like the one that had taken the life of Mael. From this rotted tree, a group of beautiful mushrooms grew. Small animals had claimed holes in the log as their homes. As the group passed, Ember could see the cycles for what they were – she was a part of nature just as much as any log, flower, or animal. One day she would lie down and die, though she hoped a small animal wouldn't use her for a home. She wondered if a beautiful flower would grow in the place where her body lay.

Her thoughts were interrupted by a slight movement to her left. The group walked through a small field just beside a great forest. Ember stopped to look and see what sort of animal had come so close when she was suddenly struck in the back by Brig'dha, who had been deep in her thoughts. This was another good reason for party members never to walk too closely together. Unfortunately for her at this moment, Brig'dha never seemed to be that far away.

"Behunas, eshe pewmeyus! You see it, umm a small animal, right there by the tree? It's following us. A squirrel? Maybe we can have a squirrel roast if we can catch it," Ember said, her stomach immediately responding to the thought with a growl. Squirrel meat was very oily and very rich, but with a little salt and some fire, just about anything could be made to taste good. Brig'dha gazed into the forest at the small furry creature that seemed to be following them. It stood a distance behind the tree line and hard for her eyes to follow, but she was pretty sure that it wasn't a squirrel. Ember accepted that the creature was probably a fox or something similar, so the two women continued walking.

It was not long before Brig'dha noticed the small furry creature was still following, always keeping its distance. When midday meal came around, and the group stopped to eat, Brig'dha again noticed the little creature was still close by. At this point, she was determined to figure out what it was and why it would not leave. She snatched a piece of roasted deer meat from Ember and slowly approached the wooded area where the creature waited. Ember nearly choked on the meat she was eating while trying to object to the theft, but she soon forgot her objections and became much more curious about what this creature was that Brig'dha had seen.

Brig'dha approached the edge of the wood until the creature began to back away. She ducked low onto her knees and held out the food twisting it back and forth in her fingers and making noises with her mouth to call the creature. By this time, several of the other group members had noticed the affair and were watching with equal suspense. Then, unexpectantly, the creature stepped from the woods and into the light where it could be seen plainly.

"It's just a wildcat. Actually, it's a very young wildcat," Ember observed, immediately recognizing the animal for what it was. These creatures did exist on the island of Inn'bry'th but were not as common. Brig'dha and her people had only seen them on occasion, while Ember's people had much greater contact with the cats. The small creature stepped from the wood revealing a small, furry body, a mixture of black, brown, and white stripes and large, green eyes. It certainly was a small cat and very tame for some reason. Ember had never known these creatures to be tame or to approach humans. Normally, they avoided humans at all costs and, at the very most, might sneak into a tribe at night and steal whatever they could find to eat. However, to approach a human was extremely uncommon.

"I would be careful priestess, that little thief is only deceptively cute. It has four sets of claws and sharp teeth to go with them. That tiny creature could shred you faster than an obsidian blade, um... a cute obsidian blade," Ember, said slightly succumbing to the creature's innate cuteness. It was more adorable than the adults simply because it was young. It looked as though it had only just recently been a kitten, which might explain why it was more agreeable to humans than its kind generally were. Ember wondered if it was a runt, given its noticeably smaller-than-normal size.

"Well, I think it's adorable, and it looks like it's hungry. We have plenty of meat to go around. Here you go," Brig'dha said, tossing the meat treat for the cat to eat. The cat approached, cautiously, with its head down, but its eyes locked firmly on Brig'dha. As it approached the meat, it paused and blinked twice at her, seemingly waiting for a response. Brig'dha mimicked the blink, which seemed to appease the cat. It slowly stepped forward and began to lick the meat, eating hungrily.

"Well, it looks like you have a friend," Ember said with a smile. Meegin suddenly lost her ability to resist the cuteness of the small animal and approached it with her hands out to pet it. The cat watched the eager woman approaching in horror. It quickly grabbed the food snack and dashed back into the trees to hide. Meegin came to a halt with her hands at her side, quite confused. She had expected the creature to let her pet it and didn't understand why the sight of the wide-eyed, intensely happy woman approaching it had scared it off. Tes and Eryi nearly fell over laughing while Aethen tried not to choke to death on the food he was eating at the sight. The group had needed some laughter, and Meegin had unwittingly provided it.

"Good job, Meegin, you scared it off," Kel snarked with a laugh. Meegin held a piece of food and called for the creature for the remainder of the midday meal, ignoring the teasing, but she never saw it return. Kel and Aethan could not help but taunt Meegin over the affair. They tried not to be mean to her, but it was simply too funny. Even Galar and Kyra could not hold back smiles. If nothing more, the small wildcat had provided everyone with an emotional release, a gift far worth providing a little food to a wild animal.

ɔ ɔ ɔ

Several tendays had passed when the group came upon a beautiful meadow to stop for the night. Just at the edge of the wood Ember caught sight of a large, brown animal watching them with mild curiosity. Horses were hardly the best food, and so much would be wasted if they felled such a large creature. Besides, the group had plenty of recently acquired food, so the warrior and would-be prey merely observed each other momentarily before the horse disappeared into the wood. Ember adjusted her leather shirt and waist cord before gazing at where the animal had gone one last time. Her urge to hunt was quite strong, yet tonight was a time of rest.

The evening slowly became night, and a beautiful pink glow filled the skies. Unfortunately, the night would be dark as the Moon would not rise. For reasons that people didn't know, the Moon would sometimes be hidden for many days at a time, only returning when it so chose. This would be one of those extra dark nights. Tes placed deer meat on a rack over the fire to cook for the group. Over the many nights, the group had eaten salted meat and other provisions. Tomorrow was a rest day, and the group had been lucky, spotting a deer just before camping. Aethen had skillfully tracked and killed the deer with a single arrow, so tonight they would eat well.

The small furry wild cat had been following the group ever since Brig'dha had fed it nearly two tendays before. Most days, it could be seen far in the distance shadowing the group, but it would approach during midday meal and in the evening when the group stopped to make camp, to receive treats. Brig'dha had taken to giving it a small piece of her meal as well as some of the leftover pieces the group did not eat. Because the creature was so small, the amount of food required to keep it happy did not impact the group, and to many of the others, the little creature was too adorable not to feed. But, for some strange reason, it had not come by this very night. Tes had a small piece of deer organ to feed it if it approached, but she had yet to see it.

Tes and Eryi had been tasked with preparing the deer for dinner. This was consuming work and took most of the evening to complete. Eryi was almost useless at the task of dressing an animal. She was an artist and created beauty with paint and anything else she could find. Gutting an animal with a knife was simply not a task she was good at. Tes was much more versatile and took care of the most gruesome parts, such as removing organs. Unfortunately, this required that she remove her ample necklaces.

As she removed a large organ, which appeared to be the stomach, Tes began to wonder whether the horns could be collected to make new forms of necklaces. Most deer shed their antlers in the harvest, regrew them while it was cold, and shed the antler's velvety softness in the thawing season. It was early for roe deer, but red deer would be plentiful. Perhaps if she could collect enough, she could trade a quantity of them in exchange for having a few of them carved. One could not have too many necklaces, and a necklace made of deer antler would stand out from the crowd. Tes continued to fantasize over what the necklace would look like as she scooped intestines from the deer. Detaching the mind was... preferable.

The task of preparing an animal was constantly shifted between people. Each member of the group had their chance to perform the horrid task. Often, they would pair up to make the work quicker and easier. There was also an unspoken rule that stated that the person who killed the animal never had to clean and prepare it. It was a courtesy in exchange for the task of hunting.

Caelwyn had agonized as he watched the two women damaging the precious leather skin and sinew from the animal, but there simply wasn't time to do anything with these otherwise valuable resources. He supposed that the sinew from the legs and back could be saved, but a good portion of the nonfood bits of the deer would be left for the carrion eaters. This was the way of a group traveling a long-distance – waste and quick work. Then, when they were done with the carcass, it would be deposited in the woods not far from the campsite. A designated refuse pit would have been fashioned if the camp had been more permanent.

"Hey Caelwyn, instead of sitting there complaining about the deer hide you couldn't do anything with anyway, why not help us remove some of these organs?" Tes suggested in a humorous tone. Caelwyn shrugged and pulled out a flint knife. He supposed the women had a point, and his stomach was already begging for the delicious taste of roasted deer liver. He stepped over to the carcass and lifted the back leg to get a good look at what remained inside of the chest cavity and abdomen. It was not long before the deer was fully prepped and ready to be roasted. Many organs could be cooked and salted to save them for the long trip.

Meat provided the flavor and fill of an animal, but cooked organs provided the nutrients.

As the Sun descended below the horizon, the group sat around a large campfire and ate their fill as they prepared to do absolutely nothing the next day. After an evening of eating their fill, they would sleep all night, then awaken only when it suited them. If the Moon had been out, some exploring around the local area might have been had, but with the darkness, it simply wasn't safe to leave the campsite.

"Brig'dha, that little cat hasn't come back today. Do you suppose it decided to stop following us? I mean, isn't it really strange that it followed us at all?" Meegin asked as they ate. Most of the people were stuffing their faces with deer meat and not joining in the conversation other than to listen.

"If it does come back, you should name it. I've heard of people with pet dogs before, but never a cat. Cats are mostly thieves, at best," Aethen said. There were many head nods around the campfire at the suggestion. It was true that dogs were common enough to find in many tribes, but nobody had ever heard of a pet cat.

"Ember, what did you say when you saw the cat? You mentioned something under your breath, but I didn't hear it well. Was that your word for cat?" Kel asked. Ember spent the next few moments quickly chewing a piece of meat she had just bitten into before answering. Most of the Isen'bryn only knew a few of Ember's words, but she could speak their language quite fluently.

"I said, 'pewmeyus,' which means 'little thief.' It's a sort of word that we use for cats, mice, and other small thieves," she said with a laugh. Brig'dha recited the word in her mind several times, "pewmeyus," "peeuuMeYoos," "Peyoo Mues." Then, suddenly, the name "Mew" came to mind. It sounded a bit like the actual noise the small cat made, and it also resembled Ember's term for the creature.

"If it returns, I will name it Mew!" Brig'dha announced quite plainly. Everybody stopped to look at her. Brig'dha didn't say that much normally, and she made the pronouncement quite loudly and unexpectedly. It was quite easy for everybody to guess how she had derived Mew from pewmeyus, and many nodded their heads in agreement. It would be a good name.

"Well, we will have to see if Mew returns tomorrow. There's something off about that cat, something strange that makes it want to follow. Perhaps it's possessed by a spirit? Maybe it isn't very smart?" Ember suggested. The discussion continued as the night grew dark.

Ɔ Ɔ Ɔ

Tes looked up from the fire and realized just how dark it had gotten. It was easy enough to forget how dark it was when standing before a well-lit fire. She had been needing to relieve herself for a little while and had gotten caught up in the conversation about which direction to head. There had been some discussion about heading slightly east or west as they headed south. Though nobody was sure, the group was generally believed to be halfway to the Blue Sea. In reality, this was nothing more than wild speculation as nobody, not even Ember, had ever actually been to the Blue Sea.

Speculation aside, one thing that Tes was quite sure of was her own need to find a tree. She had her fill of deer and plenty of spring water that had been collected nearby. The resulting task was best performed under a tree or bush a little way from others, as Tes was slightly shyer than most when it came to such things. She stood from the group and wandered off towards the trees. It was pitch black outside, and she wished dearly that the Moon was out. Several torches were sitting near the fire, ready to be used if needed. Each was a bundle of dried twigs, grass, reeds, and other materials drizzled with beeswax, an item traded for in the small village where they obtained passage across the Greatest River. They were not the high-quality torches made in some villages, but they served their purpose when needed.

Tes lit a torch from the campfire and wandered off towards the darkness to do what must be done. The layout of the land was such that she had to travel much farther from the camp than normal to find a tree. Most people would have simply done their business right in the open, without much concern. There was a particular taboo against people watching, so she didn't need to be as modest as she was. Regardless, she was always sure that somebody might be watching, and the thought made it hard for her to relieve herself.

She was not a fan of dark forests, but this forest seemed to frighten her a little more than even the colder, darker forests near the Isen'bryn. It was a strange eerie feeling as though she were being watched, and it had extended her stay in the woods as a result. Some things were much more... difficult... when the nerves were on edge. The torch was almost burned down by the time she had finished cleaning herself, a task performed with whatever available materials could be had, in this case, several small pieces of bark, followed by a handful of fresh grass. The only true way to become clean was to sit in running water and wipe vigorously, but that was not always a luxury when traveling.

She stood and pulled her clothing back up, fastening her belt quickly and with nervous fingers. Though it was possible to simply remove the back portion of the loincloth and dangle it over the front of the body when squatting, it was easier to simply remove the whole apparatus. The strange feeling of being watched was growing worse. Tes looked around in each direction, expecting to see somebody peeking at her. Of all the times someone might peek, she could not imagine why somebody would choose this time. Off in the distance, she could see the dim light of the campfire, but she had walked much farther into the woods than she had realized. This would have been much less of a problem if the Moon was out.

Just then, she caught movement far to her right. She whipped her head and looked but saw nothing. The light of the torch lit everything around her, but the trade-off was that she was blind to anything outside of its immediate light. Human eyes were marvelous with color, contrast, and quality in bright light, but they were almost useless in the dark. She quickly finished fastening her belt and turned toward camp. Suddenly, something ran past her, between where she stood and the camp... something large and gray. Tes stepped backward, away from the camp but also away from whatever it was that had just run past her. There was only one thing that she knew of that fit that profile... Wolves.

Wolves generally did not attack people in or near tribes, but they were known to strike people in the deep wilderness, people like her. They would single out children who walked too far away from a group or younger women whose smaller body size was more favorable for prey. Tes turned and headed back toward the camp when her greatest fear stepped from behind a thick shrubbery. The creature was much larger than she had realized, it's back level to her stomach. It glared at her with yellow eyes that reflected the flickering light of the torch, a terrifying flash of light. Horror filled her as she locked eyes with the apex predator.

Instinct took hold as her vision became dark to everything but the wolf, adrenaline dancing through her body. Tes stepped backward from the menacing creature, not realizing that it was instinctually herding her from the rest of the people. All she could think about was the horrifying creature slowly advancing. Then, another wolf came into view close to the first. At that moment, a new surge of adrenaline took hold, and she turned and ran from the predators. As she ran, trees and limbs slashed and cut at her face causing her to close her eyes. The sensation that something was behind her and about to grab her was so frightening and suddenly overwhelming that she accelerated to her maximum speed, a blinding run fueled by adrenaline and primal fear. Branches cut at her arms as she ran, but she felt no pain. Her body suppressed all minor injuries with the sole goal of achieving escape from the monsters that chased her.

So dark was the night without the Moon's blessing that she did not even see the small gully in front of her before she tripped and stumbled down its steep slope. The angle was steep, but the drop was shallow, and she was not greatly harmed, as she tumbled forward. By the time she stopped rolling and came to a stop, she was disoriented. She was in bad shape by herself, entirely unarmed and too far to see the light at the camp. Worse, her torch was simply not there. She could only guess that she must have dropped it at some point when her primal instincts took over or as she had tumbled. The same instincts that had worked their best to save her had quite possibly removed the only thing she had that could have thwarted the animals. Sadly, those instincts had evolved before her peoples' huntress goddess Brid'da had given them the gift of fire to slay the beast Gho'taig.

Tes frightfully looked up to see two more wolves encircling her. She knew nothing but fear and wanted only to cry, yet she couldn't bring herself even to scream. Even with the animals directly in her midst, something in her kept telling her not to move and not to make a sound, as though they would suddenly go away. More than a billion years of instinct did their best, but an unarmed human was no match for apex predators.

ↄ ↄ C

Ember was jokingly holding a stick with a deer eyeball stuck through it and offering the bright shiny bobble to anybody daring enough to eat it when, off in the distance, a scream was heard. The laughing and talking stopped abruptly as everyone went quiet to listen to more of what they had just heard. A moment later, a second scream came from the forest. It wasn't as much of a scream of terror as a cry of pain.

"Tes!" Ember screamed, jumping to her feet and pulling free her dagger. She couldn't be sure what was happening, but there was no way that she would let one of her party members be harmed if she could do anything to stop it. The problem was that the Moon had not risen, and the night was extremely dark. The dense wood was a terrible place to find anyone, especially by a scream alone. This was why most people did not venture far to do their business. Modesty and shyness were fine during the day, but the deep forest was just too frightening of a place at night.

She grabbed a fire torch and dipped it into the campfire, lighting it ablaze. Before waiting for anyone else, Ember rushed into the woods toward the screams. Behind her, Aethen, Kel, and Galar followed. Yan, Brig'dha, and the others were only a few moments behind.

Ember ran as fast as she could through the woods holding the torch high above her head so that she could see where her feet fell. After a short time, she stopped, unable to get a bearing. She stood completely still, listening for any sound that could be heard. Behind her, she could hear the rest of the party approaching through the woods, though they were still quite a distance behind. She had set off into the woods without even wearing her shoes, having no care other than to save her party member. The only other sound she could hear was her heart pumping in her ears. She was silent for only a few moments before she heard a sound which made her blood run cold, the sound of wolves.

"Oh no... No... no, no, no!" She ran towards the sound with no fear for herself. If not for the torch, she might have fallen into the same gully as it was only noticeable with the light of the fire. Ember stopped at the gully's edge only to illuminate a horrific scene below. Four wolves stood over what looked like Tes. Ember could not tell if she lived, but it would not be for long, even if she did. There was simply too much blood. The firelight was enough to see the results of the wolves. Ember could see it all in her mind's eye – Tes had made a run into the woods to get away from a wolf, but they had caught her as a pack. Ember remembered running from wolves and knew that fear all too well. This could have been her nearly two harvests before, but she had been lucky then. Unfortunately, it looked as though Tes had not been so lucky. Pure rage filled her veins, and all fear suddenly evaporated.

She leaped from the edge of the gully, landing halfway down the slope and sliding to the bottom. As she leapt, she screamed as loudly as she could and swung her torch. One of the wolves turned from feeding to challenge the newcomer. But Ember rushed straight at it with her dagger in her hand, heedless and screaming. She came upon the creatures so fast that they barely had time to react, her speed boosted by the leap down the incline. She was not trying to scare off the wolves... she was coming for their blood. The wolves quickly recognized the murderous rage for what it was – a fight they didn't need nor want when food was still plentiful.

Three of the wolves turned and fled from the torch, but the largest wolf dropped its head low into a snarl and held its ground, unwilling to let its food go to this new rival. Ember, fueled by adrenaline, rushed up to the wolf and swung her blade as the creature snapped at her. The blade cut into the creature's mouth, causing it to yelp as the obsidian blade tore deeply into the flesh. She followed the slash with the fiery end of her torch as her body slammed into the wolf, arresting her momentum. The shuddered and wounded animal issued a yelp and scampered away as fast as possible. Ember lunged from her knees at the wolf but missed. For a tunnel-visioned moment, she swung her blade in each direction as she fought to catch her breath while searching for enemies. Seeing no other wolves nearby, Ember crawled clumsily two arm's lengths to where Tes lay.

The woman was still alive, yet strangely calm. She weakly looked at Ember with a curious sort of stare. Blood was everywhere, and the wound on her neck continued to pump more. Though her mind fought to deny it, Ember knew nothing could be done for this level of injury. She had heard once of an older man from her tribe having been attacked by a wolf. He had said there was no pain initially, just a strange tugging sensation at the wound. Most people knew well that fatal wounds often did not hurt. Sometimes, the pain seemed to vanish when a person was at their end, the graces of the spirits, she supposed. As Ember looked down into the dying woman's eyes, she saw that point approaching.

She would have given nearly anything to save this woman's life. It wasn't so much that Tes was near and dear to her heart but more of a fondness for life in general. Strangely, thoughts of the deer she had eaten earlier came to mind. In some ways, humans were not unlike wolves. The only reason the wolf seemed more terrible was that it seemed more vicious. It did not have the use of weapons, and so it used teeth. Also, she valued human life more than animals, yet what might the animals think? She wanted to hate the creatures for what they had done, but would she not have done the same if she had been a wolf? She shook such strange thoughts from her mind, her brain's attempt to escape a horrible moment, and refocused on the fallen woman, her friend.

Ember gently lifted Tes's head into her lap and began stroking her light, brunette hair while she softly sang the words her people used to help the spirit of a fallen comrade leave this world for the next. Her motions were ridged as her hands and voice quivered in the moment. Most people were no strangers to death, and Ember had watched many people among her people die, a natural part of life. Yet, this did little to reduce her grief each time it happened to someone she knew. She supposed that was healthy, but that realization provided little comfort.

Tes almost seemed to relax as she gazed at Ember. It was as though she realized this was the end, but somehow, she seemed more at peace with a friend there to see her through. Tes began to softly shake and twitch, but she did not seem in terrible pain, shock fully blocking her senses. Ember continued to sing her song as tears fell upon the dying woman. It was not long before Tes stopped shuddering, and her pupils slowly began to dilate. Ember sobbed as she sang the song of the spirits. Her voice faltered as the horror of what had happened filled her with painful grief, making her chest ache. Suddenly, her voice was joined by another sound and then even more.

Brig'dha and the rest of the group had followed her into the woods and now stood behind Ember. One by one, each of them began to join in the ceremonial songs to mark the passage of the spirit into the next world. Ember, who sang in a different tongue, was renewed by their spirit and began to sing in the language of the Isen'bryn. She matched Brig'dha's words and felt them resonate far into the sky. Poor Tes may have been alone when she was attacked, but at least she had been with friends in the very end. Life and death continued their dance, as they always had.

☽ ☽ ☽

The next tenday passed without many conversations. The death of Mael had somehow passed more easily than the death of Tes. Brig'dha did not know why this was, but she suspected it was because the natural order was upset. The old died before the young; it was the way of things. Mael had not been so old that he had been expected to die, but he had lived a full life, and now he would join his wife in the next world. She had fallen victim to a mysterious illness long before, and he had never taken another wife. But Tes had been young and full of life. At only seventeen harvests of age, she would have looked forward to finding a husband within a few harvests after she got to the South. Who knows what her life might have become, yet that was not to be.

Ember had spent the rest of the night with a polished stone axe cutting wood for the pyre. Others had helped, and a pyre had been constructed by the sunrise. That morning, Ember, Brig'dha, and Geb had cleaned and painted Tes ritualistically with the ash from their fire. Her many necklaces had been cleaned of blood and placed around her neck to accompany her into the next world. Her arms and legs were bound tightly into a fetal position, and she was placed on the pyre by Aethen and Kel. While a ritual had been performed over the pyre, Ember felt that the actual ceremony had occurred the night before.

Brig'dha stopped thinking about Tes as she felt tears. Many days had passed since that fateful night, and yet the emotions were still raw. It was important to grieve but not important to dwell on the pain. If a person did not think about their loved ones, their emotions would rise to the point of breaking, and the result could be disastrous. However, if one thought too long and too often about a fallen loved one, their life could become wrapped up in what could have been and what never was. A life not lived, in some ways, was worse than a life lost. Brig'dha thought about that familiar phrase as she watched Ember walking ahead of her. She had begun to question how she felt about many parts of her life and what she might be missing.

The scenery was changing from thick forests to smaller trees. Ember and Brig'dha knew that this meant that they were approaching the South. It would not be long before they found the water and had to make hard choices. Soon they would be faced with either attempting to create a village with just a handful of people or perhaps joining a larger, established village. Brig'dha was of the opinion that neither of these two choices suited her. She hoped that she and Ember could set out for the True South or some other place and leave the rest of the group behind. It wasn't that she disliked them, though she could deal with never seeing Galar or his sister-wife again. Instead, she felt drawn to a different sort of future, one where she and perhaps the radiant redhead might be... closer.

On the bright side of things, the small cat had returned and continued to follow the group. Brig'dha had named the creature Mew and had taken to carrying it now and then. Each time that Ember caught Brig'dha holding the cat, she would explain how impossible such a scenario could be. According to Ember, cats were vicious wild creatures that could never be held. She explained that Mew must be defective in some way or possessed by an evil spirit. Evil spirit or not, the small animal had brought Brig'dha some much-needed happiness following the death of Tes. *Of course you don't like Mew... he's a cat and you're a fox,* she had thought.

The days were getting warmer, and the season was looking to become another hot one. This would make the fourth harvest in a row that was warmer than Ember remembered. She could not wait until it was warm enough to go swimming. Swimming was by far her favorite activity, other than sleeping and eating, and she was hoping to convince Brig'dha to come with her. Brig'dha was not particularly good at swimming, but she could learn. Her chaotic thoughts were interrupted when Ember slowed her pace so that she came to walk beside her. It was time for conversation, and she would initiate it as usual, as Brig'dha was never one for starting a conversation.

Mew the Cat

"So... you will go swimming with me next time we find water that's warm enough to swim in, right?" Ember asked with a catlike expression. Brig'dha turned a worried look upon her, unsure of what agreeing might entail. If she said yes, the next time they walked by a pond, the random redhead might push her in. She happened to be more chaotic than most people and was known to do sudden and unexpected things, especially without thinking first.

"I suppose I will, but only if you let me test the water first. I don't like it when it's too cold."

"Where's your spirit of adventure?" Ember asked with a sly smile. Brig'dha simply stopped walking and turned an incredulous stare at Ember. They had just journeyed across the entire known world – twice.

"Okay, I get your point. But still, I'm sure you'll enjoy it," Ember said. As she continued to chat about the finer points of swimming, Brig'dha thought about something troubling her. Maybe it was time to discuss her thoughts with Ember. She waited, much longer than she suspected she would have to, for a pause in Ember's excited swimming chatter before speaking. Not far behind, little Mew trotted along and carefully listened to what Brig'dha had to say.

"So much death and suffering have happened. I want to travel, but I don't wish to harm anyone. I hate the suffering... I hate death. I sometimes know it's needed, but it should be avoided if possible. You risk your life so much. Do you think that we could avoid such things?" Ember knew that Brig'dha hated weapons and combat. In fact, Ember never enjoyed their use either. The difference between them wasn't that Ember enjoyed violence, it was that she was willing to let loose the bowstring for the greater good. She did not know how to explain that to Brig'dha, but the look on her face told Ember that she wanted nothing more than to avoid violence at all cost.

"Sometimes, you have to take a life to save a life. If I can avoid it, I will spare you from that," Ember whispered. Brig'dha smiled, seemingly satisfied that Ember had gotten her point. It was a very emotional point and not very practical, but Brig'dha thought more with emotion than logic. It was simply who she was. Ember sensed a touch of worry in Brig'dha's smile. It was as though she sensed that the reckless redhead's ability to keep her word was at odds with the world. Ember tended to help others, often at great risk to herself. Her noble and self-sacrificing nature, coupled with her chaotic and childish side, were some of the reasons that so many people were attracted to her, but they were also a great potential for tragedy.

She's worried that she will lose me if I keep helping everyone, she realized. Ember had been the only friend Brig'dha had since her husband had died, and she feared losing Ember, too. She reached behind her neck and began to unfasten the cord that held the goddess pendant that her friend Blossom had given her over a harvest before. She had vowed to bring that pendant back one day. Ember was not sure how long in the future that would be, but she would either complete the task or die before she did. Either way, her next action would speak more than words to the emotionally minded Brig'dha. In truth, she cared deeply about how Brig'dha felt, perhaps more than she could ever let the beautiful brunette know.

"Here, let me put this around your neck. I swore to bring this back one day, and I will. If it's around your neck, you will never fear losing me, and I won't fear losing you," Ember said, placing the necklace around the stunned Brig'dha's neck. She stared back, speechless. She knew the significance of the goddess pendant, and for Ember to put it around her neck told Brig'dha that her words had not been for nothing. As she watched the brave warrior tying the necklace, she wanted nothing more than to wrap her arms around her and kiss her, but she held back, too frightened of what might happen.

She remembered their first meeting beside a pile of baskets during the trading days at Nes when the foxy redhead had stood before her excited and unable to do more than stare. It had been the first time in her life that the gaze of another had not bothered her. Ember's well defined and muscular arms, lower, nearly husky voice, and striking features left the breathless brunette with tingles when she considered them. Yet, what had really mattered was who the random redhead was. She was a friend, a quirky and accident-prone woman, sort of, with often dreadfully bad ideas, little impulse control, and a problem with inserting herself into other people's problems. But this was also why Brig'dha couldn't stop thinking about her. She had never met a man like this, nor had a man ever physically interested her.

Still, the otherwise assertive warrior had never made an overt move to be anything more than a friend. Among Brig'dha's people, a woman rarely initiated a relationship. There were some tribes where that wasn't the case, but the idea of initiating a relationship terrified her. She was socially awkward, anxiety-ridden, and mostly afraid of what might go wrong if she tried. So, she had waited, but it was becoming harder to do so when the ravishing redhead would stretch every morning in full view, her muscles each defined under her painted light, brown skin…

"Hey… you okay?" Brig'dha snapped back into the moment, realizing Ember was smiling at her, though a little concerned. Embarrassment washed over her as she realized that she had become lost in the moment. Brig'dha took a deep breath to steady herself before she let her memories and thoughts wonder too far. Luckily, Ember quickly changed the conversation topic and began blabbing away, letting the matter pass unaddressed.

For the rest of the evening, Brig'dha held the pendant tightly as Ember walked beside her. She felt a connection with Ember much stronger than just a friendship, and she was starting to wonder if such feelings were truly one way. Had she misunderstood Ember's feelings? She had wanted to ask for over a harvest, though she remained far too shy. If she were wrong, it might damage their friendship, a risk she couldn't take, so she kept silent, her mouth closed, yet her eyes and ears open. Tes had never had a chance to find love, and here she was letting such a chance walk just beside her… so close, and yet beyond her reach.

Chapter Eight

The Blue Sea People

The warm shores of what is now modern-day French Rivera, near the city of Nice, reveal a beautiful and sunny landscape rich with a bounty of food and with a reasonably temperate climate. Given the extremely hospitable conditions, a tribe of 20 to 30 individuals could live in such a location and even thrive. The only problem facing the settlers from Isen'bryn is that their numbers had continued to dwindle since they left. Even a small influx of additional people could mean the difference between struggling to survive and thriving.

The gentle winds of the warming season were already beginning to blow on what was perhaps the fifth tenday since the small group of travelers had left the shores of the Greatest River. Fifteen people had left the village of Isen'bryn, and now thirteen remained, along with the addition of the small cat. The scenery had changed from dense forests to a great multitude of small hills with grayish red dirt and small scrubby trees. The Sun had almost reached the high point of the day, though the Moon would not be expected to rise. All around, the world had become a brighter and warmer place.

Ember paused to remove her fox fur coat and leggings, and placed them in her traveling pack. It had been a little chilly that morning, but now the heat of the Sun made fox fur unbearable. This was one thing she did not like about the South, the rapid climate fluctuations and extreme range of temperatures. The mornings tended to be very cool, while the midday and evening were quite hot. She wore her roe deer loincloth, a set of freshly woven nettle fiber shoes, and her long doe skin leather shirt with a fresh coat of black doe-like spots. Exposing her legs would help keep her cool while keeping the Sun off her upper body. Besides, she always felt better when her legs were open to the air. Leggings, quite literally, rubbed her the wrong way and chafed at her skin.

Of course, this also meant that she was dressed as a man. Women among the Isen'bryn usually wore wrap skirts made from leather or entire hides tucked into their waistbands, the bottoms cut into tassels. If they wore upper garments, these were usually leather shirts made from two deer skins sewn together and traditionally decorated with extensive beadwork. Though the styles were different, her own Great River people tended to wear similar designs, though they wore a slightly larger percentage of textiles. Ember would never be the victim of the status quo, opting to wear a loincloth, occasionally leggings, and optional leather shirt in the style of a man. None had bothered her over this choice, probably not realizing that it was also out of place for her people. She was out of place for her people, she supposed.

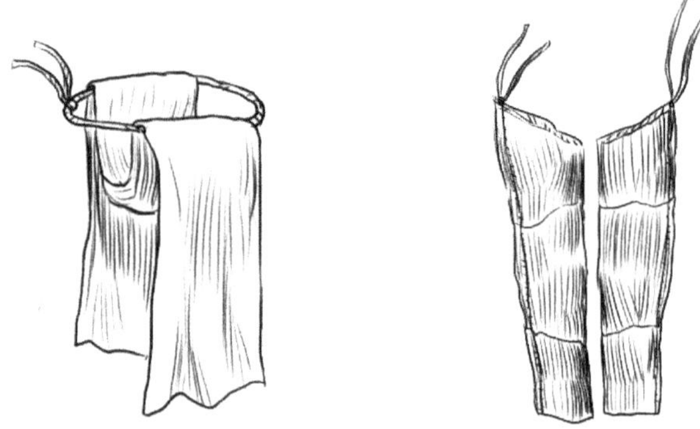

Ember's loincloth and leggings

She had never felt comfortable in the clothing of a woman, even as a child. Among her people, there were those born male who took on women's roles, called wergene – a portmanteau of "wer," meaning man, and "geneh," meaning woman. The third gender among her people was as crudely defined as the name, yet it was accepted. Of course, she had been born female, and no such group existed for someone like her. She frowned as she considered that the reason was likely her people not believing someone born female could handle the tasks of a man. It was absurd and yet another reason to stay away from her people, at least for a time. Was she some female species of wergene? Perhaps a "Genewer?" Whichever gender she was, she was now at least cool and comfortable.

She paused and sat upon a rock, quickly applying lines running horizontally around her legs. She always felt naked without paint, and her people had strict rules of decency, regardless of gender. Indecency occurred when the body was left bare of paint. Her skin did not have to be covered from head to toe, but at least a stripe or two here and there, or maybe some dots would suffice. This pleased the gods, and Ember wasn't in the mood to upset spirits or any divine beings who might be watching. Brig'dha came to stand above her, looking down and shaking her head slightly with a smile as she watched the recalcitrant redhead painting herself as the men of her people did. While her own people wore body paint, she found Ember's obsession with being painted quite amusing, though she could not help but appreciate the beautiful patterns her friend used or her strong muscles just beneath the paint... Brig'dha took a breath and looked away, trying to ignore such thoughts.

Ahead, the small brush-infested hill had a strange brightness and cheerful look, which seemed in stark contrast to the ugly scrubby plants which grew upon its sides. The small hill blocked all sight ahead. The group had just recently emerged from a valley to the smell of sea breeze. There was no mistaking the strange odor nor the birds flying overhead. All their senses told them that a great river of some sort was just ahead. Ember still did not quite understand the concept of a "sea." Mael had explained it to be similar to a very large lake, but she still had trouble with the idea. With her legs free and air blowing across the sweat, cooling her, she aimed to march forward and find out.

Brig'dha watched as Ember trudged forwards heedlessly through the brush over the top of the hill, tripping and falling once in her obsessive need to see what was on the other side. Earlier that day, Brig'dha had removed her heavy leather shirt and applied a simple reed shawl. Given a few tendays, she would adjust to the heat, but for now, her best defense against the heat was layering. Her other problem was that she had a warm ball of fur in her arms, little Mew. Mew adored being carried and would complain until Brig'dha picked him up, while Ember took every opportunity to remind everybody just how incredibly rare a cat that liked humans should be. Brig'dha had supposed that the reason for Mew's lack of fear might have to do with his age.

Either way, Brig'dha couldn't help but adore holding the small furry creature in her arms. She knew that one day he would grow too large to be easily carried, but she hoped that day would be far off. According to Ember, Mew appeared to be a bit of a runt. Brig'dha was also not quite convinced that he was the most intelligent cat. She also suspected that something might be slightly wrong with him, but it only added to his cuteness. Brig'dha's thoughts of Mew were interrupted by sudden screaming.

"The Blue Sea! We actually found it!" Ember screamed. Everyone rushed forward and up the side of the hill to behold the sight. Before them spread a vast waterway that stretched from one side of the horizon to the other. The waters were a beautiful, almost transparent, turquoise, unlike the usual dark blues the Isen'bryn were used to or the muddy brown that Ember grew up beside. It was indeed a beautiful sight.

Everyone rushed forward and down the slight embankment onto a grayish-white sandy beach. Up and down the coast, sheer rock walls prevented most access to the water, but here and there, beautiful beaches similar to the one on which they now stood emerged from the sides of the rock walls. The water was probably not nearly warm enough to swim in, but Ember didn't care. Tossing aside her clothes, she ran heedlessly into the water. It was quite cool, being only the very beginning of the warm season, but actually much warmer than she had expected. In fact, the water was only slightly cooler than the air. Either way, she didn't care. Ember swam arm over arm through the beautiful turquoise water. Then, after a few moments of swimming, she looked back to see how far out she had gotten. Nearly 20 lengths of a man separated her from the water's edge, quite a good distance.

Ember caught Brig'dha's face and saw the exasperated expression of her friend. That alone made her actions worth it. Ember laughed aloud and then took a deep breath and dove under the water. Beneath the waves, the water was so clear that Ember could see all the way to the bottom, which was, at least, three lengths of a man below her. She had never seen such beauty and clarity in her entire life under the water. She swam deeper and deeper until she reached the very bottom, though her ears began to hurt from the pressure. All around, beautiful fish of different colors swam around the strange colored rocks and other beautiful sights she could not quite describe. Ember only emerged from the water when her lungs forced her to do so.

A short while later, the reckless redhead emerged from the water, shivering almost uncontrollably but with a broad smile across her face. This small beach was very well-suited for a camp, if not a village. At least for the time being, the group would remain here until they figured out what else to do. Brig'dha was glad that Kel had the forethought to light a fire while Ember was out freezing to death in the cool water. Brig'dha shook her head at the sight. She sometimes wondered if Ember was really part fish. Perhaps she would have the upper body of a woman and the lower body of a fish. What a strange creature that would be, she pondered.

That night, the group ate fresh fish and shellfish as they camped on the beach of what could only be described as paradise. The air smelled fresh and clean, and the fish came in all manner of strange shapes and colors. It would be at least a tenday before basic huts were constructed, but they had enough people to get the beginnings of the village started. Sitting around the campfire, discussion continued over what to do next

The first task would be sending out scouts in each direction to ensure that they were not encroaching on another tribe's land.

"Galar and Yan should head East to scout, at least, a day's journey. Nael and I will head West. Caelwyn and Kel, why don't you search to the North?" Aethen said as he doled out tasks for each person. He was not the leader, but he had leadership qualities, and people naturally tended to follow his words. Normally, Galar would have at least complained some to ensure that he did not seem to be entirely reliant upon the bidding of Aethen, but he was deep in thought of what might come next, so he merely nodded his head in agreement.

"I know what I can do, but this might sound weird..." Ember said, gently touching her fingers together and looking at the rest of the group in an excited sort of way. Around her, most people's faces acknowledged their agreement with at least the last part of her sentence.

"I will scout the waters and beaches to the West. It may sound odd, but you never know what could be underwater, right?" Ember said, all smiles. The entire group just glared back at her in confusion and amusement. Of course, many considered the idea absurd as water was just water, but the fish they had eaten tonight came from Ember's spear, so no one made any arguments against her suggestion. Besides, perhaps she might indeed find something interesting.

"That's a really good idea, Ember," Aethen said with excitement before realizing that he had laid the praise on just a little too thick. Several people turned to glare at him with confusion and slightly accusatory expressions. He looked down, a little embarrassed by his own reaction. Ember had been so wrapped up in her own statements that she had not noticed what had happened, luckily for Aethen. In truth, he was attracted to Ember, and this attraction is what had prompted him to make such bold moves. Unfortunately, he didn't know whether she held any interest in him.

His hope was that he might encounter Ember alone and make an even bolder overture of his interests. Unfortunately, simply praising her idea in front of the group didn't seem to work very well. Across from him, Brig'dha sat beside the radiant redhead glaring back. Her expression was neutral, and yet it held a subtle warning. Aethen cautiously stuffed a large piece of fish in his mouth and began to chew. He didn't quite understand why Brig'dha seemed so annoyed, if not openly territorial, and he doubted he would figure it out.

ᴐ ᴐ ᴐ

Five days had passed since the splinter group of the Isen'bryn had arrived at the Blue Sea. The construction of half a dozen huts had begun, and many of the necessary tools of society were already being forged. Meegin sat before a wooden frame that held a stretched deer hide which she was scraping. Her honey-colored hair was tied in long braids to keep it out of the way, and she had stripped herself down to a wrap leather skirt and a reed cloak to ward off the Sun. Her only regret was that Geb was no longer nearby to chat with.

Having already made enough arrows for a small war band, Geb, Kyra, and Eryi foraged the local region for whatever plant life could be had. Somewhere far off in the hills, Kel stalked animals with his bow while Nael and Galar worked to build huts and other structures needed for a small village. Faenel, Yan, and Aethen constructed baskets, tools, and other things required around the village.

Not far from where Meegin sat, Caelwyn used his adze, a stone pick-like tool used to work wood, to shape wooden poles from felled trees to construct more huts. Meegin had taken to speaking to him, though he barely replied to anything that she said. Caelwyn was not one for words, and Meegin more than made up for both of them. Curiously, he found her voice relaxing, and he was beginning to realize why Geb spent so much time working near the talkative woman.

Building a new tribe with his own hands, Caelwyn could not help but feel proud of himself and the group. If everything continued to work out, he considered the chance that he might even approach Meegin at their next ritual. He stopped splitting wood for a moment and turned to regard her. With her back to him, he could see her long, honey-colored braids bobbing backward and forwards as she scraped the leather hide. The entire time he watched, only a short moment, she never stopped talking. He wasn't even sure if she breathed. Strangely, it almost made him laugh.

Unlike the well-braided hair of Meegin, his long, black hair was tied in a ponytail behind his head, he was covered in sweat, and he wore a simple loincloth. He was hardly in the condition to approach her, so he simply listened while she continued speaking about the most random of things. Meegin was certainly the kind of woman he could live with. Caelwyn shook his head with a smile and turned back toward the poles. *The tribe's not going to build itself,* he thought.

While everyone else performed their tasks, Ember spent a good portion of her time in the water hunting for building materials, anything that was shiny, and of course, catching fish and mollusks. She was a natural underwater and could hold her breath for nearly twenty counts of ten, longer than anyone else she knew. This gave her time to dive deeply and scour the land under the water for anything which could be found.

Ember carried a long fishing spear and a flint knife which was thicker than her dagger and better suited to digging or prying things loose from the seabed. The water remained chilly, but she swam in the nude as clothing made swimming difficult. Luckily, she had become accustomed to the cool water in only a short time. The secret was to take breaks and bask in the Sun on a particularly large rock that protruded from the water only a few lengths of a man from the shore.

The day before, Ember had found a massive clam not far out and about two lengths of a man deep. The clam was almost the same size as her entire abdomen and quite heavy. It took her a considerable time to pry it free from the seabed and lug it back to the shore. She would dive and lift the clam, carrying it a short distance before dropping it and returning to the surface for air. This went on and on until she finally got it to the shore. That night, everyone had eaten a handful of tangy clam meat. The shell was utterly beautiful and allowed to dry in the Sun, so it could be used either for tools or even as a "pot" to boil water. The Blue Sea truly was an amazing place.

It was probably the shells that were of the most benefit. To Ember's surprise, she discovered that the shells she found by the water could sometimes be sharp enough to cut like a knife. She had even nicked her own finger on one of them, using it to slice open a fish. The idea of a warrior armed with a giant clamshell had popped into her mind producing intense laughter, but all joking aside, a shell could be much more deadly than many realized. She was glad to have a steady supply of the sharp objects readily available for her to grab at a moment's notice.

With her fishing done for the day, Ember had walked down the beach towards the West for quite a distance. She hoped to find more of the beautiful seashells the sea held or something similar. As she stepped barefoot upon the warm sand, the warmth from the Sun on her back staved the still cool air and made for an existential contrast. The feeling was intoxicating, as was the teal blue water beating upon the rock and sand beach. Ember started to wonder why anyone lived in the Northern lands.

She stopped as she heard a strange sound up ahead. There was a very sparse beach in this area, and where the water met the land, the land rose quickly to extreme heights. Those same rock walls could play tricks on the ears and the mind. She gazed up one of the sheer rock faces and felt dizzy at its height. Ember continued walking for a short time longer before she heard the sound once more. This time, it sounded much more like a scream. Thoughts of the wolves immediately returned, and Ember began to run toward the sound with her fishing spear at the ready. If some unfortunate person up ahead was being attacked by wolves, she had to save them.

There should be nobody from her tribe out this far, especially not down by the water. Several times she had to jump in the water and swim between small rocky beaches as there were simply impassable areas where sheer rock face met the sea. As she stepped around a rock wall, the source of the yelling suddenly came into view. A small boy, likely no more than eight or nine harvests of age, sat on a very tiny rock protruding from the water, about ten lengths of a man from shore. The boy did not appear to be in any immediate danger, but this told Ember that other people would likely be nearby. The likelihood of finding an unattended child more than a short distance from a tribe was slight.

At first, Ember suspected that the small child was simply too afraid to swim back. Perhaps he had swum out to the rock and then became too scared to return. She wasn't sure how anybody could be afraid of such a short-distance swim, but the child was young. She looked towards the water's edge and called to the boy to calm him. She would merely swim out to the rock showing him that there was nothing to be afraid of. Perhaps, if there was a tribe nearby, helping this child could be the first step toward securing good relations. Ember smiled to herself, thinking how useful she would be to her people.

"Hey, little boy! It's alright! I'll swim over and get you. Don't worry," Ember yelled at the child, waving her hands with an exaggerated smile on her face to calm him. The boy looked back, shock and fear on his face. Somehow, she had not calmed him much. In fact, he looked even more afraid. He began to point at the water and scream something that Ember didn't understand. She supposed that he was frightened? Perhaps he suspected that monsters lived in the water. She had not seen any monsters in the blue sea, so she figured the best way to help the boy would be by demonstration.

Leaving her fishing spear and loincloth on the beach, Ember took a deep breath and rushed forwards, launching herself into the air and diving into the quickly deepening water. All around her, bubbles of air fluttered by, slowly disappearing and revealing a beautiful teal scene. Strangely, there were large fish swimming near the rock with the boy. Each fish was nearly as long as Ember, with a long gray body and long pointy fins that formed sharp angles. The tips of most of these fins were black, like soot.

Ember swam towards the rock and the amazing giant fish. Perhaps they were similar to catfish or sturgeon, just more angular and quicker? She suspected that the child was afraid of the large fish. She had encountered giant catfish and sturgeon many times before in the Great River without incident.

Suddenly, one of the creatures swam by her from behind. She reached out and allowed her hand to flow across its body. Strangely, its skin was smooth in one direction but extremely rough in the other. Whatever form of catfish they were, they were beautiful to Ember. She watched the large catfish-like creatures swimming for a moment longer and then surfaced for a breath of air. Using her hands to pull the hair from her eyes, she looked up at the boy with a smile to show him that she was quite safe and had nearly reached him. Nevertheless, the look on his face was dreadfully frightening, as though he expected some horror to take place. Ember began to wonder if perhaps there was some basis to his fear, perhaps something she didn't understand about these giant catfish?

Oddly enough, she saw a fin from one of the creatures break the surface of the water for a short moment before returning beneath the waves. The sight of the fin seemed to horrify the child. Ember took a deep breath and returned beneath the waves to get a better view of the creatures. She had swum almost all the way to the boy, and perhaps he could explain his fears to her in some way. He might even know some of the trade languages. The people of the True South that she had met before did know some trade language though their words were somewhat foreign.

As the bubbles cleared from view, the large catfish-like creatures returned. Ember noticed that they had increased their overall speed and now made sudden and sharp turns. One of the creatures approached, shaking its head sideways and arching its back in a strange display. The unusual display was quick, but one lasting image remained in her mind. The creature had quickly snapped its jaws open and shut, revealing a trait that catfish did not normally have – a generous number of extremely sharp and pointy teeth. Suddenly, Ember knew exactly why the child was afraid, and she began to panic. *Aeeya!*

ɔ ɔ ɔ

The young boy had no idea who the strange woman was swimming with the deadly creatures, but she seemed unafraid of them, and they seemed to respect her. Her hair color was much redder than any woman he had seen, and she swam extremely fast. Perhaps she was some kind of water spirit? He wasn't sure, but he knew that eventually it would grow dark and he would not wish to spend all night on the rock. The boy dove into the water and swam as hard as he could toward the shore. It wasn't that far away, and he hoped the strange water spirit woman would keep the sharks at bay.

☽ ☽ ☽

Ember had stopped advancing and was about to turn around and flee when she heard a splashing sound. She turned and saw that the boy had entered the water. He immediately began swimming as hard as he could toward the shore. Ember was not sure if the creatures were attacking him or not, but she didn't want to take the chance that a young boy might be eaten by one of these giant killer catfish. She pulled free the flint knife at her waist and began to swim as hard as she could toward the boy, hoping to intercept any creature that stood in his way.

Coming to the surface for a breath of air, Ember realized that she had swum so fast that she had nearly caught up with the boy. She was a much better swimmer than he was, having spent every warm season since she was old enough to walk swimming nearly every day. The boy swam by kicking with his feet and paddling with his hands, a very wasteful and slow technique. Ember dove underwater with a large breath of air and came up underneath the boy, watching a sleek monstrous catfish-thing approaching at a speed she could hardly believe. Right as the creature lunged at the boy, Ember slashed her knife into the side of its head, cutting a long gash.

The knife barely penetrated the tough hide, but it caused the creature to swim off at a high rate of speed. All around her, more than a dozen of the creatures swam, with more approaching every moment. The catfish-like creature she had attacked disappeared into the blue within moments, only to be replaced with more of the creatures coming straight for her. The blood from the first animal lingered in the water around her and seemed to entice those nearby. Ember turned and swam as hard as she possibly could towards the shore, a blinding dash. Behind her was a sea filled with giant catfish monsters.

☽ ☽ ☽

The boy reached the shore and flung himself onto the sand to escape the monsters. As soon as he caught his breath, he stood and looked back

122

at the water. He saw many tails and fins splashing in the water and even blood. That woman was in the water fighting with the sharks, or so it seemed. A moment later, the redheaded water spirit woman burst forth from the water, screaming and dancing as though a spider had just landed on her. In her hand, she held a flint knife. She dropped to her hands and knees a moment later, seemingly exhausted. The boy gazed at the woman wide-eyed. She was a hero who had saved him from sharks, quite literally fighting them with a knife. He had to bring her back to his people, or they would never believe him.

ↄ ↄ ↄ

I actually survived an incident in the water without passing out! she thought, sarcastically. Having finally caught her breath, Ember again stood before the child with one hand upon her chest as she breathed deeply and the other holding the knife. Whatever those things were, she did not want to encounter them again. They seemed obsessed with blood and were now in some sort of frenzy in the water splashing around. The boy's leg had a scrape which likely came from a piece of the strange tree-branch-shaped white rocks that "grew" underwater. It wasn't very big, but even now, a small amount of blood dripped from it. Perhaps that was what had attracted the creatures. She supposed that now would be a good time to introduce herself.

"Aes-Kaelu eahg'nom," she said to the child using the Isen'bryn words for, "My name is Ember." The boy stood before her, seemingly enchanted by her strange looks. She was taller than him and had long red hair with a different facial structure. But, unfortunately, as curious as he seemed to be of her, he had no look of recognition upon his face. She hoped that he might understand some words from the trade language, though her wide smile and large eyes seemed to have convinced the boy that he was not in any danger.

"My-name, Ember. Do you-know words?" she asked in the horrible broken way of the trade language. The trade language was actually an amalgamation of many words from different languages. The vocabulary was not very large, but it was easy to learn, and basic trade could be had with only a few words. Typically, many of the words known to one group would not be known to another, as this was not a universal language. The boy looked at her for a moment, slightly confused, as if forming a reply to her words in his mind. Ember repeated herself several times very

123

slowly and used hand gestures to emphasize her name. The boy slowly gained a look of recognition.

"Ein. Ehnim, Ein," he said using what sounded like "ehnim," which Ember supposed was a close cousin to the trade word for name, "Nhom." She had not expected that a young boy would know very much of the trade language, but the fact that he knew anything about it gave her hope. It meant that wherever his parents were, they likely would know more and could speak with her. The boy grabbed hold of her hand and began to pull her down the beach towards the path which led up the side of one of the rock faces toward the land above. He seemed excited as he led Ember happily towards his people, the redhead pausing to attach her loincloth and grab her spear.

Ember didn't mind meeting the people, but she worried that she might be a tad indecent. Her indecency came from her mostly unpainted skin. A body must be painted, and to present herself before new people without proper body paint was scandalous. Looking down, she noticed with some relief that some of her berry-based paint remained while most of the black soot paint had washed off. She hoped being mostly unpainted wouldn't offend these new people. At least the beautiful Amber of Life necklace hung around her neck, giving her a little more credibility.

ɔ ɔ ɔ

Ember and the boy walked a short distance before coming upon a group of perhaps 30 living in small makeshift huts of leather stretched across poles. The scene before Ember was not an established tribe but more like an ill-prepared nomadic group. She also noticed that there were oddly very few old or feeble people. The faces of the adults were dour and hopeless. As soon as the people took note of Ember, several men rushed forward with war clubs and spears at the ready if the strange woman proved hostile.

She could not imagine how fearful these people must be if their men were dispatched with weapons against such a terrifying sight as a barely dressed woman with a fishing spear. This was a new level of paranoia. Seeing the men approach with a resigned, fearful look upon their face as though they expected trouble, she tossed aside the fishing spear and dropped to her knees with her arms outstretched in a sign that she was completely non-hostile. The men approached but appeared to calm down at such a peaceful gesture. Slowly, some of the men encircled her while several others hurried off in the direction from which she had come, probably scouting to ensure no one else had followed.

Ember and Ein exchanged confused glances. She did not suspect that a group of tired and frightened refugees, that is what they looked like, would mercilessly kill a woman on her knees, but she swallowed hard anyway. A tall man stepped from the camp center with a rugged look about him. His body was tattooed in multiple places with black coloring in various animals shapes and scarification in different patterns. From his half-bald head grew a long scruffy mane of black hair. He wore a long loincloth and a pair of leather boots, as well as the longest beard Ember had ever seen on a man. He came to stand before her and listened as the child, Ein, quickly described the events which had just transpired.

She took note of the people in more detail. Their hair ranged from very dark and almost black to a deep brown. Like their hair, their eyes were generally dark brown, and their noses were slightly larger than her people, their faces having a slightly different shape. Their skin was a little darker than hers, but it had an olive color rather than her light brown tan or Brig'dha's people, with the very dark skin. The people wore loincloths and ornate leather aprons decorated with shell and bone beads, while the children were unclothed, as expected. Very little upper body garment could be seen, aside from a few shawls. Many of them decorated their upper bodies with necklaces and other jewelry made from bone, coral, and other baubles which could be found. They seemed more accustomed to living in a warmer climate. This area did appear to get cold, but Ember had a feeling that it never got quite as cold as where she was from, and humidity made it feel even warmer.

All around her, people from the small refugee tribe gathered to hear the fantastic story of the woman who battled the vicious giant catfish-things. She wasn't quite sure what the child was telling the older man, but given his frantic hand gestures and exaggerated speech, it sounded as though he was turning her one knife slash into a vast sea battle. She hoped the child would not over-exaggerate too much. She would try to straighten things out once she got a chance to speak to the man, who was apparently their leader.

The man listened patiently to the story Ein told and then knelt before Ember. His face had been weathered by the Sun, and he wore scarification marks across his cheeks, but his eyes spoke of a man with thoughtful intent. He looked upon her appraisingly, judging her before he said anything. He also noticed the Amber of Life necklace and repeatedly stared at it. Next, he spoke what sounded like the same basic sentence in two different languages. Each time Ember shook her head to indicate that she did not understand. The man thought for a moment and then switched into what sounded like the trade language and began again.

"You-know, words?" he asked. This time, Ember understood him and smiled, nodding her head to indicate this. The man smiled back at her, returning the gesture. For a long while, Ember sat before the man and spoke as best as she could. In all, they shared perhaps two dozen words, those she had learned from the traders from the True South in the village of Nes. It wasn't long before Ember had explained to them who she was and what had actually happened with the "catfish." She spoke of her own people building a tribe nearby and their need for people to create a stable community. Though carefully listening, the man would occasionally pause to translate to his people, most of whom did not seem to speak the trade language. His people seemed more interested in the discussion than anything else, and whatever work they performed had ceased.

It turned out that the man was named Arunden, the leader of his people. They were called the Shell People, or at least what was left of them. Ember was not quite sure that she fully grasped everything Arunden was saying, but it sounded to her as though the tribe had once numbered greater than 100 individuals. As the story went, a strange sickness had come upon the tribe during the cold season. It was believed to have been caused by evil spirits that had been offended somehow. Their elders and shaman had tried in vain to calm the spirits, but by the time the sickness had faded, two-thirds of the tribe had died.

His people had burned what was left of the tribal dwellings and set out for a new place to live as soon as the weather warmed. It was a sad tale, but Ember had heard of similar stories before. No one knew what caused spirits to attack entire peoples, but the results were usually horrific. It was known that approaching such a tribe might cause offense to the same spirits. People known to have offended local spirits were typically avoided, which explained why they were on the move. It had been nearly half a harvest since the sickness had left these people, which meant that they were probably safe to approach. Yet, spirits tended to remain in a general area. But, since they had burned their village and left that area, it should have appeased any remaining angry spirits. *Well, I did say that you could find interesting things by the water, sometimes... I found an entire tribe,* she mused.

What amazed Ember even more than the spirit story was the explanation of the giant catfish. According to Arunden, the creatures she had fought were called "Fierce-Fish," at least in the trade language. They were not catfish but a predatory kind of fish that could easily kill a man. Ember a bit concerned at the thought that the Blue Sea might be filled with these creatures. Arunden explained that they were actually not that dangerous when encountered by themselves, but they could become dangerous if many approached and frenzied or if blood was spilled in the water. This was why spearfishing underwater should only be performed for a short time each day.

As time went by, Ember spoke with several group members, telling each of them of her own journey from the North, Arunden translating. In a way, these people shared a common goal with her own, finding a place to live. However, there were too many of them to join a traditional village. Even though there might be enough to start a new community, they could use some fresh, younger members with skills. As she listened to their plight, she began to envision a way to solve their problems while benefiting her own people. *I found the salt for the pork,* she thought.

Arunden's people had been on the run since leaving their village to burn. They had been rejected by many other tribes because of their offense to the spirits, and now they only wanted a place to stop and build a new life. Arunden's own wife had been taken by the spirits early on, leaving him to care for their young son Ein and their slightly older daughter Linaren. Ember felt for their pain and remembered the effect angry spirits had on the people of Nes when she had visited that village. Brig'dha's Husband had been killed by those angry spirits of Nes, though luckily, Brig'dha had been spared this horrible fate. Moved by their misfortune and given her own small group's need for people, Ember decided to make an offer. *I'm going to get in trouble for this,* she thought.

"You," she said, gesturing to all the people to indicate the entire tribe, "you, [join] me, people. [One] people," she concluded using hand gestures for join and the number one. Ember had not discussed this with any of her own people and felt that it was quite likely that she was speaking out of place, but she had been carried away in the moment having heard of their terrible misfortune. Besides, what more could her group have asked for? Here was an entire band of people in need of a place to stay, people in need of a new tribe.

Ember stood and began motioning the people in the direction of her small camp. It would take them a little while to gather up their belongings and break down their nomadic huts, but that moment of pause would give Ember the time she needed to meet some of the people and calm their suspicions. She realized how outrageous the notion of suddenly integrating her people with these folk would be. Still, opportunities like this seldom came, and she wouldn't throw this one away.

ↄ ↄ ↄ

Aethen stood over a pile of logs attempting to attach a well-polished stone ax head to the piece of wood which generally held it. Every now and then, the handle that held the ax head in place would become damaged or just wear out and need replacement. The problem was that he did not have enough people harvesting supplies to ensure a steady supply of resources, such as ax handles. Casting the handle aside, he picked up the stone ax head and began to try and split the logs holding it with his hand. This approach worked, but sometimes a log would split with part of the wood bumping his hand, which hurt dearly. He wished there were more people in his extremely tiny tribe, and not for the first time.

Behind him, Galar approached, watching Aethen stumble foolishly with the stone ax head. The sight was almost too pitiful to behold. It was absolutely apparent to Galar that his plan to leave and take with him the necklace was by far the best choice available. There were simply too few people to ever form a village, and if they lost even one more person, their tiny "tribe" would likely collapse. What he needed now was to find the right time and place to obtain the necklace from the crafty redhead.

"Aethen, you know ax heads are supposed to be connected to a handle. Your hand doesn't really count," he said, approaching Aethen with a smirk. Aethen looked up with a sardonic look across his face. He dropped the ax head and slouched forward. Galar was right, and it wasn't the ax he was talking about. What he really was speaking of was the lack of people and resources, and Aethen knew it. Traveling was one thing, but starting a tribe took people. They initially left contemplating joining a village or perhaps taking in a few people from a larger village, but the opportunity for these exchanges of people had not come about.

Even if Tes and Mael had survived, they would have needed at least ten more people. There was still the possibility that a local tribe with significant numbers of people might be found, some of whom might be interested in joining their small tribe. What they would do next had yet to be decided, though talk among the group was leaning toward integrating with another tribe. Aethen was pretty sure that the group would have to come to a hard choice very soon. Likely, they would have to join another tribe and abandon all hope of creating a new people. Aethen heard Ember calling as she appeared on the crest of the hill above their small makeshift village. Both men turned to see what Ember had found, hopefully, some mollusks for dinner.

"Hey Aethen, the wood chopping... um… you're doing it wrong. Here, let me give you some help," she called with a grand smile. Galar and Aethen both stared at the woman expecting her to come to help them or perhaps pull some sinew out of someplace. Ember was known for surprises, often helpful ones. What happened next was totally unexpected. Over the hillcrest, thirty people appeared slowly walking with their belongings and supplies. Many men had wooden poles crossing their shoulders and dragging behind them on the ground. Stretched between the poles were leather cords and other sticks lashed across. This provided a sort of sled to carry large numbers of heavy items.

Beside Ember stood a very tall man covered in tattoos and scars with a young girl and boy at his side. Aethen and the other members of their group stood alarmed at the sudden group of people. Aethen grabbed the wooden ax handle while Galar placed his hand upon his flint knife handle. No one was quite sure what would happen next or who these people were. Aethen slowly approached as Ember casually wandered toward him, still smiling and without explaining anything. She was supposed to find food in the sea, not a caravan of people.

"Ember, who are these people? What is this?" Galar asked, genuinely more confused than angry. Ember laughed loudly before speaking, relishing every moment and look of confusion.

"These are the proud and noble survivors of the Shell People. They need a place to stay and would like to join our tribe, the Blue Sea People!" Ember smiled to herself at that last bit. She just randomly thought of the name Blue Sea People on the spot. It actually sounded like a good name for the group, and she hoped that everyone else would agree. Brig'dha stepped forward from a small, newly constructed hut carrying Mew in her arms, her gaze shifting between the people and Ember. This was going to be a lengthy explanation.

ɔ ɔ ɔ

The Great Lake to the North, one day known as the Black Sea, was connected to the Blue Sea in the South, one day known as the Mediterranean Sea, and called the Blue Lake by some, by a long and powerful water channel called The Brown River, one day called the Bosporus. The Brown River got its name because of its light brown color, which came from the sediment picked up whenever a powerful current caused a surge of water through the river. As far back as anyone could remember, water from the Blue Lake would occasionally surge down the Brown River, causing flooding along its banks and sudden bores of water through the lands and washes. Approaching the banks of the Brown River, a lowly dye trader named Idmasa walked with his strangest companion ever. Said companion had traded a beautiful bone bead necklace simply to be escorted from the city of Nara'kit to the city of Isut'na, to the Southwest and then to be traded as a wife to the man of her choice.

He had seen and heard many strange things in all his days, but never anything quite so confusing as this. Idmasa still did not quite understand her motive. She actually wanted to be traded away, or so it seemed. He continued to mull the idea over in his mind. Being traded away was tantamount to being a concubine, yet she had been the one to ask for such treatment. He assumed that she was trying to flee and hide from someone or some trouble in Nara'kit and that she had figured the city of Isut'na was a good place to hide. That part made sense, but why be traded as a wife – a concubine? And why to a man that she picked out? Why would that be a safe way of escaping her problem? He simply did not understand the logic behind her thinking, but the lapis lazuli and copper beaded necklace she had given him was of exquisite quality and certainly worth her bizarre request. It had taken four days to walk the distance between the cities, which included a short boat ride across the Brown River.

The woman walked not far behind the trader with a blank expression, her thoughts buried deep within. She had done away with the high-quality linen clothing she was accustomed to wearing in the city where she was born. Instead, her feet tread lightly on thick leather-soled sandals, each reinforced with an extra wrap of leather for the journey. Around her waist, she wore a corded flax belt made from a braid of two-ply cord, to which she had fastened a leather pouch and a stone dagger and sheath. At her waist hung a bark fiber apron, though it had extremely long tassels which hung to her knees. It was not much to wear, but the climate was warm and very humid, making heavy clothing extremely uncomfortable. Around her neck, she wore a simple leather cord necklace with a single raven feather attached. This was her secret symbol of the goddess An'an, and she would call upon its strength to guide her through her ambitious goals.

The Sun beat down upon her back as Ianmu'kimun, or Ianmu to those who knew her, strode along the well-beaten path. Nara'kit was a little larger than Isut'na but of a similar design and culture. Its inhabitants were hard-working farmers who grew wheat and raised goats. The city worshiped the goddess An'an, the mother of the world, who had dominion over life and death, as well as her consort Gumaer the Bull God. Even now, as she walked across the dirt path, Ianmu could remember the high priest Kes'etir as he advised An'sankup'Anteanar, ruler of Nara'kit and father to Ianmu, against Ianmu's priestesshood.

"Your daughter is of exceptional beauty, but the Goddess requires more than beauty from her priestesses. She requires a strong bloodline. Since her mother died soon after she was born, the bloodline on her side is less than adequate. I would recommend choosing another of your children. Perhaps young Uleti? He is a fine hunter and comes from a strong bloodline, from your current wife. He would make a fine priest of Gumaer when he grows up," the high priest had said, casting a glare at Ianmu. She doubted that beauty or bloodline had anything to do with being a priestess. Later that day, she repaid him for his treachery by choking the life from him with her legs. She wondered if he had found her beautiful or pure enough as she choked him to death. Even now, she felt nothing but satisfaction at the memory of the dead priest. Reducing her to nothing but a tainted flower had done little to endear the man to her. Some flowers had thorns.

The next morning the goddess An'an had come to her and instructed her that she had a destiny in the city of Isut'na. She would journey there and gain control of the entire city in An'an's name. That powerful vision had told her that she would change the destiny of many. An'an didn't tell her she was beautiful or pure. Instead, she told her that she had a destiny and a purpose beyond the infantile amusement of men, though she was willing to use such absurd techniques if they proved effective.

Well, father, I've always considered myself a priestess of An'an, and I will show you just what your daughter can do, she thought with mirth. It was her intention to take control of the city of Isut'na. She had told no one before she left, not only because she did not want her father to stop her but also because her plan was so foolish and brazen that she would have been thought mad. In fact, she probably was mad to think that she had any chance. She was quick with a knife, quite dexterous, smart, considered reasonably attractive, and had been born with an oddly innocent look about her. These would be her tools, sharper than any knife. All she needed to do was find the right man to control – a man in the proper position for her to strike. She had actually come up with a plan for how she could take over an entire city one day while lying in a field of flax watching the clouds drift by. She had never expected to use the plan, having only dreamed it up on a lazy day. She smirked.

The city of Isut'na was an important trading hub for the area. As a result, much was known about its happenings. The city was led by a high priest of some fertility deity named Isut and a bull deity, though she did not know the name. In many ways, this was similar to her own city. The high priest of Isut was also the de facto leader, though most cities also had a council of elders. She assumed that Isut'na was no different. The important fact that she had learned was that the leader of Isut'na was without a wife and without a male child. This presented an opportunity for some powerful individual, most likely a man, to propel himself into a leadership position.

The basic premise was simple enough – Ianmu would need to find a way to become a concubine, lover, and finally wife to a powerful and clever man and then simply convince him to try and take power when the leader died. Waiting for the leader to die could be a time-consuming event, but mandrake root was always very useful in accelerating these sorts of things. Ianmu tapped her hand against the small leather bag that hung from her waist cord. Within this bag, she carried enough mandrake root to kill just such a man. Getting close enough to poison him might be a little complicated, but Ianmu was always up for a challenge.

The most important thing that was needed for her plan to work was absolute dedication to the task. She could have no regrets and no fear of dying if she was to succeed. She would directly manipulate powerful people in a large city using only charm, poison, and the slit of a throat. It was maddeningly brazen, and its chance of success was laughable, but she also had the will of the goddess An'an. If her goddess stood with her, who could possibly stand against her? She was filled with a sense of adventure and fear as she approached the city of Isut'na. Within a few Moons, she would either lie dead or be victorious.

CHAPTER NINE

AMBER OF LIFE

Rape and sexual assault are never justified under any circumstance, and the victim is never at fault. There is no possible justification.

The concept of rape and the right of people to refuse unwanted advances varies by culture and period. In our modern society, we tend to strive towards principles of mutual respect and consent (though we often fail.) However, this has not always been the case throughout humanity (nor is it fully the case, even today), not just from maligned people but also as a social norm. For example, ancient Greek mythology is fraught with rape, the victims sadly often blamed. In some tales, Medusa was raped by Poseidon, yet his actions are excused as simply being such a creature as he, while Medusa is blamed for having been a victim – a detestable example of victim blaming.

This illustrates just how different concepts of morality can vary from group to group and how lucky we are to have advanced in our cultural understanding. Unfortunately, even in our modern world, rape, and similar acts, are still quite rampant, even though our society has come to regard them as morally repugnant. Let us hope we can cleanse these dark traits of humanity from our species.

Five days had passed since the formation of the Blue Sea People, and things had been going well. Ember had survived her intense chastisement from Aethen, Galar, and Brig'dha over having invited an entire people to join without consulting anyone first. Even better, in her opinion, they had chosen to keep the name she had come up with. The main reason that nobody held too much anger was because of how badly they needed people. The Shell People told a heartwarming story, and as a people, they were very reasonable and agreeable. Ember suspected that being broken and forced to travel the wilds searching for food and a place to sleep might have made them more agreeable. Either way, the sudden increase in people made a significant difference in the quality of life.

Ember and Caelwyn were the best speakers of the trade language. For the first few days, they worked tirelessly at forming a common vocabulary between the newcomers and their own group. Soon, they had nearly four dozen words. It was not much, but it would serve them well until they began to truly learn each other's words. With complete immersion, Ember suspected that people from each original group would speak fluently between one another within as little as a full harvest.

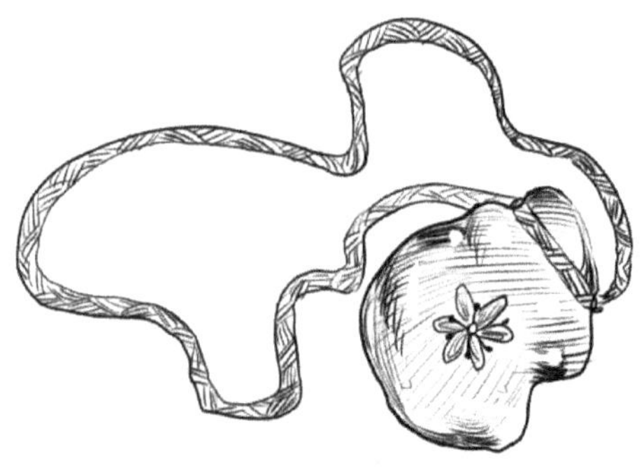

The Amber of Life pendant

All around, the new people worked building more permanent huts and settling down. With 45 people in the new tribe, Ember was sure that the Blue Sea people would grow to be a large community someday, and she was proud of what had been started here. What Ember did not tell anyone was that she and Brig'dha were planning on leaving for the True South shortly, though Ember did not know exactly when.

Besides bringing new people and extra hands to work, the original Shell People also brought with them advanced agricultural skills. Their people had formerly tended entire fields of plants before their tragedy. They had leather bags of flaxseed and wheat berries with them, which they intended to plant as soon as they settled. Flax would provide a valuable trade commodity that could be very useful when setting up a new tribe. Specialized tools could be obtained in trade for linen cloth and flax cord.

Meegin and Nael had been working with several others to slash and burn a small field to grow the flax and some wheat. They used small, controlled fires to burn the brush and sharpened antlers as slashers. The flax would grow until the warm season became full, and then just before the cold winds came, the wheat would be planted. It was expected that the first harvest would be sort of rough, with most of the food coming from gathering and hunting. However, the following growing season would see the first wheat and perhaps some of the finer products made from the flax. In time, the Blue Sea people could become a large tribe, but for now, their primary concern was merely making it from day to day.

The Isen'bryn used basic slash and burn techniques for the very primitive farming they practiced or just traded for wheat from the South. No one from the Isen'bryn group knew how to plant or grow crops in any significant sense, but luckily, many of the newcomers did. Two women, in particular, Puel and Fae, were both experienced farmers, and Meegin and Nael quickly took to their tutelage. On the fourth day of their arrival, the first field had already been picked clean and prepared. No one could believe how well the people had integrated with one another though they barely spoke familiar words. It was a partnership of necessity that was slowly becoming a friendship.

Aethen and Caelwyn had even suggested at the last group evening meal that the Amber of Life might not even be needed, though Ember thought they might be joking. In truth, she was still not quite sure what to do with the item. It hung around her neck where she had placed it following the death of Mael. There had been no reason for her to remove it at that point. Brig'dha had explained that its general function was simply to be present in the tribe as a sort of talisman. Ember wasn't quite sure how effective it was though she had to admit it was breathtaking.

Many of the new people, upon seeing the necklace, had done their best to convey their opinion of how beautiful it was. Given the language gap, this was actually more complicated than one might expect. Ember caught many people staring at the precious item. Of all the people who came by and glanced, the only one that sent shivers up her spine was Yan. She suspected that he wasn't actually eyeing the necklace but really eyeing her. She had turned away his advances so many times that she could no longer count them. The man just didn't understand what no meant, and he was growing more and more aggressive.

ↄ ↄ ↄ

"People are not watching each other as carefully anymore. I have heard talk of major villages in the direction the Sun rises, along the coast. Is this still what we want to do?" Kyra asked Galar, unsure of his motives. He had not mentioned their planned theft of the Amber of Life necklace in many tendays. Kyra had a tendency to switch from delicately passive to sharply aggressive very quickly. Galar sensed that she was simply acting calmly, hoping that he would agree with her. He had a sense that failure to agree would bring forth her sharpened and aggressive side as suddenly as a warm season's storm. The two sat by a small cooking fire in the center of a little wooden hut that normally housed five other people. He had to admit to himself, it was getting a bit cramped.

"Coming to the South was a significant change, but living in this tiny hut is not worth it. You and I cannot even be close without other people watching... Strange people whose language I do not even know. I'm sure these people will survive just fine without us – without the necklace. I, for one, would like to live in a larger tribe where food is plentiful and where we can have our own hut," he agreed. It had been five full days since the newcomers had arrived, and Ember was totally in control of the situation. Galar did not know what influence she had over Aethen, but the man was also popular and quickly rising to prominence. It was time to leave.

Kyra smiled like a wolf, having finally received such a direct confirmation that her husband was now on board with her plans. She felt a strange exhilaration, an almost frightening anticipation for what they were about to do. There was something reckless and intoxicating about plotting against the tribe. For some reason, it made her feel alive, more than anything else.

"We must pack our things today and hide them behind the hut. But the big question will be how to get the necklace from that fool girl. She wears it every moment of every day!" she said. They both began carefully packing their belongings as they pondered the best way to get the necklace from Ember. Plan after plan was proposed and then rejected for one reason or another. At one point, Kyra had even suggested killing Ember. Galar had dismissed the plan on the simple basis that they didn't need the entire tribe chasing them. They would be lucky to avoid pursuit as it was. Then, suddenly, Galar had an idea inspired by Kyra's suggestion.

"Wait a moment," he said, "I think I have an idea of how to get the necklace. Ember usually takes it off when she washes, right?"

"Have you not seen her? She eyes it like a fox. She'd see anyone trying to grab it, and she doesn't take it off when she goes for a swim," Kyra interjected, having watched the random redhead over the past few days, looking for a time when she could capture the necklace. In fact, the only time it wasn't around Ember's neck was when she cleaned, and she couldn't imagine a distraction big enough to preoccupy the warrior woman. As if reading her mind, Galar continued, his smile growing.

"You know how Yan has been trying to win over Ember since we came to the mainland? He's furious now that Ember has been ignoring him. It wouldn't take much to convince him to take matters into his own hands. I think I have a plan..." She gazed back at him, suddenly enticed by his cunning. Kyra liked a man who could match her ability to control those around him. For the rest of the evening, Galar and Kyra worked out the details of a rather vile plan to get the necklace.

ↄ ↄ ↄ

Each morning several members of the tribe would leave early, just as the Sun rose, to gather sticks to be used in fires later in the day. The following day, Yan, a woman named Aester, and a young man named Ragus had journeyed across the cliffs overlooking the water searching for sticks. They worked until the Sun was halfway to its midpoint before returning with large tied with a leather cord over their backs. Both of Yan's younger companions had returned to the tribe before him, unable to carry as large of a load. Galar had waited patiently for Yan to return but finally gave up and searched for the man.

It was not long before Galar discovered what was holding up Yan's return. He had stopped to take a break by a cliff overlooking the water. Galar approached and waved a greeting. Below he saw why Yan had chosen the spot for his break. Ember and Faenel were gathering mollusks from the shoreline not far below. Yan had an obsession with Ember, one that was probably a little unhealthy but definitely to Galar's advantage. The man had been relentless in his pursuit of the redhead, and he didn't seem to realize that she absolutely loathed him. It was a joke among many in the group though nobody ever dared to mention it aloud. Now, he would see just how pliable the man was.

"Yan, you are a good man, and you don't deserve being snubbed by her," he said, indicating Ember.

"Yeah, well, she seems to have more interest in her friends than me. Haven't seen her go for any men, not even Aethen. I doubt she's even been with a man, at least not with a real man," he sneered. For a short moment, Galar stood silently and pretended to appreciate everything Yan had said. Among those of the tribe, Yan was not the most intelligent by any stretch, and he approached problems with much less maturity than he should. His response to Galar's statement reflected this, but it also told Galar that Yan was potentially open to more radical action. The bone hook was already in his mouth, and Galar needed only tug a little to set it deep.

"Maybe you're just approaching her wrong," Galar wondered aloud, absentmindedly. Yan turned his full attention upon Galar with an accusative look. He didn't understand what Galar was saying, but if there were any chance that he might learn a better method of courting his obsession, he would drag it out of Galar one way or the other.

"What do you mean?" Yan asked impatiently. Galar bit back a smile, always amazed at how easy Yan was to manipulate. It was like holding a sweet fruit before a child.

"Ember isn't like other women. Do you see how strong her arms are? She has almost as much muscle as me," he said with a laugh, though Ember's physical strength had been one reason he had restrained himself from backhanding her on a few occasions. He was reasonably sure she would have hit back, and quite hard.

"Well, I've heard that some women pretend not to be interested... But what they really want is a man who will take action. Maybe if you come to her while she is alone and show her exactly what you have in mind, she will realize what she's been missing. You could teach her to enjoy you more than her friends. She just needs a strong hand and someone to show her how it's done," Galar suggested with a twisted, knowing smile. Galar actually felt a small pang of guilt, but he quickly suppressed it. The ridiculous redhead had it coming, didn't she?

Yan's expression switched to understanding, now realizing what he was saying. Galar suggested that Yan should be much more forceful in his pursuit and demonstrate to Ember that he was a "real man." The thought had crossed his mind, but he had dismissed it. A man who forced himself upon a woman and was caught doing so could face serious repercussions. However, Yan had always fancied himself a particularly great man, a deserving man. It angered him deeply that she had rejected him so many times. Maybe he had simply misread her? Most women put on weight, a sign of beauty among his people, yet Ember was lithe and muscular, something Yan found quite attractive, uncommon as his tastes were. She had to know he was interested, so what was she waiting for? Maybe she was playing hard to get?

"Some women only pretend that they don't want you. It's like a deer in the woods. You have to stalk them and take what's yours, or else they'll never give in. When she realizes that you're a man who takes what he wants, she will give in and be yours. She's more aggressive and independent than most women, so you have to be firm with her. She would make an excellent wife," Galar said with a smirk.

"But what if somebody sees? What if you're wrong, and she tells the tribe what I did? How can I take that risk?" This was the part Galar had been waiting for – the price.

"That's a good point, but I think I know how to get around it. I'll go and tell Aethen that you and I will be heading to the east to look for flint. If I am wrong and she says anything, I will merely say that you were with me the entire time. Who are they going to believe, her or us?" he said with a smile. Yan listened with growing enthusiasm. Galar had actually expected a greater degree of push-back, but it seemed that Yan was much more obsessed and held a looser grasp of reality than he had expected.

"If she gives in, you'll be a lucky man. If she gives you any trouble or threatens to tell, just take that necklace she stole from Mael and bring it to me. I'll hide it for a couple of days, and then you can 'find it' and be a 'hero.' Her reputation would be destroyed for losing it. It's a simple and foolproof plan. It's about time that you got a wife, and why not the one you want?" Galar paused and pretended to look around as though ensuring nobody was nearby before leaning close to Yan and whispering.

"And if I weren't married to Kyra, I would do the same," he added. In reality, Galar certainly would not make a move on Ember – he wasn't that brave – but Yan seemed to buy it, and being larger than Galar, he had a good chance of defeating her.

"She will probably go swimming after they finish gathering the mollusks, then take her necklace off to clean. When she is alone, cleaning, that is the perfect moment. I'll head back to the village to give Aethen your alibi, and you wait up here until the right moment," he finished slapping Yan on the back for reassurance. A moment later, Galar strode off, leaving Yan to his fate.

He would not condone Yan actually forcing himself upon Ember, but he figured that the likelihood of that coming to pass was nil at best. Ember was a strange woman, and he couldn't help but wonder if there was a slight chance that she might actually accept him. He suspected that the most likely outcome was that Yan would return to the village with some sort of painful injury. It would teach him a lesson about obsessing too much, and Kyra could simply sneak out from behind a rock and steal the necklace while Yan was keeping Ember occupied with his nonsense. No real harm done.

ↄ ↄ ↄ

Kyra stood on the beach behind a rock outcropping watching the women dig mollusks from the sand. She had caught sight of Yan and Galar several times on the rocks above. She did not know if Yan would be successful, but she would be ready if he failed. Kyra and Galar both knew that no woman wanted to be seized by anyone. The notion that a woman might play hard to get and accept a man who proved himself strong by having his way with her was total nonsense. He had been a fool since childhood, one reason she had always avoided him. Why Yan would believe such a foolish idea was beyond her comprehension, but she had known too many men like him to discount the likelihood that he would believe it. She shook her head at the notion. She was very likely to watch him receive a broken nose or something similar. She smiled at the thought as she had never liked the jerk.

She knew that Ember would likely get into a fight with Yan, but she might get a chance to steal the necklace during that struggle. In preparation, Kyra and Galar had placed their traveling packs with supplies on the outskirts of the village if they needed to make a hasty getaway. While she waited, Kyra wondered how Ember would react to Yan's forceful encounter. Ember might be a little over-the-top and an annoyance to Kyra, but she was also a proven warrior. If even half of the stories Brig'dha told were true, Yan's head would likely be found on a wooden pole before the day was finished. Kyra almost bit her lip, trying not to laugh at the thought. She found the man just as creepy as Ember did and was quite glad that she was not the subject of his designs. She felt a little better when she noticed that Ember did not have any noticeable weapons on her.

Ember waved goodbye to Faenel as she left the beach with a basket full of shellfish. Mollusks were easy to obtain, and their shells were very useful. The shells could be used to create patterns in clay for pottery, something the new members of their growing tribe knew how to make, and the sharp edges of a shell made a quick and easy knife. Ember would often use a shell to slice open fish she had caught without the need to dirty a knife. Besides being sharp, the shells could also be used as necklaces and even worked into fishhooks, both of which could be traded with neighboring tribes for food. For this reason, the gathering of various types of mollusks was of extreme importance and a daily ritual. Memories of the river mussels her people wore for some ceremonies returned.

Finally, alone, she gazed at the beautiful teal water and watched the waves gently splashing upon the sand. The air was beginning to become quite warm and occasionally even hot. Being considered part fish by her friends, she always made time for a good swim. She figured that she would clean the sweat off her back with a quick dip before returning to the tribe for the evening meal. The warm air and the beautiful water were simply intoxicating, and she found herself often swimming several times per day.

She removed her leather shirt and the Amber necklace, placing them on a rock not far from the water where she would not lose them. She normally swam, then cleaned herself, but she was tired and hungry, and decided to combine the activities, wanting to get back to camp to eat the shellfish as soon as she could. Standing bare under the warm sun, she stretched, digging her toes into the beach. The feel of the hot sand under her feet was always lovely. It was warm and had a wonderful texture which contrasted the cool Blue Sea. Water splashed across her feet within a few moments, adding to the sensations. Ember was an existential sort of person, and longed to simply feel the world in its tactile nuance.

The water continued to rush forward, crossing her feet and sending chills up her body. She tossed her loincloth to the sand and carefully stepped into the cool water, feeling shivers run up her body and watching tiny bumps appear all over her skin from the cold. Ember waded out until the water reached her waist. She bent over, dipping her hands into the sand and pulling out large globs she used to rub across her skin, removing dirt. Ember began to chant a cleaning song that she had learned as a child. Many women in the tribes she had visited had inquired as to why her skin was so smooth and soft. Her secret was simple, clay and sand, natural exfoliants.

ↄ ↄ ↄ

Yan was actually more nervous than he suspected he would be. He stepped out onto the beach and beheld the sight of Ember cleaning herself. She was truly a strange-looking woman, being leaner and more toned than most women, almost a little masculine, in some ways. It was normally considered attractive for a woman to have a little weight and fuller breasts. That weight helped a woman through childbirth and more closely resembled the Goddess. Ember was lithe, if not a bit skinny, but she had an exotic appeal that fascinated Yan for some reason he couldn't quite reconcile. He approached the water's edge as she finished her cleaning, ready to make her, his.

Ember stepped from the sea and carefully rubbed the water from her eyes as she bent down to fetch her roe deer loincloth from the sand where she had discarded it, securing it in place with several knots. Leather could quickly fall apart or rot if allowed to become wet, one of the many reasons swimming was done in the nude. Garments like her doe skin shirt were oiled, which provided a degree of water resistance, yet even this was fleeting. She was shaking the last of the water from her body when she looked up to see Yan standing before her.

"Aeeya!" she exclaimed, nearly jumping with a start. The last person that she wanted to be standing on the beach staring at her as she finished cleaning was that creep, Yan. How long had he been there? Had he come just to watch her naked? Nudity wasn't normally an issue, but context mattered. Yan was never a valid context. Suddenly, her cold skin began to run warm with anger and a little embarrassment. This was yet another reason why she and Brig'dha should leave. Some people were simply too creepy.

"How long have you been standing there? Go away!" Ember yelled at him. He glared back at her with a strange sort of look in his eyes. His gaze sent waves of creepiness throughout her body. The last man who had stared at her in that way was the big oaf who had tried to take advantage of her nearly two harvests before. That big oaf had been killed by an arrow from one of his own companions for his actions. What could Yan possibly expect? Did he think that this was a great place to attract her? *No wonder you don't have a woman. You're a creep,* she thought.

"It took me a while to realize what you wanted, but now I see. You play hard to get to find the strongest man. You need a man who could be even stronger than you. I get it now," he said, slowly stepping forward. Ember glared back, dumbfounded. She knew that he could be annoying, but she had never suspected that he would fully lose his mind. She stepped backward, ready to flee into the water, when her foot poked against a sharp shell making her pause with a slight yelp. The moment she looked down at her foot, he was upon her, both hands grasping her shoulders.

Ember struggled to free herself but quickly realized that Yan's grip was quite strong. She leaned forward and brought her knee as hard as she could between his legs, but Yan had expected this and simply twisted his hip sideways, deflecting her blow. He pulled her forward and roughly threw her to the sandy ground. He stood towering over her and pulling free the cord holding his loincloth. Ember looked around but could find no one to help. There was only her, sand, and some mollusk shells. She tried to stand and run, but Yan paused what he was doing and quickly grabbed her, subduing her once more. Ember wasn't even half as strong as Yan. Just then, he finished unlacing his waist cord, his clothing falling to the wayside. She had tried nonviolent methods to ward him off, but now she couldn't hold back.

Yan dropped to the sand grasping her flailing form and forcing himself atop with a frightening amount of strength. She was but a thin piece of roe deer skin from knowing this creature and the thought brought back the terror of the large man from before. Ember swung her fist as hard as she could, catching Yan just above his temple. His head jerked sideways but then snapped back, terrifyingly undamaged despite her best efforts. He leered back at her, and she could tell that something had changed. He was now entering a violent rage. Yan threw her hard to the ground and grabbed ahold of her neck, holding her down. He clenched his fist, ready to punch, but he calmed and simply slapped her across the face, causing lights to explode in her vision. Ember almost froze in shock, but she began pulling herself back together. She couldn't let fear take hold… she couldn't let this be like before.

"So you like it rough, huh? I can be rough," he said, holding her neck with one hand and trying to loosen her loincloth with the other. Ember dug her fingernails into his face, attempting to tear his eyes out. Before she could do much damage, Yan slapped her hard across the face a second time, so hard that she was left dazed for a moment as her vision darkened. It had all happened so fast. She had been standing there and then suddenly he was upon her. Her mind struggled to reset itself after such a violent slap. She fought to regain her vision as she felt his hand fighting with her waist cord. He could have just tugged the excess leather from under the cord, but thankfully he hadn't seemed to consider such an obvious act.

As her vision and ability to think returned, she began to panic and attempted to struggle, but she made little headway. How could this be happening? Why wasn't anyone around to help? She wanted to deny that these events even occurred, and yet there he was, straddled atop her waist and she was powerless, terrified, crying. Oddly, she recalled Nes and saving Brig'dha. The brunette had been powerless, terrified, and crying, yet she was not alone. Ember had taken charge and saved her. Ember was weaker than Yan, but she was also a warrior… she had to be. She couldn't stop him with strength, but she could use her wits. She would fight no matter what.

Ember let go of Yan's arms and fumbled with her own behind her head, hoping she would feel either a rock or a stick, but all she felt was a single broken clamshell. Fear raced through her as her mind struggled to accept what was happening, but she had to act. It would only take him a few more moments to unfasten the waist cord of her loincloth. She had one chance to save herself and she would take it, just as she had with the large man, the wolves, and even the Greatest River. Win or fail, she would do her best, just as she had for Brig'dha and Tes.

ↄ ↄ ↄ

After what had been perhaps the most painful courtship he ever undertook, Yan was relieved that Ember had tossed back her arms and appeared to be relaxing. It seemed that Galar was correct; she simply needed a firm hand, and had quickly surrendered to his will. The problem he now face was that her loincloth was tied with multiple knots. He had never seen someone tie a waist cord so tightly, and he was still trying to free it with only one hand. Looking down at Ember, he saw that her head was turned sideways, away from him. She had a submissive look about her – the doe had given way to the buck. He suspected that he could let go of her neck and use both hands to free the knot or just pull the cloth free and leave the infernal cord. While Yan worked to free her waist cord, he didn't notice the slow and cautious form of Kyra as she sneaked to the rock and carefully removed the necklace, retreating into the bushes. He was too preoccupied with what he suspected would be his new wife.

"Please... please don't do this..." Ember whispered to Yan, tears in her eyes. Her hand had found the clamshell, and she now held it firmly in her fingers. She knew what she could do to stop him, but she didn't want to do it. She didn't want it to end this way. Yan was a freak of nature, and she despised him, but she didn't wish him dead. Yet, she knew that if her words failed, the only way to stop Yan would be to kill him. Instead, he simply ignored her pleas. She continued to beg him to stop as she felt each of her four knots holding her loincloth coming loose. The moment that he got it free, she would have to strike. Tears flowed freely, as she remembered how much Brig'dha hated death and violence.

"Please, I won't tell anyone if you stop... Stop before what happens can't be undone," she begged, feeling more in control as her fingers found the correct grip on the jagged shell. Three knots... two knots...

"Please... stop..."

The last knot came free.

Ember slashed her hand as fast as she could across his neck with the small sharp point of the shell. Her movements were quicker than a fish jumping from the water and more accurate than she had expected. In one fluid movement, she opened his neck, and blood began to flow. Yan let go of the loincloth and grasped his neck, one of his carotid arteries partly torn open.

Blood squirted faster and faster as his heart pumped quicker and quicker. He looked down at Ember – shocked – his expression one of confusion and bewilderment. It was as though he had only just realized the gravity of what he had been doing. He had grossly misjudged Ember's feelings, which would cost him his life. Ember pushed him away and quickly fastened the loincloth cord.

"Why? Why did you make this happen? Why couldn't you just find someone else?" she yelled in anguish using her own language. She had not wanted to take another life, but yet again, she had done so. Her entire chest and arms were soaked and blood, Yan's blood. He lay on the ground holding his neck as his precious lifeblood poured free. The shell had not cut the entire neck, but it had cut open part of a major artery, which was enough. Yan stared at Ember with fear and helplessness in his eyes as he slowly bled out. Suddenly, the role of the helpless had switched. Now she was above and in control and he was powerless, terrified, and crying. But she held no interest in power and control of others. The idea made her sick. Ember turned away, leaving the man to face his death alone.

She remained on her knees, gently sobbing for a while. She had never been with a man though she had just come very close to having done so. Yan was not a common example of a man, more of a vile exception. She knew that many, if not most, were good by nature. Men like Aethen, Kel, Mael, High Hunter Nor'Gar, and even the hunter Pak, perhaps. These were all good men. Now and then, a bad one would arise. She could accept that, but why did the bad men always seek her out? All that was important was that she was alive, and she would live to see another day, but Yan would be yet another face she would not forget.

She rose, and then stepped slowly into the water and then suddenly dove in. The cool water took her breath away, but something about its purity made her feel better. The blood washed from her skin as she swam, and her body became numb. All she could feel was the soothing water as it embraced her and wiped clean what had happened. Ember emerged from the water and stood in the gentle warm breeze shivering a short time later. Warm tears flowed down her face. Yan marked the third death since they had left the Isen'bryn and the fifth man she had killed. For some reason, she did not hate Yan. What he did was terrible, but she wished so deeply that she could have stopped him without resorting to violence. He was simply too strong. In the end, there had been only one thing she could do to stop him, and if she had not done it, the results would have been too horrible to consider. It was one life for another.

Before her upon the ground lay the now lifeless body of Yan. Judging from the sand, he had tried to drag himself barely an arm's length, but he had finally succumbed to blood loss and died. Ember had been in the water swimming and trying to wipe clean from her mind what had just happened while he was dying. For a moment, she simply stared at the lifeless corpse, barely able to reconcile what had just happened. She would tell someone in the village, and hopefully, something could be done with the body before the scavengers got to it. She felt slightly in a daze as though detached from her own emotions. She knew that her emotions would return in force, but for the moment, she was in a strange sort of shock.

She returned to the rock and began to almost mechanically retrieve her clothing, her mind almost blank. She was dressed before realizing that the necklace was not sitting on the rock. She had been so shaken by the events which had just happened that she had not immediately noticed it missing. As panic took hold, Ember began to search around the rock frantically, looking for the precious item. It was not long before she realized that it was truly gone. She dropped again to her knees, now in more grief than before, when suddenly she noticed something – small tracks leading away from the rock toward the bushes.

Ember looked at the tracks and realized almost immediately that the small footprints were probably from a woman. Someone had stolen the necklace, and what was more horrifying to Ember was that they had probably done so while she was in the middle of being assaulted. Men were not the only ones who could sometimes do horrible things, and somewhere was a woman who had committed her own vile act. Ember lifted her head to the sky and screamed as loudly as she could in frustration.

ꙅ ꙅ ꙅ

Kyra hurriedly walked through the village with her head down, hoping not to attract any attention. She had stuffed the necklace into a small leather pouch attached to her waist cord and was heading toward the outskirts of the village where she hoped Galar would be waiting with their things. She found him standing beside the leather packs with some extra clothing and a nervous look about him. He was whittling a stick rapidly with a small, sharp stone when he turned to see her approach.

"What happened? I have been standing here trying not to panic, and I'm still waiting for Yan to get back," he asked Kyra in a quiet voice that was full of apprehension. She glared at him in anger. She had done all the hard work and didn't appreciate being questioned.

"I hope you are not planning on waiting too long for him. He's dead," Kyra said flatly, walking past him to pick up her pack and prepare to leave. Galar just glared at her with a dumbfounded expression. What did she mean by dead?

"Tell me, woman, what happened? What are you talking about?" She finished securing her pack and then turned to leave without a word. Galar grasped Kyra's arm and spun her around, demanding answers.

"Your man tried to force himself on Ember! He nearly did, but she slit his throat with a common clamshell and spilled his blood all over the beach. I thought he was going to be forceful... but not that forceful. As far as I'm concerned, he got what he deserved. I sneaked behind him and stole the necklace, simple as that," she said, patting the leather bag on her side.

"When I left that red-haired creature, she was covered from head to toe with blood... Yan's blood!" Galar realized why she was in such a hurry to leave. Ember wasn't a woman, she was a monster, and she would be coming for them as soon as she realized, if she realized, they had something to do with what happened. At that moment, both of them heard the scream far down the coast... It was the scream of an evil spirit, vengeance made real. They hurried from the village as fast as they could toward the East.

つ つ つ

Nearly two dozen people from the village raced over the edge of the embankment and down to where the scream had originated. A body lay face-down upon blood-soaked sand turning pale. Next to it, Ember stood seething in pain and disgust. Aethen rushed to her side to learn what had transpired. He was quickly flanked by many other people with a similar interest. Such events would quickly drag the entire tribe into the drama.

"What happened here? How did Yan die? Are you okay?" he yelled as he approached his friend. Ember held her shirt in one hand with her head pointed toward the sky. The crowd fell silent with anticipation. Most of the gathered people were new members of the tribe and did not really know the dead man very well, though many had interacted with Ember and knew her to be a friendly and happy person. Ember closed her eyes and spoke softly though most people were now close enough to hear.

"Yan is dead... because I killed him. He tried to rape me," she said plainly. All around, there were gasps of shock. The newcomers did not understand the exact words Ember had used, but most of them could guess what they had meant. The original Shell People had never witnessed a woman kill a man so effectively. Sure, accidents happened during domestic squabbles, but the man's throat had been sliced open by a single shell. It was simply beyond anything they had experience with. Ember looked up at Aethen in shame.

"The necklace... Someone took the Amber necklace. It was a woman, and I think she had something to do with Yan," she said, pointing to the rock where the tracks could be seen. Ember slowly turned and walked towards the village without a word. Brig'dha burst forth from the people and ran to comfort Ember, but she pushed Brig'dha aside, wanting to be alone. In reality, she wanted nothing more than to hold Brig'dha tightly and cry, but she didn't want to explain the details of how yet another man had died. She just wanted to be alone with her thoughts.

Brig'dha held her arms tightly to her chest as she watched Ember pass in silence. She could see the pain the woman held behind her eyes, and it brought tears to hers. The enormity of it all left Brig'dha in a state of anguish. She wanted so badly to hold Ember and tell her things would be okay, but she knew that her friend needed some time alone, and she would give her that time. Ember would come around in a little while and probably talk to her about what happened. As long as she was safe, that was all that mattered. She cared so deeply for Ember, perhaps more than a friend...

ꙅ ꙅ ꙅ

Aethen puzzled over the statement that a woman had been involved. Aethen and Kel approached the rock and began to inspect the tracks. It was apparent to both of them that the tracks had indeed been made by a woman, a woman who was trying not to be heard. The front of the tracks was buried much deeper than the back, and the stride also varied quite randomly, like a person slowly sneaking instead of the smoother stride of a person walking naturally. Kel looked up at Aethen and shook his head.

"She's right. The tracks lead away from the village, so whoever it was has probably left. We should pull everyone in the tribe together and see who's missing, assuming that this wasn't someone from another tribe," he said with a resigned look. Aethen shook his head in disagreement.

"I agree that we should put everyone together, but I don't think it was someone from a different tribe. Why would they have just stolen the necklace? How would they have even known of it?" Aethen stood and ordered everyone in the tribe to meet by the central fires as soon as possible. An official leader had not yet been chosen, but no one disagreed with Aethen's orders. He just hoped that it wasn't one of the new people, or their brand-new alliance might be torn to shreds in an instant.

A short while later, everyone had gathered at the center of the tribe, everyone that is, except Ember, Brig'dha, Yan, Kyra, and Galar. Ember and Brig'dha had been accounted for as they could be seen not far off down the coast apparently talking. Yan, was dead. It wasn't long until it was discovered that Galar and Kyra's possessions were gone. A short time later, Kel appeared to inform everyone that he had followed the tracks from the beach all the way to where a man had been standing whittling a piece of wood. The unknown female and male had then left and headed east. That was the final piece of evidence needed.

"Treachery," Aethen muttered to himself, shaking his head.

ↄ ↄ ↄ

The Sun was low on the horizon as Ember stood by the sea, throwing shells and small rocks into the water. The shock of what had happened had passed. Ember was not as upset about the attempted rape as she was about having killed a man. It had been a violation, but it had luckily never gone beyond the horror of what could have been. Perhaps if Yan had been successful, those feelings would have been reversed. Ember never liked taking a life. She could remember the faces of the four men she had killed before this day. She had fired an arrow into the chest of one man and into the neck of another. The third had fallen face-first onto one of her wooden traps and died. The fourth man she had killed just this passed cold season as he raided her village. Of these four, all had been raiders. Now there were five. Ember began to sob once more.

For a moment, she was alone with her guilt, shame, and fear, and then she felt Brig'dha gently place her arms around her. It was subtle at first, almost questioning. She had been violated, so the already gentle brunette was going to be even more delicate. This time, she didn't fight back and let herself be held. Instead, she issued a scream at the injustice of it all that trailed off into tears. She had been violated, Yan was dead, and someone had watched it all as they stole the necklace. The idea that his death and her assault might have been just a ploy to steal the necklace was a violation, an injustice beyond reckoning. Ember sank to her knees as she sobbed under the fading sunlight.

When she had finally calmed enough to return to the present, she realized that she was entirely wrapped within the arms of the now kneeling Moon Priestess. She breathed deeply, settling herself, grounding. Brig'dha's hands were soft, and her touch was welcome, something so unexpected, given the events of the day. Deep within, she felt a new feeling stirring among the ashes of her emotions, an ember of love. Slowly, almost timidly, she turned and lifted her face to see the priestess. Behind her knelt the beautiful brunette, her face so close in their embrace. Brig'dha's face was fully unmasked, her concern and friendship colored by another emotion, something deeper.

For a moment, Ember gazed into those beautiful, hazel eyes wanting nothing more than to kiss the Forest People woman. Brig'dha had felt right since they had met, yet the Moon Priestess had never made a move toward her or given any solid indication of her interest. At first, Ember had dismissed this as wishful thinking on her part, but the more she got to know the bashful brunette, the more she realized that Brig'dha tended to mask her emotions. She could appear almost neutral in expression, even when she was on the verge of screaming. The implication was that she had no real way to be sure Brig'dha liked her too.

But now, as she looked upon Ember with concern, there was something else… something just beneath that she couldn't quite identify. She licked her lips, her instincts flooding her as emotions danced in her mind, both confusing and tumultuous. She wanted to find out… to make her feelings known through body language. Yet, she could feel her earlier pain just below the surface, waiting to rise. What if she spoke and she had misread Brig'dha's intentions? No, this wasn't the time to take such a risk when her mind was in such a state. She needed to sleep, or at least to rest. As if sensing the passing of the moment, Brig'dha said nothing and continued to hold Ember tightly as the Sun slowly set in the West.

Both women knelt at the water's edge for a long while until the Moon rose in the East, though it was only a sliver and barely illuminated the land. That night on the water was one of the most beautiful Ember had seen in a long time. Both women sat at the water's edge gazing at the beauty of eternity and felt dwarfed by a sea of waves and a sea of stars. At first, beauty and companionship had worked to tame her suffering, yet, a new pain began to form deep from within, a pain spawned from anticipation and the regret of what was to come. As her mind quieted, she began to consider what had to come next and she regretted everything about it.

She would find out who had taken the necklace and if they had anything to do with Yan's death. She could feel in her gut that he had been used as a tool to some end, though she was unsure how she had come to this conclusion. Something about his compulsion towards her had seemed forced or at least spurred. She would find whoever was responsible, but she would do so without Brig'dha. She would spare her what would likely be another death. At that moment, Ember decided that she would leave early in the morning as, Brig'dha slept, and hunt whoever the mysterious woman was who had taken the necklace. She felt guilt over the idea, but she knew it had to be done if she wanted closure.

"I think we should sleep now. It's been a very long day," Ember said. Brig'dha nodded in agreement. Ember looked back at her for a moment with a strange expression, as though there was something she wanted to say.

"I... um, I just wanted to say that," but Ember stopped mid-sentence. Emotions welled up deep inside of her, but she caught herself before she let them burst free. Brig'dha gazed expectantly at Ember for a short moment, but she merely smiled and headed back towards the huts. As she passed, Brig'dha thought she heard Ember whisper words, but they were in her native Great River people language. It sounded as though she had said something like Ehg, wennus'du, but that was the best Brig'dha could make out from the whisper.

"Ehg, wennus'du," Brig'dha whispered back to herself as she watched her friend returning to the tribe. She wondered what it was that Ember had wanted to say and what those words had meant. She recognized what sounded like the word for "I" and maybe the suffix for "you." Being much better at languages than Brig'dha, Ember had learned most of the words of the Isen'bryn while she had learned very few from Ember's Great River people. At that moment, she wished she had learned more. She hoped that she could coax their meaning from Ember the next day. There had been something Brig'dha had also wanted to say, but she had felt like the moment was wrong, given what had happened. She hurried and caught up with her redheaded friend, and the two women slowly walked back to the village under the dim moonlight.

ↄ ↄ ↄ

The Moon was halfway across the sky and barely a crescent when Ember slowly sneaked out of the hut with her unpacked traveling gear in hand. Dressing and gearing up had been too much trouble to perform in the hut without making sounds. Ember did not want to wake Brig'dha, who slept nearby under a thick bear fur blanket. Ember had not actually slept, her mind awash with the day before. She had simply passed the time watching Brig'dha sleep and petting Mew. She marveled at how innocent the priestess looked while she slept, made more so by the cat sleeping on her legs. Now, as she slowly donned her traveling gear and slipped her obsidian dagger into place, she could not help but long for her long-lost innocence. With her unstrung bow in place and a small leather pack filled with provisions, Ember turned to head towards the East to begin the hunt.

Just as she stepped past the last hut in the tribe, she heard a sarcastic chuckle from behind. Quickly turning, Ember found Aethen standing near her and dressed to travel. Both wore similar clothing, woven fiber shoes, loincloths, and long shirts, the clothing of men. Ember simply stood where she was, slightly embarrassed at having been so readily caught but glad that it wasn't Brig'dha who caught her. *I should have covered myself in soot. I might have actually sneaked by,* she thought, reminded of the leather pouch of soot she carried to keep herself painted.

"So, you heard that Kyra and Galar are likely behind what happened. You have left your friend behind, and you are seeking to recover the necklace, maybe even some vengeance?" he said flatly. Ember frowned, taking his statements as accusations, more than merely factual observations. He could not help but admire the woman. She stood before him with her waist-long hair blowing in the wind and new black dots painted beneath her eyes. With a bow strap to her back and an obsidian dagger hanging from her waist, Ember was truly a force to be reckoned with. Aethen almost felt sorry for those she now set to hunt.

"What of it?" she said in a low voice. Aethen smiled at her remark, a bitter smile that held little humor.

"If you don't mind, I would appreciate settling the score too. Mael was also my friend, and he died believing in this journey. I don't think we need the necklace to succeed, but I cannot stand the idea of someone else taking it. If anything, it should be yours. As soon as we get the necklace, we can return. What say you?" Ember could not believe her ears. She didn't think anybody would understand her reasons for hunting down the necklace and possibly, assuming that her guess was correct, the person who put Yan up to attack her. A slight smile crossed Ember's face, and she nodded, turning and proceeding to the East.

"We must recover the necklace, but why not return it to the tribe?" Ember asked as they started walking together. She looked back at Aethen and saw that he wore a confused expression. He assumed that Ember would be remaining with the tribe, so if she possessed the necklace, the tribe would effectively possess the necklace. Her question left a strange wonder in the back of his mind, but he shrugged it off and just kept walking, his grey eyes narrowing.

"Don't worry about it. We'll figure it out once we find Galar and Kyra," he said.

つ つ つ

Brig'dha awoke from her dream and rolled over to see if Ember was nearby. Little Mew lay curled at her feet, enjoying the warmth of the fur blankets. Ember's furs appeared occupied with a bulky form curled up underneath. Ember did like to sleep under many furs. Brig'dha smiled and drifted back to bed with her pet cat, Mew, by her side. She decided that they would both sleep in and recover from the horrors of the previous day. Everything was falling back into place... As she drifted off, she whispered the words once more, "Ehg, wennus'du."

つ つ つ

The city of Isut'na was located near the southern mouth of the Brown River, which connected the Great Lake to the North and the Blue Sea to the South. The mouth of the Brown River opened into the Blue Sea and was the primary source of water flowing north into the Great Lake. Very few proto-cities existed, mostly due to the lack of resources required to sustain them and their large populations. The city of Isut'na was located in an ideal place, a junction separating the immense deserts of the South from the vast expanse of the plains and mountains to the North. In times past, it was said that the lands to the South were lusher than at present. More and more, the land to the South had become arid, but it was still quite fertile. As a result of its location, Isut'na was a trading hub and an intersection of cultures. At any given point, its population would vary between 2000 to as many as 2500 individuals, roughly ten times the size of the average Northern tribe.

Isut'na was one of the first cities large enough to produce goods solely for export to other cities and places. A significant amount of labor was dedicated to the production of crops, the herding of animals, and all manner of specialized craftwork. Tribesmen from a Western tribe could journey to Isut'na within a few days and trade quality raw materials, such as bone, raw metal nuggets, animal hides, and most importantly, fermented drink, and return to their people loaded with beautiful linen, bark fiber cloth, and leather to make clothing, as well as fine quality goods crafted from the same raw materials. Isut'na was indeed a modern place.

Quite a distance before the dye trader Idmasa and his strange would-be "concubine" arrived at the city, they began to encounter the signs of settlement. The path they walked was intersected by another slightly visible trail that appeared to come from the edge of a glade of trees. The closer they got to the city, the more paths appeared and intersected into the main path. The pair strode along the bank of the Brown River, water to their left, heading south. The landscape was lush with marshes and thick rush-filled wetlands. Trees were small and scraggly but green and full of life. All around, tall grass and wildlife could be seen. Isut'na was a very well-placed city, in Idmasa's opinion. The only real downsides were the heat and humidity, which only let up during the mild cold season.

Ahead, a large party of women and children wandered through the brush picking up sticks, likely to be used for kindling. A dozen women each wore large rush-reed baskets upon their backs filled to the top with sticks. Some women wore leather pouches or flax nets as slings around their necks to hold an infant child and allow nursing while collecting the wood. Idmasa was always impressed that a woman could work with a baby drinking its fill. It seemed that the women more heavily encumbered by a nursing infant relied on their older children at their feet to collect the sticks for them. Children always made the best helpers as they could turn any chore into a game. He would have to get himself a child someday if he lived long enough. *And if a woman will have me,* he chuckled to himself.

Behind Idmasa, Ianmu slowly trudged along, glad to see the signs that the city she sought was close at hand. She could use some water to clean herself and something to eat. Luckily, her sandals and apron had kept her cool in the hot steamy air. The land outside of Isut'na was even hotter than Nara'kit, and Ianmu could see the effect on the locals as they passed. While women worked, young children ran free without the need for clothing, their only tasks being to play and occasionally gather a stick for their mothers. Ianmu could vaguely remember the days when she would run around outside of her father's building and play on the dirt paths which crisscrossed the city of Nara'kit. Those glorious days were the happiest moments of her life, long before the cares of society or the position as a priestess. If not for the goal that her goddess had set for her, she would trade everything to return to those days.

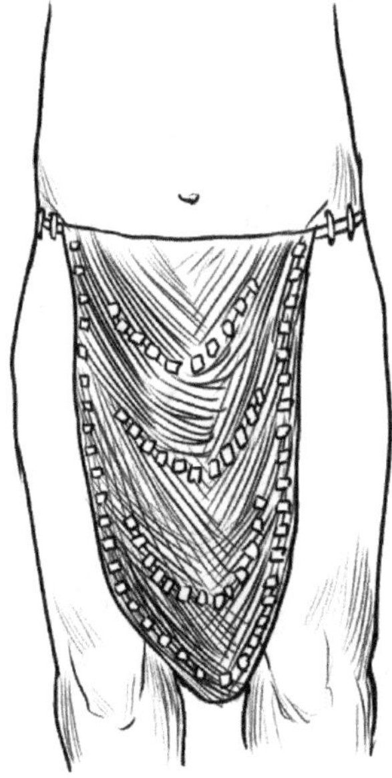

Leather apron with beadwork

Due to the heat, most women wore their hair rolled up into circular buns at the back of their heads with long hairpins made of smoothed wood. Each woman wore either simple leather boots or leather sandals with extra strips of thick hide wrapped around the bottom to reduce their wear while in the brush. Sandals were not easy to make, and extra care was always taken to improve their life span. When back in their city, most would likely opt to walk barefoot, free from brambles and the rocky ground.

Some women wore basic linen or bark fiber aprons, like Ianmu, though most wore wrap skirts made from leather or textile. While most textiles were naturally colored, one woman wore a red-dyed apron while another boasted stamped patterns from clay seals and paint. The most beautiful design was worn by a younger woman who was likely trying to catch someone's eye. Most of the women wore ample necklaces of polished stones, shells, and other adornments. These were certainly not your average tribal villagers. Only a city provided the resources for such clothing.

Another sign they were near a city was the approachable attitude of the people. Small tribes tended to be more fearful of outsiders while a city would see its citizens spread across the landscape performing various tasks. However, these women did not feel alone. As many as half of Isut'na's inhabitants would be spread out across the landscape performing their various jobs during the day. It reminded her of ants leaving an ant mound. The women and children waved at them and pointed in the direction of the city, assuming that this was their destination. Ahead, Idmasa waved back at the women as he continued walking.

It was not long before the travelers passed over the top of a small hill and Isut'na came into view. The city was nestled beside several large hills right on the edge of the Brown River and beside a floodplain. Around the city were several dozen fields with irregularly spaced plants growing with dozens of people working the land. By this time of the season, the wheat would have been harvested, and the flax harvest would be in full swing. Long irrigation trenches covered the fields and led back to the Brown River. Isut'na had a significantly more advanced agricultural base than Nara'kit.

As they approached the fields, the various crops became recognizable. Sure enough, many large fields filled with flax plants stood ready to be picked by the laborious workers. Most of the great proto-cities grew a variety of crops, though flax was not common. Du'ubria, a vast city to the Southeast grew nearly no flax, importing most of their linen from places like Isut'na and Nara'kit.

Flax was ready to be harvested when flowers had fallen, and the seedpods had begun to brown. In the fields were perhaps one hundred people with huge bunches of flax formed into neat little piles propped up against one another, allowing them to dry. As they passed the fields, they watched the meticulous work that went into the harvest. A young man finished propping his flax bundle against a few other bundles to dry and took a tired, but satisfied breath before returning to gather more. He would bend low, grabbing the flax by the roots and pulling up the entire plant, careful not to break it. He would grab a weed, pull it, and toss it to the side ever so often. Weeding was normally a job for the children, but every now and then, they missed one.

Once the man had pulled up a large handful of the plants, he would beat the ends of the roots against his leg to free up some of the excess soil. When he had a few dozen plants, he would take a single plant and use it to tie a knot around the bundle. It was in this way that a field was pulled. Ianmu could see that the fields were in different stages of growth, though mostly ready to be harvested or showing the signs of having already been. Many bundles of the flax would be left for a few days until they were dry. She could already see several women beating the flax with wooden mallets to thresh out the seeds. Ianmu had always wondered if some sort of comb, like the delicate ivory hair comb she had left back in her city, might be more useful in this process, but perhaps not. There was no wind at the moment, but she could see reed baskets full of broken seedpods waiting to be winnowed, a process where the seeds were thrown into the air allowing the breeze to blow away the excess chaff, leaving only seeds to be collected.

Several fields had been fully harvested where the flax now lay in piles on the ground, letting the moisture and humidity slowly break down their material, releasing the precious fibers from within. Each day, these fields would be tended to ensure the flax was in good condition. After at least a tenday, these bundles would be taken and bent across a wooden board. Next, they would be beaten at an angle with a flat wooden tool to tear the plant parts away from the fiber. The result would be the flax fibers, ready to be cleaned and combed. The process was laborious, to say the least. The finished products would be flax cord, flax yarn, and woven linen. Ianmu casually tugged at one of the bark fiber strands which made up her apron. It was a different sort of fiber, but many of the same techniques were used in its preparation.

Not long after passing the linen and wheat fields, as well as a young boy tending to a small flock of goats, the pair arrived at the city proper. Isut'na was made of several hundred cubic buildings constructed from mud-brick and painted with white-gray plaster. Each of the little buildings was about three lengths of a man wide, four lengths of a man long, and one and one-half of a man tall. Buildings were built atop of buildings, stacking as high as four tall in some places. Ladders could be seen everywhere to allow access to and from each little building. The majority of the buildings appeared to be entered from the roof, with no visible ground-level access, aside from a few ground-level passageways which looked as though they could be easily sealed off in the event of a raid. If the ladders were all pulled up, access to the city would be almost impossible. It made for a useful defense.

Before them stood one side of the city made up of nearly 30 buildings in length, each with at least one building on top and some with as many as three. A small and narrow passageway opened in between several of the buildings to allow entry into the city. On the roofs, people could be seen working and carrying out their daily activities while children played nearby. Some of the buildings were beautifully decorated with painted exteriors. Nearly every building on the second level and higher had several windows to let in light. When it became cold, heavy leather mats would hang in front of the windows to keep out the cold or to block the rain. Overall, Isut'na was extremely similar in design to Nara'kit, though Nara'kit was a little bit larger. Ianmu had even heard of several cities to the south that were even larger than this city, though she could not imagine how more than 3000 people could live together in any form of peace.

Ianmu, the "concubine," and her pretend "master" Idmasa approached the entryway under the watchful eye of a single man on the second-floor roof of a building holding a bow and carefully looking the group over. They hardly looked like raiders, but it was always a good idea to take note of anybody entering your village or city. They had to stop before they could enter the narrow walkway as an older man and what was probably his younger son carefully maneuvered a large cow out of the city. Livestock was often kept within the city for protection though livestock spent a significant time beyond the wall-like buildings where food could be had. Besides meat, cows provided milk which could be curdled into a soft, lumpy cheese.

Some people could drink milk directly, but this resulted in an upset stomach for most. It seemed that children lost the ability to drink milk when they finally weaned from their mothers. Cheese could be more easily digested and lasted longer with salt. Ianmu already missed the salty cheese taste but assumed she would not get much of that in her new life as a "concubine." If she succeeded in the impossible and took over the city, she would eat her fill of the best cheeses and a large cup of fermented honey drink. Until that happened, she would eat whatever her "husband" gave her. It would be difficult to hide the pride she wore as the daughter of a city leader, but for An'an, she would make herself bow to authority.

Yet another good reason why you should not fail, she mused. The enormity of the task she had set for herself was not lost upon her. She often questioned her sanity at the belief that a woman could march into a city and take possession of it. The very notion was absurd, at best. But life was an adventure to be had, and what greater adventure than conquering a city? She only hoped that her disguise would hold up. Being traded by her "father" to another man was hardly a common method of marriage, though it was one of the only ways that she could attach herself to a powerful man in the city, quickly. The other possibility would have been to woo such a man in the standard fashion. The problem in that scenario was the unlikelihood of a random woman coming from some distant place and trying to pick up a powerful man. It would seem strange, but less strange, if she were a young woman to be traded by her oppressive father instead of a loving wife to be wooed.

As she entered the city, the sights and sounds that greeted her reminded Ianmu of her birth city. All around, people lived, worked, and carried on with their lives. The inside of the city was a giant open area with a packed dirt ground and the remnants of many fire pits. Likely, this area was a ceremonial ground used for meetings, dances, and rituals. An area filled with people trading merchandise was off to one side, while the other side was packed full of people working their wares. This was the trading area and the central source of material wealth. Several other travelers from distant places could be seen wandering about inspecting the wares.

The citizens' quality of clothing was quite impressive, even by Ianmu's standards. By far, the most common garment worn by men was the loincloth – a panel of material, usually leather, but sometimes cloth, worn between the legs. The excess material was either hung down the front and back or tucked back into the garment. When colder, leather leggings might be worn – tubes of leather attached to a waist cord, one for each leg. Given the warm season air, some men wore long leather shirts or vests, though most upper bodies were bare.

Men's hair was often wrapped into buns atop their heads, though a fair number wore their hair long and free down their backs. Necklaces, earrings, bracelets of carved and polished stone adorned their bodies while large beards framed most of their faces. In general, Ianmu considered the men of Isut'na at least as attractive as those of Nara'kit, if not slightly more decorated.

Women tended to wear wrap skirts of mostly leather, with some textile versions – a panel of material wrapped around the waist and secured with a waist cord, the excess material folded over the waist cord. Many of the younger women opted to wear textile aprons – A cloth panel woven to a waist cord, usually between one and three hands wide and two to three hands long, covering the groin, with typically lengthy tassels of string hanging to the knees, and sometimes even to the ground. The buttocks were typically uncovered, though some women hung decorative strings and items from their waist cords. Aprons conveyed a woman's availability to wed, especially if they were highly decorated. However, many women seemed to wear them when obviously tending to a family, though usually far less decorated. This was why Ianmu had opted for the garment, a sign of her age and intent to be wed.

Like the men, most women's upper bodies were bare, though some wore shawls of cloth, fur, or leather, often highly decorated, and even more necklaces and adornments than the men. They tended to wear their hair in elaborate braids and buns, often using polished wooden sticks as hairpins. Though everyone could use body and face paint, the women seemed to apply more than men, though perhaps only two in five people wore any body paint.

Feathers were used often for decoration, though never vulture or owl feathers, she noted. In Nara'kit, large bird feathers, such as these, were reserved for religious purposes, and to see someone wearing them outside of a ritual marked that person as a leader, a priest or priestess, or someone soon to be accosted. Many villages and cities had similar gods, but these were mere copies of Nara'kit's real gods, obviously not as powerful as An'an and Gunmaer. She laughed at the thought of their weak gods, the unexpected sound from the otherwise quiet woman catching the attention of Idmasa.

"What is so funny to you, *daughter?*" he asked with a chuckle, emphasizing the last word. Ianmu glared at him for a moment but realized that she had asked him to call her that when in public so that nobody would realize who she really was. This was quite a juxtaposition for her, having been born the daughter of a city leader. Nevertheless, she would have to make the most of it.

"I think my 'father' should get us both a drink, something fermented and sweet, and a room to stay in while he looks for someone to trade me to," she suggested firmly. This was not a request, and Idmasa knew that his "daughter" was one who must be obeyed. In reality, he was really the servant, bonded as he was by his trader's oath to fulfil her deal, least he explain his treachery to the spirits when next he prayed. He rolled his eyes and headed toward the small vendor where one could get food and drink.

This whole business continued to perplex him. He still could not figure out what this bizarre woman had in mind. It just didn't make any sense. He rolled his eyes and "ordered" her to follow him towards a public eatery, another comfort afforded to city dwellers.

The pair arrived at a small building where a heavyset woman stood chatting with several rough-looking men who sat on a mud-brick bench eating strips of salted pork and eggs. Some drank fermented honey drink mixed with water, but most simply drank water. The men turned at first to see the man who was approaching, but then their glances became overt, gawking at the "shy" woman who attended the trader. In fact, Ianmu was considered beautiful in the eyes of her people. She was a little plump and well-proportioned with wide hips and breasts which hung slightly, a look that pleased the Goddess almost as much as men. Her skin was smoother than most women owing to a life of being oiled and cared for inside of a dark building away from the Sun. Her hair was thick and silky soft, revealing her physical health. Hair was often an indicator of a person's current and historical health, and long, thick hair was considered highly attractive in both their societies.

"Hey beautiful, why don't you smile," one of the men offered as his friends looked on, smiles all around. Men called out like that to women from even their youth, something that had always disgusted Iamnu. She had seen it many times, though none were daring enough to do so when she lived in Nara'kit. She buried her urge to retort with an obscene gesture, realizing that she had to play the part of a typical woman. Unfortunately, that part of typical womanhood was degrading.

"Well, to the jackals with you then," the man grumbled, seemingly angry that he had been ignored. To his credit, Idmasa cast the man a frown – the look going unchallenged as the matron of the food trading place slapped her hand flatly on the wood table before her, drawing the collective attention of the men. She had seen enough of such behavior and wasn't in the mood to ignore it.

Ianmu was suddenly more self-conscious than she realized. She had no interest in these men, but she felt their eyes boring into her, appraising her like a goat to be traded. She tried to dismiss their looks without care. They were obviously simple farmers and laborers. What really mattered was the eye of a powerful man. At least, she had worn a fine apron with long that tickled her knees and a good, sturdy pair of sandals. Ianmu wished she had been painted as she would have been in her city, perhaps wearing one of her beautiful linen shawls or some copper jewelry. But, unfortunately, the mistreated daughter of a man willing to trade her for beads would not have these things, so she had left them behind.

Idmasa and Ianmu sat at the end of the bench, waiting to be served. The woman in charge turned to regard the pair for a moment. Her customer skills were less than impressive, but her patrons were lifelong customers. She was the only sit-down food vendor in the city, which provided her a great degree of latitude in how she interacted with them. She eyed Ianmu and then turned a catlike expression upon Idmasa. Ianmu was less than pleased with the implications in her expression. Contrary to his "daughter," Idmasa was prideful as he smiled with an almost boastful expression.

"Honey drink for me and water for her. We are hungry from our trip and would eat some food," he said cheerfully, placing three red coral beads on the table, plenty to trade for some food. The woman flashed him a judgmental and distrusting glance. She placed two identical clay bowls full of drink before the travelers and then turned to grab some food. Idmasa quickly switched the bowls, remembering that his client had ordered a fermented honey drink. He had not wanted to tip-off anyone who might be watching by ordering her the more expensive honey drink.

The woman returned with a small plate containing roasted acorns, figs, and roasted fish. It was certainly a decent meal that the travelers shared in silence. Ianmu carefully sucked the meat from a fish bone while she observed the people in the trading area. Somewhere in this city, there was bound to be a man of influence in need of her special services. Her father had long spoken of the glory to be had in raiding a city like Isut'na. Nara'kit was known to attack villages and even other cities on occasion. If her father could do it, so could she... She just had a slightly different method.

CHAPTER TEN

A WILLING SACRIFICE

Compassion and a general interest in the well-being and the disposition of other members of a group seem to be an emergent property of social species, such as humans. This interest in how others feel and how they consider you is called empathy. The degree of empathy shared between people is based not only on the nature and magnitude of their relationship but also upon each individual's capacity to experience empathy. While people like Brig'dha and Ember are extremely empathetic to the needs of others, sometimes to a fault, there are others who experience almost no empathy, such as Ianmu or Kyra. While some might pass judgment upon their actions, it is important to consider that this is simply how her brain functions. Likely, both kinds of people benefit society in some way – the reason their genes have survived so long.

Brig'dha awoke and sat up, tossing Mew from his comfortable resting place at her feet. She rubbed the sleep from her eyes and spent a short moment stretching. Ember had taught her the art of a good morning stretch, and she had spent extra time doing it ever since. She rolled onto her stomach and continued her random stretching making strange little gurgling noises as she worked just the right muscles. After a few moments, she turned to see the big pile of furs under which Ember was likely asleep. Mew approached the pile and cautiously sniffed them, causing Brig'dha to laugh. The cat was simply too cute to ignore.

She had worried about what drastic steps Ember might take following the news that Kyra and Galar had likely been behind the theft of the necklace. Worse, it seemed that Ember believed they might even have been behind Yan's actions. She suspected that Ember might want to leave the tribe and catch them. So, she had thought about several possible arguments she could make to convince Ember not to go. She didn't wish to take a chance that she might be harmed or even killed on some foolish necklace rescue mission. Ember was simply too important to her, more important than she even admitted to herself... something she really needed to tell the radiant redhead if she could just manage the courage.

Ember had completely missed the point behind her words. It was true that violence and death upset her deeply, but the real reason that Brig'dha wanted Ember to steer clear of danger was born of her own fear of losing her. Brig'dha wished that she could have been more direct, but her words were guided by her feelings, and she always had trouble expressing them openly. That brought to mind Ember's words of the night before, half-spoken and left unfinished. What was it that she had almost said? Ehg, wennus'du, or something like that?

"Are you feeling better today? What does Ehg, wennus'du mean?" she asked as she began to poke at the bundle of furs that made up Ember's bed. As soon as she poked the blanket, she realized something was wrong. Quickly, she grabbed the edge of the furs and pulled away the blankets revealing several rolled-up deer hides in the shape of a woman. A cold chill burst up and down her spine like a flock of birds taking off from a lake. Brig'dha almost immediately knew what had happened. She had seen that stoic look in the revengeful redhead's eyes the night before. Ember had left to hunt Kyra and Galar in the middle of the night. She felt nothing but fear through her veins as the reality sunk in.

Why? Why would she do this? Why would she have left me behind? Her mind exploded in discordant thoughts. She wrapped a worn deerskin around herself and ran barefoot from the hut, frantically checking around the village, hoping that she was wrong, and that Ember could be found. She ran around the village, checking huts and calling for Ember, but all she found were confused people who didn't realize what was going on. A moment later, she bumped into Kel. The watchful man had seen her running through the camp and had quickly determined the cause of her troubles. He placed a steadying hand on her shoulder and took a deep breath. Brig'dha pulled back, reflexively, the touch feeling almost like a burn. Only Ember's touch didn't burn… and now that touch was gone.

"Brig'dha, Aethen has left, and we think he may have gone hunting Galar and Kyra," he said matter-of-factually, retracting his hand. Brig'dha looked him dead in the face, something she rarely did to anyone, her fear fully realized. Since childhood, Kel couldn't remember having ever seen Brig'dha so upset. It was as though she had lost her lover, not just her friend.

"Ember is gone too!" she said as a tear rushed down her face.

Ɔ Ɔ Ɔ

Ember and Aethen made good time as they hiked down the coast following the tracks Galar and Kyra had left in their frantic escape. The land quickly became mountainous with large rock formations and steep cliffs not far from the water. As a result, anyone hiking quickly discovered that walking along the shore was the easiest way to get from one place to the next. However, the sandy shoreline made it easier to follow them. Ember and Aethen occasionally lost the trail, only to quickly find it again.

"The only thing I can think of is that they planned to join another tribe somewhere else. Maybe they would use the necklace to trade their way in," Aethen said as the pair marched. He had spent the entire morning trying to come up with a reason why Galar might have taken the necklace and what Kyra's involvement was. Had he put her up to it? She had not seemed like a malicious woman. Aethen simply could not imagine any other possible motive for their actions, nor did he understand how Yan could have been involved. He had even toyed with the idea that the theft and the assault were unrelated, but the timing was just too close.

Ember had fewer reservations about the idea that Kyra was involved. From her perspective, Kyra was likely the architect of the entire event. True, Galar had always been more of a nuisance than Kyra, but she could sense Kyra was a manipulator. She just could not imagine that a woman would have put Yan up to such actions against another woman. Sure, women could easily be as vicious as any men, but there were some things Ember had thought were too far. Of course, Yan was ultimately responsible for his actions, no matter how much prodding he had been given. She supposed she would find the answers when they found their thieves.

Finding the thieves troubled her less than how Brig'dha might respond when she discovered that the pile of blankets was not Ember. With the Sun now risen, it was likely that Brig'dha had discovered her deceit. Brig'dha had a habit of happily waking her up in the morning with a smile. Now that warm smile nagged at Ember, making her feel awash with guilt. She had promised that "you will never fear losing me, and I won't fear losing you." She hoped that Brig'dha would remember that promise and realize that she would return, having spared the priestess what had to be done. Brig'dha was very emotional, but Ember figured that she would come around after a day or two. It wasn't as though Brig'dha would have the nerve to chase after her, she thought sarcastically.

ᴐ ᴐ ᴐ

Brig'dha spent the first half of the day wallowing in sorrow which slowly turned to anger, as she rocked back and forth. She felt lied to, betrayed. In reality, Ember had not actually lied to her and had not exactly betrayed her either, but she had left upon a dangerous trip without her. She was frightened for what might happen to her friend, but being left behind and not knowing was almost too much to bear. Couldn't Ember have understood this? She sat in her hut staring at the pile of deer hides that she had mistaken for Ember and crying from frustration. How could Ember treat her in such a way? Her emotions continued to control her thoughts, and pain raged through her.

"Fine, go get yourself killed! Join the countless victims of this world. Just throw your life away and see if I care!" she cried in anger, causing Mew to scamper off. As she lay down, she felt something poke her in the neck. Brig'dha reached down to remove the offending object only to find that it was the goddess pendant. She held the pendant before her, tremendous anger building. A full meltdown underway. She pulled as hard as she could and tore the cord free from her neck, then lifted the pendant to throw when suddenly she realized... It had been her wishes that had caused Ember to leave. She remembered the words she had spoken to Ember, "I hate the suffering... I hate death. I sometimes know it's needed, but it should be avoided if possible?" Unfortunately, Ember had seemingly latched onto her first words, missing the point. Brig'dha had gone on to say, "You risk your life so much. Do you think that we could avoid such things?"

Brig'dha screamed as she burst into tears, realizing that Ember was searching for the necklace for the sake of the tribe, and she was doing so alone, taking all this risk upon herself merely to protect her. How could she be so weak and selfish as not to have realized this before now? Ember was protecting her. Brig'dha was not a very aggressive person, and she was certainly more fearful than most, but she would not let her friend face the uncertainties of the wilds tracking dangerous people by herself. If Ember died, it would be her fault. She would have nothing more than her own selfishness and weakness to blame. Brig'dha decided that she would find Ember herself, somehow.

"Yes, Mew, I have lost my mind..." she said to her confused cat as she wiped tears from her eyes. Mew had sat on a deer fur, watching her as she anguished. The animal seemed largely insulated from the troubles of the human world, a casual observer at best. However, mew did offer some distraction, pawing at her possessions as she stuffed them into her bag. Then, quickly, she donned her traveling clothing and packed her gear to leave. Little Mew stretched in anticipation of a trip where he would be carried much of the way. That was the purpose of people, right?

The Sun was already past the midway point when the daring priestess stood ready to go. She had painted the entire upper portion of her face black with soot paint in mourning over her actions. The process of applying the paint had taken a little while as she chanted to the Goddess for every form of blessing that could be given to Ember. Paint in place, she adjusted her clothing in preparation to leave. She wore her soft leather shirt and her leather wrap skirt, with her woven nettle fiber shoes. At her side was strapped a flint knife. She carried a sort of backpack across her back with food and supplies. She had even attached a feather to her hair for luck.

The door to the hut burst open, and Brig'dha, the Tracker, stepped out, Mew, her faithful cat, at her side. It was only a few moments before she realized the enormity of what she had planned. Gazing across the coastline to the East, it became apparent what a difficulty tracking Ember would be. She wasn't even sure of where she would find footprints to begin with, but she had faced greater dangers than this with Ember by her side. Brig'dha took a deep breath and started walking, Mew trotting along beside her. Kel saw Brig'dha and approached to stop her and make sure that she wasn't about to do what it looked like she was about to do.

"Are you seriously going to leave by yourself and try to track down Ember and Aethen?" he asked, incredulously. Brig'dha stopped and regarded the man, Mew standing firmly beside her.

"Do not make fun of me. The Goddess will protect me, and I will find her," she said with as much gusto as she could muster. Kel looked deeply into her eyes as though measuring her willpower. Though she was hardly a seasoned tracker and wore an almost fearful look, Kel could also see her determination – a look he deeply respected. He had already considered tracking the pair and joining their hunt, and with Brig'dha this adamant, it seemed like as good of a time as any. Besides, she was likely braver than half of the men in the tribe. After a moment, he nodded as though he had seen something. Brig'dha was unsure of what his gestures meant, so she and Mew continued to frown at him.

"Well then, priestess," he said in his usual jovial tone, "it looks like you'll need a tracker if you're going to find anything. If you give me a short moment, I will ready myself and come with you." Brig'dha was surprised at the sudden offer. The chances that she would find Ember would be ten times greater or more with a tracker as proficient as Kel, widely known as the best tracker in the village. Brig'dha rested her pack and sat on the ground, praying to the Goddess for a safe journey while Kel returned to his hut to quickly collect his traveling gear. All around, other tribe members gathered to ask what was going on and to watch the happenings. For her first prayer, Brig'dha thanked the Moon Goddess for providing her with a seasoned tracker.

☽ ☽ ☽

"I keep looking behind me expecting to see them coming," Kyra mumbled, worry clearly tainting her voice. Ahead, Galar replied without turning as the two marched across the sandy beach.

"I wouldn't worry that much. Ember may not be grounded, and she would have attacked us if we had stayed but following us would be quite a grudge. A man might have done it, but not her. Women don't hold grudges like men," he said matter-of-factly. Kyra's worry over being followed was suddenly sidelined at the bizarre comment. She nearly burst into sarcastic laughter at his words, curious to hear Galar's absurd explanation of how men and women held grudges differently.

"If a man holds a grudge, he might travel a tenday or more for revenge. Women are not like that. They'll scream and yell at you while you're there, but if you leave, they usually won't follow. They tend to fear the wild, being weaker," he said with authority. Kyra stopped walking for a moment and just glared at him. Was he joked or was he actually this delusional?

"For a big strong man so sure that the red-headed monster won't follow, you certainly ran out of the village fast," she said, causing Galar to momentarily pause. He had no rebuttal for that, so he merely grumbled under his breath and continued making quick time away from the village. Bravado aside, deep down, he knew that she was correct. His words had been as much to reassure himself as they had been based in any truth he believed about women.

Part of her wanted to correct him, to show Galar the err of his ways. They had both grown up in a mostly male-dominated society, where women were not regarded at the same level. Every woman was aware of it – it was a source of constant complaint – yet it was also accepted as a fact of life. Kyra was a product of this environment, latching on to Galar to elevate herself in a world that prevented her from achieving the same level of power as a man. Strangely, she had some form of respect for Ember, having easily matched, if not exceeded, the status of most men from where she came, by her own hand. Unfortunately, she would cling to the methods that had worked for her in the past and continue to manipulate Galar until someone better came along.

The thieves had made excellent time following the coastline heading east towards the place where the Sun rose. They had walked nearly half of the night and slept only a short while before continuing the next morning. The goal was to put as much distance between them and the People of the Blue Sea as possible. Pausing a few more times during the day, they continued making progress along the beach, using the Sun to guide them.

The day had grown long, and night approached when Kyra again had a strange feeling that they were being followed. An irrational and nagging feeling deep in her gut told her that the red-headed monster was not far behind. After a short rest to drink water and quickly eat some food, they resumed their quick-paced walk down the coast. It was not long until Galar stopped and ran off to a bush to relieve himself. Kyra wasn't quite sure why he ran so far. The two slept together and were married, but Galar held reservations about certain things. While Kyra waited, she absentmindedly looked at the strange stones on the ground. One of her footprints in the sand had uncovered a beautiful red stone that... Suddenly, she realized to her horror that there were deep and distinct tracks trailing behind them and heading all the way down the coastline. How had she not thought of this before?

"The sand!" Galar emerged from behind a bush tugging at his loincloth and trying to get it back into position when he noticed that Kyra was distraught, her hands twisted and entangled in her hair as she looked at the ground. He knew she disliked bad smells, but when he sniffed the air, he couldn't smell any odor from his recent activities.

"Look!" she said, pointing to the tracks. His blood ran cold as he realized that she was correct. It wasn't a smell upsetting her. It was the tracks... their tracks. They were leaving a perfect trail to follow, and half of the men in the tribe could probably track them. The problem was that the only place to go where they wouldn't leave tracks was either in the water, which was obviously not going to happen or higher up in the cliffs, which could be dangerous. He looked back at Kyra and realized that she had the same thought.

"We could walk along the edge of the cliffs for a while and then maybe return to the shore. If we did this from time to time, it might throw them off." Kyra nodded in agreement, and the pair began to hike to higher ground. It was not long before they walked across the steep hills above the sheer rock face that ran along the coast. The hike was more difficult and much slower, but they were not producing as many tracks, and Galar hoped nobody would follow. The last thing he needed was the red-headed monster finding him. If he were lucky, she would trip and fall from one of these cliffs. Then again, perhaps Kyra was incorrect, and nobody was following. Some things were best left unknown.

The Sun was low on the horizon as the pair navigated a cliff above the beach. There was very little sand, and mostly rocks and scrub brush. It provided a means to walk without tracks, but the trade-off was the perilous, steep ledges and sudden drops. Both Galar and Kyra had long brown hair, which the wind tended to catch, blowing hair in their faces. This was a significant danger as the pair hugged the side of the rock wall, moving ever so slowly around, the ground quite a distance below. They were carefully stepping around the edge of the rock wall when Galar suddenly felt something nick him in the leg. It felt as though somebody had struck him with a small stick. He was so startled that he tripped and nearly fell off the cliff. Instead, he tumbled onto his side, holding his leg where he had been jabbed. Behind him, Kyra screamed and jumped back pointing.

"Snake!" He glanced at his leg and found two puncture wounds just above his ankle. Galar turned in horror to see the creature, a brown-colored snake with a strange pattern down its back. Kyra and Galar both turned their attention to the wound. Galar was beginning to panic as pain grew in his leg. He had never seen a snake exactly like this, but he knew that snakes that left two wounds were much more deadly than snakes that left many small marks. They matched eyes, shock and fear in his, fierce calculation in hers. Would he die in moments, or would he live through this? There was no way to be sure, but now wasn't the time to keep hiking. The small snake had quickly slithered away, wanting nothing more to do with the creatures that had surprised it.

Kyra dropped to her knees and grabbed ahold of the leg. She wasn't sure what to do as snake bites were not common where they came from. She had heard a story once of venom being sucked from a wound, but she didn't see how that made any sense. Wouldn't the venom harm her too? Her mind raced to find a solution, but nothing came to mind. If Galar died, she would be forced to wander the wilds looking for a tribe to join by herself. Kyra poured water from a deer bladder over the wound to wash it clean with little interest in experimentation. Galar lay back against the rock wall while Kyra quickly built a small fire as shielded from view as she could. If his symptoms grew worse, the fire could be useful, and it might mean life or death.

ꓛ ꓛ ꓛ

Ember and Aethen continued to follow the trail down the coast. The best tracker in the village was a younger dark-haired man named Kel. Both of them would have appreciated his company, but he had not been available when they left. Ember was not a superb tracker, and in all truth, Aethen was only a moderate tracker at best, but these tracks were easy to follow. The tracks suddenly veered off towards the hills and disappeared not far ahead. Aethen stood looking around the area for a few moments to see if the tracks reappeared while Ember collected her hair into a ponytail. They were both tired and hot from walking.

"Dammit, one of them had a good idea," Aethen complained.

"First time for everything," Ember added. Tracking them would be much harder now, and the Sun was low on the horizon. It was time to camp. Ember quickly scavenged some driftwood for a fire as well as an armload of mollusks, which seemed to be quite easy to find near the Blue Sea. She was still having trouble with this idea of a "sea," a large body of water like a lake, but so vast that you couldn't see the other side. She had wondered if the Greatest River might actually be one of these 'seas.' Nobody had ever explored it fully, and so no one really knew. Of all the trips that she and Brig'dha might plan, that would not be one of them. Neither of them was very interested in water travel.

Given the darkness, a nice fire was of more importance that night. It was a new moon, and even though it rose through the night, Ember could only barely see it to the South as the faintest shape. The water was nothing more than blackness, and the fire became a single pinpoint of security. Ember placed the little mollusks in a semicircle around it as the fire grew. She slowly rotated them with a stick as they cooked. As always, they opened their mouths when they were done. Mollusks were one of the only foods that announced when it was cooked. Ember suspected that she found this cuter than the mollusks did.

Ɔ Ɔ Ɔ

Kyra glanced over the edge of the cliff upon which they now sat. The sheer drop was nearly ten lengths of a man. She had done her best to hide the fire, but it was hard to keep it hidden yet warm enough to aid Galar. Worse, he was not doing well. His eyesight had become foggy, and his leg had swollen, painfully. Kyra did not know how long it would take him to recuperate, but now he was becoming a liability. Out of desperation,

171

she had placed the Amber of Life necklace around his neck in the hope that its magic might help heal his wounds, but that had not seemed to help.

"Kyra, where's the Moon? I can't see the Moon. I think I might have gone blind!" he said in a panic though his words were strained as he was obviously weak. Kyra ignored him as she began to plan what she might do in a post-Galar world. She could still find a tribe without him and take a prominent role. Perhaps she could proclaim herself a traveling priestess and gain a prominent position using the necklace. The possibilities were quite impressive for a wily woman with a necklace of life and fertility around her neck. In truth, she had a slight fondness for Galar, but it had never mattered as much as what that fondness could bring her. It didn't make much sense to her why a person would entangle themself in the long-term with another person without some significant gain. Yet, this was how everyone else seemed to behave. She had always done her best to hide this opinion from others, but no one was watching, now.

Beside her, Galar moaned in agony. His mind had become foggy, and he had lost control of his leg. He could tell by touching his leg that it had badly swollen. Luckily, Kyra had helped him remove his boot before it had to be cut off. The problem was that they might be under pursuit though they didn't know for sure. Perhaps they could hide on the small cliff, and the pursuers might pass them by if they came at all. How could he have been so stupid to step without looking first? At the very least, he could have been beating at the ground with a stick to ward off such animals.

Back on the island from which they came, snakes were not a major problem. How could he have known? His eyesight was fading in and out, and the darkness didn't help. Galar barely made out the form of Kyra, though she looked to be sleeping. He did truly love her though he was pretty sure that she didn't love him. She had always been very manipulative and never seemed to be moved by what most people would consider a sad or emotional event. He raised his hand to her head and ran his fingers through her hair. For better or worse, he loved her despite this fact. She simply was who she was, and he had accepted that long before. At least, the snake had spared her.

As he lay, he considered his many mistakes and choices leading up to his present situation. Perhaps it was an altered state from the venom, but his mind seemed to clear of its usual emotion, focusing on the past. He remembered fighting with his father, teasing Brig'dha for being so quiet when they were children, and even stealing a necklace from a trader once as a child. Most of all, he remembered how vile he had been to

Ember, the stranger from the East. She had cost him his chance at the early respect he would need to become an elder... maybe. In fact, he wasn't sure of that now. As he slipped into the darkness of sleep, he considered just how reasonable his actions of late had been.

Kyra awoke startled with a burst of adrenaline. She had not meant to sleep the entire night and had intended to keep watch in case she had to leave Galar behind and flee. When she opened her eyes, she could see the faintest glow on the Eastern horizon, signaling that soon the Sun would rise. Beside her, Galar snored, indicating that he had not yet passed, though a quick look at the size of his swollen leg showed no sign that he would be ready to leave anytime soon. She stood and climbed above the cliff a short distance to give herself a better view down the coast, ever vigilant of snakes.

As she arrived atop the cliffs, the vastness of the world came into view. Towards the East, she saw no evidence of any tribes. To the West, she saw something she had dreaded. Along the beach was a tiny point of light, an orange glow. It was the kind of light made by a small campfire on the beach. For a moment, she stood in the budding dawn trying to make out details from near the fire, but it was simply too far away for her to determine anything.

"Damn them... Damn that redheaded monster," she whispered under her breath as she saw the pinpoint of light not that far away, which signaled the camp of her pursuers, most likely. She didn't know for sure that it was Ember, but she could almost feel it. There was something inhuman about that woman. Now she had a real problem to deal with. Just below on the cliff was a liability with a damaged leg. If she left him alive when she fled, the pursuers would continue to follow. He would likely tell them everything when the monster put her blade to his throat, or lower. At the rate they were moving, she would not be able to escape, having very little skill in the wilds. Quickly, a plot formed, a way to trick Ember and keep the necklace. Much of it hinged on the fact that the shore was rough with rocks below the cliff and most certainly a place where water-filled periodically. Impassible.

Kyra had always believed that every disadvantage was nothing more than a potential advantage in disguise. Galar was certainly a liability, but there was a way that she could use him to her advantage and perhaps rid herself of pursuit. She took a deep breath to prepare herself for what would have to be done. It was a calculated plot, but she would be free from the pursuit and completely free of all attachments if she pulled it off.

Strangely, the thought of what she was about to do caused her a brief moment of what might be described as guilt, though it was fleeting.

Kyra stepped down to the cliff edge where Galar lay. His leg was even more swollen than last time she checked, brown with dark shades forming around the bite, and he did not look so well. He made strange whimpering sounds and shivered now and then. Kyra wasn't quite sure that he would live, even if she had cared for him back at the tribe. Perhaps this would be the simplest way to put him out of his pain, but either way, he would serve her purpose. She removed the necklace from his neck and placed it over hers. Her plan was deception, but the hardest part would be the physical act of pushing him off the cliff.

☽ ☽ ☽

Ember awoke with a stretch and was pleased to find that the fire had not yet burned down. She had experienced significant nightmares from her encounter with Yan, but her sheer exhaustion from the rapid hiking had spared her much of it. It would be a long time, if ever, before such intrusive thoughts ever fully left. Even now, she still had nightmares from the men who had captured her, the night the wolves had attacked, and the men she had slew. She saw their faces some nights as her arrows slammed into their chests. A strange look of confusion, shock, and rejection of their sealed fates – a truth few could accept – as their lives flowed away like water in hand. Even now, she was sure they had deserved their fates, yet their guilt did little to keep their shocked faces from her slumber. Unfortunately, scars of the mind took just as long, if ever, to heal.

She missed the beautiful brunette who should have been sleeping beside her. Some nights, when the images and the dreams were especially bad, she would sit up and watch the Moon Priestess merely sleeping. Even now, the thought of lying beside Brig'dha sent a tingly wave of euphoria through her body. She knew what she would need to do about this, but not yet. First, she needed to take care of the thieves and recover the Amber of Life pendant for the Blue Sea people, and then confront whatever came next.

That night, she and Aethen had taken turns adding more wood. Ember did not expect wolves on a beach but given her past experience and what had happened to poor Tes, she wasn't going to take a chance. She and Aethen slowly stood and prepared to resume their task. Aethen unpacked some dried meat strips for breakfast. There was a limit to how long their rations would hold out before they would have to pause and replenish their food and water, but they had another day or two before that occurred.

Ember wandered out into the cool water for a quick morning swim before resuming the hunt. Her mind was awash of human interactions and how to understand them. There was Brig'dha, who by now was cursing her name and for whom she had so many unresolved thoughts. Then there was Galar, a pig of a man though she couldn't help but wonder how many of his actions were influenced by Kyra, his wife who strangely looked almost like a sister. In truth, Ember had no real evidence that Kyra was manipulating Galar. She could be an innocent bystander in all of this. Perhaps she had seen the attack upon Ember and had been too frightened to say anything, retrieving the necklace because she had been commanded to do so by Galar under some threat.

Around and around in her mind, the various possible scenarios continued to play out. This was one of the reasons why she enjoyed her morning swim. The other reason was that it gave her a place to relieve herself in the morning where no one else could see. Bushes were fine, but other creatures could be found in a bush. Ember was not interested in getting bitten by a snake or another animal. She cautiously gazed back at the shore where Aethen was preparing the food. She hoped that the fish wouldn't be too displeased, but this was a pretty standard action when in the water. *Good morning to you, vicious giant catfish*, she thought with a giggle, remembering the black-tipped vicious fish she had seen not so many days before. She left them a good-morning surprise, then cleaned and left the water.

A quick morning bath completed and her body fresh and clean, Ember emerged from the water, quickly applying her loincloth. She stepped over to the campfire to dry off. In front of the fire, she rubbed dry sand across her skin, taking with it the excess water and having an exfoliating effect. As soon as her skin was mostly dried, she used some of the charred wood from the fire to apply a dark coat of soot and lines around her arms and legs before dawning her shirt and boots. Behind her, Aethen couldn't help but watch. He shook his head and turned his attention away from Ember and toward the cliff where Galar and Kyra had likely traveled.

"Do you see that cliff up there? I bet you that's where they went. It's the most accessible place along this route. Hopefully, we can pick up their tracks on the trail leading up. I doubt it will be easy with all the rocks," Aethen said as the pair began to walk down the beach heading for the cliffs. Ember was quite pleased with how fast Aethen moved. He didn't spend long dawdling in the morning though she had to admit that she could regress into the laziest of creatures if nobody were watching. Strangely, just before the Sun rose, she thought she had seen a bit of light from the cliff, but it could have just been in her mind. There was no way that Galar would have set his camp so close to theirs.

Ember began to march towards the cliffs, with Aethen falling behind. He admired her bravery and willingness to go after the necklace at all costs. She had plenty of flaws, such as laziness and inappropriate spontaneity, yet bravery was not one of them. Not so long ago, he had vowed to reveal his true feelings for her if only they could be alone for a short time. Now they were traveling through the wilds, and the most he had done was hand her a piece of dried deer meat. Aethen shook his head in frustration. He suspected that battling a large bear to the death would be less troublesome than speaking his feelings to a woman.

◠ ◠ ◠

Kyra tugged and pulled at Galar until she could roll him. She was always astounded by how heavy men were. She wondered, and not for the first time, how was it that they were able to stand and walk with such weight? As she got him to the edge of the cliff, Galar awoke from his stupor and realized that he was being rolled to the edge. Frantically he grasped at Kyra, trying to stop her, but his strength had failed him. Given many tendays, that strength would return as his wound healed, but if Kyra pushed him over the edge of the cliff, that would never happen.

"Kyra... What are you doing? Stop..." he plead weakly, but he could do nothing more than mount a token resistance. Kyra merely stared at him with the expression of a person having trouble pushing a heavy object. There did not seem to be any other trouble in her eyes. He had always known that she held no real affection towards others, but he had not realized to what extent her apathy extended. He reached forward and found only her smooth skin with his hands. Unfortunately, he could not grasp that skin with his fingers, so his weak hand slipped. She looked him in the face right before giving him a final push. For one moment, their eyes met. Galar realized that she saw only an expendable liability. At that moment, he wished that his wife had been more like Ember.

Kyra pushed, and Galar rolled off the edge of the cliff but not without grabbing a small clump of her hair. The hair tore free and fell in strands upon the rocky ledge causing her to scream. His body slammed into the rocks below with a horribly twisted bounce from which nobody could have survived. She jumped back and grabbed ahold of the painful injury. It was only a little hair, yet many strands lay on the cliff. For a moment, her anger flared, but then she realized that the hair strands only added to her story. Looking over the edge of the cliff, she noted that the little point of light had vanished. If Ember were coming, she would be here soon.

Quickly, Kyra took the necklace and climbed to the rocks above. She lifted a rock and gently placed the necklace underneath. Next, she climbed back down, careful to remove any trace of her movement from the dirt. She pulled her leather wrap skirt loose so that it was almost torn off, but not quite. Using her bald fists, she rubbed her eyes over and over until they became red and puffy. She needed to look as though she had been crying. Once that was completed, she kept an eye out for her pursuers. This would be a dangerous ruse.

ↄ ↄ ↄ

Ember and Aethen hiked the slope of the gentle hill, which became a cliff with a steep drop. For the most part, tracks could not be found on the rocky ledge. There were a few patches of sand here and there where Aethen believed he might have seen a track though it was hard to be sure. Their only hope was that the trail they currently traversed was really the only way to navigate the cliffs. The tracks in the sand had led toward the cliffs. Tracking their prey was now more guesswork than following a trail.

Up ahead, the cliff became completely rocky with a sharp corner and a narrow ledge to pass. As they rounded the corner, both of them stopped to take in the sight which befell them. Lying on the ground curled in the fetal position was a woman who looked like Kyra. Her hair was a tangled mess and her leather skirt looked to be torn halfway free. Beside her, two traveling packs lay with their contents spread across the ground. Aethen and Ember pulled loose their daggers and rushed forward to find out what had happened.

"Kyra! Kyra!" Ember called as she ran to the woman's side and gently tried to roll her over. Kyra maintained her fetal position with her eyes closed though she seemed awake. It looked to Ember as though she had spent most of the night in this position and had cried herself to sleep, judging by her eyes. On the ground nearby were several long strands of Kyra's hair. Ember was not liking the scene that she saw. Her own assault was fresh in her mind, and it didn't take much for her to jump to conclusions.

"Kyra! Are you already? What happened to Galar? Where is the necklace? Why did you do it?" she rattled off, shaking Kyra with the hope that she would speak. Kyra looked away in shame, but she slowly began to speak. Her words were haunted with pain and regret.

"The gods knew... They knew..." she said in a whimpering voice. Ember waited until she spoke again.

"Last night... they came, two men came. They saw our fire... they found us. Galar... Galar convinced Yan to attack you. I could have stopped him, but I didn't. I just wanted the necklace," she paused for a moment, seemingly grief-stricken, before continuing. "They took the necklace, but they pushed Galar over the cliff when he tried to help me. The gods knew, and they punished us," she buried her head in her arms and made muffled sounds of whimpering. Ember couldn't believe what she was hearing. Two men, probably from a local tribe, had attacked them and taken the necklace just the night before. Ember could guess what else they had done, judging by the scene before her.

She glanced back at Aethen, who had a similar expression. The primary goal was to recover the necklace, and that's just what they would do. They had to move quickly before the men got too far north. Ember felt bad for what had happened to her, but Kyra had walked her own path, and this was the result. Their village was not that far away, and she could walk back by herself to face the consequences of her deeds. Ember was unsure if she believed Kyra's story of limited involvement with Yan, but this didn't seem like the right time to bring that up. The woman had lost her husband, and it appeared that the two men who had attacked her may have done even worse, though Kyra had not stated this. These events made it hard for Ember to hold any deeper of a grudge.

"Kyra, you have angered the gods, and now you have felt their wrath. Tell us where the men went, and we will follow them," Aethen said. For a short moment, Kyra simply sobbed before speaking.

"They came... from the North, one day... that's what they said," she answered weakly. Ember and Aethen stood and left the woman to her misery and headed north as fast as they could to capture the necklace from the thieves. As soon as they left, Kyra sat up and breathed a sigh of relief. Her plan was going much better than she had suspected. Ember and Aethen were so interested in recovering the necklace that they left her only moments after finding her. It really wasn't that far if she were to return to their village. But of course, returning to the village was not her intention. She had bought herself at least a day of head start or more. Now, all she had to do was recover the necklace and head East. There simply had to be a tribe before long.

◯ ◯ ◯

The first half of the day saw Ember and Aethen making excellent time north along what looked like a deer trail. Many inland villages had small and well-beaten trails providing access to large bodies of water, such as the Blue Sea. That part of Kyra's story made sense. It was certainly reasonable that two men from an inland tribe might wander past the cliff where she and Galar had slept. The deer were also known to follow these small paths though Ember was unsure whether deer had made this path.

The land was a beautiful mix of scrub brush and small trees. Ember and Aethen hurried along the trail in constant anticipation that they might see the men ahead. As time progressed, Ember began to think more and more of her interactions with Kyra. She felt slightly guilty that they had not taken the time to retrieve Galar's body, but right now, finding the necklace and catching the men who had assaulted Galar and Kyra was much more important. Still, her mind mulled over inconsistencies.

As the Sun rose high in the sky, some aspects of her encounter with Kyra began to really trouble her. If the two men had performed such a wicked deed and had killed Galar, why had they not either abducted Kyra or just thrown her off the cliff? Why leave a witness behind who could return to her tribe and speak about what they had done? How did they even know about the necklace in the first place? Ember supposed that they may have seen it, or perhaps Kyra had offered it to them in exchange for her life. But that still brought up other problems. The kind of men who would do such a thing were not the kind who would honor such an agreement.

More troublesome was the lack of footprints. Ember and Aethen had headed out at such a rapid pace across the natural trail without thinking too deeply about the details of her story. They had hoped to catch the dangerous men before they had gotten too far. Half a day had passed, and they had yet to find any tracks. Piece by piece, the story Kyra had told was breaking down as their minds scrutinized each little bit. Later in the day, Ember finally put her hand on Aethen's shoulder, stopping him to talk. He turned to see Ember looking slightly confused and perhaps a little sheepish.

"Has it been bothering you too? Something about that story just didn't add up," she said, self-doubt poring over her. It had been bothering Aethen as well, but he had kept his thoughts to himself until now.

"It has also bothered me. Why didn't the men kill her or take her to be a wife? Why leave her? She could easily return to her tribe and speak of what the men had done. And why tell her where they came from? I doubt she watched them leave, either. When we found her, she was on the ground and did not look as though she had stood since the attack," he agreed.

"And how was she able to understand them in the first place? Dammit! You don't think that she still has the necklace?" Ember said in frustration. She was trying to wrap her mind around the deception. If it were true, the next question would be, how did Galar die? Aethen came to the same conclusion at almost the same moment.

"Perhaps Galar only slipped and fell. Perhaps he wore the necklace, and right now, she's down there retrieving it. Her tears may simply have come from her grief over his death. We should head back now before she gets away," Aethen spoke hurriedly. Ember was embarrassed and extremely mad with herself for being so easily fooled.

☽ ☽ ☽

Brig'dha and Kel had made good time heading east. Both had been well-rested before they left and had marched through the night. Walking at night under the dark sky was dangerous, but they had followed the shoreline, which gave them a point of navigation. Starlight was their only guide as they trudged forward. It was a calculated gamble since neither would be able to follow footprints in the dark, but if they were right and if everyone had stayed close to the shore, they would emerge from the darkness almost dead on top of Ember's group. As the Sun rose, Kel quickly spotted four tracks heading down the beach, two sets older than the others.

"It looks like we have them, and half of these are really fresh," he said, kneeling over the tracks. Brig'dha was very glad that Kel had come. She had no skill at hunting or tracking. Unless the Goddess sent her a sign, she would have wandered aimlessly without help. Ember had always provided that service for her, and now Kel took on that role. Besides being a tracker, he kept her mind occupied and off what had happened. She realized now why Ember had left, but part of her was still heartbroken.

As she walked, Brig'dha continued to think about her friend. They had been together for greater than a harvest and had shared so many life-and-death experiences. She had come to rely on Ember and could not imagine her life without her. When they got past this event, Brig'dha worried over what Ember might do next. Would she find some man and start a family with him? She supposed that she would be relegated to best friend status. Still, somehow the thought of ending their adventures together left her with a growing void in her heart and a slight depression. After the loss of her husband, Mohdan, Brig'dha could no longer imagine any other man at her side. In actuality, her marriage to Mohdan had been more of an arranged event than any real love. He had been a good man, but she never felt a strong attachment to him nor physical attraction. Brig'dha sighed and trudged along. Not far behind, Mew trailed. His biggest concern was what he would eat when next they stopped.

Not far ahead were some cliffs which passed above a place where the beach became almost nonexistent. Kel realized that the tracks led from the beach and up onto the cliffs, as he expected they would. He and Brig'dha began walking up the hill towards the cliffs. It was not long before they found the campsite in all its gruesome detail. Galar's possessions were scattered all over the rocks and heavily picked through. Scattered on the ground were long brown hairs which might have belonged to either Galar or Kyra.

The scene was ominous, and neither had a good feeling about what they would learn. Kel began searching for tracks and trying to learn what happened while Brig'dha carefully examined the campsite. The fire had cooled, but the charred wood was still warm, which told Brig'dha the fire had only been lit the previous night. The ground was covered with so many scuff marks and conflicting tracks that it was nearly impossible to get a good feel for what happened. It was obvious to both that a significant amount of movement had occurred at this place, perhaps even combat.

As Kel wandered around, Brig'dha examined the edge of the cliff. Below her was a drop approximately ten lengths of a man in height. The bottom was punctuated by large rocks emanating from the water. This was certainly not a place anyone would like to traverse, which might have been one of the reasons why Galar and Kyra had traveled across the sheer cliffs. Brig'dha couldn't help but notice an object bouncing up and down in the waves. The closer she looked, the more she realized that the shape was human, though the skin appeared to be mottled and discolored. She looked more closely when suddenly the waves turned the shape over against a rock.

"Galar..." she whispered in horror.

Brig'dha spent a short time offering prayers to the Horned God for the safe journey of Galar's spirit to the afterlife. Unfortunately, the Goddess was not in power due to the new moon. Moreover, the Horned God would be a better choice for helping the body of Galar in the wilds during the day. If they had more time and more people to help, she would have buried his body, but he was in a terrible place to approach, and around his neck, she clearly saw no necklace. Likely, Kyra had fled with the precious item.

"It looks to me like a man and a woman, likely Ember and Aethen, headed north along this deer trail. A single woman, probably Kyra, climbed up to this rock and headed east. So, the question is, do we follow Kyra or Ember?" Kel asked. Brig'dha was at a loss. Part of her wanted to catch Ember, but at the same time, that necklace was the reason that Ember had left. If she let Kyra escape with the necklace, all of Ember's actions would have been for nothing. She had to weigh in her mind the best option, and retrieving the necklace continued to seem like the better route.

Brig'dha stood and used her foot to trace the line of an arrow pointing to the east. She hoped that if Ember and Aethen returned, they would see the arrow and head in that direction. She wished that there was an easier way to inform them of the details of their journey, but unfortunately, on one could not use symbols to communicate words, or, at least, she had never heard of anybody doing this. Determination overtook Brig'dha. For once, she would adopt the role of Ember, and she would be the hunter.

"We head east to find Kyra," she said with determination, turning and abruptly walking to the East. She didn't even look back to see if Kel was following. She didn't want to take the chance that she might lose her nerve.

ↄ ↄ ↄ

Kyra was glad when she saw smoke ahead, just over a slight rise, which indicated a village. The night had been dark, and she had slept by herself against a rock face without a fire. It was warm enough that she didn't need a fire, but something was comforting about the light and heat that warded away the fears of the night. Feeling the weight of the heavy amber necklace bumping against her chest was somewhat reassuring as she stumbled over the rocky ground, and the village came into view.

The village was much larger than she had expected it to be. A wooden palisade wall surrounded the majority of the village though some of the dwellings existed outside the wall. All the houses were made of poles and buried partly into the ground. The roofs were a mixture of thatch and thin wooden poles, likely reinforced to survive the storms from the Blue Sea. The sides of many of the buildings were painted with artistic shapes and designs, a common practice among most tribes. The design seemed friendly enough. Kyra hoped the friendly artwork portrayed the attitudes of their creators.

As she staggered across the rocks, people from the village began to notice her presence and rushed forward to see who she was. Kyra tugged at the necklace to ensure that it was evenly shifted across her chest. With her skirt in poor repair, her boots scuffed and dirty, and not even a feather in her hair for decoration, she suspected that she would not make a superb first impression. She had no idea how she would speak to these people, but she figured that she could make her intentions clear using hand gestures. It was how traders spoke when they did not know the trade language. As was the custom, Kyra stopped approaching and waited for the people to come to her. Most people considered it rude to just simply walk into a foreign village unannounced.

ɔ ɔ ɔ

Ul'uer heard the commotion at the front of the main palisade gate and couldn't resist the opportunity to see what was going on. He had been chopping wood with a large stone ax for much of the morning, and the prospect of something new to do filled him with hope. With the ax in hand, just in case, Ul'uer walked toward the palisade gate to see why everybody was making so much noise.

As soon as he exited the palisade, he saw the source of the commotion – a single woman stood atop a small hill in front of the village. She had long brown hair and piercing eyes, or at least, that's what it looked like from where Ul'uer stood. He wasn't that young, but he wasn't past his prime either. It wasn't that he couldn't see the distance due to age, but more due to the orientation of the Sun's light. It would have made things much easier if she had approached from the East. He supposed it was time to live up to his namesake and do something for the village. With a deep breath, he began to approach the woman.

Ul'uer was the son of the high priest Ul'na'har. He had never become a priest himself, but his family was among the leading families of the tribe, which gave him a certain degree of latitude in the chores and tasks he chose to do. He never seemed to connect with the spirits in the way his father did, which was likely why he had not expected an encounter like this. Yet again, the high priest had been correct. He would have to give his father credit for his accuracy later. Ul'na'har had just stated two days before that a strange time was upon them. According to Ul'na'har, the new moon had come early, which signaled the need for a sacrifice to appease the sea goddess, Mear.

Some questioned his proclamation, and few believed that the new moon had come early, but very few were willing to argue with Ul'na'har aloud lest they be found worthy of the sacred honor of sacrifice. Ul'uer chuckled at the thought of the last man who had dared to cross Ul'na'har, just a few harvests passed. That man had appeased the Sea Goddess in one of the most outrageous ceremonies he had ever seen. Perhaps she was a sacrifice delivered into their hands or maybe a member of a trade group who got lost. One could not always tell.

He approached the woman and was surprised to see a gorgeous amber necklace adorning her neck. Her face was shaped slightly different from his, being rounder and with thinner lips. Her eyes had a slightly sharper appearance than the more oval-shape of the women from his village and her skin was much darker, a forest person. She stood there waiting for him to approach with a strangely pleasant look upon her face. Women were not known to wander the wilds alone, especially not a woman with such a large and beautiful amber necklace.

Ul'uer was of reasonable height with short dark hair, dark eyes, and a slightly intense complexion. He wore a pair of leggings with a leather wrap around his waist and a pair of sandals, holding an ax in his right hand. He wasn't sure if he would intimidate the woman, but she had politely stood watching him so far. He came to a stop once he was within arm's reach and waited for a moment, a smile on his face, before continuing. He could tell that she was nervous, and he did not want to make things worse by acting rashly. The woman made no move to stop him or flee, so he continued. He was careful lest he be struck down by spirits from the woman. For all he knew she was a spirit from the sea, or perhaps even the Sea Goddess herself.

He had heard a story at the last harvest festival of a tribe who had been visited by a minor god. Supposedly, the minor god had been enraged by the tribe failing to properly honor him and had brought a plague upon their people. He had heard several variations of that story while at the harvest festival. Still, whether it was spirits or a god, the results were always the same. The afflicted tribe was cursed and made sick. He kept that story in mind as he carefully spoke to the seemingly innocent woman.

"Hello, do you speak my words?" he asked her slowly and cautiously. Behind him, several dozen villagers stood ready to fight or flee, should the woman turn into a spirit or something worse. She looked back at him, confused. He was pretty sure that she had not understood what he had said. Spirits knew all languages, which immediately told him that this was a flesh and blood person. Her eyes were still a little red and puffy, and she looked as though she had been walking for days. If ever a sacrifice had been delivered straight to the gates of the village, this was it.

"Aelae... aes-K-eye-rah eahg'nom," she said, stressing the word "K-eye-rah" as she pointed to her chest. Ul'uer assumed that K-eye-rah was the woman's name while the rest of her words were foreign to him. He pointed with his finger towards her necklace and gestured, requesting permission to touch it. At least, that's what he thought his body language was saying. The woman smiled and nodded. He reached forward slowly and lifted the beautiful necklace. The large amber pendant held a small flower forever preserved inside. Ul'uer let go of the pendant, suddenly withdrawing his hand. It may have been his mind, but he swore that he felt a tremor from the item. He pointed at the amber and provided a questioning expression hoping that she would explain by some means what it did.

Kyra seemed to understand what he asked as though she had expected the question. She dropped to her knees and held her hand over a patch of empty dirt in which nothing grew. She lifted a handful of the dirt and then sprinkled it on the ground while casting him a sad expression as though she were upset at the lack of life. Next, she removed the necklace and placed it on the patch of dirt, circling her hand over the necklace while chanting. When she was finished, she replaced the necklace around her neck and then pantomimed a flower growing from the ground. When she was done, she looked up at Ul'uer with a smile, pointing to herself and then to the tribe.

There was no doubting her message. The previous poor harvest had taken its toll on the tribe, and many prayers had been issued to tempt the spirits of the land into becoming fertile once more. Out of nowhere, a beautiful young maiden had come bearing a magic item that contained what looked like the essence of life itself. Ul'uer felt a wave of emotion pass over him as he realized how fortunate his people were. He had heard stories of the Goddess' deeds and of the gifts that the spirits of the land would sometimes bestow upon the people, but this was well beyond even those tales. A willing sacrifice. He stepped forward and embraced the woman tightly and with reverence. She stared back at him, shocked but was seemingly pleased that everything was going well. His people would not go hungry this coming cold season… her blood would ensure this.

CHAPTER ELEVEN

BRIG'DHA, I...

Love is a complex emotion experienced by higher-order sentient creatures. It manifests in many different ways, only some romantic or sexual in nature. Love is one of the most powerful expressions of compassion and empathy known to any sentient creature. It is a great equalizer, bringing together factions and superseding differences. It is both the source of our greatest joys and greatest sorrows, the great primal catalyst. Love is perhaps the most significant manifestation of evolutionary group dynamics, the pinnacle of sentience.

It wasn't long before Ember and Aethen arrived at the place where they had left Kyra. It was just as they had suspected. While she may not have been guilty of whatever tragic accident had befallen Galar, she certainly had taken off to the East. Aethen really wished that Kel had joined them. Neither Ember nor Aethen were expert trackers, but they could easily see the footprints heading east. Strangely, it almost looked like there were several people headed east, but neither Aethen nor Ember could make heads or tails of the differences in their footsteps. Perhaps the greatest oddity was what looked like an arrow pointing to the East and traced upon the ground. Ember and Aethen glanced at one another with confused expressions.

"Well, I'm glad this isn't getting stranger in any way..." Ember said with a sigh. Aethen smiled, and the pair turned towards the East in the hope of catching Kyra before she encountered another tribe. *Now I know why predators have really good noses... following tracks is hard!* Ember mused. In their haste, both failed to notice little wildcat paw prints also heading east.

Ↄ Ↄ Ↄ

Brig'dha crouched low in the bushes on a hilltop above the tribe. They had left the main path which led to the village and climbed the hills to the North. Below, she could see enough buildings to house at least 200 people in what looked like a large fishing village with small fields for growing crops. There were many small boats mostly made from stretched hide, though a few dugout boats could be seen. Kel knelt beside her, watching for any sign Kyra had made it to the village. This was the most likely place for her to have gone. The only real possibility that Brig'dha could imagine was that Kyra would come here and attempt to trade the necklace in exchange for acceptance and a decent place to live.

They had been lying on the ground for quite some time, and Brig'dha had already been bitten twice now by ants. The only reason they had not moved along was the strange behavior of the people they watched. They were cooking large amounts of food, hurriedly, more than one might expect to see in a tribe of this size. Below, she kept seeing people frantically observing a primary structure as if something were going on inside. If something interesting were inside, it might involve Kyra. Suddenly, the doors to the central building opened. People started to emerge caring what appeared to be a woman on their shoulders, holding her high above for all to see. The woman had long brown hair.

As they watched, the woman was carried around the village three times while dozens of people followed behind yelling some sort of chant. On the ground in front of the main building, hides were being placed in a long row while the food was brought to place upon them. It appeared that a feast was being prepared, perhaps for the woman being carried around. Brig'dha could not imagine that the necklace would have brought this level of praise, but she had to give Kyra credit for making a great first impression. Perhaps they would sneak down closer when the night fell. Behind her, mew carefully approached Brig'dha's feet to sniff. Smelling feet was one of the many tasks he engaged in.

ɔ ɔ ɔ

Aethen held his hand up and gestured for Ember to drop down as they approached the edge of the hill. Ember crept up the side of the hill on her stomach to see what Aethen had found. Before them lay a large tribe with a vast palisade wall of wooden poles. This was definitely the sort of place where Kyra might have gone. They quickly hurried off the main path that entered the village and sneaked around the South for a better look. Ember was just glad that Aethen had seen the village before they had been spotted. It was best to have a good look-see before making themselves known.

There wasn't much space between the rocky cliffs that quickly descended into the water and the palisade wall. Ember and Aethen hugged that small space as they sneaked beside the village. From where they stood, they were directly against the palisade wall hiding on the outside.

This let them see the happenings of the village through the cracks in the wood without being seen themselves. Ember sat against the wall looking through a crack between two poles where the mud that was caked between the poles had broken free. Behind her, only half the length of a man was a rocky cliff with a drop-off high enough to likely kill anyone who fell.

As they looked through the cracks, they saw Kyra being carried on the back of a large man and surrounded by a procession of dozens of villagers. She was smiling, her body adorned with flowers, and the villagers seemed jubilant to have her in their presence. Even more interesting, the necklace was still around her neck. Ember would have suspected that she had given it up to have received such a greeting, and yet there it was. Ember and Aethen exchanged incredulous glances.

"You vicious deceiving little..." Ember began in total rage at having been deceived when Aethen abruptly clamped his hand over her mouth, silencing her. It was at that moment that she remembered why they were being quiet. When next they spoke, they did so in a whisper.

"Well, you can't say anything bad about her form. I knew that she was manipulative, but an entire tribe is a bit of a stretch. There has to be more to this," Ember whispered plainly, a bit irritated. Aethen grunted acknowledgment. For now, they would simply watch and see what happened. If they could find a moment when Kyra was absent from her fans, they could grab the necklace and be gone. Ember was not against the idea of punching her in the face and running. The problem would be if they were forced to enter the village and explain the situation to the locals. Things could get dicey, fast.

ɔ ɔ ɔ

Kyra could not believe her luck. It was becoming rather painful sitting on the back of the large man below her as she circled the tribe for the third time, but could she really complain? These people had accepted her with open arms, almost as though they desperately needed her. They had not even taken the necklace, though many of them had looked at it intently. They didn't quite pronounce her name correctly, but that didn't really bother her as long as they showered her with gifts of flowers and herbs. More impressively, a feast was being created in her honor, at least, that's what she figured.

Her strange procession came to a halt after the third circuit and carefully put her down. An old man stepped forward and spoke rapidly to her though she did not understand what he said. The only thing he said that she knew was his name, as he simply pointed and spoke it plainly. Oolhana'harr, or perhaps it was Ul'na'har. He looked like an elder shaman. The man was nearly bald and wore strange tattoos across his skin in the shape of little dots. Around his neck was a necklace made of some of the most beautiful clam shells she had ever seen. He had a long beard that reached nearly to his belly button. He wore an extra-long wrap skirt made from some sort of woven textile, leather sandals, and a reed cloak.

Around and around, he walked, examining Kyra. She simply stood and let the man do as he would. Then, after a few moments, he became satisfied with whatever questions he had and proclaimed something very positive to his people. He was almost excited as he spoke, and all the people looked very pleased to hear what he had to say. She supposed that this ritual was designed to bring her into the tribe. It seemed that the feast was to start soon, but before that could happen, a group of the tribe women came to escort Kyra to a smaller building.

The women washed her hair and body with water scented with flower petals. They rubbed her skin with precious walnut oil scented with herbs, then applied intricate designs to her body with black soot and oil-based paint. Across her face, beautiful geometric shapes were painted with red paint made from ocher. Kyra simply relaxed and enjoyed the treatment. It had been a long time since she had been pampered in any sort of way, and this was the pampering a headman's daughter could expect. Upon her feet, a new pair of leather sandals were placed. Around her waist, a flax string girdle, basically a waist-cord with long strings hanging down, was tied. It covered the front and back mostly, though she found it a little more revealing than she was used to.

Around her neck, a beautiful necklace made of dozens of clamshells was placed. Each clamshell was fastened to the next, making a triangular necklace that hung down the front of her body. Clamshells seemed to be important to these people. Kyra decided to name them the Clam People as she did not know their actual name. Other pierced shells were tied in her hair, and various armbands and necklaces were applied. Kyra was dressed like a goddess by the time she stood ready for the feast.

She stepped from the building and into the village with over 180 people watching her from the feast mats. It was slightly disconcerting with this many people and especially when her clothing was so elaborate, but how could she frown on hospitality of this magnitude? Kyra came to sit at the head of the feast where food was brought to her by the basket load. She did not go hungry. As the night came upon the feast goers, groups of people danced while song and music filled the night. Nothing was held back from Kyra. She was offered the finest meats, ate fresh berries, and even drank magical fermented honey water, one of the rarest drinks to be found where she had come from.

ↄ ↄ ᴄ

The following day Ember and Aethen awoke from their precarious hideout on the cliff's edge. Ember had watched the entire feast and had been amazed by how beautifully Kyra had been decorated. She kept wondering what prompted such actions from these people. She could not shake the feeling that something was wrong. There was too much religious activity involved for her to be calm. Drastic and dangerous things could happen whenever religious fervor was at its height. Ember remembered being sent on an epic quest across the world simply because of a sign at one of these types of festivals. She remembered the near-sacrifice of Brig'dha out of the fear of the spirits. What could these people have in mind?

As she watched, the tribe began to awaken and begin their daily work. Not far ahead was a cliff that jutted out quite a distance over the water with a sheer drop. The ground on the cliff was made of rock and dirt and well-tread. All around the cliff were what looked like painted wards against spirits, as well as offerings. Ember concluded that rituals occurred on this cliff and wondered what gods these people followed. Since the cliff dropped directly into the sea, nearly ten lengths of a man below, she concluded that they worshiped sea spirits of some variety. Her own people worshiped the spirits of the Great River, but she wasn't quite sure if sea spirits and river spirits were the same.

ↄ ↄ ᴄ

Brig'dha and Kel approached the village cautiously. Mew had left early that morning to hunt, and would likely not return until the night, at that earliest. They had hiked a short distance away and spent the night in a place between two large outcroppings where they could light a small fire without being noticed. Brig'dha was getting the feeling that there was something religious about the happenings below. Three times around the village, Kyra had been carried. The mats for the feast had been laid out in five large areas. The dances had occurred seven times. Whenever specific numbers like this occurred in patterns, it often implied religion. It was known that the gods appreciated numbers and held some numbers sacred.

191

Three, five, and seven. Everything about this felt like a great ritual, but a ritual to what end?

If Ember had been with her, they might have crept closer or perhaps even sneaked into the village at night to learn these truths. Though she trusted Kel's ability to track, Brig'dha was not brave enough to do something so daring. Instead, the pair would have to remain outside of the village and wait for their opportunity to make a move. Brig'dha wondered how many days they could camp waiting before they simply had to leave.

ɔ ɔ ɔ

Kyra awoke late in the afternoon, having spent most of the day sleeping and then lounging on soft, delicate rabbit furs sewn together into a large blanket. Two women had stayed with her the entire night, singing her to sleep and then remaining nearby to care for any need that she had. Even she was beginning to suspect something was wrong with this level of treatment. As she awoke, one by one, people came to the building where she slept and brought her gifts. She had small, eloquently crafted pots, a lamp made from a large clamshell with beeswax and a wick already inside and ready to burn, several containers with scented oils, and multiple statuettes of a goddess she had never seen before. All the gifts unnerved her, seeming too votive for her liking. But she decided to go along with it a little longer. Perhaps it would make sense in due time.

She looked down and saw that the necklace was still around her neck. That was probably the strangest part. They had not attempted to either barter for the necklace or simply take it. She was pondering this when her two servant women, she supposed that's what they were, came to escort her to a place where food was prepared. If she ate too much more of the rich food, she was worried she might explode. She had never eaten so much delicate and tasty meat in her life. The pieces she was fed came from the most tender and finest parts of the animal.

The evening had descended upon the village when the women came for her again. This time, they came to prepare her for what seemed like another event. They carefully washed her and then reapplied her extremely intricate paint. Other women were helping this time to apply the pigment faster, which was good considering that the women skillfully decorated every square inch of her body. She could not imagine what she must look like. She looked down at her body and saw beautiful geometric forms across her skin, the likes of which she had never beheld. The women replaced the shell necklace, but this time, they removed the amber necklace and then placed it back so that it lay over the shells. She wondered if that had some sort of significance. Perhaps they intended to take the necklace from her tonight during some ritual?

☽ ☽ ☽

The waxing Moon would not rise that night, and the Sun was nearly set when Brig'dha saw Kyra exit the hut. She could not believe the intricacy of the paint that covered Kyra's entire body. The flax string girdle was dyed a blue color, one of the rarest color dyes. Brig'dha was almost jealous of Kyra's outfit though she had to admit that there wasn't much of it. She flatly refused to let herself consider how stunning the woman looked, given what she might very well be guilty of. Everything she was seeing looked more and more like a religious ceremony.

☽ ☽ ☽

Ember and Aethen watched as Kyra was carried three times around the village, once more. Ember was shocked to see the level of detail of the paint that adorned Kyra. Though she didn't like the woman, she had to admit that she looked gorgeous in her complex ceremonial garb. What really troubled her was the high priest and several men who were ritually painted standing together and discussing something. Not far from them, a wooden table had been placed on the ledge where Ember suspected rituals were performed. She was beginning to get a bad feeling about what might be happening. If these people tried to harm Kyra, thief or not, she would have to stop them.

☽ ☽ ☽

The Sun was low on the horizon and nearly set as Kyra was led ever so gently by the two women who had attended her the night before. She felt light as a feather as she passed around for all the people to see. Her heart fluttered with anticipation as she stood before the priest like a goddess herself. Carefully, the two women escorted her to the cliff and the table. She was confused at the sight of the table on a cliff over the sea, an unnerving feeling passing over her. The Sun was already halfway into the sea as the priest stepped forward with a beaming smile, the entire tribe at his back. He began to chant while four men came forward, each wearing a simple loincloth and painted with a similar design to she wore.

Standing before the table on the edge of a cliff over the sea was disturbing in many ways. Her worry increased as she tried and failed to understand what was happening. As the men advanced, she became frighteningly aware of how precarious she was on the cliff. If this were a ritual of taking the necklace, why the table? She should have questioned that earlier, but she was so wrapped up in the beautiful ritual. Her fear piqued when the four advancing men passed the rest of the spectators headed straight for her.

The men suddenly grasped her arms and legs and began to lift her. In horror, she fought against them, tugging, and pulling as hard as she could, panic filling her veins. It finally dawned on her what was going to happen. Either this was a fertility ritual, and she would get to know one of the priests very well, or it was a sacrifice. Neither of these prospects appealed, but she wasn't strong enough to fight four large men off. They carried her to the table and laid her, arms and legs spread wide, over the wooden structure. Holding her down, the two attending women gently fastened her arms and legs to the four corners of the table with a braided cord. She tugged as hard as she could when they released her, but the triple-ply double braided bast fiber rope would not break.

The elderly priest stepped forward to stand over Kyra. He began to chant as the men flicked seawater from little cups across her body. The two women who had attended her came forth caring a large clay bowl and a dagger made of beautifully flaked obsidian. She was to be a sacrifice to their gods, likely to ensure a harvest or the sound health of the tribe. Kyra struggled against her bonds, clamshells clinking against one another as she tugged. Finally, the priest reached down and removed the amber necklace holding it up for the crowd to see. There were cheers from the people. When Kyra looked into the eyes of her captors, she saw an odd mixture of admiration and respect. These people had treated her so well because they had suspected her of being a willing sacrifice, perhaps sent by their gods. Kyra began to scream in terror.

Their duty completed, the four men left the ritual area leaving only the two women attending Kyra as the elder priest stood a short distance away chanting and speaking to the crowd. Each of the men was proud to have served their tribe, but they were almost envious of the woman to be sacrificed. Within a very short time, she would be in the loving embrace of their goddess, a hero to their people.

ↄ ↄ ↄ

Aethen reached forward and grabbed Ember's arm, stopping her from rushing out to stop the events unfolding. She glared at him in desperation. While both had planned to do something on Kyra's behalf, Aethen believed that this was not quite the moment to attack. Having earlier witnessed the preparations for what appeared to be a sacrificial ritual, the pair had already taken steps to give them an upper hand. It appeared that the ceremony would take place either at sunset or at night, given the number of fires prepared beside and near the altar. Ember and Aethen were covered from head to toe in ash and soot paint, something Ember always carried along due to her people's custom of always being painted. They had used all the soot she had left, but the dark disguise made them harder to see at night.

"She may be guilty of stealing the necklace, but she's already lost her husband, and now they mean to take her life! We have to do something to save her and the necklace!" she said. Aethen did not disagree, but simply rushing into the ritual was not the best idea. Even if Ember ran and took the necklace, she would not be able to set Kyra free before she was attacked. From their hiding place overlooking the water, they stood to the side of the altar in the shadow of the palisade wall. Due to their position, they would be able to sneak almost directly to the edge of the rocky ledge without being seen, but the moment they stepped out of the shadows, they would be right in between the priests and torches, and Kyra.

"I know, but we must think this through. If we rush in and grab the necklace, how will we hold them back long enough to save Kyra?" he asked. What they needed was a diversion, a distraction behind the mass gathering of the people to make them turn away. Ember suddenly had an idea, though it was extreme. Unfortunately, it was times like these that often called for drastic measures. She gave Aethen an apologetic glance before speaking, which caused him to swallow hard in expectation.

"If you sneak around and behind the village with a torch and set fire to several of the buildings, the people will rush back to put out the fires. I can sneak up to Kyra and cut her free during the distraction. Once she is completely free, their ritual will be ruined, and the necklace will be safe. We can sneak back in a few days and steal the necklace. I can't see any other way," she said. Aethen thought about her plan, mulling it over. It was actually a pretty good plan and bolder than he would have come up with. He nodded and grabbed the last beeswax torch from his traveling pack, quickly heading off. He stopped only to pat Ember once on the shoulder for good luck.

☽ ☽ ☽

Brig'dha and Kel had sneaked, from the North where they were hiding, around the village's east side to come up beside the ritual place. They now knelt concealed in the bushes and barely a few lengths of a man from where Kyra was now tied. Brig'dha had determined what would happen even before the men had grabbed Kyra. This was a ritual sacrifice, but she did not know the exact details, of course. Currently, they had no plan, but they hoped that the ritual would take a long time, as they often did, allowing them to make a move when the time was right. Kel had strung his bow, and Brig'dha nervously held her flint dagger.

She absentmindedly muttered a chant to any spirits or gods in the area who would listen and help Kyra. She so desperately wished that Ember was with her. Her friend would know what to do in this situation, likely some extremely bold and risky maneuver that might save everything. But, instead, Kyra's fate now hung in the hands of Kel and a priestess who was almost too terrified to move. She began to pray even more aggressively. What she needed now was a miracle from the gods.

Mew had disappeared, likely to hunt for dinner, and wouldn't be seen until morning. That was probably for the best, Brig'dha figured. There was no way the two of them could take on an entire tribe, even with a cat. She continued to pray to the Goddess for a sign or perhaps intervention. The real problem that she had was that the Moon was not visible. The Goddess was personified by the Moon. During a full moon, she could have expected more assistance, but on this dark night, she had only the local spirits to call upon, and she suspected that they might side with this tribe.

Brig'dha was meticulously watching the ritual, trying to guess what might happen next, when suddenly screaming erupted from far to her right. Confusingly, she saw a fire raging at the backside of the village. Perhaps someone had left a torch or hearth unattended? Brig'dha could not be sure, but its effect upon the ritual was instantaneous. The high priest pointed, and many people began to rush in that direction. A fire in a village could cause vast devastation if not immediately put out. Buildings might need to be quickly demolished, lest they catch fire and worsen the situation, and water was thrown on the embers as they flew through the air.

196

She could not help but be amazed at her luck as everyone ran forward except for the old priest and one of the female attendants. It made sense as the entire village was surrounded by a palisade, aside from the main entryway and an opening at the edge of the cliff for the sacrificial altar. Technically, someone could sneak along the outside of the palisade on the edge of the cliff and enter through the open sacrificial ledge, just as Brig'dha was doing, not to mention Ember and Aethen on the other side, though this was unknown to Brig'dha as the shadows hid them both from the villagers and each other. But it seemed these people had little worry about this. The sacrifice, the attendant, and the priest were not really well suited to stop a fire, so they waited for the rest of the village to put the fire out.

An old man and a woman made for vastly better odds than an entire tribe. Brig'dha grasped at her goddess pendant and quickly whispered her thanks to whatever spirits or deities had intervened at this critical moment. The task of freeing Kyra was still terrifying to her, and she took many deep breaths as she slowly stood. She began to sneak with Kel following behind, arrow at the ready.

They were nearly to the cliff when Brig'dha noticed movement from the other side of the altar, just at the opening in the wall for the cliff. A dark female form with long hair slowly crept from the shadows maneuvering stealthily and directly for Kyra. Brig'dha halted, unsure of what to do next. Ever so slightly to her right, the high priest stood watching the fire, seemingly unaware of her presence as she stood just outside his peripheral vision. To her far right, almost to her back, was the village with its people rushing to extinguish the fire. In front of her was Kyra bound to the platform with a single attendant standing watch. Who was this unknown person painted black? She could ruin everything. Brig'dha wished that Ember was there. She would know what to do.

ᴐ ᴐ ᴐ

Ember slowly approached the table with Kyra. In front of her, not even two lengths of a man, stood a single heavily decorated woman, probably a priestess. She was watching the fire raging in the village with her back to the table. Ember reached the table with Kyra, standing precariously less than the length of a man from the priestess. She barely breathed for fear that she would be heard. Luckily, the Blue Sea made some background sound, which drowned out minor noises. As Ember came into view, she slipped her hand over Kyra's mouth and put a finger to her own mouth, indicating that Kyra should be very quiet. Ember lowered her mouth to Kyra's ear and whispered.

"Shhh. Tell me, why did you do it?" she asked, wanting an answer right then and there. She wanted to know why the necklace was stolen and if Kyra really had anything to do with Yan. Kyra looked up, fear in her eyes. She suspected that Ember knew about Galar and what she had done. There was no point in lying. If Ember had wanted to kill her, she would have already done so. If she didn't answer quickly, Ember might not save her life. Fear motivated her now, and she spoke in a breathless whisper before she thought her words through, so lost in the terror of the moment.

"I... I had to kill him... He was wounded... He would have slowed me down... He would have died anyway..." she said, her words frantic. Ember stared at her in horror. She had wanted to know why Kyra had stolen the necklace, but she had just admitted to having killed her husband, and it would seem that she had done so because he was simply slowing her down. For a brief moment, Ember glared back at the woman, who suddenly looked very different to her. Instead of Kyra, who was guilty only of theft and perhaps of being a less than good person, she was now a vicious murderer in Ember's eyes.

"You killed Galar because he was wounded?" Ember asked, unable to accept such a motivation. It actually made little sense to Ember, but this entire affair had boggled her mind, anyway.

"You would have done the same in my place. He was dead already... in another day or two from a snake bite. But I did it quickly. His journey to the next life helped me stay in this one. Now free me before they see," she whispered. Ember looked down at the woman in a different way than before. She had left her once before, and now she would prefer to do so again. It would appear that Galar had been bitten by two vipers. Ember stood back in disgust, shaking her head in shock. She had killed her husband and likely watched while Yan tried to have his way with her. Any sympathy she had for Kyra died right there.

"How could you have killed your husband and watched a man try to rape me while you stole the only thing our people had to see them through the next harvest?" she said aloud... too loud. The attendant spun around in shock to find the black soot-covered woman standing behind her. Ember didn't hesitate and pulled her dagger out, stepping forward and quickly touching it to the woman's neck as she put her finger to her lips, indicating the universal signal for "shut up or die." Some words did not need a translation. The woman said nothing but slowly stepped backward as Ember continued moving forward, keeping the dagger close to her neck. Ember could see in her eyes that she was about to turn and make a run for it. Stabbing her would make too much noise, and this woman did not seem evil, merely a priestess performing the same sort of ritual performed by so many other tribes.

Ember suddenly switched hands with her dagger, tossing it into the air and catching with her left hand. The fluid movement distracted the woman for just a moment. In that moment, Ember stepped forward and punched her in the stomach as hard as she could. The woman dropped to her knees and doubled over with one hand on the ground and the other clutching her stomach as she gasped for air. She would be all right though she might have a bruise the next day. Ember rushed for the priest as he turned to hear what all the noise was about. She reached out and grabbed the necklace from his hand, tearing it free. She jumped back from the priest, holding the necklace in her right hand and her dagger in the left. She backed away from the man menacing him with the blade. Strangely, behind the man, she noticed a woman that she had not seen before rising from behind the rocks. *Great, another person to deal with,* she thought.

⊃ ⊃ ⊂

Brig'dha approached the priest and the women wanting to get a better look. Only moments before, she had witnessed an exciting, if not short-lived, fight between the soot-covered woman and the attendant. The soot-covered woman's actions were chaotic, to say the least, but for some reason, she had not seemingly come to save Kyra, only to retrieve the necklace. Could she be some sort of thief? Though it was very dark, she swore that she recognized the soot-covered woman. The closer she got, the more she suspected that she knew who it was. But how could what she presumed be possible? The soot-covered woman held the necklace and stepped back from the high priest. At the same time, the attendant continued to kneel, holding her stomach and trying to regain her composure. Suddenly, a group of armed men came rushing toward the high priest, apparently noticing what was going on. The situation was deteriorating fast. Kel stepped forward and grabbed ahold of Brig'dha's shoulders.

"Come, if we don't leave right now, we will be captured!" he whispered frantically. It was at that moment that Brig'dha fully recognized who she was looking at...

"Ember! Run!" she screamed.

ↄ ↄ ↄ

At first, Ember did not recognize the woman behind the priest in the darkness, but the woman screamed her name, revealing herself to be Brig'dha as she had alerted her to the approaching men. Horror consumed Ember as her plans suddenly endangered more than just herself. They endangered someone she cared for. How had Brig'dha come to be here? It was nearly impossible to believe. The only explanation her mind could derive was that she had mounted her own rescue mission. It made little sense to her, but what she did realize was that more than a dozen men with weapons had just appeared behind Brig'dha and the priest. There would be no way that she and Aethen could fight this many warriors. Worse, if she returned to Aethen, he would be found too. She had to figure out a way to lure the attention of the men away from Brig'dha and towards herself. She had to hope that the moon priestess would get away. She would rather die than allow Brig'dha to be harmed.

Ember slipped the necklace over her head and dashed forward to grab the priest around the neck. Luckily, the man was quite old and unable to resist her as he once could. With the priest as her hostage, dagger to his throat, Ember started screaming at the men to stay back and acting as frantic as she could. Her irrational screaming stopped their advance, but she doubted it would hold them back for long. Brig'dha was still partially in the shadows, and Ember was so blatant with her movements that it was quite possible the villagers hadn't seen the priestess. She had to hope for this.

She began to back up toward the edge of the cliff, passing Kyra along the way. Ember could think of only one way to get Brig'dha out of this, one action she could take which might divert the onlookers' eyes from where Brig'dha stood, buying her time to flee. It was risky, to say the least, and it would only work if Brig'dha turned and ran. There were too many villagers for both women to run in different directions with any chance of either surviving, nor was there any real hope for Ember to fight so many opponents. Brig'dha's only real hope was that it did not appear that anyone from the tribe had seen her. Ember continued menacing the men from the tribe while holding their priest captive, effectively keeping all attention to herself.

She knew that she might die in just a few moments. It had not been a long life, but it had been fun. The best part of that life was when she was next to her beloved friend, Brig'dha. There had been something she had wanted to say for a very long time, but she always held back out of fear. She had almost said it a few nights before, but now with her death a very real possibility, she supposed she might as well speak her mind. It didn't seem like she had very much to lose. She looked at the approaching people and not at her friend, fearful of them realizing Brig'dha's position.

"Kyra killed Galar! Leave her to her fate!" she screamed while looking at the villagers and hoping they would mistake her unknown words as threats to them. Brig'dha heard the words as panic filled her. She had worried that Ember might choose such a rash course, and now it seemed that she was about to do it. Brig'dha felt a hand grasp her from behind and begin pulling her into the shadows. Stunned as she was, she barely resisted. Beside her, Kyra began screaming, realizing that Ember intended to leave her to the crazed tribe.

"Run! Run into the night and live! Brig'dha, don't die here... promise me!" At that pronouncement, Brig'dha's heart felt as though it had stopped. Ember closed her eyes, ready to say something she had wanted to say for a long time. Emotions welled up in her, adrenaline filling her veins for what she was about to do. She wasn't sure if her impending death frightened her more than what she was about to say, but at least, in her peripheral vision, she could see Brig'dha backing away into the shadows. She felt relief that Brig'dha had heeded her words.

Brig'dha, I...

Ember's final words were muffled by the sound of waves crashing against the rocks. She shoved the priest forward and reattached her dagger to its sheath. Giving Brig'dha one more glance, Ember turned and ran, leaping from the cliff into the darkness. There was enough time to count to three before a splash was heard, so far down was the fall.

Brig'dha stared blankly as though her entire world had just ended. She had not heard Ember's last word... She was in shock. She felt nothing but numbness. She wasn't even aware when Kel came up behind her and slowly dragged her away and down the cliff making a quick getaway. Kel lifted Brig'dha into his arms and literally carried her down the shoreline, running as fast as possible with the woman over his shoulders. Brig'dha did not even make a sound.

ↄ ↄ ↄ

The priest returned to the wooden platform to continue the sacrifice with the village under control. Ul'na'har had not been too harmed by the strange woman who had attacked him, but he knew that he would be quite sore the next day. His body was simply too old to be tossed around like that without suffering the consequences. The fire had turned out to be a large pile of wood lit by a beeswax torch and nothing more sinister. It had been easy enough to explain away the events of the evening as a clash of spirits sent forth by the lands themselves to test his people and their worthiness. In reality, he suspected that the people who had attacked were motivated by some other interest, perhaps the necklace. He would like to have sent men after them, but to do so would be to admit that they were real people and not spirits. It was best not to let the people become angered by such calamity.

At least not everything had been destroyed. As he approached, he found that the sacrificial woman was still tied to the altar. Of course, the loss of the necklace would reduce the potency of the ceremony, but the death of the willing sacrifice would still be of extreme importance to his people. One of his daughters stood beside the woman while the other leaned against the wood, clutching her stomach.

"Kenis, that spirit woman hits pretty hard, doesn't she?" he said with sarcasm. His daughter glared up at him with an annoyed expression.

"She almost killed you, so don't make fun of me. Let's get this over with. This woman gives me a creepy feeling," Kenis, the attendant, said. Ul'na'har agreed and approached with the sacred dagger. Whoever this woman was, the spirits had left her. Therefore, it was absolutely for sure that she was a perfect sacrifice to the Goddess of the Sea. The dagger would be used to ritualistically kill her, and some of her blood would be drained into a bowl and poured upon the crops. When her body was fully drained, it would be weighed down with rocks and cast deep into the sea. The priest looked down at the squirming woman with deep respect for her noble sacrifice.

"Do not worry, my brave woman. There is nothing in the world that will prevent you from completing your destiny," he said.

CHAPTER TWELVE

I AM ALIVE

It may seem easy to condemn a person for knowingly using the presuppositions and bias of her time to advance her goals. Ianmu is a young, unmarried woman living in a time when equality and equity were not always assured. She desires power, like so many others, yet her options to achieve it are limited. Like so many women in ancient times, she must use atypical methods to achieve this power. If that meant using a deeply flawed and misogynist system against itself, who are we to judge?

"I am not sure that I see a purpose behind the construction of a wall. A stonewall is for livestock, not people. We have not needed a wall, nor do I know of any city or village with a wall... well, maybe a small palisade, but not a full wall." Kamar spoke in a dismissive tone. Kamar was a master hunter and the man charged with the city's defense. Isut'na was built from many small buildings stacked upon other small buildings. Its very form resembled a vast wall. To Kamar, the idea of building a secondary stone wall around an intrinsically walled city was a ludicrous waste of resources.

This was not the first time that Sar'Tawas had brought up the notion of building a wall around the city to defend it. He had heard of a great city to the South and several villages which had raised defenses encircling them. While it was true that most small raiding parties would avoid a vast city for fear of being totally outnumbered by its defenders, Sar'Tawas worried that one of the larger settlements in the South might one day set its designs upon Isut'na. Perhaps even a city like Nara'kit, the Great Brother Tribes of the West, or perhaps even Du'ubria. It seemed like a pretty straightforward notion to Sar'Tawas, so he again had brought up the idea.

Kamar stood slightly taller than Sar'Tawas with a strong muscular frame honed from many harvests of hunting in the dense forests to the North. His skin was tanned darker than most men, and he bore a vicious scar on his left abdomen from a spear thrown by a raider many harvests before. He had been lucky to live from such a wound, but the chants of the priestesses and a little yarrow ointment had spared his life. The scar was clearly visible as Kamar's upper body was completely bare, a constant reminder of his bravery, and pretty much the standard for everyone in the city until the deepest part of the cold season came. Around his waist, he wore a leather cord with a long leather loincloth reaching to his knees. Around his left leg and just above his sandals hung a scabbard with a knife. Kamar never seemed to be unarmed, though Sar'Tawas doubted that a man with such a reputation even needed a blade.

He flicked a bug off his shoulder as he turned away from Sar'Tawas. He held little interest in the man's "tactical" viewpoint. Sar'Tawas was the leader of the Guild of Crafters, and he would be surprised if the man had ever even fired a bow, let alone decided the strategy for protecting the city. Isut'na had repelled many raids before. Children would take turns standing on a wooden platform raised above the tallest building and watching the land. The eyesight of adults tended to fade when middle-age hit, around thirty harvests of age. Children had the sharpest eyes and could see approaching raiders long before they struck. People could be alerted to leave the fields and return to the city. With the very few entryways to the city quickly blocked by stone and objects, raiders would be confronted by an encircled city of buildings. First floor buildings had no outward-facing windows and would require a ladder to reach.

From the tops of the buildings, the men could fire arrows, throw spears, and launch sling rocks at the targets below while the women tended to the wounded and protected the children. This technique had worked for as long as anyone could remember. The only weak points in the entire city were the three alleyways that led into the central part of the city, generally open to the outside. These alleyways could be blocked off with large stones, quickly pushed into place. Kamar just could not support the notion of multiple harvests of people laboring day in and day out to build a wall when their own city's design functioned effectively as a wall.

"My words have not swayed you, have they? You remain ever stubborn on this issue," the guild leader lamented with a hint of a smile. At one point, he had been more aggressive, and perhaps held a grudge against Kamar over his reluctance to accept the plan. Still, this debate had resurfaced so many times in the past that it had become almost a mock argument between the two. Sar'Tawas hoped that one day he might convince the man as the building of the wall would see his craftsman working day and night. Enterprise itself could benefit a city's defense though he doubted that explanation would fare any better. The economics of proto-cities were a new concept, and few seemed to grasp the greater implications the future held.

Kamar stood with Sar'Tawas in the central trading area at the southernmost point of the large open area, which sat in the city's center. Kamar had been waiting for his wife and son when Sar'Tawas happened by and again tried to strike up the same old conversation. The mighty hunter sometimes felt harassed by the sleazier backroom dealing guild leader. He didn't trust people with hidden agendas, people who would say one thing when they really meant another. He supposed that Sar'Tawas was simply a city product, much like any bolt of linen cloth or leather good.

It was said that long ago, Isut'na was controlled by no leader, only a group of elders. Over time, the city's spiritual leaders gained more and more power until they effectively reached the point of being leaders. The Elder Council remained, but they had become more of an advisory group. Isut'na, like so many other large tribes and cities, had switched from an egalitarian democracy into a theocratic autocracy. Sar'Tawas, and people like him, were an emergent property of such a system.

"If we are ever attacked by raiders, I will simply have you go talk to them. After listening to your arguments on and on, I would suspect that they would flee and leave us alone," he quipped in a playfully sarcastic tone as he caught sight of his wife entering the open area that served as a ceremonial ground and a public place for people to do their business.

The guild leader watched with slight envy as the beautiful Zah'namu and her young son Kam'ir crossed the ceremonial ground heading in their direction, each laden with baskets full of wheat recently harvested. Zah'namu was not so tall for a woman, but she had nice round hips and was not too thin. Unlike most women, she kept her hair short and not in a bun. Today she wore a leather wrap skirt decorated with lapis lazuli beads, held by a thick leather cord. At her waist was a sheath with a knife handle protruding. Her feet were protected by soft leather shoes, and she wore a harness made from two loops of flax cord which looped over her shoulders and crossed around her solar plexus and the middle of her back. A basket could be attached to the harness, allowing her to carry items hands-free.

"Are you hassling my husband again? Whatever business you have with him can be brought up to the council, not when we are trying to be a family. Besides, I wouldn't want my son to become interested in your silly dealings," Zah'namu said as she knelt beside her son, placing her hands on his shoulders and giving him a big smile. He had barely seen six harvests, but already he stood with a basket of wheat in hand, helping his mother carry it home, even if only a token amount.

"My brave little hunter Kam'ir. One day you will grow to be strong and courageous like your father. Then, raiders will flee in terror from your presence. But today, you will help mommy as she gets this wheat ready," she said with a beaming smile as the small boy laughed at the attention. Kamar flashed a smile at Sar'Tawas and turned to leave with his family. What bothered Sar'Tawas the most was not the rejection of his plan for the dozenth time but that Kamar had such a beautiful wife and already a strong and healthy son. Sar'Tawas was one of the most influential men in the city, but all his power and wealth, he had neither wife not child. By the measure of age among his people, Sar'Tawas was long past his prime at the age of 31 harvests.

While Kamar was a skilled and efficient hunter, his wife was quite a force as well. He was actually a little intimidated by Zah'namu. He had watched her cutting wood on many occasions and knew how proficient she could be with an ax. Zah'namu came from a family of strong warriors, and she had grown up with many brothers. When it came to being a warrior, Zah'namu was nearly the equal of Kamar. He shuddered as he considered how powerful their young child would grow to be.

Sar'Tawas was of average height with short, wavy black hair and a slightly receding hairline. He sported a well-groomed goatee and mustache. Like Kamar, he wore a knee-length loincloth made from soft leather and ornately decorated with beads of bone and lead. Around his neck, he wore a long flax cord necklace with beads of lead, copper, gold, and bone. It was obvious to anyone who saw Sar'Tawas that he was a man of many possessions and resources. The reason Sar'Tawas had no woman was not so much because of his looks or even his age, but mostly because of his personality. He was reclusive and manipulative, having no real-time to form a relationship. Relationships required attention, something Sar'Tawas was unwilling to share. What he needed was a woman who needed no real love or affection and who would bear him many sons. *I'm less likely to find someone like that than I am to get my wall built,* he laughed to himself.

The guild leader watched the family go with longing. Anyone who looked at him could see that he was a lonely man whose only friends were power and possession. But not just anyone was watching. At the opposite end of the trading area stood the trader Idmasa and his "daughter," Ianmu. Idmasa was trying to bargain with an older man who was selling a polished deer tooth necklace while Ianmu watched the people in the trading area, attempting to find her mark. They had been in the city for three days, and Idmasa had nearly completed trading his small jars of dye for various trinkets he could trade when he returned to Nara'kit. Unfortunately, Ianmu had found very few men who seemed to have the correct status and none without wives. She had already turned away nearly a dozen younger men in fine condition, the sort of men she wouldn't have minded getting to know. Yet, they likely had little power.

Her luck had changed the day before when she noticed a particular man with a well-groomed mustache and goatee. He was adorned lavishly and seemed to spend most of his time speaking with people politically rather than working. Ianmu recognized this behavior as common for the men who hung around her father. Very few people in the city could afford to spend their entire day barely working, but there were a few who could, and they were typically the leaders. She had yet to see any woman come to this man or show him any interest. Some men were interested only in other men, or many genders. While that practice was perfectly acceptable to her people, it would be a problem if she tried to pick up such a man. Luckily, she had witnessed the lavishly decorated man gawking at many a young maiden. Ianmu believed that she had found her mark.

As soon as the merchant finished trading, Ianmu poked Idmasa in the ribs to get his attention. Stepping out of the center of view, she leaned in closely to speak to him. She had to keep her voice down as the language of Nara'kit was an extremely close cousin to what was spoken in Isut'na. She could readily understand most of the people around her, which implied that they might understand her as well.

"Idmasa, do you see that man with the well-groomed mustache, goatee, and the flashy necklace?" she whispered as soon as the pair had stepped away from the trader. He nodded that he did see the man, wondering if Ianmu had found the man that she was looking for. He had been to this city many times before, and he had seen that man at several major events. Whoever he was, he was someone of importance.

"Is that the man you wish me to sell you to?" he asked, still unable to grasp exactly what bizarre idea this woman had in mind. He had even entertained the notion that she had some strange need to be owned. Perhaps a weird fetish or some other oddity? Whatever the reason, she had apparently picked quite the mark. He wondered if he would have any success trying to sell her to such an important man, unsolicited. Such a transaction out of the blue could get messy, really fast.

"Yes, he is definitely the right one. When you go to him, tell him that you traded several flax fishing nets to villagers near the Brown River for me. Tell him that my family needed fish more than they needed yet another daughter. Most importantly, tell him that you have a wife, and she would not appreciate me. This is why you're willing to trade me for much lower of a price than might be expected, and quickly. Once I am traded, you are free to leave and never speak of our arrangement to anyone, or An'an will curse you unto the next world," she concluded. The original plan had called for Idmasa being her "father," yet she had just changed the plan, slightly. He wondered why, yet he decided to leave such questions unspoken.

Idmasa looked the curious woman over once more and saw her determination as she spoke with the determination of an elder. Perhaps he did not want to know what she had in mind. There was a strange manipulative look behind her innocent face. He made his profession from reading people, and one obvious thing he read from this woman was determination. He suspected that she was much less innocent than her face implied. In fact, Ianmu had judged her target to be connected with trade in some way, which meant that he might have met Idmasa before, or might inquire about him. That meant being his "daughter" could open her story to… questions. So, a tiny tweak to her story was all it took.

Sar'Tawas stood by a bone tool worker inspecting the clay seal the man and his wife used to indicate their work. He would arrange for some of their goods to be traded next warm season with some of the villages to the West in exchange for other needed goods. One of his primary functions as the leader of the Craft Guild was to ensure that the exchange of goods and services was, at least, equitable between foreigners and the city, if not more so. As far as he knew, Isut'na was the only proto-city in the world where trade was considered so critical that an elder oversaw it.

His thoughts scattered like startled birds in a field as someone fell against him. Catching himself, he turned just in time to hear and then see the clay seal shatter. This was not a major concern as more seals could be made easily, but such a rationalization did little to quell his flaring anger. He was an elder and not the sort of man to be run into… at least, not without consequences. Spinning to face the fool who hit him, he began to issue a rather vicious rebuke. The words faded to breath as his eyes fell upon his "attacker."

Lying on the ground where she had fallen was a beautiful woman. His anger evaporated like water on a hot stone roof. The woman was lying on her back and slightly propped up on her arms. Her arms and legs showed reasonable muscle tone while her overall form was curvy with plenty of body fat, the pinnacle of beauty among his people. She wore a loosely woven bark fiber apron whose excess hung halfway to her knees, becoming long tassels. Around her neck hung a single black feather attached to a thin leather cord. Had her beauty not captivated him, he might have noticed how oddly staged she looked, as though lying in such a way as to display herself. The woman cautiously looked up at him, revealing medium-length brown hair, large brown eyes, and a strangely innocent expression.

"I'm sorry. I didn't mean to bump into you. I wasn't paying attention," she said in her thick Nara'kit accent and trying to sound absent-minded. Ianmu hoped to portray herself as not being very intelligent. If this man thought that she was simple minded, it would make her plan to control him so much easier. As she lay on the ground, she stared at him as if in awe at his presence. In truth, he was reasonably easy on the eyes for a man of his age. This made her task slightly easier. A moment later, she heard the sound of Idmasa coming up behind her.

"I am very sorry. Did my property bump into you?" he asked Sar'Tawas. The guild leader looked at the man, then back at the woman. Slavery was extremely uncommon, though women were taken in raids, becoming concubines, of a sort. Sar'Tawas had only known of two other concubines in the city's history though he could not think of any moral reason against the idea. It was simply not practical for most people as concubines and slaves cost time and effort to care for. They were sometimes held as barter between cities or spoils from a raid but rarely as traveling companions.

"A trader?" he asked Idmasa.

"That's right, I trade dye. I'm from the city of Nara'kit. I'm sorry this woman bumped into you. She's been nothing but trouble since I traded several flax fishing nets for her in a village on the Brown River, on my way here. Her father said that he had too many daughters and not enough sons. She looked good, but she's about a smart as a fire in a rainstorm," he laughed, using a local vernacular to indicate her low intelligence. Sar'Tawas could not think of any reason to own such a concubine as it did not look like she was much in the way of a worker. Of course, she could take care of a house, but what other good could she be besides a house cleaner?

"I had thought to trade her to someone who wanted to make some children with her. I already have children, and my wife wouldn't take well to me bringing this one home if you know what I mean," Idmasa said with a lascivious smile. Sar'Tawas looked the woman over again. She just sat on the ground watching the two of them talk. She certainly didn't seem that intelligent, but she was one of the most beautiful women he had seen, and she certainly looked quite capable of producing many children, by his measure. Luckily, it was a well-known fact that a child's intelligence came from the man and not the woman. Sar'Tawas smiled back at the trader, having just thought of another possible use for such a woman.

If she could produce children for him, then he could have his bread and eat it too. Within the city, women had approximately the same rights as men. If a man mistreated or ignored his wife for too long, she might simply leave him for someone else. Being a concubine, he wouldn't be morally required to provide her companionship, and she would be compelled to do whatever he wished. Judging by her vacant expression, keeping her happy wouldn't be that difficult. If things didn't work out, he could trade her to someone else and perhaps still make a profit, depending on what this trader wanted for her.

She would be a concubine – a woman he was joined with but not wed to. The status of her freedom would be somewhat dicey, as she technically could leave him, as women were not owned, yet she was also "property," by the rules of trade. According to the city's rules, there was no real moral issue with this, but it reminded people too much of raiders and would be frowned upon. In short, she could "free" herself if she wanted to, but if he treated her well and she never inquired about it, she would remain his. A strange grey area he was eager to exploit. She would likely remain by his side once she carried his child, which he suspected would be quite soon.

"What were you looking for in trade for the concubine?" he asked absentmindedly as if more curious than interested. Idmasa and Ianmu both held their breath for a moment. This powerful man pretended that he wasn't really interested, but both the merchant and "concubine" knew better.

"Well, I really need to leave for Nara'kit, but I would trade a good copper knife or a few bolts of fine linen," he offered. Ianmu had told him to start low, but Idmasa smelled a profit, and he was not willing to walk out of here without something good. A very perceptive man, Idmasa could already tell just by looking at him how interested he was in the woman. Sar'Tawas frowned at the offer. A copper knife was not a common object, and only a few existed in the entire city. Linen was much easier to get. For a moment, he wavered. Ianmu saw the wavering in his eyes and realized that Idmasa had bargained too high. This was a pivotal moment when the entire trade could fall apart. She smiled at the guild leader and made a giggling sound as though she found their discussion amusing, an act that forced her to physically restrain her urge to sneer. Regardless, such sounds always had their effects.

"I will trade you four bolts of linen, each the length of a man and the width of an arm, one of them is dyed red," the smitten guild master said. Idmasa held out his hand, palm up. Sar'Tawas placed his hand over Idmasa's, palm down. They touched hands, signaling the confirmation of a deal. Ianmu breathed a sigh of relief. The very first part of her plan had come to fruition.

"I will return in a very short time with the linen. Wait for me here," Sar'Tawas said, turning and walking toward his building to fetch it. He was trading enough material to make several high-quality garments, but he had a feeling that he was getting something good in return. His only worry was that he might not be thinking as much with his mind and more with baser needs. He had always been a cunning individual, and he hoped he had not made a mistake, yet memories of Zah'namu drove him onward.

Ianmu sat on the ground, watching the man leave. Lowering herself to mere property was denigrating, as was listening to the men speak of her as they had. Denigration aside, she also used these men as her tools to reach her goals. Long ago, she had dreamed of standing up and seizing power with her own two hands, much as men did. As the sun beat down on her skin, she wondered what it would be like to be such a woman, a woman who took control in her own right and not from the shadows.

Ↄ Ↄ ↄ

She awoke on the floor of a small hut with a fire burning beside her. Furs covered her body, and a terrible headache tore through her head. She sat up and felt the room spinning. For some reason, she couldn't remember who she was or why she was here. All she knew was that her head hurt really badly. The woman closed her eyes but found that she could not sleep. It felt as though she had slept for days. Her body was stiff, and she had sore places where she had slept awkwardly. She again sat up and tried to stretch but found her left arm was pained and did not wish to move.

Examining her arm, she realized it was bound with sinew and sticks, holding it straight. The arm tingled and throbbed. Perhaps it had been broken, but she could not imagine how that had happened. She wore a simple loincloth made of leather with a beautiful amber pendant necklace hanging between her breasts. Many cuts and bruises covered her body, though each of these appeared to have been tended with herbs. The woman tried to stand but immediately sank backward, weakly. She thrust her arms out to slow her descent, but she buckled when pressure was applied to her left arm. She slumped back upon the bed, moaning aloud as tears welled in her eyes from the pain.

The leather flap door to the hut opened, and in stepped a middle-aged woman wearing a sleeveless leather dress with white beads sewn at various lengths from top to bottom. It was an odd garment, but she was not interested in fashion at the moment. The woman gently helped her back into a comfortable position on the bed. Next, she brought her some water in a cup. The older woman knelt beside her and spoke comforting words though she had no idea what the woman was saying.

"Ese, ese... Suneh henhent," she said in a soothing voice. The confused woman had no idea what this meant, but she felt at ease with this woman. Something about her came across as being goodly though she had no real basis for such judgments. The woman began inspecting her various wounds with great care. By the sounds that she was making, they were coming along quite well.

The hut walls were made of leather stretched over a wooden frame. The hut had the feel of being old and not of good repair. Hanging within were flax cords with various herbs and other foodstuffs attached. Near the door was a bundle of long wooden poles waiting for some unknown task, while on the other side of the door was an old wheat grinding stone. The hut reminded her more of a spare utility room than a normally occupied home.

"Who are you? Who am I? How did this happen to me?" she asked, confused. It would be much easier to understand what was going on if her head would stop hurting. It felt like she had bumped it, but she couldn't quite remember what had happened. Suddenly, she had a flashback of cold water, and a strange nauseating feeling washed over her. The older woman gently stroked her hand as the younger woman recovered from nausea. She had fragments of memories, but she couldn't remember who she was or where she came from. Then, slowly, sleep took her again.

ɔ ɔ ɔ

Nemanar emerged from the hut to find her daughter Ninrea'mu and her son Gel'nar standing at attention, desperate for any news. Both children had been ordered by their father Ketamir not to enter the hut until the wounded woman had healed enough to stand and walk. Now, every day when Nemanar entered the hut, the children would appear like insects to food. She couldn't blame the children for being curious. Living as a simple family without a tribe, they were not used to this level of intrigue.

There was nothing else around them as interesting as the mysterious woman from the water.

"If you must know, she is awake now and even speaking. I don't know her name, and she can't seem to speak our language, but I think she's going to make it," she said to the excited children.

"She is certainly doing a lot better than what I found washed ashore," added her husband, Ketamir. He recalled two days prior when he and his son Gel'nar had taken their stretched hide boat fishing early in the morning. Somehow, Gel'nar had noticed what looked like a person lying against the shore halfway out of the water, a woman by the look of her. He always had sharp eyes. Upon landing their boat nearby, they discovered that it indeed was a woman. Her head was matted with blood from what looked like a vicious head wound. Her left arm appeared to be bruised, and she was cut in many locations. Her shoes were gone, but her loincloth had remained as well as a very well constructed obsidian dagger, traveling pouch, bow, and quiver lashed to her body with flax cord, and a strange, yet beautiful amber pendant necklace.

Who she was, no one knew. She did not even resemble the local inhabitants. Oddly, she was dressed and equipped as a man, her body showing indications of having been painted, though the water had removed most of it. Was this woman a warrior from some distant land where women fought battles? Was she part of a raiding party? Had her fellow raiders left her for dead? He would learn in due time, but at the moment, she was far too wounded to be a threat. They had brought her back to their hut to care for her, hoping she might regain life. If she were a raider, others might wish her dead, but she had not harmed them. Their goddess, An'an, honored warriors and strangers, and so would they.

Stranger still was what they had found when they opened the traveling pouch. Wrapped in a waterlogged rabbit fur was a large blue crystal the color of the sky. The gem was the size of a balled fist. Such an item, not to mention the amber necklace, could be traded to a nearby village for unknown wealth. Perhaps an entire herd of cattle, or even many dozens of bolts of fine linen. Nemanar and Ketamir were not thieves, and they would return the items to her if she survived, though they had discussed the possibility of keeping them if she had not. There would be no use in letting such objects go to waste. Besides, would she really need such wonders in the next world? The matter had been settled, or so it now seemed.

"She looks really confused, and the fact that she can't speak our language makes things worse. Ninrea'mu, why don't you go in there with her and see if you can help her learn some of our words," Nemanar said to her daughter. She was a gentle sort of girl; soft-spoken and easily the most well-behaved of her two children. If anyone had the patience to instruct this new woman in their language, it was her. She seemed excited by the prospect of speaking with the new woman from the sea and quickly hurried into the hut, leaving her dismayed brother behind.

Ketamir wondered what story she would tell when she learned to speak in their tongue. A fisherman by trade, he, and his small family, lived by themselves in a hut slightly east of a larger village. They had come to this land from a place far to the East, hoping to find a peaceful life for themselves outside of the city where they were born. The people of these lands called their villages large, but they had never seen villages of the likes Ketamir came from. Far from small wooden palisades, the city from which he came had vast cubic buildings which formed a wall against invaders. He did not miss that life for a moment and much preferred the simple life on the shores of the beautiful Blue Sea.

ↄ ↄ ↄ

Aethen had spent the rest of the first-night hiding by the shoreline searching for Ember. He suspected that she had jumped, hoping to swim, but the fall had been so much farther than she had realized. If the height was great enough, the water felt like hard ground when you landed. Worse, many large rocks jutted from the shore and emerged from the water below. The chance that she would miss them was slim at best. Ember may have been a good swimmer, but in that black water, Aethen could find no trace of her, alive or dead. There was no clear answer. The shock slowly vanished throughout the night, replaced by tears and anger. He had never told Ember that he cared for her. Now it seemed that he never would. He did not even know if she would have returned his feelings, but he could have at least tried.

The next day while searching, he had come upon Brig'dha and Kel, also sneaking across the shoreline near the village. He had seen them the night before after returning to aid Ember. Setting the fire had been easy enough, simply tossing the beeswax torch into a large pile of kindling. However, there had been several huts nearby which may have held sleeping people. It had taken him an extra moment to find a place where a fire could be set that would not endanger anybody sleeping in the huts. Aethen had wanted a distraction, but he wasn't a murderer.

214

Once he was sure that the fire was started, he had sneaked back around to the sacrificial rock, ready to provide support with his bow should Ember needed. It was at that moment that he saw Ember standing upon the rock, begging her friend not to die there. Aethen would have rushed to Brig'dha and Kel's side, but they disappeared down the other side of the hill and had been effectively cut off from him. Kel was also in shock over what had just happened. He nearly broke his leg sliding down the hillside, hoping to find Ember in the water, but there was nothing in the blackness. Perhaps the strangest part was that the villagers did not pursue them. Aethen had more unanswered questions than he knew what to do with.

Aethen and Kel were exhausted from searching as the Sun set. It had been three full days and three nights since Ember had jumped, presumably to her death. They had searched the area by the village and up and down the coast for any sign of her. This had been difficult since the people from the village were active fishermen. Sneaking past their boats had been a feat in and of itself, but now they were beginning to realize what Brig'dha had initially refused to believe. Finally, the pair returned to the small camp they had made not far from the village, nestled in the rocks where no one would see.

With each passing day, it was becoming more apparent that they would never see Ember again. Brig'dha had sat in an almost catatonic state the entire night and most of the next day, comforted by little Mew, who eventually returned. She would not take water or even interact with the men. It had been the second night when she finally came out of her trance-like state and began crying almost uncontrollably as she rocked back and forth. Throughout the night, she agonized over the loss of her friend. Neither man knew what to do with her other than to leave her by herself and provide water and food if she would take it. They simply had no idea how to console her.

When both men returned from their latest scouting trip by the water, they found her kneeling by their small fire and gently rocking back and forth, chanting a never-ending mantra. Her words sounded to the men like a plea to the Goddess of the Moon for the safe passage of Ember's spirit into the next world. Brig'dha's body was lightly covered with soot, which suggested a funeral rite. Neither man was pleased, but they hoped that perhaps Brig'dha could move on with her life once she got some closure. It was partway through the night before Brig'dha finally fell asleep, Mew at her feet. Kel sat beside her and tried to lend comfort as best as he could, though she was nearly inconsolable. Even Mew had not attracted her attention.

"In the morning, we should return to our village. There's nothing more to be done," Aethen finally admitted.

"Ember was her best friend. I'm not sure how long they knew each other before they came to our village, but it's almost like they were sisters or grew up together," Kel said. In truth, he had never seen somebody so distraught over the loss of another. It would likely do Brig'dha well to get away from this place and return to people she knew. Aethen agreed, and the two men slowly drifted to sleep while Brig'dha lay curled by the fire having cried herself to sleep.

As she slept, Brig'dha dreamed of beautiful blue waters with fish of every color swimming through them. She floated over the water, smelling its salty tang, and feeling the warmth of the Sun on her skin. The coast was rocky though quite pleasing to behold. She watched the fish swimming below her when suddenly somebody stepped in the water in front of her and scattered the fish in all directions. Brig'dha looked up to see feminine legs, smooth yet well defined. Her eyes rose, following the legs all the way up to the face. Ember looked down at her, towering above with a smile and a fishing spear in her hand. Brig'dha wanted to speak and say something, but she could not. The Ember of her dreams gazed at her with warm affection and merely breathed five words in her native tongue. Brig'dha knew few of her words, yet she knew all five of these, fortunately.

"Eag kah'giae" - I am alive
"Stehk, kieag" - Wait for me

Brig'dha suddenly awoke covered in sweat, adrenaline surging through her body. From her arm, a butterfly quickly beat its damp wings and fluttered away, its perch suddenly not so steady. For a moment, Brig'dha watched the insect as her mind fully awakened. How had she understood the words so well? When Ember had spoken in her language not so long before, Brig'dha had not understood more than a word or two at best. There was only one explanation. Aethen and Kel looked up from their groggy sleep, slightly alarmed and reaching for weapons.

"Did you hear something?" Aethen asked, alarmed and looking around for intruders, yet missing the insect as it flew over his head. They were close to the village where Ember had died, and being so close unnerved both men.

"Ember... She's alive! I know she's alive. She is safe... but we must wait for her," Brig'dha exclaimed, cryptically. Aethen exchanged a glance with Kel. Both men had heard of the dead speaking to the living. Women were known to be exceptionally good conduits for spirits, but what Brig'dha was saying sounded a little too far-fetched for them to believe.

"We all miss her, but how can you be sure that what you say is true? She fell from such a great height, and there were many rocks in the water below, rocks that we couldn't see until we searched," Kel asked. Brig'dha was not as good as Ember at speaking her mind, and both men looked quite doubtful. She could not blame them for their doubts, but she had to convince them to stay. She had no room for doubt, and she knew of only one form of magic which would satisfy the men and give her a clue of where to look for Ember. Brig'dha grabbed several of the driest pieces of wood they had and dropped them onto the fire, quickly converting the hot coals back into a small but hot flame. Both men watched as Brig'dha began to chant in the quick and repetitive way of a priestess.

"I will ask the spirits and the Goddess. They know the fate of Ember," she pronounced, reaching and grabbing Aethen's dagger. Then, before he could stop her, she held up her left hand and slit a cut across her palm. At that moment, Aethen and Kel knew what Brig'dha meant to do – blood magic. This was among the most powerful and dangerous forms of magic, but it was also effective. The problem was that blood carried a person's spirit energy, and exposing one's spirit energy directly to the spell was known to be dangerous.

Kel had heard of a man who had cut his arm for a blood ritual. Not long afterward, the wound had become red and sore. With each passing day, he had grown worse, and no amount of prayer or sacrifice could appease the spirits. Eventually, the man had died a gruesome death. It was said that spirits had found their way into his body and would not let the wound heal. This was a distinct possibility for anyone who performed blood magic and why it was normally forbidden.

Brig'dha held her hand over the fire while chanting and squeezing her palm, letting droplets of blood fall in the fire with a sizzle. Neither man could hear what she was saying as she chanted softly and rapidly. She continued to chant at an almost feverish pace for a short while as droplets of her blood fell into the fire to be consumed by its flames. Suddenly, she threw her arms wide and yelled, causing both men to jump.

"Spirits, tell us where we should wait for Ember! Tell us if she lives!" For a few moments, everyone stared at the flames and waited...

nothing happened. After a short while, Kel looked at Brig'dha, hoping to console her, when he realized that she was still staring intently at the fire and had not broken any concentration. Suddenly, the fire popped, and a hot ember flew straight past Aethen, landing on the ground half of the length of a man away and in a northwesterly direction. Fires were known to pop out embers, but the timing was quite suspicious, and the ember was rather large. Neither man could deny such an obvious sign. Brig'dha smiled, smearing her bloody hand across her face and thanking the spirits. Ember lived, and Brig'dha would get a chance to ask her what it was that she was about to say before she threw herself from the cliff.

Brig'dha turned to face both men, her body covered from head to toe in soot, and fresh blood smeared across her face. Her anguished expression had been replaced with tears of joy and a smile greater than either man had seen. There was something magical about a priestess that could be a little unnerving to many men, and Brig'dha definitely reinforced this notion.

ᴐ ᴐ ᴐ

Sar'Tawas awkwardly led the concubine into his building. Every family had a building with a primary room two or three lengths of a man wide and three or four lengths of a man long. Attached to the primary room were often smaller rooms that might be used for storage, altars to the gods, and serving other more specialized functions. Like most buildings, Sar'Tawas's primary room contained a small oven for baking bread as well as bull horns upon the wall in praise of the bull god, Gunar. The walls were plastered white with a long red stripe surrounding the entire room, purely for decoration. Hanging from the ceiling were many different plants drying and bone chimes. In addition, there were nearly a dozen clay jars filled with various fermented drinks in one corner.

Along the walls, several plastered stone benches extended for people to sit upon, as well as a small wooden table in the center of the room, quite a luxury indeed. It wasn't the greatest accommodation in the city, and he could have obtained an even larger multi-roomed building, but Sar'Tawas simply had no need for the extra space. Choosing a smaller dwelling had also afforded him the right to berate other people for using too much space, a useful political tactic. Other than his main room, the only other room was a small storage space with a low ceiling, which would likely be large enough to house his latest acquisition.

"What should I call you? Do you have a name?" he asked the woman as she stood there pretending to be amazed by the room and its possessions, as though she had never seen something so fine. Ianmu had once lived in a much larger place than this, though she had to admit that this was a pretty nice building, quality-wise.

"I am called Ianmu. What is it that you want me to do?" she asked innocently. She could tell that he was attracted to her physically. Oddly, his seemed to make him a little nervous. Ianmu delicately adjusted her stance to be more provocative, mostly because it amused her to watch him shifting uncomfortably. There was something wonderful about causing this man discomfort. She supposed it was some sort of power trip, but she seemed to be able to pull it off very innocently, and she suspected that it wasn't hurting her disguise.

He was not sure what to do with the woman. He had traded for her with the express purpose of bearing a child. The need for a child was a strange instinct that overcame most people. The technique required to create a child was well known to Sar'Tawas, but something was holding him back. He glanced at the woman, and she looked back at him with a playful expression. He looked away suddenly, a little embarrassed. It had been a long time since he had laid with a woman. He felt indecisive, but his instincts quickly provided him with some tempting suggestions. He was not a beast, and he would not be led by his body, so he took a deep breath and motioned Ianmu to the oven.

"Your work each day is to keep this building clean and ready for my use. You will bake bread and make me food in the morning and evening. In every way, you will perform the actions of a wife. Do you understand?" he clumsily asked, unsure of what to do next. Having a concubine had seemed like a great idea until suddenly, here she was. It seemed somewhat awkward to him, but he figured that he would get used to it. He wasn't quite sure how he would bring up the issue of children, but maybe he should wait a little bit. Sar'Tawas decided he would return to the trading area and see if any new traders had come since last he checked. He would leave the concubine to become acquainted with her new home.

Ianmu stood alone in the room a short while later. She had expected him to try and force himself upon her as soon as they entered, yet he had mostly stood awkwardly, unsure of what to do with her. It seemed that she merely needed to stand before the man and appear as though she did not understand his intentions. His own awkwardness and unwillingness to speak his true thoughts to her seemed to be troubling him greatly. Nevertheless, there was something strangely exhilarating about pretending to be somebody she was not, and she could not help but enjoy the effect she was having upon Sar'Tawas.

Of course, she knew that her deception would likely lead to an intimate encounter with the man... likely more than one. The sudden thought of such an eventuality filled her with dread, but she quickly mastered her thoughts. She had chosen this method because it was the fastest, safest, and most likely way to achieve the goals of her goddess. Just as a warrior accepted the risk of death when he lifted his spear, she would accept whatever came of her choices. If her actions were the will of her goddess, then nothing she did could be immoral, and nothing was beneath her dignity. An'an's word was all that mattered to Ianmu, and she would die before she failed her goddess.

She examined every piece of the small building, looking for clues about her new owner. From what she could tell, this man, this Sar'Tawas, had significant material wealth and apparently many connections. The entire storeroom was filled to the top with fermented beverages, from honey-based to fruit-based, and everything in between. He had rough bars of copper and lead, and entire wooden containers full of jewelry and tokens from merchants. Perhaps he was the leader of the merchants, though she could not tell. Either way, she became more and more confident that she had selected the right man. Best of all, he seemed to have a weakness when dealing with women.

For the next part of her plan, she would need to figure out a way to kill the man who ran the city, a man by the name of Isut'Sanup'ra Utiakur. The most important part of the plan was to ensure that she was the wife or lover of whoever stepped in to fill the vacuum of power. She hoped it would be this man, but she would need to scout around and ensure that she had chosen well first. The city likely had a fertility festival at the end of the warm season, just before planting the wheat. If that were so, it would be a good time to poison Utiakur. Until that time, she would need to keep this Sar'Tawas fellow happy and see where all the pieces on the board lay.

CHAPTER THIRTEEN
ROMANTIC INTENT

While there is evidence that many species, including humans, have enjoyed naturally fermented honey, fruit, and grain for millennia, some of the earliest evidence for fermented drinks comes from ancient China, 7000 BCE and older. During the time Ember lived, the knowledge of the fermentation of grapes, honey, and cereals might have been available from the Middle East, China, and some portions of Eastern Europe. Transport of such exotic and perishable substances would have been sparse. What little may have been traded would probably have been reserved for significant events and found in small quantities. In the warmer regions of Anatolia, just north of the Middle East, access to fermented drinks would be significantly more widespread while still likely costly in trade. Critically, the reader should understand that there is no current evidence for the quantity of alcohol consumed in the story, though it is certainly possible, given human nature and what technology existed.

The sign revealed to them by fire and blood magic suggested a place to the Northwest, where they might once again meet Ember. Aethen continued to roll the idea around in his mind. On the one side, the sign had been so direct. On the other, it made no sense to him that Ember would jump off a cliff and suddenly appear far to the Northwest. They might have to give up if she didn't appear before the cold season hit. Luckily, they were not that far from the Blue Sea People, perhaps two days journey Southwest.

Only two days journey inland and northwest from the village where Ember had jumped, Brig'dha, Aethen, and Kel had encountered a small farming village with perhaps 50 people. The huts were small and made mostly of poles with stretched skins or wattle and daub, more like forest people than river people. Many had been capped with bark to keep the water out in a heavy storm. With a small field for growing limited crops, much of the food came from a nearby river which broke off into many small streams passing the village. Besides fish, wild game could be obtained from the dense forests while other pressing foodstuffs could be traded from local tribes to the North and the West.

The people wore mostly leather clothing, though the heat and humidity were quite intense in this part of the world, land just northwest of what would one day be known as Genoa, Italy. Some women had even taken to fashioning clothing from light bast fibers or even linen when it could be traded. Due to the heat, many people would spend a significant portion of time in the local streams with their cool mountain waters until the cold season came. The group was planning on leaving before that time, and with any luck, they hoped that Ember would arrive very soon.

Given the small size of the tribe, much work needed to be done during the warm season in preparation for the cold season. They had found themselves quickly welcomed in exchange for aid with the village work. Small communities desperately needed labor. In return for that help, Aethen had secured a small hut where they could remain until the harvest festival – a river and farming people sort of event, though forest people also had similar regional festivals. They would need to leave at that point, lest they burden the tribe during the cold season. It was a fair exchange and a very common one among most people. The only real difficulty they encountered was the language barrier, though hand gestures and a little patience had prevailed.

Kel spent the first few days trying his best to comfort Brig'dha. He really liked her, and he had been quite impressed by her spiritual abilities in divining the location of this small village. He had not wanted to make any sort of advance on her when she was in mourning for her friend. Now it seemed that Ember might be alive, and if that were true, it would open the way for Kel to form a relationship with Brig'dha if she would have him. Life was short, and it was important to find love where one could.

He had brought her food each morning and tried his best to be friendly. He would have done this for her whether or not he had been courting her, but it helped either way. The problem was that all she cared about seemed to be waiting for her friend to return. He had to admit that it was impressive to see somebody this devoted to a friend, but he wished she would turn her eyes towards him from time to time. Sometimes he worried that he might be a little selfish, one of the main reasons he had maintained his distance. He wanted to balance his own interests with her needs.

Kel entered the hut one morning not long after they had arrived to find Brig'dha sitting on a wooden bench in the corner, lost in thought. In his hand was a small wooden dish with a piece of duck meat and a variety of fresh greens, a delicious breakfast by anyone's standards. Brig'dha was sewing together two furs with the ultimate goal of making a large fur blanket. It was tedious work, but the result would be an extremely warm blanket for the cold season. Sewing required a bone punch, called an awl, to make a hole in the leather and then a delicate bone needle to pull nettle fiber thread through the soft rabbit pelt. Each group member had taken up such a task since they had arrived. With Kel hunting enough food to supply his own people and with extra to spare the village, Brig'dha and Aethen had taken some of the most needed and yet most time-consuming chores off the hands of the locals and earned themselves a place to stay. Brig'dha looked up from her sewing to see Kel entering. Her eyes quickly fell upon the proffered food.

"You brought me food? Thank you," she said, glumly, before returning to her work. She still had trust in the spirits, but time had continued to pass without Ember arriving, and there had been no new dreams. It had been wearing thin on her hopes and leaving her more and more stressed with each day. Kel sat beside her and watched what she was doing with passing interest. Brig'dha was so lost in her own thoughts that she didn't even notice him as she performed the lengthy and mind-numbing task.

"Is that a rabbit fur blanket you are sewing?" he asked. She waited a moment before replying, and she didn't even look up when she did.

"Yes, it's for a woman who carries a child. The soft blanket will make things easier for her," she replied absentmindedly. Kel continued to press to get some kind of reaction from Brig'dha, but she continued to look glum and began to fidget with a broken thread. Given the heat, he could not understand why she remained in the hut. Down in the South, the warm season truly earned its name. Kel decided to ask more direct questions, the kind that he hoped would spur some reaction.

"Remember when we played by the water as children?" he asked. Brig'dha merely nodded, focusing on her stitching.

"You avoided most of the others, but you liked younger children."

"They don't bother me as much," she replied, cryptically.

"Have you ever thought of having children?"

"A few times."

"Maybe settling down and finding someone special?" Brig'dha remained silent, but began to slightly rock back and forth, her sewing becoming more of a fidgeting.

"The South is truly a beautiful place, isn't it?" he asked, hopefully.

She nodded in agreement, but her thoughts were clearly elsewhere.

"The weather is so hot you could almost walk around without clothes, right?" he asked jokingly.

"Maybe."

"I bet the locals would be annoyed, right?" he said with a forced chuckle.

Brig'dha said nothing, now rocking much more.

Kel slowly stood and left the hut in silence, sensing he had likely said something wrong, but at a total loss for what it might have been. This was not the first time he had tried to speak to her for several days, and she had rejected him every time. He had tried everything he could, but he was beginning to realize that Brig'dha had no interest other than finding her friend, and he had to accept that. As a hunter and tracker, he knew that sometimes you could follow the deer until the end of your days and never catch it. Sometimes it was better to abandon the deer that would not stand still and look for one that would. It pained him, but these things could not be forced. He would remain by her side as a friend. It was the least he could do.

ↄ ↄ ↄ

Espe looked up from her work gathering edible plants to watch the dark-haired man leave the hut and slowly walk off towards a stream nearby. She had been eyeing him for some time now, but she had not approached. Fear played a major part in holding her back and the worry that he and the brown-haired woman in the hut were a couple. It had been a tenday since the group had arrived at her tribe, the People of Rene, and they had been quite helpful so far. Unfortunately, the language barrier had allowed only the taller, long dark-haired man to speak with a trader among their own tribe named Gren.

It was uncommon for them to have visitors, and so many people had been interested in getting to know the two men and the woman, but the woman seemed reluctant to show herself. It had not been long before Espe had noticed the man, a peculiar-looking fellow with dark hair, rich brown skin, and blue eyes, so different from her own people. He had caught her eye almost immediately, and she had glanced his way ever since. If only she could determine his relationship with the brown-haired woman.

She had been walking around the village looking for any edible plants as well as picking weeds for much of the morning. Most edible plants could be found much farther from the tribe, but she always took a quick peek around the huts before heading out of the village. As she walked past the newcomers' hut, she heard their conversation. She did not understand what Kel, that was his name, had said to the woman, whose name she didn't remember. Espe sighed as she dropped to her knees to pick a mushroom beside a hut. If she were ever going to have a chance, she would have to make her move and see what happened.

After so many days of anticipation and having spent an unhealthy amount of time spying on the dark-haired man, it was time for her to make a move. The last thing she had waited for was confirmation that he was available. The brown-haired woman's disinterested replies had seemed good enough to her. Her worry was that the travelers would leave soon, and with them, her best chance of finding someone before the harvest festival, or worse, letting her mother find her a man from a neighboring tribe and having to settle…

In truth, she was of age to find a man at the coming harvest festival, but there was something to be said about a woman who brought her own man rather than just looking for one. A woman who married too young could suffer problems with childbirth, yet she had passed the age of concern. She had bled for several harvests, and her body had grown as needed. She could still remember the itching and soreness as her chest had grown, not to mention the painful little bumps on her face that had thankfully gone away, but flowers took time to bloom. Unfortunately, flowers lasted for only so long, and she was hardly the only bloom in her people's field. As she rehomed her focus, she shook her head to banish the bee metaphor emerging from her vivid imagination. This was a great opportunity if she could merely keep her focus.

There were so few travelers passing their village, and the likelihood of her finding a man with such a good disposition was quite small. She might be forced to wed a much rougher man if she didn't act quickly. All she had to do was conjure a mental image of the other men who lived in her tribe if she needed any help spurring herself to action. Firstly, she needed a timely incident to bring the man to her. The day was hot and sweat beaded upon her skin. She had a feeling that she knew exactly where Kel was headed.

Espe lifted her reed basket with a lighthearted laugh and quickly headed north of a nearby stream that provided water to the tribe. She could wander downstream and bump "accidentally" into Kel from that point. They spoke only a few words in common, mostly trade words, but in the tendays length that the foreigners had been in the village, a few additional words had been exchanged. Along the way, she stopped to look in an old used clay pot by a hut that had caught rainwater to see her reflection. One's face paint needed to be correctly applied. With a small rush of adrenaline, she headed to the north of the stream.

ↄ ↄ ↄ

The little tribe was full of hard workers, it seemed. Kel saw two women skillfully making pottery from lumps of clay. At the same time, a man standing near them banged away at a large piece of wood relentlessly with the stone tool. He wasn't quite sure what the man was doing, but there was always something to carve or build. Behind him, young children played while their mothers dyed delicate bast fiber fabrics in large clay vessels. Two women passed by Kel, smiling and waving at him as they carried large bundles of sticks from the forest. A bit shy, Kel smiled back at the women and hurried toward the stream.

He passed Aethen on his way to the stream, happy to see a familiar face. Aethen was busy binding large bundles of sticks together with reeds. It was important to have lots of kindling on hand for whenever it was needed. Aethen had spent much time gathering logs, splitting them, and gathering kindling. His next task would be to char the wood into charcoal. Charcoal could be used to make fires very hot, which aided in creating pottery, a form of magic that river people used to shape mud into complex objects, such as containers. He glanced up at Kel and shook his head.

"Rejection again, huh? I told you. In the sea, there are many fish," Aethen said, laughing. Besides, it was generally rumored that Brig'dha liked women, though it seemed Kel had forgotten this childhood rumor, though they had grown up in the same tribe.

"There is not a deer in this forest safe from my arrow, yet I cannot seem to find a woman," Kel said sarcastically. In truth, it was starting to look like he could hunt 100 deer more easily than attract a single woman. He had mostly resigned himself to the idea that Brig'dha would not pay him any mind, but if that turned out to be the truth, where else mighty look for a wife? The newcomers to his own tribe, who had formed the Blue Sea People, had few young women among them. If he didn't find a woman in a nearby tribe, he would have to develop a relationship with one of those deer in the woods. He chuckled to himself at the thought.

"There is no prey quite as difficult and dangerous as a woman," Aethen said, laughing. He sympathized with Kel, having sought the affections of Ember for so long, only to watch her cast herself into the darkness. If she did not return, as he was beginning to suspect that she wouldn't, Aethen would also need to find a woman to wed, given both men were of the proper age. The problem was the Blue Sea People simply had too many men and not enough women.

"And if you think one is a handful, wait until two or three of them group together. They become an unstoppable force of gossip and laughter. Worse, you can't look at one without one of her friends noticing. They are more cautious and more aware than your common deer," he concluded. Kel laughed and continued along the path to the stream where he would swim and try to cool off in the heat. Not long after he passed, Aethen watched that same woman with long wavy brown hair he had seen eyeing Kel for days heading to the North of the stream. She headed in a different direction but constantly looked back to see where Kel had gone. She kept her distance and stayed at a slow, cautious pace, but her intentions quite obvious to Aethen.

"The Mighty Hunter is now the prey, hunted by the same doe he cannot find," he joked to himself as he watched. Life was the funniest joke of all.

Kel was dying in the heat. He came from a cooler place where the rain fell often, and fog blanketed the landscape. The only reason he wore his leather shirt was to keep his skin from blistering under the Sun. As he reached the cool spring with its beautiful trees along the sides providing ample shade, he removed the leather shirt and unfastened his loincloth. Within a few moments, he stood completely nude in the water. The stream split into two parts with a smaller, faster-moving branch up North. That was where most of the villagers obtained water and performed their chores. The slower moving and deeper section was more often frequented by bathers.

The thought of swimming in the cool water was more intoxicating than he could imagine. Below him, he saw small fish darting back and forth in the water while strange insects landed on its surface and then flew away. There was something peaceful about the water of the small stream, which put his mind at ease. Quickly, Kel ran and jumped into the air tucking his legs against his stomach and wrapping his arms under them. This resulted in the largest possible splash that could be made.

Normally, a man would do this when the water was full of women, one of the best ways to irritate them. But he was by himself, and yet it was still enjoyable. At first, he dove under the water and ran his hands through his hair, rubbing clean his scalp with his fingers. It was important to be clean, and the hair was the first step. A short time later, he sat on the bank, rubbing mud across his skin to remove oils and dirt. The Sun found its way through the canopy of trees and began to beat down on him once more. Soon he found himself back in the water with just his head bobbing in the refreshing stream.

Ↄ Ↄ Ↄ

Espe slowly approached with her large basket full of herbs. She actually picked many of them along the way, not just so that she would have an excuse to be here but also because they were needed by the tribe. Up ahead, she saw the man swimming in the water. To make a direct move upon him would be frowned upon by the other women and was not the way of things. It was better to lure him to her by pretending that she did not realize he was nearby as she bathed on a hot day. The distinction was a fine line, but Espe was always one for splitting hairs. She walked a little bit closer to ensure that he saw, but not so close that she could not easily pretend that she had not realized his presence. Her heart beat fast as she prepared to make her move. She would seize life in her hands and do so with a smile.

Ↄ Ↄ Ↄ

Kel emerged from the water after seeing quite a large fish go by. He shook the water from his face when he suddenly noticed movement to his right. A hunter by training, he slowly sank low in the water and turned his head to see what it was that had moved. Not far away was a woman from the tribe. She slowly approached the bank carrying a large basket full of fresh herbs overhead. Kel had seen the woman before and had thought her quite pretty, but he had ignored her in his quest to win over Brig'dha. Now he wondered if he had been ignoring someone wonderful while chasing someone he could never have.

The woman did not seem to realize he was there, and he did not want to startle her, so he kept his head down. Kel was reasonably sure that most women were not natural hunters, unlike men, so he suspected he could avoid her by simply staying still. He suddenly felt a little ashamed as he recalled how good of a huntress Ember had been. So many men carried misconceptions that the quirky redhead had challenged repeatedly. He would certainly miss her. He turned his attention back to the woman at hand, hoping to bury his pain over Ember's loss.

She placed the basket on the ground and then untied the waist cord which held a knee length piece of leather which wrapped halfway around her waist with a large opening on one side, letting it fall to the ground. A moment later, her sandals were off, and she slowly waded into the water. She dove under the surface, only coming up for air a few times, very likely washing her hair just as Kel had. Most people similarly cleaned themselves during the warm season. He felt slightly guilty watching her and wondered if he should make his presence known, but for some reason, he did not want to give himself away. Just as he considered standing, she emerged once more, whipping her hair backward.

The woman waded over to the bank where there was clay to be found. She scooped small globs of it to paint across her skin. Her face had started with a very detailed paint job that now began to run, but Kel had seen it before she had stepped into the water and was quite impressed. It had been made from long bands of red paint streaking out from her eyes in every direction. He watched her as she applied the clay to her skin and vigorously rubbed it off. As he watched, his heart pounded and exhilaration flooded his body. It wasn't the nudity, as semi or wholly nude bodies were common to see in any tribe. It was something more sensual about watching her clean, which seemed to excite him on a primal level. Perhaps it was the voyeuristic nature of it, or maybe the context?

Ↄ Ↄ C

Espe really did appreciate the chance to wash after working under the hot Sun all morning. The cold water felt absolutely fantastic, and the mud left her skin silky smooth. What made this bath so much more incredible than others was the strange adrenaline-fueled exhilaration she felt as she performed her display. If the man had not been watching, her cleaning motions would have been far less graceful, and she would have scratched the nagging itch she had on her butt. Regardless, something was intoxicating about putting on the display – a strange exhilaration. She had sneaked up upon the hunter and thoroughly entrapped him. Most amusingly, he probably suspected that she didn't realize he was there. Many men believed that women could not hunt, but Espe thought differently. She almost giggled aloud. *The doe stalks the buck... too easy.*

Ↄ Ↄ Ↄ

After rinsing her body free from the bulk of the clay, she gingerly removed the little extra bits that stubbornly remained. The woman placed her hands in her hair to pull it back to remove it from her face. Then, suddenly, she turned her head and looked him dead in the eyes in a quick but smooth motion. It was as though an arrow had hit him between the eyes. *She knows!* Immediately he became worried that he had blown his only chance to get to know her. If a woman caught a man staring at her, she might become quite angry. Worse, she would tell every other woman what had happened, and soon that man would become the enemy of all women. His best bet would be to apologize and hope she had not been offended.

Kel slowly rose until the water was at his waist and approached the woman. She turned towards him but continued moving her fingers gently through her hair, sort of combing it. She did not seem angry, but he couldn't take the risk. Women were far too complex to be dismissed lightly. They could become affronted in ways that a man did not even understand and had no hope of grasping. She put her hands down as he approached and waited for him to say something. He only knew a few words in her language as they had not been there very long. This was going to be an interesting apology. Oddly, he noticed her eyes lingering on his abdomen, then rising quickly back to meet his.

She had long wavy brown hair and beautiful hazel eyes, an uncommon color among these people, as the majority of this tribe had darker eyes and hair. He realized that he was staring at her face and not apologizing, so he looked down and closed his eyes for a moment, thinking of exactly what to say. He looked back up and found her smiling back and waiting.

"Ekh... ta'gea..ma..." he said, which he suspected to mean, I apologize, though he had only heard Aethen use the word for apologize, once.

The woman looked at him blankly in the face for a moment, her much lighter skin turning red. Suddenly she burst into uncontrollable laughter. Kel was unsure of why or if he even said what he thought he had said. She stopped laughing after a moment and looked back at him with her finger on her lip and a smile on her face.

"Eekh t'garea, meh'ekh ta'geama," she said, emphasizing the last word. He looked back blankly with absolutely no idea what she had just said. It sounded like two variations of what he had said. She giggled, realizing that he was completely lost, and decided to work harder towards his understanding. She pointed at him and said, "Eekh," then placed her hands together in an apologetic sort of way and slightly bowed her head, saying, "t'garea." Kel assumed that she had just spoken the words, "I apologize," correctly. But if that was how she said it, what had he said? It sounded similar, but not the same.

She looked back at him, turning even redder, and giggled even harder. Now it was time for her to explain what he had originally said.

She pointed at him and repeated the word he had used for sorry, "ta'geama." She took her fingers and hooked them around one another, producing the symbol for two people joining. The entire encounter was quite confusing, but unfortunately, Kel thought he understood what she was saying. This was reinforced by her persisting giggling and blushing skin. Instead of apologizing, he had asked to marry her, more or less. Kel applied his hand to his face in a rapid fashion.

Languages were not his strong suit, and if he kept trying to speak in the strange language, he couldn't imagine what the next thing he might ask her to do might be. For some reason, it was always this way – common words, like "hello," always seem to sound very similar to something terrible or insulting. He might walk into a tribe and say, "hello, tribe," but it would translate into something more like, "I have come to eat your babies." This was why Kel wished that a simple language could be used for all people. He guessed that the world would be boring that way, and he did strangely enjoy listening to this woman speak her language, though he didn't understand what she was saying. So, he decided he would make his intentions more obvious using the universal language of the body.

The woman was still laughing at him, so he splashed water in her face. She stopped laughing and just stared at him for a moment in shock. Then she splashed water back at him. Though it was a bright day, both of her pupils were quite dilated, a more subtle sign of affection. Espe dove into the water, and surfaced beside him, lingering a moment beneath the water to open her eyes. She felt a mixture of longing, fear, exhilaration, and a different sort of tingle more unexpected than she cared to consider. This was a path she had chosen to walk – a path with far-reaching consequences. Yet, she was brave, like her mother, and she would not back down. Forcing her wandering mind aside, she splashed the man, playfully. Her path was also fun.

They played like children in the water for a short time, splashing and having fun. Kel jumped from the water onto the shore and grabbed one of her sandals, quickly returning to the water holding it above the surface. She had been splashing him relentlessly, and this sandal was to be a hostage to prevent the splashing. It was all good fun as both of them enjoyed the cool water. Finally, the woman lunged forward to grab her sandal, reaching with one hand for the sandal and the other to push Kel backward. He tripped and fell back, but not before grabbing her to share in his underwater fate.

Instead, Kel fell into a shallow area full of mud, landing in water that did not fully cover him, and the woman landed on top of him. Both were laughing like children until they felt their bare bodies pressed tightly together, and they realized that they were not boy and girl – they were man and woman. That same tingle returned and Espe swallowed hard, her more primal instincts suddenly at war with her rational mind. For a short moment, they lay against each other, their faces far too close for childish play. The woman should have rolled off, yet she remained, hesitating as though she didn't want to leave what should have been an awkward situation. Kel could feel his body reacting, a signal he couldn't hope to hide with her body atop his. Yet the woman seemed unbothered. Instead, she gently reached forward and brushed the hair from his blue eyes.

Her hazel eyes held an intoxicating sort of look, as though she was overwhelmed. Was this her first time in such contact with a man, he wondered? Just then, she leaned forward ever so lightly, her pupils dilated and her cheeks red with blood. Kel made no move, yet his own sea-blue eyes eclipsed at her proximity. The brown-haired river woman pressed her lips to his in an instant. Her lips were as soft as ripe fruit. Pleasure danced up and down Kel's body, all worry over their accidental conjunction lost in the moment. This was the most forward he had ever seen a woman act, and yet here she was, and he had no complaints.

Suddenly, she rose and stepped quickly back. Kel lay confused in the mud, unsure of what had just happened. She turned and skittered out of the water, stepping upon the shore to put her clothes on, her lighter river people skin turning red from head to toe. She quickly fastened her leather wrap half-skirt around her waist with a cord, then tied her sandals, all the while looking away from Kel.

Damn it, I messed up, Kel self-admonished. He didn't know what it was that he had done, but it appeared that he had greatly upset this woman. They had so much fun in the water that he had truly forgotten that they were man and woman. He had not been trying to woo the woman but merely enjoying her company. Now that was over and due to some unknown grievance. He decided he would try to apologize once more. This time, he tried to remember the words she had spoken.

"Eekh t'garea," he shouted, standing in the water. The woman had been looking away shyly, but what Kel didn't know was that she had been smiling the whole time. Falling upon him had been rather exciting for her as well, and she had even kissed him. Yet she had been embarrassed as their bodies pressed, the first time she had ever been so close to a man. The embarrassment caused her to flee, but now she had regained herself, and she was not quite ready to end their fun. When she heard the words, her smile broadened. He had apologized, and he had done so with the correct words. She could not help but appreciate his earlier offer of marriage, however mistaken it had been. Her first kiss, intimate contact, and marriage proposal, all in a short time. It was turning out to be a good day.

No longer able to take the suspense, Espe approached the man, light on her feet. She walked over to the bank where he sat and kicked at his clothes, indicating that he should get dressed. She wanted to show him something, but he would need clothes if they were to go wandering around. She had watched him for a tenday and satisfied herself many days before that he was a good man. There was only one last thing to be sure of. Her small tribe had nearly no men her age who were not taken. Her selection was extremely limited and was not likely to improve. She had not wanted to rush things, but deep down, she knew that this might be her only chance at real love. She appreciated that her one chance appeared to be a good catch.

Of course there was always the coming harvest and fertility festival if he turned out to be a dud. There were plenty of men there, but it was troublesome to get a feel for their real personalities. All too often, they put on a show for the women, which hid who they really were. Espe had to know for sure that he was not brutish. She wanted a strong and brave man, but she did not want a man who was unwilling to see the beauty in the world. So many men were embarrassed to admit beauty or felt uncomfortable around flowers and simple butterflies. She knew that these were not the affinities of men, and yet to see his reaction would be telling. This would be the final test, and she hoped that he would pass.

"Euh! Gem'ke'meh! Gema, gema!" she said excitedly, motioning him to follow. Kel stepped from the water and applied his loincloth and boots. He figured he would carry his shirt for a while, letting himself dry. Unfortunately, water and leather never mixed well. He walked with the woman for a short distance before stopping, waiting for her to notice. She turned to see what was wrong. He did not even know her name, and he figured it was about time that was corrected. He pointed to himself and clearly spoke.

"Kel... Aes-Kel eahg'nom," he said, which literally meant "Kel... (it is)-Kel, my'name," but he hoped the playful woman would figure out what he meant, though her language and even the way she ordered words were different. She playfully stepped towards him with a smile and poked her finger into his chest.

"Kel," she all but purred back. She then put her finger to her chest and said, "Espeee! Eg'ehneme Espe!" emphasizing the long ee sound at the end of her name. Espe was not a name he would ever hear among his own people though it was quite pretty in his mind. It certainly seemed to match her personality, lighthearted and overly happy.

Espe and Kel wandered through the forest on the other side of the stream passed a large rock outcropping. They entered a vast field that stretched in every direction, all the way to the small mountains to the West. Espe pretended to look at the field, but instead, she pointed her eyes sideways to witness Kel's reaction. In some ways, she felt sort of silly bringing a man to a field of flowers simply to see how he would react. Worse, she was about to make a major life decision based simply off the reaction of one man to a field of plants. What if he sneezed? Espe lived in the moment, and right now, she wasn't breathing in that liminal moment...

The scene before Kel was so vast and amazing that he came to a stop to take it in. He stood before the vast field filled with many different flowers of every color he could imagine. On the ground in front of them grew many purple and blue flowers, orchids. Kel dropped to his knees before the orchids to gaze at them. Truly, he had never seen a flower so beautiful as this in his entire life. Most of the men of the Isen'bryn did not seem to care for flowers, a womanly pursuit. Kel had always had a soft place in his heart for beautiful things. He considered them the art of the forest spirits. He assumed Espe had brought him here to show him the magnificent view of the mountains, but the flowers inspired him even more. He hoped that she wouldn't be upset.

He reached forward and gently touched one of the flowers. Its delicate beauty was overwhelming. Behind him, Espe watched him with growing affection. This was definitely the man for her. She had an extremely limited selection, and the likelihood of ending up with a plain and reserved man was extremely high. Kel was as rare of a find as any flower. Why the other woman who came with him could not see this, she could not tell. She wondered if that woman were into women, or perhaps no one? Her elder brother had joined a man from another tribe, and she had felt so happy for them. Espe did find some women beautiful, but she could never imagine herself joined to one. *Oh well, that will be her loss,* she thought to herself as she dropped to her knees to look at the flowers.

Kel picked some of the flowers and tied them into a chaplet, placing the beautiful creation in Espe's hair. He regarded the woman, finding her beautiful and accentuated by the flowers. He had spent so long looking for a woman, harvest after harvest, and now suddenly there was Espe. She wasn't just beautiful; she was also fun and easy to get along with. Of course, he had only just met her, but he hoped this wasn't just a fun escape for the wavy-haired brunette. He hoped it could be more.

Just then, Espe placed her hand on his chest, her fingers slowly lowering to linger against his well-defined abdomen. Her hazel eyes returned to his, her intentions too plain for confusion. Slowly, they sank into the flowers with the mountains as their only witness. She would seal this love as fast as she could, lest her one chance at happiness escape.

ɔ ɔ ɔ

For three days, Sar'Tawas had made no advances towards Ianmu. In that short time, she had learned that he was indeed the leader of the Guild of Craftsmen and a member of the city's council of elders. She had also learned that he was highly critical of their current leader, Utiakur. Sar'Tawas tended to pace back and forth in the evening. He would mutter to himself and occasionally even talk at her. It was more of "talking at," because he never solicited any response from her. It was a strange habit obviously born of a man living alone. Nevertheless, it had the benefit of feeding her a wealth of information, however annoying it might be.

The life of a concubine turned out to be relatively easy for her. Far from a harsh ruler, Sar'Tawas treated her in a laissez-faire sort of fashion, allowing her a great degree of freedom with what she chose to do at any given time. She was almost more like a wife than a servile concubine in many ways. Each day she would awaken and ensure that he was fed and that the fire was kept burning. Each night she would ensure that his cup never ran dry and generally stay out of his way. It was actually not that difficult to work though she was beginning to become bored with it. She had concluded that Sar'Tawas was definitely the right man for her to control. He was easy to work with, already interested in ruling the city, and best of all, he had a weakness when dealing with women.

With her decision finally made, she needed a way to cement their relationship and possibly grow it beyond master and concubine. Additionally, she wanted to make sure that people knew that she was associated with him. This would be important if he attempted to ascend to power. If she were unknown, he could easily leave her behind. If people thought of her almost as a wife, she could become that wife when the time came. On the morning of the third day, Ianmu learned of how she might accomplish both of her goals and ensure the hook was firmly in the mouth of her big fish. Sar'Tawas came to her in the morning as she was sweeping the floor with a hand broom made of rush strands.

"Tonight, I'm going to have some important people come by to talk. I need you to take this," he handed her a flax string with polished bone beads running down it, "and trade it in the marketplace for walnuts, goat meat, and berries of some variety. Maybe figs... yes, get some figs. I'll need you to make enough food for at least five people. Prepare the food and have it ready by sundown. You will serve me, and you will serve my guests, and don't mess it up," he said awkwardly. Suddenly, he realized that he was looking her body up and down rather than addressing her directly. He turned slightly red and wandered off a little embarrassed.

"I hope I will please you," she said absentmindedly as he left. She almost doubled over in laughter. Sar'Tawas was a smart man, almost cunning. It always amazed her that a woman could cause even the most intelligent and powerful men to feel awkward and make all manner of mistakes. Sar'Tawas had this problem worse than most men. He had some sort of behavioral flaw involving women, and every day that she lived with him, she felt more and more at ease with her choice. His behavioral flaw could be easily exploited to gain additional control over him.

Ianmu wandered down a short mud-brick staircase into the low ceiling storeroom beside the main building. This was where she stayed most of the time. She had built a small clandestine shrine to An'an in one of the four corners where she knew Sar'Tawas would never be bothered to venture. She knelt before that now and prayed to her goddess repeatedly for strength and assistance with her plan. She had been taught to dance as a hopeful priestess; she was the daughter of her city's leader, after all. The harvest before she had even taken part in her city's fertility dance, though she was not a priestess. Fertility and harvest dances tended to be quite evocative, with significant hip-swaying and body motion. These were designed to show off parts of the body and bring forth the spirits of love and fertility, something she had always found odd given the fertility in question was usually livestock and crops.

Ianmu planned to use these very same moves tonight when the guests arrived. She would make her grand entrance in such a way that no one forgot who she was. It was a risk, but a calculated risk. If Sar'Tawas did not react negatively to what she was doing, she would likely bed him this very night and endear herself upon his guests. First, she would go to the trading place and get what she had been requested to pick up. Then, she would prepare the food and have it ready, but after that, she would make some black soot-based pigments to apply to her body in preparation for the dance... the dance that would place the bone hook – and bedding him would set it.

ɔ ɔ ɔ

Sar'Tawas entered the main room of his building. Only buildings directly facing the ceremonial grounds in the city's center had ground-level access. All other buildings were accessed through their roofs. As an elder, many special privileges were afforded Sar'Tawas. The term "elder" was quite literal in most smaller tribes, and even in Isut'na in the past. More recently, the term was applied to anyone of significant power and influence. The distinction wasn't trivial, as the old usage of the term drew influence from wisdom, while the new usage drew influence by power and control. Regardless, this was the way large populations seemed to be headed.

One of his primary duties was to keep the trading equitable and remove troublesome bits of commerce, just as a craftsman re-honed a blade. Today he had brought three elders and several select friends to discuss the prospect of obtaining more fermented fruit drink from the North. The majority of citizens consumed fermented honey drinks or locally obtained fermented fruit drinks, but Sar'Tawas felt that these were of lesser quality.

"Please make yourselves at home. We will eat, and then we will talk," he said as he beckoned his guests to enter. First in the door was Kamar, the lead hunter, and an elder, as well as his wife, Zah'namu. Behind them entered Katakar, a very old, nearly bald man with sparse white hair and a pronounced limp. Katakar was the master of the wheat fields and charged with ensuring there was enough grain for the city, though Sar'Tawas was unsure how well the man could even see. It was rumored that his daughter and son provided his eyes though they were not present tonight. Given his position, Katakar wore a small ceremonial wreath in his sparse hair made from wheat.

Cereal crops were essential for the city. If anything happened to the crops, the mass suffering that would result could destroy the city. What little cereal crops that could be imported from other villages would be done at great cost to prevent such catastrophes. As a result, only someone as old and wise as Katakar could be charged with such a duty. Luckily, wheat had grown well for many harvests, all which Katakar took credit for.

Next through the door was the elder Isu'mamu, an elderly woman who wore beads at various intervals in her hair. She was mistress of the flax fields, one of the smaller, yet lucrative crops grown by the city. In some ways, Isu'mamu was second to the great Utiakur. She had started as a lowly born daughter of a flax worker. However, her luck changed when she was chosen by the high priest of Isut, the late Anatiakur, father of the current leader, Utiakur, as the fertility festival divine vessel. She had been young, but she had birthed a strong daughter following the fertility festival, which ensured the fields were overflowing with wheat, barley, peas, and flax the coming harvest. It was not long before she was chosen to be a priestess of Isut and then eventually the master of the flax fields. Isu'mamu rarely passed judgment on any issue, but when she did, people listened. It was said that the key to influencing any decision in the city was simply to convince Isu'mamu of your opinion. She slowly entered with the help of her grandson Kilumar, a farmer of flax and controller of an entire field – nepotism, in Sar'Tawas's opinion.

With his five guests seated on soft, wooly sheepskins, Sar'Tawas came to sit as well, pausing only for a moment to offer a quick prayer to his bull god statuette. His guests glared at Sar'Tawas with confusion – normally, it would be the duty of his wife or the children to serve the guests, but without a wife or children, that duty should fall upon Sar'Tawas. Did he expect the guests to serve themselves, they wondered? Sar'Tawas enjoyed their confusion and hoped to leave them wondering for just another few moments before he showed off his new toy... and then the moment grew longer. Sar'Tawas began to wonder where Ianmu, the concubine, had gone. Could she have run off? That wasn't likely as there really wasn't any place for her to go, and he smelled cooked food. He began to fidget as the silence lingered and what had started as a meal, was quickly becoming awkward.

ɔ ɔ ɔ

Ianmu had tilted a small, polished obsidian mirror on a table so that she could see the guests from the storeroom where she now sat with the food without being seen herself. She needed to maintain Sar'Tawas's belief that she was slightly airheaded and not very intelligent. She could use this as a cloak of deception more effectively than any other tool. Besides, she liked making him nervously wait. When she saw that Sar'Tawas was about to stand up to go look for her, she lifted a basket containing fruit and placed it on her head, and then stood with a jug of fermented honey drink in her right hand. She stepped out from the storeroom and walked into the main room in such a way as to be very conspicuous.

As soon as Ianmu stepped out with the food and the jug, there were immediate gasps and intrigue among the guests. Nobody had attended a wedding between Sar'Tawas and such a beautiful woman. Who could she possibly be? Everyone turned their eyes to Sar'Tawas, expecting him to explain, but instead, he sat back with a smile on his face and waited to be served. Ianmu could see her "master" was enjoying himself, and, strangely enough, she found the ruse to be somewhat amusing as well, but she contained her laughter and maintained her innocent expression. She was unsure why the Goddess had blessed her with a strange innocent look. It didn't often work on women, but men typically seemed to assume that she had only good intentions. *Thank you, An'an,* she thought.

"Sar'Tawas, do you pay this servant of yours flint and obsidian arrowheads for her service? There is no way such a pretty girl would hang around with someone of the likes of you without payment," old Katakar said with a laugh. Sar'Tawas was surprised that Katakar could even see the woman in that much detail, given his old, withered eyes. Ianmu was holding the guests' attention so well that they had not brought the full weight of their questioning upon their host yet. She bent over low and placed the basket on the reed mat that everyone's sheepskin mat sat upon. She then put a series of small clay cups in front of each person and poured a generous serving of fermented fruit beverage in each.

"All right, Sar'Tawas, you've had your fun. Explain to us who this person is and why she is serving us, or I will just ask her for myself," said Kamar, the hunter. Zah'namu did not wait for Sar'Tawas and took the initiative.

"My dear, who are you, and how did you end up serving Sar'Tawas? Perhaps your father owes him a debt which you are paying off with work?" she asked politely. Ianmu stood up with the large serving jar and smiled at everyone as if confused and thinking of what to say. She enjoyed drawing the suspense out as long as possible, and she hoped what she was about to say would put Sar'Tawas in an even more uncomfortable position. Deep down, she realized that torturing the man was not her smartest move, but for some reason, she utterly adored it.

"My name is Ianmu, and I am the concubine of Sar'Tawas. He bought me for several bolts of linen to bear him children. I'm from a village on the Brown River. I will bring the roast meat now," she said with a smile before turning and leaving Sar'Tawas to fill in the details. Kilumar nearly choked to death on a piece of fruit he was trying to eat, and Kamar merely shook his head. Then, everyone turned to stare at Sar'Tawas. Their expressions were a mixture of amused to disgusted.

"You bought a young woman? Do you plan to force her to have your children?" Zah'namu accused, anger stirring behind her forcibly neutral visage. She was outspoken and often took the lead in any conversation. It was said by many that the reason she had married Kamar was simply that he was the only man in the city who could stand up to her. Old Katakar simply produced a low chuckle as if laughing to himself over a private joke. Nervous, Sar'Tawas quickly spoke, hoping to settle the matter.

"There is nothing wrong with having a concubine. As the trader explained to me, her father was trying to get rid of her anyway. He had too many daughters, and he had no room for this one. Fathers trade their daughters into marriage all the time," he said matter-of-factually. He dropped his voice a little lower before speaking the next part. "She's... Well, she's not the sharpest flint in the lot, if you know what I mean. But she does good housework, and she may bear me a son," he finished. Everyone stared in shock. It was true that there was no real rule against owning a concubine or a slave, but it was rare.

While male captives taken in raids were usually ritually killed, female captives were often forcibly wed or ritually killed. Traders spoke of powerful men who took women into their households to increase their chances of heirs, effectively concubines, but this happened only in proto-cities to the far Southeast, such as Yarehk, one day known as Jericho. Zah'namu couldn't help but suspect that the woman was more of a slave than a concubine, having been purchased rather than accepting the role. She had to fight to keep the snarl of anger from her politically neutral visage. The disparity between men and women – accepted as the status quo by many women – was a major source of resentment for her. In her estimation, raiders and people who took slaves, concubines, and captives were the sand in the sandals of humanity. She stuffed food in her mouth lest she say something that would cause a major upheaval.

Ianmu returned with a large basket containing roasted meat drizzled with walnut oil and surrounded by berries and figs. She placed the delicious food before her guests and then ensured their cups were full. She quickly disappeared into the backroom to prepare for her performance, having heard their discussion and hoping it continued, given how delightfully awkward it was. Oddly, causing such a stir had been more exciting and amusing than she had expected. She supposed that growing up seated behind her father as he spoke with the gathered elders had long prepared her for such events. She wondered if a typical woman would have found them as mundane as she did.

◯ ◯ ◯

Ianmu knelt before the small obsidian mirror illuminated only by a clamshell oil lamp. She hastily dipped her finger into a small clay pot and removed some of the black ash and oil pigment she had made earlier. Crushing charcoal from the fire and mixing it with some leftover walnut oil had provided her with an extremely rich pigment. She would have used a fine brush made of wild horsehair or a fine slice of reed to carefully apply beautiful and complex lines, but her finger would have to do in this ad hoc environment.

Quickly, she rubbed some of the walnut oil over her body, though just enough so that the firelight would reflect off her skin. Sometimes, her people would mix ground obsidian into paints merely to make them sparkle. She had thought to do that, but it took time to grind the obsidian finely so that it did not harm the skin. She simply had lacked that much time. Looking down at the reflection of the oil lamp's soft red glow upon her skin, Ianmu was pretty sure that she would captivate her audience.

Delicately, she painted black horizontal stripes from her feet all the way to her head. It was not a standard design, but she hoped to seem natural and naïve. Her dance moves were carefully honed from many harvests of ritual events in her city though she planned to use random improvisation now and then to prevent anyone from suspecting this. She took a deep breath and slowly let it out. This would be the second pivotal moment of her plan.

◯ ◯ ◯

"All of these questions about the concubine woman and none about the drink from the North. I assure you, there will be plenty of time for you to meet her another day. She's actually not that interesting, anyway. She has not done anything but cooking and cleaning since I obtained her. Just think of her as my wife, sort of," Sar'Tawas said, having been exhausted by a deluge of questions from his guests as they hungrily ate the roasted meat. Most meals involved rough wheat bread, porridge, roasted vegetables, and various concoctions made from the organs of the animals. It was only on a special occasion when food like berries and quality roasted meat was served. As tasty as it was, a person could not live merely on roasted meat.

Kamar reached for another piece of meat when sudden movement caught his sharp hunter's eye. He looked back toward the storeroom

241

expecting to see Ianmu walk out with more food. But, instead, Ianmu lightly danced out from the storeroom into the main room, coming to a stop before the guests. Her entire body was painted from top to bottom with black horizontal stripes, and the light from the fire danced off her lightly brown skin. Everyone stopped eating and talking, unsure of what was about to happen. Dancing was commonplace, especially at social and religious events, but a personal dancer in a home was, unexpected.

"Please keep eating. I will dance for you," Ianmu said and began to twirl around in very tight circles, all the while singing a folk song that she had heard the lowest farmers of her city sing on many full moon nights. She knew much more beautiful songs, but she did not want to risk giving away her knowledge of their intricate words, some being magic. As she danced, Ianmu shifted in and out of various techniques and used random improvisation, which she hoped would make her appear as somebody who had watched dancers but who had never been formally trained. The guests sat back and watched the amazing show with expressions of awe, envy, and bemused confusion.

"Sar'Tawas... You lucky man! You have a woman who will dance for you every night while you eat, and serve you as well. All I have are my wheat fields and my memories," joked old Katakar. While his reaction was one of amusement, Isu'mamu's grandson Kilumar was absolutely captivated. Sar'Tawas noticed that the boy was fully entranced by the performance. He glared at the concubine as her hips rotated around in tight, quick circles, her hands held high above her head. Seeing the young man staring at her enthralled nearly caused Ianmu to laugh aloud, but she held back her thoughts and continued singing her song. She had danced at many of Nara'kit's religious festivals, often entirely nude, and was unbothered by the many eyes.

Like what you see? And why shouldn't you, boy? I doubt even you will attract a woman quite like this, Sar'Tawas thought to himself with selfish pride. He was beginning to realize that having a concubine would make him the envy of most men. He liked to be the envy of most men.

Ianmu continued her dance, ensuring that everyone was fully hooked. Most importantly, she could see that Sar'Tawas was beginning to appreciate just how much of a woman she was. It was important to bed a man, or his loyalty might remain in question. Ianmu had noticed over the past three days that Sar'Tawas did show an interest, but he was held back by a mixture of distractions and some strange form of awkward embarrassment each time he had nearly approached her. She would need to drive these distractions from his mind so that he could think of only one thing. She had spoken her prayers to An'an to ward off any children from her actions tonight, and she was pretty sure she would be safe. An'an had always protected her before.

She slowly approached Sar'Tawas with her hips swaying rhythmically. She descended to her knees just in front of where he sat. It hurt her knees a little to gyrate her hips at such a speed while pressed against the rush matting, but the effect it had upon him was apparent. She continued her hip swing dance looking him dead in the eyes as if nothing else mattered. Sar'Tawas almost seemed to forget that he had guests as he began to reach forward towards Ianmu. Right as his hand was about to touch her waist, she suddenly stood with a giggle and danced away and back into the storeroom. Sar'Tawas stared with a crazed look upon his face, as though he would leave his guests and chase after her right at that moment. Old Isu'mamu coughed, breaking the silence.

"I could dance like that once, long ago. Sar'Tawas, my eyes are old and do not see well, but I think that she likes you. You can always tell when the field is ready for sowing," the old woman said matter-of-factly before bursting into laughter at her own crudity. Kamar looked uncomfortable, and young Kilumar coughed his drink from his mouth, choking for a moment at the comment, while Zah'namu frowned, displeased by the power imbalance.

"She certainly seemed to have a romantic intent," Zah'namu said, though her tone was skeptical. A woman's consent was hardly a common concept at the time, yet it was something Zah'namu considered key to any healthy relationship. She doubted a woman who was somewhere between a wife and a possession could properly consent. The power dynamic was dubious at best, and likely much viler. Unfortunately, such ideas of mutual consent would not be considered of great importance for another 7500 years. Of course, unknown to the mighty Zah'namu, Ianmu was hardly a victim, and perhaps even more of an apex predator than her "master."

Morality and ethics aside, she secretly felt a mix of thankful and envious emotions toward the woman. Her envy was simple enough to understand, but thankfulness was a more complex emotion. It had been quite a while since Kamar had been this excited, and she appreciated his feeble efforts to hide it. After such a display, she hoped that he might be in the mood to provide her with another child. She had a son, but she hoped to have a daughter. For a moment, she began to ponder the ethics of a nearly captive woman providing her a benefit, and if that entailed some sort of guilt on her part. Zah'namu took a sip of fermented drink and tried to push the ideas aside, lest they give her a headache. Sometimes, she suspected that those without morals were the ones who truly slept peacefully.

☽ ☽ ☽

Ianmu sat on the sleeping mat she had laid out for herself in the storeroom pretending to nap while Sar'Tawas finished escorting the last of his guests from the building. She hoped that he would return for her, but only time would tell. She adjusted her position on the sleeping mat to appear as enticing as possible. It wasn't a very natural sleeping position, but she doubted that if Sar'Tawas came for her, he would notice. She was pondering her next actions when suddenly the dim light from the fire was occulted by somebody standing in the doorway to the storeroom. She rolled over onto her back and looked up at Sar'Tawas in much the same position they had first met in the trading area.

"Do you wish for me to dance for you again? If you don't mind, I'd like to..." she said as innocently as possible. Sar'Tawas had not been with a woman for too long, a fact which seemed to make him less able to see through obvious ploys. As he knelt before her, Ianmu smiled, still amazed that her plan was working so well and ever thankful of her goddess for granting her the boons she needed to have made it this far. *First, I will be yours... then, Isut'na will be mine.*

CHAPTER FOURTEEN
THE GODDESS ISUT

In stark contrast to the many sexually repressive religions of the modern era, human sexuality and fertility were often openly celebrated and even encouraged in ancient times. From Aphrodite of Greece and Haumea of Hawai'i to Inanna of Sumer and Asase Ya of Ashanti, fertility, love, and even lust deities can be found throughout the ancient world. Given the vast numbers and varieties of such deities and the critical nature of sex and fertility to childbirth, plentiful livestock, and fertile farming land, it can be supposed that such sex and fertility deities were not uncommon in the Neolithic. Though it is important not to attribute all Neolithic religious beliefs to fertility and sex, a reductionist and all too common mindset.

Nearly three Moons had passed, and Brig'dha had all but lost hope. She sat on a deer hide, watching a village dog gnawing on a bone. She was supposed to be cleaning tubers, but she had been staring at the dog for quite some time. It wasn't so much that it was interesting – it was that she didn't know what else to do. Mew had not shown his face that day, but he really wasn't keen on the dog. She suspected that he would return that night for some food or to bring her a gift. He tended to deposit dead rodents and birds outside of the hut. It wasn't the best gift she had ever received, but she appreciated the sentiment.

She had come to the tribe of Rene, a small tribe just northwest of the village where her friend had jumped into the water, expecting Ember to return with her stories of survival and how she had swum to safety. Instead, most of the warm season had passed, and Brig'dha had all but given up hope. The people of the tribe had been very polite and accommodating to her group. They were hearty folk who didn't seem to have any particularly special trade-ware or commodity. Many of the inland tribes were not particularly specialized, merely self-sufficient. Nevertheless, existing between multiple large villages provided trade opportunities.

Her friends Aethen and Kel had worked very hard at cheering her up, and she felt sorry for having ignored them. Aethen had obviously been a strong friend of Ember and had taken her loss pretty hard. She wished she had been more supportive of him, but she had been wrapped up in her own grief. She wasn't entirely sure, but when she recalled what had transpired over the past few tendays, she began to wonder if Kel had been attempting to become more than a friend. If that had been the case, it was too late now. Not a tenday after their arrival, Kel had fallen for a local woman named Espe.

Brig'dha actually didn't mind Espe. There was a sort of innocence about her that reminded Brig'dha of Ember and prevented her from having any negative thoughts towards the woman. Kel and Espe had become closer each day, and Brig'dha was pretty sure that, if things continued as they were, they would become married before long. With the way they looked at each other, Brig'dha supposed it was probably for the best that they got married soon... before, Espe carried a child. Strictly speaking, there had never been taboos among the Isen'bryn or many other smaller tribes concerning a child born out of wedlock. Children were the lifeblood of the people, and a healthy child was an asset, never to be shunned.

Aethen approached her, dropping a stone ax to the ground. He was covered in dirt and had obviously been cutting wood most of the day. He had brought up the subject of returning to their tribe a few days before. By the look on his face, Brig'dha knew what he was about to discuss. Aethen was tired of chopping wood and longed to return to people he knew. The prospect of journeying into the great unknown had intrigued him, but the loss of Ember had dampened his spirits.

"We have been here for most of the warm season," he said.

"I'm sorry," she replied softly.

"We all cared about her, but now we must care about ourselves and move on."

"I know, but perhaps if we waited just a little longer until the Sun is not quite so bright. The walk home will take at least two days, and this place is sweltering," she said. Aethen couldn't argue that point. The South was hot, but he enjoyed the relaxing weather and this beautiful small patch of scenery. It was actually much nicer than where his own people had settled though he wasn't about to tell anyone that.

From around the hut strode Kel and Espe, each hand-in-hand. Aethen had suggested that Kel find a woman, but this was just impressive. Theirs was a love affair to be carved in stone for generations. Espe ran over to Aethen and Brig'dha, excitedly telling them about something happening, oddly reminding Brig'dha of a chittering red squirrel. The moon priestess had learned virtually none of their language as she had spent most of her time lamenting her own loss. Aethen had learned more of the language but not enough to understand the excited Espe. Kel stepped behind her and placed his hand on her shoulder, bringing her back to reality.

"If Espe takes a breath before speaking, I will try and translate for you," he said. Over the past two Moons, Kel and Espe had spent much time together, and they had learned some of each other's words. Espe excitedly spoke her news while Kel translated.

"She says that in about a moon, there will be a harvest festival held about halfway between where we are now and our own people's village. Everyone regionally will come to celebrate. It is a harvest, fertility, and equinox festival of sorts. It's normally where people find lovers and exchange wares," he finished. Espe stared at Aethen and Brig'dha with wide eyes, awaiting a response. No translation was needed to guess what the excitable woman wanted to know.

"Well, it might be a good idea to wait a little longer and attend the festival. It would give us a chance to meet other tribes from the area, and then we could simply walk the remainder of the distance back to our tribe," Aethen reasoned. Brig'dha let out a deep breath and nodded. She didn't want to leave, but she couldn't spend the rest of her life sitting in this tribe peeling tubers waiting for someone who would never return. She took another deep breath holding back the sudden urge to cry, and forced a smile.

"Then we will go and try to let go of what we cannot have. We will be reborn," she said.

ɔ ɔ ɔ

Over the past three Moons – one-fourth of a full harvest – Ember had lived with Nemanar and her family, fishing and hunting in the warm waters on the coast of the Blue Sea. It had been nearly a tenday before her memory of who she was had finally cleared. She had no memory of how she had ended up in the water, only that she had been trying to find the woman named Kyra. The necklace around her neck told her that she had indeed found her, but why did she still have it? Somehow, she felt that Aethen and Brig'dha were safe. She had no knowledge of where they might have gone. She suspected that they likely returned to the new tribe, the Blue Sea People. She hoped that he and Brig'dha were well, but there was not much she had been able to do as she waited for her arm and head to stop hurting. Her arm had not seemed broken, and yet only now had she been able to use it, after three Moons. Her head had healed a little faster, but the dizzy spells had only just finally left a few days before.

Ember stood in the cool, salty water, which rose to her waist, holding a fishing spear and waiting for fish to get close enough. The weather was hot and beat down on her skin. She had fashioned a rough hat from reeds using basic basketry skills. She had taken to simply wearing a loincloth and nothing else, given the heat of the day this far South. This had not been much of a problem, as her new foster family dressed similarly though they were more accustomed to the hot weather than Ember. The only trouble she had was the Sun on her face and shoulders, which the hat sometimes failed to block. This could be easily remedied with ocher paint, in which she was constantly adorned. *I'll be as tanned as tree bark by the time I return,* she thought.

"Ember! Father say wheat *Aza'n* is held in just two tendays! Will you come to the *Aza'n*?" Ninrea'mu excitedly asked Ember. Ninrea'mu was the daughter of the fisherman Ketamir and his wife, Nemanar. Her thick dark hair and dark eyes seemed commonplace among people from the True South. It was through her careful instruction and absolute immersion that Ember had picked up their language so quickly. She remembered her nights spent with her friend Kistra of the Tornhemal. Ember supposed that people became better at learning new languages when they learned how to listen to the differences in speech.

In truth, she had not understood every single word she heard, but she was smart enough to assume the other words based on their context. She realized that the word, Aza'n, probably meant some sort of gathering, though she did not quite understand what it exactly meant. The problem only occurred when somebody spoke so quickly that she became lost. Ember paused for a few moments while Ninrea'mu used hand gestures to indicate a great gathering of people, thus clarifying for Ember that Aza'n did, in fact, mean "festival." She sometimes wondered if she might begin speaking multiple languages randomly after learning so many words from so many tongues.

"Yes, I will come. You go to *festival* every harvest?" she asked using that word, now understanding its meaning.

"There are festivals in close villages, best festival near is harvest festival. Not in village, near village. Many people come. Many different places, to meet," Ninrea'mu said, using words she knew Ember had learned. The girl bounded into the water excitedly as though she had some important news to add. She seemed totally unaware that she had scared away all the fish nearby. Ninrea'mu suddenly developed a strange, dreamy look and held her hands tightly together. She was a little young to find a lover, but love was all that seemed to occupy her mind. Ember didn't feel like spoiling her dreams by reminding her she still had a few harvests left to play as a child.

"There will be strong hunters. The best dance in rituals. Maybe hunter will choose me! We sit, talk under the stars," she said, using hand gestures to make up for any words Ember did not understand. Ember chuckled to herself. She remembered when she was this young. Love and romance danced through her mind like a beautiful song, and the worries of the world seemed far away. A strong hunter would emerge from the woods and deposit a massive beast they had slew in the center of the tribe. The hunter would walk forward and call out to a maiden in front of everyone with no fear in their eyes. She had been that hunter. Yes, she remembered her dreams. There had recently been someone she felt that way about, but she would not be able to do anything about that until she returned to the village of the people of the Blue Sea.

"Ember? You hear what I say? You just stare at sea," Ninrea'mu asked, confused. Ember realized that a few moments had passed, and she had not been paying any attention. It was easy to become lost in the dreams of childhood.

"Yes, I hear. I think of friend I want meet at festival... but will not," she said, with difficulty having such a small, shared vocabulary.

"Oh! Tell me, tell me of him? Strong, brave? Meke'assaetarsu?" Ninrea'mu asked in a young girl's excited way and used the word "Meke'assaetarsu," which Ember did not understand.

"Meke'assaetarsu?" Ember asked, slightly confused. Ninrea'mu used her hands to indicate that "Meke" meant great or big, while "assaetarsu" meant love. In the context of finding someone at the festival, the words made more sense, perhaps indicating a romantic or great love. This was certainly more direct than the girl had been several Moons ago. When she had first met Ember, she had been meek and very reserved. Luckily, it had not taken long for her to open up. The girl seemed to appreciate a younger woman she could speak with, even though their age gap was still significant. How could she explain how she felt to a child? Ember was not even completely sure of her own feelings, let alone explaining them in detail to someone as young as Ninrea'mu and with a tiny vocabulary. She figured she would explain as best she could.

"It hard to describe person. I give my life to save them. I think they do the same," she said. When she looked back at Ninrea'mu, the girl's eyes were massive and fixated upon her. Ember endured the rest of the day filled with relentless questions. This was her punishment for speaking of romantic things around the starry-eyed girl. *Wait until your strong hunter snores,* she thought with a laugh.

ↄ ↄ ↄ

The city of Isut'na had a population of nearly 2500 individuals, but not all those people would attend every major ritual or event. This was not only due to the limited space available but also due to practical and logistical necessities. For example, people were needed to watch the herd animals or keep an eye on the fields, day and night. At the city's center was a large gathering area where perhaps 1500 to 2000 people could easily attend rituals and other meetings.

The ground was made of packed dirt with a central fire pit boasting a main blazing inferno which rose nearly two lengths of a man into the air tickling the very sky with its flames. Around the perimeter of the ritual area, at least a dozen smaller pits were dug to allow smaller fires, more for light than heat. The square mud-brick houses and buildings surrounding the gathering area caused sound to be reflected back into the dance area and created a sort of amphitheater. The effect was a cozy-feeling and large dancing area where songs could be heard without great effort.

The mud-brick houses and buildings surrounding the dance and trade area rose two stories in the air and even three in some places. This late in the warm season, the night air was extremely hot, though this night was a little less humid than normal. The firelight from each fire bathed the surrounding white plastered buildings in a flickering orange glow, contrasting strikingly against the black star-filled sky. The Moon was not to be seen that night, and the contrast between the orange and the black gave an almost magical and surreal feeling to the night.

People danced and sang to the sound of flute and percussion as cooked goat meat and fish were served, as well as many other delightful dishes. If clothes were worn, men wore simple leather or linen loincloths while women wore aprons, wrap skirts, or string skirts made from bark fiber, flax, wool, or nettle fiber. Everyone decorated their bodies with intricate and beautiful geometric shapes using paints, each trying to outdo the next. They adorned their hair with complex braids, bird feathers, beads, and other ornaments. Due to the excessive number of wares to be traded to obtain complex and ornate clothing, most people relied on their ability to paint their bodies to show off skill or status. It was not practical to wear large or complex pieces of cloth, and it was simply too hot for much covering. Moreover, the festival to Isut was a fertility festival – thick and heavy clothing never seemed to contribute well to fertility.

Situated on the top of a building directly in front of the temple of Isut were small leather mats with a series of soft goatskin cushions. Upon the center cushion sat the proud leader of the city, the great Isut'Sanup'ra Utiakur. Utiakur was an ancient man having lived 72 harvests. He had fought off many raiders to the city and had outlived most of its inhabitants. None of these things detracted from his legend, and even now, in his old age, he was still regarded as an almost supernatural figure among his people. Many people had been born under his reign, lived a full life, and died. Unfortunately, long life was not a common occurrence.

Utiakur sat back against the wall behind him and watched the festivities and ritualistic dancing below. He could feel his body was coming to its end, and he wondered how many more of these events he would witness before his darkness came and Isut flew down to claim him. He had long white hair, mostly balding in the center. His eyes were a sharp brown, but he found it very difficult to see out of them at this point. Most of what he saw was a strange blur of movement, especially in the dim light. Though his body was still functioning, his teeth had mostly disappeared long ago. Growing old was the punishment for being lucky too many times. There was always a price to be paid.

Utiakur reached down and adjusted his short linen wrap. The weather was quite hot at this time of the harvest. Three tendays before had been the hottest point of the entire harvest, but even now, as the stars blanketed the sky, the temperature was still hard to bear. Utiakur looked down at his cup and noticed that it had run dry. He was about to stand to get some more drink when a younger woman approached him carrying a large clay jug. He openly regarded the woman for a moment. She stood before him wearing a simple linen apron with extra-long tassels in the front and rugged leather sandals, a single black feather hanging from a leather cord around her neck.

He had seen her several times before with the leader of the Craft Guild, Sar'Tawas. If he was not mistaken, she was a concubine to the man or perhaps a slave? The sleazy man had traded for her from a neighboring tribe or trader, though he was unsure of the details. Her body was full-figured, a form more pleasing to the gods. She had a beautiful complexion with strong cheekbones and thick eyebrows framing her determined look. Her skin was a little darker than his, and her richly dark hair was a little thicker than most, likely owing to good health. She stood with a certain elegance of stature which reminded him slightly of his own daughter.

Sometimes he wished his daughter might eat a little more to better attract a husband. Being skinny was not as pleasing to the gods as a woman with a fair amount of body weight.

The woman stepped forward and indicated his cup without saying a word. He nodded and held the cup forward while she poured some of the fermented honey drink his people obtained from the Northwest in trade. Utiakur wasn't particularly fond of the idea of owning a slave or a concubine, but it happened from time to time, and he had never received any signs from the gods to suggest that the practice was wrong. Perhaps this concubine would keep Sar'Tawas occupied so that he might leave everyone alone. Utiakur chuckled to himself as he closed his eyes and began to sip on the delicate beverage. This particular batch had an odd flavor, but no two batches were ever quite the same. The creation of fermented beverages was a manual process, and the results varied widely. Nevertheless, the drink would help him tolerate the warm air this night.

On hot nights such as this, he missed his now long-dead wife, Yari'aya. She had left this world for the next to take her place with the goddess Isut so long before. Utiakur closed his eyes, allowing her visage to return, a comforting thought. He could see her playful smile and her beautiful waist long shiny black hair twirling as she danced on a night like this. He remembered most fondly those intense eyes, darker than the darkest night. It was those eyes he had fallen in love with so long ago. After many women before her, he had settled upon Yari'aya as his wife, even though she never bore him a son.

Utiakur had been with many women as his role as high priest of Isut demanded. He would attempt to sire a male heir every harvest to take his place one day. It was a major ritual and had to be performed every single harvest to ensure a full crop, if possible. In fact, it had not been that many tendays since the last time the ritual had been performed. It seemed that no matter which woman he was with, they never quite compared to his beloved Yari'aya. She had been mother to his only child, a woman named Aya'tar. He shook his head as he thought of how many rituals and prayers he had made, and still no luck. What would his only daughter do when he died? Could she lead by herself? Who would perform the ritual to sire a child?

His thoughts were disrupted by a change in the music. Men played sound sticks and bird bone flutes while women sang and shook bone rattles. The pace had changed from a slow festive beat to a more rapid ceremonial rhythm. Utiakur slowly opened his eyes for a look. For a moment, he was confused as the image of his long-dead wife Yari'aya remained... no, this was not Yari'aya – it was her daughter, his one and only child. She stood before him, adjusting her clothing before taking part in the important ritual dance. Oh, how she looked just like her mother. Many men would have lamented having only a daughter and not a son. Some had even said that this was his only failing as a leader. But, son or not, Utiakur simply could not feel any loss as he gazed upon his daughter preparing for the ceremonial dance. She was his greatest accomplishment, as far as he was concerned.

"Aya'tar," he said with a smile. Isut'Sanup'ramu Aya'tar, or "Aya'tar" to her closest friends, turned her wide smile towards her father. Her face was painted completely red with thin black lines forming beautiful and intricate geometric patterns of triangles from one ear to the other, crossing her face and eyes. Her title of Isut'Sanup'ramu meant Priestess Vessel of Goddess Isut. Without a wife, the duties of the High Priestess of Isut had fallen upon Aya'tar at a young age. Isut was a fertility goddess, so her worship was directed by all sexes and genders. Upon this very night, Aya'tar would perform the ritualistic dance to invoke Isut. It was important to invoke Isut several times a harvest to keep the Goddess' interest in the city. If she were not properly entertained, she might take her graces elsewhere.

"Do not worry, father, I felt sort of tingly all day. I'm sure the Goddess will fill me tonight," she said with that wide smile she always had for him, pausing to take a heavy sip from his cup to calm her nerves. Aya'tar turned away from her father to look at the events before her – the main dancers had cleared the center of the festival area, leaving an empty void in which Aya'tar could dance right beside the central fire. Several men stood with bull horns by the edge of the fire awaiting the dance. Their role was that of the spirit of the mighty bull, Gunar. The men had removed their clothing and painted completely black with ash and oil paint. It was a complicated dance, but its proper completion would ensure the Goddess remained interested in the city.

Isut'Sanup'ramu Aya'tar praying to Isut

Leaving her father with a thoughtful smile, Aya'tar trotted forward and down the mud-brick steps toward the people. She had performed this dance many times before though she was still nervous in front of many people. She wore a long linen apron roughly two hands in width and similarly long with the shape of a vulture, the most sacred of birds, woven into the panel. The excess flax string tassel, made from the vertical strings, called warp threads, of the loom upon which the garment was made hung nearly to her feet. The beautiful garment was dyed red and black and hung from a waist cord woven into the apron.

Her upper arms, shoulders, chest, and back were painted in one giant horizontal stripe of red paint extending from just below her neck to just above her solar plexus. Her arms and legs had red painted lines with black borders and black circles in the middle. Around her neck, she wore a leather cord with a series of copper discs attached. There was a row of three discs spanning her neck, two discs below that, and then finally one disc at the bottom. The necklace was joined using a leather cord and formed roughly an upside-down triangle. Around her ankles and wrists, she wore copper bracelets made from crude copper strips. Her loose hair was black and shiny, reaching all the way to her hips. Fastened to the back was a fan of sacred vulture feathers arching high over her head. In each of her hands, she held a long beautiful black feather with its tip painted red.

When Aya'tar stepped onto the dancing ground, she felt the warm packed dirt beneath her bare feet and felt a connection to the land and the Goddess above. Aya'tar held her arms out and began to softly chant to Isut, asking the Goddess to fill her. She approached the fire with her eyes closed but felt its warmth, her rare and precious copper jewelry clinking loudly and catching the light of the fire for all to see. The entire crowd of nearly 2000 people made no sound as the priestess slowly walked, chanting. She came to a stop when she began to feel a strange sensation welling within her body, a euphoria. Aya'tar had felt this many times before and knew that this was the presence of the Goddess. She had seen old women jerking and convulsing with the presence of Isut, but for her, it was always a gentle feeling of bliss.

She opened her eyes and slowly gazed at all the people as she turned to let her eyes settle on one young man deep in the crowd. The young man had long dark hair with tanned skin which glistened with a light sheen of sweat from the hot night. He wore a simple leather loincloth that hung to his knees and a set of worn leather sandals. Across his chest was an upside-down triangle in the same shape as her necklace and made from the same ocher paint Aya'tar used. Many of the elders had recommended using the red rock paint, which came from a reddish rock that could be crushed and mixed with oil, but Aya'tar had always preferred the color of red ocher.

She smiled as she realized that the young man had worn that symbol and the color solely to attract her attention. Imkanar had no need to wear colors to attract her, though. She only gazed at him for just a brief moment. This dance was supposed to please the Goddess, but she was a goddess of fertility, so what could be more pleasing than also dedicating the dance to her lover? With a brief flash of a smile and a longing look, Aya'tar's body language told Imkanar that this dance was for the Goddess and for him, but no one else. She hoped Isut would not mind.

Aya'tar began to dance in wide circular twirling motions creating spiral shapes around the dance area with the fire in the center. As she danced, she recounted the story of the world's creation loudly in the form of a song. The black painted men with the bull horns slowly danced in the opposite direction, occasionally repeating what Aya'tar would say as she continued the story. Sometimes one of the men would suddenly rush toward the crowd with his bullhorns, emphasizing some portion of the story. It was quite theatrical but also taken very seriously. Aya'tar danced harder than she ever had, needing to make up for having dedicated a portion of this important dance to someone other than the Goddess. If anyone knew she had done so, the consequences would be extreme.

∋ ∋ ∋

Not far away from the place where Utiakur sat stood an older man with a goatee and mustache, Sar'Tawas. He spoke for the crafters of the city whenever decisions needed to be made. In truth, the city's leadership was split up among several important people. The position of high priest and leader of the city was more of a figurehead than a true chieftain. Like many of the other elders, Sar'Tawas had a significant say in the goings-on of Isut'na. He glanced over at Utiakur once more, wondering how much longer this great leader would live. It was very rare for a man to live to such an age, and it was very likely that he would die without a male heir.

Sar'Tawas felt some pity for the man in this respect. He also had no children, but he aimed to remedy that problem with the help of his newest acquisition. Turning his attention toward the dancing area and the young Aya'tar, Sar'Tawas considered yet again if it was time for him to make a play for the role of high priest. He had the backing of the crafters and many of the field workers. The concubine would be of use, but there was a sweeter fig on the tree. If he could simply father a child with Aya'tar, he could take over as leader and let Utiakur step down from such a tiring position.

The problem was that Aya'tar had many times in the past shown her displeasure towards his advances. It was true that he was much older than her, but did she not understand the benefits of a man of his power? As the leader of the Craft Guild, he never had to labor. He spent most of his days settling disputes between crafters and traders. He had no interest in taking away her position of power. She could dance for the Goddess all she liked, as long as she danced for him now and then. One day her father would journey to the next world, and perhaps then she would see the wisdom of his proposed union. Besides, he would be doubly happy if he could have Aya'tar and keep the concubine.

With a lascivious smile, Sar'Tawas turned his attention back towards the woman he had recently purchased from a trader. Ianmu had a strange exotic beauty about her. She was physically beautiful, and she was just a little bit heavier set than Aya'tar. That was the one thing that bothered

Sar'Tawas about Aya'tar. She spent so much time dancing for her goddess that her body was skinny. Being supple and lithe wasn't a bad thing at all, but she was just so skinny. As a result, Aya'tar was nearly the exact opposite build of the Isut figurines she worshiped each day. The irony was not lost on many.

Ianmu stood not too far to his right with a large clay jar in her arms which she had been using to serve him. Her long dark hair was tied into thin braids, and around her neck, she wore a simple leather corded necklace featuring a small feather. Many nights since her first dance with the dinner guests, she had visited him. He did not know how long it would take until she bore a son, but the effort was not without its merits. Sar'Tawas was quite sure that the coming harvest would bring some major changes, hopefully in his favor. Oddly, in the light of the fire, he noted that Ianmu actually did remind him of the Isut figurines.

Ɔ Ɔ Ɔ

Imkanar stood with everyone else and cheered the priestess as she danced around the fire, recounting the world's creation from the darkness of the previous world. He had heard the story many times before and wasn't really paying much attention to the words though the sound of her voice captivated him. His attention was mainly focused on Aya'tar's beautiful movements. They had met two harvests before when he had delivered the very copper anklets she now wore. His teacher, Kuwar, the copper worker, had created the anklets.

Imkanar was of lowly origin, having been orphaned at a young age when his mother and father were killed in a raid by the rival city of Nara'kit while working the fields. Having been raised by Kuwar's family, he had been put to work helping Kuwar and quickly learned the copper working trade. Working copper was quite uncommon, and he and Kuwar were the only two in the city who could perform this task. Besides copper, lead, gold, and silver could also be turned into beautiful treasures or useful tools. So uncommon and difficult was copper to obtain in the quantities and purity required to make tools and treasures that perhaps only a few items per harvest could be manufactured.

His attention was returned to Aya'tar as she screamed, signaling the end of the dance. As was customary, she dropped to her knees, holding the feathers out toward the stars in the sky. It was all Imkanar could do not to rush out to her right then and pull her into his embrace, but that was not to be. He was of low birth and would never be allowed to be with somebody as high in rank as the daughter of the great Isut'Sanup'ra Utiakur, so long as she remained the priestess of Isut. His only hope was that her father would sire a male child with one of the younger women this coming growing season.

A son might free Aya'tar to choose whom she wished. Until that happened, their love would have to be secret. Imkanar felt a little guilty as he thought of how many times he had prayed to Isut to let her favored priestess go. Imkanar wondered if he prayed for Utiakur to have a son more than even the great leader himself. He took a steadying breath and simply waited with anticipation as Aya'tar's two younger priestesses came to help her up off the dance ground. Even copper took time to melt and melt it would.

ↄ ↄ ↄ

The high priestess stood on weary legs. She was not that exhausted, but the exertion of dancing for as long as she had while singing took her a short time to recover from. She was helped up by the two younger priestesses Isha'kau and Hullamu. Both had deep hazel eyes and long brown hair though Hullamu's hair was lighter. What set Isha'kau apart from the pair were her intricate scarification marks placed in circles around her shoulders and running in lines down her arms. They were painful to make, but she had applied them in ritual sacrifice to the Goddess. Aya'tar and Hullamu had made the cuts themselves. Once they had healed, they were a beautiful reminder of her devotion.

Hullamu was a gabby woman abandoned at the temple when she was just a baby and raised by a close relative of Aya'tar, who was still nursing her own child. When she was old enough, she had joined the temple as an initiate priestess. She was younger than Isha'kau and not quite as good at remembering the rituals, but Aya'tar believed that one day she would make a good priestess to Isut. Hullamu spent most of her days tending to the temple and performing the basic work needed to keep things going. When she was not cleaning, she spent the rest of her time gossiping or making the large amounts of paint required for rituals.

Isha'kau was much stricter than Hullamu though she seemed to have a romantic flair, especially when it involved other people's relationships. Isha'kau was the youngest daughter of a family of leather workers. Her mother had been the ritual maiden of a fertility festival, and Isha'kau had also shown signs of Isut's blessings as a young child. As a result, she had taken on the role of an initiate priestess. It was Aya'tar's hope that

Isha'kau might take the place of the virgin avatar to Isut this coming growing season and provide her father with a male heir. Though she had brought the matter up many times with Isha'kau, the woman had never wanted to discuss it.

Aya'tar assumed that it was because Isha'kau was worried about overstepping her bounds or damaging her friendship with Aya'tar. If Isha'kau allowed the Goddess to fill her and then provided Utiakur with a son, things might become a little awkward. Isha'kau would technically become Aya'tar's almost-mother-in-law, even though she was younger. Isha'kau's son, if she had a son, would become Aya'tar's stepbrother. It was complicated, but the benefits to the city and its people far outweighed any awkwardness from the arrangement. She would have to bring up the issue again, perhaps after Isha'kau had had a few cups of the fermented honey drink.

"That was one of the most intense dances you've ever performed," Hullamu said with a slight giggle having a suspicion as to why the dance was so passionate and intense. Aya'tar gave Hullamu a sly glance, but she wasn't in the mood for talking. She had only one goal on her mind, and if a certain man got a certain message, that man was waiting for her right now in a secret room. Isha'kau handed a clay cup of the sacred fermented fruit drink to Aya'tar, who accepted it and quickly consumed the beverage.

It was tart and acidic, but that made sense considering it was made from the small fruits that grew in large bunches on vines to the Northwest. The juice from these fruits could be left in jars until it eventually fermented into a tasty drink, sped up with a little water and wheat berry mixture, and lasting a lot longer than the fruit by itself. Most importantly, it left the imbiber feeling calm and relaxed. Aya'tar handed the cup back to Isha'kau and her two feathers, then promptly left the two junior priestesses behind. She headed for an alleyway behind the main temple, where few people ever ventured. Hullamu and Isha'kau exchanged amused glances.

ↄ ↄ C

Imkanar stood in the center of a deserted building just behind the main temple absentmindedly fidgeting with the end of his loincloth as he waited nervously for his lover. Above, moths danced in the warm air. He had thought about getting a linen loincloth recently. Some of the men in the field had told him that they were much more comfortable than leather.

The real trick was getting a strong two-ply fabric. The older the woman who made it, the better quality it would be... His mind was wandering as he waited impatiently.

The building where he now waited had been used to store large pots full of grain as well as water. The food stores had recently been cleaned out so the walls could be re-plastered. This meant that, for at least tonight, this room would be completely empty, and no one would expect to find anyone here. Finding a place where two could be unseen was a precious gift in a city where everyone lived so close to each other. Through the doorway and a small window, light from a nearby fire meant to illuminate the dance area filtered into the room, filling it with a gentle flickering orange glow. Suddenly, the light drifting through the doorway was blocked. Imkanar quickly turned to see who the intruder was.

The silhouette before him bore the unmistakable shape of a woman. After a few moments, his eyes accounted for the darkness, and the powerful form of Aya'tar came into view. Her hair and her eyes were as black as a starless night, and her smile was wide and welcoming. Aya'tar's body was covered from top to bottom with a glistening sheen of sweat from her dance causing her body paints to run, but Imkanar did not care. Sweat did not smell good, but somehow her smell was sweet to him. He began to reach forward to embrace his lover, but she pushed his hand aside and motioned for him to sit on the small goatskin blanket he had placed on the floor.

For a moment, she stood there watching him sit. Forging copper was a laborious pursuit which left his arms tight and solid, as though made from stone, and his body, lean and defined. His own sheen of sweat caught the firelight reflecting off his tight skin. As he sat and looked back, his dark eyes regarded her with such open anticipation that she felt her self-esteem spike. He wanted her, and there wasn't anything masked in his expression. While he was so enticing to look upon, his so blatant desire for her felt intoxicating. She wanted nothing more than to slip into his arms, yet she had greater plans... a temptation for them both.

"My love, I still feel a little of the Goddess within me. It would not be proper for us to continue until I have satisfied her. Let me dance for you, my Imkanar," she whispered. Aya'tar took a deep breath, preparing herself to move once more. Her vision was still a bit blurry, and she felt a little dizzy. The fermented drink felt warm in her belly and took away some of the pain in her feet, the result of dancing on the hard ground. Her heart pounded, and her mouth was dry, but it had been a long night. Imkanar sat back against the wall of the little room with a smile on his face. There were some things that power and privilege simply could not afford. He may not own much, but he was the richest man in all Isut'na tonight.

Aya'tar slowly danced around the room in delicate circles, much like the greater dance. In a low, whispered voice, she sang her spells and songs. As she slowly twirled around the room, she let her excitement build. The smells of the wheat and the scent of oils filled her nose while the warm night air drifted across her skin, bringing with it the existential epiphany of Isut's grace. She wasn't just a woman dancing before the man she loved, longing for his closeness, his warmth – she was the mortal vessel of the fertility goddess who created the world, quite literally. The thought of her power and the effect she was having on Imkanar sent waves of warmth through her body, an arousal she could hardly control. Yet, she would hold her composure until she broke, dedicating her struggle to the Goddess.

Imkanar marveled as the warm firelight danced off her damp skin, sending faint shadows dancing around the room. The muscles in her legs flexed, their vital definition so clear in the soft light of the fire. Her body flowed with the essence of femininity as she dominated the room. She wasn't just a woman. She was the agent of Isut, the body of the Goddess made manifest. So exhilarated was Imkanar as he watched the dance that he felt the Goddess' presence in the room and began to feel the spirit of the bull within him – he felt himself becoming Gunar, the mighty bull.

"And the world was a barren field. Isut lay in wait until the mighty Gunar, great bull of the West, came upon her. She lay naked, her body was the world. He despaired that she would be so baren. Gunar toiled for seven days and nights until he had sown his seed of life. Then, with a cry, Isut brought forth the trees, the birds, the fish, and animals…" she sang as she danced. Her apron had fallen to the wayside, yet her naked skin still burned with the heat of her exertion. She danced on and on as she recited the story of the world's creation, bare before Imkanar.

"From her body, the waters of the world flowed…" She had become so excited by the dance that she failed to consider the powerful fertility magic involved in the very words she spoke. It was as though the Goddess were taking control of her body. Before her sat Imkanar, his own garment cast aside. She could see his interest, and she could feel his presence. He was a man who appeared possessed by the spirit of Gunar. An inner voice cried out to stop… that she had initiated the great fertility festival's highest ritual at the wrong time and place, and yet her body was too far gone. Sometimes, one couldn't smell sweet fruit without a taste, though to invoke this ritual in this way was a forbidden fruit.

The penalty if she were caught performing such a ritual during the wrong time, and improperly initiated, would be death. She was the next in line after her father to perform the ritual and she knew how it was done, yet here she was breaking the rules. Imkanar, turned Gunar, should have prepared for seven days, and where were his horns? If the gods took affront to her acts, they might strike her down for it, but she felt the passion of Isut, the same lust that had created the world. She wouldn't stop until she had gone all the way… but hopefully, not too far.

All her fears and apprehensions disappeared as the sweat beaded off her skin, the inner voice dying in the heat of the warm season. As she looked closer, she saw bull horns emerging from Imkanar's head, his mighty body lying in wait. Aya'tar, now possessed by Isut, stepped forward and knelt to join with him. Together, they completed the ritual without care of being overheard. As she felt her desires filled, Aya'tar began to sing the invocation of Gunar the mighty bull, a powerful spell meant for the highest fertility ceremony when the high priest was joined with a maiden. But tonight, Imkanar would be her high priest, and she would be his maiden, she would be Isut, the maiden of the barren world. Tonight, he would be the bull. He would sow the seeds of the world. Tonight, she would not act upon thought but instead upon her most basic needs. She hoped the Goddess would not mind. After all, she was a fertility goddess...

> *Isut, Isut, the winged maiden of the stars so bright,*
> *Gunar, Gunar, the bull of the fields whose horns so fright!*
> *Isut, Isut, the maiden who becomes a mother soon,*
> *Gunar, Gunar, the mighty bull, and maiden's delight!*

CHAPTER FIFTEEN

ALL OR NOTHING

Throughout much of recorded history, fertility festivals and fertility deities have been regarded as extremely important to many societies from nearly every part of the world. The underlying cause behind this importance is the simple evolutionary drive to reproduce, while the festive and religious manifestation results from the belief that human actions can either directly or indirectly, usually with the help of a deity, affect the likelihood and outcome of this reproduction. Fertility and reproduction are also related to a fertile world full of plants, game, and other foodstuffs. Fertility means new life from the womb, and plentiful food from the lands, therefore, life-and-death. Beyond simply celebrating fertility and a possible, and supposed mechanism, for altering its outcome, major festivals also provided an opportunity for various peoples, regionally, to meet and exchange ideas and trade.

Ember and her foster family had arrived at the festival grounds before the Sun was at its midway point. The grounds were located in the floodplain of a piece of land that jutted slightly from the mainland. It was about half the distance between where she had been recovering and where the Isen'bryn had settled to become the Blue Sea People. The trip had taken three days, but the walking had been easy enough, though hot. The weather had remained warm and had forced Ember to either cover herself with a large basket-woven reed hat or use dried mud to keep her skin from burning. Her foster family had a more tanned, olive-colored skin and did not seem to have the same troubles she had, though her own skin was reasonably tanned. Over time, her skin would darken and be less affected, but it had not quite been long enough for such a change.

The gap in her memory had been a cause of concern for Ember. She could now remember more of her hunt for Kyra and Galar, as well as discovering that Galar had died. She even had a strange feeling in the back of her mind that Kyra had been dealt with and perhaps had even been at fault in some way. Everything became extremely dicey whenever she tried to remember anything from that night. Now and then, strange images would appear in her mind, such as a large feast and a woman being carried on the shoulders of a man. Ember guessed that she had left Aethen to perform some solo task, and he had simply returned to the tribe by himself. Whenever she thought about the safety of her friends, she always got the feeling that they were all right. How could she possibly know that? None of it made much sense, but she supposed she would get her answers when she returned to the Blue Sea People following the festival.

Ember missed Brig'dha most of all. If she could have returned earlier, she would have, but her dizzy spells and wounded arm would have made her nearly defenseless by herself. It had not been broken but perhaps overextended or sprained. Whatever the cause, it had taken many tendays to heal. Ember now felt confident in its strength, but she had waited to return just a short time longer so that she could attend the festival. She felt like she owed Ketamir and Nemanar for their kindness, and helping them bring their tent and supplies to the festival would be a step toward repaying that. Besides, she hoped that she might find a gift she could trade something for to help appease Brig'dha when she returned. Perhaps a golden pendant, like the one Kis'tra had worn? She expected that she would be heavily chastised, and she knew she deserved it.

Brig'dha was the only person on her mind, and she had decided that she would bring up something that had been bothering her for a long time. Ever since she was a child, Ember had not felt right with the way men and women were joined by the tribe. She had taken part in teasing the boys and had even chased after them with her friends, but it all felt like an act. It felt like she was simply performing the motions because they were expected. After all, there was really no other choice. Whenever she noticed someone who interested her, it was always the wrong kind of person. She began to panic a little at what she had planned to say when she returned to her people. Ember quickly pushed those thoughts from her mind and returned to thoughts of the festival. It wouldn't do to worry before it was time to worry.

The strangest thing had happened when the group had passed the large village of Koneh, west of where she had been staying. Koneh had a massive wooden palisade that surrounded it and had been built right on the edge of cliffs overlooking the water. It looked like a beautiful little village, but Ember felt apprehension as they passed it for some strange reason. She had been glad when Ketamir, the fisherman, had chosen not to stop, insisting on a slightly more direct route. Why that village, which she had never been to, disturbed her, she could not say. *Such a beautiful village... and only slightly creepy*, she had mused at the time to banish the worry. But now, she was finally at the festival ground and ready for fun.

Clearing her mind of the jaunting journey, creepy Koneh, beautiful Brig'dha, and all the other worries she had to deal with later, Ember turned her sights to the festival grounds before her. She stretched her muscles in preparation for what she would do later that night. Ember loved dancing, and she was already excited at the prospect of seeing so many beautiful costumes and eating all the tasty food which always accompanied festivals. Before she could do anything, she would need to help unpack and set up the tents.

The festival grounds were quite vast, and hundreds of people had already arrived from various tribes. A similar festival occurred close to where Ember grew up, every few harvests. Many places held them to allow people to exchange ideas and find partners. These sorts of events were extremely important to the entire region. They were the basis for the formation of many trade routes and the exchange of new crafting techniques and other forms of interchange. Perhaps most importantly, they were the best place to find a spouse beyond one's own tribe.

Ember gazed across the open fields seeing the vast array of people arriving. She could not even see the faces of the people on the other side of the festival grounds, so far away were they. In the center, a vast dance area had been set up and was now being picked clean of rocks and debris by small children while their parents stood and talked. To the South, traders flaunted their wares. To the North, where Ember's group was headed, food had been prepared communally. Most people seemed to Ember to be of the same basic appearance and culture. However, her own foster family looked a little different from the locals, as though they came from a different location.

Nemanar and her son, Gel'nar, began to set up a small leather tent on the northern grounds while Ketamir met with the elders in charge of the event to offer salted fish for the feast. Ketamir attended the festival every few harvests for trade and general news. This time, he hoped that his daughter Ninrea'mu would get a good feel for the people and what was to be expected. He would bring her here in two harvests time, hoping that she might find a good man. She was not quite ready to find a mate, but this chance would give her the upper hand of experience. He had left Ninrea'mu under the watchful eye of Ember, a woman whom he had come to rely upon.

Ketamir respected Ember both as a good person and in her abilities as a hunter. He thought of her more like a man than a traditional woman in many ways. The distinction between sexes and genders was quite stark in most northern cultures. Chores, religious activities, and general cultural attitudes divided the genders, so men, women, and other genders did not share many activities. It was extremely uncommon to find anyone who stepped out of this norm. The split between genders was less defined in the South, with a more egalitarian lifestyle being accepted. Unfortunately, Ember was a woman from the North.

Physically, she was very feminine with an athletic, female form and dazzling waist-length red hair. The difference was in her personality. She enjoyed more traditionally male-oriented activities, such as hunting and exploring. Ketamir felt a little guilty about the way he thought of her. Judging her as though she were a woman who acted like a man made him feel awkward, as though he were raising her value to that of a man, a backhanded compliment. He had decided that it was best to think of her as just Ember.

She simply was unlike anyone he had met, not quite man nor woman. They had journeyed together into the wilds on several occasions to hunt deer. Ember was surprisingly good at hunting, once her arm had healed, more often than not killing a large prize animal when Ketamir could find nothing. He didn't mind the competition, and his wife seemed to find it ever so amusing. It was always refreshing to see a woman breaking the traditional gender bonds, though many men would not see it the way he did. The most curious aspect of the woman was that she had washed ashore fully armed like some sort of warrior dressed for battle, yet wounded and broken – perhaps a casualty the spirits of war had chosen not to claim?

When he had found her, she had an obsidian dagger tied at her waist and a bow and quiver attached to her back. The bow and quiver had been lashed with flax cord, the only reason they had not come loose. She had worn a simple loincloth with no leggings or anything heavier than a light leather shirt, which had probably saved her life in the water. She had likely swum to shore extremely delirious and bleeding from her head, and the extra weight would have killed her. More strangely, she had been painted rather crudely from head to toe in black soot paint. She looked more like a woman dressed for battle than some lost maiden.

What was most impressive were the two items that she carried which were not like any other he had seen. Around her neck, she had worn a beautiful amber pendant, larger than any he had seen and with a tiny and delicate flower forever suspended in the frozen honey-like material. If that wasn't impressive enough, the large blue crystal in her traveling pouch most certainly was. Larger than a balled fist, it was a marvel that it had not been lost in the water. Everything about the woman struck him as bizarre, but in time, he realized that she was not like most people. He hated to think that she would leave after the festival, but he would not dare stand in the way of somebody a strong-willed as Ember.

She did not seem to remember the days just before she was found, but her memories from before that time had come back almost immediately when the fogginess of her mind had left. She had not mentioned any husband though she was certainly of the age to have one. Ketamir hoped that she would find someone at the festival though he would hate to lose her. Whenever he held his beloved Nemanar, it filled him with a sense of purpose. He hoped that Ember would find such a purpose. To that end, he had asked Nemanar and Ninrea'mu to decorate Ember as elaborately as they could. It would give Ninrea'mu ideas for what she would wear when her time came and also give Ember the best hope of attracting a good man, a man worthy of such a woman. Offhandedly, he wondered if he might start bringing his daughter when he hunted. Perhaps she might also grow to enjoy hunting?

ɔ ɔ ɔ

The festival lasted two whole days, with the first day's night being the most important. It was still early in the day, and the tent had already been prepared. Ember and Ninrea'mu had already toured most of the vendors a short while before. Young Gel'nar played with several of the other younger children nearby the tent while Ketamir unpacked the fish leather he hoped to trade at the event. Ember stepped into the small family tent to find Ninrea'mu and her mother Nemanar eyeing her intently. She raised an eyebrow at their predatory looks.

They planned to do something, and she realized that she was the target. Ember was lying on a mat being carefully cleaned and prepared a few moments later. Nemanar was enjoying the vicarious action of preparing Ember for the event. She was too old for such things, but Ember was a valued companion and full of youth. This was like an appetizer for Nemanar. She would soon be preparing her own daughter for the festival and possibly marriage. Among their many roles, nitpicking and matchmaking were some of a mother's most important.

Ninrea'mu was absolutely mesmerized by the notion of decorating Ember to become as beautiful as possible. Of all the games she liked to play, dress-up was number one on the list. She carefully combed Ember's long red hair with a four-tooth bone comb and then tied small, tight braids separated by varying distances. The majority of Ember's hair would be left long and free, but a few thin braids here and there would add to her appeal. Next, she tied small songbird feathers throughout Ember's hair using tiny pieces of sinew. Ember simply lay back and let it happen. There was no arguing with them, and she couldn't help but nearly drool with pleasure as her hair was played with. She always loved the feel of somebody messing with her hair.

When her hair was completed, it was time for the body paints. Mother and daughter worked relentlessly applying the paints made from nut oil and twice burned bone ash, much darker than soot. They each chanted the same song as they worked. It sounded like a prayer to some goddess known as "An-an." Ember sat perfectly still and faced down on her stomach as they meticulously painted her back. She could probably attract a whole tribe of men by the time they finished with her, but there was only one person she had wanted to dance with tonight. Unfortunately, that wasn't to be, at least not until she returned to the Blue Sea People.

The feelings that she had were not common among women or men, but they were known to happen from time to time, perhaps one in twenty. Normally, a man fell in love with a woman, and a woman fell in love with a man. Yet love was a much more complicated emotion than most people realized. In her time spent traveling through the wilds, Ember had met so many different people that she had come to realize that what one group considered normal, another would find bizarre. She had met tribes where sacrificing people was commonplace and not considered particularly wrong. Still, she grew up in a tribe where the very thought of human sacrifice would be considered the vilest of acts. Ember had truly become pluralistic, embracing or, at least, understanding the differences between many different types of people. More impressively, she had broken the boundaries of her gender in a misogynistic world through her deeds. Ember believed life was what you made of it – though she was still not entirely sure what to make of hers.

She had seen so many people die, but she had seen so few people live. Most people did what they were told and followed the rules outlined by their culture. If they were told something was wrong, then it simply was. No thought need be applied. No… she had something left to do in this life, and she was going to do it. She had a person she need to speak her feelings to, and to the depths of the Greatest River with anyone who stood in her way. There had been something that she had wanted to say for a while now, something she felt so deeply about that her chest ached to think of it. She would dance tonight and let herself go, for when she returned to the people of the Blue Sea, she would speak her truth. Whatever happened, happened.

"May the spirits strike with lightning anyone who stands in my way," she whispered… it would be all or nothing.

☽ ☽ ☽

Aethen stood on a hilltop on the Western grounds of the festival area. All around him, hundreds of people gathered preparing for the night's festivities. The Sun was over halfway across the sky, and the Moon had recently risen in the East. The Moon was hard to see in the daylight, but he could tell it was nearly full. According to Brig'dha, who kept a keen eye on the positions of the Moon, it would remain in the sky for nearly half of the night. Most people would be ready for sleep by the time it set. The festival grounds had been chosen because the Moon would rise and set so that it was not obscured by the mountains and trees that dotted the landscape. Aethen was quite impressed by the amount of thought that had gone into planning such an event, but people like Brig'dha would spend their whole lives learning the phases of the Moon.

Their group had no tent to prepare though some other groups had arrived similarly. Some tribes brought dozens of members and set up quite sophisticated little makeshift camps. This was turning into the largest event that Aethen had ever seen. Beside him, Brig'dha sat carefully applying paint to her body with little enthusiasm. Behind her, Espe and Kel were setting up bedrolls made of leather as well as the rest of their supplies. Theft during such a large event might be a concern, yet another one was finding a place to sleep after a night of dancing.

Aethen and Kel had painted each other with intricate patterns of lines that hashed one way and then the other as they rose up their bodies. Both men wore simple leather loincloths and sandals, though nudity would be commonplace during such an event. It was certainly the end of the warm season, but the air was still warm enough at night for such garb, and they planned to work up a sweat dancing. Aethen and Kel wore their hair in long braids down their backs in the way of their people. It was long known that the Horned God appreciated men wearing their hair in braids, while the Goddess preferred that women let their hair fly free, like the wind. An older man whose hair was still long might even put it up in a bun, but Kel and Aethen were far too young for such decoration.

They had brought some items for trade to obtain a place at the feast for the night. Brig'dha had produced several sewn mittens, a small fur hat, and several simple bone beads. These were common things, but they would trade for a few days' worth of rations and a good portion of food for the feast. Aethen and Kel felt a little bad for not bringing anything while Brig'dha had made these objects, but they had put their backs into hard work at the tribe where they had stayed. It all balanced out in the end.

Brig'dha was feeling somewhat dour as the Sun sank lower in the sky. Creating paint wasn't very complicated, but she had little in the way of festival clothing or much inspiration in paint designs. She was simply depressed. Even Mew had shown himself at the edge of the wood, and promptly ran off when people approached. She doubted she would see him until after the festival. In many ways she envied the cat and his life of freedom from the rules of people.

She wore her simple leather wrap, though she was considering removing it. At a fertility festival like this, covering up was not the goal. Ember would have worn something amazing on a night like this, something that would make everyone's mother blush. Brig'dha felt a terrible loss as the thought crossed her mind. Ember would have known what to wear. Brig'dha had decided that she would dance this night in her memory and then move on. She couldn't spend the rest of her life in regret, though she had a feeling that she might. If only she could have heard what it was that Ember had said before she jumped. Deep down, she suspected that she knew... perhaps had always known.

Suddenly, a bundle of strings landed in Brig'dha's lap and startled her from her thoughts. At first, she was momentarily aggravated, her emotional mask undone, but then she became thankful that her darkness had been temporarily banished. She looked up to find Espe standing over her. The woman was absolutely gorgeous. Her long hair had been tied into little braids, dozens of them, at varying lengths using tiny pieces of sinew. Her skin had an incredible paint job made of red hand-prints which covered her entire body. It was an extremely creative design and would probably not be seen on any other woman. As Brig'dha stared in confusion, Espe held up her hands, showing her red palms. Behind her, Brig'dha noticed that Kel also had red palms.

Her feet were bare, but she wore flower garlands around both ankles, her wrists, neck, and even her head. The flower garlands probably wouldn't last the night, but, judging by how fertility festivals normally unfolded, they were not likely supposed to. Around her waist, she wore an apron-like drape made from nettle fibers with flowers tied all the way down. The back of the apron would normally be completely open, but she had looped a small strip of soft leather hanging down the back to keep her backside covered. Overall, her outfit was about as revealing as something

Ember might wear. It made sense as she was technically still courting Kel. She wondered if Kel would be able to control himself the entire night with such a beauty dancing exclusively for him. Brig'dha was suddenly jealous of their love, and she felt ashamed of it.

Looking into her lap, she lifted the most bizarre creation. The item was a simple bark fiber woven belt with strings hanging down the front and back, knee length. This was certainly something not to be worn during the day and possibly one of the most revealing outfits she had seen. This was the sort of thing Brig'dha needed on a night like this. She needed a rebirth, the renewal of her feminine energy, and this was exactly the kind of garment she needed to wear. She looked up at Espe, who smiled back at her.

"Eusbuh," she said, using one of the several words Espe's people used to mean *thank you.* As she gazed at the beautiful garment, a profound notion came across her. This was her last night to dwell on the memories of Ember before she cast them aside and moved on with her life, and she would go all the way. She would not devote this dance to the memory of Ember... she would dance as Ember. She grabbed her bowl of black paint and the string garment and left for the trees where she might be alone to prepare. The rest of the group watched her go with some confusion at her sudden impetus but hoping she would return and have a good time.

Ↄ Ↄ C

The Moon rose in the Southeast when the Sun had set. Ember emerged from the hut just as the last red glow faded. Ketamir turned to see how good of a job his wife and daughter had done, but he had to step back at what he saw. Ember's waist-length red hair had many tiny braids at various lengths, and small songbird feathers tied all the way down. Her body bore tiny little lines all the way around, running horizontally. Each line was actually a series of very small dots perfectly drawn. In between the lines, circles had been painted representing the faces of the Moon going all the way around each arm, leg, and her body. It had taken the entire evening and both mother and daughter to apply this complexity of body paint.

Ketamir was stunned at the detail. Ember's face had been covered with the same beautiful designs. In the center of her forehead was a full Moon with a crescent Moon painted in each of the four quadrants around it. Around her arms and ankles, she wore many beaded bracelets, while around her neck, she wore six leather cord necklaces with various beads and various lengths. The centerpiece hung between her breasts, the large Amber of Life necklace. Otherwise, she was wholly nude. Ketamir suddenly wished he were young again. Tonight, some man would know the embrace of a goddess. Ember was so decorated that she didn't even look like herself unless he stood very close and carefully regarded her, so complex was her body paint.

His wife Nemanar blushed as she stepped from the hut and saw the expression on his face, but she really couldn't hold it against him. He loved her too deeply to ever leave her, and she couldn't help but feel pride that part of his reaction was her handiwork. Besides, she had to admit that Ember truly was a thing of beauty. Young Ninrea'mu's eyes beamed with admiration. She had made it very clear to her mother that this was how she wished to look in two harvests time. The only apprehension Nemanar had to this plan was that in two harvest time, when her daughter arrived looking like Ember did now, a man would quickly take her away. It was the way of things, and she would not deprive her daughter of such pleasures. Instead, she would use this event and watching Ember fall into some lover's arms to ready herself for what would come. It was the will of An'an that lovers find each other.

Nemanar caught her son Gel'nar hiding behind their tent and staring intently. He was still young, and she was unsure if he stared in amazement or because he was slowly becoming a young man. Either way, if it had that kind of an effect on him, it should just about rip the heart from the chest of a mighty hunter. She smiled, positioning herself between Gel'nar and Ember simply to be mischievous.

A short time later Ember and Ninrea'mu left the tent and headed for the dance area, which had just been ritualistically purified by a group of priests and priestesses. Young Ninrea'mu wore a beautiful, beaded leather skirt with ample necklaces. Given her age, it was designed to be pretty but not particularly showy. Younger children would dance on the outside while the adults danced on the inside. As things became a little more heated, the children would be sent to sleep. The adults would eventually follow though not all of them would make it back to their tents. Normally, the woods were not the safest place for two lovers to disappear into, but the level of commotion, fires, and people patrolling the woods meant that there would not be a wolf within a day's travel.

Ɔ Ɔ Ɔ

Ul'na'har, the high priest of the village of Koneh, arrived with his eldest son Ul'uer and his daughters Kenis and Vestra. They were accompanied by nearly three dozen members of their village. Ul'na'har was getting old, and he knew that this might be his last trip to the festival. His hip had finally stopped hurting him after that troubling spirit woman had thrown him to the ground all those moons before. During his time recuperating, his son Ul'uer had slowly taken over most of his priestly duties and would likely replace him when the time came. Some men would fight to the bitter end and never let their children excel past them, but Ul'na'har was not such a man. After so many long harvests having the entire health of the tribe laid upon him, he was glad to let his son take the reins. Perhaps he would be guided by his young but knowledgeable sister, Kenis. Neither his son nor daughters had been wounded by the spirit woman though Kenis had been punched pretty hard in the stomach.

He smiled as he considered his walking staff. The staff had allowed him to take the weight off his wounded hip, making the burden of walking much easier. At the top of the staff where his hand would rest, the arm bone of a human had been attached. The bone had been intricately carved with magical symbols, but what truly made it a blessed item was that it came from the arm of his willing sacrifice, killed not so long before. With her blood poured across the fields, they were sure to have a good harvest.

Fertility festivals, such as this, were a great place to meet and greet those of power and influence. This would be a good chance for his daughters to find men of purpose, important young men who could be brought back to their village. As a result, both women wore elegant outfits made of raven feathers and shells, while his son wore a plain linen loincloth as he already had a wife and child back at the tribe. Ul'na'har suspected that his daughters would have a good time, and perhaps even his son might loosen up a little.

ɔ ɔ ɔ

Brig'dha stepped from the woods, depression, anxiety, and exhilaration racing up and down her body. Her emotions at this point could be described as confusing, but she would see this night through. She stopped just outside the tree line and looked to the South at the Moon. It was nearly full, and it bathed her in light. She and Ember would stare at the Moon on nights like this. She held her hands out to the Moon, hoping the Goddess might channel some of Ember's spirit through her. She felt a strange tingly sensation throughout her body and attributed it to the Goddess, a feeling reinforced by the presence of so many moths and flying insects as they darted about the edge of the woods.

Tonight, she would be clothed in paint, wearing only a simple bark fiber string skirt she had received as a gift from Espe. She had painted her entire body completely black, even coloring her hair black with soot. Using water from the stream, she delicately placed dozens of little stars across her body, simply removing the soot on her skin to make them. She stood under a starry sky, looking up at the Moon and hoping to channel the spirit of her dead friend. Around her neck, the goddess pendant hung as the only other object adorning her body. She felt strangely liberated, though a bit risqué. Surprisingly, standing there painted from head to toe left her in an almost altered state. It was as though she were no longer the priestess Brig'dha, and instead, an empty vessel waiting to be filled with the spirits from beyond.

This empty vessel had one spirit she wished to invoke, one persona she wanted to take on. Abandoning the usual complex dances and invocations, she took a more direct approach. Looking toward the Moon, she screamed as loudly as she could in her native language.

"Kaelu Kree'yeh!!!"
Ember, where are you?

ᴐ ᴐ ᴐ

Ember gazed toward the Moon, which had risen to the Southeast. Oddly, she thought that she briefly caught sight of a small wildcat in the woods, but it quickly vanished before she got a good look. In the sky, the glowing disk all but called to her, screaming her name like a warrior's cry… demanding that she act. She would heed that call and dance like the Goddess of the Moon until she collapsed from exhaustion. The next morning, she would return to the Blue Sea People and seek out the person she loved; the one she had loved for so long yet couldn't bring herself to tell. This had gone on long enough, and she would speak her true feelings regardless of the cost. Tonight, she would focus her dance to the Goddess of the Moon asking for her blessing, using the mass ritual for her own purpose. She had nearly died, yet now she was restored. This dance would mark her rebirth – the end of her old fears and the start of something new, Goddess willing. With an excited smile, Ember faced the Moon and screamed her invocation for the world to hear.

Goddess of the Moon, show me your light!
If the answer is no, I will lose a friend.
If the answer is yes, I will gain everything!
I beg you, make that answer yes!
It is all or nothing...

It was a bit sappy, and it sounded more like a demand than a prayer, but Ember didn't care. This dance of rebirth was the start of a chain of events that she had planned that would lead either to an ultimate love or a final rejection, always a risk when love was confessed. But she was a warrior, and such terrible risk was part of that, and she would face her fears as a warrior should. Tonight, she would dance and let completely loose, all inhibitions lost. She would dedicate all of this to the Goddess of the Moon, hoping that she would be led to the one she loved and who waited for her back in the village of the Blue Sea People. *I hope she's not still mad I ran off...*

◡ ◡ ◡

Kel and Espe danced into the firelight, a huge raging inferno towering two and a half times the height of a man. Strong men had carried massive logs and propped them into a large pile. Near the main fire, the second humongous log fire stood ready to be ignited when the main fire burned down. Nothing would stop the event, not even rain, though the night looked absolutely clear, and the sky was gorgeous with more stars than could be counted.

Espe danced circles around the fire, her flowery apron catching the air while her hair spun in circles around her body. She excitedly danced around the fire disappearing into the mass of people, only to return from the other side a short time later. Many other young men were dancing with Espe, as many women danced around Kel. This was to be expected and even encouraged. However, no matter who danced with them, the two lovers would again meet in the end. The event had a component of random chaos and ordered discipline, not unlike a river.

When Ember stepped into the firelight, quite a significant number of eyes trained on her. She began to spin in circles, her hands high above her head and a song from her Great River People on her tongue. The music was loud, and many different songs were sung simultaneously, but all to the same basic cadence. Most songs could be adapted to fit whatever beats were available so dancers and musicians would not interfere with one

275

another. Ember's hair flew through the air as she spun, with its long strands flying high in the night. Many marveled at the beautiful Moon shapes decorating her body as she began to dance. Faster and faster she spun, slowly working herself into a frenzy. Excitement filled her veins, and goosebumps crossed her skin, the vitality of the night outright intoxicating.

ↄ ↄ ↄ

Close by, Espe danced past a man who was oiled from top to bottom and then passed another man who had been decorated with strange, striped patterns which covered his body. Some of the art made her laugh, while other designs caught her eye and kept her in place for a short time. Nearby, she watched two men flirting with each other, one dressed as a deer and the other as a hunter. She watched them for a moment, until the "deer-man" bounded off into the darkness, pursued by his "hunter."

As she danced around the fire, she felt her excitement building like the raging fires. When she finally finished this dance, she would find Kel and make sure he knew her exact intentions. He would be forever hers. Espe's thoughts were briefly interrupted as she circled around the vast fire when she nearly bumped into a gorgeous woman with long red hair, her body painted in intricate moons. Espe danced an entire circle around the woman, simply amazed at the detail of her paint. Of course, she was a little envious, and she would have to make sure Kel didn't venture too close to such a woman. She doubted that she had anything to worry about, but competition was competition.

ↄ ↄ ↄ

Ember watched a younger woman dance a single orbit around her, obviously jealous of her moon paint. Her entire body was clad in red handprints. *Flashy,* she thought, quite impressed, though she knew her moons were yet to be outdone. This festival and the dancers' costumes so vastly outdid anything she had ever seen at her tribe's dances. Some of the clothing even more impressive than the glorious apron she had worn the night that she became a woman. After a single orbit, the younger woman danced away purposefully. Ember supposed that she would take up a position on the other side of the fire. It would not do to have two beautiful women in such close proximity, as they would do nothing but compete. She laughed loudly at the arbitrary absurdity of it all.

ɔ ɔ ɔ

After a short time, a second fire was lit, and the dancing area had swelled to nearly two hundred people. Music played loudly into the night as Brig'dha approached the fire. Her heart pounded, yet her mind was almost numb. This was her rebirth, a liminal demarcation when she would let go of the old and move forward with the new. It was a strange mix of exhilaration, sadness, and allure, and it was absolutely intoxicating, driving away her normal dislike of so many people… as long as no one touched her. As she stepped into the firelight, dozens of people turned to see her fabulous design, with far too many eyes for her comfort. Brig'dha looked like the very night sky – a woman adorned in a blanket of stars. She was an incarnation of the night, so dark and lonely, even in the face of so many. She was darkness without her moon.

Flinging her hands free, Brig'dha began the mournful swinging dance of her people. She sang a funerary song of love and loss, her words of passing flowing into the night sky, hoping the spirits of the stars or the Goddess of the Moon would carry her funerary prayers through the night to the beyond. Her song was her emotion, and her dance was a plea to the spirits of the dead. It was an invocation of Ember's spirit for a final dance among the memories and essence that had been her friend... whom she had hoped might become so much more… This was the conclusion. This was her funeral dance – a votive offering to be consumed, forever.

Tears began to streak her face as she chanted the death rites for the woman who had saved her twice and given her life in the process. Her dance was one of death, and her words and her movements were unlike any other dance, spoken to the very gods without reservation. Hers was a song of loss, a wail of mourning, a plea of want, and the resignation of a love which could never be. Her mask was undone, and the raw emotion called upon everyone nearby to hear her plea, though they did not understand the words. It was not long until many were dancing around her, simply listening to the emotive and beautiful chant, some moved to tears while most simply listened.

Nearby, Aethen danced with two identically painted women when he saw Brig'dha stepping into the dance area. As she began to chant, a lump caught in the man's throat as the worlds of a rite of death filled the night. The singing and music drowned most of them, but Aethen knew the missing words far too well. Worse, he knew who they were for. As he listened, Espe spiraled her way past him and danced a full circuit around

Brig'dha, taking in her friend's amazing, if not ad hoc painted body designs.

"Go get 'em, priestess!" she yelled, though Brig'dha didn't understand her words as Espe danced away laughing, entirely missing the crying woman's expression through the clutter of people.

ɔ ɔ ɔ

The identical twin priestesses Kenis and Vestra both danced together, as they usually did, the pair nearly inseparable. They had decided that they would either both find men this night or not at all, neither willing to be alone while the other took a lover. As they danced, they pointed out various possible candidates, men of good standing or who at least looked to be of good standing. Suddenly, Kenis caught sight of the woman with long red hair and Moons covering her athletic body. As the woman glided past, she gazed at each twin for just a moment. Kenis could not help but feel that she had seen the woman before, but she couldn't recall from where. She was distracted a moment later when a smaller woman danced by her in a figure-eight, circling both women and then dancing off. The strange woman was covered in red handprints. Kenis shook her head and tried desperately to remember where she had seen the long-haired redhead before... the sudden realization struck her like a fist to the stomach... again.

"Vestra! The spirit woman is back!" she said to her sister in horror. Her stomach began to ache at the very thought of the water spirit.

ɔ ɔ ɔ

Ember danced closer and closer to the fire, the heat dancing off her naked skin as her ecstasy roared to life. When someone danced long enough and with enough conviction, they could enter a trance-like state, a state Ember was rapidly approaching. She held her hands high above her head and rotated her hips at an alarmingly fast rate causing everyone around her to watch in amazement. Nearly two harvests spent hiking all over the known world had done much to leave Ember's body in an athletic condition. She was simply nimbler and held a higher endurance than most others at the dance. She had become so much stronger than the young woman who had left her tribe those long moons before, both in mind and body. This realization struck her as her dance of rebirth continued.

The faster she went, the more detached from reality she felt. Sweat began to drip down her face as she gyrated her hips in a circle while her body rotated in the opposite direction, all the while she danced a vast circle around the fire. Three circles occurring at the same time. When she was younger, she could not have held such a dance for long, but tonight the Goddess of the Moon seemed to fill her as sweat ran down her body. She only hoped she would not become dizzy and accidentally fall into the fire, turning her rebirth into a cremation. Ember laughed aloud at the notion though she probably should take it more seriously.

All around spun a dizzying blur of people dancing and chanting. Men danced by her wearing intricate masks painted with complex shapes and adorned with feathers, while women wailed into the night, their bodies painted from head to toe in a dazzling display of colors and designs. Some people had even come in animal costumes. Dancing around the fire, she saw a woman wearing an entire set of bird feathers attached to her arms, resembling a bird. Behind her, a man stalked by wearing the skin of a wolf and taking on the persona of the very creature. It was as though the spirits of nature filled the dancers. She even saw a woman standing fully painted while her child lay comfortably in her arms, drinking its fill of milk, every stage of life represented before the fire.

☽ ☽ ☽

As Aethen danced in close proximity to Brig'dha, he continued to listen to her mournful song. Aethen's chest ached at the subject of her pleas to the night. He, too, had lost a friend and someone he had hoped would become so much more. Life was short, yet how precious were love and friendship to create such pain? As he listened to Brig'dha's chant, he let go of what could not be and began to think of what might become. He wasn't sure where he would find love, but he decided at that moment that he would take whatever steps were required to achieve what Kel and Espe had. His thoughts of pain were interrupted when a beautiful redheaded woman danced into view, her body soaked with sweat. Something about her was strangely familiar.

☽ ☽ ☽

A woman painted from head to toe in Moons drifted from around the other side of the fire. Her arms and body rotated to dance to a rhythm known only to her. She was detached from the other dancers, a spirit

279

locked within her own world. The fire and the moon's light danced off her wet skin as sweat gently rolled down her painted body. The strange gyration of her hips caught Brig'dha's eye, temporarily breaking her attention from her own sorrowful song of mourning. Before her, a woman danced in a circle, within a circle, and yet within a third circle if she counted her rotation around the fire. It was so unexpected that her chant drifted into silence, her eyes lightly blurry from tears.

Her shadow of her sorrow was momentarily banished by the moon woman's magnificent form, her muscles plainly visible in the firelight. There was something familiar about her, a feeling that tugged at her memories, causing her to blink to remove the tears from her vision. The hip moving and the rotations brought with them a compelling comfort, a strange feeling of wholeness. The woman twirled with a smile on her face that was infectious, causing Brig'dha to smile her first smile in so long. She had found someone who instantly captivated her, and it startled her. She decided to slowly dance closer in the hope the beautiful dancer would improve her mood and give her a chance to remember where she had seen that dance before.

The strangest part was her lack of guilt, which made no sense to Brig'dha. Yet, she felt none as she watched the dancer. Part of her wanted to feel guilty as this had been a dance to Ember's memory, yet wasn't she supposed to move on? The feelings were too volatile to touch, and she would rather place her hand into the fire than dig deeply into the morality and emotional chaos that filled her body. She had sung the funeral rites and begun her closure, yet this beautiful dancer had caught her eye, and she couldn't turn away. Why was she so alluring? It was almost as if the woman had cast a spell of love upon her, yet how could she feel love for a stranger? Her subconscious cried out for her to see, yet her pain had left her nearly detached from the night.

The beautiful dancer's body flowed with a goddess's grace and the fire's passion. She was filled with such vitality that Brig'dha felt compelled to stare, her emotionally wrecked mind utterly fixated. Within a few moments, both women danced beside one another. Brig'dha bit her lip as her eyes finally cleared of tears, and she realized that the gorgeous woman was painted from head to toe in intricate moons, illuminated by her glistening body as she twirled. Brig'dha slowly danced her own circle, turning her back upon the beautiful rotating dancer just before her face came into view, each dancer missing the other as they spun.

Ↄ Ↄ C

Before Ember stood a woman black as the night and pinpointed by stars. She slowed her dance and stopped spinning enough to take in the marvelous sight. She was already halfway into a surreal state of euphoria caused by the dance. Even so, something about the woman's form reminded Ember of Brig'dha, though there was no way they could be one and the same. Her form was relatively easy to take in as the woman wore only a simple string skirt, playful strings hanging down the front and back. This one was sure to pick up a man this night with such a brazen outfit. Of course, she doubted Brig'dha would participate in such a crowded event as this, yet that didn't matter to the recherche redhead. Ember liked Brig'dha for who she was, shy or not. But this dancer wasn't Brig'dha, and tonight was her rebirth – a time to banish the old and move forward.

Ember turned her head to see the strange, red-painted hand-print woman pass by once more with a quirky-looking expression. She couldn't imagine what a handful that woman would be for whoever became her chosen lover. She was simply one of the most carefree people Ember had seen. A woman with a personality like that was likely quite fun to hang around, quite dominant, yet probably a bit taxing after a fashion. She laughed aloud at the thought of some poor hunter's paradigm firing without an arrow when he married her, only to realize that he was no longer in charge. As she spun, caught up in the moment, Ember looked up at the beautiful stars. She didn't want to think of other women – she wanted to think of Brig'dha.

Overhead, a shooting star flew passed, producing a small streak. Ember continued laughing and spinning as she looked straight at the milky stars above. Then, suddenly, she felt her feet coming free from the ground. All the spinning had disorientated her, and it appeared that she was beginning to fall. She had not even realized it until the pressure against her feet changed. This was one of the reasons that a spinning dancer should not look up.

꙲ ꙲ ꙲

Brig'dha rotated once more, her emotions a flutter with her declared purpose at war with the strange feelings the moon dancer had lit in her mind. Glancing up, she caught sight of a line trailing across the sky. It was a shooting star, and it left a small trail behind it, which quickly faded. She spread her arms wide to the sky, beckoning the spirits to aid her dazzled mind. It had all just been too much, and soon she would be tired, and her last night thinking of her friend would be spent, never to be thought of again. Ember's last words came to mind as she resumed her chant of mourning. *Ehg, wennus'du...*

"What was it that you said..." she whispered.

"Oh no... Aeeya Aeeya Aeeya!" Suddenly, Ember stumbled back, the spinning leaving her dizzy. Her nimble feet had caught her before she fell, but she overcorrected, still disoriented, and slumped forward out of control, though avoiding an untimely cremation. Ember reached forward, trying to grab hold of something or someone to prevent her fall, and fell right into the outstretched and raised arms of the pretty woman wearing the night sky paint. The crash took the night sky woman by surprise, but she grabbed Ember, preventing her from falling, and helped her up. Ember held on tightly, her head hung as she waited for the world to stop spinning. The night sky woman politely held her without a word, where some women might simply have let her fall, a swift end to the competition. The moment the world stopped spinning, Ember raised her head to face her savior and thank her for the effort, Ember's free hand wiping her long hair from her face as she beamed a foxy smile. Her head rose, and her eyes fell upon the woman. The world stopped…

☽ ☽ ☽

Brig'dha barely kept from falling as the Moon woman fell across her from out of nowhere. She had been dancing in circles just moments before and then suddenly tumbled forward. The Moon woman appeared slender and lithe, but she bore significant muscle tone, making her much heavier than she looked. Brig'dha held her tightly, allowing the Moon woman to get her bearings. Too much spinning could have this effect on a dancer. She could tell this woman would need a few moments, but that was alright. Oddly, the woman's touch didn't offend her senses. In fact, something about the embrace felt comforting, perhaps even familiar. Only one other person had ever held her without causing her stress. Stranger still, the woman smelled familiar, a primal and powerful memory evoked by her very scent. Brig'dha simply waited a few moments for the woman to regain herself, her thoughts far too jumbled from grief to understand the odd sensations.

After a moment, she felt the weight easing as the woman gained her balance. Slowly, she began to raise her head. Brig'dha could not help but regard her beautiful long red hair as the woman brushed it from her eyes. Her bright, green eyes barely illuminated by the fire. It couldn't be... it simply couldn't be. As she stared, the world held its breath. It was her. The world began to melt away as cold chills flowed down their spines. They grasped each other, unable to move, for fear they might fall – for fear that it was an illusion. Above their heads, the Moon gently cast its light through the beautiful starry sky. Tears welled in their eyes, and Brig'dha made a strange sound, not a word, not even a moan, something much more primal. None of it made sense. No explanation even began to surface. They simply gazed into each other's eyes just as they had when they had first faced each other in Nes.

At that moment, Ember realized that the time had come. How it had come to pass, she didn't know. None of this made sense. Yet, she would seize the moment and figure out the impossible details later. Some things were better just done in the moment. Yet, this wasn't just any moment – this was the moment when her fate would be sealed, one way or another. She had not finished her ritual, nor was she prepared, yet she had fought raiders and wolves with far less preparation and wouldn't back down. Yet, not even the wolves terrified her as much as what was to come. If she failed, she might just let the wolves take her. It was simply all or nothing. The beautiful hazel-eyed woman stared back, equally dumbfounded, her star-spangled eyes smeared with tears.

"I... I thought that you died... I... waited... Are you a... Are you a spirit?" Brig'dha asked, her lips trembling and tears making their way down her starry face like shooting stars. The resurrected redhead gently cradled Brig'dha's face and held tightly. All or nothing.

"Brig'dha, I love you..."

Brig'dha could not speak. Words would not form in her mouth. Her lips trembled as her mind twisted, trying to understand this. The joy of her friend returning had seemed like the greatest possible happiness she could have felt this night, but now there was another. Ember loved her. She had not used the Isen'bryn word for the love of a child or the love of a friend, "Koeseu." Instead, she used the word reserved for a lover, "Leau." Brig'dha had to be sure – she had to know the feelings were shared and that the word was chosen with care. Her mind was a blur, her heart thundered, and her body felt light. She had to be sure this wasn't a dream, an illusion, a spirit… she had to know, and her hypolexic brain had no words to ask, so she did the only thing she could. It was all or nothing.

Brig'dha grabbed Ember's face and pulled tightly against hers in a kiss, the kiss reserved for a lover. The kiss for a leau. As their lips met, her heart leaped in existential release as she felt Ember instantly press into the kiss; nothing held back, no hesitation. It was a beautiful surrender of the individual as two became one. Ember wrapped her arms firmly around Brig'dha, gently pulling her tight, smearing stars across Moons in the most intense and passionate act she had ever performed. Both women felt the flames of love dancing through their bodies and burning brighter than any fire. The entire world washed away, but for their embrace, tears streaming from their eyes. The Moon passed overhead as the two lovers held each other.

As their lips parted, they stood alone in a bare field, raging fires burning under a starry, moonlit sky. Time was for other people, and this night was for them alone. Brig'dha cried while Ember laughed, tears in her eyes. It made no sense, and Brig'dha's legs quickly grew weak. But before she could fall, she felt the strong arms of her warrior, her fox, her Ember. With great effort, Ember lifted Brig'dha in her arms and carried the priestess away from the flames, their lives leaving the ashes of what was and emerging as something new.

A moment later, they sank to the ground on the outskirts of the dance without thought or care for the other dancers, who simply didn't exist. Above her, Brig'dha felt Ember's body touch her gently as the warrior… her warrior lay beside her. Their lips rejoined, pressing tightly, no words able to express their feelings. A moment later, Brig'dha pressed her tongue forward, finding no resistance as their kiss became so much more profound. Under a blanket of stars and the blessed light of the Moon Goddess, it was there that they became one. Neither had ever known the touch of another woman, yet they would never forget their first. It was an escape, a release born of deep and profound love, a truth both had long felt. That old life was now passed.

CHAPTER SIXTEEN
THE GREAT ISUT'SANUP'RA UTIAKUR

Poison and toxic substances were well-known in ancient times, though not always readily accessible, from Socrates, the philosopher who died upon drinking hemlock, to Cleopatra VII Thea Philopator, who experimented with various poisons on her prisoners to determine lethality and dosage (though this is debated). For as long as history has been recorded, and very likely long before that time, poison and toxic substances have been a favorite method for arranging the untimely departure of inconvenient acquaintances. Among the possible poisons available to those in Isut'na with the connections and material wealth to trade for them were mandrake root and belladonna berries, known to Isut'na's people as "Dark Berries." Both contain highly poisonous alkaloids capable of sickening, debilitating, and even killing an imbiber.

Her linen skirt had worn a little at its edge. Aya'tar twisted and turned a small piece of loose flax thread which had come free from its frayed edge. The thread was two-ply and spun by hand. Aya'tar had spent long days as a child spinning flax thread from the strong fibers produced from the plant. It was long and tedious work, but the task could be performed mindlessly if you were skilled enough. She would sit with her friends and discuss the latest news as the thread was slowly spun. This process was often performed by older girls and young women, too young to marry. Like most tools and materials people used, flax thread was of great importance and required significant physical labor to produce.

"He stirs again," whispered Hullamu. Aya'tar turned her gaze back to her father. Her mind had been wandering, mostly to cope with the stress of watching her father die. As his daughter and the high priestess of Isut, she had prayed for two days and nights for whatever ailment had stricken her father to leave him. His pupils remained dilated, and he shifted in and out of delirium and hallucinations. She could not tell if he had been infested by an evil spirit or if dark magic was at work. Whatever it was, the old man's health simply could not tolerate this great of an assault.

Suddenly, Utiakur lifted a quivering hand and grasped his daughter's arm. He turned his head and looked at her as though she were a ghost, his eyes darting frantically. She could not tell if he was hallucinating again or if he really gazed upon her with his faculties intact. Aya'tar's eyes were red and puffy from tears, but to see him look her right in the eyes brought tears anew. She held her breath awaiting what she knew deep down would likely be the last thing he would ever say to her.

"My daughter... Isut calls me," he spoke upon quivering tongue, barely any breath behind his words. His lips whispered as he strained to finish. His eyes had a strange yellow coloring, and he had lost the ability to control any activity of his body. The once-great leader now struggled simply to tell his only daughter goodbye. It was his final battle, and he would win this battle even at the cost of his life.

"She calls... and I must leave you behind. You carry the spirits of 100 leaders before... in you. We will meet... again," he said. His skin had a yellow tint in the light that drifted through the main temple's windows. For a moment, he simply gazed at her, his pupils slowly dilating even more. Suddenly, Aya'tar realized that he had passed. The moment of death was unclear, but he did not seem in pain. For a moment, she simply stood, barely able to come to terms with what had just happened.

As reality began to overcome her, Aya'tar knelt beside her father's body and quietly wept. The man had lived twice the average age of any man she had known. She could not curse the spirits who took him, for he had already been blessed to have seen more sunrises than most people who lived. He had survived battles, raiders, and strange illnesses which had swept the city in times past. At least, his last few moments provided him with the clarity to say goodbye, a clarity most people would never be afforded.

The temple was hot with the smell of moisture and dust. Around the priestess stood perhaps a dozen people of various import, each here for the final moments of their great leader. Beside his bed, the junior priestesses Hullamu and Isha'kau continued to chant, wearing their ceremonial masks made from woven reed and painted in such a manner as to ward off evil spirits. Both women were painted completely white with clay and wore a ceremonial feathered headdress, their feet bare to aid their connection to the world. They needed to continue actively maintaining the room's protection lest evil spirits corrupt the final departure of the great leader's spirit into the arms of Isut and off into the next world to be born again.

Behind her stood Zah'namu and her husband Kamar in a show of support for the legendary leader and his daughter. Zah'namu held her husband close. Watching the death of a beloved leader had the effect of reminding everyone present just how short and fragile life was. It was important to live life to its fullest and to experience all the joys and sorrows it held for that brief moment each person lived.

With the death of their great leader, a power vacuum had emerged within the city. By the law of the land, Aya'tar was the ranking member of the city, the ipso facto ruler. The Council of Elders oversaw much of the day-to-day activities, but they were more legislative than executive. Zah'namu had suggested to Kamar that he should step in as the leader, but he had rejected the notion for Aya'tar. She did not understand what he saw in the priestess, but she respected his opinion though it differed from her own. She would broach the subject with him in a few days when death was not so fresh in the air.

"Someone must make a statement to the people. I shall do this," Kamar said as he left his wife's side and placed a firm hand on Aya'tar's shoulder. She turned to face him and simply nodded. Her tear-stained face made Kamar swallow hard, a lump forming in his throat. Mighty hunter or not, Kamar had a soft heart, and the sight before him was difficult to watch. Far from the great man who would speak for the fallen leader, he simply wanted to step from the room while maintaining his composure.

ɔ ɔ ɔ

Kamar stepped down from the ladder which led to the temple's roof. Most buildings were entered through their roofs and required ladders. Removing his foot from the final rung, he turned to see hundreds of people gathered to hear the news. The rumor that the leader was close to death had traveled through the city faster than he had expected, and this was the result. Below him, many people had painted their faces white with clay in the traditional manner of mourners. Utiakur was not a member of their families. Still, somehow, he had been thought of as a father figure to everyone in the city.

Kamar waited for a moment, taking a deep breath before speaking. Behind him, he could hear the soft crying sounds of Aya'tar emanating from the rooftop entrance, so silent had the crowd fallen. He lifted a small clay pot and held it for everyone to see. Placing his right hand within the pot, he removed a large clump of white clay. All the gathered people held their breaths, knowing what was to come but unable to make a sound until he finished. Kamar, the hunter, smeared the white paint from the top of his face all the way down his body ending at his loincloth. Ritualistically, it was the sign given to everyone that he had officially entered a state of mourning. It was the message given without word.

"The Great Isut'Sanup'ra Utiakur journeys from this world into Isut'nesis upon the wings of birds. His only daughter, Isut'Sanup'ramu Aya'tar, born of Isut'San'ramu Yari'aya, is the high priestess and leader of Isut'na!" announced Kamar loudly from the roof of the temple overlooking the dance grounds. Through the rooftop entrance leading up to the temple, Aya'tar heard the words but could barely grasp them. Behind her, she heard the wails of women in the screams of men. Few alive could remember a time when the great Utiakur was not their strong and fearless leader. Fear and sadness were felt by all, an entire city in mourning.

ɔ ɔ ɔ

Sar'Tawas stood toward the back of the room, watching the events unfold. Several elders were in attendance, but he had kept to the rear where he could observe the interactions between people and gauge their willingness to accept or reject the priestess. He held no ill will towards Aya'tar and even thought her to be a competent priestess, but not the city leader. It wasn't that she was a woman, but that she was young and had no real experience with leadership. The city needed a strong leader, a cunning leader who would do what was needed. The city needed Sar'Tawas, and he would figure out a way to make sure that happened.

Simply put, if the people backed the priestess, he would have to find a way to convince her to take him as her husband. If the people did not back her, he would need to push her out of the way and assert himself as the leader. The only real problem standing in his way towards the second course of action was his own lack of a child. Isut'na was the city of the goddess Isut, a fertility goddess. In the city, having no child was simply a liability. Aya'tar was an unwed woman, young and full of potential, so her lack of a child wasn't an immediate problem, yet Sar'Tawas would be viewed much differently.

Many long harvests past, his wife Meki'kmu had died of the sweats brought on from a pain which started whenever she tried to urinate. Pain from urination sometimes afflicted women, though rarely a man. Commonly, the afflicted woman would sit by a hot fire and ensure that she drank plenty of herbal fluids. It was not common, but a person could die from those sorts of pains. Even after so much time had passed, the thought of her slowly slipping away still made him uncomfortable. He had loved her, and she had been snatched from his grasp for reasons no

288

one understood. Was it the will of the gods that he have no child? Such an argument could be made and could prevent him from taking charge.

He had no real family to back him up, a very uncommon occurrence in a proto-city where most people came from large extended families with dozens of members. In fact, his only other family member was his older sister Nemanar'Tawas, who had left Isut'na to marry a man from Nara'kit when she was barely a woman. Last he heard from traders, she and the man were well, and they had left and traveled far to the West to start a new life in some distant land. Unfortunately, this left Sar'Tawas as the last living member of his family line, his relatives far too indirect to count.

While he thought it very unlikely that Aya'tar could be convinced to marry him, even if she did, there was a distinct possibility that she may also be barren. Utiakur had died with only one heir, a woman. The same argument that might prevent his ascension could also be made against Aya'tar. In short, the key to every possible victory lay within the womb of a woman. Sar'Tawas needed a child, and it did not matter whether it was a boy or girl.

This was where the concubine Ianmu came in. She was young, healthy, and with very little will, or so it seemed. These were qualities that would make her a simple and effective concubine. On the other hand, Aya'tar would be a handful, strong-willed and intelligent as she was. The last thing he needed was a woman scheming behind his back and making demands of him rather than producing an heir. On the other hand, having both women would double his chances of an heir. He had never known anyone to own a concubine, but there were no rules in the city that forbade it. Having multiple wives was also not unheard of, at least among those powerful enough to support such arrangements. Besides, the arrangement had other benefits. Sar'Tawas had many thoughts in his mind, all of them pressing.

Ianmu stood behind Sar'Tawas carrying a clay vessel of water. Standing there watching the old man die was a time-consuming and annoying process, but it was also one step closer to her goal. She could see that Sar'Tawas was brooding over how best to advance himself and what his next move might be. That sort of behavior was to be encouraged as it propelled Ianmu closer to a position of power. If Sar'Tawas could take control of the city and then suffer a sudden accident... Sar'Tawas turned to gaze upon her for a few moments, his eyes wandering. His unexpected stare snapped Ianmu from her own plotting designs. She stared at the floor with as vacant of a look as she could achieve. Pretending to be less than intelligent was actually quite difficult, but she seemed to have pulled it off. Sar'Tawas was no fool, and the slightest slip-up on her part would be detected. This was a dangerous game, but the sort of games with the largest prizes always carried the greatest risks.

Ɔ Ɔ Ɔ

The Sun's beautiful rays danced warmly across the open fields as Brig'dha opened her eyes. Her skin was a strange smear of soot and sweat from the night before. On top of the sweat and soot, a thin layer of dew coated her body, adding to the coolness of the morning breeze. The night had been chilly but still warm enough to sleep on the open ground. In just a few tendays more, the land would be too cool for such delights. As it was, her skin felt sticky from dew, and her back itched from top to bottom, the result of dirt and grass. But none of that mattered…

The night's events had changed her life forever and for the better. She had found true love, discovered that the most important person in her life was still alive, and felt the soft touch of a lover, all in the same night. Even now, memories of what had happened flowed through her body like her very blood, pulsing and tingling. Tears danced in the corners of her eyes as she lay surrounded by memories too beautiful to fully understand.

In some ways, the very foundation of her world had been shaken, but in other ways, she felt more at peace than she ever had. Brig'dha and Ember had experienced more over the last two harvests than most people experienced in their entire lives. She remembered lying on her back and gazing at the stars with Ember's head in her lap as they floated across the Greatest River, their lives in the hands of the spirits of the water. She remembered the night that she had looked up with tear-stained eyes, bound to a wooden pole and waiting for death in the village of Nes. When her eyes had opened and come into focus, her savior Ember stood before her, cutting her free. This love had grown for a long time, but she had never realized its true nature until that night.

She rolled onto her side to gaze upon her sleeping lover. Ember lay on her back with her limbs sprawled in random directions. Her skin had been decorated with extreme intricacy, beautiful shapes now smeared in the throes of passion. The woman, if that term even applied to Ember, was beautiful to her in spirit and personality, yet her form was also undeniable. Her entire body was strong and muscular, like a man, yet feminine. Her small breasts and slight curves were so unlike that of a man, though she was far from her people's ideal of a woman. In fact, Brig'dha's wide hips, larger breasts, and ample body fat were considered marks of beauty among her people.

Though the physical appearance of the warrior woman was enough to send tingles through just the right places when she was in the mood to consider them, those were simply not the parts she cared the most for. One day, if they lived long enough, both women would age into wrinkles and hunched backs. Yet, Ember's personality and spirit would remain, growing richer and more lovely with age and experience. Brig'dha decided that those features were Ember's most beautiful and attractive – though her corded arms and clearly defined muscles were hardly easy to ignore. Uncharacteristically, the usually bashful brunette giggled as she considered her lover… her warrior… her fox.

Brig'dha delicately cleared stray hairs from Ember's face as she looked tenderly upon her, a mere friend no more. Such love between two women, or two men, was not common in the tribes to the West and North. There were no taboos against it, but due to the lack of people and the need to have children, such arrangements were often frowned upon. Brig'dha had known of two such traders a few harvests before who had come to her village. Each man had a trade specialty that complimented the other. Of course, she had seen several such couples at the dance, as well.

Brig'dha smiled at the possibilities as she tended Ember's hair. She still had no explanation for where she had been or how she had lived. A quick examination of her body revealed the red marks of an injury to her left arm. It appeared that the arm had mostly healed, but it would likely be several more tendays until the marks faded. Otherwise, the quirky redhead looked to be in good repair and well-fed. Brig'dha nuzzled her face against Ember, taking in the smell she recognized. She was simply happy beyond her wildest dreams.

Ember suddenly awoke as the light of the Sun blazed across her eyes. The hair Brig'dha had parted from her face allowed the piercing rays to beat upon fragile eyelids. She rolled over onto her side, making strange mumbling sounds, and attempted to curl back up for more sleep. Ember was known to many as one of the lazier human beings around. Brig'dha tried to hold back a laugh. She returned to lying beside Ember, curling up behind her in a spooning fashion. Simply lying in the field and holding her tightly was one of the greatest feeling she had ever known. Her only lament was not learning that Ember had felt the same way about her earlier.

"Now that I have you back, I'm not letting you go," she whispered.

つ　つ　つ

Kel sat up and stretched. He needed to urinate, but he was too sleepy to stand. Beside him, he heard the sound of snoring. Looking to his left, he found Espe lying face-down in the grass. Her garlands of flowers were all tatters now, and whatever piece of leather had been covering her backside had fallen off at some point. The small nettle fiber apron that hung down her front did little when lying face-down. What impressed him most was how thoroughly her beautiful red ocher hand-print body paint had been applied. She actually had two red hand-prints on her butt. Kel shook his head, trying to hold back a laugh. *If a squirrel had been born as a woman,* he thought.

He figured that she was snoring because of how she was sleeping. To remedy this, he carefully rolled her over onto her back. Sure enough, the snoring diminished. The Sun would soon awaken Espe as it beat down on her skin. As he watched, a spider crawled across her stomach and back into the grass. She rubbed her stomach and mumbled something Kel didn't understand. He smiled, thinking of what effect the spider might have had were she awake.

People lived their entire lives around bugs. As a result, it was quite common to find a spider, insect, or other unwanted guest crawling in your bed. Soil was often built-up around the edges of huts, cracks sealed with mud, and beds elevated from the floor to combat this. Unfortunately, it did little to keep out their creepy little friends. Though most people did not panic at the sight of a spider, Espe seemed to have a strange fear of them and would react explosively if she saw one anywhere near her. Spiders were an unfortunate side effect of sleeping in a field. Luckily, it was late enough that ticks were not also counted among the unwanted guests.

She was not much of a morning person, but neither was he. Luckily, she had very aggressively made her feelings clear the night before. Espe wanted to remain with Kel. Taking the hint, he asked her if she would marry him. It was strangely abrupt, but that was just the kind of relationship they had. Espe's answer had come more through her sudden and immediate actions than through any real words. As he sat there in the grass, he had no doubt in his mind that his soon-to-be wife lay beside him. If they were really lucky, they would have a child come the thawing season. Oddly, his hips hurt and his skin was a little raw… *What a painful "yes,"* he mused.

☽ ☾ ☽

A short time later, Ember sat on a rock in the middle of a stream near the fields where the event had been held. Several dozen festivalgoers could be seen along the stream cleaning and freshening after the festivities of the night before. It was already past midday, and the Moon would soon rise in the East. She stretched, considering how well she had slept the night before. It had been the best sleep she had experienced since leaving to chase the thieves so many tendays before. Even now, she felt relaxed and freer than she ever had. Her chest was sore, her body ached a little from the hard ground, and she was quite sure that she had a few new marks on her back that would slowly heal, yet the pain reminded her of her new reality – she and Brig'dha were lovers.

Ember had never laid with a person before. She had always expected it would be with a man, an experience she had not looked forward to but had expected. She remembered the many times she had developed a crush on one woman or another, often the infrequent visitors to her village. Yet she had never considered how they might be intimate, at least in a practical manner. It had not been important to her fantasies at the time. But instead, her first experience had been at the edge of a fertility festival dance surrounded by hundreds of dancers. She almost laughed at how unlike her expectations it had been… in more ways than one.

In her village, a large, extended family occupied a longhouse. It was common to see lovers joining in open view of the rest of the family. Just as every other animal in the world, this was normal and expected. Though one was supposed to ignore the sounds and certainly not watch, she had, of course, watched several times to see what sex was and how it worked. It seemed that her expectations only applied between a man and a woman, as what she had experienced the night before bore no relation to what she had watched one of her distant cousins and her new husband do a few harvests before. She mentally thanked the spirits for that. Still, the feel of Brig'dha's soft body against hers as the unexpectantly bold brunette nibbled on her neck… Ember stopped herself with a calming breath. She would have plenty of time to consider that later. For now, she needed to wash and take a cool dip in the water to calm her inner fire.

Much to the chagrin of her friends, Ember suddenly dove into the stream and completely submerged herself in the sudden act. The water was cool, and most people would only bravely wash small portions of their bodies at once. *Great, she fell off a rock and into the water again. She needs to stop doing that,* Brig'dha thought with mirth.

Ember opened her eyes to see the strange creatures and sights to behold in the deep stream when her body was entirely submerged. The water differed very little from most streams and rivers she had swum in. Rolling around, she could see the light bouncing and reflecting off the surface of the water and feel the current as it steadily pushed her along. Little glittery speckles illuminated the bottom while strange matter floated by. Mostly, she saw people's legs, but every now and then, very tiny fish would swim by, most smaller than her little finger.

Ember had once captured a similarly tiny fish when she was a child, and she had eaten it out of curiosity. It had actually been strangely tastier than she thought it would be though it had a few flavors that she was not quite pleased with. She had never told her mother as she knew what sort of trouble she would be in. It had always been considered inappropriate to eat raw meat, at least among her people. However, Ember always enjoyed trying new things, such as swimming in the stream. She suspected that if more people would simply go for a swim and open their eyes underwater, they might appreciate the world just a little bit more.

Besides the troubles of the overly cool water, it was also considered bad luck to clean ritual paint from one's body. Normally, paint from dances and rituals would be left until it faded. This was especially true for Ember's people, who believed the body should always be painted. To be unpainted among her people would be similar to being undressed. Some paints could survive a quick rinse while others could not. Luckily for Ember, fine soot from charred animal bone had a tendency to withstand being lightly washed when mixed with oil. She had been painted with a much higher quality pigment than what she normally applied to herself.

Brig'dha sat upon the shore barely the length of a man from the rock Ember had used before she dove in. She vigorously cleaned herself in a slightly less intense manner. Splashing her skin with water, applying sand, and then rubbing herself clean allowed her a more comfortable solution. Not far from where she sat, Aethen aggressively scrubbed at his scalp as he lay on his back with his hair dangling in the water. The oil in hair never really left, but a good scrubbing would make the hair softer and cleaner. The previous night had left everyone with sweat which needed to be removed.

Kel and Espe had yet to arrive, and Aethen suspected they were probably still rolling around somewhere in a field. He had never seen two people grow so attached in such a short time. Most likely, they would wed after the festival and likely return to the Blue Sea People. Aethen was happy for his friend, but it was sometimes annoying to be around them.

Their love was simply too exaggerated for him, and it reminded him that he was still alone. What he needed now was to get away from it all, to find his own love, his own purpose. He had come to terms with the fact that Ember would not be part of that purpose, but, at least she was still a friend.

There had been many questions that morning. For starters, Aethen and Brig'dha explained to Ember what had happened the night that she had jumped into the water. Ember was beside herself upon hearing the story. She could not believe her own actions and had even wondered if they were joking. Strangely, it would explain her apprehension passing that large tribe to the Southeast, as well as how she came to be washed ashore. Learning of something you had done when you could not recall the events for yourself was a little distressing.

Ember felt a little guilty over the pain she had caused her friends while she recuperated, and they were left thinking she had died. She had supposed that they had known that she was okay for some reason. As she sat back and logically thought it out, this made little sense. Those first few tendays had been confusing, to begin with, possibly due to her head injury. Had she known that they had been left in mystery, she might have been tempted to brave the wilds and return even with her wounded arm. Brig'dha assured her that she had made the right choice to fully heal before returning.

The part of Brig'dha and Aethen's tale which was most troubling was the death of Kyra. Brig'dha had supposed that the woman had been sacrificed, likely with a dagger. Ember had told her just before jumping that Kyra was guilty of the murder of her husband and that she even played a role in Yan's actions. Ember was troubled because she had no recollection of how she had concluded Kyra's guilt. She simply had to trust that she had made the right choice, but she couldn't imagine having told Brig'dha something like that unless it were true, nor Brig'dha making up such a story.

Ember, Aethen, and Brig'dha had experienced some of the best and the worst that the world had to offer. As they sat cleaning and talking, Brig'dha decided that it was time to bring up something she had been thinking of for a while, a change of pace. She was not one for speaking aloud, especially in the company of many people, but she was still feeling exhilarated over Ember's proclamation of love, which filled her with the motivation to speak. It was time to propose something radical, a new beginning.

"I'm tired of the West and the North. I am tired of the old. I want to see the lands below where the Sun rises," she said. She had felt rejection since she had returned to her people without her husband. Though she felt no real ill will toward her people, something had changed. Brig'dha no longer felt like a member of the Isen'bryn or the Blue Sea People. In some ways, the death of Tes had been the final blow. To journey to the lands below where the Sun rose and perhaps even South of that could be dangerous. But, if Ember were by her side, she felt that she could climb to the very clouds themselves.

"The lands to the Southeast are the birthplace of the family who saved my life," said Ember right before she stuck her face back into the water. She pulled her head from the stream and began to swish water around in her mouth. She spit after a moment, which saw an arc of water projected dangerously close to where Aethen was cleaning his hair.

"I'm sure they could tell me how to get back to their lands, and perhaps you could learn whether or not this is truly what you want to do," Ember said as she slowly turned to look Brig'dha in the eyes. Ember suddenly became more serious.

"If you wish to go Southeast, to the True South... know that I will follow. I do not want to leave your side again," she said. Brig'dha smiled warmly at the thought. The Goddess of the Moon had answered her prayers and delivered Ember into her arms. *Brig'dha, I love you...* The words still danced in her mind and brought with them exciting warmth which blanketed her body to the core. She had the feeling that they were about ready to begin a new adventure.

Aethen stood and began to sling his hair back and forth, freeing it from much of the water it had absorbed. He had been listening to the women and was considering his own pursuits. At nineteen harvests of age, it was about time that he found a woman to love. Kel had found Espe, and surprisingly Ember had Brig'dha. He couldn't help but be happy for the couples, even though there was a part of him that mourned. He had longed for Ember's affections, but he had never made his feelings known. In the end, their love seemed so natural that he was almost glad that he hadn't. Aethen had little attachment to the remnants of his people, part of the reason that he had journeyed south in the first place. Perhaps his future wasn't with the Blue Sea People but might be found in the adventures of these two quirky and yet inspiring women. Aethen chuckled as he squeezed the water from his hair.

"I will go with you if you will have me. Perhaps the South is full of beautiful women. Maybe I should find one who takes me to her liking," he said with a smile. Brig'dha became more enthusiastic the moment she heard the support of Aethen. Ember simply laughed in her lighthearted way. The prospect of playing matchmaker between Aethen and some True South woman appealed to Brig'dha and Ember. It would be a fun game to play.

"You are a good man Aethen. You will need the support of two strong women to save you from the vast swarm of southern women who will try and claim you as their own," the redhead laughed. She turned to see Espe and Kel approaching. They both looked just as dirty and messy as everyone else who had woken up in a field. Everyone immediately noticed how they held hands and how relaxed they were. They had "the look." Ember turned to Brig'dha, and both women exchanged curious expressions. When Brig'dha peered back at Espe, she looked down with a smile. Brig'dha returned her gaze to Ember, and both women began to giggle. Aethen wasn't sure what strange mental exchange had just occurred between the women, but he was pretty sure they had exchanged information in some fashion. They had divined something humorous.

Ember glanced at Espe, recognizing her as the younger dancer who had spun semicircles around her the night before. Both of their faces lit up in mutual recognition. In the daylight, each woman regarded the other with mutual respect in appreciation for both their dance ability as well as their passion for life. Ember was glad that the beautiful dancer was apparently deeply in love with Kel. She hoped that Kel had explained who she was to the mysterious handprinted dancer.

Aethen stood with his hair mostly slung free of excess water. He reached down and double-checked the cord attaching his loincloth and turned to regard Kel and Espe as they approached. Ember and Espe gazed upon one another with an intense stare indicating that they had met during the dance or sometime before. He figured it was probably best that he introduced everyone before things became awkward. Suddenly, Ember and Espe both broke into laughter and smiles. Glad that they were not about to pounce on one another in some kind of bizarre fight, he decided to introduce them promptly.

"Ember, let me introduce you to Espe of the Rene people. She and Kel are a pair," Aethen said with a laugh.

"We have met several times," Ember said, remembering the dance.

"Kel, how was your fortune last night? Did you and Espe have a good time... at the dance?" Aethen asked with a humorous smirk. Kel was all smiles, but he said nothing. It took Aethen only a moment to realize what that meant. The two lovers began to clean themselves in the stream, neither wishing to go into any more detail about the events of the night before, but Ember wasn't paying attention anymore as she stood and attached her sandals.

"Red-hair, Brig'dha, good night, eh?" Espe said in broken Isen'bryn and gesturing at each woman as she spoke. Espe had learned a little bit of Kel's language, though it took everyone gathered a few moments to realize what her words meant, so terribly accented where they. Ember stopped lacing her sandals for a moment and gazed at Brig'dha with a smile. Brig'dha looked down, her dark skin turning slightly red with embarrassment. Even Aethen could pick up on those sorts of signs.

"Eh, kaes'aegge, Brig'dha esu'nuku, ehe? Smae-guoi... Makh'luh!" Espe said and abruptly burst into laughter as she stuck her feet in the water to clean. Kel tried not to laugh, but he began to turn red at her comment. Ember frowned and cocked an eyebrow looking him dead in the face. She slowly approached Kel with a serious look. He stepped back, slightly worried.

"What did she just say?" Kel paused for a moment attempting to think of the best way to explain the comment, not all of which he understood, to be honest. He would prefer not to explain it to Ember, but she was actually quite an intimidating person when she looked irritated.

"She thinks that you and Brig'dha had a... um... 'great' night and thoroughly enjoyed yourselves..." Kel said with a slightly guilty look. Ember frowned more deeply with her hands on her hips. Kel lost his ability to hold back his laughter. Now Ember was sure that she had said something else entirely inappropriate, yet very funny. The younger woman seemed to have a sharp tongue but in a good-natured sort of way.

"Smae-guoi means smeared stars," he said, a reference to Ember and Brig'dha's smeared paint jobs. At that, everyone burst into laughter. Ember could not really be mad at Espe. The woman had a similar personality to her own. Ember now stood and addressed Kel in a more formal tone. There was something important that needed to be done, and he would be the man to do it in light of Aethen's request to accompany them.

"Kel, is it your intention to return to the Blue Sea People?" Kel looked up from what he was doing and re-spoke the words to Espe so that she would understand. As soon as he did so, she became extremely interested in what he had to say. It seemed to Ember that Espe and Kel had also discussed this very issue. It also seemed that he had not given her an answer. Kel stood nervously with all eyes trained on him for the second time in only a short moment. He thought for a moment and then seemed resigned to some decision.

"Espe's people join as our people. Some leave or join her tribe by marriage. It is the way of things. I offered to join Espe's tribe, but she desperately wants to start a new life in a new place. She wants a change. We will journey back to her village, but only to say goodbye. We will then return to the Blue Sea People. There we will be joined and have many children. Espe likes children," he finished awkwardly. He turned and spoke to Espe a moment later, informing her of what he had just said. Ember was pretty sure by her reaction that at least some part of this plan had not been agreed upon before he had said it. Either way, Espe reacted pleasantly to the news, suddenly embracing Kel.

Learning that Aethen would be joining them on their new quest to the True South and learning that Kel was, in fact, going to return to the Blue Sea People, Ember realized that one last action needed to be performed. The time had come for Ember to do something she had waited for almost half a harvest to do. Around her neck was a cord with the Amber of Life pendant. This was the very item that she had traveled all the way to the village of Koneh and nearly died to recover. The item was magic, a fertility necklace that could bring prosperity to any land or fertility to any person. It was a powerful magic item. She stepped forward, removing the necklace, and approached Kel.

"Take this necklace back to our... your people. If I were you, I would keep it on and perhaps assert yourself as leader. The Blue Sea People are a young tribe, and they need a strong leader. Anyone willing to do the things you have done would serve nicely," she finished. Kel held the necklace in his hand for a moment and considered the significance of the precious item. The necklace had cost the lives of four people. The only life it seemed to have saved was Ember's. In fact, she had nearly died trying to recover it, twice. Something about returning it did not feel right to him.

"Mael gave you this necklace just before he died. You were the only person whose life the necklace has ever saved. It belongs around your neck, not wasting away in some hut. Our new village is built on land with ample food. I do not think that we will need the necklace to thrive," he said, holding the precious item in the light so that he could better see the flower. All around him, there were murmurs of agreement. Aethen had suggested to Ember several times that she should keep the item. The Amber of Life had served the Isen'bryn for a long time, but that tribe was no more. The Blue Sea People now lived in a land of plenty, a fertile paradise nestled on the shores of the great Blue Sea. Aethen stepped forward with his own thoughts.

"Ember, you have changed the lives of many people. Because of your actions, Kel and Espe will become one, and the Blue Sea People have been avenged. You have even brought hope to the Shell People. Kel is right, this necklace favors you, and it saved your life. I think that you should keep it and continue to spread hope wherever you travel," Aethen said, more stoic than anyone in the group had seen him. Kel simply nodded his agreement.

Before Ember could speak, Kel placed the necklace around her neck. Its weight felt good, somehow natural. It was strange to Ember that she would be chosen by a necklace of fertility when her love was for a woman. She would never be able to conceive a child with Brig'dha, and yet the necklace had saved her life, or so it seemed. Truly she did not remember the events of that night, but it sort of made sense. Perhaps the only person who should possess such an item is somebody who does not desire such a thing. *Why does life always give food to those who are full?*

Ember suddenly had a thought concerning the necklace. They would remain here for another night before doing anything, at a minimum. There was one use Kel might make of the necklace before they parted ways, perhaps forever. Ember removed the necklace from her neck, drawing confused glances from everyone. She turned and approached Espe holding the necklace out before her.

"Kel, you said that Espe wanted children, right? Ask her if she *really* wants children," Ember said, dangling the fertility item in front of the curious woman. Espe's eyes followed the necklace, almost in a trance. It was a thing of beauty.

꩜ ꩜ ꩜

With Brig'dha and Aethen's interest in the True South piqued, Ember decided it was time for her foster family to meet the team. Espe and Kel also came, more out of curiosity than any other reason, as they had already decided to return to the Blue Sea People. Luckily, the tent erected for the family was merely on the other side of the dance grounds, a short walk from where they now washed. The entire dance area was full of hundreds of people going about their business before the next dance. There were even people still lying on the ground sleeping from the night before. If any of the magical brews had been brought to the dance, they could have this sort of effect on people.

The Moon was finally rising when the group approached the family from the True South. Ember introduced Ketamir, his wife Nemanar, and their two children Ninrea'mu and Gel'nar. Ketamir and Nemanar had left their ancestral lands far to the South when they were as young as Kel and Espe. Ember never pressed them to learn why they had chosen to come northwest, but she had always gotten the impression that they were interested in seeing new places far from where they were born. The need to explore seemed to be a general trait among some people, though it was expressed much more liberally in Ember.

Young Ninrea'mu watched as Ember held Brig'dha's hand tightly. The way the two gazed upon one another did not escape her sharp eyes. It was not long before she realized that the brown-haired woman with hazel eyes was the person Ember had been longing for. Her eyes gleamed with youthful romantic thoughts. True, her own romantic ideas involved a dashing hunter saving her from a pack of wolves and then carrying her off to his tribe far to the North, but love was love, and she envied Ember for it. Luckily, she had a mere two harvests to wait before she would find her dashing hunter. Ninrea'mu's eyes turned toward Aethen, a man who fit her hunter fantasy quite well. She knew that it would never be, but that wouldn't prevent her from daydreaming.

What troubled Ember most was figuring out how to make it to the South, having never been there. She had been told of mountains that reached the sky and other complex obstacles which stood in the way of her goals. Having spent the entire warm season with these people, she had learned how to speak their language well enough to ask such questions. Regardless, having Ninrea'mu provide nearly real-time translation would allow Ember to speak almost as she would to anyone else. The young girl had a knack for languages, an extremely useful skill.

Ember, Brig'dha, and Aethen sat down with Ketamir and Nemanar on leather mats placed in front of their tent to discuss the perils of a trip to the True South. They were joined a moment later by Espe and Kel, who had followed out of curiosity. Before any discussion was had, Nemanar brought forth roasted vegetables and meat, and water for everyone in attendance. Nemanar was originally from a place called "Isut'na," before joining with Ketamir and living in his home, a place called Nara'kit, far to the Southeast. In Nara'kit, it was considered customary to offer guests food. Though they were in a new place, there were some traditions that they always kept.

Speaking was reasonably easy, with Ember glossing over words she didn't know or making accurate guesses of their meaning, given the context. She was pretty good at doing this and seemed to have a natural knack for languages as well. For example, Nemanar's first sentence was full of unknown words and sounded to Ember like, "Kaou this [nod indicating Brig'dha] you talk many times, sare'assaetarsu you left behind?" From this, Ember understood the sentence to actually mean, "Was this the person you spoke of so many times, the sare'assaetarsu [friend?] you left behind?" She supposed sare'assaetarsu meant friend or maybe even lover. Nemanar had asked with a motherly smile. In truth, Ember had mentioned a person she loved many times, but she had never told them who it was.

"This Brig'dha. We walk long, fight, swim Greatest River, far west. I fear tell Brig'dha I like. I fear Brig'dha no like," she replied, as best as she could. Ketamir gave an approving nod at Ember's choice though he too had to ponder her words for a moment. Many misunderstandings were quickly corrected with hand gestures, possibly one of the most useful tools for teaching another language. Ember hated speaking like a young child in a broken language, but she had not lived with them long enough to understand every individual word.

"Truth, I expected man meke'assaetarsu," he said smiling. Ember cocked an eyebrow, almost slightly frowning at his statement. She understood more words than she could speak, yet one word had been used that she didn't know, once more. Hadn't Ninrea'mu used this word once before when she was fishing? Ember was sure that she had, but she couldn't remember if it meant lover or something similar.

He paused, realizing that Ember had not understood his words. She had learned most of the words he used in his sentence, common words. He looked to his young daughter Ninrea'mu to aid him in translating before the confusion became more awkward. Ninrea'mu could understand enough of Ember's words that she could facilitate their common speech as a translator. With Ninrea'mu actively translating, Ember and Ketamir could speak with a greatly enhanced vocabulary at nearly their normal speech rate, simply pausing after each sentence to allow Ninrea'mu to translate.

"Assaetarsu," he said, holding his wife tightly in a loving embrace. Ember believed she understood that "assaetarsu" simply meant love or fertility. Next, he said, "meke'assaetarsu," explaining through hand gestures that "Meke" meant something much greater. The second word was again the word for love. If Ember understood him correctly, it seemed that he might be explaining the idea of romantic love. This was definitely what she had heard while fishing, though the memories were vague. If that were the case, then Brig'dha would certainly be her meke'assaetarsu.

"Brig'dha is my meke'assaetarsu. Very meke," Ember said with a smile, hoping that she was correctly using the words. Ninrea'mu quickly assisted with filling in any missing parts and using the larger, shared vocabulary. Ketamir had truly expected Ember to return with a dashing hunter, but he could find no fault with her choice of Brig'dha, the priestess. In the lands where he had come from, such forms of love were even more commonplace. Large cities had as many as 3000 people. As a result, there was much less pressure upon an individual to marry for the purpose of having children.

The next topic was perhaps the most important question on everyone's mind – how to get to the True South. Ember was not against the idea of simply journeying toward the South and finding what could be found, but she truly hoped that Nemanar and Ketamir could provide a better explanation. Nemanar and Ketamir sat for a short time pondering Ember's inquiry into a route to the True South. It had been many long harvests since they had arrived from the Southeast. Ninrea'mu continued to translate in real-time, allowing for conversation to flow more naturally, though some words still required a few moments to explain with hand gestures and body language.

"Why do you wish to go to the True South?" he asked Ember.

"Because it is there," she answered cryptically, though quite accurately. Ketamir thought about her words for a moment before responding.

"The True South has great beauty, large cities tens of hundreds of people, but also, great danger."

"Tell us how to find the great cities." Ketamir and Nemanar exchanged glances for a moment, and then Nemanar spoke.

"The trip will take nine tendays," she said soberly. Seeing that Ember and Brig'dha were not discouraged by the vast length of the journey, she closed her eyes for a few moments recalling the way as best as she could remember. Nemanar had always been better with directions than her husband, having an almost photographic memory when it came to traveling.

"You will walk one tenday toward the sunrise. Stop when the land curves southeast. Head southeast for four tendays, maybe five. The Blue Sea will be on your right the full way. Follow the coast until you travel entirely south," she said, pausing for Ninrea'mu to translate, "Once you have reached this point, walk east for a tenday. You will reach a lake called West Lake."

"It was named by people who live to the East," she said, noting Ember's skeptical expression at the name.

"West Lake is very wide. You must cross it by boat, though many villages will take you. After that, walk directly east. For a tenday, there will be land on your right and to south. For two more tendays at least, there will be water to your south. This water to the South is called the Great Lake. Eventually, you will come to a mighty river called the Brown River, which empties north into the Blue Lake. Along the way, ask people the way to the Brown River, the city of Isut'na, my birth city, or the city of Nara'kit, where my husband is from. They will know."

Ember suddenly bent forward and pulled her into an embrace. She had just provided the key information that would allow her small band to travel to the most amazing place she could have ever dreamed of, the True South. For the rest of the day, everyone remained with Ember's foster family laughing and socializing as the Moon rose in the sky and the Sun set. There would be one more night of dancing and festivities before they parted ways, possibly forever. Ember was becoming regrettably used to the idea of leaving people that she cared for. It was, unfortunately, one of the prices to be paid to see the world. But now, she would bring someone with her, a person she didn't have to leave, a lover, and a companion.

CHAPTER SEVENTEEN
THE SUN, THE MOON, AND YOU

The cover of the book depicts Brig'dha wearing a skirt made from flax cord strands connected to a single flax cord belt. While most Neolithic clothing was likely not textile, some quality textiles were known to have been made. Beyond hypothetical string skirts, whole panels of cloth were woven using different forms of loom, allowing for the possible creation of more sophisticated clothing, such as shawls, skirts, and perhaps even rudimentary dresses. The amount of time required to make even a single square meter of cloth could be quite extreme, as was the amount of time needed to grow the plants, obtain the wool, or collect the bark that made the fibers used in the cloth. As a result, good-quality textile clothing would be worth a significant value in trade.

A full moon had passed since the death of the great Isut'Sanup'ra Utiakur. As was customary, a full moon of mourning had been observed before the next leader was officially named. However, Aya'tar had already been unofficially proclaimed as the leader by Kamar. Among the people, the word of Kamar and the natural succession of Aya'tar had seemed an unshakable wind. People did not like change, but as time had passed, the seeds of doubt began to sprout. Concern had grown among many over the ability of Aya'tar to lead. She was without heir or husband, a great concern for the ruler of any city. Worse, her father's perceived infertility was of concern for any high priestess to a fertility goddess, such as Isut.

There had been significant discussion among the Elders of the city over the matter, but without a collective decision. Sar'Tawas had made it clear that he believed the highest-ranking man who was unmarried should join with Aya'tar. This took into account Utiakur's wishes that she find a husband, as well as the proper order of succession. While many in the Elder Council agreed with his logic, they also heard the undertone of control in his words. It was obvious to everyone as he argued his point that he would be that man. This very issue had brought the Elder Council to meet this night. From the meeting room window, Sar'Tawas could see the Moon in the Southwest. It was waning but still quite bright. He hoped that this was a good omen.

Behind Sar'Tawas stood Ianmu with a clay pot full of water. Though the notion of concubinage was still quite new to the city, many of the Elders had taken note of the utility provided by the concubine. It was a convenience having someone else do the work for you. Ianmu stood patiently with the water maintaining her ever-vigilant expression of vacant disinterest. In reality, her interest in the proceedings before her could hardly be understated. She needed Sar'Tawas to marry Aya'tar or simply seize leadership himself. Only then would she be in a position to take final possession of the city by dagger, accident, or poison. She was still amazed that she had gotten this far alive. *My thanks, An'an,* she thought with conviction.

"She is young, but we could guide her. This would increase the position of the Elder Council and prevent any possibility of angering the gods," argued Kamar. Sar'Tawas waved his hand dismissively while old lady Isu'mamu, mistress of the flax fields, sat patiently awaiting a strong point to be made. The arguments had been continuing since earlier in the day and had yet to achieve any momentum, either way.

"She needs a strong man to guide her. She will wander free without a firm grasp and lead us all into danger. I'm just not sure that Sar'Tawas is such a man," said Gurmar, the master of the herds, all the while glaring at Sar'Tawas. Kakamu, Elder of Lore, laughed as she listened to Gurmar's words.

"Spoken like a true shepherd. Aya'tar is no cow to be lost in the marshes. Legend speaks of a time when a single woman ruled the city and called no man her husband," she said proudly.

"That may be true, but if I recall the story correctly, this woman had several sons. I doubt the spirits fathered them. Perhaps some of the duemuas aided her," Gurmar said with a laugh drawing the ire of Kakamu.

Duemuas were known as the third sex, those born with both the male and female physical aspects. Even more highly regarded than those who could hear spirits speaking in their minds, duemuas were treasures of the city. Very uncommon, such children were considered to be the result of the male bull god Gunar and the goddess Isut inhabiting the parents during conception, the other possible outcomes being incredibly rare female and male twins or a narmu. A duemuas would often be afforded the position of priest within the temple and was considered sacred in body. To harm one was considered blasphemy and a direct attack on the gods, punishable by death. There had been few duemuas born within the city over the last few harvests, and the last duemuas offered, Utu'raru, had declined a position as a priest a few harvests before.

Next to duemuas were Narmu, those whose gender differed from what was commonplace. A narmu might have a male body, yet the spirit of a woman, vice versa, somewhere in between, or perhaps no apparent masculine or feminine gender traits. While not as sacred as a duemuas and numbering a few dozen at any given time, they were considered touched by the goddess or the god and typically given a measure of respect as having been directly affected by the gods.

"To speak that way of a sacred duemuas and a priestess! Such hubris serves only to anger the spirits! What we need now is the good fortune and favor of the gods, not their spite over your joke... it wasn't even funny," Kakamu said. Certain things were inappropriate to make jokes about. Besides, Kakamu was a narmu and looked poorly on such maligned attempts at humor. The gods, duemuas, narmu, and those endowed with the ability to hear voices from beyond or to see what others did not were among groups too sacred for humor. Anyone foolish enough to commit such hubris could potentially be struck down by the gods.

"I shall make my apologies to the gods tomorrow morning with the sacrifice of a goat. I'm sorry... the meeting is long, and I'm weary of argument. It seems that I spoke without thought," said Gurmar. Taking a second thought at what he said, he realized the great danger he could put himself and his family in if he made such jokes. He hated backing down and capitulating to Kakamu, but messing with the gods was too frightening.

Old Katakar, the master of the fields, listened to everyone speak before finally clearing his throat. He had heard Sar'Tawas restate his position and saw some value in his words. He felt it was time to make his intentions clear, the oldest of the elders as he was. Katakar lifted his hands and waited for everyone to come to order. He had not spoken on the issue more than a few moments in all the days since the death of their leader. Everyone sensed his intent and quickly quieted. Ianmu paid special attention to what this old man said as she could sense that everyone in the room held him in high regard.

"Many of you have made your points. In fact, in some ways, you are all correct. Aya'tar is young and inexperienced. Her fertility remains to be seen. The best course of action may be for her to marry someone who would bring her balance, like the fletchings of an arrow. I believe that removing her would bring the ire of the gods upon us. I have seen no sign that she is personally disfavored. If any wish to court her, this, I would suggest. Yes, Sar'Tawas, even you. Aya'tar will choose you if she wishes," he said with a smile. Behind her master, Ianmu also smiled.

"And if time passes and she does not have a child or make her choice?" Sar'Tawas asked, slightly annoyed.

"Then a new ruler to the city may need to be chosen, though I still believe that Aya'tar must remain as leader of the temple unless or until the gods themselves speak against her," Katakar finished. Sar'Tawas smiled, having obtained the sort of answer that he had been looking for. He needed now only to court Aya'tar. Behind him, Ianmu found it difficult to keep from smiling. Things had just become a little bit simpler.

ↄ ↄ ↄ

That night, everyone remained on the festival grounds for the final night of feast and dancing. Kel and Aethen moved their camp next to Ketamir and Nemanar's tent. It made little sense to split their group, given their newfound familiarity. Most importantly, it allowed for sharing resources, such as food, water, and labor. Sadly, three of them would be leaving in the morning. Though the primary festival only lasted two days, much trading and smaller events would continue a few days more. Kel and Espe might continue to remain in the event one or two more days, but they would eventually leave for the Blue Sea afterward, making a stop in Rene.

The Moon was high in the Southwestern sky, and the night was free of clouds as the singing and dancing for the second night continued. Espe and Kel had returned to the dance, though not quite as made up as the night before. Aethen had remained behind with young Ninrea'mu, who seemed quite interested in helping him learn their language, the language of the True South. Ember now stood at the doorway to the hut watching as Ninrea'mu slowly spoke a word while Aethen listened. He seemed oblivious to the girl's obvious crush on him though she was far too young.

"There is much dancing to be had. Would you waste your night learning to speak like a child?" Ember asked Aethen with a smirk. Watching the young girl apparently trying to hide her crush on Aethen was extremely amusing to Ember though she thought it innocently sweet.

"If I can learn a common tongue, then I might find a wife in the South. This girl speaks the language of the women where we travel. With her help, I can do more than just use hand gestures. Besides, she seems keen to help me. Perhaps she's not one for dancing," he said, entirely oblivious. Ember had to contain her laughter over Aethen's apparent

308

inability to see the crush written all over the girl's face. He was a nice person and a true friend, but his perception was lacking.

"If you hang around her for too long, you may already have a wife," she said, laughing as she left the tent. Aethen turned to regard the girl, suddenly realizing what Ember found so humorous. He had not recognized the expression upon her face for what it was until Ember had brought it up. He would have to be careful not to lead the young girl along, as he wouldn't want to break her young heart when he left. He decided that he would explain to the girl as best as possible that he was traveling south to find a wife. He hoped she would take it okay. Unfortunately, she continued to stare at him with a dreamy look in her dark eyes. He sighed at the new problem.

Ↄ Ↄ Ↄ

Ember stepped from the tent to find Brig'dha waiting for her. Both women were still reasonably well painted from the night before, though slightly smeared. They walked hand-in-hand, barefoot, towards a small hilltop not far from the celebrations. As long as they stayed within shouting distance, they would have nothing to fear from wolves and other creatures. The commotion made by the people filled the night and would ward off any such problems.

Tonight was a night when they could relax and completely let go. At a fertility festival, very little would be disapproved of, and what little modesty was required on a typical warm day was tossed to the wind at such an affair. Besides, Ember had quite literally lost her virginity the night before lying on the edge of the dance area, surrounded by untold numbers of dancers. They were hardly the only couple who had failed to make it more than a stone's throw from the dance before losing their self control, yet their passion had been perhaps hotter than the fire itself.

A light breeze carried a fresh wind that was utterly intoxicating against their flesh. They had each held back their feelings for over two harvests, believing them not shared and unwelcome. Now, they walked through the grass hand-in-hand, feeling the love they had rightfully earned through sweat and blood. This was their prize to be had after all they had done, a night to simply let go of all fears. The night before had been so emotional and intense, that it had become a blur of pure love. Tonight, they would take their time and savor their love in the most intimate way they could.

Upon arriving at the hilltop, they gazed out over the festival grounds to take in the sights. It was truly amazing to see so many people dancing around such a huge fire. It was quite a dramatic scene. They could see the bodies of hundreds of dancers moving rhythmically to the sound of percussion and flute. Orange firelight danced off their bodies and adornments. The entire dance brought with it an almost spiritual feeling, a life of its own that was intoxicating. Somewhere below, Espe and Kel danced while Aethen tried as hard as he could to learn the words to court a woman in a faraway land from a girl with a hopeless crush upon him. Ember was suddenly taken by the amusement of it all and laughed loudly, drawing a bemused expression from Brig'dha.

Showing no signs that she would explain what was so funny, Brig'dha tugged upon Ember's arm. Both women knelt onto the ground and then collapsed, rolling onto their backs. The ground was still warm below them, having been heated by the Sun. The fresh air blowing across their skin was slightly damp, and there would be dew before the morning. There was a new freedom in their actions, a liberation which Ember had only before felt as she had stood on the sandy beach all alone in the wilds not long after she had first left her people. The only difference between her feelings then and now was the ever-present warmth of love.

They both lay back in the grass and gazed upon the beauty of the sky. Neither woman knew what the specs of light were, but there were always people with opinions. Ember's friend Blossom had once told her that the stars were the teardrops of the spirits. Ember wondered if each of them might actually be similar to the large chunk of frozen water that she owned. Whatever they were, they were beautiful and slowly twinkling. Most were white, but some had a bluish or reddish color. There were four special stars out tonight. The special stars moved, unlike the others. Many believed that they were spirits or possibly somehow kinfolk of the Moon Goddess. Ember pointed out each of the special stars to Brig'dha, one at a time.

"Directly overhead is the Red Star. It's one of the hardest to see, and you can only see it on a really clear night like this. Over toward the East, where the Sun rises, you can see the tiny orange one. Next to that, just slightly to the East, is the Bright Star, one of the brightest in the sky. It likes the Sun and tends to stay near it. Lastly, the smaller bright star over there really loves the Sun, even more than the last. I know priestesses normally only care about the Sun and the Moon, but don't you think that these other stars might mean something too?" Ember asked. Brig'dha huddled closer to Ember and wrapped her arm behind her head.

Right now, stars were not on her mind though she couldn't help but appreciate their beauty. Ember was the only person she had ever met whose touch didn't feel unnerving, and whose eyes Brig'dha could gaze into, at least for a moment. She had never liked human contact, preferring solitude, yet the radiant redhead just felt… right. Perhaps that was the most significant part of their connection. Ember was someone that she actually could hold, and be held by. She still had sensory issues, one of the reasons for avoiding the dance area, but, somehow, Ember made her feel calm.

"There are many beautiful things in our world. I concern myself with three, the Sun, the Moon, and you," Brig'dha said, rolling onto her side to look at Ember. It was a mushy thing to say, but Ember appreciated it just the same. They had only professed their love for each other the night before. It had been a stirring emotion deep within both women for more than a full harvest, ever since their first journey across the Greatest River. Even now, anticipation danced up and down their bodies, tingling in their toes. Both women were overtaken by a giddy feeling as they rolled closer. Ember again laughed as the giddy feeling danced through her body, a delicate and wonderful joy. She adored the anticipation and longing and wished to delay it as long as possible.

"It is cooler tonight than last night, so let us make a small fire and lie together under the stars," Ember suggested, standing suddenly and heading off to the woods to grab some wood. Brig'dha rolled onto her back and stared at the beautiful stars whispering prayers of thanks that she had found love again. She had known too many women who had lost husbands and had been forced to live the rest of their lives alone. It wasn't fair, but it was the way things were. She thanked the gods yet again for her good fortune.

Even as a young girl, Brig'dha had always found some women attractive. She had found several men somewhat attractive, but it felt more like she appreciated them as being attractive rather than actually being attracted to them. Any person could realize that another person was beautiful and appreciate this even if they were not attracted to that person. It wasn't until she approached adulthood that she realized that other women did not feel the same way she did. It was true that a woman would gaze upon another woman whom she found beautiful, but this was often borne from envy or self evaluation, not actual attraction.

Her marriage to Mohdan had been as much of her family's doing as anything else. Brig'dha's mother had died when she was much younger. Her father had never been known to her. According to her mother, he was a visitor from another tribe engaged in trading. As a result, Brig'dha was raised by her extended family. They had been very interested in setting her up with a man who might gain them some additional position within the tribe, somebody like Mohdan.

Part of her did love him. Mohdan always treated her well and was a decent person, though she was pretty sure that he realized that she did not find him desirable. This might have been the reason that they had never had a child. Children required not only intimacy but repeated intimacy. It was possible to have a child upon the first encounter, but it usually took many for most couples. Though Ember had brought up the possibility that the Amber of Life necklace might be powerful enough to allow any two people to conceive, Brig'dha was quite sure that it was not possible between two women. That certainly made things a lot easier. She lay back continuing to think about her past and what had led her to this point. As she thought, she caught sight of a small shooting star streaking across the sky.

A short time later, Ember appeared with an armload of kindling and a few small, felled logs. It was all she could carry, given their weight. Ember was strong, but wood was heavy. Ember strategically piled the logs and kindling into a small. She had learned much since she had left her people, including properly setting a fire. It was not long until a small flame bathed both women in an orange glow, a private sphere of warmth and protection.

Ember sat beside Brig'dha and watched her as her skin formed little bumps from the difference between the cool night breeze and the radiant flicker of the warm firelight. Both women held hands and simply gazed upon one another for a short while. Something was relaxing about opening up and letting love loose. Brig'dha decided that she would ask Ember a question that had been troubling her since the night before.

"Have you always liked women?" Brig'dha asked, gently rubbing her fingers through Ember's long red hair. She wondered how much longer she could hold back. Ember thought about it for a moment. She had never really given much thought to the subject and sat back for a moment staring at the stars as she searched for a reply. Her life had always been filled with swimming in the river, shoving as many berries in her mouth as possible, and having as much fun with her friends as she could. She often chased after boys and even some men who had journeyed to the tribe but always more for fun than anything else.

"I've looked for love before, but I never really thought of where I might find it. I guess I've never really been that attracted to men. I've never found a person I could truly bond with until you. There was one young man two harvests ago. His name was Pak, I think. I could never have loved him, but I feel like he could have been a friend if things had been different," she said. Brig'dha frowned at the explanation.

"You think? How can you not even be sure of his name?" the priestess asked, confused. Ember laughed.

"Well... he had threatened to kill me just a few moments before. He never really spoke my language, but he pointed to himself and said his name," she answered absentmindedly. Brig'dha rolled over to stare at Ember, her eyes the size of the Moon. She was a strange woman indeed.

"It's okay. It was his leader who was trying to kill me. It's a long story," she said. While she had told Brig'dha of her adventures before they met, including the men who captured her, she had glossed over much of the details of that part of the story, not quite comfortable speaking of them at the time. This did not clarify anything for Brig'dha, but if they planned to walk to the True South, there would be plenty of time to cover this encounter's details. The time for speech had ended, and Ember could sense Brig'dha's frustration at wasting such a beautiful night in conversation. Though shy during the day, the priestess had proven quite bold at night.

She placed a silencing finger on Ember's lips, then leaned in to kiss them. The radiant redhead's lips were as soft as a flower petal. Brig'dha took her time kissing them as her fingers traced a line down Ember's abdominal muscles. Ember's swimming, running, and other activities had seen her body become tight with definition, a fact Brig'dha had waited all day to explore. As she kissed, her tongue probing deeper, her fingers delicately rose and fell as they passed over each abdominal muscle, then up and over her chest. The warrior's voice, typically so strong, became weak in the moment as Brig'dha's fingers found just the right place to sap her strength.

"Kaelu... Ehg, wennus'du," the moon priestess whispered as Ember's hands found her fuller body. It meant, "Ember, I love you," yet it was a shadow of her true feelings. Brig'dha left the softness of her lips, kissing down Ember's arms, each strong and defined from drawing her bow, yet distinctly feminine. Brig'dha gasped as Ember became bolder, ever the explorer. A moment later, the moon priestess lay on her back, watching the Moon above, feeling joy beyond her wildest imagination, her body locked in the warm embrace of the beautiful warrior Ember, her best friend, and lover. She surrendered to the night and let herself go to the sounds of music, dancing, and the most tender kisses of all. How could anything feel so right?

ɔ ɔ ɔ

Not far away, Espe and Kel strode past a group of merrymaking folk from another tribe. They had been headed for a secluded little hill when they saw the firelight and the shapes of two lovers. Seeing that the hilltop was occupied, they turned to head toward the stream where they had cleaned during the day. Hopefully, this would be a secluded place where they could use the magic of the Amber of Life. Both of them felt a wonderful excitement coursing through their veins as they left the dance for the joys known only to lovers. They had expressed their mutual wish to wed only the night before.

More even than Kel, Espe felt a freedom that she had never known. She had only recently been made a woman, and in that time, she had never done anything on her own or outside of the tribe. She had lived with her parents, as young unmarried women were supposed to, and had little say in her destiny. Now here she was walking hand-in-hand with the man she wished to marry with no one to tell her what to do but the stars themselves. She had discovered him, hunted him, caught him, and now she would marry him. She let out an almost giggly laugh at the exhilaration of freedom. Growing up was both liberating and a little intimidating.

It was only a few moments before they reached the hidden shores of the stream. Kel came to a halt pulling Espe from her thoughts. He turned to face her. She was beautiful, but more importantly, she cared for him. He couldn't quite explain to himself why that meant so much more. When he was younger, he had chased after women like most men. Love was not always the intention. Now, when he looked into her eyes and saw only love in return, he realized that love was the only important part. Love was what truly fulfilled him. He knew that not every man would see it the way he did, but that didn't matter. The only thing which mattered to Kel was the woman standing before him. This course of action could lead to only one result, and he aimed to ensure the greatest luck at that result.

"Espe... this is the one night we can use the Amber of Life. It is what I want, but is this what you want?" Espe looked upon him with a slight shock at the question. It wasn't so much that she hadn't expected it, but that she had not expected it at that very moment. So many men were strong and brave, but not that many as good as Kel. Sure, he was strong and skilled but also kind and compassionate. He was open about his feelings, a rarity among the men of her tribe. She knew the consequences of their actions the night before and the action they intended in moments. She would not have laid with him in the field of flowers, at her tribe, and the night before had she not considered the answer to this very question. She simply had wanted to hear him ask it.

She looked him in the face and giggled, slowly tilting her head from right to left as she gently touched his cheek with her hand. Kel became unsure of himself as she simply stared without answering. She continued to look him over for a short time longer, jealously savoring his look of confusion. The more horrified his expression grew, the more weight she realized that his words had carried. Espe stepped closer and reached for the string holding her linen skirt in place.

"Yes... We shall be one," she softly spoke as the skirt fell and she stepped forward wearing only the Amber of Life. Kel – his heart racing – placed his hands gently on her hips and looked deeply into her eyes. The pendant hung between her breasts, and she felt warmth rush through her body, which she attributed to its power. Neither was sure of how powerful the object was, but somehow the night seemed more magical than before. Kel embraced his lover thanking the spirits for their grace. Espe closed her eyes, asking them for twins, a boy and a girl.

ᴐ ᴐ ᴐ

Aya'tar sat atop the temple building, watching the Duya aza'n, literally "in between festival." There were two periods when the day and night came at equal length for each harvest. One occurred in the middle of the thawing and growing season, and the other came amid the late harvest. Like the majority of the other festivals celebrated in the city, this festival was a fertility festival aimed at ensuring that the following growing season's crops, which had just been planted, were bountiful. Between these, many festivals of harvest, purification, and other such important events occurred. The festival took the entire day and lasted into the night. During the early parts of the ceremony, intricate dances would be performed to appease the spirits and the Goddess. At the end of the festival, a general dance would open up for everyone.

The early night air was filled with the smells of scented oils, large fires, and the sounds of dancing. Below Aya'tar was the main dance ground with hundreds of people gathered outside. In the center, a dozen men danced wearing only bullhorns upon their heads and painted from head to toe with intricate patterns. These men each represented the spirits of male fertility. A series of women would dance in between them similarly decorated but wearing flowers and wheat instead of horns in a few more moments. In times past, Aya'tar had been one of those women, but tonight she was the high priestess and leader of the city. Her duty was to observe and to be observed.

She had been feeling strange ever since the last time her pains had come. They had come at the wrong time and had been unusually weak, but she assumed that this was simply the result of the stress she had been under. Normally, her pains came nearly once a moon and were of average strength, though this was not the case for all women. Hullamu always seemed shocked when her pains came upon her, and Isha'kau claimed hers were almost nonexistent. What possessed a woman's body to bleed was anyone's guess, but Aya'tar never spoke poorly of the pains as they were part of Isut's will.

She laughed to herself as she thought of a proverb told by the older women:

When men bleed, they prepare to end life, but when women bleed, they prepare to create life.

It really wasn't a fair proverb, but it was certainly something to think about as boredom seeped in from every direction. She wondered how her father had dealt with these nonstop ceremonies. They had never before troubled her, but she had always been a dancer. Below danced hundreds to the beat of rhythmic percussion and the sound of flute and song. Soon, the dancing competition would begin, and youth wishing to impress their peers would compete.

Aya'tar was simply happy that no one but Isha'kau and Hullamu sat with her on top of the temple building, watching. She had felt sick when she had awoken and spent a short time that morning over a clay jar dry heaving. It was only a short time after that when lore master Kakamu had stopped by to see how she was doing. It did not take long before Aya'tar realized Kakamu's real intentions – to determine if she had found a suitable candidate for a husband. For some reason, every single person in the city always seemed to have an ulterior motive for everything they did. It could be burdensome trying to guess all these unknown purposes.

Everyone wanted her to marry and bring forth a child. The child part was slightly frightening, but that part almost seemed easy compared to the other. She had fallen in love with a young copper worker named Imkanar, a man of low birth. If they became married, he would become co-leader of the city and at least a priest to Isut or Gunar, by default. If the people did not support this decision, it could tear the city apart, some siding with her and others with the Council of Elders. All she wanted were Imkanar's warm, strong arms wrapped around her, but even as the ruler of the city, their love had to remain a secret. She wondered if some of the other great cities were smarter for not having an established ruling class, such as Du'ubria, one day known as Catalhoyuk.

She needed to leave and meet with Imkanar, but that seemed less and less likely. Aya'tar turned her attention to the female dancers as they burst onto the scene, their bodies painted with red and yellow stripes. She loved the dances, seeing all the beautiful costumes and the intricate moves. Somehow, tonight the dance was not as lovely to her as it normally was. She suspected the problem lay with her darkening mood more than the actual dancing. She would almost cry if she had not already exhausted all her tears at the death of her father. His body had first been placed upon a wooden tower for one full moon for vultures, the sacred messengers of Isut, to carry his spirit to the Third World. After that, his remains had been cleaned, painted with ochre, paint, and plaster, then buried within the temple under one of the stone benches not too many days before.

If the spirit chose to remain, he would be resting barely the length of a man from where she slept. Being surrounded by the spirits of the dead was comforting. Sometimes, their skulls would be dug back up and placed in prominent places where they could see and influence the happenings of the world. She wouldn't know for quite some time if his spirit remained, though the signs pointed to his departure to the next world.

Just beside the high priestess, Isha'kau could see the frustration and the worry in Aya'tar's eyes. She had loved the high priestess as a sister since they were children, though they were unrelated. Isha'kau could not tell what the source of her frustration was and suspected that there was more to it than simply the loss of her father. Life was hard, and death was common, but the emotions that Aya'tar displayed suggested a deeper problem – a festering problem. In the meantime, the high priestess' cup had run low on water. She could, at least, fill the cup if nothing more. Isha'kau lifted a clay pot full of water and moved to fill the cup. Moving too quickly, she accidentally bumped Aya'tar's arm, causing her to drop the cup. Aya'tar's face flared with anger as she turned upon her childhood friend.

"Watch what you're doing!" she blasted. The look on Isha'kau's face was one of shock more than anything else. Her friend was not known for yelling, and she could not recall the last time that Aya'tar had ever raised her voice since they had become adults. Aya'tar quickly realized that her outburst was not proportionate to the situation. How could she have become so instantaneously angry? What was wrong with her mood? Her face flushed with embarrassment, and she suddenly felt ashamed of her actions. The night was going poorly, and everything seemed against her. Above all, she really needed an excuse to leave and see Imkanar.

"I... I'm sorry. I don't know what has come over me tonight. Please forgive me," she said humbly. Isha'kau stepped forward and embraced Aya'tar in a sisterly way.

"There is no worry. You've been through a lot recently. Think nothing of it," the lesser priestess said. Aya'tar suddenly had a thought, but she felt slightly guilty for it. The night was going poorly, and an escape from the current festival would do her good. Isha'kau was similarly built to Aya'tar. From a distance and wearing a linen shawl against the cool night air, who could tell the difference? After yelling at the woman, the suggestion she was about to make made her feel even worse, but she had to get away if she wanted her mood to ever improve. A simple swapping of roles might do the trick.

"Switch places with me, quickly!" Aya'tar said as the two women rotated in their embrace, quickly swapping shawls. Isha'kau sat, totally confused, while Aya'tar stood back as a humble servant. It took only a moment for the quick-witted Isha'kau to realize what had just happened. For a moment, both just stared at each other, waiting to see whether or not anyone had noticed the sudden exchange. At that very moment of the dance, the main dancing woman and man had entered into a close and very exaggerated series of moves. Everyone's attention seemed to be captivated by their movement. The only person who seemed to notice was Hullamu, who was trying desperately to restrain herself from laughing.

"I can't stand the ceremony anymore. I just want to be alone for the rest of the evening. I'll be okay, but do you mind being the ruler of the city until the festival is over?" Aya'tar asked Isha'kau in a playful tone, a tiny piece of good humor returning to her at the prospect that she might soon be away from it all. The priestess thought about it for a moment and then smiled. It was not often that she had a chance to be the city's ruler. Realistically, nobody would see, and she need merely sit on the nice stool and drink fermented honey wine. It was really a win-win situation.

"Fine, my servant! I command you to leave us now and go rest. Don't make your leader angry!" Isha'kau said in jest. Aya'tar bowed her head at the order and left with a sigh of relief. She did not know why she had yelled at her friend a few moments before, but she had been overreacting lately. Worse, she felt worn out, and then there was the sickness in the morning. If she had not so recently had her pains, she would have thought that she carried a child. If only she could get enough sleep, maybe she would feel better.

"Why do you get to be the leader? I'm the one who does all the hard work," Hullamu protested. Isha'kau waved her hand dismissively.

"Quiet my servant, and fetch your leader a cup of drink... and perhaps one for yourself. Am I not benevolent?" she said in a playful tone. Hullamu rolled her eyes and reached for the jug.

ɔ ɔ c

Sar'Tawas sat at a table near the main dance area eating a delectable dish of roasted duck while his concubine stood beside him, keeping his drink topped off. The fertility festival had always stirred him at a primal level. He suspected that it had the same effect on most people, which might have something to do with the large number of children born during the wet season. Tonight was no exception as he watched the women dance before him, their bodies painted white and intricately designed beaded necklaces flying with their movements.

By his side stood the concubine woman Ianmu. She was perhaps more annoyed than anything else. Tonight would be a great night to get information about the intentions of the high priestess Aya'tar. She needed to be following the priestess instead of filling her "Master's" cup. It had not escaped her notice when the priestess had swapped places with one of her helpers. Sar'Tawas was no fool, but a dancing area filled to the top with beautiful dancing women had taken his attention faster than a bolt of lightning. Like many men, his weakness was women. It seemed to be the only thing capable of defeating his otherwise exceptionally cunning mind.

She was not a slave and could leave any time she wished. A concubine was more of a lesser wife in rank but without the benefit of station and say in family affairs. Unfortunately, she needed to maintain her appearance of being thoughtless and dim. To leave Sar'Tawas and run off for a while would quickly alert the man that she had some ulterior motivations. She rolled her eyes at the annoying facade but quickly regained her composure, needing to think of a strategy.

She needed to get him away from the ceremony and asleep. She had been keeping his drink filled, hoping that he would become drunk and leave for bed, but so far, he had managed to stay sober. Only one other technique came to mind, and she again rolled her eyes at the thought. If only there were some other way... but Sar'Tawas could not be intrigued by her intelligence while she tried her hardest to mask that same intelligence. She would make use of more simple pleasures, a quality she had not concealed. Luckily, the dancing women seemed to put him in the perfect mood.

Sar'Tawas was initially annoyed when his vantage of the dancers was suddenly blocked by his concubine. She stepped forward to refill his cup, making sure to do so in as enticing of a manner as possible. His anger quickly faded as he realized that before him stood a willing concubine. She was much prettier than the women he now gazed upon. What's more, he had learned that she could dance well, and an alluring dance at that. He felt a little rundown, having consumed so much fermented honey drink. That fool concubine of his seemed to keep his cup ever filled. If she had been one of the Elders of the city, he would have suspected something, but when he gazed into her eyes, he saw nothing but innocence.

"Come, enough of this dancing. I would have a private dance and whatever else comes with it," he pronounced, slowly standing as he quickly imbibed the remainder of his cup. Ianmu stepped backward and looked as confused as she could. Deep down, she was withholding a smile over how easily her plan was working. Sar'Tawas had two vices: women and drink. This was convenient since she was a woman, and she carried a very large clay vessel full of fermented drink.

ↄ ↄ ↄ

Ianmu rolled over and took a deep breath. She had danced for a little while and then laid with the man until he was satisfied and had fallen asleep. This entire process had taken surprisingly less time than she had expected, considering the amount of drink he had consumed. Perhaps she had laid the dance on a little thicker than usual. In truth, Ianmu found that she enjoyed dancing. She would have preferred a different audience, but there was something sensual about dancing in such an alluring way. Something about the effect it had upon Sar'Tawas felt empowering. Though he commanded her to dance, in reality, she was the one in control.

Reattaching her loincloth and wrapping a linen shawl around her upper body for warmth, Ianmu left the building and headed to where the high priestess slept. She would need to remember to make an offering to An'an after she finished to ensure that nothing came of her activities with Sar'Tawas. A woman always had to take proper precautions. It had been a while since the priestess had left the dance, and the Moon had moved four finger widths from the Northeast to the eastern sky. With the Sun having set not long before, she quietly moved through the alleyways passing house after house full of festive people. In fact, Nara'kit had no alleyways, nor did Du'ubria, if she recalled what she had heard of the other great proto-cities.

ɔ ɔ ɔ

Aya'tar stood near a midden building not far from the temple, waiting for Imkanar. He had told her that he would meet her when the Moon was in the East at this very location. Unfortunately, the temperature had dropped, and she would not wait much longer, lover or not. She had been feeling ill recently, and spending a significant time away from a fire was an unwelcome feeling.

"Hey, Aya'tar!" came the welcome voice of Imkanar as he stepped from around the corner, looking to make sure that nobody had followed.

"I'm sorry that I am late. The old man had me heat some copper for tomorrow. He likes to get working as soon as he comes in," he explained. Copper required heating and cooling before it could be worked. After only a short time of working with the metal, it would become hard again and require more heating and cooling, one of the very strange properties of copper. The techniques to melt and pour copper into molds had not quite made their way to Isut'na, yet. One of Imkanar's jobs was to maintain this heating and cooling process.

She could tell that he had been working before a fire as he smelled strongly of wood smoke. The smell of oil, wood smoke, and leather was common upon everyone's body, but Imkanar had a strong musky sort of wood smoke about him tonight. Strangely, she felt slightly attracted to the smell for reasons she could not explain. This was a good thing as she had discovered just two days before that walnuts suddenly made her extremely ill to be near. She was glad that his scent had not triggered the same response. Semi-peculiar things had happened to her recently, and she was beginning to become worried about her health. If a person became sick, there was nothing other than prayer and ritual that could help them.

Aya'tar came to stand before Imkanar. She wore a finely dyed bark fiber skirt with a soft and well-worn linen shawl. Around her wrists, ankles, and neck were many fine strings of beads, customary to wear at a festival. Her feet were bound in leather sandals, and she wore ceremonial body paints. By comparison, Imkanar was truly a peasant. He wore a simple leather loincloth and a pair of old sandals. He had not even worn a shawl against the cold. She could even see soot upon his chest from a hard day's work. What attracted her to the man was the way he looked at her and the way he spoke to her, though his handsome form was undeniable. She was deeply in love with the copper worker.

This made what she was about to say to him even more troubling. She had been worrying about how the Elder Council would react if they learned of her relationship with the low-born man. Many powerful people either sought to wed her or play matchmaker with somebody from their families. As a result, Imkanar's very life could be in jeopardy if their love were allowed to continue. For right now, she hoped that she could convince Imkanar to keep his distance for a short time until she could figure things out.

"My love, things have become complicated. It's not safe for us to see each other now," she said, her emotions running wild and her composure harder to maintain than normal. For a moment, she waited in anticipation expecting Imkanar to react negatively to what she had said. Instead, he smiled, his chest filling with confidence.

"I fear no man and wish only to be by your side. I don't care about titles or ruling the city. If things are dangerous, then why don't we run away to one of the northern villages. With some of the items in your possession, we could easily trade for a decent standing in one of the tribes. It would not be such a bad life, and we would be together without complication," he pleaded. To Imkanar, everything seemed so simple – If the city was a danger, leave the city. The problem facing Aya'tar was a responsibility beyond anything which Imkanar understood. She was not just a leader. She was the spiritual link to the Goddess for her people.

She doubted Isut would rain down fire from the sky merely if she left, but she owed it to the people, her people. Besides, she had met with several elders, and they had discussed the importance of her finding a man. If only she could sway them to understand that the man she needed was Imkanar, but she doubted that would come to pass. Why did it all have to be so complicated? Why couldn't love simply be?

ɔ ɔ ɔ

Ianmu lay on the rooftop above, carefully listening to the conversation. She casually adjusted her loincloth strap and scratched a nagging itch on her butt as she lay uncomfortably gathering priceless information. It appeared to her that Aya'tar had just increased the stakes by finding a man, and nobody realized. Even better, it was the wrong type of man. She rolled over onto her back with nothing but stars above. It was difficult to hold back laughter, but this was exactly the sort of information she needed.

All she would need to do was figure out how to allow Sar'Tawas to discover the information. He would act quickly, removing the unwanted male, and he would do so discreetly. Learning that Aya'tar had already found a man on the side could have no effect other than spur Sar'Tawas to move more aggressively. What's more, this low-born man was likely the only reason Aya'tar had not given in to Sar'Tawas's persistent petition to wed. She was already convinced that he was taking too long, and she didn't want to lose her chance. If Sar'Tawas failed to take control of the city or marry Aya'tar, she would have to switch to an alternate plan.

ɔ ɔ ɔ

"Please, consider what I've said," he finished, looking the high priestess dead in the eyes. She returned his gaze. She wanted to tell him that there was no way that they could be together, but she didn't want to harm what little hope he had. Secretly, she harbored the same dreams. These were the foolish dreams of a child, but she would cling to them for as long as she could. Part of her just wanted to die or perhaps run away. It was all so painful and so complicated.

"Here, I made something for you, something for you to remember me by." She looked at him, confused by his words. His resigned look of sadness told her full well that he was no fool and harbored the same doubts that she did. Perhaps his request had been his last hope in delaying or avoiding the inevitable. Either way, his wording was upsetting and added to the already defeated and hopeless feelings that had plagued Aya'tar of late.

"I want you to consider what I said about running away together. We both know that it is likely that our love will never be, but we can hope. No matter what, I want you to keep this to remember me by... No matter what happens," he said, pulling free an object from his loincloth strap. He presented the object in the moonlight for Aya'tar to see. It was a long copper hairpin. The narrow copper shaft was one and one-half the length of her finger, the end hammered flat with what looked like the etching of a bird feather upon it. Such an item would have taken many long days to make from a single copper nugget and was no simple gift.

"Let me help you with it," he said. She was stunned by the gift. Jewelry made of metal was of extreme rarity. Copper was difficult to work with, and only two methods were known. The metal could be heated and cooled and then worked with stone tools. This process was repetitious and took significant time to perform. The other method involved melting the copper into a mold, but she had only heard of other cities doing this and no one in Isut'na had yet figured out how. The small dent marks on the copper suggested that most of the work had been performed by small stone tools and hammering. This made the copper very hard but was also extremely difficult.

Imkanar stood behind Aya'tar and carefully bundled her hair into a ponytail and then proceeded to roll it around and around until it eventually became a circular bun on the back of her head. The hairpin fit through the bun holding the hair in place quite tightly. As soon as her hair was pinned up, she could hear better and even see more of her surroundings. Though she enjoyed her hair being loose and down, there was a benefit to having one's hair in a bundle. A hairpin like this would mean the difference between profuse sweat or cool tolerance on a hot day.

ↄ ↄ ↄ

The festivities had ended, and most people had left for their beds or each other's company when Ianmu reached the dance grounds near Sar'Tawas's building. Though there was a more direct way back to his building, she had taken several side-passages looking for just the right person to satisfy her new goal. Sar'Tawas was useful, but he was also very intelligent and, therefore, dangerous to her. What she needed was a man she could fully control, someone who would not think too deeply about it. If Sar'Tawas failed to eliminate the boy or if Aya'tar became a liability, she needed someone who could do what must be done, especially if she were around other people at the time.

It was not long before Ianmu noticed a single drunken man urinating against the side of a building. She had seen this man several times before and noted that he was never with any friends or women. Everything about his demeanor suggested someone who was not a deep thinker. She would have to take a risk as there wasn't a huge selection of men to choose from, and, given her strategy for controlling this person, a woman was simply out of the question. She offered a quick prayer to An'an that her words and actions might be guided.

She stepped from around the corner and placed her hands upon her eyes, rubbing them to provide the illusion that she had cried. As she walked into the open moonlit area, the man finished adjusting his loincloth and turned to see her. To the man, she appeared to be a woman in distress. He wasn't sure what had happened to her, but he figured he might as well ask. He was quite confident he would fix whatever it was.

"Hey, what's wrong with you? Had a bad night?" he asked. Ianmu could not tell yet whether or not this was the man, but things were going well so far. She stopped and looked down as though too ashamed to speak. The man stepped forward and placed his hand on her shoulder, turning her roughly to see her face. Such roughness was not an endearing feature, but it was certainly the kind of brazen and brutish attitude Ianmu was looking for. His demeanor might also explain why she had never seen him with a woman.

"Hey, my name is Pedar. I've seen you before with that guy, Sar'Tawas. Aren't you his lover or something? Shouldn't you be with him?" he asked. Ianmu's hand reached behind her loincloth to where her small flint dagger was tucked away. If she gave away too much information and he proved not to be the man she needed, she would have to slice his throat. It was a risk, but as a priestess of An'an, she could not let fear stand in her way.

"I am the concubine of Sar'Tawas. Tonight I tried to please him... he rejected me. He threatened to beat me if I didn't get out of his sight. He was angry about some deal that failed," she said, feigning tears. Pedar looked at the woman, confused. He could not understand why any man would reject such a woman, but he suspected Sar'Tawas had some other reasons that he didn't understand. He certainly knew that he would never reject a woman like this. Though he honestly felt bad for her, his care over her state was born more of objectification than thoughtful empathy. Ianmu ironically considered that the man she had seen with Aya'tar would likely have come to her aid out of empathy rather than objectification. *Such irony,* she thought. This was why she could not use good men.

"Maybe, you would let me stay the night with you? Please, I don't want to sleep alone," she asked with her most innocent expression. It always seemed to work, though the idea that an abused woman would desire to sleep with a stranger was absolutely absurd. Yet, the innocent look clouded the minds of the foolish and weak-willed. Only women seemed immune to her innocent look, though she had witnessed them fall victim to men with similar charm. It always irritated her having to use this technique, but her objective was quite immense, and she needed to use whatever worked. Nothing was below her when the will of An'an was concerned.

ɔ ɔ ɔ

Sar'Tawas awoke to find his concubine lying beside him where she had fallen asleep after their short but intense encounter. His head ached from the fermented brew, and wondered again why he drank something that caused so much pain. For the 100th time, he swore to himself that he would never drink another cup, but he knew that later that night, he would have another. It was a vicious cycle that many people succumbed to. As he sat up, he let his eyes wander up and down the concubine. She looked so peaceful as she slept. He couldn't help but appreciate that there was one person he could trust not to be a danger. She was far too innocent and beautiful to be anything but a butterfly on his finger. A thing to be admired.

Ianmu awoke and rubbed the sleep from her eyes. She had finished satisfying Pedar's "compassion," then returned to pray before her secret altar of An'an, finally lying down in the same position she had been in once she had finished with Sar'Tawas. She had not had enough sleep after the previous night's escapades, but she would trade sleep any night for the information she had obtained and the patsy she had found. She would need to maintain her relationship with Pedar every few days and continue the story that she had begun to weave of how her master beat her and rejected her. She would eventually have to move the story towards whatever purpose Pedar would play, but that would be in times to come. For now, she had a more pressing concern.

For her next performance, she would have to drop information right into the lap of Sar'Tawas without him suspecting her involvement. He was a cunning man who had a tendency to notice things that didn't add up. This presented a problem as there was no real way to be anything but direct. She took a breath and prepared herself for what was to come. Ianmu had long before accepted that her treachery and her lies might bring her death, but she was in the service of her Goddess who had come to her and directly given her a task. She would rather die in the service of An'an than live a safe life void of purpose. Therefore, every detail had to be perfect.

"I am quite sure that we will need more clay next warm season. That damned fool Kitnar thinks he can pull a fast one over us, but I'm confident he has access to more dried clay than he claims," Sar'Tawas ranted as he paced back and forth, apparently angered by some trade deal. He rounded on Ianmu, pausing momentarily to take in her visage.

"You don't really care about clay, do you? Well, at least you listen," he said, slightly amused by the concubine's apparent lack of understanding. She stood before him with a smile, casually brushing the hair from her face.

"Master, I will get water and food from the trading place if you wish. You want to celebrate, right?" she asked as innocently as possible while standing completely nude, having just awoken and for effect. Sar'Tawas was mildly distracted by her form, but her words caused him to frown. Luckily, her form seemed to have distracted him enough to be more concerned with what she had said and not too concerned by how she had known to say it.

"Celebrate? And what exactly will we be celebrating? I am still deficient at least 12 pots of clay," he asked incredulously, though trying not to stare. Ianmu stood back and clasped her hands together in front of her body, looking down slightly to show the body language of someone who felt that they had made an err.

"I'm sorry, Master, but I thought that you would want to celebrate that the priestess woman had found a man. I remember hearing in your elder meeting that this was what they wanted," she said. She barely drew her next breath before Sar'Tawas rushed forward, grabbing her by the arms. This was exactly what she had wanted him to do, though he came at her so fast that she was genuinely surprised when he grasped her arms, shaking them.

"Found a man!? By the spirits of the snakes, what are you speaking of? What have you heard, and how did you hear it?" he asked. Ianmu looked as timid as she could, all the while trying to hold back a smile that could make a wildcat envious. She timidly replied, making sure to look as ashamed and fearful as she could while doing so. Playing with Sar'Tawas was dangerous, but oh, so much fun.

"I'm sorry. I did not mean to say the wrong thing. Last night on our way back, I saw the priestess in the embrace of a man, a young man who works with copper. He handed her a copper hairpin. I saw him once before when you visited old man Kuwar, the copper worker," Sar'Tawas listened to every word, looking his concubine in the eyes to see the truth of her words. She seemed almost frightened by his sudden aggression, and truthfully, he felt slightly embarrassed for having reacted so aggressively. Regardless, this news was not welcome. He had seen that young boy who worked with Kuwar eyeing the priestess once before, though he had never suspected anything more than the boy fancying the woman. He couldn't hold it against him for finding Aya'tar beautiful; no one could. However, he could hold it against the little bastard if he made a move on her.

Sar'Tawas let go of the concubine and rushed into the small storeroom to get his sandals. He had things to do, given the severity of the news he had just learned. Ianmu waited, pretending to shake with fear until he left. Afterward, she replaced her loincloth and sat down on the bed. She was still quite tired and figured that Sar'Tawas would likely be preoccupied with her news for much of the day. This would give her a chance to rest. Besides, satisfying both of her "lovers" had left her sore, and a chance to skip a night would be welcome.

"What was that master? You said you wanted me to drink the rest of the fermented drink and take the day off? As you wish," she said to herself, laughing. She felt like she needed a good relaxing nap.

Ianmu the "concubine" or Ianmu'kimun of Nara'ki

CHAPTER EIGHTEEN

A FERTILITY GODDESS

Isut'na is often referred to as a Neolithic proto-city, yet it could be classified as a Chalcolithic proto-city, given the use of copper and other soft metals. The Chalcolithic, or "Copper Age," followed the Neolithic, existing for a short time before the Bronze Age started. In fact, Catalhoyuk, the real proto-city Isut'na is loosely based upon, was deep into the copper age at the time of our story. Of course, only a small number of copper items are being produced at Isut'na, and most of the populace continues to use stone-age technology, making the categorization of Isut'na a bit gray.

Brig'dha opened her eyes and looked up at a bright blue sky harboring a few puffy clouds. She lay atop a small hill by the remainder of a burned-out fire. At her side, Ember lay softly snoring. Strangely, she felt something fluffy at her feet. Sitting up, she noticed that Mew the cat had arrived sometime late that night and curled into a small fluffy ball between her legs, just above her feet. He had done this a few times before and seemed to find feet the best place to sleep. She just could not understand why any animal chose that location, but it did keep her feet warm. She was surprised that he had come out of hiding, given the number of people, but Mew had always been a strange cat.

Today was the day for the group to leave for the True South. Brig'dha quickly attached her bark fiber string skirt Espe had lent her and began to poke Ember in the stomach to wake her. It was hard to do so when she would rather curl back into the redhead's strong embrace, but they would have many more nights together. Perhaps a greater task than the journey to the True South was the simple act of waking Ember. Brig'dha tried tickles, poking, and even shaking her. Eventually, the reluctant redhead rolled over and began to climb to her feet. Brig'dha was unsure what words came from her lips as they were in her native tongue, but they sounded less than enthusiastic. Ember was not a morning person.

"I've had a drink that makes you feel warm and relaxed and then fall asleep. I wish they had a drink that woke you up. Maybe they have something like that in the True South," she grumbled. Neither woman was a morning person, but Ember was exceedingly lazy. While Ember fiddled with her loincloth cord, Brig'dha poked at the remainder of their fire to ensure that none of the remains were still hot. It wasn't considered good form to start a forest fire. It wasn't long before they were both walking down the path toward the stream to wash.

ↄ ↄ ↄ

The women were mostly clean by the time Aethen wandered to the stream. He had spent a good portion of the night with Ninrea'mu learning the language of the True South and had then slept to let the knowledge sink in. At least among his people, it was known that the key to learning was a good night's sleep. He now felt that he was ready to at least greet a woman from the True South and perhaps say a few things. He had been glad that young Ninrea'mu had taken it well when he had explained that he would be using the words he learned from her to find a wife. Her crush on him did not seem to diminish, but it seemed that she understood his reasons.

Just as Aethen stepped into the cool water to wash, Kel and Espe approached all smiles. Around her neck, Espe wore the Amber of Life and strangely held her hand on her lower abdomen. For a moment, Ember stared curiously at the hand position. The only reasons she could imagine for a woman rubbing her lower body in that position would be either stomach pains from something she ate, the pains that women went through each moon, or the belief that she was pregnant. Ember discarded the last possibility as it would be impossible for something like that to occur in one night.

"Why are you holding your belly? Is something wrong?" Ember asked out of curiosity. Espe stopped and smiled back at her in an almost motherly way. Kel restated the words to Espe in her language, though it appeared that she might have already figured out what Ember had asked. Espe giggled and then replied in her own language and with the tone of an expectant mother, a sort of reverence in her words.

"Eekh syeenkh. Eekh mater'muks!" Neither Ember nor Brig'dha required translation as they knew what she had meant by her tone, even though they did not know what she had said. Both Ember and Brig'dha stared at the woman with confused expressions, Ember's right eyebrow cocked.

"I am pregnant. I am a mother, soon," Kel translated, though even he too had a cocked eyebrow. Nobody was quite sure what to say, nor did anybody wish to object to her proclamation. It was simply too early for anyone to know, but women sometimes had strange feelings about things,

330

and everyone simply assumed that was what had happened. Besides, she *had* worn the Amber of Life, so it wasn't outside the realm of possibility. Anything was possible with magic, though Ember suspected it was simply more of Espe's squirl-like antics.

Brig'dha stood, still dripping with water, and approached Espe. With a permissive nod from Espe, she placed her hand gently over the flighty hazel-eyed woman's lower abdomen. She could feel a strange warm sensation with her hand, which she attributed to being the feeling of life. She whispered prayers to the Moon Goddess that the baby would be born safely and that Espe would survive the birth. A pregnant woman was always something to celebrate, but a hidden danger came with birth. All of them knew of at least one woman who had died in childbirth and many children who died before birth or even soon afterward. Those old enough to have children were simply lucky, the survivors.

☽ ☽ ☽

It was midday when Ember stood by Ketamir and Nemanar's tent, hugging each of them goodbye. She had lived with their family for over a quarter harvest, and they had saved her life, but now she would leave them and journey to the lands where they were born. Ember would journey to the vast cities in the South to witness sights that few from the North would ever see. The trip had a strangely romantic and whimsical feel that was not lost upon anyone. Ember was ready for a new adventure, a new place to see. With Brig'dha at her side, she felt she could take on the world.

Ember and Brig'dha were similarly dressed, wearing long leather shirts with wide loincloths and nettle fiber, leather soled boots. Ember had recovered her doeskin shirt with spots which Aethen had kept after she had removed it to paint herself black before her near death a quarter harvest before. Almost the inverse, Aethen carried his shirt in his traveling pack, instead donning a pair of leather leggings and a loincloth, leaving his upper body free to the cool air. The group had cold-weather clothing in their traveling bags, but it was still too warm to wear, especially when walking. Luckily, Ember had obtained some old and used travel gear from Nemanar. She could not wait to meet more people from where these generous people hailed.

Everyone in her "foster" family was sad to see Ember go, but no one was quite so sad as young Ninrea'mu. Ember and the young girl had experienced many days of fun and fishing in the warm Sun, as well as

331

learning to speak each other's words. Ember held back her tears as she took one more glance over her shoulder before the group left, heading in the direction of the rising Sun. Everyone hated goodbyes, especially if they were long. Ember had left a string of people in her wake who were friends and who she might never see again. It was always bittersweet. This was a price to be paid for one who wished to see the world. At least she now had a friend by her side whom she would never have to leave.

Based on Nemanar's directions, they were to head east for a full tenday where they would encounter the land abruptly turning south, though a little easterly. At this point, they were to head south, following the shoreline. Ember was unsure how warm the trip would be, though the temperature had not really dropped that much. The group carried a small amount of provisions they had traded for before leaving, though it would not be long before they either needed to pick up more provisions at a village along the way or simply hunt for some food. Either way, remaining near the coast would make things easier. Behind them, Mew, the cat, slowly trudged along, hoping desperately that someone would pick him up.

☾ ☾ ☾

Aya'tar sat on her bed, waiting for the nausea to end. Isha'kau had spoken with her the night before and had suggested quite strongly the possibility that she might be pregnant. Aya'tar had dismissed the notion explaining that she had recently felt her pains, though they had been light. She had been shocked when Isha'kau explained to her that some women occasionally had their pains even after they were already carrying a child. She had dismissed the statements and gone to bed, but now as she sat with the clay pot in hand and hoping the nausea would end, she realized that the younger priestess was probably right. *Isut... am I carrying a child? The child of my...* her thoughts suddenly ended in another wave of vomit.

"It's definitely a child. Likely two children with the way you're vomiting. These things can be divined, of course," Hullamu said. She sat in the corner of the room, slowly spinning flax fibers into flax thread, a common daily chore. The younger priestess had long dark hair, which she kept loose, and hazel eyes. The room was illuminated from a gentle light entering through a window and from the crackling warm fire from the hearth off to the side of the room. The heat from the fire kept the room warm, and so Hullamu wore a simple leather loincloth, her sandals sitting by the door waiting to be used. Comfort was always her major concern, and she liked the feel of the beaten rush matting under her feet. Hullamu had decorated her arms with long streaks of white clay paint, though Aya'tar assumed that it was purely aesthetic. Hullamu was more likely to wear paint for aesthetic purposes than any ritual.

Aya'tar watched her spin thread, hoping to take her mind off the strange queasiness that came in the mornings. Hullamu had a large bundle of long flax fibers on her right and a wooden spindle on her left. The long wooden rod had a clay cylinder at the bottom which acted like a fly wheel. She would spin the spindle while feeding the flax fibers with her other hand. They would twist upon themselves becoming a strong thread as the spindle twisted. After enough had been made, she would unroll it from the spindle shaft and twist it tightly at the bottom, like a bobbin, then repeat the process. Isha'kau suddenly appeared at the ceiling entrance breaking her thoughts.

"Are you feeling better? Do you need something?" the more extroverted priestess asked. Aya'tar looked back at her in desperation. It felt to her as though things had just become so much more complicated, as though they were not already complicated enough. Isha'kau had nearly the same hair length as Hullamu, though her hair was much darker. Unlike Hullamu, she wore a wool apron with a pair of sandals, but she also wore a heavy fur wrap around her upper body and several long feathers in her hair. Isha'kau was not one for enduring the cold. If it got cool enough, she could be found wearing the sort of clothing one would expect of a northerner.

"What am I to do? So many people don't think I can lead, and they wish to take the city from me. I'm not even sure that I want to lead the city. All I ever wanted to do was to help the people and to make people happy... to do the right thing for Isut," she despaired. Isha'kau climbed down the ladder and came to sit beside Aya'tar. All three women had grown up together and were effectively sisters, though not biologically. The two lesser priestesses were Aya'tar's advisers. The notion of three younger women sitting at the head of a city, ipso facto leaders, was so unexpected to the city that no one had really known what to do.

"That is the very reason that you should be the leader. You don't want power for the sake of power. You wanted to help people. That's probably why Isut chose you. If you ask me, things did not just become more difficult. They just became much simpler," she said. Aya'tar glared back at her, nearly angry at what seemed like a poor joke. She had been working on controlling her emotions, but this still wasn't a good time for humor. She had just come to the conclusion that she was likely pregnant. In what way could that possibly help the situation?

"How could things possibly be simpler? Now I have to look out for the health of the baby!" she said.

"Babies," Hullamu added, drawing a frown from the high priestess.

"Stop that… It's hard enough pushing one out," she chided.

"If you don't want anything coming out, then maybe don't let something go in," Hullamu shot back with a twisted grin, causing Aya'tar to all but snarl.

Isha'kau, realizing that Aya'tar had not put the pieces together, and wanting to end their silly back and forth, decided that she would explain. Isha'kau picked up a small clay pot with red paint and came to kneel on the bed beside Aya'tar. She dipped her fingers in the pot removing a small amount of paint. She began applying it to Aya'tar's face. As a junior priestess, one of her jobs was to help Aya'tar keep her priestly look, including body paints. Aya'tar took in a deep breath to let her anxiety diminish. Pregnancy caused her such a fluster. However, she always found having her face painted to be relaxing.

"You are the high priestess of a fertility goddess. The most important thing in swaying the people is having the Goddess on your side. How can anyone doubt that you are in the good favor of the gods when your belly swells? Stand before the people and proclaim that you are pregnant. At a very minimum, nobody would dare lay a hand on you until the warm season. In that time, you will have a chance to come up with a different strategy, and perhaps people might simply just accept you by then!" she said with a smile.

Aya'tar was stunned by the proclamation. The craziest part of it all was how much sense it made. She was, in fact, the high priestess of a fertility deity, so what could possibly be better than pregnancy, the purpose behind fertility? In her current condition, somebody could make a move against her, but if she publicly announced her pregnancy, nobody would dare as it would be seen as a direct attack upon the Goddess.

So suddenly relieved was Aya'tar that she swatted Isha'kau's hand from her face and embraced the junior priestess in a deep hug. Unfortunately, the act nearly caused her to vomit once more. For a short time, Aya'tar remained holding Isha'kau, unwilling to let go lest she vomit. In the corner, Hullamu continued laughing at the entire event. This whole morning sickness thing was really becoming troublesome. Within a few moments, Aya'tar was sitting once more, having gained control of her stomach. Some women didn't experience the sickness. *Why Isut? Why did you have to add that little extra part?* she wondered.

"I will wait a few more days to be sure, but then I will make a speech before the city. Isha'kau, you may have just saved everything," she said. It had been many tendays since Aya'tar had anything resembling a plan or hope. Perhaps the people would accept her and even her choice of a lover in time.

"Don't thank me, Hullamu was the one who suggested the idea to me last night," the younger priestess said. Hullamu looked up from her flax and waved at the pair with a smile. Hullamu often had good ideas, but she was never keen on expressing them. She usually told Isha'kau and let her do the explaining. The only speaking Hullamu liked was gossip, something Aya'tar disliked.

ɔ ɔ ɔ

A thick piece of leather served as a doorway into the building where old man Kuwar worked. Sar'Tawas pushed aside the leather "door" and stepped into the room, a small dog rushing between his legs into the warm daylight. He never liked dogs. It was dark and full of smoke. The temperature difference alone was a stark contrast with the cool outside air. Sitting on a leather hide before him was old man Kuwar, a metal worker. Behind him, a young man stood by a heavy stone hearth fanning the fire, sweat pouring down his face.

Metalworking was a new idea, and very few places engaged in it. The technique of simply beating a nugget of gold into a shape that could fit around a necklace had existed since the days of old, but in this room, the most advanced crafting techniques were being put to use. Gold, lead, and occasionally silver was heated to melting and poured into a shape. Even copper molding had been attempted. True three-dimensional molds had not been figured out, but crude sand molds were doable. The heat required to do this was simply amazing. Logs were converted to charcoal, which was used to get the temperature hot enough. Constant fanning was required, and even then, the heat only barely reached the point where metal would melt. A lower temperature fire was often used to make the metal more workable, as the beating of a rock hammer would quickly bring its strength back, one day known as "work hardening."

"What brings you to my workplace, Sar'Tawas?" old man Kuwar asked. The old man did not like the leader of the Crafting Guild. Still, he understood the importance of keeping a working relationship with the man. Very few metal objects were produced each harvest, and each would have to be skillfully traded. Kuwar relied on the skills of Sar'Tawas to ensure that he always obtained the trades he needed.

"How comes the copper blade? I received word that a city far to the South would trade heavily for such items." Kuwar nodded his head in appreciation. For a city to be willing to trade for an item meant that his work was held in even higher esteem than he realized. He was also glad that he did not have to deal with the seven cities to the South that worshiped strange gods. Apparently, they were so confused that they even mistakenly believed the Moon was ruled by a god and not a goddess. At least these were concerns for Sar'Tawas and not for him.

"The blade is coming along. I believe it will be ready just before the flax is planted. Perhaps I can etch a simple pattern upon it which would please the city." Sar'Tawas nodded his appreciation of the comment. He walked past Kuwar and approached the younger man tending the fire, feigning interest in his work. Imkanar turned to face Sar'Tawas. He kept his face neutral, but deep down, he had a seething dislike of the man before him. He knew that the guild leader had the intent of marrying the woman he loved, though he dared not say anything. As long as his love for Aya'tar was unknown, both of them would be safe.

The guild leader stood for a few moments observing the younger man's work. He watched the embers brighten to a glowing orange with every wave of the reed fan, a small blue flame dancing over each of them. He leaned in close before speaking, hoping to keep their discussion from the ears of Kuwar.

"You seem to have a good feel for the flames and the heat of the fire. You do fine work, and I would like to see you one day take over for Kuwar. Until then, a young man like you should find a good woman to live with. A woman of your means, perhaps one of the farmers or one of the women who makes pottery. Be careful that you don't reach for any coals beyond your means, or you might find yourself burned," he said cryptically, but emphasizing the last few words strongly.

Imkanar looked back at the man with a confused and slightly alarmed expression. Did he know? Was that a threat he had just been given? He didn't want to give too much away, but he had to determine if Sar'Tawas was just being strange as normal or if he knew of his relationship with Aya'tar.

"The farm women and some of the potter women are quite beautiful, but I already have a woman I love. She burns brighter than any of the coals in my fire. And like you said, I have skill with fire" he said, watching Sar'Tawas carefully to see what his reaction would be. The guild master glared back at him with what could almost be described as a mixture of disdain and respect for his boldness. Any doubts Sar'Tawas had were now gone. Somehow, this boy had done what he could not. He would rid him of any delusions.

"This is a dangerous game you play, metalworker. If you continue to see her, you might find yourself having an unfortunate accident. I have more eyes and more daggers than you see before you. Let it go and live a long life," Sar'Tawas said, slowly turning to leave. Imkanar stood beside his fire, his rage burning hotter than the coals he worked. All he wanted to do was grab a knife and attack the man, but he knew that nothing could be done. The guild leader was simply too powerful and had too many under his control. Sar'Tawas stopped at the door and turned to say one more thing before leaving.

"Oh, and Imkanar, the hairpin was of exquisite beauty," he said with a smile before leaving. Old Kuwar looked back and forth between his younger worker and the older guild master. He wasn't quite sure what their exchange had been about, but he suspected that the guild master had asked for something custom-made on the side. It had not escaped Kuwar's attention that Imkanar had worked on some small copper item each night. In truth, he was glad to see the younger man establishing himself. He knew that he did not have that many more harvests before he journeyed to see Isut and he needed someone to carry on his work.

"Moon god... Southern fools," Kuwar mumbled with a laugh.

ↄ ↄ ↄ

Isha'kau and Hullamu made their way back to the city, each with a large clay pot in their arms. Toward the evening, both women would take a walk to the marsh nearby to fetch water for the next day. The river was very close, but the marshes were much closer and provided water, reeds, amphibians, shellfish, and small fish. While what they were doing was important work, it provided a good opportunity to stretch their legs after a day sitting and working on crafts and a chance to gossip.

Both women were wrapped in heavy leather shawls, and Isha'kau had gone so far as to wrap a heavy leather skirt around her waist. It wasn't really cold yet, but it certainly wasn't comfortable, and an apron was not enough in this kind of weather. Hullamu had elected to simply bear the temperature, loincloth or not. She had pure disdain for this time of the seasons. During the day, it would become warm, and any exertion performed would cause a person to sweat. The moment that the Sun set, the temperature would follow, and she would quickly become cold. The temperature was just too dynamic.

"So, do you think it will be a boy or girl?" Isha'kau asked. Hullamu let out a long moan at having to carry water such a distance, but she knew the answer to the question without thinking about it. She always had feelings about things that tended to become true.

"A boy, of course, and perhaps a girl as well. Have you not seen Imkanar? He shares more in common with a bull than you might realize," Hullamu said, bursting into giggles.

"I'm not sure that is what determines if it is a boy or girl. I guess Aya'tar will pray to Isut for whichever one she wishes. I'm betting she will want a girl. Girls are easier to deal with than boys." Hullamu stopped dead in her tracks, causing the water in her clay jar to wobble dangerously.

"Girls... Easier to deal with than boys? Have you ever met a girl? Boys are much easier to deal with than girls," Hullamu said incredulously, "besides, I am sure she will have one of each," she finished.

The two priestesses continued debating when suddenly they noticed another woman within earshot and standing by the marsh picking reeds. They both became quiet and continued along, hoping they had not been heard. The woman picking reeds glanced at them casually for a moment and then returned to her job. It was difficult enough to pick reeds when it was warm, but it was simply a miserable job when it was cold.

"Hey, do you recognize that woman?" Isha'kau asked Hullamu. Both women had indeed seen her before.

"She's that woman that Sar'Tawas bought, the slave or something like that," Hullamu responded. She held disdain for the idea of owning another person. But, of course, if she were a concubine and not a slave, she would not be technically "owned." Hullamu couldn't understand why a man would purchase a woman. It was... bizarre.

"I've heard of people being taken as slaves in battle or as payment of a debt, but I heard that she was just traded for, like a piece of flint," Hullamu continued.

"Well, Sar'Tawas *would* have to buy a woman. Hope she has good eyesight. She'll need it to find..." The two women continued rambling and joking as they passed. Their laughter could be heard all the way down the path back to the city.

Ianmu stood by the water with reeds bundled in her hands. She had awoken that morning feeling refreshed after taking the previous day off.

As she had expected, Sar'Tawas had been so stirred up by what she had said that he had paid her almost no mind. She had hoped to pass the time soaking the reeds to make a basket later this evening, but now she had other problems to deal with. She had heard every word the two babbling priestesses had said and had quickly put two and two together.

It seemed that the mischievous priestess had somehow become pregnant, probably spreading her legs for the young and aimless copper worker, though she couldn't entirely blame her for that. Telling Sar'Tawas would be a mistake. For starters, she had already divulged information to him just the day before, and she didn't want to break her disguise of being a foolish and innocent concubine. Secondly, for all his fanaticism, he believed in the will of Isut, and he would not lay a hand on a pregnant woman. Part of her was angry at him for that, though a small part of her respected him a little bit for it.

If she waited perhaps a Moon, Aya'tar would eventually show the signs of pregnancy, and people would learn naturally. During that time, she would convince Pedar to kill the high priestess, though she was unsure how to steer him in that direction. If the high priestess were killed while pregnant and her Goddess did nothing to prevent this, it would show that she had fallen into extreme disfavor. Perhaps in the confusion, Sar'Tawas could step forward and become the leader. There were many details of her plan to work out, but she had at least a Moon to wait and scheme. For the time being, she would return to her home and pray before the altar of An'an for wisdom. An'an was above all a goddess of war and change, and she would have none of this sacred fertility business.

☽ ☽ ☽

Hullamu and Isha'kau approached the main temple with clay pots full of water. Both women were in a jovial mood, having allowed their humor to descend to the lowest depths of depravity, which always made for a good laugh. However, as Isha'kau stepped from around a corner, she bumped square into a younger man and nearly dropped her water. She stumbled backward, sloshing some of the water across one of her legs. Surprised, the man stepped backward and dropped several stone beads to the ground. He was tall with dark brown hair and dark eyes, and he had the unmistakable smell of wood fire about him. The smell was not unpleasing to the priestess.

"Oh, I'm so sorry, priestess. I wasn't looking where I was going. My apologies," the man said as he bent down to pick up the beads. Isha'kau immediately recognized him as Imkanar, the high priestess' lover. She put her water jug down and dropped to her knees beside him to help pick up the small beads. Several times in the past, he had used similar tactics to deliver a message. Her only problem with the messages was his method. He needed their encounter to appear accidental to avoid any suspicion, but she wished that he didn't always have to bump into her. As she bent onto her knees and placed her head close to his, he began to whisper.

"Sar'Tawas knows of us. Until the next Moon, she will not see me other than in passing. Tell her I will visit her on the night when the Moon is full and sleeps below the horizon," he said as he gathered the last of the beads into a small bag. He stood and reached forward to help the priestess stand. As they stood, the pair eyed one another for a short moment. Isha'kau was disturbed by the message she had just been given, and Imkanar looked no less upset. Aya'tar would not see him again until the next full Moon, though that full Moon would not be visible.

"Thank you for your understanding, priestess. I will watch where I'm going in the future."

"May the blessings of Isut be upon you," Isha'kau said with a serious expression. This was most unwelcome news, and she would make sure Aya'tar heard it as soon as possible. The man quickly left, leaving the two lesser priestesses standing with their water and worries.

ↄ ↄ ↄ

They had been walking for nearly a full Moon when it became apparent that the land was truly changing. According to their instructions, it was at this point that they were to turn East and again head toward where the Sun rose. The land was flat with small trees and bountiful rush growing by the water. Beautiful mountains rose to the East, and a generously sized river flowed before them. It seemed to Aethen that this might be the right time to head east. It would prevent them from crossing the river and allow them to pass over just the very beginning of the mountains. He wished Ketamir or Nemanar would have mentioned more detail, but according to their story, it had been a very long time since they made the journey.

"Were you thinking that this would be the right time to head east?" Ember asked as she watched Aethen staring at the horizon. They had spoken on this very issue the night before, though no decision had been made. He pulled his shirt off and lashed it to the side of his traveling pack with a leather cord. The nights were cool, almost cold, but the days could become quite warm. One thing that he hated was the sticky feeling that came with being sweaty and wearing leather. Aethen looked toward the river and the mountains once more before turning to the women.

Ember stood before him with her shirt draped across her shoulders. This was also her way of dealing with the heat, which only existed for a short time during the midday. Unlike Aethen, Ember had stripes painted across her skin to maintain her modesty, a cultural attitude that did not afflict Aethen or Brig'dha. She also had the habit of bathing every day, an uncommon habit among most tribes. Only river tribes tended to do this. Soon, she would dawn the shirt as the temperature dropped. Aethen shuddered at the notion of cleaning himself in ice-cold water.

Behind him, Brig'dha stood holding Mew, the cat in her arms. She had taken to carrying the animal not only because he preferred to be carried rather than walk but also because it provided her warmth, allowing her to simply stow her shirt in her traveling pack. Cats produced significantly more heat than people, which Aethen found useful late at night camping under the stars. Mew would sit on one person for a while and then move to another. There did not seem to be any rhyme or reason governing his actions, but Aethen loved when the small furry animal chose his feet to sit upon. Ember had finally given up trying to explain how impossible it was that a cat could be tamed, empirical evidence to the contrary so apparent.

So far, they had made excellent time exceeding the original estimates of Nemanar. This meant that they would get to their destination quicker, but it also meant that her explanation of tendays was not of much use. Part of their urge to move fast was to encounter and cross the water they knew was looming before it became too cold. The party had experienced the dangers of water crossings, and none were too interested in repeating it in the dead of the cold season. In fact, they were not too interested in crossing it at any time.

Aethen thought a little more about Ember's question. His mind had wandered as they came to a halt but now it was time to focus on an important turn in their quest. If they headed east and were incorrect, all the relative directions would be useless. However, this did feel like the right place for them to turn East. He wasn't entirely sure why he felt this, but sometimes one simply had to act upon their instinct.

"I guess so. I know that you are part fish, but the rest of us don't swim so well in icy water. Besides, those mountains go on for a distance, and I would hate to cross them during the cold season. My luck, I'd wind up dead with an arrow in my back from my own party for complaining so much," he laughed.

"We have been lucky that the weather has been so warm of late, but now the nights are too cold to sleep without a constant fire," he continued, droning along. Aethen had been lost in thought, and his wandering thoughts influenced his wandering mouth. Then, suddenly, Ember interrupted him.

"So, what you're trying to say is, 'yes.' You just felt that we should journey to the answer in a roundabout way," Ember said with a laugh. Aethen didn't say much, but he tended to do so in a less than precise manner when he did speak. Ember found it much more funny than annoying, but she sometimes wondered if Brig'dha agreed. She could understand why he was lost in thought. The very land had a strange feel to it. It almost felt as though something was waiting to happen here. It was a strange feeling that Ember had, but she couldn't quite place it. Pushing the thought aside, she turned toward the direction of the rising Sun and prepared to leave. Little did she know that in nearly 5000 years, the very ground she stood upon would be known as the city of Rome.

CHAPTER NINETEEN
WAIT FOR ME IN THE THIRD WORLD

Avian Excarnation is the act of leaving a deceased body open to the elements, specifically scavenger birds. Sometimes called a "sky burial," this mortuary practice is used in many cultures worldwide. While the sky burial can be a primary burial, meaning that the burial site is untouched once used, such burials are often secondary, meaning the de-fleshed body is reburied after being rendered nothing but bones. Catalhoyuk, a famous Neolithic proto-city and real-world analog of Isut'na, was found to have what appeared to be depictions of Avian Excarnation. Interestingly, osteological analysis of the burials at Catalhoyuk does not support the common usage of this practice, which should have left gnaw marks on the bones. Perhaps only high-status individuals were provided such a burial?

The Sun was low on the horizon when Ianmu caught sight of the farmer, Pedar. He was standing in a small open area between several buildings absentmindedly breaking a twig into ever smaller pieces. The man had heavily tanned skin with short brown hair and deep brown eyes, not so troublesome to look at. Ianmu had been grooming Pedar for many tendays, and now his utility was finally at hand. She had considered keeping the priestess alive at first. However, during the previous Moon, she had reconsidered her options, realizing that a child would do nothing but complicate an already delicate situation. She needed to be rid of Aya'tar before the woman could announce her coming child. This goddess Isut would look well upon a woman carrying a child, and the sooner that Aya'tar died, the better for her plans.

In truth, killing the priestess as she carried a child had also not been an easy decision for Ianmu. She knew something about it was morally wrong, though she was quite sure that this would put her closer to achieving the goals set forth by her Goddess. The hardest part had been stealing the dagger from that annoying fool, Imkanar. The boy possessed a plain flint dagger with a simple rough ring of copper around the shaft separating the blade from the hilt. It was not an amazing weapon, but it was distinctive. If Pedar were caught or killed, the blade could be useful in implicating the boy.

Ianmu wore a rough linen shawl to stay warm, along with her apron and leather sandals. She had painted her skin with black zigzagging lines

343

hoping that the pattern would be more enticing to Pedar. She needed him to have no doubt – to be absolutely ready to do what she asked. Most men were more thoughtful and moral than he. They would either turn down requests like the one she was about to make or perhaps even take action against her for even having made it. Finding someone as morally bankrupt as Pedar had been challenging but fortuitous.

Pedar had spent all day in the fields collecting the last of the harvest before the cold winds came. He disliked this time of the harvest because the temperature changed so wildly from morning to the high-sun, and to night. Already, the temperature was dropping, yet he only wore the simple leather loincloth of a field worker. He would need to find a leather cloak soon enough. He had even been considering the possibility of obtaining a necklace, perhaps a leather cord with a large bead. He had been existing from day-to-day for quite some time now, and he felt like it was time that he increased his standing.

His attention was suddenly taken by movement to his right. He turned to see the beautiful concubine approaching. Pedar could not believe his luck at having somehow attracted this beauty. She may be the property of the powerful Sar'Tawas, and he might be just a simple farmer, but when she needed true love and companionship, she came to Pedar. He was now sure that he would trade for a necklace and a leather cloak or perhaps steal. His fortunes had been changing of late, and his wardrobe might as well change along with them. He turned to face the approaching woman.

She seemed slightly different tonight. She was painted in a more intricate pattern than normal, which made her so much more enticing. Strangely, she held in her hand what appeared to be a flint dagger with a simple copper ring around the handle. He doubted that she was coming to harm him, but her worried look and timid demeanor suggested a problem he could help resolve. She was not the most intelligent woman he had ever met, but he was pretty sure that once he solved whatever was troubling her, she would help him warm the night.

"So, what is the trouble? What is on your mind, and why are you carrying that dagger? I am not in trouble, am I? You wouldn't kill me, would you?" he chuckled playfully. Ianmu almost paused, but suppressed her natural predatory look. She approached him slowly, holding the dagger sheepishly, as though she did not know how to correctly use it. Ironically, daggers and knives were her preferred weapon. She had grown up using them and was extremely proficient with a blade. She looked away, hoping that Pedar would press her for a little while longer before she told him what was on her mind. It was always best to make her victim beg for the information. She had witnessed many women using such techniques to control their husbands, when her father would gather the elders for discussions.

"Well, out with it. What possible trouble could a concubine have?" Ianmu looked up at Pedar with her innocent expression and allowed her eyes to focus on his, but then to dart around as though searching for answers. She had planned out everything, from her body language to her words.

"Sar'Tawas has asked me to do something that I'm afraid to do. It's something that I know must be done... It's something the Goddess herself has all but commanded. Yet I am afraid... I..." Pedar grasped Ianmu's shoulders firmly as though he intended to shake the details out of her. This was the level of frustration she was hoping to build in him.

"What has that old wretch asked you to do? How bad could it possibly be?" Ianmu pretended to be unwilling to say as Pedar pressed her for the details. Finally, when she could see that Pedar was obviously approaching his limit of frustration, Ianmu said it plainly, hoping to deliver just the right amount of shock. She slowly lifted her head to meet him eye to eye as she spoke. Every single facial gesture perfectly articulated.

"I am to kill Isut'Sanup'ramu Aya'tar... I am to murder the priestess herself," she said with mock fear in her eyes. His look of shock was exactly as she had hoped. Before he could say anything, she continued, "I do not know his exact reasons for her murder, but it makes sense, doesn't it? The high priest has died, and now his daughter is without a man or child. How can she be a priestess to a goddess of fertility? How will our crops grow next harvest? How will we survive? Even a concubine has to eat... but... I am afraid." Ianmu looked like she was on the verge of tears as she paused to let her words sink in. Now, the important part was to attach an alluring bait to her trap, and she had just the perfect bait... a lovely concubine.

"But why you? Why send a woman to murder another woman? He could have found someone else," Pedar reasoned. To his people, women were considered the creators of life, not the takers. Only in dire situations would women join men in battle or similar pursuits. The idea of sending a woman to murder the priestess baffled Pedar. It went against the grain of his society and the social norms he had grown up around. Nevertheless, this was what Ianmu was waiting for. When a person became confused and too many questions were left unanswered, providing an easy solution to one of the questions could provide the illusion of an answer to all of them, at least to somebody like Pedar. Neither Sar'Tawas nor even Aya'tar's handsome lover would have fallen for such a weak story. She nearly shook her head at a loss for how anyone could be quite so gullible.

"Sar'Tawas has lost interest in me. He has not been with me in several tendays. If I were caught or killed, it would be of little loss to him. If only I could complete my task, surely Sar'Tawas would be pleased. He might even offer me freedom so he could find another concubine..." Pedar suddenly had a look of inspiration. Manipulating him and playing her part was almost amusing to her. Far from intellectual battle with the insightful Sar'Tawas, Pedar was almost juvenile in his thought patterns. Ianmu hoped that he had the right inspiration, or she would be here all night trying to steer him in the correct direction.

"What if I killed the priestess for you? Sar'Tawas might give you your freedom, and then we could be together. You could be with a man who knows how to please you," he concluded. Ianmu had to be careful not to laugh as she thought of how little skill this man actually had at pleasing her. Strangely, Sar'Tawas was much better. She could not deny that he had several interesting virtues, though she typically found herself playing the part of the loud and satisfied lover more often than not. Regardless of Pedar's romantic shortcomings, this was exactly what she hoped he would say. If Pedar committed the crime, she would be free of suspicion. All she had to do was make sure that she was in a very public place for the rest of the night.

There was a slight chance that Pedar might get caught and try to implicate her, but who would believe that a concubine could somehow compel a farmer to kill the priestess? He would likely inform whoever caught him that the gods had turned against Aya'tar. This was something believed by many already. She would simply play dumb if that were to happen, and everyone would believe that Pedar was grasping at any chance to save himself. If society foolishly thought that she was harmless, so much the better. The only trouble she now had was what to do with Pedar if he completed his mission.

ↄ ↄ ↄ

Imkanar walked briskly down the narrow passageway between the buildings, hoping nobody would see him. The Sun had set not long ago, and Isut had just laid her feathered wing of darkness across the city. It had been many days since last he had seen Aya'tar, and he could feel himself growing impatient for her embrace. The path he now traced led to a wooden ladder made of square poles which would take him up one story to the level of the temple. Entering the temple would require that he walk across the roof and climb down the ladder in the ceiling. Though some buildings had doorways at the ground level, most of the buildings were entered through the roof.

He had cleaned himself thoroughly by the river before the Sun had set in preparation for the night. It would not do for him to smell bad upon meeting the woman he loved for the first time in so many days. Imkanar had rubbed soot around the edges of his eyes, darkening them, and lightly oiled his skin with scented nut oil. He wore a simple goatskin loincloth and leather skin shoes. He had spent many long days planning what he would do or say when he saw his beloved next. He had thought to wear something more ornate, though as a mere craftsman, he had very few pieces of clothing to choose from. In the end, he had settled upon the simple leather and oil, hoping Aya'tar would not be displeased.

The ladder climb was only two lengths of a man and very easy. It was possible to enter the temple from the ground level through the storage room beneath, but this would mean passing through the area where Hullamu slept. Because she had been adopted by the temple as a baby, Hullamu lived in a small room under the main temple, technically within the storeroom. As Aya'tar had explained, Isha'kau and Hullamu were both known to use the storeroom as their personal recreational area and hangout. Imkanar wondered if the two gossiping women were watching him from some vantage point, even now. It was only a moment before he found the square opening in the roof to the temple with the ladder slightly poking from the opening. He stopped and took a deep breath. It had been a while since he had held his lover, and now the time was at hand.

Ↄ Ↄ ↄ

Aya'tar paced nervously in front of the statuette to the Goddess. All around her was the comforting sight of the temple with its goddess statuette on one side and its bullhead statuettes on the other. She had spent a large portion of her life in this very building surrounded by the graves of her ancestors and now even her father. As the thought hit her, she turned to see the sleeping area over to one side of the temple. Atop the sleeping area, several clay pots sat, filled with herbs. Underneath that stone platform lay the body of her father. It comforted her to know that his body was nearby, and with it, a link to his spirit. Her people did not fear the dead, and often relatives were buried beneath the floor of a family dwelling to be close to the living.

She brushed aside her sad thoughts as she began to worry again over the matter at hand. She was awash with anxiety over what was to come. She knew it would be best to send him away to live in a different village until she could sort her problems out, but how could she convince Imkanar to leave her alone for a while? Men always wished to solve any problem presented to them. It was both one of the more annoying, yet also one of the most charming characteristics of men. But in this case, she had to convince him to leave, or he would be made a pawn in Sar'Tawas's game. Then there was the matter of the baby...

Aya'tar heard a creak from the rafters above, and a slight wave of panic rushed through her. She had spent the entire day wondering what she would tell Imkanar, and now suddenly, all her rehearsed words were gone. She turned and quickly glanced at the small, polished obsidian mirror on a wooden stand against the wall. She could see a little bit of her reflection, but not much. The mirror only worked when all the lamps in the room were burning or when direct sunlight shone down through the windows and doorway above. She hoped that she at least looked all right for her lover.

The priestess' waist-length hair had been braided down the sides, leaving the back tied in a bun and secured with the copper hairpin her lover had given her. Around her waist, she wore a simple flax wrap, dyed green and fastened by a leather cord. A flax cord was wrapped around her waist above the leather cord. Attached to the very front of this thinner flax cord were a series of knee-length flax strings, each dyed red with bone beads hanging from different lengths. The girdle of strings surrounded her waist like a string skirt. Wrapped around her upper body was a soft sheepskin shawl, also dyed red. She had spent time affixing small songbird feathers to her hair at various lengths. Her face and entire body were carefully decorated with intricately drawn black lines and bands, courtesy of Hullamu.

Aya'tar stood back from the ceiling door and watched the light from the stars above as it was slowly occulted by the shape of someone entering. She hoped that it wasn't a late caller to the temple for a blessing. Slowly, feet appeared and then legs. Within a few moments, Imkanar had come to stand on the floor. He turned and let his gaze fall upon the priestess. Aya'tar's heart felt like it had missed a beat as she stood before her lover. She wanted nothing more than to run to him and throw herself into his arms, but how could she do that with so many doubts and questions in her own mind? For what felt like an eternity, he simply stood there and took in her beauty. Aya'tar felt awkward before him, but she slowly approached, her mind going blank. She wanted nothing more than to surrender to his love and to lay all her secrets bare... but she knew she could not.

Imkanar felt his breath escape for a moment as he took in the sight of the woman who stood before him. Every time he saw her, he felt as though nothing else mattered. How could she stay in this temple and give herself to the Goddess, ignoring him for so long? Deep down, he knew that wasn't the case. Half of the city had called for her to marry one of the highborn men and create a child before the end of the next warm season, while the other half called for her to be cast out of her role as a priestess and for someone else to take her place. She was in more precarious of a position than he could possibly imagine, and yet she could still find it in herself to greet him looking like an incarnation of the Goddess. He could feel nothing but respect as he stood before the high priestess, Isut'Sanup'ramu Aya'tar.

Aya'tar approached her lover, forcing herself to live in the moment. She had so many problems, yet she pushed them aside. She decided that she would hold him close once more before she asked him to leave. Her only worry was that their romance could harm the unborn child. Men could be pleasantly strong, so she would have to convince Imkanar to be gentle. Aya'tar stretched her arms into the air letting the shawl fall aside, and quickly found herself pressed against him, feeling his strong embrace. He reached behind her head and pulled the hairpin, letting the hair spill down her back. He tossed the hairpin onto the floor by her sleeping bench with one hand while his other hand gently found the cord holding the flax wrap around her waist. Aya'tar never broke eye contact with him. This was the moment she had been waiting for – the close physical connection that gave her the strength to go on.

"Please, be gentle," she purred.

ᴐ ᴐ ᴐ

Not far below the temple room stood Hullamu and Isha'kau, listening to the romantic parts of the conversation and trying desperately not to whisper too loudly as they rapidly gossiped among themselves. This was the sort of romance that both women lived for, and they were not going to miss a single word. The floorboards did a decent job of blocking sound, so much so that Hullamu had even suggested that they both climb up the small staircase and enter through the small door in the back of the temple. There they could stand just out of sight and listen, but Isha'kau had rejected the notion. She wanted to hear what was said, but she didn't feel right watching the high priestess during her most intimate moments. After a short time, the few words exchanged became nothing but indistinguishable sounds.

"I expected them to say a lot more than they did," Isha'kau said, slightly bored by the lack of dialogue.

"When she's had her fill with him, I suspect that she will tell him about the baby... When she asks him to leave the city, you can bet that words will be exchanged. I bet it's going to turn into a screaming match!" Hullamu stated with slightly more enthusiasm than she had meant.

"It sounds like it already has become a screaming match," replied Isha'kau with a sly grin. Both women felt a little embarrassed, but such sounds were normal and heard throughout the city on a given night. Besides, it was a fertility temple, after all.

ↄ ↄ C

Pedar stood atop the third story of a building watching the entrance to the temple. He had covered his body from top to bottom with ash from a fire until his skin was almost completely black. He still wore his leather loincloth and leather sandals. In his hand, he nervously clutched the flint dagger with the copper ring around the handle which Ianmu gave him. Pedar did not know that the dagger actually belonged to Imkanar, only that this was the weapon his lover had handed him along with her dark task. He would wait a little longer to make sure that no one entered the temple, and then he would sneak in and do what must be done.

The act of killing the woman did trouble him, but he realized that Ianmu was correct. The Goddess had likely forsaken the priestess. This was evident as she had no child and refused all suitors. What he did now would help the city, much like pulling a weed from the field, or so he rationalized. More importantly, this deed would open the path for him to be with Ianmu. This was his chance to finally get a little ahead. In one stroke, he would achieve a wife and perhaps even something of value on the way out the door. The longer he waited, the more easily he rationalized what he was doing.

ↄ ↄ C

Sar'Tawas sat on a mud-brick bench on one side of the large central room of his dwelling, watching Ianmu slowly dance and sway. He had invited several other important people from the city to discuss what was to be done about the wayward priestess. Each of the men sat captivated by the sight of the lovely Ianmu as she lavishly performed the beautiful dance of the Dancing Birds. This was a dance that she had seen performed many times in her city, though usually, the performer would hold a fan of bird feathers in each hand. Now, wearing a simple flax girdle, she was leaving the bird feathers to the imagination of her viewers, and not much else. The most important part of her presentation was that so many men were watching it – or, more importantly, providing her with an alibi.

Around and around, she danced, feeling the plastered floor and rush matting beneath her feet. All around her swirled a plastered room with red and black decorations adorning the walls, illuminated by the soft orange flickering light of a fire. The smell of oils, sweat, honeyed drink, and incense filled her nose while the warm air danced across her skin. It was quite cozy, if not slightly intoxicating.

"If we make enough trades with this harvest's flax, I'm going to see if I can convince my wife to let us trade for a concubine like yours from one of the small villages to the West," said field master Akanar, the man charged with overseeing the day-to-day harvesting and production of the many flax-based goods the city produced to export, under Isu'mamu. Of the people in the room, Akanar certainly had the material wealth to trade for a concubine, but Sar'Tawas knew that his wife would absolutely never allow him to do so. Akanar had two sons and a daughter already and had no real need of a second wife or concubine, like Ianmu. Several of the men chuckled while sipping their fermented honey drink. Sar'Tawas glanced with a smile at Katalar, the master of the fields for growing food. Concerning edible crops, he was the equivalent of elder Isu'mamu, the field mistress of flax, and by far the oldest man in the room.

"What say you, Katalar? Do you think you could handle someone like my Ianmu?"

"Huh? Are you trying to kill an old man? Is your ambition that great? If your concubine started to dance for me in private, Isut would finish it by carrying me to the next world," Katalar said with a big smile, revealing very few remaining teeth. Ianmu continued to dance in her circles as the men continued their idle conversation. She could not help but enjoy being the center of attention to the most influential men in the city, but she couldn't forget how precarious her situation was as her assassin crept through the night with full knowledge that she had put him up to it. Ianmu sang a warrior's prayer softly to the goddess An'an under her breath as she continued to dance. While these powerful men sat and discussed what they might do, she was actually doing it.

ɔ ɔ ɔ

Aya'tar lay on her back, held tightly in the strong arms of Imkanar. Her hand gently glided over her lower abdomen as she thought of what lay inside. Their child was a seed within her, slowly growing as wheat in a field. She wanted so badly to tell him, but she knew that telling him of the child would just put him at even greater risk, as well as the child. Aya'tar had waited long enough, and now it was time to bring up the painful subject. She rolled over until she was partially on top of Imkanar and looking him deeply in the eyes. He gazed back at her with nothing but unbridled love, which forced her to look away with the shame of her own deception. The sight of the altar to Isut gave her a small measure of strength.

"What's wrong, my love? Does my face offend your eyes so much that you must look away?" he asked with a half-smile and in a playful tone. Aya'tar took another deep breath and carefully pulled her loose, sweat-damp hair from her face before speaking.

"I must tell you something... Something which hurts me to say. Something that must happen. Please let me explain before you reply," she said, gently placing her index finger over his lips. She wavered, wanting nothing more than to embrace him and quietly slip into a deep sleep, but she had to continue.

"There are many in the city who wish to force me to marry someone like Sar'Tawas or who wish to drive me from the temple of Isut." She could see the objection on his face, but he held his tongue as she spoke. She took a breath and summoned the courage to continue.

"I need you to leave the city, at least until the warm season. I think that I can get enough support by that time, but if you stay here and anyone finds out that you are my lover, it will place you and me in great danger. I need you to leave for both of us... until the warm season..." She wanted to say more, but tears welled in her eyes, and she needed to hear how he would react to what she had said so far.

Imkanar propped himself up on his elbows and looked Aya'tar squarely in the face. Her words seemed almost foreign to him as she spoke them. She was asking him to leave the city where he was born, the city where he worked his craft of copper and fire, but most importantly, the city where his true love stood on the edge of a cliff with her entire world hanging in the balance. The emotions welling within him were too complicated to be given a name, but anger, betrayal, and tremendous sorrow were among them. He wanted to hold her tightly and never let go, but also to grab her by the shoulders and yell at her.

When she had stood before him, she had appeared as a strong and glorious high priestess of Isut. As she looked upon him now with a tear in her eye, she looked like a frightened woman on the verge of weeping. He could not believe that she would ask him to leave in the moment when she might need him the most. He wanted to yell, but the fear in her eyes told him that she had dreaded saying what she had said. She had known how he might react. He just sat there for a short while, looking down, unsure of what to say. After a period of silence, Aya'tar reached over and picked up a small leather bag that contained many beautiful pieces of obsidian as well as lead beads. She had taken these items from the temple's private store of materials to provide him with a means to secure a place in a village to the West. His copper skills would be of little use in a small village, but the high-quality obsidian pieces and lead beads could be traded at any village to the West for lodging for at least a harvest.

"Here, please take this. It will help until you can return," she said, handing him the bag. He took it from her, examining its contents. He was dumbfounded. Not only was she trying to prevent him from helping her through the most terrible period of her life, but she was tossing a handout at him. He felt belittled, and anger was beginning to seep in. Deep down, a tiny part of him realized that this was the only way, but that part was crushed by the weight of anger and unchecked emotion.

"You want me to leave and stay away until the warm winds come again? Am I such a burden upon you? Does my love cause you that much trouble? Perhaps you are worried that your enemies will find a way to use me against you?" he asked. As soon as he had said it, he wished he could take it back. His words had cut her deeper than even an obsidian blade. A second and third tear joined her first as she looked down in shame.

"I... I didn't mean what I said. I will return when the warm winds come..." he whispered, turning his head away in embarrassment at his own actions. He was just overloaded with emotion and unable to think clearly. He stood and quickly tied his loincloth before grabbing the bag and his leather shoes. His mind was awash with emotions, and he feared that he might say something else in anger. He headed to the ladder to climb out before he could. Imkanar stopped with his foot on the first rung and looked back to see his lover weeping. His emotions were a whirlwind of betrayal, love, anger, and misery. Imkanar quickly climbed the ladder and fled into the night. He would leave the city and return when the first warm winds came, just before the flax harvest. He had not meant to say such wounding things to Aya'tar, and he hoped she would forgive him, but right now, he was too pained to speak to her. He had to hope that she was right... He had to trust her.

◌ ◌ ◌

Not far away and lying flat atop another building, Pedar watched as the man he had seen enter the temple climbed out and walked away. The man appeared extremely troubled, holding his head and talking to himself under his breath. Pedar wasn't sure if the man had seen some vision from the gods or if he was merely burdened by some personal dilemma, but this was not something for him to worry about. He stood and climbed down onto the roof of the temple. If the priestess died, he could rescue the poor concubine from her miserable existence. Deep down, he knew that he was rescuing Ianmu more for himself than for her, but he felt like he deserved her. The rationalization wasn't too difficult given the low quality of existence his life had been. He was quite sure that he was doing a good thing. He had one goal now, and he wasn't about to fail.

◌ ◌ ◌

Isha'kau and Hullamu sat by the narrow mud-brick stairs leading to the temple floor. Their mouths were open, and they only glared at one another. The drama had been intense though not unexpected. Both initiate priestesses felt a terrible loss for their friend, but they agreed with Aya'tar that it was best for her lover to leave until this was all over with. Initially, Isha'kau had wanted to go to her friend and comfort her, but Hullamu had stopped her. Hullamu believed that Aya'tar needed time alone simply to cry and regain her mental strength. They would come to her in the morning and offer whatever support and condolences she needed. Until then, they would both sit at the bottom of the stairs and softly gossip about what they had heard and what could be done.

Hullamu was discussing possible contingency plans for the baby when Isha'kau stopped her with a raised hand. Hullamu paused what she was saying for a moment staring at her friend. It only took a moment before she realized that there was a new sound above them.

354

"Shhh! Do you hear something? I wonder if Imkanar is creeping back in to apologize.... listen," she said.

"He did leave pretty hot. It would be great for him to return and say something nice. They shouldn't part on bad words," Hullamu added. The women were unsure, but it did sound as though somebody might be creeping down the wooden ladder. Carefully, the women climbed the staircase as quietly as possible so they could hear the juicy details of what might come next.

ↃↃↃ

Aya'tar lay on the bed where she and her lover had reached new heights of passion just a short time ago. Now she felt only sorrow as she slowly curled into a ball. She knew that Imkanar had acted out of anger and not out of his true thoughts. She had wished that their parting could be on better terms. Sorrow filled her as she thought of the baby's father, who was probably right now gathering his things to leave the city. Would she ever see him again? Would he fall for some pretty woman from one of the western villages while he waited for her? Why shouldn't he? She offered him nothing but a dim future full of unfulfilled promises, her intrusive thoughts tormented. She absentmindedly pulled her rabbit pelt blanket over her body and began to cry herself to sleep. Her mind screamed at her that she had been wrong and a fool. The intrusive thoughts had been coming more and more of late, something she attributed to her stress. So lost in her thoughts and emotions was the priestess that she didn't hear the creaking of the ladder as a dark painted man slowly climbed down and into the temple.

ↃↃↃ

Pedar had been in the temple only once before, as a small child. At that time, the grandmother of the woman he now stood before had been the high priestess. She had long since died, as had this priestess' mother and father. In fact, she was the last of their line. Soon she would journey to meet them. The room was cool and dark, with only the dim light from the main hearth slowly burning down. Pedar stopped to face the goddess statuette. In his mind, he knew that the priestess had to die. If she continued to lead their people in religious worship when she had no mate or child, it would simply mean pushing the people further from Isut's embrace. Within a tenday, Pedar would be standing in the doorway of his home holding his new wife, Ianmu. This was the way of things, life, and death.

If he slit her throat, she would die quickly, and this entire matter would be over with her merciful death. He crept ever closer until he saw her nude form halfway emerge from under the rabbit fur blanket. Finding her like this made it harder for him to forget that she was a living and feeling woman and not merely some problem to be rid of. It became more difficult for Pedar to confront what he was about to do. He kept thinking of Ianmu and how poor this harvests crops had turned out. He was starting to banish his doubts when he heard the priestess sniff her stuffy nose. She was softly crying. Pedar was beginning to stiffen up. He did not consider himself to be an evil man, and this woman was unknowingly undermining his will simply by his observation of her suffering. With a deep breath to banish unwanted thoughts, he stepped forward and placed his hand over her mouth and the dagger against her throat.

Aya'tar rolled over with a look of sheer horror. She had been half in and out of a sad, semi-dream state when suddenly she had been returned to a reality of terror. She grasped the arms of the man who held a dagger to her throat only to find that those arms were thick and strong. She looked up with pleading eyes at her attacker, hoping that he would not slice his dagger, but she simply did not have the strength to free herself. For a brief moment, she considered kicking with her legs, but the blade rested so perfectly against her neck that she feared how easily he could slice it open if she tried. Who was this man, and why was he holding a blade to her throat? If he had come to kill her, why had he not done so? She fought to calm herself, to think.

"I just wanted you to know that I don't blame you for losing the love of the Goddess. I have to do this because we cannot all die for your failure... But I want you to know that I will make it quick and that I'm sorry," he said, removing his hand from her mouth and placing it on her chin, forcing her head back so the cutting would be easier. Aya'tar could not believe what was happening. She had to say something – anything – or she would be dead in moments. If she delayed him long enough, Imkanar might arrive to help...

"I carry a child! Please, don't kill me... please..." she cried softly. Pedar heard the words but could not force himself to believe. The woman would say anything to save her life, he supposed. He couldn't blame her for trying. He looked down at her body, just below her navel, and saw not even the slightest bulge to indicate a child. He felt sad, but he would do what must be done. He pressed the blade firmly and prepared to make one quick deep cut.

The small wooden door which led to the storage level below the temple suddenly burst open as Hullamu and Isha'kau entered the temple in a state of panic. They had heard his proclamation and the pleading of their priestess. Before them lay Aya'tar sprawled across her bed with an unknown man standing over her painted all black and holding a dagger to her throat. Isha'kau wasted no time and ran straight for the man grabbing ahold of his hand and pulling the dagger away from Aya'tar's throat before he could even make a sound. The man swung his arm wildly, trying to free it from the grasp of the temple priestess. Suddenly, Hullamu slammed into his legs, toppling him backward and onto the floor. Aya'tar seized the opportunity and crawled off the bed and climbed towards the man's arm to try and wrestle the dagger from his hand.

Pedar had gone from a man in total control of the situation to sprawling on the floor with three women clinging to him. He was instantly filled with rage, and a burst of adrenaline rushed through his body, giving him strength. He used his body and weight to sling the first woman who had attacked him off his arm. Isha'kau flew across the room and smashed into a table, landing hard on the floor. Next, he pulled free his legs and kicked the woman at his waist off him. Having released his body, he rolled over and shoved Aya'tar backward, her head striking the edge of the bed. He would deal with these two lesser priestesses before finishing off the main priestess.

Hullamu lifted her head up and shook the stars from her eyes. The man had kicked her in the chest pretty hard, but she knew that she had to get back in the fight. This man was stronger than all three women, and if he got the upper hand, they might all die. Beside her sat a small flint dagger on the bench, which she used when spinning her flax. She grabbed the short knife in desperation and held it out before her. She knew that she was no knife fighter, but the man before her did not hold his dagger very well, either. Isha'kau was still trying to pick herself up off the floor, so Hullamu crouched low and waited for an opportunity to strike.

Pedar stood to his full height like a monster towering over the smaller priestesses. He did not believe that she would even swing her knife, let alone hit anything. If she wanted to play with knives, he would accommodate her. He stepped forward and swung his dagger, but somehow, she ducked sideways, dodging it. Continuing her motion, she rolled along the outside of his arm towards his body using the same dance moves the priestesses used on ceremonial nights. Two rotations later, she was beside him. She stabbed her knife into his side, causing him immediate agony as she twisted the knife around. Her initial attack had used finesse and agility, her dexterity giving her the advantage. However, she did not have the skill to use this edge. As she pulled her knife free from his side, Pedar turned suddenly and slashed his dagger across her lower abdomen.

Hullamu felt herself being punched in the stomach as hard as she could possibly imagine. She tried to stand back as everything went black, but she felt something cold across her abdomen and a strange sinking sensation. She stepped backward with most of her vision blackening. She looked down and saw blood... lots of blood. It was on her hands, running down her legs, and it was already on the floor. Her bare stomach revealed the long and deep slash. Pieces of what lay inside of the body slightly protruded from the wound. Gone from her mind were any thoughts of attacking the man or anything at all. She could not move other than to slowly sink to her knees and double over. Her hand, which had once held the small flint knife, now grasped an open gash in her lower abdomen as if she would somehow hold the blood in. She heard nothing, and she couldn't seem to breathe...

Isha'kau saw Hullamu stepping backward away from the attacker, clutching her abdomen. There was blood coming out. She realized that her friend had been wounded and that if she didn't act drastically, it would be the end of them all. Isha'kau rushed at the man and jumped into the air latching her legs around his waist and her arms around his neck. Being a lighter woman than Hullamu, Isha'kau was able to jump quite high and clamp herself around him in a vice-like grip, pulling the man to the floor. Isha'kau landed on the floor, holding the man from behind as tightly as she possibly could. He lay on top of her struggling to get her arms off his neck. A life of carrying large and heavy pots of water and other chores had given Isha'kau more strength than Pedar could have expected. Recognizing the life-and-death reality of her situation, her brain overrode the natural inhibitors which prevented her muscles from over-exerting themselves. She squeezed so hard that the attacker began to gag from lack of breath.

Pedar could not seem to pry the impossibly tight grip of the woman who now held him to the floor. He took his bloody dagger and began stabbing behind himself at whatever flesh he could find. He felt the blade dig in and strike bone. He pulled the dagger out and stabbed it again and again. Each thrust caused the woman behind him to scream in pain. She was beginning to weaken, and in a few more moments, he would break free and put an end to this one as well. Suddenly, he saw movement by the bed.

Aya'tar stood and shook the blackness from her eyes. Her head throbbed from where it had hit the side of the bed. Hullamu, seemingly holding a wound, lay on the floor to the right, though Aya'tar's vision was blurry, and she could not make out the details. Before her was the attacker held fast by her faithful friend Isha'kau. She looked down and saw the copper hairpin given to her by her lover, Imkanar. She seized the hairpin and slowly approached the man, hoping not to fall over from dizziness. She dropped to her knees and held the hairpin like a dagger. The man wiggled his head frantically, trying to get free of Isha'kau, who had released his head and was now trying to hold his arms pinned. Aya'tar grasped his face with her free hand and brought the hairpin to his eye.

As Pedar struggled to remove the vice-like woman from behind, all he could see above him was the ceiling. Suddenly, a woman came to stand over top of him. She seemed dazed and slightly confused with a small trickle of blood coming from the side of her head, but in her hand, she held a weapon. She reached forward, grabbing his head and plunging the weapon downward. As she screamed, the woman before Pedar ceased to be a young, frightened priestess, and she became like the goddess Isut herself.

"In the name of the goddess of life and death – almighty Isut – I remove you from this world and curse you from entering the next!" she screamed as she plunged the hairpin through his eye and into whatever lay beyond. Almost immediately, Pedar ceased stabbing and fighting, making one strange and final gurgling sound. Isha'kau let go of the man though her arms were very stiff and hard to move due to overexertion. Aya'tar quickly helped role the man off her friend. His body quivered and shook as though it were still alive. In truth, Aya'tar did not even know if the man was actually dead or not, but she knew that he was no longer a threat and would be dead very soon. Objects penetrating deep into the head always seemed to kill.

The high priestess looked around the room in a total state of shock. Isha'kau lay on the floor holding what looked like multiple wounds to her right hip and thigh. Hullamu lay on her stomach, faced down in a pool of her own gore and shaking. Aya'tar, too weak with adrenaline wearing off to stand, crawled over the convulsing man's body to her friend Hullamu's side. She gently rolled the priestess over to find a horrible sight. Hullamu's lower abdomen, slightly to the right of her navel, had a deep slice as long as a hand. It looked deep, and dark blood ran from it.

Hullamu looked up at Aya'tar with a weak smile, though she appeared slightly pale and gently shook.

"Is he dead?" she whispered. Aya'tar nodded her head. The scene before her was surreal.

"Ish... Isha'kau?"

"She has been hurt, but I think she will be fine... By the Goddess, you've been slashed open!" Aya'tar said as the shock of the moment began to wear off.

☾ ☾ ☾

Ianmu lay on a leather cushion filled with short flax fibers. Beside her lay the sleeping form of Sar'Tawas. Her dancing seemed to have quite the effect upon him but not so strong of an effect as the fermented fruit drink he had consumed. A strange mixture of excitement, fear, and a little shame passed through her as she thought about the plot that she had set into play. At this very moment, as she lay on her back having just finished feeling what it meant to be alive, not far away, the priestess Aya'tar was most likely dead. Life and death were very important to the goddess An'an and represented the cycle of the world. Regardless of how many times Ianmu tried to reconcile her deeds with these facts, she could not help but feel shame.

She sat up and propped her back against the plastered mud-brick wall. She reached down and picked up the clay jar which held the fermented fruit drink. Sar'Tawas would not let her have any of the drink as he believed her to be a low-born woman, worthy only as a concubine and laborer. She casually drank the slightly sweet brew as she laughed to herself, sardonically. She had grown up eating better food than most and drinking fermented drinks nearly every day. Now she had to please Sar'Tawas until he slept if she wanted a sip. Luckily, pleasing Sar'Tawas was not a lengthy endeavor. *If this tasted as bitter as life, I'd spit it out,* she thought.

Slowly she felt the effects of the drink. Sar'Tawas traded very well and obtained very good quality brews. The average citizen of the city would be lucky to have a single cup of fermented drink per harvest if any. As she sat cross-legged while sipping the remainder of the pot in the dim light of a shell lamp, she became more introspective than normal. Her emotions were quite complex, a mixture of anger, shame, and sadness. Part of her wanted to scream at her petty deception. It was humiliating and ridiculous, though unfortunately, it seemed a necessity. If that wasn't enough to keep her conscience on edge, thoughts of Aya'tar lying dead on her bed, her seed never growing to maturity, continued to surface. She shook her head and guzzled more of the drink to banish them. She turned to glance at the peacefully sleeping Sar'Tawas.

I bet you think that you are truly a man among men. Somehow you have obtained a concubine as beautiful as a leader's daughter. Surprise that is exactly what you have. You only think that I'm stupid because you think of me like a beautiful figurine and not a person, a slave for your delight. But my herbs killed the great Isut'Sanup'ra Utiakur, she thought with sarcasm. She began to chuckle to herself when suddenly it occurred to her that this man, who objectified her, was the very man she would have to marry if she wished to conclude her plot to take over the city. If only she could find another man who was powerful but who would treat her better. Many good men in the city might treat her with respect and dignity, but these were the kind of men who were hard for her to manipulate. Perhaps after taking control of the city, a tragic accident might befall Sar'Tawas, and a more thoughtful and respectful man could be found.

Ianmu closed her eyes and felt the cozy fire in her stomach as she sipped more of the drink. She would savor every moment of her life as the game she now played was very dangerous, and she could end up dead as easily as the winds changed. Yet, this fear of death brought exhilaration to the life she led. Perhaps she was hooked on the danger and the power that came with it in the same way Sar'Tawas was hooked upon the fermented drink. She looked over at the snoring man and put her fingers into his hair, slowly feeling the softness.

"You have your dark spirits and your vice, and so do I..."

ɔ ɔ ɔ

Isha'kau carefully stood and helped Aya'tar lift Hullamu, placing her on the bed. Isha'kau was in such agony from her hip and leg wounds that she nearly passed out from the pain. Yet, she had a strength that Aya'tar had never realized before, all the while hidden within the otherwise soft-spoken and carefree Isha'kau. Shortly afterward, Isha'kau climbed onto the same bed to lie beside her friend. Aya'tar was the only one of the three who was not seriously wounded, and it would be up to her to do what she could to help them. The problem was that Hullamu had an extremely deadly wound, and the likelihood of her surviving was almost nonexistent. Aya'tar wanted nothing more than to curl up into a ball and scream, but she was a high priestess, and right now, she had to hold it together, or her friends might die.

Her first task was to treat Hullamu's wounds, the worst by far. There was really no established technique for taking care of such a deep wound. Men who received such wounds defending the city from a raid almost always died. Most effort was made to make their final moments as comfortable as possible or end their suffering mercifully. Aya'tar hoped it would not come to that, but as she looked upon Hullamu, she saw death creeping in. Feelings of panic and hopelessness filled her, and her head throbbed in pain. She banished them as best as she could and concentrated on the present.

Wasting no time, Aya'tar ran to the side storeroom to get what she would need. She grabbed a leather bag full of clay powder and a clay jar containing a mixture of beeswax and yarrow mixed with a fermented honey drink. The wax had solidified over time, so Aya'tar returned to the remnants of the central fire and placed the jar close enough that it would heat up without breaking. She stopped to throw a few more logs on the fire and hoped they would catch without too much work. She didn't have time to stoke a fire. She grabbed a second large jar full of water and placed it by the fire. If the water were close to boiling, it would mix more quickly with the clay powder.

Aya'tar returned to Hullamu to see how she was doing. She was still breathing, but the blood flow was reducing, and she was looking paler. Her skin was cold to the touch, and she began twitching. Aya'tar stroked her fingers through Hullamu's hair as she looked her friend in the eyes. Hullamu peered back at her with tears but with no words to speak. Suddenly, Aya'tar remembered the water and reluctantly left her friend to fetch it. She carefully poured boiling water into a clay dish filled with the clay powder using heavy leather mittens. She let this sit for a short moment to mix and cool off while she grabbed the honey and yarrow mix. The mix had cooled a little, though it still burned her fingers a little when she dipped them into the pot to extract a glob of the medicine.

She used her fingers to ensure that anything protruding from the wound was pressed back inside. That act alone was one of the most horrifying things she had ever done, almost surreal. She delicately applied the medicine to the deep wound. It pained her to see Hullamu flinch and twitch in pain. She was too weak to even lift her hands, let alone make much protest against the pain. Yarrow could reduce bleeding, but the closer Aya'tar examined the wound, the more fear and sorrow filled her. She pushed her apprehension aside and grabbed the clay. After quickly mixing the powder with a stirring stick, she caked it over the wound, hoping for the best.

"Will she make it?" asked Isha'kau in a hushed voice while Aya'tar bent over her with the remainder of the medicine. Aya'tar opened her mouth to speak but could not find the words. Somehow deep in her mind, she knew that Hullamu's fate was sealed. When she found her, she was lying in a pool of her own blood... It was too large of a pool. Aya'tar simply ignored the question and carefully coated the stab wounds on Isha'kau's hip and thigh with the wax and yarrow mixture. Isha'kau bit down on her hand from the pain, but she lay back, drained of energy after the application was complete. Aya'tar knelt beside Hullamu and began to pray to Isut to spare her. Aya'tar prayed over and over, frantically imploring the Goddess until sweat poured down her face and her voice became hoarse.

Death was not necessarily bad as it hastened the journey into the next world. Everyone knew that the world in which they lived was actually the Second World. The First World was the world of the gods and spirits. After many long debates over which spirit and which god were the most powerful, the mother goddess Isut became fed up with the constant bickering and the never-ending challenges for supremacy. She stepped forward and cast into existence the Second World, much as she had created the first world with Gunar. All spirits were compelled to journey into the Second World and live out lives as people, animals, and all manner of life. The Second World served as a trial ground for spirits to prove their worth as mortal creatures. Isut next created a third and perfect world. The Third World would be correctly constructed to accommodate the spirits who deserved to inhabit that paradise.

When people died, their spirits might remain within their bodies, or they might depart for the Third World and the Goddess' embrace. Either way, the body would typically be buried within the family home under a stone bench where people might sleep or under the floor itself. It was comforting to the family and the spirit of the deceased to remain close by until the end of the Second World. If a spirit was of exceptional quality, the Goddess herself might call upon that spirit to immediately leave. Either way, the bones would remain as a constant reminder to the family, a comfort. Only a priest or priestess, such as Aya'tar, could sense whether the spirit remained or had been summoned.

ↄ ↄ ↄ

Hullamu opened her eyes and felt no pain. Gone was her wound as she lay in a field of grass that stretched as far as the eye could see. Above her, white puffy clouds floated effortlessly in the deep blue sky. She lay back under the warm Sun and felt the simple joy of being for a while. She could not think of why she was here or what the purpose was behind these visions, but she felt a calmness that she had never felt before – a strange sort of certainty about what was to be. Then, above her, the clouds broke apart, and the enormous and beautiful form of Isut appeared in all her glory. The Goddess had deep blue eyes like the sea and long black hair dotted with stars that filled the sky. Between her eyes was the very Moon itself. Isut spread her arms wide and from her bosom came forth a flock of the most beautiful birds Hullamu had ever seen. So many birds came in shapes and colors that did not even exist. Most important of all the birds were the vultures. Vultures were the only creatures that seemed completely immune to even the most rotting and foul death. They were the blessed messengers of the Goddess. In fact, the Goddess' wings were vast vulture feathers. Hullamu raised her arms and slowly floated towards Isut, with birds lifting her into the air. She knew at that moment pure euphoria.

ꙩ ꙩ ꙩ

Aya'tar awoke early that morning to find Hullamu in much worse condition than the past night. Hullamu looked as though she didn't still live. Her skin was much lighter, and her breathing was so shallow that it hardly registered until Aya'tar put her ear against her lips. Isha'kau was still sleeping, but Hullamu was in some sort of strange trance. Every now and then, a tear-streaked from her eyes, and she would mumble something. When Aya'tar placed her ear against her lips to feel that her breath still came, she heard what Hullamu was saying. Her words were weak and without breath.

"Isut... The birds lift me... I'm yours..."

Aya'tar sat back onto her knees and stared at her friend with a stunned look. Shivers danced down her neck and back. Hullamu spoke to the Goddess and was accepted into the Third World, right before her eyes. If ever there was a sign that Hullamu was one of the few the Goddess called directly, this was it. Even her own father had not shown a sign. She could tell that Hullamu was in pain, and it was clearly obvious that she was close to death. Still, the final painful departure to the Third World was causing her agony... agony which she could be spared. Aya'tar

364

decided at that moment that she would do the only thing that she could. She would end the suffering of her precious friend. The Goddess had called her, and anything she could do to hasten her trip to Isut was a good deed. If Hullamu could not be brought back to this world, she could at least be cut free to enter paradise and the loving embrace of Isut.

Aya'tar got up and stepped to the storeroom solemnly to get what was needed. She returned with red ocher and white paint made from clay, the rest of the large jar of water, and a jar full of yarrow and fermented honey drink. The yarrow and fermented honey drink were meant to be used in small amounts to heal wounds. Aya'tar had been told once that consuming enough of the mixture would cause a person to become still, like death. She was unsure how true this was, but she hoped this would help ease Hullamu's spirit into the next world. She paused for just a moment, nearly losing her composure, but deep breaths helped her refocus. There would be time for tears when she was done. There would be oh so many tears.

She wasted no time cleaning Hullamu's body with the water and a small linen towel. As she cleaned, she gently sang a soothing song, half-whispered and half hummed, pausing now and then to whimper in anguish. She was not sure if the song was for her or for Hullamu. After her body was washed, Aya'tar covered her in white paint. She painted white every part of her body but her face, hands, and feet. Next, she painted the hands and feet red with the ochre. Aya'tar quickly painted ritualistic lines across Hullamu's face. She peered vaguely back at her with a knowing and yet strangely relaxed expression. Hullamu appeared to know what was going on and seemed somehow comforted by it. She knew that she was about to join Isut, her goddess.

The high priestess continued to breathe deeply, trying to keep composed, but Aya'tar could feel tears welling within her as the final part came. The high priestess lay on the bed in between Hullamu and Isha'kau, who was thankfully still sleeping. She carefully lifted Hullamu's head and helped her drink the yarrow and fermented brew. She only barely swallowed the liquid, some of it dripping down her face. After a short moment, she choked and coughed some of the liquid up, which compelled Aya'tar to stop. The drink would relax her and ease the final moments.

Aya'tar waited for a short moment for the drink to take effect. She could barely keep herself together as her mind fought against the absurdity of it all. How could this be? How could it have come to this within moments? Just the day before, they had all been healthy and sitting in this very room talking. Now she knelt over her childhood friend, ready to aid her passage into the next world... she took a deep breath. It was now time. Aya'tar gazed deeply into her fading eyes, her vision blurring with wetness. The initiate priestess whispered something Aya'tar could not make out. She moved her ear against the woman's lips to hear her final words.

"I... will ask Isut... help you... send help... will... see you again..." she breathed. Aya'tar bit her tongue to keep from crying. Here she was on her deathbed, and Hullamu offered to ask the Goddess to help her personally. No level of thanks could be offered to equal such words. Aya'tar took a deep breath to steady herself. Her eyes were now blurry, and tears began to trickle down her face.

"Are you... ready, my sister?" she asked. Hullamu had a strange clarity in her eyes as she gently and almost imperceptibly nodded. Aya'tar took deep breaths of air to keep herself from bursting into tears, but she wanted to keep her face as strong as she could for what she must do next. She gently placed her hand over Hullamu's mouth and then pinched her nose with the same hand, cutting off all air to her beloved friend. Aya'tar could feel tears running down her face as she gently stroked her friend's hair and sang her a child's lullaby. Hullamu looked back with a strange mixture of conviction and love for her friend. It was not long before she began to struggle gently, though she was so weak from the drink and the tremendous blood loss that she could do nothing more than provide token resistance. Aya'tar knew that her body would fight even if her spirit wanted to leave. This was the way of all living things. Hullamu's legs wiggled, and her head pulled back and forth, requiring Aya'tar to push her hand much harder... And then she simply stopped, her body giving out more from blood loss than suffocation.

"Wait for me in the Third World, dear Assi'duma Isutmu, Hullamu," she said, finally losing her composure and bursting into uncontrollable tears. She was the high priestess of a goddess who governed life and death, the most natural cycle in the world, and yet she couldn't accept it. Why Hullamu? Among her people, it was perfectly acceptable to openly question the gods' intent. Only a weak deity would consider questioning its actions as hubris. She had not cried this hard for her father when he died, but that was because his death felt more natural. He died after a life lived longer than most people in the city. Hullamu's life was taken in the quick slash of a dagger by an unknown assailant whose body still lay on the floor where she had left it. *WHY Her?! Why didn't you save her! WHY!!!* Aya'tar curled up beside her beloved friend and held her close. *Why...*

For the rest of the morning, Aya'tar lay in the bed holding on to her deceased friend, almost a sister. After a while, Isha'kau awoke from her deep wound-induced slumber and joined Aya'tar in grief. By midday, the first person entered the temple to discover what had happened. As soon as she entered and saw the scene, Zah'namu screamed loudly in shock. At first, she thought that all three women on the bed were dead and that their attacker lay dead on the floor. It was not long before she realized that the other two women on the bed were grieving for their fallen priestess. Isha'kau sat up on her knees and wiped her tear-stricken face.

Hearing that somebody had entered the temple, Aya'tar forced herself to stand. She was simply out of tears and emotionless. The priestess slowly stood from the bed, covered with the blood of her comrades, and still shaking. Taking in the sight of the high priestess, Zah'namu realized that Aya'tar truly had within her the ability to lead. Gone from her eyes was the visage of the younger and frightened woman. Instead, Zah'namu saw before her Isut'Sanup'ramu Aya'tar, a woman ready to handle anything life threw at her. Though she still agreed with the Elder Council that a more powerful leader should be installed, those thoughts were beginning to waver, and her doubts were evaporating slowly.

"Zah'namu, please gather some people to help us bury Hullamu. That man who lies dead on the floor killed her. She... She died trying to save us," Isha'kau stammered out with a shaky voice. Then, suddenly, Aya'tar spoke, her mind lost in some waking dream no one else could see.

"No... I saw the signs. Hullamu will be offered directly to the Goddess. Afterward, she will be buried under the temple. That man, that horrible man... Somebody must know who he is. He will be buried with no possessions. He will be buried, head pointed down and in an open field. We will need someone to dig a hole," she said softly. Zah'namu knew that the Elder Council was on the verge of replacing Aya'tar with someone else or forcing her to marry, but by technical definition, she was still the acting leader of the entire city. It would be unwise not to follow her commands until she was properly removed from power. Zah'namu nodded in affirmation, turned, and hurried up the ladder. It was not until this moment that Zah'namu began to regret that possibility.

"I will make my speech tonight, just before the Sun sets. I will do so before Hullamu leaves for the next world. I want her to hear what I have to say... for her to know that it was worth it... Was it worth it?" Aya'tar whispered as she knelt beside her fallen friend. She had stopped crying at this point more from lack of tears than a lack of pain. The cycle of life was always full of immense joy and terrible pain. In her arms, she held the now cold and still body of her beloved friend, a woman she had been friends with since either of them could walk. Now, she carried a young child in her womb who would soon burst into the world. This was the very cycle of joy and pain that her people celebrated.

CHAPTER TWENTY
I CURSE YOUR SPIRIT TO OBLIVION

A common source of information archaeologists use when determining the nature of ancient civilizations is the treatment of the dead. While an analysis of human remains is of great aid in learning how a person died and how they lived, the nature of the burial itself can be extremely telling. Grave goods, the configuration of the body within the grave, the means of deposition, and even the location of the grave within or outside of a community can reveal so much about the ancient people who left no account of their own history in writing. Interestingly, burials within the living areas of buildings, sometimes directly underneath sleeping areas, were quite prevalent in many Neolithic societies. Such a practice might be considered bizarre today, yet it tells us much about people who, at one point, thought it proper.

It was not long before the majority of the citizens had gathered in the ceremonial dance area in the middle of the city. News of the attack and the death of a priestess had spread like wildfire. Fields were utterly abandoned, activities halted, and nearly everybody now stood within the ceremonial grounds staring up at the building which served as their temple. From the central temple ladder, a single woman slowly climbed.

Her face had been painted a bright red. This was more to hide her sorrow and puffy eyes than for any other reason. She wished she could have worn a painted reed mask, like the other people on top of the building. Unfortunately, the reed masks they used to ward off evil spirits were never worn by the presiding priest or priestess. Her body was painted entirely white with clay, and she had donned a ceremonial feathered headdress. She wore a linen skirt and a shawl made of sewn rabbit furs and walked barefoot, as was customary during funerals. Aya'tar was a striking woman, even in her grief.

She came to stand before everyone gathered and merely waited while several men carried the body of Hullamu carefully up the ladder and out of the temple. The men gently placed her body upon a wood and leather litter to carry. Then, delicately holding her body so she wouldn't move, they lifted Hullamu in place as they inclined the litter to about a 45° angle so that the crowd could see the priestess and that she was well prepared.

Isha'kau painfully climbed her way up the ladder with the assistance of a friend named Erinar, a younger woman who had spent much time in the temple the previous harvest as the sacred virgin for the fertility festival. Erinar had not produced a child with Aya'tar's father, but soon afterward, she had fallen for a farmer and was already showing signs of a child. Isha'kau came to kneel beside Aya'tar, her wounds too painful for her to sit or stand. There were gasps among the gathered people at the sight of the wounded priestess whose side was covered with deep wounds. Isha'kau had left the side of her body that had been attacked entirely unpainted so that the gathered people could witness what had been done. She had painted the rest of her body white and had donned a reed ceremonial mask and a bright, red-dyed linen loincloth, as well as a feathered headdress.

The last people to leave the temple were a hunter and the leader of the hunters, Kamar. They roughly lifted the attacker's body from the temple and brought him before Aya'tar. His body was still a little stiff, but the freeze of death had almost left him. Aya'tar continued to take deep breaths hoping that she would not become a ball of tears or lash out in anger when she spoke to her people. She was about to change everything, and she knew that this would present a blow to whoever had sent this man. That alone was the driving force behind her need for composure. She took a deep breath, her head still throbbing.

"People of Isut'na. You respected and followed my father, the great Isut'Sanup'ra Utiakur. With his passing and without any other heirs or wives, I am now the high priestess of Isut and the city leader. I know that many of you think that I am too young and that I have fallen out of the favor of the Goddess. I will answer these two charges here and now... You have a right to hear them answered," she said as loudly and as clearly as she could for everyone to hear. Below her, she saw Sar'Tawas staring back at her with an odd mixture of curiosity and contempt. Near Sar'Tawas gathered the rest of the Elder Council. These people were the real day-to-day leaders of the city, coming to Aya'tar only when a major decision needed to be made or the gods counseled. Aya'tar knew that some of the people supported her, mostly because of her father, while the rest wished her gone or married to a powerful man, like Sar'Tawas.

"Isut is the goddess of life, death, and rebirth. Now I stand before you representing all three of these aspects, and I tell you, the Goddess is with me." She waited a few moments for the words to sink in. Those close enough could see the living priestess and the dead priestess, representing life continuing past death, but no one knew of the child. Then, once dramatic effect had built up to a reasonable level, measurable by the gossiping, she continued.

"Within my womb grows a child. I do not know if it is a boy or girl, but I do know that it was conceived during the ritual to the gods this past warm season. If he is born a boy, he will become the next high priest when he grows. If she is born a girl, she will grow and marry the city leader to become a high priestess. If they are duemuas or narmu, they shall become the high priest or priestess upon my death, and potentially the leader of the city, if the Goddess shows this to be her will. My family's connection to the Goddess has been pulled as thin as the threads of flax on a quick-fingered spinner, but that long strand has not broken," she paused for a moment to let her words sink in. She had just reasserted her position, a hard line to take. Now she needed to provide concession to weaken any who would rise up against her.

"Those on the Council who believe that I am young and perhaps naïve in the ways of ruling are correct. They are right to think that I may not be ready, yet I am still your leader. As a leader, I need to make decisions that serve the city's best interests and not my own. As long as I carry a child within me, I will remain priestess of Isut and let no one be foolish enough to cross the Goddess on this point. The last man who did lies dead and cursed at my feet," she said, indicating Pedar. She paused for a moment taking a deep breath to steady herself after briefly thinking of the wicked man.

"However, until the Council thinks I'm ready to be the leader, I wish the Council to govern the city as they have already done since the death of my father. I will remain high priestess," she concluded. The council members glared back at her, some with scowls, but most with looks of respect. She had changed the game in such a way that she could hold her position and remove the need for anyone to challenge her, at least until the warm winds came.

"Who is the father?" screamed someone from the crowd. This was followed by other people yelling the same question. She knew that this would come up, but she was unsure how people would take to it. She held up her hands, calming people so that she could answer them. This was the part that everyone waited to hear. Only Sar'Tawas stood shaking his head, having already deduced the father.

"The father is a man of crafts from the city. He is not of a high family, nor would most of you know him, but he is my lover. If the child is born and healthy, this will be a sign from the Goddess. I would then wish to marry him. If the Council eventually chooses someone else to lead, I will live with this man and bother you no more. He has been sent from the city on a task by me, and he will return in time for our child to be born," she finished. She hoped that her last statement was true, but there was no way she could be sure. Before anyone could begin asking more questions, Aya'tar switched focus to speak of the man who had attacked the temple and taken the life of her friend, Hullamu. She motioned the men beside her to hold up the attacker. They grabbed his body and roughly lifted it.

Aya'tar leaned over and raised a large clay jar full of water and splashed it across the face of the attacker, washing soot away. His mouth hung open with his tongue hanging out. His one good eye was still open, but the other had a nasty wound where the hairpin had been inserted. The front of his body was already darkening as the blood pooled from lying on the floor. Typically, a body was painted to hide these discolorations and aid the spirit's passing. No such rites had been afforded this man. Aya'tar refused to look at the body, her anger at his actions threatening to make her cry out.

"Who here knows this man? Who here knows of any reason why last night he sneaked into the temple and tried to kill Isha'kau and me? It was his dagger that wounded Isha'kau... His dagger that killed the priestess Hullamu. If you know anything of this, please speak," Aya'tar begged the crowd as people gasped, staring at the lifeless corpse of the murderer. Suddenly, a woman who worked in the fields recognized the man and pointed.

"Hey, that's Pedar. Yeah, that's Pedar for sure. But why would Pedar try to kill the priestess?" the woman spoke aloud. It was only a few moments before other people realized that she was right. The man was named Pedar, and he worked the fields along with many others. Slowly, more people spoke up, adding details of who the man was and anything that might explain why he had done this most heinous act. It turned out that Pedar once had a family, but he had been estranged from them due to an incident they did not wish to discuss. He had lived by himself without a wife or child ever since. Several people mentioned having seen him a couple of times recently with a woman, but nobody could remember who.

Aya'tar turned and faced the man. He had brought her so much misery, and yet very little was known about him. She could not imagine what would have driven him to do this, but she felt nothing but hate for him. There were few punishments to be handed down for many crimes, each of these codified within the collective memory of the citizens. Families handled their own justice for minor offenses most of the time, and somebody like Aya'tar or the Elder Council would handle major infractions. One of the few crimes with a prescribed punishment was murder. Murderers were ritualistically killed and sent to the next world with no possessions, their bodies often mutilated. Aya'tar wished to go a step further.

She held out her hand, and Isha'kau handed her the very flint dagger which he had used to kill Hullamu. The handle had a thin copper ring. Aya'tar could swear that she had seen a blade like this once before, but right now, her mind was too focused on what she had to do to consider where that might have been. She reached forward and used the dagger to cut the waist cord holding the man's loincloth. Next, she bent down and cut the straps of his sandals, removing each, while avoiding the soiled cloth. She nearly gagged at the smell, yet she held her composure. He would be buried uncleansed, unpainted, unblessed, and with no possessions, an act of malice against any spirit. It was Aya'tar's hope that his spirit just vanished into oblivion, but if it somehow found its way into the next world, it would do so with as low of standing as possible.

Last came the hardest part. In the unlikely event that Pedar's spirit did journey to the next world, ritualistic mutilation might continue to curse the spirit beyond. Such acts were performed upon enemies and the greatest of criminals. Aya'tar had seen this sort of act performed several times before, but she had always had the luxury of looking away. Today, it would be her hand that made the cut. Using the dagger, Aya'tar castrated the man before the gathered thousands. The act was quick but drew gasps of horror and agreement from the audience. Then, standing before the ruined corpse of Pedar, she screamed her curse to Isut and stabbed his corpse in the gut – the same location where Hullamu had been cut.

"Pedar, I curse your spirit to oblivion. In the name of Isut, I've taken your life, your seed, your eye, and now, you will be buried with no possessions. You will have a restless sleep with your feet pointed toward the sky. You will rot in the ground until the Second World ends. Perhaps, by then, my spirit will forgive you for what you have done, but not in this world. In Isut's name, I curse you!" she screamed as she pushed the dagger in deeper and then pulled it out, suddenly. Strange fluids leaked from the wound, but they were not blood. Dead bodies did not usually bleed. The two men picked up Pedar's body and carried him down the ladder and out of the city to a hole that had been dug earlier that day at Aya'tar's request. He would be placed headfirst into the hole and buried without ceremony.

Aya'tar wasted no more time on Pedar, leaving the cuttings from his body lying on the temple roof for the Goddess to collect if she wished. Next, she turned her attention to the body of Hullamu, dropping the dagger to the ground. The main reason for painting the body was to spare the living the sight of the discoloration after death. While waiting for the ceremony, Aya'tar had prepared the body of her dear friend. She had washed, ritually purified, and painted her body. Next, she had wrapped her best bark fiber string girdle around Hullamu's waist and adorned her neck with several beautiful strings of bone and obsidian beads. Over a dozen small items had been placed upon her stomach by friends and by Aya'tar. These items included a large spool of flax cord, a jar of dye, a pot containing fermented honey drink, but most importantly, a small clay figurine of the Goddess.

With the murderer now dealt with and her speech heard by everyone in the city, it was time for Hullamu's spirit to be accepted by the Goddess. Aya'tar came to stand before the body of her fallen companion and placed her hands upon Hullamu's abdomen and head. She began to sing the long and mournful song of the dead. This was the highest honor afforded the dead and had only recently been performed for her own father. She sang the first verses by herself, barely loud enough for those around her to hear. Aya'tar's voice began to waver when suddenly she heard the sound of a second singer. She turned to find Isha'kau, weakly and apparently in pain, standing by her.

Together, the priestesses sang their loud and mournful song imploring the Goddess to accept Hullamu's spirit directly into the Third World, as Aya'tar had foreseen. It was not long before Erinar joined to build their song to new heights. Only those consecrated by the Goddess could sing such songs, and Erinar was just such a person. When the funeral rites had been performed, Aya'tar stood and climbed the final ladder to the highest point on top of the temple: a small wooden platform raised one story greater than the temple itself. From this vantage, she could see the entire city and some of the lands beyond. Not far to the West, the two men carrying the body of Pedar could be seen slowly dragging the corpse unceremoniously uphill toward the site where a small hole had been dug.

Aya'tar closed her eyes and held atop her head a vulture's feather in her right hand and a single stalk of wheat in her other. She gazed at the sky toward the beautiful red glow of the setting Sun. A light breeze blew across her skin as she held the symbols for life and death, imploring the Goddess to act.

"Please, Isut... it is time," she whispered. Aya'tar released the wheat and the feather, which slowly fell to the ground. Suddenly, the wind picked up, catching both items and lifting them into the air, blowing them away from the temple and toward the East, where the dark wing of Isut slowly blanketed the world as night fell upon the land. All around, there were gasps as people witnessed what was surely a sign, yet more proof of Aya'tar's standing with the Goddess. Hullamu's spirit would begin its trip to the Third World and into the Goddess' warm embrace.

ↄ ↄ ↄ

A full tenday had passed since Imkanar had arrived in the small village of Karut. With around one hundred people, the village supported itself primarily on fishing and as a trade stop for people en route to and from the major cities to the South. As he had expected, the people had no use for copper working, but they did have a use for a man skilled at making charcoal, as well as another hand at fishing. As the priestess had suggested, the villagers had accepted his offering of obsidian pieces and lead beads in exchange for a space in a dwelling to share with two other men who were unwed, as well as the essential items he would need to begin a new life.

Imkanar had become a less bitter man in just a short time. At least as far as he could tell, the feeling that women needed to be protected was commonplace among men. At first, he had been angered that Aya'tar had been unwilling to let him help her. He had felt that she was in over her head and needed someone strong to protect her. Part of him was ashamed that he had believed Aya'tar too weak to handle her own problems. She was the high priestess for her goddess, not some child. As he passed the time fishing and making charcoal, Imkanar had slowly come to accept that if he truly loved her, he needed to have trust in her ability to lead. Unfortunately, he could not shake the feeling that she needed him and was all alone.

Having just cast his net, he stood on the edge of a small lake to the West of Isut'na. Fishing was not the worst life, but he longed for the embrace of the priestess. To wait for her until the warm winds came was almost too much to bear. Worse, he knew that she was in danger, and at any moment, her enemies could swoop down and attack. He bit his lip until he tasted blood at the thought of waiting there though he knew that she would never forgive him if he went back on his word. His frustration and anger were driven by love and pride. As time passed, his pride was slowly beginning to relax, and his frustration and anger were being replaced by worry and longing.

"Isut, goddess of the Moon, Gunar, god of the bull, watch over my love," he prayed.

ↄ ↄ ↄ

Fortune finally turned its smile upon the group as they came to the crest of a small hill overlooking a village by the water. Ember, Brig'dha, and Aethen had walked for a tenday heading mostly east through a valley that cut in-between the large mountains, which ran like a spine across the land. Ahead lay a beautiful coastline, which likely indicated the waterway that they must cross. It was the ominous and broad expanse of West Lake. As far as Ember was concerned, the "Lake" appeared to be the same size as the Blue Sea or the Greatest River. She could not even see the other side.

"Oh look, another giant expanse of water we can cross... Doesn't that look fun? I hope I pass out and nearly die again! Won't it be a grand time?" Ember said sarcastically. Aethen laughed at her comment though he shared her sarcasm. None of them were interested in crossing the vast body of water, but they knew that their goal was regrettably on the other side. Brig'dha looked down at the bundle of fur she held in her arms. Mew, the cat, had not seemed particularly fond of water, and she wondered how well he would take to crossing such an expanse. At the moment, he seemed more interested in toying with a lock of her hair, bringing a smile to her face.

"Well, let's head down to that village and see if they have a way across the water," Aethen said, lifting his traveling pack and beginning to walk down the hill toward the village on the edge of what would one day be known as the Adriatic Sea.

The village turned out to be a group of small wooden houses that were slightly elevated using stilts, with heavily thatched roofs. The walls were made of small wooden bundles of sticks lashed with sinew and coated with mud. The poles had been painted with a mixture of clay and ochre paints, giving them various white, brown, and red appearances. All in all, the design was very similar to other buildings throughout the mainland, though it appeared that flooding might be a problem. Most interesting were the large wooden masks resembling animals attached to the sides of most buildings, just above the entryway. Brig'dha wondered what their significance might be, perhaps a homage to local spirits.

Judging by the look of the people, Brig'dha supposed that the villagers were a mixture of farmers and fishermen. Small fields had been erected near the village, though it was too late in the harvest for anyone to be attending them. Standing on wooden platforms, which extended into the water, several women could be seen spearfishing. A man knelt before a loom beside one of the nearest houses, spinning some sort of wool fiber yarn as he slowly worked a panel of cloth. Not far from him, wooden pens had been created to hold pigs. Brig'dha was still amazed by the difference between her northern people and these southern people. The difference in their technology and how they fed themselves varied so greatly.

Brig'dha was just glad that the town didn't seem to have any dogs. Mew had returned to her arms to be held, and the sight of a dog would likely scare him away. She wasn't sure if the cat could be taken across the water, but she would certainly try. Ember had also grown quite fond of the small animal, even though their relationship was standoffish at best. The cat was hardly domesticated and would scratch Aethen if he got too close. It seemed that Mew would continue to love only Brig'dha. Strangely, she was okay with that arrangement.

"I'm not sure exactly how we are going to trade for passage across the water. What do we have to exchange of value?" Aethen asked. Ember began poking around in her small traveling bag while Brig'dha put Mew onto the ground so that she could look in her own bag.

"I do have this, though I'm nearly out of things to trade," Brig'dha said, removing a small golden nugget from her traveling bag. Such gold and copper nuggets could be found in streams and riverbeds in the North, but this was her last such item. Ember had always called them yellow rocks and only recently adopted the term "gold" from those in the South and from her short-term adopted family from the True South. The word Espe had used was Melnea, basically meaning honey. The word Nemanar had used was khusken, which merely meant "shiny metal." It was easier than saying shiny yellow rock.

"If that is your last trade item for passage, what will we do at the next place?" Aethen asked. He supposed that he would end up chopping more wood, but he wished there was a better way. Ember felt the weight of the large blue rock in her traveling bag. It was a fist-sized, blue-colored stone, or perhaps warm ice? No one was quite sure. She had held onto the item for so long, and yet it served no real purpose and contributed nothing. She had nearly died several times without ever realizing any benefit from it. Life was too short to waste holding onto something when so much could come from its utility. She decided at that moment that she would trade it at the next major town they came to. It would provide many minor items for trade and perhaps a gift for someone she cared about.

Ɔ Ɔ Ɔ

Isha'kau stood behind high priestess Aya'tar within the temple. Before them lay the northern side of the temple with its freshly plastered foundation. Buried underneath the plaster was the body of Hullamu, entombed one moon before. It was customary for a second ritual to be performed after the first moon to ensure the purity of the burial. Isha'kau's leg was sore and puffy, but it seemed to be slowly healing. The first few days after the incident, Isha'kau had been worried about the mental state of the high priestess, but she had slowly come around, having accepted what had become. In some ways, Isha'kau thought Aya'tar might even have become more stoic since the attack.

Aya'tar stood over the plastered floor holding the painted skull of her grandfather in one hand and a vulture feather in the other. It had been determined long before that the spirit of Anatiakur, grandfather of Aya'tar, had never left his body and would likely remain until the end of the Second World. The skull had been removed from the burial site, carefully cleaned, and ritualistically plastered and painted to resemble life, long before. Whenever she held his skull, Aya'tar could feel the presence of her grandfather, and it comforted her. The spirits of the dead who had been purified and buried brought comfort to those they cared for. Only the spirits of those who had died un-purified were of any danger.

Underneath the North and East floors were many graves of important people, each buried within the building. The initiate priestess had been placed in a flexed, fetal position as best as her remains could be. She had been laid to rest wearing a beautiful linen string girdle and necklaces made from bone and obsidian beads around her neck. A dozen objects had been placed on her, uncommon as most bodies were buried without adornment or attire. Aya'tar knew that the items had not left this world to journey to the next. Everyone knew that items would wait until the end of the Second World to travel into the third, but when that time came, they would be ready.

Standing around the fallen priestess were most of the members of the Elder Council and several people who knew her. To be buried in such a place and first be given to the vultures to carry away her spirit directly to Isut was perhaps the highest honor anyone could have. Not only had Aya'tar detected the signs, but Hullamu had given her life to protect the leader of the city, a pregnant woman. To harm a pregnant woman was considered extreme hubris and despicable in the eyes of the gods. All of these reasons alone would be enough to warrant a special burial.

Standing behind Sar'Tawas, one of the many elders gathered for the burial, Ianmu waited. She felt remorse over the death of the priestess. It had not been her will that Hullamu die. Ianmu had never wished to kill anyone, but every life in the world was forfeit if An'an called upon them. No act, however immoral it might seem, could truly be immoral if the Goddess called upon it to be done. The gods were above the morals of mere mortals, for they had a timeless will and goals that the living could not understand. It was unfortunate when someone died unexpectedly, but at least, this woman had played her part in what was to become the will of An'an. Ianmu found herself whispering a prayer to her goddess for the woman's spirit as she blinked back a tear.

ↄ ↄ ↄ

Ember cautiously stepped from the wooden dugout boat, placing her bare feet into the cold water and feeling relief as they touched the sand beneath, slowly going numb. Feeling that she could tolerate the water even as cold as it was, Ember climbed from the boat and helped pull it to shore. Their party had crossed West Lake in a long but shallow dugout boat. There had been many other deeper boats available, but the only person willing to take them in the cold season was an older man named Inoin. The man's tattooed skin was tanned almost as badly as aged leather, and Ember had yet to see a tooth in his mouth, but he seemed like a friendly sort and had accepted the single gold nugget in place of more proper payment.

It had been one of the most uncomfortable experiences of Ember's life. The boat was small and cramped. Worse, relieving oneself required leaning off the back of the vessel while everybody sat just a few arms lengths ahead. It had been cold, though at least the Sun had remained during the day and the wind had not been too strong. Ember wore her long doeskin leather shirt, a pair of leather leggings, her roe deer loincloth, and leather wrap around her upper body for additional warmth. She left her leather boots in the boat where they would not become wet. She had initially thought her clothing would be adequate as they were heading into the warm True South, but as the cold season came upon them, she started to become worried that she would need much warmer clothing. It seemed that even the True South could become cold.

Aethen and Brig'dha were similarly garbed, as well as worried over the cold air and their less-than-cold-season clothing. While Ember and Aethen had both taken to wearing the leather they slept upon wrapped around their shoulders for extra warmth, Brig'dha had found a better utility for her bed mat. She had found that wrapping it around Mew seemed to calm him. She had used this technique when she had brought the cat onto the boat to cross the water. That and a combination of fish pieces throughout the journey appeared to work. Unfortunately, the cat would barely relieve itself or take water during most of the trip. She felt sorry for Mew, but she could certainly understand why the water was so displeasing to him.

A moment later, Aethen jumped from the boat to help pull it onto the shore, quite glad to have the journey over with. If Mew thought his journey had been troublesome, Aethen had suffered a much worse time. At one point, poor Mew had gotten loose from the large leather wrap Brig'dha had kept him wrapped within. It was the first time he had realized that he was on a boat. He had run around the boat trying to find a way off only to discover, to his horror, that the water fully surrounded him. When Aethen had reached to seize the cat, Mew had reacted quite negatively. His arms and legs still had cuts which would likely remain for many more days.

Ember dropped to her knees in the sand, thanking the gods and spirits they had passed across the water without any mishap. Best of all, she had finally discovered what a conscious arrival from a boat trip was like. She dug her hands into the cool, wet sand and felt the joy of the firm ground beneath her. She loved swimming and loved the water, but crossing it was a horrible adventure that rarely seemed to end well.

How can there be people who spend their lives doing this? It's a nightmare! she wondered.

Not far ahead, Mew ran free, apparently just as pleased to be ashore. It was only a moment before the cat entered into the strange little dance that he performed before relieving itself. Brig'dha knelt beside Ember and began a prayer to the gods and spirits. Mew completed his preparatory movements and finally relaxed. He was not the smartest cat, perhaps less intelligent than most. He didn't understand what had happened to him, but he was pretty sure that he would scratch the next person who tried to put him on a boat.

With the boat pulled ashore, Inoin had collected his payment and hidden the boat behind some bushes where it would remain until he was ready to return. They supposed that he would likely head either north or south to find a village to trade the small gold piece for something of real value and perhaps even find another willing traveler to trade for the return voyage. The man seemed reasonably familiar with where he was and confident that he would quickly find such a village. Either way, Ember and her friends would be heading east until they found a place to remain for the cold season.

382

CHAPTER TWENTY ONE

MATERIAL WEALTH

While metalworking would not come into common practice for a few hundred to several thousand years after Ember was born, depending on the location, the practice of working soft and relatively pure metals, such as gold, silver, copper, and lead, was likely known around the time she lived. Extremely rare and relatively un-worked, jewelry was likely produced from these soft metals. Perhaps one of the most well preserved and ancient sets of golden jewelry comes from the Varna Necropolis In eastern Bulgaria, barely 450 miles walking distance from where Ember and her group now stand. The golden items found within the necropolis date back to as early as 4600 BCE, barely 900 years after Ember's birth. Among the items were necklaces, bracelets, and many other intricately worked golden items. Perhaps more amazing than even such works of metal is the 10,000-carat topaz crystal Ember carries.

As the Sun slowly rose in the sky, Brig'dha and Ember stood hand-in-hand surveying the landscape. Aethen had stepped aside to relieve himself and to allow the women to stare at the beauty of the land alone. The land had a romantic feel to it, and he longed to stand and gaze at its vast beauty with a woman, hand-in-hand. Perhaps that would come to pass, but right now, he made sure to give his companions alone time every now and then. It seemed like the proper and polite thing to do. For now, he would bide his time and wait until he found the vast cities to the South. There, he would try to find his own love.

They had passed over a mountain range, though they had crossed through valleys for the most part. Surrounding them was a gigantic semi-circle of mountains with what appeared to be a giant valley in the middle. To the Southeast, a vast body of water approached the mainland. It was yet another body of water so gigantic that its far side could not be seen. Ember wondered how there could be so much water in the world. Her Great River felt like a tiny stream compared to these massive bodies of water. Residing next to the water was a vast tribe with dozens of structures and a palisade built around it for protection. Ember suspected that 300, maybe even 400, people lived in that tribe.

In the distance, many other small tribes could be seen not far from the largest one. The entire area was filled with swamps and marshlands surrounding the major waterway. Such land would be infested with annoying insects come the warm season. Worse, they could tell that the humidity would become terribly unpleasant. Both women were glad that they had arrived during the cold season. Beside them, Mew, the cat, stood licking himself clean and having seemingly recovered from the nightmare which had been their water crossing.

Since that passage, nearly three tendays had passed. The group was almost empty of supplies. Every two or three days, Ember and Aethen would hunt for more food while Brig'dha gathered anything edible that could be found, but there was a limit to how much could be foraged. The cold season made the likelihood of finding any edible plant life nearly nonexistent. Even more troubling, none of them were entirely sure of what plants could be eaten in the True South, and randomly testing what they found was a quick way to meet the spirits in person. According to Brig'dha, the winter solstice was nearly on top of them, though it was tough for her to say exactly.

"This seems like a good place to wait out the worst parts of the cold season," Brig'dha said. At her feet, little Mew pawed gently, wishing to be held. Unfortunately, he had grown a fair measure since they had found him and was no longer quite that small. She bent down, grasping the animal and lifting him in her arms.

"This is exactly the kind of place I was hoping we could find, a place where I could do some good quality trading!" Ember said with enthusiasm. Brig'dha turned to regard her inquisitively.

"I have been thinking of trading the warm ice for something useful. Perhaps we could trade for some new clothes or even some beautiful jewelry! I don't know about you, but my loincloth is getting stiff and ragged, and I would really like something nice to wear." Ember's face had lit with excitement at the prospect, but Brig'dha looked concerned.

"But you have carried that stone for so long. Doesn't it mean something to you?" Ember pulled the item from her bag and unwrapped it from the rabbit fur, which kept it safe. She held it up to the Sun and watched the beautiful blue lights dancing within the stone, a 10,000-carat blue topaz crystal of the highest quality.

"I stole this from a man who tried to have his way with me and tried to kill me. It will forever be tainted by those memories. I'm not really sure I wish to keep it. It doesn't do anything for me, but somebody in a large village like this might have some use for it. If I traded it, I could get everything that we need. Why keep the damn thing when it doesn't have any magical powers I can detect or any other real utility? Besides, there are much more beautiful things in this world," Ember said, turning her fox-like gaze at Brig'dha. The priestess was a victim when it came to such comments. Most people would have gagged over the sappiness, but Brig'dha always became flushed red and moved. She began to reach for Ember, suddenly caught in the moment.

Aethen stepped from behind the bush, adjusting his loincloth and coming to find Brig'dha clamped tightly against Ember in a deep embrace. He stepped quite a distance from the pair and turned to regard the scene before him. Every single day brought Aethen closer to his goal of finding a woman from the True South. When that day occurred, he too would share in such moments. He just wished that they wouldn't rub it in so often. Aethen merely sighed and began collecting his traveling pack. He would be glad to finally relax in a large village. Spending so many tendays walking was taxing on the body, as well as the mind.

The village seemed not so far when standing so high up and surveying it from a distance. The actual journey down to the village took quite a while, and they did not arrive until midday. All around, people worked and lived out their daily lives just like everywhere else. Ember watched as laughing children ran by, kicking a sewn piece of leather with stuffing, resembling a ball. One of the small children had a tiny leather sewn doll in her hand while another carried what looked like a little toy bow with a single leather tipped arrow. Ember smiled as the children ran by, waving to them.

Nearby, women worked with large, warp weighted looms weaving yarn into textiles while the men chopped wood for the fires, which would keep them warm. Many women had their hair rolled into large elaborate buns at the sides of their heads while the men tended to braid their hair. Everyone in her group had long hair, Embers being loose while Brig'dha's and Aethen's sporting several small braids at various intervals. They would indeed appear odd to outsiders, but that was always the case when different cultures met.

The village was made of large houses built upon sturdy stone foundations. Their walls were made of poles caked with mud and clay, with cut wooden poles forming the roofs. This was much sturdier than the construction of Ember's home village or any that she had seen so far. The wooden palisade surrounding the village had its top painted red with many entryways to allow reasonably easy access. Ember wasn't sure how dangerous the local tribes were, but it did not look like the people who inhabited this tribe were terribly wary of raiders. A village this size might have had a reasonably large group of warriors to defend it.

The temperature was not quite cold, but it was too cool to be comfortable. Most villagers wore fur or beaded and painted leather wraps around their upper bodies, while a few wore textiles of wool with beautiful woven designs. Under their wraps, upper bodies were either bare, but for adornments of beads and paint, or clad in leather shirts featuring intricate beadwork and designs. Around their waists, short loincloths or leather wraps and leggings were common, as well as a few textile wrap skirts, mostly made from wool. The variation in attire was much greater than she was used to. Far from the homogeneous styles found in the North, many different clothing patterns could be seen. This certainly seemed to be a good place to pick up some better clothing.

Sitting on the stone stairs which led into a slightly elevated house was an older woman carefully repairing a fishing net. She wore large, beautifully carved bone earrings, and intricate scarification across her face. She smiled at the group as they passed. Ember could not stop looking at the older woman's scarification, finding it immensely beautiful, though likely painful. She came to a full stop and merely stared. The older woman seemed confused at the looks she received, but she quickly smiled when Ember pointed to her own skin in the same places where the older woman had scarification, indicating her interest. The older woman smiled and removed a flint knife, indicating the cuts used to make the scars, then gave Ember a catty wink. Ember glared back in worry holding her hands out and indicating that she was not ready for such pain. The old woman burst into laughter and returned to her net.

Brig'dha shook her head at Ember, always amazed at how easily she interacted with people. The shy priestess would be terrified to talk with someone out of nowhere. All in all, they seemed like a friendly sort and apparently friendly to travelers. Ember had discovered long ago that large villages were usually quite used to travelers. They were often very accommodating, assuming that they didn't have obsessed religious people trying to sacrifice you. The question would be, could any of these people speak a language that they understood?

Ember approached a small building that had the look of a guesthouse. Guesthouses were often undecorated and not usually of the same quality as the more continually-occupied houses families used. Standing out in front was a man with a large reed basket full of clay and a wooden tool in his hand, which he was using to apply the clay to the side of the building, making a repair. Repairs were constantly performed on most buildings to keep them in good order. Over time, a building without regular maintenance would slowly deteriorate. It was about time that the group found a place where they could stay for the winter, and this building looked about as likely as any other.

"Excuse me. Do you understand my words?" Ember asked in her native tongue, expecting to fail. The man turned to see who was speaking and appeared delighted at the sight of the stunning redhead. His rich, dark eyes were framed by dark, curly hair and lightly tanned skin, though still not quite so dark as the True Southerner people Ember had met once before. He merely shook his head to indicate that he did not understand, but he waited patiently, hoping that Ember might speak a different language. Next, she tried the language she had learned from those of the True South.

"Do you know my words?" The man smiled upon hearing words he understood.

"Traders?" he asked in a heavily accented and broken version of the southern language.

"Travelers," she answered.

"You need place, stay for cold?"

"Yes. We trade,"

"Bring trade tomorrow? You help repair?" he asked, hopefully. Aethen begrudgingly nodded his head yes. He had only understood a word or two from the man, but somehow, he knew exactly what he was asking… It was what everyone always wanted, an extra set of hands. Ember turned to see Aethen looking dismayed at the prospect of more labor.

"Cheer up, Aethen! Brig'dha and I can help too. It's not like you have to do this all yourself," she said. The group picked up their belongings and headed into the small building to deposit them before proceeding to the trading area. The man put down the clay and his tool, seemingly happy that he had found someone else to work on coating the walls. He paused for a moment noting the furry animal nestled within a leather-wrapped hide and carried by Brig'dha. He had seen people with dogs, but never a cat. The animal was certainly curious, and it seemed friendly, almost tame. He reached to try and touch the animal, but it made a hissing sound and swiped at him with its paw. The man withdrew his hand rapidly and looked to the woman holding the animal for an explanation.

"Stheagh... Mew meh'prae tuh," Brig'dha said to the man, causing Ember and Aethen to laugh. Brig'dha glared at the man as she carried the animal into the building. Ember shrugged apologetically at the man.

"Mew does not like you," she said and stepped into the building with a laugh, unsure of how many words he understood.

ↄ ↄ ↄ

It was not long before the group made their way to the trading area toward the water. There were many different people from what looked like many different places, all likely here to trade. This was evident as some people had different skin coloration and hair than the locals. Some people's clothing was also different, varying from more textile and exotic to more traditional leather and fur, many with very different designs to the cut and decoration of the clothing. People within a tribe and region tended to look similar. This was obviously a major trading hub for the region. Everyone was amazed to see so many different people gathered in one place. Sure, there were trading hubs in the North, but nothing as large as this. Ember counted, at least a dozen traders who appeared to be from different places though she did not know from where.

The village turned out to be known to the locals as Taerhem. Strangely, that word seemed to also mean "warm," or something similar to these people. It certainly didn't feel warm to any of them, but they suspected that when the hot season came, this village became miserably humid and uncomfortable. Part of Ember wished to remain in the town until the warm winds came so that she could swim in the bright blue waters not far from where they now stayed. Fortunately, the call of adventure in the True South outweighed her urge to swim.

The trading area was an open ground near the water where several dozen small huts and a few permanent mud-brick buildings had been set up. A few people were trading their wares, which sat upon leather mats to be inspected. People wandered by examining the items while several individuals apparently haggled for bargains. On the ground kneeling before a mat, Ember spotted a local woman holding what looked like a small leather bag containing some unknown substance. Her shiny dark hair was rolled into two large buns, one on each side of her head. She had tiny scars across her cheeks in a decorative pattern as well as running down her arms, which were bare. On the ground behind her lay a fur shawl that she had apparently set down. Around her waist was tied a leather skirt with painted decoration. Her feet were bound in fur boots to stay warm, the kind suited more for warming feet when sitting, than any serious walking. Ember was impressed to see bone jewelry and earrings, and many necklaces around the woman's neck.

She appeared to be trading the bag and its contents for a large and very ornately decorated clay pot. The man trading the pot wore a leather vest with carved designs throughout the leather. He wore leggings and a heavy loincloth with a pair of leather boots. Upon his bald head was a woven reed hat, while around his neck, he wore many necklaces containing beads of many different types of materials, likely his material wealth. As she watched, the woman haggled back and forth with the man until suddenly they reached forward, grasping each other's hands in what appeared to be some kind of agreement. Both smiled as the woman took possession of the large pot and the man eagerly snatched the small bag examining its contents.

Their first stop would be a place where Ember could exchange the large blue object for something more manageable. Toward the center of the village was a building where it appeared that communal goods were being traded on behalf of the people. Such collective trading was reasonably commonplace and involved the material wealth of the village being overseen, commonly by an elder. This was a place where grain or whatever else these people produced in mass could be traded for, and likely the best location for Ember to trade such a precious item as her blue stone.

Overseeing the trading was a man who looked to Brig'dha as though he might also be a priest. He wore a long leather sleeveless tunic that descended to the ground and possessed many intricate designs, each painted. Atop his head sat a reed woven sunshade hat, an apparently commonplace item among these people. As they approached, the man completed his business with what appeared to be local traders, though they could not be sure. The man turned his attention from his previous business toward the three strange individuals who now approached.

"Excuse me, do you know my words?" Ember asked, hoping that the man understood the words of the South.

"I do, I do. I know many words. Do you wish grain? What do you trade?" he asked enthusiastically though his speech was not perfect. The man looked directly at Aethen, expecting him to be the source of conversation and commerce while Ember slowly removed the rabbit fur from her bag. The man continued to stare expectantly at Aethen, who merely looked back at him with a cocked eyebrow as Ember fidgeted for the object. She held the rabbit fur wrapped crystal up for the man to see. At first, he only saw the fur and began to reject the idea of any trade.

"No furs, we have plenty..." His words were cut off as Ember unwrapped the fur enough for the man to see what was inside. She again wrapped the fur and indicated that they should go elsewhere to speak. The man regarded her for a few moments with an acquisitive look. He then ushered all three into the small building directly adjacent to where he had been trading to discuss this most special trade.

The small building was full of big woven baskets and clay vessels containing various bulk stores. Many of these had a symbol either painted or carved into them, which Ember supposed indicated their contents. Though the floors were musty and dirty, several old leather mats had been placed on the floor upon which they now sat. It wasn't the most pleasant accommodation, but it was private and a good place to make a trade. Many tribes had similar small huts or even buildings where they stored grains and other materials for the cold season, but this village was so large that it apparently had storage not just for their survival but for trade.

Once inside the hut, Ember unwrapped the fur to reveal the giant ball of crystal. The man stared astounded at the beautiful blue bobble. It looked like a large piece of fallen sky or ice at room temperature. It was the color of a beautiful blue sky and larger than the balled fist of a man. He reached forward, removed the object from the fur, and held it near a small fire, which warmed the room, to examine it more closely. Brig'dha took a deep breath to banish her anxiety and leaned forward to offer her opinion in the language of the True South, words she had been learning along the way from Ember. Now seemed like a good time to speak up, or so she hoped.

"It magic, big magic. Too much magic. Better for tribe," she said, indicating that the item was magical and too much trouble for the likes of her. At first, Ember stared blankly at Brig'dha, almost unwilling to believe that the shy priestess was actually attempting to pass a lie. Ember had to hold back a laugh knowing that Brig'dha was attempting to play the man. The surprising part was that she looked so serious that the man appeared to be believing her story. He turned his attention from the engrossing priestess' painfully forced stare and gazed again at the unusual item. The light from the fire reflected and refracted through the crystal covering the man's face with blue light.

"Bring good crop. We no need crop," Aethen said in broken words. The man seemed to understand. This magic item was something that a tribe would control, perhaps a group of priests. It was the kind of item that would become the magical centerpiece of an entire people, an item of wonder. Such items were few in number and highly prized by those few tribes lucky enough to find and poses them. It provided very little benefit to a few travelers. However, the many goods which could be traded for it would. This could very well be the most critical trade the man ever made, and doing so might lift his standing, as well as the fortunes of his people.

The man was no fool, and he understood immediately what they wanted. The man reached over and opened the lid of one of the many large clay pots closest to him. He placed his hand into the pot and removed it, holding in his hand grain from the previous harvest, or so it looked. Then, using his hand, he indicated that all the remaining pots along the walls on one side of the building contained the same grains. He pointed to one of the large clay pots full of grain and held up eight fingers. Brig'dha began to smile, expecting that trade had been made, when suddenly Ember made a loud huffing sound as though she were upset.

"We are sorry, we thought you wanted to trade," she said, standing to leave and returning the item to its rabbit fur. Ember kicked Brig'dha's foot, then Aethen's foot signaling them to come with her. They were utterly confused, but luckily, they didn't ask questions hoping that Ember knew what she was doing. They were halfway out the door when the man spoke again.

"Wait! Better trade!" he said quickly. Ember turned and glared at the man, waiting to see if he would offer something more reasonable. She really didn't know if the trade was good or bad, but traders were almost always known to start with a bad trade hoping that it might be taken. Deep down, she didn't hold it against him. He had likely hoped when he had first met them that they would be easy marks and that he would make a tremendously inequitable trade. She was about to dissuade him of such a notion. The man held up one finger of his left hand and pointed to five fingers of his right hand. This indicated that each finger in his left hand was equal to five. He then held out five fingers of his left hand to equal 25 clay vessels of grain.

Brig'dha and Aethen turned nervously toward Ember, hoping that she would agree to this much better-sounding offer. Unfortunately, neither of them knew any particular trading skills Ember possessed. If she continued trying to bargain with the man when she really didn't know what she was doing, she could potentially lose out. It was a risky business, but if either of them spoke up attempting to encourage Ember to accept the trade, it might undermine any sort of deception she was using. Both friends waited, holding their breath. The reckless redhead slowly turned her gaze back upon the man, unearned confidence in her eyes. She had no actual need to trade the item, so she was willing to push as far as she could, if for no other reason than the pure fun of it.

"Do better. There are other villages who will offer more. Maybe Isut'na or Nara'kit," she said, dropping the names of the two cities Nemanar had mentioned and hoping this man believed her. She actually did not know how badly he had initially tried to cheat her. For all she knew his second offer was fair. The man simply thought about what he would say next for a short time. Ember could tell that he was weighing his options, and she would let him stew until he came back with something of substance. While he brooded over the price, Ember held the mysterious item before the fire letting its light spill over the room, further enticing the man. Brig'dha was nearly in a panic over the interaction, and Aethen barely breathed.

He held up his hands, indicating the same offer as before, 25 clay vessels of grain, then a second hand, increasing the number to 50. Then, he stood and walked to a wooden box. He opened the box to reveal many bolts of linen cloth dyed with vibrant colors, difficult to obtain as linen notoriously didn't take well to dyes. Now they were getting deep into something. He removed 12 bolts of good quality linen cloth, each well-made with a high thread count. Ember caught sight of several necklaces of shiny beads within the box and pointed them out. The man now looked slightly annoyed as he continued to hold the cloth out, hoping that would suffice. Ember held the crystal between the man and the light of the fire letting its beauty fill the room with blue flickers of light. She stared past the crystal toward the man in the most alluring look she could muster without bursting into laughter.

"Big Magic!" Brig'dha suddenly said, catching everyone off guard. The man regarded the priestess carefully. Even Ember had to admit that Brig'dha strangely looked entirely truthful. It was somewhat disturbing how good Brig'dha was at lying, especially since this was the first time Ember had ever seen her do it. Realizing that this was his one good chance to find a powerful magic item, the man capitulated. He rolled his eyes and reached down to hand them the many necklaces of rare beads, a fortune in handmade wares.

A short time later, the group stood in the marketplace, ready to trade for whatever was needed. Ember and Brig'dha had two or three dozen or more necklaces of fine beads of lapis lazuli, jet, and copper around each of their necks, while Aethen carried ten clay discs with symbols upon them, each indicating a group of five units of grain. None of them had ever encountered the idea of carrying a token that could be traded instead of the actual merchandise itself. It seemed that if they traded a token to a merchant, that merchant effectively took possession of five large grain vessels, including the costly ceramic vessel, but without the need to store or carry them. The idea was abstract and bizarre, but each of them could see the utility to be found in such an arrangement.

Ember and Brig'dha both carried in their arms bolts of linen cloth. By the currency of their time, they were now richer than most small villages. Only a village this size could have afforded such a transaction. Ember was quite happy to convert grain and linen into more minor items that they could carry as quickly as possible. They would finally be able to trade for all the clothing and tools they needed. More importantly, Ember could finally get a gift for Brig'dha, something she had wanted to do for a while. She paused for a moment to glance at the timid priestess, fully impressed by her actions moments before. Deep down, she knew that the priestess had tipped the scales, and she would have to reward her with a truly amazing gift to even the score. Brig'dha glanced back, unsure of why Ember was staring, becoming slightly worried, Mew brushing against her feet.

The market was full of many beautiful items to trade for. It was not long before Ember found herself examining a long and soft linen loincloth that hung to just below the knees. The material was deliciously soft with a very high thread count. The woman who was offering it was saying something to Ember, probably trying to encourage the trade of the item, but she couldn't understand the woman. Brig'dha stood behind her examining other cloth items in wonder. In the northern tribes, textiles were very costly in trade, especially linen, if it could even be found, the latter almost always coming from long-distance trade with the South. The priestess had never seen such beautiful wears. She gently ran her finger down a piece of soft linen feeling its delicate texture.

"You should get this and a beautiful leather belt to go with it. If we are going to stay here during the cold season, we really don't need to get heavy cold weather clothing, do we? Maybe we should get something for when it warms up," Brig'dha said. Her suggestions were probably influenced by the beautiful warm weather garments she saw before her though Ember heartily agreed with her. Their current cold weather attire would probably suffice as long as they remained within their heated building for the cold season. Either way, with this many trade wares available, they could just trade for what they needed when they needed it.

"Fine, but I will get you something too… Something different," she said with an evil grin. Brig'dha seemed slightly worried at what she had gotten herself into, but she nodded reluctantly while Ember began digging through the wears, looking for something to fit the priestess. Brig'dha had slightly wider hips than Ember and stood a little taller, but Ember was sure she could find a beautiful outfit for her. Trading was turning into a fun adventure itself, something neither had experienced coming from cultures where everything was do-it-yourself.

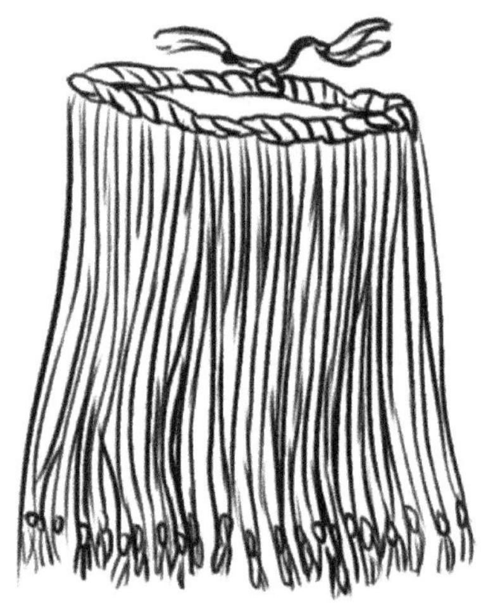

Flax string skirt

"Ahhh... this is exactly what you need," Ember said, lifting an item and holding it up for Brig'dha to see. It was a string skirt made from flax cords. Unlike the decorative skirt she had worn at the fertility festival, the number of strings was tremendously higher. In addition, each string was much thicker, being made from two-ply flax. The strings hung halfway down the legs and thoroughly covered the wearer, avoiding any unwanted exposure. Brig'dha was unsure of what to say at first as the rambunctious redhead held the beautiful garment out before her. Suddenly, she dropped to her knees to hold it against Brig'dha's hips and see how it would look. The priestess reeled at the item, finding it beautiful but a bit too open for her tastes. She was a strange mixture of horrified and enchanted at the same time.

"Oh, come on, you need to live a little. Take a risk!" she said. Brig'dha stared back at her incredulously, almost shocked. Had Ember already forgotten the three trips they had taken across the vast expanses of water, or perhaps the events which led to Ember jumping off the cliff, or maybe the lie she just spoke to the trader?

"Okay, I take back the risk part. Trust me, it will look great." Brig'dha took a deep breath and nodded her assent. She knew there would be no way to sway Ember, and deep down, she did find the string skirt to be quite beautiful though she normally associated such items with ritual and not daily wear. She hoped that the stories of the extreme warmth of the True South were accurate. Ember finished trading several quality bone beads before grabbing Brig'dha's hands and dragging her away toward the next location. The priestess suspected that this would also be quite a perilous adventure.

Aethen left the women to their fun, a bold of linen and a single grain token in hand. Ember had generously handed him the token, unwilling to hear any expostulation. He was a part of their group, had done his part, and so he got linen and a token. Giving up any protest, he had left with his own agenda. He had something he needed to find, something to give him an edge when finding a woman in the True South. What he needed was a gift, something to offer a would-be lover.

Ɔ Ɔ Ɔ

Aethen stood with a pair of quality leather sandals and a new linen loincloth in hand. Ember had explained to everyone how warm it would be in the True South, and he wanted to be ready. The strangest thing he had so far traded for were the sandals. A sandal turned out to be a piece of leather that the wearer stood upon protecting his foot from the ground. Leather thongs were attached to the leather bottom sole and wrapped around the foot so that the sandal was held tightly in place. The result was a foot nearly completely exposed to the elements while providing protection, a must in the heat. According to Ember, this was the proper footwear for a True Southerner. Aethen hoped that all her numerous proclamations were correct. She made such proclamations with the confidence of a seasoned elder, having only learned the information from her short stay with the True Southern family.

Suddenly, something caught his eye. He approached a small vendor who was trading jewelry. There was a necklace with a leather cord and a strange, very beautiful shell hanging from it. The shell was slightly round, though a little longer than wide. He had never seen anything like it before, with its strange spotted pattern. The shell would one day be known as a cowry shell, but to Aethen, it was strange and beautiful. More impressive was a second necklace with a string of many of these small shells. There was also a matching set for the wrist, the ankles, and the waist, each with many of the little shells placed around a cord of leather. In his mind's eye, Aethen could see his beautiful wife-to-be wearing these amazing shells. He was becoming wrapped up in a romantic love affair with a woman he had never even met.

Perhaps it was strange, the notion that a man would buy a present for an unknown woman he had not yet found, but Aethen always liked to be prepared. He decided that if he found a woman he could truly love, a woman who would love him just as deeply, he would certainly wish to bring her such a gift. Aethen held out a string of lead beads for the man running the shop to inspect. He pointed to several beads, offering half of them for the jewelry. He had already traded one bolt of linen for all the clothing he had obtained and received the beads as the difference. He appreciated Ember handing him the linen and a token since the rock had not belonged to him, but she was a very giving sort of person, and arguing with her was like arguing with a rock.

He placed the jewelry within his traveling pack, except for a single larger shell on a leather cord, which he tied around his neck. He would need to stop by someone trading for food and obtain something for the group to eat. Whether he killed the animals himself or just traded for them, he liked to provide for others and hated for people to have to provide for him. It wasn't a male versus female issue, either. He would object to anyone having to take care of him. It was a pride issue he knew that he would need to overcome one day.

ↄ ↄ ↄ

A short time later, Ember and Brig'dha emerged from a small hut where they had been arguing with an old woman who worked within over the value of some high-quality body paints. The old woman had wanted too many beads in trade, so they had left. Besides clothing, Brig'dha had also obtained a small leather pouch full of a smelly yellow powder. Supposedly, the powder could be used to cast out evil spirits, though

Brig'dha wasn't quite sure when she would use it. Having the material wealth to trade for random things not really needed made her feel a little guilty. They were headed back toward the communal hut where they would stay when Ember suddenly spotted something to her left. Brig'dha walked along for a short time before realizing that Ember was not at her side. Turning to look back, she saw Ember gazing at something far behind them. Ember looked back at her with a slightly coy expression.

"You should probably head back to the hut. I saw something back there that I wanted to take a look at. I'll be just a moment," she said with an expression on her face that reminded Brig'dha very much of what little Mew looked like when he was going to be fed. Brig'dha knew immediately that she was up to something; her green eyes were almost catlike. Unfortunately, there was not much she could do, and she had every confidence that Ember would eventually come back... mostly in one piece. She had long ago learned that when the riant redhead was about to go do something risky or stupid, she would display a strange, stoic look. As long as that stoic look did not appear, it would be okay. Right now, she was looking catty. The priestess wandered back toward the hut taking deep breaths and hoping nothing bad would happen. Would Ember return with some poor orphan child, a river priestess fleeing capture, or perhaps it would be a sacrifice she must prevent, or maybe…

Ɔ Ɔ C

Ember skipped away with a devious smile on her face. She certainly had seen something that she wanted to look at more closely, something she really wanted to obtain. Ember was not a big shopper, but she had spied something quite beautiful, and she was pretty sure that Brig'dha had not. Ember had often seen women in her tribe happily presented gifts from the men hoping to win their affections. She had put Brig'dha through so much pain and trouble this past harvest, and she wanted to apologize with a gift. She also hoped that if the gift were beautiful and could be worn, it would solidify their bond. It occurred to her that she was almost playing the role of "man," at least by the standards of her culture, in their relationship, though she didn't mind. Ember barely thought of herself as a woman, at least by societal standards and social norms.

It was only a few moments before she found herself standing beside the dwelling where the beautiful items she sought could be found. As she came forward, a large man stepped before her holding his hand out and preventing her entry. He said something to her in an authoritarian-sounding tone. She did not know what it was that he had said, but she suspected it was along the lines of "trading customers only." She scowled at the man, slightly angry that he would judge her not to be a trader. Trading seemed to be vastly more common among the men though Ember suspected that this was more cultural than due to any abilities. *I probably have more grain and linen than any of you,* she thought to herself sardonically.

She held up a small stack of grain tokens doing her best to hide the delight she felt at witnessing the man's eyes bulging at the sight. She pushed his hand out of her way and boldly stepped into the structure. Many gold, copper, and lead items could be found on a large deerskin draped across the floor. Worked metal was perhaps the rarest possession to be owned, aside from a unique item such as the Amber of Life or the blue rock. Ember had only heard of advanced metalworking by legend, and she had seen metal possessions only a few times in her life. The memory of the golden pendants crudely formed by the people of Tornhemal, with whom she had lived for a short time, came back to her.

Most of the items before her looked to have been crudely constructed from some sort of mold or just hammered from the metal itself. Metalworking was almost unheard of, and only a few places had developed techniques to do so. Unknown to her, the traders with whom she now engaged had walked nearly three tendays from the Northeast, a place where some gold and copper working existed. Ember lifted a gold and copper item from the leather for a closer inspection. The item she held was made from one long thick wire of gold and two long thick wires of copper, braided around one another. The braided piece wrapped around the neck with an opening in the front to allow it to be donned as a sort of torc. It was truly an amazing craft item. Moreover, beside it sat several similar items, each made from copper and gold, all matching.

As she stared at the objects, watching as the light from the small fire nearby danced off their shiny and beautiful metal, she noticed what appeared to be a projectile point made entirely of copper, probably an arrowhead, based on the size. Carved upon the arrowhead were what appeared to be magical symbols, small shapes carved into the metal using pressure from a rock and carrying with them magical significance. She could only imagine how deadly such an arrowhead might be and felt the overwhelming need to obtain it. *Who knows what could be in the True South!* she thought as her eyes danced across the beautiful copper and potentially magical arrowhead.

"Which interests you, my jewelry, or this magical arrowhead?" the trader inquired, hungrily.

"Both," she said with an excited smile, recognizing his accent as similar to the travelers she had met from the True South.

The man looked up with a smile on his face knowing that he was about to make a trade. He traded only the finest metal items to be found and was well known in the region for his wares. He did not know how such a strange woman had obtained enough material wealth to trade for his rare items, but he was not concerned with such questions. The many grain tokens in her hands and her brazen attitude told him of a woman not to be dismissed lightly. Ember held up two-grain tokens and began to negotiate. She hoped that Brig'dha would not strangle her to death when she returned, having spent a small fortune to trade a few useless items of immense value for several other useless items of immense value.

ꝋ ꝋ ꝋ

The light had dimmed as the Sunset low on the horizon, though the Moon was out in the Southeastern sky and would be out for most of the night. Brig'dha sat in the hut waiting for Ember. Aethen had finished cooking some small game he had traded for and had already eaten his share. Brig'dha had been waiting for Ember to return before eating hers, though she was worried it might get cold before that happened. Both had become concerned and would soon go looking for the chaotic woman if she didn't appear shortly. Only little Mew seemed unconcerned with the present situation. Turning her mind from Ember, the priestess considered the necklace Aethen had traded for and his reasons behind it, which he had explained at length.

Brig'dha could not help but find the necklace, bracelets, anklets, and waist cord that Aethen had purchased quite beautiful. She liked shells and found the entire set breathtaking, though not her own taste. She thought his explanation of the necklace's utility, as a future present for some yet-to-be-found lover, quite romantic, though she was ashamed that she had not expected him to be so romantic. She longed for such romance and hoped to find a way to experience it with Ember, though she was unsure of how to approach the problem. Their reunion night at the dance had reached romantic levels unheard of, but what else could they do? The big problem would be finding a way to engage Ember in a romantic outing or perhaps...

Suddenly, the leather flap opened, and Ember stepped in with a large leather hide held out in front of her in an awkward sort of way. The hide seemed to cover the front of her body all the way up to her chin, almost needlessly. Brig'dha immediately suspected she was hiding something, but knowing Ember, it was best to simply wait and see what it was. It barely seemed that she could hold back whatever this strange surprise was she hid behind the leather hide.

"Aethen, don't you want to go for a nice walk? The Moon is so beautiful tonight... Don't you want to go see it for a little while?" Ember asked with a coy, almost frantic smile on her face. Aethen and Brig'dha exchanged nervous looks. Finally, he rolled his eyes and grabbed his leather wrap to walk outside. Ember's hint was less than subtle, and he was not interested in the frustration that would be caused by remaining in the tent while Ember did whatever she was going to do to Brig'dha. It was hard being the third person, and while he hoped to alleviate that as soon as they reached the True South, for tonight, it would simply be Aethen and the Moon. *Perhaps the Goddess will keep me company,* he grimaced.

As soon as he left, Ember turned her wide-eyed smile toward Brig'dha. The priestess took a deep breath as she slowly turned to face whatever madness was about to ensue. Not far behind, Mew, the cat, sat yawning and watching with waning interest. The humans were always interesting, but if they didn't have food for him, he was more likely to simply fall asleep.

"I got you a gift... the sort of gift that a husband would give a wife," she said very awkwardly.

"But you're not my husband," Brig'dha said, matter-of-factly. Ember rolled her eyes at the technicality.

"True... that is true, but lovers should still exchange gifts." Brig'dha swallowed hard. Whatever was about to be unveiled could be anything from a pet animal to a giant weapon or some magical implement with a dark, secret past.

"What sort of gift did you have in mind?" the priestess asked, fear building.

"Why only the most amazing type, of course," Ember said, dropping the leather hide to reveal what she was wearing. Ember dropped the hide, revealing a gold and copper braided torc as well as braided copper bracelets around her wrists. Brig'dha stared at the items, almost in shock at their beauty. Before her stood the rousing redhead wearing her new jewelry, catching the flickering hearth fire and filling the room with a dazzling specular display. The only thing more stunning to Brig'dha was the look of delight on Ember's face at seeing her so marveled. Only the leader of a large village could afford such an item, and certainly not a full set. In fact, there might not be a single person anywhere with anything so grand,

Was this the gift? Did Ember mean to give her one of these precious items? The redhead dropped to her knees and shuffled over to face Brig'dha merely a hand's length from her face, still sporting her catlike grin. The priestess continued to stare at the beautiful metal items enchanted by their luster. Of course, this was exactly what Ember had wanted, but she still had one more amusement with which to delight herself. Brig'dha reached a gentle hand out to touch the beautiful metal torc. It was cool to the touch, smooth and firm. She licked her lips at seeing it.

"Are… are you going to give me one of those?" the priestess asked. Ember withdrew suddenly with a mock look of shock.

"Of course not! These are all mine," she said, waiting just a few moments for her words to stun her lover before she completed the thought. Brig'dha had a sudden look of shock. It was time to bring out the real surprise before her little stunt caused any real troubles. Ember hated being mean-spirited, but sometimes it was fun to play with poor, literal Brig'dha.

"But, I will give you this matching set!" she announced, removing from her bag two golden bracelets and a second braided copper and gold torc. Brig'dha sat bewildered, almost expecting this to be a dream. She just remained still as Ember quickly applied the jewelry.

"How much did you trade for those?" Ember paused before replying and looked a little guilty when she did.

"We couldn't actually carry all of that grain with us, anyway. We still have plenty of linen, beaded necklaces, and some other things... just no grain." Brig'dha had a strange urge to become angry, but at the same time, the blue rock had belonged to Ember, and she hadn't really traded all their material wealth. More importantly, Ember's explanation that they could not carry the grain actually did make sense, even though she knew that it was only a hastily concocted excuse for what had likely been quite a spontaneous and impulsive action. Unknown to Brig'dha, Ember had traded her three remaining grain tokens for a large leather bag of necklaces, beads, gems, and other small items of value, effectively cleaning out the metal seller's inventory, and the inventory of the other traders nearby.

Gold and copper torc and matching bracelets

Brig'dha stood wearing her brand-new jewelry and feeling the weight of the pieces against her neck and wrists. She was entirely enamored by the gifts though she still had the odd urge to throttle her lover. Strangely, she felt a giddy feeling all over her body at just the sight of the beautiful items. She might very well be the only forest person in the world to wear something so amazing. She turned to find her red-haired warrior standing behind her with a sly grin. Brig'dha rolled her eyes, guessing where things were headed. She had to admit, Ember had indeed set the mood.

"I sure hope Aethen is enjoying the Moon," Ember said with a chuckle, "it's going to be out all night!"

Ɔ Ɔ Ɔ

Aethen stood beneath a waning gibbous Moon, now high in the southern sky. Twice, he approached the hut, and twice he had realized that it was not the time to reenter. He could not wait until he had his chance to find true love and experience it for himself. It was apparently a loud and joyous thing, that involved a lot of vocal agreement.

Ɔ Ɔ Ɔ

Isha'kau lay on a bed of furs resting. Not long after receiving deep wounds to her hip and leg from the knife wielding Pedar, she had taken ill with a fever. Aya'tar had waited by her side day in and day out, tending to her wounds, applying salt and herbs, and dancing the sacred dances of healing. Over time, the priestess had fought off the evil spirits which had invaded her body, causing the red sweats. The red sweats and the fever that came with them were well known to be caused by evil spirits, and they could easily take a person's life within just a few days. Luckily, Aya'tar had known the right rituals to perform to drive the spirits from her body, and she was already recovering. She would be back to normal within a moon by her own reckoning. Her body was young and strong, which along with the Goddess' good graces and the motherly care provided by Aya'tar, had been the difference between life and death.

She gently pulled back furs to examine her hip. There were three red wounds made by the stabbing dagger. They had closed but would leave scars, both physically and mentally. She could not help but be thankful that she still lived to have those scars. Her furs and cushion sat upon the very stone shelf under which Hullamu was forever buried. Both women had been knocked to the floor. If she had stood first, it would have been her lying dead now. A tiny part of her envied that Hullamu had been so readily accepted by the Goddess, and she hoped that one day she would be taken into the loving arms of their deity, or perhaps even Gunar. Isha'kau was not sure if she was ready for eternity in the arms of the Bull God, especially not with hips that hurt like hers. Luckily, Hullamu's body buried beneath her brought a sense of peace.

"If you're interested, I can bring you something to do. I have several small pots that need to be decorated as well as beads which need to be counted. We wouldn't want you sleeping all day, right?" the high priestess joked as she stepped into the room. Isha'kau covered up her wounded hip and smiled back. It had been nearly half a harvest since the night when Aya'tar had lain with her lover, and she was now showing the results of that encounter most plainly. Observing the customs of her people, Aya'tar had decorated the bulge in her abdomen with images of the Goddess. Except to ward off the cold, her midsection would be left bare that all would see the gift of a new spirit entering the Second World.

Aya'tar stepped before the altar and knelt to pray, as she did multiple times per day. The lesser priestess could see that she was troubled. All humor aside, Aya'tar had been out of sorts ever since the death of Hullamu. It had bothered her even worse than her own father. Death was no stranger to the people of Isut'na. It would strike without reason and often without warning, but something about the brazen attack had left her disturbed. She was also under stress over her own predicament, as well as the act of carrying a child. Isha'kau decided it was time to bring a little cheer to the priestess.

"You are going to make a great mother, you know," she said, interrupting Aya'tar from her prayer. Aya'tar glanced over toward the bed with an eyebrow raised.

"Oh? Did the Goddess provide you some insight into the future?" she asked, jokingly.

"When the sweats had almost taken me, and I drifted in and out of life, you sat beside me and did whatever you could to comfort me. I am just your lesser priestess. Imagine how much you would love your own child. My own mother has only come by a few times to see me, and yet every day you hover over me like a sister." Aya'tar was touched by the comments. It had troubled her how little Isha'kau's mother had stopped by, though the woman had her hands filled with her many other children.

"Have you come up with a name yet? Do you even know if it's a boy or girl?" she asked.

"I have received mixed signs and cannot tell you if it is a boy or girl, but I haven't felt anything which would make me worry. As for the name, I have had a few thoughts about that." Aya'tar finished praying and stood, turning to face her friend. Perhaps it was time they discussed the proper name for a child.

☾ ☾ ☾

The man stepped out of the hut, having concluded his business. This was the third small tribe he had stopped by, yet he had found no evidence of the copper worker. Sar'Tawas had sent three men searching for a young copper worker with the express purpose of ending his life. According to the Guild Master, the boy had stolen the payment for a trade and fled the city. He suspected the real reason was that the boy was indeed the lover of the high priestess. That did complicate things, but if he killed the man far enough away from the watchful eyes of Isut, everything should be okay. There was still no proof that the high priestess truly was in the good blessings of the gods.

There was only one more village he could check, but the cold season had finally caught up with him, and he had been forced to remain where he was until warmer winds prevailed. It never really got that cold in the Southern lands, but he could use a break, and Sar'Tawas had given him plenty of trinkets to trade for a place to stay and food to eat. When the days were not so cold, he would head towards the last small tribe before returning to Isut'na. He felt confident that he would find the boy and return with his head.

"That son of a jackal is going to owe me a storeroom of wheat and flax when I return," he mumbled under his breath.

ↄ ↄ ↄ

Ishayan came to a stop at the peak of a small rise and gazed upon the city of Isut'na. Behind him, four men stood thankful for the break. Dunu'lekal'Ishayan, or less formally Ishayan to those who knew him, was the eldest son of An'sankup'Anteanar, ruler of Nara'kit. He had achieved early middle-age, 32 harvests, and had yet to take a woman as his bride. His father had been complaining about this fact for quite some time. The laws of succession required a long steady line of offspring. If he did not soon find a woman and bear children, there would be significant repercussions. Only just that previous harvest, his younger sister Ianmu had fled from the city after murdering the high priest of An'an. The loss of a child had only served to increase the stakes. He had only one task before him, and Isut'na would be the setting for that task. As he stood before the beautiful city, this, and his other reasons for making this journey rolled through his mind.

Tall and strong, he had long dark hair with dark eyes and very sharp features, striking indeed. He was desired by many women and even a few influential men. He had always sated his desires with women on the side though his father was right about the need for children. If the rumors were true and Isut'na was now under the control of a young unmarried woman, what better opportunity could he find? He would walk in as the dashing warrior he was and sweep her into his arms, and with her the city. His father might be right about him needing a child, but he was wrong about the need to use his warriors to take Isut'na. A strong hand could crush a delicate flower-like Isut'na. Sometimes, all that was needed was a little finesse.

Anteanar, his father, was a violent and oppressive ruler. He excepted nothing but the best and would hear nothing but his own opinions. It had been arguments with the aggressive and overbearing man which had driven him to leave Nara'kit in an attempt to take Isut'na with a strong but gentle hand rather than with a knife. Action alone would sway his father's opinion. It was that same dominating personality coupled with the treachery of the former high priest which had apparently driven his younger sister to flee. She had been weak and likely fled to the South. It was of no matter, he would take Isut'na and continue his family's legacy.

"Now remember, no fights, no arguments, and no trouble... or you will find my dagger at your throat faster than their city's warriors. We are to be on our best behavior. In your own way, each of you are warriors helping me conquer Isut'na for Nara'kit, just in a more subtle way," he said with a smile.

"If we are successful, I will reward each of you with a prominent place of status, a beautiful wife, and all the respect you deserve," he said to his men. It was always a good idea to spread a little honey on the end of any stick. Behind him, he could hear the men speaking to one another of what they would do when they became influential. That kind of loyalty was what he needed, whether he let them live or not.

"As soon as we enter the city, I need the four of you to find us a building where we can stay. After that, I will make my way to the temple to pay my respects to the gods. It wouldn't do to be rude now, would it?" he said, flashing a smile at the men. They did not know what he had in mind, but anyone is ruthless as Ishayan was to be obeyed. They suspected that he had an elaborate plan and would inform them of his needs when the time came. Until then, the men hoped they could eat and drink on the trades of the eldest son of Nara'kit.

ɔ ɔ ɔ

Isha'kau and Aya'tar stood by the altar of Gunar, placing a small offering of the previous harvest's wheat in a tiny clay pot of fermented honey drink for the bull god. The temple primarily made offerings to the goddess Isut, but it was never a good idea to ignore the Goddess' lover. To this end, Gunar had a miniature shrine on one side of the temple. Many villages worshiped a bull god and a fertility goddess, though often by different names. There was much debate among people over whether or not these were all names for the same deity or similar deities. A bull god was revered above a fertility goddess in many places, but not in Isut'na. Aya'tar found that she liked this arrangement. Sometimes she wished that life mirrored it a little more closely.

Isha'kau was still having some trouble with the pain in her hip, but she was recovering quite well for the most part. Aya'tar had even begun to cheer up a little seeing her friend recovering. With any luck, the warm winds would come within a short time and with them the return of

Imkanar. It was possible that everything might even work out and the two might become wed, though no one could be quite sure of what sinister plots might be hatched within that time. The high priestess adjusted the bowl of fermented honey wine and stood back with a deep breath. It had been a long day, and her feet hurt. All she wanted to do was take a nap.

"May I help you with something?" Isha'kau asked, causing Aya'tar to turn-in response. It took a moment to realize that the initiate priestess was speaking to a man who had just stepped down the ladder and into the room very quietly. Aya'tar stood back and waited to see what the man might say. He stood before her with long dark hair and striking eyes which shifted back and forth between the women as though searching for something. She could not help but note how sharp and dark his features were, a not unpleasant ending to a long day. She would accept no man's touch but Imkanar, but she could find no fault in having a good look. The man turned to face Isha'kau and began to speak.

"Hello, my name is Dunu'lekal'Ishayan, eldest son of the great An'sankup'Anteanar, ruler of the city of Nara'Kit," he said in one long, continuous string. Aya'tar listened to the entire title, seemingly impressed. Isha'kau stepped forward as the man completed his title.

"Wow, you have a really long name. I'm not sure what all that means. Did you come for a blessing? I am an initiate priestess, but I can help you. My name is Isha'kau, much shorter than yours!" Isha'kau smiled at the man as she spoke, unconsciously manipulating her hair with two of her fingers. Aya'tar sat back for a moment to watch as the junior priestess attempted to flirt with the man whom she was pretty sure might be out of her league. It was simply too amusing to interrupt. The man merely stared at her, slightly confused.

"Ih-shah-kah-oo," she slowly spoke once more, just in case he had not heard her.

Ishayan blinked, slightly taken aback. He had believed that he had found the high priestess when he had spoken to the woman who initially approached him. He turned his attention instead to the woman lingering in the shadows, the woman with a very obviously protruding abdomen decorated with magical paints, a woman with child. Seeing that the amusement was over, Aya'tar stepped from the shadows to stand before the man.

"Excuse me, are you the high priestess of Isut, the ruler of the city?" he asked directly, wanting to get to the point more quickly. As she stepped into the light which drifted through a small window, Ishayan was taken aback by her beauty. Pregnancy had left her hair shinier and darker than normal, though she was beautiful by anyone's definition. It had taken only a moment before he realized the answer to his question. She carried herself as a high priestess should, stepping forwards with her arms out wide, palms up. It was the proper way for a high priestess to behave. Aya'tar slightly bowed her head and politely introduced herself, still very confused over why the son of the most powerful man within a tenday's journey had paid her a visit.

"Greetings Dunu'lekal'Ishayan, I am Isut'Sanup'ramu Aya'tar, ruler of Isut'na, the city of Isut, but you may call me Aya'tar," she said with a smile. Ishayan was impressed by her looks and her obvious command as a leader. She had formally addressed him by his full title, Dunu'lekal, which meant "son of a ruler," essentially a prince. Her own title of Isut'Sanup'ramu meant priestess vessel of goddess Isut. Most of all, he was glad that she had afforded him the courtesy of calling her by her short name, generally reserved for friends and family. Isut'Sanup'ramu was otherwise quite a mouthful.

"Greetings, Aya'tar, and you may call me Ishayan," he replied, stepping forward to examine the Gunar altar.

"May I ask your reason for visiting our city?" she asked, watching Ishayan carefully and noting how easy he was upon her tired eyes. She was tired and rejected most visitors, but she would be happy to spare significant time for such a man as this Ishayan.

"I have come here upon hearing a rumor, perhaps something that I can help with," he said, leveling his gaze upon the high priestess. Pregnant or not, he found her to be a strange mixture of intriguing and beautiful. In Nara'kit, the idea of a woman controlling a city would be beyond belief. Perhaps it was this juxtaposition that intrigued him so. He had debated with himself over the right way to approach Aya'tar. In the end, he decided upon a direct and blunt approach. It might initially fail, but as the high priestess thought upon his words, once he had left, she might see the wisdom in them. It was a risk, but Ishayan liked risks.

"Oh? And what rumor has brought you so many days journey?" she asked dismissively, turning to bow before the altar of Gunar once more. Isha'kau stood back, watching the delicate exchange between the two but mostly watching Ishayan.

"It has come to my attention that the city of Isut'na is being led by an unmarried woman. To be simple, I wish to marry you. Your beauty is legendary, and I am humbled by your presence. With our two families united, our people would prosper and control trade over an even larger area. Most importantly, your position would be secure as high priestess," he said flatly and looking at her plainly the entire time. Aya'tar simply glared back at him with wide eyes. For a short moment, she couldn't even say anything, so dumbfounded by his bluntness and offer. She turned to look away from him, slightly overwhelmed.

"Who are you to come here and say such a thing to me?" she asked, continuing to look away.

"Who am I? I am the eldest son of the most powerful man in the region," he said calmly and with confidence. His confidence was like a stone wall, a force imposing itself throughout the room. It was as though Gunar had entered the room in spirit.

"How can I answer such a question?"

"You could simply say, yes."

"But I don't know anything about you... just who you are."

"I will remain in the city until the warm season comes. Please, take your time and think about it, and maybe you could get to know me in that time," he added smoothly. Aya'tar made an exasperated sound but had no real words to follow. She had no defense against such blunt words other than anger, and she would hold that in check so she would not show weakness.

"Just one more thing, high priestess, consider that if you say yes, your child will become our first child and keep the right of succession. It is my interest in you that brought me here, not power... Something I already have," he said with a smile before bowing to leave.

Aya'tar knelt before the altar of Gunar, a mixture of horror and shock replacing her usual prayers. Strangely, something about the man attracted her while other parts of him repelled her, causing her confusion. His extreme confidence was strangely enticing, making him feel to her as though he exerted some form of control, though he did not. Isha'kau waited for a few moments before rushing forward and grabbing Aya'tar by the shoulders to force her into an immediate discussion. If ever there was something to be talked about, this was it.

"Audacious... Arrogant... Presumptuous..." Aya'tar fumed.

"Tall... Sharp... Competent... A solution to your problems..." Isha'kau added.

ↄ ↄ ↄ

For seven tendays, the group had remained camped in the village of Taerhem, which had turned out to be a great place to spend the cold season. Their assumption that the large village was a trading hub had been correct, and there had been a constant influx of people. Ember always loved trading hubs as she would constantly meet different people. In a traditional village, traders would only arrive a few times a harvest, at best. More importantly, traders from the True South had taken up residence in the same guest house. This had given everyone a chance to practice speaking the words of the True South, as well as for Ember to confirm their route towards the city of Isut'na.

Ember wanted nothing more than to see this thing called a "city." It was said they were vast establishments of people, larger even than the biggest tribes to the West. Allegedly, a city could be so large that it had vast scores of people who just worked on one project or another – complete job specialization. Amazingly, cities had their own protection forces of warriors, large temples, and vast markets. The idea sounded absolutely exciting to a woman raised on the shores of a muddy river in a small tribe. She felt giddy every time she thought about it.

Over the past two tendays, the group had walked nearly dead East until they had finally come upon the beautiful expanse of water known to the locals as the Blue Lake. Ember thought that the Blue Lake reminded her very much of the great Blue Sea, having no distant shore to be seen. From the small hill where they now stood, Ember, Brig'dha, and Aethen saw below them a small village of perhaps 100 people built beside the shoreline. If what they had been told by the traders from the True South was correct, they were very close to the cities. Perhaps these people could point them in the right direction?

The party slowly approached the small village, having grown weary of walking and needing at least a tenday of rest. Perhaps the most tired of the group was their small cat, Mew, who now perpetually fussed to be held by Brig'dha. Ember supposed it was because his legs were so tiny, and had to move so often to keep up with the group. At least, Mew had the benefit of being able to more easily find dinner, though that never stopped him from complaining until he was given handouts.

The village turned out to be composed of twelve mud-brick and stone dwellings with wooden pole roofs. Around these buildings, dozens of people labored at daily tasks such as skinning animals, decorating pots, and grinding grain. A small slash and burn field was not far from the buildings where at least ten people labored at some agricultural affair. Ember still didn't quite understand how complex agriculture worked, but she suspected they were harvesting or planting something. More surprisingly, there were even pens for pigs. Two men chanted on the roof of one of the buildings, holding clay dishes in the air, probably observing some minor religious ceremony.

"Well, they don't look too dangerous," Aethen said with a chuckle.

"I don't see any dogs, so Mew can come too," Brig'dha said, holding the large fluffy cat. She still did not know why the animal followed her, but she fed it generously every night. The only time it would leave and not return was when the group had stayed in villages with a significant population of dogs. Mew always returned once they had left. They suspected the cat would remain close by in the woods and await their departure. At this point, Mew was large enough that Ember believed he was more than a match for any dog, having a set of what appeared to be polished obsidian claws. She suspected that the cat was significantly less intelligent than other cats and would likely have died on its own. *Perhaps that is the reason you are so friendly. Poor little Mew, at least you found yourself a mother,* she thought as she watched Brig'dha lift the creature into her arms.

"I could use a tenday of rest after that long walk," Ember said, stretching. It had been a pretty rough trek, and they had not taken many breaks, wishing to get to the Blue Lake with much haste after having spent so many tendays cramped up during the cold season. Brig'dha had a pulled muscle, and Aethen had a pretty bad sore on his foot. Perhaps it was time that they took a break. Walking, especially long distances, was much more strenuous on the body than most people realized.

The group approached the village slowly and remained calm with the hope of making a successful entrance without any commotion. Villages not used to trade tended to be more aggressive, and this was a small village that likely saw few visitors. Ember stepped forward as many local people turned to see them approaching. She held her arms out wide, indicating that she was not carrying a weapon and friendly. She attempted to speak the language of the True South, hoping that somebody would understand her.

"Hello! Do you understand my words?" she asked more confidently than before. The 70 days spent throughout the cold season had given her ample time to learn so many more words. Ember was the most proficient, but Aethen and Brig'dha had picked up enough words to get by. A man with a thick leather wrap around his waist and a leather vest stepped forward with a spear in hand though he did not look aggressive. He held his left hand out to sign that he was open to friendship.

"Hello to you, woman! I do understand. Are you from the North?" the man asked with a slight accent. Ember smiled back at the man, hoping to ease his tension, though she was annoyed at being called, "woman," something other women seemed unbothered by.

"We are from the far Northwest. We need a place to rest for a tenday before we continue. We can work or trade for our stay," she said, hoping that everything would go well. Twice before, they had been turned away from small villages, but generally, the farther south they traveled, the more hospitable the villages seemed to be. The man stepped forward and examined Ember, Aethen, and then Brig'dha, looking them over carefully. They couldn't help but notice how long his eyes lingered upon the beautiful gold and copper jewelry Ember and Brig'dha wore, as well as the large and fluffy animal which Brig'dha held in her arms. They were truly an uncommon sight.

"You must stay with us. We wish to learn where you obtained such beautiful jewelry," the man said with a laugh. For small tribes, stories and information were their own form of currency. These strange visitors from a faraway land wearing amazing jewelry would provide several harvests worth of discussion. The man motioned them forwards but then stopped to look back for just a moment.

"Oh, my name is Mimnar. Welcome to Karut," the man said, leading the group to a place where they could stay.

As the group entered the small village, a young man with long black hair and deep brown eyes glanced up from a large pile of charcoal he was making using a small clay brick oven. He thought that the foreigners looked quite peculiar. He would have to see if he could speak to them later that night. Imkanar had always been interested in foreigners, and there was not much else to do in the small village while he waited for the warm winds to come and carry him back to his lover.

CHAPTER TWENTY TWO
THE TRUE SOUTH

Ember's people refer to the lands beyond the southern mountains, namely the Pyrenees, Alps, and Carpathian Mountains, as the "True South." There, her people's terms for Mesolithic, "Forest People," and Neolithic, "River People," hold little meaning. Ember's people lack a complex understanding of race and ethnicity, and much knowledge of what exists beyond a few ten days' travel. To Ember and Brig'dha, these new lands to the South are exciting and adventurous.

The place where Ember had spent the cold season was very close to modern-day Thessaloniki, Greece, while the fictional city of Isut'na is situated almost directly on present-day Istanbul, beside the Brown River, known as the Bosporus in modern times. Each of these locations featured different cultures with varying levels of advancement, though the majority of these southern cultures were deep into the Neolithic period, Isut'na and Nara'kit being on the edge of the copper age and significantly more advanced than the cultures that Ember, early Neolithic, and Brig'dha, Late Mesolithic, were born into.

The fire felt good against their skin as Ember, Aethen, and Brig'dha sat in the central stone building eating a large meal with many of the village's inhabitants. A few shells and several beads had been all they had needed in trade to secure a full tenday of relaxation in the village. At first, Ember had thought this an unfair trade until the village leader, Elder Mimnar, had clarified things. In the nearby city of Nara'kit, their small beads and shells would trade for precious flax, flax seeds, and wheat. Agriculture and trade seemed vital to these people, much more than her own.

Around them sat many people, mostly observing watching. Ember and Brig'dha had decided to wear their more traditional deer leather clothing with more traditional northern body paint, hoping that they would seem more exotic to these people, which might get them more information in favor. Being exotic seemed pleasing to many people, so Ember would be as exotic as she could. Sitting beside her was a young girl who kept reaching up and touching the dark feather in her hair. She realized by looking at the little girl's face that she was related to Elder Mimnar. She shared his eyes, as well as sitting close to him.

"Here you go, this comes from a great bird from the Northwest. Wear this in your hair for protection," she said, removing the large and beautiful feather and placing it in the hair of the little girl. The girl became a bundle of giggles, exceedingly pleased with her gift. She turned to show it to everyone in amazement. As Ember suspected, the Elder and his wife, Kesanu, reacted quite positively. In Ember's opinion, it never hurt to suck up to the leaders.

"You have told us about the land where you come from, but where is it that you are headed?" asked a middle-aged man sitting across from them. Ember had explained the lands to the North at length and was now stuffing her face with fish, and Brig'dha was never one for words, so Aethen figured he would take on this question. His vocabulary was much less refined than Ember's, but there was no way to improve it without speaking.

"We travel to find city. We want to see city. We hear of Nara'kit, Isut'na. Do you know way?" he asked, hoping his broken words were not too laughable when compared to Ember's highly articulate speech. Several people seemed to be thinking about what had been said as if trying to decide how to answer. Finally, Mimnar turned to face a younger man with long dark hair sitting toward the back of the room. The dark-haired man looked as though he had expected to be called upon, for some reason.

"We know of these places, but this man, Imkanar, is from the city of Isut'na and can tell you much more." All eyes fell upon Imkanar. He took a deep breath, not having expected to become a speaking figure. He had only attended out of interest in the exotic new people. The problem was that every time he thought of Isut'na, images of his beloved Aya'tar flooded back into his mind, and with them, the pain and fear of leaving her to face the wolves of the city while he labored over charcoal in this tiny remote village. Luckily, the warm winds would soon be upon them. Imkanar waited for everyone to become silent and then began to speak.

"If you wish to see a city, I recommend Isut'na. Unfortunately, Nara'kit has a more aggressive ruler who may find some reason for your sacrifice, and Du'ubria is too far of a journey." Ember, a fish hanging from her mouth, lifted her head in surprise at the words. There was no way she would go anywhere near a place involved in human sacrifice. Several times they had already dealt with that horrible practice, and they were not going to put themselves knowingly into such a situation again. Imkanar saw her alarm but continued to speak.

"I see you understand what I mean when I say sacrifice. Isut'na is the city of the fertility goddess Isut. I have lived my entire life in that city and will return as soon as the warm winds come. If you remain here until that time, I will take you," he said. Aethen glanced at Brig'dha and Ember. It would be nearly a Moon until the warm winds came, which would mean yet more time would pass. As much as they wanted to finally get the walk over with and arrive at the city, having a local guide would make life much better. Ember grabbed another piece of fish and shoved it into her mouth. She decided she would bring the issue up with the group that night.

The drama of Imkanar's words was soon over as an older woman and a younger girl began to sing a chant-like song for the guests. Ember continued cramming food in her mouth while Brig'dha cautiously eyed the man from Isut'na, looking for any hidden deception. Aethen leaned back, enjoying the atmosphere, and the night passed by smoothly. Outside, Mew skillfully stalked a small "true south" mouse hoping for a tasty meal, too.

ꙅ ꙅ ꙅ

Ishayan sat on a small wooden bench on the roof of the modest building they had traded to stay in for the cold season. It had been quite cramped with four other men, but he had until the end of the cold and wet seasons to complete this task, and he would not fail. He had initially shocked the high priestess with his blunt declaration of his wish to marry. He suspected that his initial request would not have met with acceptance, but he had wanted to leave an impression on the woman strong enough that it would keep coming up in her mind, visiting her in her sleep. He knew that she was under pressure to step down or to take a husband, and whenever that pressure came up, so too would the memory of the young, dashing man who could solve her problems simply by her saying "yes." He did not need to pressure her. She would pressure herself.

He laughed at how daring his own play had been, but deep down, he was sure that Aya'tar and the city would be his soon. He had remained away from her for two full tendays allowing his words to stew a bit. As the pregnancy grew and the politics continued to burn in the back of her mind, he would simply make himself available as the easy way out. It wasn't the most aggressive strategy, but it was a good plan. Ishayan had always believed that the best course of action was the most successful course of action.

After two tendays of absence, he began frequenting the temple to pray before the altar every few days. He never brought up his request nor any other such topics, sticking strictly to praying and then leaving. The priestess would glare at him each time he entered, but though she waited expectantly for him to say something, he never did. He suspected that his infuriating actions were slowly wearing the woman down.

Today was yet another day for him to journey to the temple to pray, but before he did, there was one other dirty piece of business he had to rid himself of. It had come to his attention not long after he arrived that an older man was apparently in charge of some guild of craftsmen, a strange invention of the ever-industrious Isut'na people. This older man also competed for the hand of the lovely Aya'tar. Though Ishayan was younger and much better looking, in his opinion, the older man apparently had most of the Council of Elders behind him. This would be something Ishayan would have to rid himself of before it became a nuisance.

From the ladder came one of his men with important news concerning a plan Ishayan had put into play just earlier that day. Not long before, he had sent one of his men to scout the dwelling that the older man competing for Aya'tar, a man named Sar'Tawas, inhabited. Hopefully, this business would be concluded without any trouble.

"Are the men ready to remove my problem?" Ishayan asked the man, casually looking off into the distance. He noted several large griffon vultures off in the distant sky, circling.

"They are ready," the man replied.

"One man will slip into the old man's building this night and remove the competition. Two will stand outside and keep watch. Perhaps, they may even set up that woman who follows him. Maybe drop a knife beside where she sleeps," the man added with a laugh. Ishayan frowned, not completely convinced that the second part was as good an idea as the first.

"No, just kill the woman. Too many people make the mistake of complexity. Keep your plan simple, and we are likely to succeed. Now, if you'll excuse me, I must take care of my religious duties," he said with a smirk, standing and straightening his linen wrap. The man chuckled behind him, always amused by the great Ishayan's schemes.

Ɔ Ɔ Ɔ

Aya'tar knelt before the altar to her Goddess, praying for luck. A tiny spider crawled over her leg and scurried off toward the door drawing a smile. Nearby, a large fire burned in the room, warming her spirit. The priestess was close to the end of her pregnancy, her body transformed, and her abdomen swollen. She could feel the baby moving inside of her, a gift from Isut. She knelt upon a leather cushion stuffed with short flax fibers. Isha'kau was at the market collecting food, a menial task to make the lesser priestess perform. After she had recovered from her wounds following the death of Hullamu, Isha'kau seemed almost paranoid about leaving the high priestess for even a moment. However, if she could be convinced to leave, she would stay out for only a short time.

She lifted her hands from the ground to her head and ritually brushed the evil spirits away from her body as she knelt before the altar. Often, prostration was the next step in the daily ritual, but with her abdomen so large, there was no way she could perform such a maneuver. Since her complication was in itself related to fertility, she suspected the gods would forgive her. Her brushing was suddenly interrupted by the familiar sound of Ishayan entering the temple. His soft deer soled sandals had a distinctive sound. Though her initial instinct was to slap him, she instead ignored him and continued chanting and brushing.

Ishayan approached, dropping his linen shawl to the floor and kneeling on the rush matting before the altar. Aya'tar was unsure if the man truly followed her Goddess, being from the city that worshiped a similar deity named An'an. She could not help but admire his skill at ritual though she still doubted the truthfulness of his words. He began to perform the same basic maneuvers the priestess had performed, finishing with a full prostration. Afterward, he returned to a kneeling position and began to speak to the Goddess out loud where Aya'tar might hear.

"Mighty goddess Isut, matron of the city of Isut'na. I call upon you to help sway the mind of a certain high priestess," he spoke quite seriously. Aya'tar paused her chanting and turned to look at him in shock. If he were not speaking so seriously, what he now said could be taken as blasphemy, pure hubris. To mock a deity at her primary altar was extremely foolish. This meant that the man was a fool, bolder than a great hero or speaking the truth.

"She is the rightful ruler of your city and even carries the gift of a child, your gift. Unfortunately, she is in great danger, and many in your own city wish to harm her and cast her down from the position that you have rightfully given her," he continued. Aya'tar could not keep from speaking at this point, so brazen was this man. She could not tell if he was serious or not. The problem was that if he was serious, then she had no grounds to stop him. Were she not pregnant and a child not involved, she would have bashed his head with the clay pot over such hubris. While normally non-violent, as the high priestess, she could not allow the Goddess to be mocked in her own temple. Further, her word was effectively law, and she had the power to order the death of anyone who offended the gods.

"What is this that you say to the Goddess? Who are you to say these things? Do you joke before the goddess Isut?" Aya'tar screamed in rage. Ishayan ignored her and continued to speak to the Goddess in absolute seriousness, as far as anyone could tell.

"I have left my fair city of Nara'kit where I am the eldest son and next in succession and offer myself as her husband to protect the natural succession of Isut'na and to save your priestess from her own people. I asked that you help her consider what is best for her people, for her, and for her child," he concluded. He bent forward and held out a handful of feathers to deposit on the altar as an offering. Aya'tar towered before the kneeling man, staring obsidian daggers into his very spirit, wanting to know for sure if he truly prayed to the Goddess for these things or if he was simply speaking hubris.

"How dare you say such words! Do you make fun of the Goddess in her own temple?" she spat at him. He glanced back at her with an almost apologetic, if not slightly sad expression – very calculated expression.

"You are in danger from your own people. You are the ruler of the city and may do as you wish, but when they come for you, know that I will accept you as my wife and the co-ruler of the city. You may hate me for it, but I offer you an easy way out," he said. Aya'tar slapped the man across the face. As soon as she had, she stepped back, wishing she had not. Part of her felt guilty for acting so quickly and out of anger when the man had truly offered her a way out of her situation, self-serving or not. The other part of her feared that he might harm her. Her word was law, but he was much taller and much stronger than she, and her word would mean nothing if he choked the life out of her before she could give it. Worse, she had no one with her for protection, and she carried a child.

"I can see it in your eyes. You fear that I might strike you back. I will not. I have never struck a woman, nor do I intend to start now. Perhaps that slap was well-earned though my words to the Goddess were true. I apologize if they have harmed you. I do not wish to upset you this close to your child's birth, and I will leave now. May the gods protect you, high priestess," he said, standing and heading toward the ladder to leave, pausing only to pick up his linen shawl.

Aya'tar watched the man slowly climb the ladder. She was in a state of total confusion. She wanted to believe that he was actually a good man with good intentions, but there was something just so opportunistic about his arrival and offer. On the one side, she suspected him of simply wishing to take power, but on the other hand, it was true that he would naturally take control of the city of Nara'kit, anyway. She grabbed her head, feeling another headache coming on. Deep down, a weak voice cried that she should just accept his offer and let all the struggles disappear. He seemed to be a reasonably good man and much more handsome than Sar'Tawas. Unfortunately, such voices in her mind had been growing louder of late, and harder to ignore.

A few moments later, the ladder made another creaking sound as Isha'kau climbed down with a large basket full of provisions. She wobbled a few times, nearly tripping with the large basket, but she caught her balance and made it safely. Isha'kau had always wished that the temple could be one of those few buildings entered on the ground level. When she got to the floor, she looked to see the distraught priestess.

"Did I miss something?" she asked frantically, looking around, worried that an intruder had attacked. *I can't even leave to go to the market for even a short moment,* she thought, exasperated.

"No. I'm just more confused now than ever. Should I just accept what Ishayan says? Am I the wrong one?" the priestess asked. Isha'kau put her basket down and stepped forward to embrace the priestess in a reassuring hug. She wasn't really looking for answers to her questions. She just needed somebody to be there for her. Aya'tar wished those arms belonged instead to Imkanar.

ↃↃↃ

Ianmu lay beside Sar'Tawas, slowly drifting off. Things had not been going well of late. Sar'Tawas had seemed to be the most likely candidate to marry Aya'tar, but that was until the powerful Ishayan had arrived. Unknown to anyone else in Isut'na, Ishayan was her older brother and next in line as the ruler of Nara'kit. She sighed at the irony. Most likely, their father had decided to finally begin his conquest of Isut'na. Ishayan had probably taken the opportunity to try and win over the high priestess with his charm and take the city without bloodshed. Though many might see him as a broker of peace, Ianmu knew Ishayan far too well to be so easily fooled.

She knew just how cunning the man could be, and she feared his actions more than anyone else in the city. The thought that he was out there even now, plotting and scheming, sent shivers up and down her spine. All her scheming could simply be undone if Ishayan took control of the city as the husband of Aya'tar. Besides, bedding Sar'Tawas so many times to reach her goal had been less than an appealing task. She realized exactly why the man had no lover. Like a torch made from dried grass, he was intense and short-lived. The fact that the man thought of her as somewhere between a concubine and a slave might have something to do with his lack of grace, she suspected. Her thoughts were abruptly interrupted by the sound of the door quietly opening.

If she had been asleep, she would never have heard the quiet sound, but ironically, her sleepless deliberations had provided her the opportunity to hear the intruder. She reached for the flint dagger Sar'Tawas kept beside the bed and quietly stood. Sar'Tawas had a reasonably large building by most people's standards. He had recently separated the main room into two sections with several large, heavy hides hanging from the ceiling as a partition. It kept the sleeping area much warmer than the other side, which Ianmu had to admit wasn't a bad idea.

The "wall" of leather hanging down did not quite touch the floor, and she could see the shadow of an individual moving toward the right side, likely trying to sneak into the sleeping area with as little disturbance as possible. Ianmu crept to the left side of the leather, her bare feet making her much stealthier. The cool air danced across her naked skin, and she wished she had worn something more. She stood by the leather opening against the wall and waited to step into the other room when the intruder came into the sleeping area, switching positions. The leather would be disturbed by Ianmu at the exact same instant the intruder disturbed it, preventing them from noticing.

The moment that the leather pushed aside and the intruder began to step in, a man carrying a knife, Ianmu gently slipped beyond the leather to where the man had come from. She dropped to a low crouch as she gracefully moved into the main room, quickly looking to ensure no one else had accompanied the attacker. The intruder might have been merely a thief, but the crude flint knife he grasped suggested otherwise. She held her own dagger for a moment feeling its weight and preparing to do what must be done. It was very likely that her cover as the barely competent concubine would be blown, but if Sar'Tawas died, what would it matter?

The men of her family trained from a young age to be warriors, mastering club, spear, bow, and knife. Unlike most women, Ianmu had spent much of her time using a dagger. Copying her brother and the other warriors, she had quickly mastered its use. She appreciated how graceful and quick the blade could be – a truly feminine implement. Many had said that she was a natural. Unfortunately, her brother Ishayan was also quite adept with the blade. She suspected that the man she now stalked had been sent by him, though there would be no way to be sure. She stepped forward, gracefully pushing aside the leather wall and approached the man from behind. He approached Sar'Tawas's sleeping form with his knife held blade down, ready to stab the man over and over, and not really holding nor preparing to use a stone blade properly, she noted.

"An'an, please guide my hand," she whispered, stepping forward and coming up behind the attacker, matching his speed. Her heart beat fast, and adrenaline flowed through her body as she prepared to make the kill. In one quick and precise movement, she placed her hand delicately against the left side of his head and stabbed her flint dagger into the right side, just under his jawbone where the neck connected to the head. She grabbed his hair with her left hand and held it tightly as she wiggled the knife around, blood pouring down her right arm. The man-made a series of strange gurgling sounds, then dropped to his knees. Sar'Tawas awoke and rolled over to find the man with blood squirting from his neck, horror across his face as he fell to the ground. Behind him stood Ianmu, covered in the man's blood and holding a dagger.

"By Gunar, what is going on here?" he asked, reaching around frantically for his dagger, and not finding it. Suddenly, a man burst from behind the leather... a second man. Before Ianmu could react, he grabbed her hair and placed his knife at her neck, ready to kill the concubine. Ianmu threw her right arm up, catching the man in the elbow and bending his knife arm high into the air and away from her neck. Then, in one smooth motion, she spun around twice, the first time slicing the man's stomach completely open and the second time forcing the dagger up through his neck and into his head from directly under his chin, almost like a ritual dance move.

As her own blade was buried to the hilt in the man's neck, she reached out and took the dagger from the man's hand as he dropped to his knees and then onto the floor, dying in a pool of his own blood. Behind her, she heard a third man approaching. Whoever had sent these men to kill her master had been quite serious. She turned to a confused Sar'Tawas and put her finger to her mouth, indicating that he should be quiet. Then, already covered in blood, she quickly dropped to the ground and curled into the fetal position holding the dagger by the blade against her stomach as though she had been stabbed. She fought to control her breathing, though her fear and exhilaration were almost overwhelming.

The leather burst open, and the third and final man stepped in. At his feet lay the foolish concubine clutching a dagger to the gut and slowly dying. Shuddering and whimpering in pain, a mere woman was of no concern to the man. Instead, he set his angry gaze upon Sar'Tawas. Somehow, this older man had killed his other two companions, probably using the concubine as a distraction. He was immediately filled with rage, as his two companions had been friends of his from his village – men he had grown up with. Sar'Tawas recognized the man, a frequent trader in straight shafts used for arrows.

"You? The arrow trader? Why have you done this? Who put you up to this?" Sar'Tawas asked, hoping that the concubine had some sort of plan. Deep down, he could not even begin to consider how she had switched from a woman who he valued only for her beautiful dancing and skills in bed to a deadly violent killer who dispassionately slew two men in front of him. He would have to address that if he lived through this. Behind him, the "wounded" concubine slowly stood preparing to use her blade as Sar'Tawas held his hand forward. The man also stepped forward with his knife at the ready.

"Wait, not just yet," Sar'Tawas said, speaking more to Ianmu than the man, though the man didn't realize.

"I'm too old to fight you. I killed those two because they didn't realize that I was awake. Please, tell me who has defeated me, tell me who sends me into Isut's arms!" The man frowned for a moment at the oddly forced and awkwardly worded plea but realized that his words could be used to cause a little extra harm before he killed the defenseless old man. It wouldn't bring his friends back, but it might sate his growing need for vengeance. Besides, he never liked Sar'Tawas, anyway.

"It doesn't really matter if I tell you. I was given many lead beads by a man loyal to Ishayan of Nara'kit. Tonight, you will rot on this floor while he laughs at your death. You always screwed me on trades, anyway, you old bastard. When I finish, I'll take your seed so you enter the next world gelded, you son of a goat. Now, death awaits!" The man's smile suddenly vanished as Ianmu shoved the crude flint dagger deep into the back of his neck just below his skull, breaking the blade off by the sheer force of her thrust. Flint blades were not for thrusting, but she would replace the blade, later. As she watched, the man slowly dropped to the floor, making strange quivering motions.

Before him stood his "concubine." She wore nothing but a second skin of blood and held the broken dagger in her right hand. Sar'Tawas could tell the moment their eyes met that he had been deceived. Gone was the blank, clueless stare of his concubine, replaced with a knowing and experienced look of a woman who had killed before. With three assassins lying dead before him, it troubled Sar'Tawas that the woman with the broken blade significantly terrified him more than even the men had. Something about her seemed almost unnatural. For a short moment, both "concubine" and "master" regarded each other, unsure of what to say next. It had all happened so fast.

"Ianmu? Who are you really?" he asked, hoping that she had not been sent to kill him too, though that made little sense considering how long she had been with him. Ianmu thought carefully about what to say. She knew that she could not go back to being the illusion of a foolish and not so intelligent servant, but she did not want to give up her true motive. She needed a second story, a quick story that was believable. If she spoke some truth, her words might be "seasoned" so they would taste true. She took a deep breath, thinking fast. Yet, Sar'Tawas was a man who built his world on knowing what was true and what was not, and so he watched her eyes moving as she thought.

"I was not born a fisherman's daughter. I had myself sold to you to complete my task. The Goddess came to me and told me that I would be instrumental in bringing change to this city. You are to become the husband of Aya'tar, and I am to help you make that change. I am a faithful servant of the Goddess, and I will die or complete her will," she said.

t

Sar'Tawas carefully regarded the woman. He was pretty sure that she had spoken truthfully though he couldn't help but believe that she held something back. Long ago, there was a legend of a man Gunar had come to and instructed to create great change in the city. He had killed many ruthless people who plotted against the Goddess and brought prosperity to the city. Could this woman be like the man in that story? He couldn't help but appreciate that she claimed to be willing to accept death itself to put him in charge of the city. Other than by divine mandate, he could think of no other reason why somebody would undergo what this woman had apparently suffered. Something about the bloody woman standing in the darkness lent credibility to her tale.

Their relationship had just entered a new dimension. He might call her concubine in public to keep up appearances, but never again in private would he be able to regard her in the same way. There was no doubt in his mind that she could kill him at any time that she wanted, and that alone unnerved him more than a little. Perhaps he would continue their relationship as they shared common goals. If he were careful, he might even be able to determine what she might be hiding. With that in mind, he casually stepped over the still twitching bodies and pooled blood, reaching for a clay jar. A moment later, Sar'Tawas turned and offered the jar to the bloody woman, the literal "Hand of the Goddess," who stood before him.

"I think we could both use a drink…"

☾ ☾ ☾

Eight days had passed since the group had arrived in the small fishing village of Karut when a vast storm had come with heavy winds and rains ushering in a wet period of nearly fifteen straight days. Initially, Brig'dha and Aethen had not agreed with Ember that waiting for the guide, a man named Imkanar, was worth their time. They had both argued for leaving after a few days of rest, wanting very desperately to reach their final destination. Once the rains arrived, they had changed their minds. Walking through the muddy, humid, and marshy ground in the rain was a less than appealing notion for any of them. Additionally, spending time off their feet gave Brig'dha the time she needed to fully heal her leg. At the same time, Aethen allowed the painful sore on his foot to disappear, leaving nothing more than a tiny reddish spot where it had been.

Over the Moon that they had waited, they had spoken only a little with the man named Imkanar. He was somewhat aloof and strangely did not like to speak much about the city to which he had offered to take them. This was ever so slightly alarming to Ember, a woman used to traps and other bad situations. Brig'dha had come to the opinion that the man had some sort of emotional baggage invested in the city. Perhaps he was running away from somebody or had endured some tragedy. Ember wanted to believe that was the truth and that there was nothing more nefarious, but something worried her.

While the two women worried over the dangers ahead, Aethen kept his eyes on the local women. He knew that they would be leaving these women behind very soon, so he would merely observe them and gauge what was to be found in the city. They had long black hair, dark as the night, with beautiful eyes of many colors. Many of the women had a strange hazel, almost green color to their eyes, striking and contrasting against their dark hair and rich, brown skin. Aethen was a man who cared more about who a woman was on the inside than what she looked like on the outside, but he wasn't above enjoying their beauty, and it seemed by how many women he caught looking his way, that the feeling was mutual.

ↄ ↄ ↄ

As the night fell on the 24th day since their arrival, Ember and Brig'dha stood atop a hill not far from the village, watching the stars. It was the first clear night since the rains had ended. The Moon was full that night, toward the Southwest, but it had slipped below the horizon, and only the tiniest bit of a glow could be seen. This left the night sky as a beautiful dark sea of stars with a lightly pale-colored band of stars through the middle. The women held each other close, feeling excited at the prospect that within a mere tenday, they would likely be standing in the true southern city of Isut'na.

Ember was beginning to slide her hand behind Brig'dha's shoulders when she noticed, off in the distance, a shape in the darkness moving toward the village. It was odd for people to be sneaking around a village late in the night, though the pair were technically semi-up to the same deed, themselves. The shape resembled a person creeping through the darkness, perhaps the reason Mew had seemed spooked, before vanishing just a few moments before. In that way, the cat was a bit like a dog. Village dogs kept pests away and alerted people to intruders. Of course, the cat simply left them to their fates, but at least he provided some warning to an observer.

"What do you suppose that is? It's much too big to be a wolf," the roused redhead said, pointing at the menacing creature. Brig'dha squinted at the dark form as it slowly moved towards the village, her night vision slightly better than Ember's.

"Oh my! Do you suppose it is some kind of raider? Maybe from another tribe?" she asked. Ember frowned, unimpressed.

"If it's a raider, he's pretty new at this. It looks like he left the rest of his companions behind. I suppose we should go down and figure out what he's doing and perhaps thunk him over the head with something," she said with a laugh.

"If it is a raider, I sort of feel sorry for him," Brig'dha chuckled. With that said, the two women proceeded toward the village to encounter the "raider."

ↄ ↄ ↄ

The man approached the small village covered in black paint. He had watched this very village the day before in the rain from atop a nearby hill. He had seen a young man who fit the description of Imkanar. He couldn't guarantee that this man was his quarry, but he was running out of small villages within the area to search. He had waited for so many tendays during the cold season, but now it seemed that it would finally pay off. The warm winds would come soon, and he wanted to be back in Isut'na when they did.

There were only two buildings that looked like possible locations to find the boy. One appeared to accommodate unmarried men, based on the kinds of people he had seen walking in and out. The other house held three different people who appeared to be foreigners, judging by their hair color. He had never seen a woman with red hair before, but it marked her as someone exotic from afar. Quietly, he crept past the pig pens and approached the building where the unmarried men lived. He wasn't interested in fighting a group of men, so he would make a small hole in the side of the wall and spy inside. Hopefully, he could find the boy through the crack as well as an easy path to slip inside and slit his throat as he slept. It would be a delicate maneuver, but reconnaissance through the hole in the side of the wall would make the difference.

☽ ☽ ☾

Ember and Brig'dha slowly approached the form, which indeed turned out to be a man covered from head to toe in some kind of dark paint. He came to a stop outside of one of the buildings, the one where the man who had offered to lead them to Isut'na stayed, if Ember was not mistaken. The strange man pulled forth a knife and began chipping away at some of the mud in between the wooden planks of the building. Both women stopped and dropped low, becoming more cautious as they approached. Ember pulled free her obsidian dagger while Brig'dha clutched her flint knife, all the while praying to the Moon Goddess for luck. She hoped the Goddess could hear her from just below the horizon.

☽ ☽ ☾

Imkanar awoke from yet another nightmare in which he held his lover as she died in his arms. Sometimes it was from a slit throat, while other times, the cause of death was mysterious. He knew that the dreams were omens from the spirits, reminders of what was probably happening

426

as he hid in the village. It brought shame upon him, but at the same time, he had promised Aya'tar, and he respected her far too much to go back on his word. It was less than a tenday until he could leave, and leave he would, and if that group of travelers from the distant North wished to follow, he would gladly accept their company.

There would be some use in the group beyond just companionship. If he were to cloak himself, he could enter Isut'na as a member of their party, which would be significantly easier than trying to sneak in under cover of darkness. Either way, at that very moment, he needed to relieve himself. *Just a few more days, my love,* he thought. He stepped towards the door, oblivious to the tiny hole that appeared against the wall and the eyeball now peeping through it.

ↄ ↄ ↄ

The man peered through the small hole in the wall he had just created. A man stepped toward the door to leave the building only moments afterward. Seeing that one of the men was about to leave, the darkened man dropped low and braced himself against the building, hoping not to be seen. After just a few moments, the young man stepped from the building and walked only a short distance to a small bush, where he issued a long arc of liquid. The assassin could not believe his fortune. Before him stood the young man who might very well be his target, unarmed and unsuspecting.

It would be too risky to determine if he was the right person before killing him, but it would be easy to check once he stopped breathing. The assassin crept forward with his knife in hand, slowly approaching the man by the bush. All these tendays of waiting would be over in just a few more moments, and then he could return to the city to be compensated greatly for his time.

ↄ ↄ ↄ

Ember and Brig'dha crouched low as they slowly approached the man who had dug the tiny hole on the side of the building. He was now peeping through the hole as they approached when suddenly a younger man stepped from behind the building, walking toward a bush. He paused before a bush relieve himself. They both immediately recognized the younger man was none other than their would-be guide. Suddenly, the strange peeping man began approaching with what looked like a knife in his hand. Offhandedly, Ember wondered why men often strode about entirely nude when the night air was cool. She supposed they didn't get as cold, yet the idea sent a shiver through her spine.

"Is he really doing that? Is he actually going to kill our guide?" Brig'dha asked, exasperated. Ember quickly looked around and found a fist-sized rock sitting on the ground. She picked it up and took aim.

"Son of a wolf! Oh no, you don't!" she said, and tossed the rock as hard as she could at the man. The rock flew true and struck the man on the side of the head. He made a strange, almost coughing sound and then fell over. Brig'dha stood with a wide-eyed expression, quite impressed that Ember had hit the man though she had always been pretty good at throwing things.

"Ha! That's what you get, raider!" Ember screamed, slapping her hands together and then rushing toward the "raider."

"I still don't really think he's a raider," Brig'dha said as she followed behind.

ↄ ↄ ↄ

The next morning, the majority of the village stood around a tied-up man with a large red welt on the side of his head. He seemed disoriented and had vomited many times, but Ember suspected that he would pull through. He had been dumped in water to wash off the paint and now sat bound, soaking wet, and none too pleased. Next to the man knelt Elder Mimnar, a deeply troubled man with many questions and short patience regarding possible raiders.

"Well, my friends, I do not know who this man is, but he would have killed a member of our tribe. You have done us a good service, and this will not be forgotten. If you need to remain here for longer or if you need our help, we will offer it to you," he said to Ember and Brig'dha.

"At least you didn't kill this one," Aethen said with a smirk, before receiving angry glares from both women. It looked to him like the man had a headache so bad that he probably wanted to die. The big question on everyone's mind was why he had sneaked into the tribe and attempted to kill Imkanar. Was he a thief? Perhaps some sort of scout for a raiding party? All around, members of the tribe chatted with each other, tossing back and forth conjecture. Finally, Imkanar ended their discussion loudly.

"No!" he said. Everybody stopped and looked at the man, much more confused by what he meant by "no" than that he actually yelled it.

"No, what?" Ember asked.

"No, he is not a raider nor a scout. He is a wheat farmer from the city of Isut'na. He was probably sent here to kill me... Sent here by Sar'Tawas. It's time for me to leave. If I stay any longer, I'll simply put all of you in danger, and I won't do that," he said, turning and storming off.

"Hey, what's a Sar'Tawas?" Ember yelled after the man as she skipped off, following Imkanar, completely unsatisfied by his explanation. Brig'dha had considered trying to stop her, but Ember seemed way too curious about the drama which had unfolded before her to let it go that easily. Aethen shook his head and then turned his attention to the wheat farmer.

"So, what are we going to do with you?" he asked.

It was not long before Ember caught up with Imkanar next to the water. He regarded the rambunctious redhead with an odd mixture of anger at her intrusion into his personal matters but also with respect for someone who had likely saved his life. Then, realizing that she would demand a greater explanation, he looked around to ensure nobody else was watching. Imkanar let out a deep sigh. Perhaps it was best that he told somebody anyway, as the secrets slowly ate him alive. Ember was as good as anyone else, and she didn't have any connections with the city, which made her the safest person to hear his tale.

"The city of Isut'na is ruled by the high priestess Aya'tar. She is about my age, maybe a season or two older than you. The problem is that her position is not secure. Some want her to step down and let another lead... they want a man. Of course, some wish her to marry. The problem is that she loves none of the men worthy of being the leader. She loves me, and I love her!" Ember listened to him speak and slowly knelt upon the sand, hoping he would say more. It was difficult for Ember to listen as she was always full of so many questions, but she bit her tongue and hoped the man would finish before she started interrupting him.

"The most powerful man in the city is in charge of the Craft Guild, a man named Sar'Tawas. He knows that I love Aya'tar, and he probably sent that man to kill me. This is not good news as only Aya'tar knew where I had gone. She asked me to leave to make things easier for her, politically," he dropped his head in shame. Ember felt sorry for the man knowing that it was his foolish pride causing him more trouble than it should. It seemed odd to her, but it seemed to her that most men believed it was their job to protect women from everything. Sometimes it could be charming, but it was often very annoying, especially when the men treated women like children to be coddled. Still, she felt some respect for him.

"I will leave tomorrow morning for Isut'na. If you wish to come with me, this is where I am going. I cannot take the chance that Sar'Tawas won't try something more drastic if I wait. Even if we can never be together, I would rather die than let something happen to her," he said stoically and looking off into the distance. Ember felt moved by his resolve, her expression growing stoic. She was a hopeless romantic, and every part of his story touched her. Not far behind, Brig'dha stood, having listened to the whole thing from a slight distance. She shook her head, knowing full well what was going to happen next.

"Ember, my love, you are going to involve yourself in their problems... aren't you?" she asked herself, rhetorically. Well, that was the reason that she had saved Brig'dha from death and one of the very reasons they had fallen in love. She couldn't hate the essence that made Ember who she was. She just hoped that they would make it out of this next affair alive. Suddenly, Brig'dha felt something fuzzy pushing up against her leg. She looked down to see Mew pawing at her boot and wanting to be fed.

"It's about time you finally showed up."

Chapter Twenty Three
I Will Name You Hullamu

Most twins are not identical, and those born identical are almost entirely the same sex. However, a few rare circumstances exist where identical twins can be born with differing sexes. One such example is sesquizygotic twins. In this case, a single egg is fertilized by two sperm, potentially resulting in a male and female child who are nearly identical. They share the same maternal DNA but roughly half of their paternal DNA each.

It should be noted that such "semi-identical twins" are exceptionally rare, though entirely possible. Of course, even after beating such overwhelming odds, giving birth presents a massive risk to both the child and the person giving birth. The likelihood that a child would die at birth or within the first year might easily have exceeded 30%, though the actual rates would vary considerably from place to place. It should be noted that these estimates are still debated in the field of Paleodemography.

It was midday under a clear sky with a slightly warm breeze as hundreds of people gathered in the ritual area waiting for news. Early the night before, high priestess Aya'tar had entered into labor. Word had spread like wildfire, and everyone had camped out waiting to find out if the baby was born alive, if the mother survived the birthing, and if it was a boy, girl, or duemuas. With Aya'tar as the official leader of the city and with the mortality rate of a woman's first pregnancy being unacceptably high, everyone awaited the results on bated breath. The entire future of the city could be changed in just a short time.

Sar'Tawas and Ianmu sat on a leather mat out in the open, waiting for results along with everyone else. Early that morning, screams had been heard coming from the temple window. Since then, occasional sounds had emerged, but nobody knew what was happening. Several elder women had been allowed in along with initiate priestess Isha'kau, but no one else. Standing by the ladder leading up to the roof, three of Kamar's best men stood, preventing any from attending the priestess.

"Waiting is always the hardest part, don't you agree, Sar'Tawas?" Ishayan said, approaching from behind. If the guild master had been startled, he made no indication of it.

"Why yes, I do find waiting to be difficult, but some things are worth the wait," he replied coldly. The two men regarded each other for a moment. Ianmu kept her head down and away from her brother's gaze. She had taken to wearing heavy body and face paint, and her hairstyle was much different than it had been back in Nara'kit. So far, he had not seemed to notice.

"Oh, Ishayan. I wanted to warn you of possible danger," Sar'Tawas abruptly said, causing a side glance from Ianmu.

"Oh, and what would that be?" the younger man asked with an entirely pleasant facial expression and tone.

"Not long ago, I was attacked by three men. Luckily, whoever sent them was a cowardly fool and sent worthless, low-quality assassins. I can always spot quality just as easily as petty trash. I wanted to let you know so that you can be sure and watch your back. I wouldn't want you to wake up with a dagger in that handsome face of yours," Sar'Tawas said politely, his face entirely neutral. Ishayan's right eye twitched ever so slightly, but then he bowed deeply.

"I appreciate your warning. I wouldn't want to find you emasculated with your throat slit, and face down in a ditch, either," the younger man replied coolly, lifting his head from the bow and slowly walking off. Neither man was under any misapprehension – this was all-out war.

"I know of that man. I warn you, do not underestimate him," Ianmu mumbled under her breath.

"Do not worry, I have been watching him carefully. Also, I have you to defend me," he said. Ianmu closed her eyes at the irony that he didn't even realize. Their discussion was interrupted by a loud cry to the gathered masses, from the temple.

"The babies are born, and by the Goddess, the high priestess lives! They are twins, one girl, and one boy, like the goddess Isut and the god Gunar!" screamed a tearful Isha'kau to the crowd. To produce two children in her first pregnancy and do so in good health could do nothing more than prove that the Goddess was on her side. This made the task of securing the city all the more difficult. Ianmu, Sar'Tawas, and Ishayan all closed their eyes in regret, unknown to each other, and simultaneously.

ↄ ↄ ↄ

That night, massive celebrations filled the central courtyard. Honey drinks were passed out from the city's reserve stores, and the food was cooked en masse while beautifully painted dancers filled the night with song and dance. Lying in a makeshift bed of furs atop the temple, Aya'tar lay with her two new children. Making it up the ladder to sit in front of all the people was difficult, to say the least, but showing that she was strong and with two children would help secure her position and deal yet another blow to those who worked against her. In truth, she felt like passing out from the ordeal, and her body quivered upon the edge of exhaustion.

Aya'tar had never experienced such pain and was so surprised when two children had come forth, one not that long after the other. She lay there with both children as the elder women helped clean and check the babies. They appeared to be healthy and of good form. Not long afterward, she delivered the placenta. Strangely, there was only one for two babies. She had thought there would be one per baby. The elder women seemed to consider this normal, for twins. But what wasn't normal were their sexes. The elder women spoke in hushed tones as they noted that one child was male and the other, female, while sharing a single placenta. None of them had ever heard of such a thing, let alone seen it. Regardless, the babies had been cleaned, and their umbilical cords cut with a sharp obsidian tool and tied off with flax cord.

Too tired to consider sexes and placentae, Aya'tar lay back breathing hard. She had heard the stories of all the terrible things that could happen and how wrong things could go. With each breath, she whispered her prayers and thanks to the Goddess that things had gone well. If the child had been born ill or she lost too much blood, there would be no one to save them. All she had was the belief in her gods and her body's ability to fight off death to the bitter end. Only the strong survived.

The high priestess lay on a large bundle of soft furs as the cool night air slowly drifted across her skin. On each side, large fires burned to provide the priestess with any heat she desired. Clutched in her arms were her baby daughter and son, each suckling its fill of whatever food could be had from the priestess' body, though her primary milk flow wouldn't start for another day or two. As she looked up toward the sky, the stars above twinkled, and every now and then, one of them would fly by. For some reason, lying underneath the sea of stars holding the children as they suckled brought tears to her eyes... oh so many tears. She was too weak to truly cry, but the emotions danced in her mind. She was simply that thankful to have lived and even more grateful that her children were healthy.

"You couldn't just have one? No, you had to go have two."

As she looked up, Isha'kau came to stand over her, looking down with a beaming smile. The younger priestess could not hide the puffy redness around her eyes as she had been worried about Aya'tar's health and that of the children, almost as much as Aya'tar had. Isha'kau ignored the small line of blood that had run down one of Aya'tar's legs. She really should be lying down until she healed, but she understood the woman's need to be seen. Besides, who would have believed her claim of identical twins with opposite sexes without seeing it for themselves.

"Have you finally decided upon the names of the children?"

"I had thought to name the boy after my father, Utiakur. I have since changed my mind," she said, staring up at the sea of stars above. Isha'kau cocked an eyebrow in confusion. Aya'tar had seemed so sure of her decision not so long before.

"His name carries so much weight with it that he would forever be caught in my father's shadow. Instead, I will name him Ikanar, after the brightest star in the sky. This very evening I watched as the Sun set, the star Ikanar, right beside it. It's a beautiful name and the beautiful star for a beautiful child," she said, looking at the boy. She turned her head to the girl suckling happily, and her eyes became wet. At first, a lump formed in her throat, but then the high priestess swallowed hard and spoke as tears again began to flow.

"I will name you Hullamu, in memory of the woman who gave her life so that you could have yours," she spoke quickly as her voice wavered and she became a sobbing mess. Isha'kau joined Aya'tar in tears, moved by the memories of Hullamu, who had been like a sister to both of them. Together, they cried as the babies licked, too fresh from the womb to properly suckle for long, and let the people of the great proto-city of Isut'na see their high priestess in all of her maternal glory.

ɔ ɔ ɔ

The Sun was high in the sky as the four weary travelers, and one small cat, approached the city of Isut'na. They had awakened not long after the Sun had risen, just before the Moon had set in the western sky. The four travelers had marched at nearly double their average speed hoping to reach Isut'na before the end of the day. They had been walking almost non-stop for many days, guided by Imkanar, a man obsessed with the need to reach the woman he loved. Ember was beside herself with romantic sappiness over the story, as well as the desperate urge to reach the new lands. Even Brig'dha had eventually been won over and become enamored with the story. She was quite interested in meeting this amazing priestess who ruled a city.

The air was warm and extremely humid, made worse by small marshy ponds near the city. Vast fields filled with workers could be seen not too far away. Ember had never witnessed so many people working collectively to harvest and plant crops. All around were hundreds of people working on scores of projects, collectively. Just outside of the city, she saw more people than she had ever seen gathered in her entire life, aside from the harvest festival. Brig'dha and Aethen were equally dumbfounded by what they saw. Even Mew, the cat, safely bundled within Brig'dha's arms, stared lazily at the scene before him with mild interest.

All four travelers came to a stop with the city towering before them. Imkanar looked as though he might begin to panic having come this close and yet suddenly stopping, but even he understood the significance that a place like Isut'na could have on people who had never witnessed anything larger than a village. He stood there tapping his foot impatiently, hoping they would get over themselves quickly so that he could slip into the village unseen. Rushing in right now would do nothing more than get him caught by some of Sar'Tawas's men.

The city stretched perhaps 100 lengths of a man wide from where they stood. It was nearly four stories tall in some places, with women and children carrying out their daily lives on the roofs of the buildings while men could be seen carrying wood and herding animals below. Ember saw a woman on a building close to her working some sort of loom to make cloth while children played beside her. A man stacked large rocks on the ground below, apparently working on some kind of small wall outside of the city, perhaps for livestock? There were more people gathered just outside of the main entrance to the city than existed in her entire tribe.

"Well, Aethen, if you can't find a woman here... there's something wrong with you," Ember said, drawing an incredulous look from Aethen. However, in Ember's defense, there were nearly two dozen young women of the proper age to marry sitting on mats outside of the city, apparently weaving reeds into some sort of baskets as they happily chatted and passed the day. Aethen was excited at the prospect, but finding women was a far different act than finding *a* woman.

"This is it, the city of the goddess Isut, Isut'na. Remember what I told you about finding guest quarters near the trading area. I can't help you when I'm keeping my head down and hidden," Imkanar said. He had completely decorated his face in the ritualistic paint of a man questing for enlightenment from the gods. He wore a rough wool covering over his head that covered his shoulders and ran partially down his back. It made him seem a little top-heavy as he only wore a simple loincloth at his waist and a pair of sandals, but it hid his face and would allow him entry into the city, unseen.

Before arriving, Imkanar had explained to the group how to trade for a stay in one of the very small single-room buildings available for traders by the trade area. He would be unable to speak for fear that he would be recognized. He had initially hoped that in exchange for being a guide to the city, his companions would provide some reconnaissance for him to help determine the status of things before he revealed himself. Instead, Ember and Brig'dha had become completely wrapped up in the drama surrounding his love affair with the high priestess. Not only would they provide reconnaissance, but they wished to take an active role in helping him reclaim his love. How could he say no?

The quartet of adventurers stepped through the narrow passageway between buildings and into the city proper. All around, people worked tirelessly at various trades and crafts while children ran and played. Here and there, dogs ran free, which discouraged Mew from leaving the safety of the priestess' arms. The walls of the buildings were coated with plaster and paint depicting many different scenes, though bulls and birds were commonplace. Hair could be seen tied into buns or hanging loosely in various configurations, some quite elaborate. Loincloths and woven aprons tended to dominate as the primary clothing while upper bodies were sometimes covered with shawls of textile or leather, and even an occasional shirt or vest.

As they stepped into the city, their presence was immediately noted. Above them, watchful guards with bows observed but had decided them to be either travelers or traders. While they were not considered a threat, Ember's beautiful red hair and Brig'dha's and Aethen's rich, dark brown skin stood out from the locals. Luckily, all the attention was focused on the three foreigners and none of it on the hooded man. As they wandered down the narrow passageway into the city and came to stand in the marketplace, many people stopped what they were doing to eye the newcomers.

They were glad that their clothing at least matched what the locals wore. Brig'dha wore a pair of sandals with her new flax string skirt, which Ember had all but forced her into buying, her otherwise bare skin painted with black swirl body paints. At first, she was worried that it had been a little too flashy, but she had seen other women wearing similar items, though of lower quality, and was beginning to warm up to it. Across her shoulders, she wore a flax netted shawl and, of course, her gold and copper jewelry and the Amber of Life, which Ember had given her to wear, it being magic and she being a priestess. Beside her, Ember wore a long and soft linen loincloth which hung just below her knees, the warm-weather garb of men from most places she had been. On her feet, she wore a pair of sturdy sandals, and around her neck and wrists she wore her matching gold and copper jewelry. Aethen also wore a linen loincloth along with a pair of light boots and his cowry shell necklace, a large traveling pack slung over his back.

The robust redhead, never being one to follow gender norms, had gone so far as to decorate her entire body with stripes of black and white paint made from burned bone char and white clay, the paint of men among her people. That, coupled with her feathers and striking red hair, made her stand out like a bright torch on a dark night. Standing together with the heavily cloaked and hidden Imkanar and with the priestess holding an agitated and large furry animal in her arms, the group wasn't exactly incognito. As they came to stand in the trading area of Isut'na, the party regarded the citizens while the citizens equally regarded them.

Ember quickly spotted a small bench with people sitting and eating. Food and drink were being traded for, freshly made. She quickly headed that way to bargain for a place to stay and a bite to eat. Imkanar had explained that this outdoor eating establishment also maintained several small rooms to be rented. Ember had never before heard of a place that traded goods for hot and ready-to-eat food, as well as the idea of having multiple little rooms available to be traded for. These capitalistic ideas were quite unheard of in Ember's world though she couldn't help but appreciate the benefit of being able to trade for freshly made food. As she approached the bench, several farmers turned from their wheat porridge and drink to see the strange woman approaching. From behind the table, a heavyset woman with a warm smile and a no-nonsense look spoke.

"Well, you don't look like a regular trader. Dressed like that, you look like a narmu," she observed, obviously looking at Ember's masculine clothing, yet female form, "Where are you from?" Ember took a moment to process a few words she didn't quite know before replying with a thick accent. She would have to ask what a narmu was, later. Each of the men sitting on the bench glared at Ember, having never seen either a redheaded woman nor such beautiful golden jewelry. Even in Isut'na, such items virtually did not exist.

"My friends and I are from the Northwest. We come in search of new things to trade. We need a room for a few moons," she replied. The woman behind the counter glared at her for a few moments as though judging her worth. The woman's eyes lingered upon her hair and the beautiful jewelry she wore. Ember suspected that the woman was finicky about whom she rented a room to, probably for a good reason. Ember smiled and hoped she would be judged worthy.

"All right, what do you have to trade for two full moons for a small room?" the woman asked. Ember was completely over her head, having never done anything like this before. Guest huts typically involved a work-for-stay arrangement, and rarely was bargaining involved. She placed her hand in her pouch and fingered about for lead beads. She produced the beads and put them on the table, adding extra smiles. The older woman looked back at her with a flat expression, not in any way impressed by the smiles of a younger woman. For a moment, Ember considered dragging Aethen over and seeing if his smiles worked better.

"Got some more because that's barely enough for a single Moon." Ember frowned and found herself producing several obsidian pieces, several more beads, and a small bone needle. Eventually, the woman seemed satisfied, and her flat expression became a smile, though Ember wasn't quite sure how genuine that smile was. Everyone had skills and activities they were good at. This woman was obviously good at making a profit. While convenience seemed great, it seemed that these capitalistic ideas also had a significant downside.

"Hey, what's a narmu?" Ember asked, causing the woman to pause her quick inventory of new beads. She once more glanced at the strange woman as though unsure how to explain.

"Well, when you dress like a man, but you have a pair of those," she said, glancing at Ember's breasts.

"Or when you dress like a woman, but you have… you know," she said, using her finger to suggest common male physiology. Ember thought for a moment, considering her words and their implications. It sounded sort of like a narmu was the Isut'na language equivalent of a wergene, the third gender. She suspected the term implied a lot more meaning than the woman's crude explanation conveyed. Still, the notion felt a bit more agreeable than calling herself a woman, or a woman who acted like a man.

"Well, maybe I am a narmu," Ember began, but Brig'dha cut her off, having understood parts of the speech, at least enough to generally know what was being said. Grabbing Ember's shoulder and pulling her close for a whisper, she voiced her concerns.

"What if they kill these 'narmu' here? You must be careful, just in case," she frantically whispered, though Ember suspected no one else but Aethen would understand the Moon Priestess. For a moment they made eye contact, then Ember smiled and nodded, turning to face the woman once more.

"Do your people sacrifice narmu?" she asked, plainly. Brig'dha's mouth opened in shock at how little tact Ember was using, as usual. The local woman cocked an eyebrow as though Ember had just asked if water was wet.

"No."

"So, a narmu is safe to live here?"

"Yeah… hey, you want the room or not?" Ember nodded, and the woman shook her head, wondering if agreeing to host this party of strange folk had been a good idea.

"Hey Salar, watch the food while I'm gone," the profiteering woman yelled at a younger man who looked like he might be related to her. The woman stepped from behind the table and motioned Ember and the group to follow her toward a series of small single-room buildings at the ground level by the trading area. As they left, Brig'dha sighed, realizing that she would never change the chaotic fox of a person Ember was. It was not long before they arrived at the very last building toward the corner. The woman stopped before the building and pushed aside the heavy leather skin hanging across the doorway to show them inside.

"Well, here you go. You have this for two Moons. If you damage it, we will have a problem," she said with a smile, turning and leaving. Aethen looked at the group, unused to such curt discourse.

"Well, I guess we didn't trade enough for a personality," he snarked.

"That seems true," Brig'dha agreed.

"She called me a narmu," Ember said with a smile.

"Well, are you?" Aethen asked, honestly not sure what a narmu was, as he had understood so little of the original conversation. Ember merely shrugged, tossing the idea into the tiny fire of ideas in the back of her mind that she would consider sometime later.

Everyone but Imkanar glanced at one another, confused. This was truly a new world to them, a completely different environment than they knew. Imkanar was the first to step into the room, quickly pulling free the woolen cloth and stretching. He had endured enough wearing the disguise and was quite glad to be in a familiar form of building. To him, this was the way things should be. The other three simply stood at the entryway, gazing at this most bizarre little building.

"It's not as good as the building I grew up in, but it's not bad," Imkanar said, apologetically. Truly, it was not the worst hut they had ever been in. There appeared to be a round mud-brick oven in one corner, with several small beds fashioned upon stone benches. The most different aspect was how every piece of the room was plastered in a single and uniform manner.

"White…" Brig'dha said, observing the almost entirely white plastered room. Ember thought the place quite pleasant and much sturdier than what she was used to. While she walked around the small room examining its form, the priestess stood anxiously. Brig'dha was anxious to find out how this priestess Aya'tar fared. She wanted to see this woman that had driven the young Imkanar so mad with passion, this woman who somehow controlled this entire city. Coming from a forest people village, the idea perplexed her. She put down Mew, the cat, who ran to the door, smelled a dog or something similar and then ran back into the room to hide on one of the beds.

"I don't think that he will be going outside, at least during the day, so we will need to remember to feed him. I'm going to go and see this Aya'tar woman," Brig'dha said softly. Ember looked back at Brig'dha with a sly expression.

"Don't look too long. Remember, she's already taken, and so are you," Ember playfully teased, smiling. Brig'dha looked almost alarmed by the comment but quickly relaxed when Aethen and Imkanar burst into laughter. Truly, Brig'dha was deeply in love with Ember, and no priestess of any city would break that up. She was really more curious than anything else and had become swept up in the romantic notion of the love that could not be between Imkanar, the lowly metalworker, and Aya'tar, the high priestess of the city. Though, being quite attracted to women, she had to admit that the mysterious high priestess was… intriguing.

The torpid redhead quickly removed her sandals and flopped onto one of the beds to take a nap. Far from her earlier comment, Ember had absolutely no worry over Brig'dha. The priestess looked like she was ready to rush out of the door and satisfy her curiosity, and Aethen could barely hold back the urge to scout the city. She would let those two run around while she took a nap. She knew what was important in life, and food and sleep were both high on that list. Besides, she would enjoy the city better after having rested. Seeing that they were the only two ready to leave the room, Brig'dha and Aethen both crept out of the door and into the unknown of the city.

"I can't believe she has journeyed half of the harvest across the known world and the first thing she does is take a nap," Aethen said to Brig'dha as soon as they left the room.

"I can't believe you've journeyed with her for half a harvest and expect her not to," Brig'dha countered as the pair headed in the direction of the temple, according to Imkanar's instructions.

"Well, you love her and you never acted normal. Not even growing up. So you are both in good company," Aethen mumbled as they split up to go their separate ways.

◓ ◓ ◓

Brig'dha held her flax netted shawl tightly as she stood atop the building which housed the temple. Before her was a ladder that led down into a room controlled by powerful foreign gods. Part of her worried that stepping into such an unfamiliar and magically charged area could be dangerous. She hoped to learn more about the status of this amazing priestess named Aya'tar, and offer prayers to the local deities to appease them. The problem was that she would be slightly deceptive as she obtained information about the priestess, and she doubted the local gods would miss this. Would they inform the priestess, or would they simply strike her down? It was always a risk to be taken when standing before the most religious altars of foreign gods. Brig'dha took a deep breath and prepared herself for the task.

She cautiously climbed down the ladder, a foreign task to begin with. Where she had come from, very few ladder-like structures existed. Most things were built on the ground. Access to a roof was performed with either a crude ladder or a pole with notches carved into it. This ladder was extremely rugged and made from aged and polished square timbers. The roof itself was plastered white with various designs all around the outside depicting what appeared to be religious events. She took a breath and descended beneath the entryway.

As she first stepped onto the cool floor, she was nearly blind in the darkness. It would take her eyes a moment to adjust, as the inside of the temple was dark, musty, and lit by two small fires. At one end was a wall decorated with symbols depicting birds from the sky carrying what looked like the departed souls to some afterlife. Before her was an altar to a fertility goddess, most likely Isut. At the top of the altar was a small stone statuette of a plump goddess with an enlarged bosom and hips, a very common symbol to be found among fertility deities. Off to the right were several bullhorns connected to the wall as well as a small altar to what appeared to be a bull god. This reminded Brig'dha of the Moon Goddess and the Horned God.

The floor was covered with rush matting, and there were many stone benches and even wooden shelves connected to some of the walls with lots of small clay pots containing various substances. As her eyes adjusted to the darkness, she began to notice that the entire room was covered with religious symbology. In one corner sat a warp weighted loom, while in another was a large clay pot full of some unknown substance. Brig'dha felt tingles dancing up and down her spine, which she attributed to the magical energy in the room. This was certainly the temple of the powerful deity.

Hearing a slight noise, Brig'dha turned to her left toward the stone bench, suddenly realizing that there was a person on it, someone she had not seen initially as her eyes had yet to adjust. Brig'dha instantly stepped backward with a slight gasp. A long and dark-haired woman lay upon the stone bench covered with skins and furs. She was also wrapped in furs and nursing two young children. She wore copper bracelets and an intricate ash pattern of black lines painted across her lower face, with a simple loincloth at her waist.

It seemed that Imkanar was right. She was absolutely beautiful, and her presence was undeniable. Her body was slightly heavyset, probably the result of her children, and exactly how he had described his beloved Aya'tar. Oddly, her beauty was almost secondary to her commanding presence, something Brig'dha noticed immediately. The woman regarded Brig'dha, quietly watching her, but said nothing. For a short moment, they just gazed at one another in curiosity. Brig'dha suddenly felt conspicuous, staring at the woman in what was probably her home, not just the temple.

"I... My name is Brig'dha of the Blue Sea People... well, the Isen'bryn before that. I worship the Goddess of the Moon, but I have come to pay my respects to the local goddess of the city, Isut?" she said clumsily and with a thick accent. The woman with the two children smiled back at her, patiently waiting to see if she would continue. Brig'dha found herself looking down, unwilling to make eye contact for long. Worse, she was absentmindedly holding some of the strings in her string skirt, tugging them, and feeling awkward. Something about the way this woman gazed upon her made Brig'dha feel a little inadequate. The long dark-haired woman was a fertility priestess, most likely, lying regally in the middle of a fertility goddess' temple and nursing two children. The symbolism was powerful and not lost upon Brig'dha. The fertility priestess was at her greatest power in this setting and might curse her if she misspoke.

"Are you the high priestess Aya'tar?" she asked, hoping the woman would say something. The nursing woman cleared her throat to speak, satisfied that it was now time to introduce herself. Usually, it would be considered rude to call her by the shortened version of her name before having even been introduced. Strangely, the exotic-looking brunette standing before her, and wearing an outfit which might be found on the ruler of a city, seemed so nervous and worried that she could not help but find her humorous. For some reason, while she was nursing the babies, she tended to feel exceptionally relaxed and had difficulty becoming angry. She took a deep breath and began to speak.

"My name is Isut'Sanup'ramu Aya'tar, high priestess of Isut and ruler of the city of Isut'na. These are my children, Ikanar and Hullamu. Please, use the temple. I'm sure Isut would appreciate the gesture," she said, continuing to lie on her bed and nurse the children. Brig'dha smiled back and nodded, thankful that her introduction had gone well. With the high priestess watching, she piously positioned herself before the statuette of the foreign goddess. She held before it a long and beautiful hawk feather she had found along the way. Imkanar had explained that such a feather would make a great offering and would certainly please Aya'tar. Brig'dha stepped forward and knelt before the altar holding the feather out and placing it before the statuette.

"Goddess of the Southeast, goddess Isut, goddess of the city Isut'na. I am priestess Brig'dha. You know why my friends and I have come, and you know that we mean no harm. Please accept this gesture and forgive my prayers to my own goddess in your midst," she said. Aya'tar was slightly intrigued by the cryptic nature of the prayer, strangely spoken in her language and not that of the foreigner. No one would be fool enough to attempt harm to the city and yet make such a statement before the Goddess. This told her that whoever this Brig'dha woman was, her intentions were likely pure. Brig'dha stood and nodded to the priestess and prepared to leave. Aya'tar suddenly spoke, wishing to delay her departure.

"Brig'dha, would you mind staying for a little while and telling me about yourself? I don't have a chance to get out often, and I'm curious to hear of your Goddess and where you come from." This was exactly what Brig'dha had hoped for and feared: conversation. Ember was a much better conversationalist, but people had a tendency to confide in Brig'dha for reasons that she still didn't quite know. If she were lucky, the bedridden and apparently bored Aya'tar might confide information that she could share with Imkanar. With the luck of both goddesses, she would rekindle the love between these two people. Besides, she really wanted to hold one of the babies.

She could also most definitely see why Imkanar found Aya'tar so attractive. Her hair was long and black as the night, and her eyes were dark pools which gave the illusion of being much larger than they actually were. In her arms and suckling mercilessly were the two small babies who were the children of Aya'tar and Imkanar, if the stories were to be believed. The high priestess' skin was decorated with many complex painted shapes. Brig'dha stepped forward and cautiously sat on the edge of the bed, reaching out with a finger to touch the head of one of the babies.

"That is little Hullamu," Aya'tar said. Brig'dha had never heard Imkanar say anything about children. She was unsure how she might bring this topic up, but perhaps Ember could help her decide on the best course of action. Instead, she sat on the edge of the bed and let the gabby high priestess speak.

CHAPTER TWENTY FOUR

YOUR GIRLFRIEND'S A PRIESTESS!

The fictional city of Isut'na was situated on the Bosporus close to modern-day Istanbul, Turkey. While Isut'na is wholly fictitious, the city's culture, layout, and design are all loosely based on the ancient Anatolian city of Çatalhöyük (roughly pronounced Cha-tahl-hoy-ewk). Çatalhöyük was Inhabited between 7500 BCE to 5500 BCE, making it slightly older than Isut'na, 6500 BCE to 5000 BCE. While Isut'na had a population of between 2000 and 2500 citizens, the real Çatalhöyük, known as Du'ubria in the book, housed perhaps as many as 8000 to 10,000 inhabitants at one point.

Like the fictional Isut'na and Nara'kit, several real prehistoric proto-cities flourished in Anatolia, levant, and the fertile crescent, such as Uruk, Eridu, Mureybet, and Jericho, called Yarehk in the book. We may never truly understand exactly how life was lived in these proto-cities, but, through fiction informed by careful study of these historical treasures, we may well imagine a close approximation. It is critical to note that Çatalhöyük, the proto-city that Isut'na is most closely based upon, does not show evidence of a significant social hierarchy or a unified leader, as are depicted in Nara'kit and Isut'na. This power structure was imagined for the purposes of the story.

Aethen stepped into the marketplace to get a good feel for the people and what could be found. There were many small trading areas set up. All around were leather mats with various goods and individuals pursuing them. It seemed that there was some kind of thriving economy that allowed for the extreme specialization of labor. These sorts of concepts existed in every single location Aethen had been, but never to this level. In a place like this, you truly could only make arrowheads, or only carve bone tools, as a trade. More impressively, all the food needed for the day could be picked up in this trading area in exchange for goods or little clay stamps that seemed to convey some kind of worth. Immediately, something dark and shiny caught his eye, and he approached a trader to see what could be had.

He found a mat containing a set of obsidian blades when several merchants arrived, crowding in front of the wares. Slightly annoyed, he stepped backward without looking where he was going. Suddenly, he felt the impact as he bounced off somebody, causing him to nearly fall forward into the merchants. Aethen's good sense of balance kept him from falling, but he felt slightly annoyed and turned to see who he had run into. On the ground on her knees was a striking woman with long dark brown hair and brown eyes. Aethen was taken aback by her beauty and immediately lost any notion of anger, realizing his own fault in the incident. In truth, he actually didn't know who had bumped into whom.

"I'm really sorry! Let me help you up," he said, extending his hand to help the fallen woman. She grabbed ahold of his hand and pulled herself to a standing position, bending over to wipe the dirt off her knees. The woman stood almost as tall as Aethen, wearing a short bark fiber apron and a pair of sandals. If her stunning, long hair was not amazing enough, she had a series of beautiful and intricate scarification marks set in small circles across her shoulders and running down her arms. As soon as his eyes left the marks, they fell upon her face. Aethen could not help but gaze into her eyes, captivated by the dark brown beauty they held. The woman stood for a few moments looking blankly back at Aethen as he blatantly stared deeply into her eyes. Normally, he did not stare, but this exotic woman completely captivated him, and he forgot himself.

"Do I have something on my face?" the woman asked, abruptly drawing Aethen from his mesmer. Suddenly, he realized what he had been doing and became extremely embarrassed, turning quite red. Gawking at people was considered extremely impolite among his people, but her eyes had simply enchanted him on the spot. He held his hands out, worried that he would come across as some kind of deviant. Though his skin was brown and tanned, the woman could clearly see the blush forming as a slight darkening of his skin, his pupils dilating, and a drop of sweat beading right where his hair began.

"I am so sorry. I did not mean to stare at you. Your eyes are just so beautiful. I'm sorry... Um, oh, and I'm sorry again for knocking you over..." The woman laughed at him for just a moment but continued to look at him with her bright brown eyes. Aethen couldn't help but notice that her pupils had also grown even larger, though he was trying desperately not to glare at her. The problem was the more she smiled, the harder it became for him to look away.

"You are not from around here. Are you from the North?" she asked, smiling back at Aethen and straightening her hair. He again thanked the lessons of young Ninrea'mu, Ember, and the people he had stayed with over the cold season for helping him pick up a working vocabulary. In truth, not every word was understood or likely spoken correctly, but it was enough to be reasonably fluid.

"Um, yes... Actually, from the Northwest. My name is Aethen... and you are?" The woman giggled and stepped back from Aethen in a playful manner.

"Who am I? I am late; that's who I am," she said laughing and wandering off abruptly, turning for a moment to regard the strange man from the Northwest once more. Aethen was left confused as strange tingles danced up and down his spine. Had he said something wrong? Everything had seemed to be going well until suddenly it wasn't. Was asking a person's name a taboo in this place? He was pretty sure that he would spend the next few days reviewing in his mind what had just happened. Most importantly, he hoped that he would catch sight of the beautiful, brown-eyed woman with the amazing body scarification once more.

ᴐ ᴐ ᴐ

"Aya'tar! Aya'tar! You will never guess what just happened!" Isha'kau climbed down the ladder and hurriedly plopped onto the floor to tell the high priestess what she had done and who she had met. Suddenly, she caught sight of the silhouette of a person sitting on the bed beside the priestess, apparently speaking with her. Isha'kau came to a stop waiting for her eyes to adjust to the darkness. This was most likely somebody stopping by to ask the high priestess for advice or prayer. Either way, it would not do to rush in and cause her any trouble. As her eyes adjusted, Isha'kau could clearly see that the person sitting on the bed was female and that she was gently petting the head of one of the babies. The initiate priestess relaxed at the sight.

"That is the priestess Isha'kau, my faithful companion," Aya'tar said, indicating the woman who had just burst into the temple excitedly. Brig'dha turned to regard the newcomer. Like Aya'tar, she had long shiny hair, but it was a very dark brown accompanied by dark brown eyes. What caught Brig'dha's eye immediately were the beautiful scarification markings across the younger woman's shoulders and arms. She suspected that such complex and extensive markings probably hurt quite a lot when they had been made.

"Hello, my name is Brig'dha of the Blue Sea People. I'm a traveler from the Northwest and a priestess of the Moon Goddess," Brig'dha said timidly. She became shy around many people, and encountering each of

447

these new people within their own temple was a little overwhelming. She could imagine Ember standing, then walking over to the woman and slapping her on the shoulder in a friendly sort of way. She was more content to sit on the bed petting the baby's head and smiling. Aya'tar turned her attention to the initiate priestess, now curious what she had begun to say.

"What was it you were saying when you came in? What was it that happened?" the high priestess asked. The initiate priestess wasn't quite sure how to answer the question. Before her sat a woman with a similar facial shape and skin coloring to the man she had bumped into. She had even declared herself to be from the same direction as the man. If the two of them were together, it would be an odd coincidence but also troublesome depending on how she spoke. But, unfortunately, all eyes were now upon her, and she felt compelled to speak.

"Well, I bumped into a man in the marketplace. Actually, he sort of knocked me down to the ground, but he helped me back up. It was an accident. Anyway, there was just something about him that caught my eye. I felt a strange sensation, perhaps an omen from the spirits," she said, leaving out all the important details that might give away who the man was. Aya'tar frowned, but she suspected that Isha'kau was holding back information for some unknown reason. She would pry that information from the initiate priestess after their guest had left.

☽ ☽ ☾

Imkanar finished adjusting his hooded cape and prepared to exit the room. He had been trapped in the small room for the entire day, hiding from the city where he was born and at the mercy of his companions. As the night approached, he desperately wanted something to eat. It was risky stepping out to obtain food and drink, but hunger and thirst were powerful motivators and beginning to win him over. The redhead had met up with the priestess Brig'dha as soon as she had returned, and the pair had left to discuss some important topic. At least, he had learned from Brig'dha that his beloved Aya'tar still lived and was apparently in good health. For now, that was enough. He would have to figure out what to do next, but first, he needed something to eat and drink.

☽ ☽ ☾

Ianmu stood by the drink merchant, clumsily lifting four clay pots full of fermented honey and fruit drink. Sar'Tawas certainly drank the stuff fast enough, and she was constantly sent to the merchant to trade for more. Fermented drinks were amazingly costly in trade, and only someone like Sar'Tawas could afford to consume them at such a rate. Besides simply being annoying, carrying four large clay pots was not an easy task, and she wobbled ever so slightly trying to hold them all in her arms at once. The night was almost upon her, and she wished to return with the pots before it became too dark to see.

"Do you have it, or do you need me to help you take them back to that grumpy old sow, bull?" asked the drink merchant with a laugh. Ianmu flashed a smile at the man, always ensuring that everybody believed that she was merely a foolish concubine. She didn't mind help, but she hated having to be helped, however tedious that distinction was. Feeling that she had finally gotten a handle on the weight, she turned to leave. Suddenly, one of the jugs leaned slightly, and the liquid inside sloshed, causing it to nearly fall. She compensated by adjusting her weight, which made the other jugs move in the opposite direction. That was it - she was going to either drop one jug and save three or drop three and save one. It all happened in a moment.

Ianmu cursed the wretched city of Isut'na in her mind as she watched the one jug slip from her arm and fall to the ground. Sar'Tawas would not take kindly to this though at least he seemed to fear her more than he used to. Watching her kill several men with only a dagger would have that effect. Suddenly, a man stepped forward out from the crowd and caught the jug before it hit the ground. He held the jug out without a word, allowing Ianmu to re-position the other three and take hold of the fourth. The man wore a woolen cloak and heavy face paint, making his identity difficult to discern. She felt like she had seen him before, but she couldn't quite place the face.

"Thank you. My master would be angry with me if I had broken that jar," she said in her mock naïve voice.

"It was no problem," the man said before turning and walking toward the drink merchant, himself. Ianmu turned to leave. As she walked toward her home, the man's voice continued to trouble her as well as his difficult-to-view face. Never one to forget a face and a voice, she pondered the oddly cloaked man. She had heard that voice and seen that face before, but where?

Ↄ ↄ Ↄ

The man came to stand before the drink merchant thinking back upon the face of the woman he had just helped. She was lovely though he hadn't gotten a very good look at her through his heavy cloak. Something about how she spoke and how she stood reminded him of someone... then it hit him, that was the woman-owned by Sar'Tawas... Ianmu, the concubine. He spat a curse of anger under his breath at having come so close to an agent of the very man who wished him dead.

ꝺ ꝺ ꝺ

Imkanar! You son of a jackal, you returned to the city, haven't you? I thank you for your help, but that won't stop me from killing you, she thought as she stepped into the building, having just realized who had helped her in the market. Surely, this was the work of the Goddess. The moment she entered, she placed the jugs upon the floor and dropped to her knees with her arms spread out wide in thanks to An'an. Sar'Tawas turned from what he was doing to gaze upon the extremely deadly "concubine" as she descended deep into some sort of prayer. He knew better than to interrupt a holy woman in communion, so he waited. She was oddly as intriguing as she was terrifying, but at least, she had gotten the drink.

ꝺ ꝺ ꝺ

"Each of you has seen Imkanar before. Each of you understands what it means when I say discretion, right?" Sar'Tawas asked a few days later while standing behind a large wheat storage building. Three men who worked the wheat fields stood before him. He had called upon them to meet him at this location as soon as he had decided what to do after hearing from Ianmu that the little bastard of a jackal, Imkanar, had returned. He had heard little from the men he had sent out to find the boy, but perhaps they had passed one another in the wilds. It didn't matter at this point. He would send these three men to either frighten the boy out of the city or to leave him dead in an alley.

Actually, Sar'Tawas hoped that Imkanar would leave the city and never return. He didn't really hate the boy, and he completely understood his love for the remarkable Aya'tar, but he was in the way and would have to disappear one way or the other. He had felt slightly guilty having sent men to kill the boy, a rash decision at the time. Deep down, he was

450

somewhat impressed that he had made it all the way back to the city alive. These three men were about as brutish as they came and were known around the city for getting into brawls. If anybody saw them fighting, it would be easy to explain away their actions. Most importantly, all three of them knew quite well what Sar'Tawas would do to them if they ever tried to implicate him in anything.

"Yeah, we hear you. We will hurt him a little bit and see if he leaves. If he doesn't get the point, we'll leave him someplace where they won't find him until he smells. We'll come to see you tomorrow for our payment," the lead thug recited. Sar'Tawas nodded and turned to leave. Ianmu stood for a few moments more, glaring at the three men. They had heard the rumors that this woman channeled the powers of a goddess and became one with a blade. They were more than a little unnerved by her glare, which was exactly what she wanted. While useful to a point, she would have to ask Sar'Tawas how these rumors were getting spread.

Ɔ Ɔ Ɔ

Imkanar sat on a bench-bed with a small piece of flax string carefully mending a tiny cut in the cloak he had been wearing. Brig'dha and Ember had left for the evening to walk together outside the city. It was strange living without having to work every single day, but for some reason, these two women had amassed enough material wealth to do just that. Sitting in several traveling packs over in the corner, they had the finest bolts of linen and literally thousands of beads of various types, obsidian pieces, and many other useful bobbles. What they had done to obtain this level of material wealth was beyond Imkanar's understanding.

They had been in the city for several days, and Brig'dha had traveled to meet Aya'tar on more than one occasion. It seemed that Brig'dha had learned some piece of information that she had not shared with Imkanar. Her continued assurances that the priestess was in good health and even describing her and the initiate priestess had calmed his suspicions, but eventually, he had cornered the woman demanding to know what other information she had. Brig'dha and Ember had left that evening to speak, and they had assured him that they would explain everything when they returned. Imkanar hated secrets, and he hated waiting.

On the bench next to him, Mew, the cat, slept in a bundle on a pile of deerskins. He would leave the building sometimes late at night when the population of dogs seemed to be the least visible, but he would remain inside during the day. On the floor next to the bench was a small clay dish of water and the remnants of something from their dinner the night before. Lazily, he lifted his ears and pointed them towards the door. It was as though he heard something. Imkanar watched the cat for a few moments assuming that he had heard someone walk by, perhaps a dog. He paused to consider the possibility that Ember was some sort of warrior for hire. It would explain her weapons, material wealth, and brazen attitude.

He had heard of men who would sell their skills with death to the highest bidder. Such men would kill whoever needed to be killed and protect whatever needed to be protected. Sometimes they would be brought along with trade caravans to guard against raids. He couldn't wrap his mind around the idea of the beautiful redhead being one of these people. A woman trading beads for blood? It didn't seem logical to him. It wasn't that Imkanar believed that women were incapable. His own lover ruled the entire city. It was just that women were always seen in his culture as the creators of life, not the takers. He suspected that this stereotype was more cultural than anything else. Nevertheless, she couldn't be all that bad at it, with the number of beads and flint that she possessed. Mew stood, stretched, and then began sniffing the air, cautiously.

What interested him the most were the beautiful metallic works around their necks and wrists. He had never seen anything crafted quite so well, and from gold and copper, no less. Imkanar wondered just how hot fire would have to be to melt something like...

"Well, well well, if it's not the little boy back from the wilds," said Arhar, the thug, as he pushed open the leather door and stepped heavily into the room with his two accomplices behind him. Mew hissed, fearful of the men. Each of the three men carried a large war club. There was no confusion about their intentions. These men had come for blood. Imkanar stood and grabbed a small flint knife from the table. He wasn't sure he could defeat three men, but he would cut one of them pretty good before he fell.

"Looks like he's got some fight in him," laughed Tarapar, the thug. He stepped forward, pushing aside Arhar, with his club in hand and savoring the moment. More so than either of the other two men, Tarapar loved violence. This wasn't just a way to keep himself fed. It was a lifestyle.

"She's too pretty for you. Sar'Tawas will show her what a real man looks like... maybe give her another child... maybe dispose of the two you already made. Those are yours, right?" Tarapar taunted. Imkanar was suddenly struck as though by a war club. Children, Aya'tar had children?

This could not be. For a moment, Imkanar merely stood contemplating the words he had just heard. The men paused for a moment seeing that the news was unexpected and relishing Imkanar's look of confusion.

"She has children? How many, are they okay?" he asked, so shocked by their statement that he forgot that they had come to kill him. He stepped backward, almost dropping the knife. It all made sense. That must have had something to do with why she had sent him away. She did not fear only for his life but also for the children. His not being there would avoid complicating things even more. This must have been the secret that Brig'dha had learned but feared telling him. He was angry at the priestess, and he would have likely lashed out at her had this occurred many moons before. In all the time he had spent with the tribe to the Northwest, he had come to ponder the severity of Aya'tar's situation, the true nuance of it all. Perhaps that was why he was not immediately angry at Brig'dha and Ember for withholding this information.

"You can ask those questions to the Goddess herself in just a few moments. Or perhaps your wicked deeds against the city will see your spirit to oblivion. Either way, you don't need to know any of that information in this world. Well, boys, it looks like he rejected our polite request to leave. So now we have to leave him in a ditch," Arhar said with a laugh, stepping forward with his club. He paused for a moment as though one last jab had come to mind.

"Oh, I'll tell you one last thing… There will likely be a wedding soon, and Sar'Tawas will be taking your woman," he said with a vicious smile. The three men began to advance when suddenly a clay vessel smashed over Tarapar's head, spraying melted fat lamp oil all over all the three men. They rounded to find an enraged-looking redhead painted from head to toe in striped body paint and wearing jewelry fitting a city's leader standing behind them. She held a small clamshell lamp with a little flame flickering just above its edge in her right hand. Two men began to menace the woman holding their clubs, ready to strike her down, when their leader suddenly threw his hands out wide, stopping both of them.

"Wait, she holds fire!" he yelled.

"I didn't think you were that smart. All I have to do is touch this flame to your oily skin, and the fire will do my work for me. Do you think it will hurt?" Ember asked in a teasing tone. She held the lamp out tauntingly though she was quite willing to let her dagger deal with these three fools. People like this could be dangerous to the unskilled, but Ember was quick and dexterous, and she had fought bigger men.

"I'll stand to the side now, and all three of you are going to walk out the door and leave. If you even flinch, I might just become startled and drop my lamp on your face," she said with a laugh, making a mock gesture of startled fear. Standing behind her, Brig'dha glared at the men in anger. She had just as much hatred for these sorts of bullies as Ember, but she would never have done something quite so brash. Worse, Ember had broken the entire clay vessel of oil which had cost a large obsidian piece, large enough to make a small knife, and hundreds of burin tools. Brig'dha rolled her eyes at the loss. The only thing Ember could do faster than obtain rare items was lose them.

"You won't live through another..." began one of the men, but Ember suddenly thrust the lamp at him, causing the man to step back and nearly fall on the slippery oil.

"Yeah, yeah, I know. All three of you want to kill me now, and I feel so bad for you. Now run away like little children before I set you on fire," she said mockingly. She wished she could kick dirt at them as they left, but regrettably, sandals made kicking tough. Otherwise, she had to admit they were very loose and comfortable on the feet. Ember continued to contemplate sandals as the three men rushed past her, cursing under their breaths and disappearing into the slowly darkening night.

"Are you all right?" Ember asked, stepping into the room to ensure the men hadn't harmed Imkanar. Brig'dha just about knocked everyone over, rushing in to check on her cat.

"Are you all right, Mew! They did not harm you, did they? Come to mother!" she said in her native tongue, frantically grabbing the cat and holding him tightly. Everyone turned for just a moment to watch the scene. Ember laughed, and Imkanar glared, exasperated. He had nearly been killed by three men, and words could not express his thanks to the reckless redhead. She had sacrificed a valuable container of lamp oil and placed herself in danger to save him. More impressively, she had gotten rid of the men without ever pulling her weapon. If she truly were some kind of warrior for hire, he had no doubt she was the best. Yet he had bigger troubles to worry about... Aya'tar had given birth to children.

ɔ ɔ ɔ
ɔ ɔ ɔ

Aethen stood under the nearly moonless night staring at the stars above. He was less interested in what stars actually were than Ember, but he certainly appreciated their beauty. The day had been quite warm, but the night was becoming cooler as the Sun disappeared. He now understood why most people wore so little and used layers, the climate being simply too warm for the humid environment. His skin glistened with sweat, water lost through the heat. Luckily, he had seen a well not far from where he now stood. It would do for him to get a good drink of cool water before returning to the building for sleep.

He had spent the last few days trying to find the beautiful, brown-eyed woman he had knocked over. He had seen many of the same people repeatedly, but never that woman. Something about her struck him as different from the farmers and crafters. She was more elegant and had carried herself well. He would stay here for as many days as it took to find her once more. Deep down, he was sure that a woman as striking as she would already have a strong and important husband. Perhaps that was the reason she had run off instead of introducing herself. He expected to be let down, expected to fail, but he would continue to search. A hunter didn't give up so easily.

As he stepped around the corner, he suddenly froze at the sight before him. A woman stood off to the side behind a large stack of clay pots, lazily cleaning herself from a small bowl of water and using a drying stick to scrape the excess water from her skin. Her back was to him, and she did not appear to have heard him. Aethen felt slightly awkward approaching the woman as she privately cleaned, though she was fully dressed wearing a loincloth. This was slightly more covering than the apron garments so many women wore which didn't even cover their buttocks, not to mention the large numbers of wholly nude men working in the hot Sun he had seen each day. Still, the mood felt private, so he hesitated. The woman had long black hair reaching to the small of her back. Her hair reminded Aethen of the woman he had been looking for though he had seen other women with similarly long hair. Of course, it was hard to make out the details in the low light.

He stepped forward, making enough noise with his footfalls that the woman apparently heard him as she paused for a moment and then continued washing. Aethen turned his gaze away from her not just out of respect but out of the memory of the scolding he had given Kel over having ogled a woman in the village they had stayed in while waiting to find Ember. He stepped forward and lowered a water pot on a short braided cord into the well and then lifted it up, feeling the weight of the water. In his peripheral vision, he could feel that the woman had glanced at him several times, but he had already looked at her, so he kept his eyes on what he was doing out of respect. If she spoke to him, perhaps he could ask her if she had any idea who the woman he sought was. Her beautiful scarification marks were quite distinctive, which would help.

The mineral-flavored water was cool as he hungrily drank his fill. Dropping the pot once more into the well, he again filled it with water. As he removed the pot from the well, he turned to see the woman standing beside him, suddenly turning her head away. He smiled, finding it amusing. Playing this little game was fun, and it made the evening more pleasurable, even if it never went anywhere. Aethen poured the contents of the pot over top of his head, letting the water drain from him and wash the sweat free. He dropped the pot back into the well to get more water a moment later.

He removed the pot from the well once more and poured it over his head, trying his best not to look at the woman that he knew was standing beside him cleaning. He placed the pot down and shook the hair out of his eyes. He would turn now and politely introduce himself, lest he seem rude. Aethen rubbed the water from his eyes and turned to find the woman facing him. It took him only a moment to realize that this was the same woman he had been looking for, the brown-eyed woman. He stood before her, dripping with water and unable to look away from her eyes.

She began to smile once more the same way she had the day she had first met him. Something about his stunned look seemed humorous to her. She casually glanced down and then back up again, noting the man's body was completely soaked with water, but at least, that meant the sweat was washed away. His skin was much darker than hers and tanned, his face was shaped slightly different from the people of Isut'na, and he had long dark hair with the strangest colored gray eyes she had ever seen. He truly was an exotic man from the North, and she was just as enchanted by him as he seemed to be with her. Perhaps it was time that she answered his question. She had left before simply because she didn't know what to say at the time as he had caught her off guard.

"Ih-soot San-nup ra-mu-man Ish-aah-kah-oo," she said, slowly and with a smile. Aethen looked back at her, unsure of what the words had meant. He had learned enough of their language that the words sounded familiar, but perhaps it was the slow speed at which she had enunciated them. She smiled, seemingly finding his lack of understanding amusing.

"What does that mean?" he asked, never once letting his eyes leave hers. She continued to smile back at him, though she had trouble keeping her eye contact, being shy in his presence.

"It is my name and my title. Isut'Sanup'ramu'man Isha'kau. You may call me Isha'kau. Your name is Aethen, right?" He nodded his head.

She was thoroughly pleased with how much she had put him on the spot, a welcome change from how awkward she felt a few days before. Unexpectedly, Aethen reached his hand into his traveling bag and pulled from it a necklace made from many of the beautiful shells similar to the one which hung around his neck. The lesser priestess stared at the beautiful shell necklace in amazement. Aethen stepped forward, abruptly holding out the necklace and offering to place it around her neck. Isha'kau looked back at him, confused and finding herself breathing more deeply. Seeing no signs that she rejected the gift, Aethen reached forward and gingerly placed the necklace around her neck, fastening the ends with a simple knot.

Isha'kau looked down at the beautiful item as it hung across her chest. She thought that she had stunned him, but it was he who had, in fact, stunned her once more. She looked up at the man slightly in shock. A gift of an exotic shell necklace such as this was nothing simple, nor anything less than a major trade. It was a glorious gift, and she felt the need to repay him in some way. She had nothing on her to give in the way of a gift, but one thing came to mind.

She stepped forwards and embraced the young hunter. She could feel his beautiful shell necklace pressing tightly against her chest as his warm, soft skin pressed firmly against her breasts. He was taller than her and built solidly, yet his eyes conveyed a gentleness. He looked down and into her eyes and felt a strange sinking sensation, an overwhelming anticipation. What was going on here? What might happen? She released him and danced backward, suddenly, quickly turning and snatching her drying stick from the well. She hurriedly stepped away and began to head off into the city, pausing for a moment to look back with a smile.

"Good night Aethen of the North, and thank you for the necklace. It's beautiful. When I see you again, you can tell me about where you're from," she said in a playful tone and then disappeared into the darkness. Aethen might as well have been hit over the head with a war club. He leaned against the side of the building and savored the feelings that surged throughout his body, anticipation, exhilaration, and even arousal. He could still feel her warm body pressed against him. For a while, he just stood there remembering how she felt, how she smelled, and those beautiful brown eyes.

ɔ ɔ ɔ

Imkanar sat upon one of the bench beds with his hands on the sides of his head, deep in thought. Men being sent to kill him was one thing, but what really upset him was that Aya'tar had children but had not even told him before he left. If that was not bad enough, she would become married to Sar'Tawas. He had not been gone but so many moons. She would likely have been pregnant at the same time that she had asked him to leave. She had lain with him that night in passion, knowing full well that she carried their children.

"Please be gentle," she had said, and now he understood why. Part of him wanted to explode in anger, but another part of him wondered if perhaps there was more in play than he understood, risks that Aya'tar knew and that he had not even suspected.

In just those few moons, Imkanar had changed from a young man who would have lashed out in anger and reacted with his emotions rather than thinking through a problem, into a more responsible person who considered the possibility that there might be more going on than he understood. All those long moons of introspection and constant contemplation had helped him tame himself. He would approach the situation as cool-headed as he could. Unfortunately, deep down, there was a slowly simmering anger threatening to burst forth.

He had been pleased with himself at keeping a cool head as Brig'dha profusely apologized for having not mentioned the children to him before now. Breaking the news of the children had seemed more touchy of a subject than she had known how to approach on her own. She eventually told Ember, but she had no idea how to tell him, either. They had both decided that they would sit down with him that very night and give him the news, but the armed men had beaten them to it. He had been mad at Brig'dha for not mentioning it, but he could understand how such news might be a difficult topic to broach. The sheer shock of having two healthy babies, a boy, and a girl, was so overpowering that it blew away any anger he might have had.

"I'm sure she did it in the best interests of the children," Ember said, sitting down beside the troubled Imkanar. Brig'dha sat on the floor by the door, mopping up the remaining oil with dried grass. The oil-drenched grass could be squeezed to partly recover the oil, and the grass itself could be used later on to burn, oil being far too valuable to be left on the floor, though, luckily, it was fat oil and not precious nut oil. Not far behind her, Mew, the cat, had fallen back asleep. His ability to switch between content slumber and utter terror, then returning once again to content slumber, always perplexed everybody. Ember was quite convinced that he was not the brightest, though he was oddly pleasurable to pet.

"I just wish that she had told me. Are you sure that they are healthy?" he asked?

"I saw a girl and a boy happily suckling. They looked to be in good health," Brig'dha answered from across the room. Ember took hold of one of his hands and held it tightly to comfort him. She felt sorry for the man, especially considering that children were involved. As she held his hand, he became more and more agitated. He was beginning to suspect that all of this was simply his fault for reaching higher than a man of his low birth had any right to reach.

"We will come up with some plan to get you back together with the priestess. All we have to do..." Ember was interrupted as Imkanar suddenly stood, filled with anger, his emotions shifting rapidly. He spun around and pointed his finger at Ember, his composure finally having been lost.

"We have nothing to do! I am lowborn and can never be with her! Sar'Tawas can protect her and the children, which is all that matters!" he yelled with a faint glint of wetness in his eyes. He stormed to the other side of the room and slammed his hand into the wall, his anger slowly fading to be replaced by sorrow.

"There must be some way, some rule that would let you be with the priestess," said Ember. The young man walked around the room for a few moments shaking his head before finally coming to a stop next to Brig'dha.

"The only way would be for me to be adopted by an influential family and to live with them for at least several harvests, or for the Goddess herself to approve of our union," he said, the second part of his sentence being more sarcasm than a real plan. For a short time, no one said anything. Ember began to think of a radical plot, something so brazen that it might just work.

"How was the priestess? How was Aya'tar? Was she okay?" he asked for perhaps the tenth time. Deep down, he realized that if he truly trusted and loved Aya'tar, he had to assume that she had his best interests and those of the babies at heart when she had deceived him. She may have been wrong to lie, but truly it was the thought that counted. She simply understood more of the complexities of the city than he did. It was hard for the proud many to admit that, but he knew it was true. Brig'dha looked up with a handful of oily grass and a rosy smile on her face. She was happy that Imkanar was finally calming down.

"She seemed to be quite healthy. When I met her, she was lying on a bed of furs nursing the babies. I also met somebody caring for her and helping her with day-to-day tasks. It was a younger woman."

"She has two assistants, Isha'kau and Hullamu. They are both about your age, initiate priestesses," Imkanar mumbled. Brig'dha was now thoroughly confused.

"Hullamu… That is the name of one of the children, I think." Brig'dha had not been able to remember the two children's names as she only heard them one time until that moment. As she thought about it, their names came back to her, "Yes, that's right. The girl is called Hullamu, and the boy is called Ikanar," she said. Imkanar knelt down beside her, suddenly alarmed. Behind them, Ember continued to think carefully about some quickly forming plan, ignoring the growing drama.

"Ikanar is the male form of the name of one of the brightest stars in the sky, Ikana, it's where my name comes from, too. But Hullamu is the name of her assistant. It's considered bad luck to name someone after a living person you know, but a great honor to name someone after a person who has died. I hope nothing has happened to Isha'kau or Hullamu. This worries me even more. Tomorrow, would you return to the temple to learn more of what has happened?" he asked, slightly calming at hearing the names of his children.

"Of course. I will go to visit the priestess as a concerned fellow priestess. I'm not as good at speaking to people as Ember, but I think she will continue to tell me things," Brig'dha said, piling the oily grass into a clay pot. Imkanar sat back, speaking the names of his children over and over in his mind. He was such a wash of emotions that his mental state could not be accurately described. Everything was suddenly interrupted when Ember burst to her feet, pointing her finger into the air.

"I have it! I have a plan to get you two back together. We don't need to stop the wedding, we simply need to wait for it to happen, and that's when we make our move..." Brig'dha sighed. This was an Ember plan – everyone would somehow come to the brink of death and then be saved at the last moment. Her lover never made a plan that didn't dance on the edge of a blade, so she began chanting prayers to the gods for luck.

☽ ☽ ☽

Over the next tenday, Brig'dha spent a short time each day in the temple of Isut learning about the local gods while subtly learning more about the priestess Aya'tar. The high priestess told her the story of how her initiate priestesses Hullamu and Isha'kau had saved her life when she was attacked by a man who broke into the temple attempting to kill her. The high priestess believed that this might have been an attempt on her life for political reasons though she was never able to link the killer to anyone who would have wished her dead.

Each day Brig'dha would return and inform Imkanar of what she had learned. The notion that his beloved Aya'tar had come so close to death and only barely survived, all-the-while pregnant with their children, only served to further horrify the already exasperated man. Worse, it seemed that the most powerful man in the city knew of Imkanar's presence and wanted him dead. There had been no attacks since the first one, but everyone had remained on the lookout.

If Imkanar's troubles were not by themselves enough, there was Ember's plan. She had proposed that Imkanar wait until the upcoming wedding and then challenge the man who would marry Aya'tar for her hand. Even as she had said it, Ember held her hands together, staring at the ceiling as though she were surrounded by beautiful motes of romance. Upon opening her eyes, she discovered a room full of detracting glares instead. No one could deny that the plan had a chance of success, nor how romantic such a challenge might be. The problem was the actual fight itself.

Ember had suspected that Imkanar could easily best the elderly Sar'Tawas. The man was not in bad shape for his age, but there was simply no way that he could outperform the younger copper worker. But there was a problem with this plan. According to Imkanar, Sar'Tawas could ask someone else to fight in his place, given his age. This was the right of any middle-aged combatant, over 25 harvests of age, though Imkanar had always suspected that rulers had created the rule simply to excuse themselves honorably from combat.

As though the prospect of fighting an unknown stand-in warrior for Sar'Tawas wasn't already bad enough, Brig'dha had learned that a second suitor was attempting to woo the high priestess. A man named Ishayan. If what she had heard was true, he was the son of the ruler of the city of Nara'kit. He would likely be skilled with weapons and not easy to defeat. He had not publicly announced any formal intention to marry Aya'tar, but spending a day in her presence had convinced Brig'dha that this was his plan, as the annoying Ishayan was a common source of complaint from the priestess.

Brig'dha was just glad that she had been able to get so close to the priestess. So many in the city would like to spend their day with somebody so important, but Brig'dha benefited from being exotic. She came from a distant land with amazing stories to tell. Unfortunately, socializing was not something she enjoyed, and she found each visit quite stressful. Luckily, the dark temple was quiet, allowing her senses to calm, their easy overstimulation made worse by the stress.

Brig'dha didn't feel as though she were misleading the priestess as she was serving her best interests, deep down. If Imkanar was believed, she was doing the woman a great favor. Either way, speaking each day to Aya'tar had brought up many unfortunate downsides to Ember's plan. As usual, none of these points seemed to matter to Ember, who had a counterargument for everything. And so Imkanar found himself spending each day fighting with Aethen or Ember one-on-one using sticks. He wasn't sure that this would work, but it was the only plan they had... As long as it didn't get him killed.

A tenday after the plan had been suggested, the young copper worker stood with a small stick in his hand, which was meant to resemble a dagger, contemplating just how badly he was likely outmatched and all the interesting ways he could be killed. Imkanar sighed as he again thought of the downsides of their plan. Distracted as he was, he didn't notice Ember diving in with her small wooden stick. She jabbed him right in the abdomen and then danced away before he could do anything. Looking down, he saw that he now had a long red mark across his lower stomach just above the hip. He sighed again.

"Don't worry, that probably wouldn't kill you... Well, maybe it would. Lucky for you, this is just a stick. You need to pay attention," she said, standing back and stretching.

"You could have just a few days or perhaps a full harvest to train. We don't know. I bet you at tomorrow's big announcement we will find out... and you're going to stay right here when we go!" Ember said, referring to a major announcement that was to take place at midday, the next day. Several times the group had discussed the prospects of Imkanar sneaking into the announcement, but in all likelihood, whatever was said would pertain to the high priestess. He would simply be goaded into saying something, or worse, standing up and acknowledging himself publicly.

"I've already agreed that I will stay here. But you must tell me everything that is said and hold nothing back from me. I understand why you did not tell me things in the past, but that must not happen again," he said roughly. He stood back quickly, calming down. He shouldn't be so hard on his three friends. They supported him as no one else had, or would, and he found it so difficult to believe that their only reason was that of friendship and interest. He had never met people like this. Ember stood there holding her "knife" and peeling the bark from it as she waited for the man to finish.

"I just want to thank you again. Without you, I wouldn't even have this tiny bit of hope that I do have... Let's continue," he said, lifting his stick. Ember looked back at him with a wide smile. She was glad to see that he was beginning to come around.

"Okay, when I stab at you, try blocking my hand at the wrist and then rush at me before I can react," she said, hoping her own meager dagger skills would suffice.

☽ ☽ ☽

The next day Ember, Brig'dha, and Aethen stood in the middle of the large ceremonial area just in front of the temple, waiting for the high priestess to make her announcement. According to Brig'dha, she had recuperated from her childbirth and could freely walk around, though she never seemed to leave the temple, as far as Brig'dha could tell. The sad part was that she used to be a talented dancer, but the sorrows of her predicament, as well as her pregnancy, had kept her stationary for almost a full harvest. She hoped that the high priestess could marry Imkanar and dance again as she used to, as she would love to see the high priestess dancing.

While Brig'dha lamented the priestess' unwillingness to dance, Ember decided to have a little fun with Aethen. She had seen him talking with a beautiful woman with long brown hair and dark brown eyes the night before. Ember had stepped out of the building to take care of a personal matter and had caught sight of the two speaking to one another not far away near the well. She had even seen the necklace around the woman's neck, the very one that Aethen had traded for. She randomly wacked Aethen in the shoulder to get his attention.

"Hey, that woman I saw you with last night..." Aethen turned to regard his friend with a skeptically raised eyebrow. At first, he said nothing, but it only took him a moment to realize that Ember somehow knew. Sometimes he wondered if she stalked him like some kind of predator as she always seemed to know all his secrets. He could imagine her covered in dark warpaint and hiding on top of a building, looking down and watching his every move. Looking back at her, she regarded him with a catty smile. Aethen rolled his eyes.

"Yeah, what about her?" he asked defensively.

"She's beautiful. Do you like her?"

"I do. I have met with her now several times, and we have talked," he said plainly.

"Wow, such detail... But really, is she the one?" Ember asked, bumping into Aethen with her shoulder playfully. Aethen looked back, frowning.

"I would like her to be, but I don't really know much about her. I know her name, but I don't know what she does each day, nor do I know where she lives."

"Well, what's her name?" Ember asked, now totally focused on dragging all details out of the man. Brig'dha stood behind Ember, listening casually to their conversation. Aethen thought for a few moments as though trying to recall the woman's name. In reality, it wasn't her name that was the problem, but her long title.

"Her full name and title are, Isut'Senep-ra... um, raymo-men Ishaakahoo. Something like that. Well, the important part is Ishaakahoo. Her actual name is Ishaakahoo. The rest is some sort of title." Ember's eyes widened upon hearing the title. Having the largest vocabulary of the True Southern words of anyone in the group, Ember believed that she understood what those words meant. Aethen had murderously butchered the woman's formal title, Isut'Sanup'ramu'man. At that very moment, high priestess Aya'tar and her initiate priestess Isha'kau stepped forward onto the temple's roof overlooking all the people, each one of them carrying one of the two children.

"Aethen, do you realize what that title means? Isut'Sanup'ramu'man means 'Lesser Priestess vessel of goddess Isut'... that means that your girlfriend is..." but she was cut off as Aethen threw his arm out pointing at the woman standing beside high priestess Aya'tar.

"There she is! She's standing right beside the high priestess! I wonder what she's doing there?" Both Ember and Brig'dha glared incredulously at the man. Somehow, he had found and become romantically involved with the ruler of the city's only handmaiden. Ember facepalmed while Brig'dha shook her head.

"Aethen, it's time you invited your new girlfriend over for an evening meal... I insist," Ember said. The discussion was suddenly ended as Aya'tar began to speak loudly for all to hear. She stood proudly atop the temple, wearing a skirt made entirely of layered dark feathers, a pair of woven reed sandals, and a feathered headdress. Her chest was adorned with dozens of necklaces. She carried one of her babies in her arms while Isha'kau held the other firmly.

"People of Isut'na, the chosen of the Goddess – I stand before you with not one, but two children. I am proof that Isut'na is still favored by the Goddess. I understand that many of you had worried that my family line had ended, but now you see that it has not. However, the Elder Council still worries that I am too young and inexperienced to lead the city. I do not believe this, but I do not wish to risk all of you on my pride. To this end, I have decided to take a man as my husband, a man who will become my equal, a fellow ruler of the city," she concluded.

She placed the baby Hullamu against her breast to suckle. The suckling child underscored her claim to be in the Goddess' grace. It was widely known that the milk from a mother was a gift from the Goddess. She proudly stood before nearly 2000 people and let the baby have its fill and letting the people have theirs. Seeing the woman standing before everyone feeding her child and addressing the entire city filled her people with a sense of calm. Many of their doubts at her inner strength melted away at that simple gesture. After a few moments, it became time to answer the most important question on everyone's mind, who would the man be.

"All of you are probably now wondering which man I will marry." Ember and Brig'dha nodded their heads, all eyes, and ears on the priestess. "Our rules say that I cannot marry the father of these two children as he is not of high birth," she said, pausing for a moment to take a deep breath and maintain her composure. That was one of the hardest parts of the entire speech. Aya'tar closed her eyes for a moment and banished all thoughts of Imkanar before continuing. It was at this time that Ember was glad that she had convinced Imkanar to remain in the building. She was pretty sure that he would have lost his composure at her words.

"I will marry when next the Moon rises to at least half brightness, which for those of you who do not observe the Moon, will be in three tendays time. On that day, the man I will marry is Dunu'lekal'Ishayan, eldest son of the ruler of the city of Nara'Kit, the Great An'sankup'Anteanar." She waited as the gasps and comments continued for a short time. Truly, no one had expected such an announcement, Sar'Tawas being the most logical candidate of anyone dwelling within the city. Somewhere off in the crowd, Sar'Tawas spit his drink out of his mouth and nearly choked as he heard the words.

"Ishayan has met with me many times since his arrival, and we have come to an understanding between our two cities. The union between us is a union between Nara'kit and Isut'na. We are the largest trading cities within many tendays in each direction, north or south. The union between our cities would be an end to any chance of war and bring an increase in our trade. Ishayan has agreed to adopt both of my children as his own upon our marriage, and the succession of the city will follow my children first. I hope all of you will celebrate with me in three tendays time. Thank you for standing by me when everything seemed against us," she concluded, turning and slowly walking back to the ladder which led into the temple. Everyone turned to look at each other, stunned by the news.

"Aeeya…" Ember whispered as Brig'dha frowned.

"Indeed," Aethen agreed.

CHAPTER TWENTY FIVE

YOU HAVE TO DEFEAT ME!

Humanity has always been obsessed with detecting and analyzing signs and portents of future events. Though often religious in nature, numerous methods for divining truth, fate, and the will of gods have been used by humanity as a tool to craft an uncompromising destiny out of the chaos of life. It is likely our brains, evolved over millions of years to be pattern-seeking, are the real source of our portents. In ancient times, unusual events, such as comets and meteorites, as well as more mundane but well-timed events, such as a bird landing before you or the howl of a wolf, might be interpreted as signs. Ember lives in a time when the world is magical, and the mechanisms which govern it are unknown to humanity. People of this time must watch their environment and simply guess what is to come. Before we pass judgment upon their divinations, we must first consider the luxury that is science.

"This cannot be! Damn that son of a jackal! Curse his bones to eternity!" Sar'Tawas burst into his building and threw a wooden frame, used to dry herbs, onto its side. He proceeded to knock over one object after another, smashing jars and ripping hanging herbs from the walls. Ianmu stood by the door, not wanting to get too closely involved with the incensed man. She, too, was enraged at the proclamation. If her damn fool brother married the priestess, she would be back at square one. Ishayan was a formidable fighter in his own right and nearly as devious as she. If he took control of the city, she would have virtually no chance. Suddenly, Sar'Tawas had the look of insight.

"Wait a moment. There's still one way we can salvage this!" Sar'Tawas spat from his mouth as he rushed forward and grabbed Ianmu by the arm, a little more roughly than he had intended. Given her desperate need for a solution, she ignored her initial urge to slice his throat open with her flint knife. Ianmu was not in the mood to play silly concubine today. Sar'Tawas saw the sudden flash of rage in her eyes and let go, standing back. He had not forgotten how easily she had dispatched those three men not that long before. Worse, she stood beside a small altar to Isut and Gunar, near the door. Such close proximity to the gods could make things worse.

"If we wait until the wedding, I can come forward in my capacity as one of the elders and directly challenge Ishayan to single combat for her hand in marriage. If he refuses, he will be dishonored, and the priestess will likely break off her wedding!" he said, a devious smile forming. Ianmu bent forwards and picked up a clay vessel full of fermented honey drink to take a sip. Taking a long and deep swig of the pricey beverage, she glared at Sar'Tawas as though he were a fool.

"And if he accepts your offer for combat, he will eviscerate you like a newborn lamb for the slaughter. This clay pot of drink will last longer in my hands than you would last before his blade," she said with a sardonic laugh before taking another deep swig of the drink. Sar'Tawas frowned, still finding the notion of his "concubine" making herself so comfortably at home a little unsavory, but he wasn't about to stop her.

"That is the part where you come in. By our laws, anyone over the age of 25 harvests may call upon a champion to take their place in any formal combat. So often, our leaders are not young and not in the best of health, so a champion is often needed. You will be my champion," he said with a smile. Ianmu coughed her next swig of drink onto the floor, taking a few moments to gain composure. She glared at the old man with a stupefied look, both impressed by his cunning plan and yet also furious that he would volunteer her for such a dangerous task. On the other hand, this was likely the only way to fulfill An'an's will.

ɔ ɔ ɔ

"The plan is absolutely deadly! This Ishayan guy is likely to be an excellent fighter. He will kill Imkanar before he lands a single hit!" argued Brig'dha, pacing back and forth through the room. Imkanar had been defeated yet again by Ember and in a very short time. It had been a tenday since they had started training, and the man had made very little progress. As skilled as he was with copper, he simply was not a very good fighter. Imkanar looked up at the two women from the floor where he sat, having just been thrown there by Ember as she easily blocked his slow and obvious strike. He had a feeling that he knew what the women spoke of, even though they did so in some unknown language.

"It doesn't matter. If I don't win back Aya'tar, I would rather not live. As long as she lives and the children are safe, that is all that actually matters," Imkanar said valiantly. Ember was touched by the sentiment, but she was beginning to agree with Brig'dha. It seemed at this point that nothing would prevent him from fighting, but it also appeared that nothing would prevent him from dying. Ember was beginning to feel very guilty for having even suggested the idea.

"If you fight against the man like that, you certainly won't live," she said.

"Have you no faith in the training that you've given me?" Ember frowned at the statement. It was true that she had been training the man, but she was no expert fighter. Most of the time, she felt that luck had played a greater role in her survival than any combat skills.

"I'm not an expert with the dagger. I have just used mine many times. I think you value my training too highly," she said, sitting down and taking a sip of water. Next to her, Mew, the cat, sat purring, having just recently stolen some food to eat.

"The goddess Isut filled Aya'tar, and the god Gunar filled me on the night that the seeds of our children were sown. The gods will not fail me. I will call out Imkanar upon their wedding day and challenge him. There is no other way!" the young copper worker said with finality. Brig'dha sighed with worry while Ember sat back, pondering a possible alternative solution. One extremely outlandish idea came to mind, but even Ember thought it might be too far. She smiled as the details started to fill in. For the first part of the plan, Aethen would need to employ the woman's skills he was now attempting to court. For the second part... well, she would have to keep that to herself until she was sure that it was a smart move. *Maybe the gods do favor you... they surely keep giving me odd but great plans!* She thought.

Ↄ Ↄ Ↄ

That evening, Aethen wandered around the courtyard near the temple, looking for Isha'kau. There was a strange smell in the air, the smell of a dead animal. He assumed some mouse or bird had died in one of the alleys. Such smells could be found in a forest, but he had not realized that they might exist in cities as well. It would likely soon attract carrion eaters, such as vultures and rats. It was an unpleasant odor, so he quickly left the area where he was standing and began to walk around the temple building toward the ladder, which headed up to the roof, hoping that he might encounter her.

He had been interested in meeting up with the initiate priestess all day to give her the rest of the gifts he had traded for in the town where he and his group had spent the cold season. Giving her the necklace had been an impulse, but giving her the rest of the ensemble now seemed proper.

He had been seeing the woman for a moon. In that short period, they had become close, often meeting in the evening as she came to the well to clean and even a few times near the temple for an evening meal.

He knew it was fast, but somehow, he had the feeling that she was the one. He knew of men who courted women for multiple harvests or moved from one love interest to the next before finally settling, but something about the priestess felt special to him. He was surer each day that she was the one, and most importantly, it seemed as though she felt similarly about him. That made what he was about to do feel slightly wrong, as well as risky. He was to inform the priestess of Imkanar's wish to challenge Ishayan during the wedding. It was Ember's hope that she could help even the odds.

At first, Aethen had objected to telling Isha'kau for fear that it might complicate the situation, but Ember assured him that the priestess was likely skilled in the art of being discreet. It was Ember's hope that Isha'kau might be able to give Imkanar a fighting chance when he challenged Ishayan at the wedding. According to the reckless redhead, a person could be made ill if certain uncooked bits from an animal were deposited within his food or drink. The idea offended Aethen as being dishonorable, as well as nasty. Unfortunately, Ember and Brig'dha would hear nothing of such prideful dilemmas. As far as they were concerned, true love was more important than any pride, and all was apparently fair in such scenarios.

Isha'kau had declined his invitation to meet with his friends for an evening meal, necessitating Aethen's current search. For some reason, she seemed unwilling to venture too far from the priestess, though he suspected the attack upon her and the death of the other temple priestess might have something to do with it. In fact, she never seemed to be willing to leave the temple or the high priestess' side for very long. He hoped to find her soon, as the wedding was scheduled to occur in the coming morning, so there wasn't much time left. He passed by a group of men playing a game where they tossed wet rolled grass balls against a painted target, the water leaving a mark, and continued his search.

It was not long before he found Isha'kau standing by a ladder leading up to the temple roof and inspecting a clay dish full of cracked acorns, perhaps part of the night's meal being prepared. For a few moments, he stood just out of her sight, watching. He knew that staring was not very appropriate, but she was simply beautiful to him. After a few short moments, he began to feel awkward and cleared his throat, causing her to turn. She smiled upon seeing the exotic northerner with his strangely darkly tanned skin and more rustic body paint. Isha'kau stood wearing a bark fiber apron and a pair of worn sandals, as well as a beautiful cowry necklace adorning her neck. Aethen could not help but feel guilty once more.

"I'm sorry that I did not come to see you today. Aya'tar has been depressed all morning with the coming wedding, and I've been doing my best to keep her happy. Will you be attending the wedding tomorrow?" she asked, apparently slightly depressed herself. Aethen took a deep breath, worried over how he would approach his task but unwilling to back down from the challenge.

"I've come to tell you something of great importance. It's about the wedding..." he said cryptically. Isha'kau stepped forward with a smile. She assumed that the exotic northerner had some concern over the ceremony. Perhaps his people did not wed? It seemed that Aethen was extremely confused and worried about the upcoming event. She found this reaction adorable and did her best not to smile at his frustration. As she came to stand before him, Isha'kau placed her hand on his cheek with a reassuring smile, enjoying the brief distraction.

"Do your people not wed? Do they not join together for life?" she asked. Aethen frowned, realizing that his pause in explaining himself was leading the priestess to the wrong conclusion. He decided to be blunt as he didn't like misleading Isha'kau.

"Imkanar has returned," he said. The priestess glared back at him in shock, suddenly lost for words.

"He has been hiding and waiting for the right moment to make his move. During the wedding, he plans to challenge this man named Ishayan for Aya'tar's hand." Aethen stopped speaking for a few moments to allow his words to sink in. The priestess stepped backward, looking confused. She did not understand how this man, apparently until this moment unrelated to anything occurring in the city, somehow knew of Imkanar. None of this made any sense, and she felt herself becoming filled with dread.

"How... How do you know of these things? How do you know of Imkanar?"

"My companions and I came upon a man named Imkanar in a village to the Northwest on our way here. A man was sent by someone here in the city to kill Imkanar. My friends Ember and Brig'dha saved his life. He agreed to bring us to the city as a guide, but in exchange, he wanted us to sneak him in as a fellow traveler and provide him a means to learn what was happening with Aya'tar while he stayed hidden. He has been staying with us ever since," Aethen finished, looking down in shame at his inadvertent deception.

"Did you use me to get information about Aya'tar? What is this?" Isha'kau asked, stepping backward and looking hurt. She was beginning to suspect that she had been used for information. Perhaps even Aethen's apparent feelings for her might be nothing more than a ruse? Her heart began to race, and she felt a terrible sinking feeling. She placed her hand upon her chest, trying to calm herself. Aethen approached, realizing that his words had caused the priestess pain and worry but unsure how to convince her that his feelings were not a deception.

"Isha'kau, I didn't even know that you knew Aya'tar. It was my two companions who were trying to find the information for Imkanar. When I met you, I had no idea who you were. My feelings for you are true. I swear on my honor!" he pleaded, though the look upon her face was a mixture of doubt, betrayal, and growing anger. Isha'kau heard the words she wanted to hear, that this man was interested in who she was and not what she was. The problem was that the words were too convenient. The timing was just too perfect, as was his involvement with Imkanar. She turned from him as her eyes misted, unwilling to show him how much hurt welled within. Aethen looked on in utter horror as she began to flee. Just as he was about to follow and make one final plea, he was distracted by something large and dark that landed right beside him.

"I… I need to leave now," she said, moving hurriedly away from Aethen as her chest ached. Isha'kau was awash with emotions. The man she had been falling in love with over a very short period had, in fact, turned out to be too good to be true. Worse, he picked the day before the wedding to confess his treachery and then went so far as to deny it, when even a child could see it was treachery. His story that he wasn't aware of her relationship with Aya'tar was just too unbelievable, unless the Goddess herself had sent him, yet she had seen no such signs. The news of Imkanar made things much worse if it was even true.

Suddenly, behind her, she heard the unmistakable and almost chirping-like sounds of a vulture, the handmaidens and messengers of the Goddess. Isha'kau swung around to see the magnificent bird in all its glory standing upon the ground not two lengths of a man from Aethen with its wings spread wide and facing him. The vulture was an animal touched by the Goddess. They were immune to all sickness and all evil, and even the vilest and deadly spirit-infested corpse could be picked clean by the creatures without care. The largest vultures were not even afraid of humans, though their massive size might have been part of the reason

– some having wings spanning almost twice the length of a man. Isha'kau watched as Aethen and the bird stared at each other. If he truly intended harm against the high priestess of Isut, the vulture before him would likely indicate this. In fact, its very presence might indicate Isut's desire to protect her, that last thought bringing tears and a mix of emotions.

The magnificent bird stood before Aethen with its wings unfolded and seemingly waiting for him to do something. If there had been some sort of dead animal nearby, he would have suspected that the bird was simply trying to scare him off so that it could have its fill in private, but he saw no dead animal. He suspected that the bird had been attracted by whatever dead creature had produced the smell he had earlier smelled, but its presence before him was odd, to say the least. Only a large raptor would be so bold as to face down a human. Aethen recalled Brig'dha telling him how vultures and other large birds were considered sacred to the people of Isut'na. Having the animal attack him in front of Isha'kau would do very little in helping him convince the woman that he meant her no harm.

He considered leaving before the animal did just that, but it went against every fiber of his being. He was a hunter, a defender of his people – who seemed to now be just Brig'dha and Ember – and a man. He had been raised from birth to stand before his enemies and face death. Just ahead was the large animal with wings two arm's length, each facing him like an elder warrior. Glancing to his left, the most interesting woman he had ever met stood there watching, her face streaked by tears… tears he had caused, even if by accident. He had to face his fears if he wanted to win her trust. If that meant risking the large bird tearing his hand off, which it looked capable of doing, he would risk it. It was time to be bold.

Aethen dropped to his knees before the animal and removed a piece of semi-dried deer meat he kept as a snack in his small traveling bag. It wasn't much, but he hoped the animal might accept it. The bird watched intently as he proffered the meat snack. He suspected the bird would snatch the meat and flee, like a dog, but it didn't. Instead, it began to waddle back and forth on the ground, almost like performing some little dance, while Aethen simply waited to see what would happen. He swallowed hard, unsure what would happen, yet realizing that his entire future, and perhaps the future of Isut'na, might very well be in the hands… or perhaps claws and features… of the magnificent raptor.

Isha'kau watched as Aethen tossed the food before the bird, expecting rejection. For such an animal to land so close to people in the first place was extremely unusual, and the idea that it would eat a piece of food tossed to it was even less likely. She held her breath waiting for the vulture to charge or fly away, either confirming Aethen's treachery. Suddenly, the vulture began to perform the waddling little dance they were known to do before eating. She had seen them do this before, but never so close to a person. In fact, the movement was the basis for two of the sacred dances of her people. The bird abruptly came forward, snatching the food piece and eating it in one quick gulp. At this point, it was nearly the length of a man from Aethen and looking him intently. A moment later, it turned to regard Isha'kau, and she felt a shiver across her body as if the Goddess had run her finger down her spine. She issued a gasp as powerful feelings rushed through her body, a sure sign that Isut had directly touched her spirit.

Suddenly, the vulture expanded its mighty wings to their maximum width, and took flight, but not before dropping a single large feather to the ground. Aethen stepped forward and lifted the large feather, examining it. The feather was actually quite beautiful, long and dark, with a fluffy base. He slowly stood with the feather and turned to approach the initiate priestess. She had leaned back against the ladder to the temple, her legs weak and her heart racing. He came to stand before her finding the woman entirely silent, her tear-steaked face now in a state of shock. He dropped to his knees and offered the feather to the initiate priestess just as he would have offered the antlers of a prized deer to old lady Glea, the priestess of the Moon for his former people.

"Goddess Isut of the people of Isut'na. I swear to you that I met this woman without knowing who she is or who she knows. I swear that my friends and I wish to help Aya'tar and Imkanar. I swear that my love for Isha'kau is pure. I swear this before you, and you may strike me down and take the very spirit from me if I lie," he said, looking Isha'kau dead in the eyes with every word. For a moment, the world was silent.

The priestess felt a wash of tingles and warmth across her body as Aethen spoke, holding the beautiful feather before him. She suddenly remembered to breathe, her legs growing weak. Reaching out, she touched the feature, her fingers tingling as they contacted the shaft. This was the clearest sign she had ever received from her goddess – if not a direct commandment. The signs had been provided, and the Goddess herself had vouched for Aethen's story. In fact, more and more, it was looking to her as though Aethen and the two women he traveled with were unwittingly agents of Isut. Not only would she have to trust her lover, but as a priestess of Isut, it was incumbent upon her to do what she could to help them.

Isha'kau dropped to her knees before Aethen and wrapped her arms around him, pressing his chest to hers and nuzzling her head against his face. Not all people around the world practiced kissing, and the people of the city were one such people. Intimacy involved physical proximity and the nuzzling of faces. In fact, her legs were too weak to stand and her need for someone to hold were key motivators. Aethen laid-back with Isha'kau resting atop him, gently nuzzling her face against his. This was the most physical interaction they had yet performed, and though it aroused him deeply, his greatest passion this moment came from the knowledge that she trusted him and was not going to leave him. Her eyes held fresh tears, but they were tears of joy, no longer sorrow.

"Aethen... Please tell me what it is that you wish me to do. In Isut's name, I will not fail," she pronounced. The two lovers lay together beside the ladder to the temple a moment later, unsure of what tomorrow would bring. Not too far away, a dead mouse lay awaiting the hungry beak of a vulture circling overhead. Poor Mew, the cat, had caught the mouse, only to be chased off by a local dog, leaving a meal that a particularly hungry vulture had awaited far too long to consume.

☽ ☽ ☽

The morning was hot and extremely humid when Aya'tar awoke. She lay on her bed for a short time with her two young children savoring the feeling. It was with great sadness that she contemplated how soon her bed would be shared with a man that she did not actually love. In truth, Ishayan did not appear to be a particularly bad man. He was certainly pleasurable to look at, and when she had finished taming his more aggressive nature, she suspected that he would be reasonably entertaining to be around. The problem was that she did not love him, and she knew she never would. There was only one man she loved, but she had not seen him since the warm winds had come.

She looked down at the children, Imkanar's children. She hoped that one day she would see the man again and provide some means by which he could meet the children. The idea filled her with hope, but it also filled her with immense sorrow and a strange sense of terror. She felt slightly ashamed and even a bit afraid of her decision. The emotions didn't make very much sense, but they were present, and she couldn't seem to ignore them. She had learned long ago that it was best to just accept the emotions as they were, no matter what they were. Fighting against them was a hopeless battle and a denial of how one felt.

"High priestess, you're awake. It's time for us to begin preparing you for the wedding," Isha'kau said, stepping forward with clothing and the other materials required. The priestess placed the children on a bed made of rabbit furs atop a soft bed of short flax fibers, the lot in a basket, to sleep. They had recently fed and would likely nap for quite some time. Aya'tar looked back at the children once more as a single tear dripped from her eye. *I am doing this for you so that your future will be better than mine. Please find love and don't let it go,* she thought as her fingers gently caressed their delicate heads. She turned to her initiate priestess. This preparation would need to be taken care of soon, as the babies would need to be fed before long, and she trusted no one else but Isha'kau.

Aya'tar sat a short time later on a stone bench holding both babies to suckle. She was pretty fortunate that they both seemed to get hungry and even sleep at about the same time. She had heard so many stories of children being completely asynchronous to the point where their parents slowly lost their minds. Isha'kau had taken long enough preparing the priestess that the children had become hungry once more. She could always tell as they would place their hands in their mouths and suck on their fingers. It was encouraged by fellow mothers to feed children as often as possible. Everyone knew that this was because some of the mother's spirit energy would flow into the children causing them to become more healthy and stronger as they grew. This was one of many reasons that breastfeeding was considered to be a divine act of purity.

Placing the children aside once more, Aya'tar stood before a small, polished obsidian mirror the size of a hand to see what she looked like on her big day. As was tradition, she wore a long skirt made from reeds which hung to the floor. A reed skirt didn't seem particularly practical, but it was some ancient tradition, and she wasn't interested in challenging any more ancient traditions. The wedding did not call for any particular upper body garment other than basic body paints. This was beneficial as she constantly had to feed the babies, and keeping herself open would make that much easier. More importantly, it would prevent anything painfully rubbing against her more tender parts. Having two children meant that she never gave either breast a break as there was always a child who needed milk. She was lucky that some of the other nursing women would occasionally stop by the temple and give her a break.

Women often shared the act of nursing, which was critical as some women could not produce milk, or enough milk. Generally, within a typical family, there would be perhaps ten to fifteen women within the age to birth and nurse children. Often, At least a third of them would be nursing. When a woman's child no longer needed constant nursing, she would often help other family members who needed a break. Sadly, Aya'tar was alone with no one else but Isha'kau. Of course it was possible to induce lactation in the younger priestess, but she had not thought it polite to even suggest this. Luckily, mothers coming to the temple to be blessed sometimes took the responsibility from her, giving her body a much needed rest.

Upon her head, a vast array of feathers had been affixed, some of them hanging down and some of them pointing straight up. It almost looked as though a bird had perched itself upon her head though the arrangement was quite beautiful. The feathers traveling down her hair were mostly songbird feathers, while feathers that popped up and stuck out in each direction mimicking the rays of the Sun were all from vultures, a powerful symbol. In fact, only a priest or priestess could wear vulture feathers. Around her neck, she wore almost a dozen necklaces of every sort of bead and color one could imagine, as well as anklets, bracelets, and any other jewelry that could be affixed to her body. Jewelry was a status symbol, and today she would play the part of the city's ruler.

"You have not taken any fermented drink since the day that Imkanar left. Would you not like some today?" Isha'kau asked as she lifted a large clay pot full of the precious fermented brew.

"While I was pregnant, fermented drinks seemed to bother me a little, even the smell. I will stick with water for now, but you might want to bring some down to Ishayan," Aya'tar said.

"Do not worry about Ishayan... I had planned to bring him a drink just now," said Isha'kau. The lesser priestess waited a moment for Aya'tar to become preoccupied with the babies before she acted. She had poured a large clay cup of fermented drink. On her way out the door, she paused for a moment to sprinkle in a tiny drop of dark berry powder into the cup. Dark berries, one day known as belladonna, came from the West and were against the city's rules to possess. However, Aya'tar's collection of herbs contained a tiny sample. The berries could be harvested, chopped, dried, and then ground into a powder that could easily kill. Isha'kau hoped that her memory was correct. If she got the dose wrong, Ishayan would die and she would become a murderer. It was a risk, but it was also the will of Isut, and she would do anything for the woman who had saved her from an agonizing death from her wounds.

Isha'kau paused with the drink and turned to Aya'tar, her determination slightly wavering as she began to second-guess her actions. Was she right to poison the man to marry the high priestess? Was she doing a favor and potentially saving Aya'tar, offering her another way out? If the man died, she would be a murderer and a traitor, and if he killed Imkanar, Aya'tar would be devastated. She watched as the high priestess stood before her children, gently petting their heads. Abruptly, Aya'tar turned to face the initiate priestess. Tears slowly rolling down her face. Isha'kau held her breath.

"I tell you now that if cutting off my arm would bring back my love and save me from this fate, I would ask you this moment for an ax. I do this for my children. I hope that wherever Imkanar is, he will forgive me for what I am about to do. The Goddess has not seen fit to deliver me from this fate, and so I will abide by her will. Thank you so much for helping me... You've always been such a good friend." Aya'tar finished with a another tear. Isha'kau released her breath and then found herself deeply breathing once more to prevent her own tears from flowing. *Do not worry, Aya'tar. The Goddess has not forgotten you, nor has Imkanar. Aethen was that sign, and I am the hand of the Goddess*, she thought, quickly turning, and leaving with the cup before her emotions got the best of her.

ᴐ ᴐ ᴐ

Isha'kau found Ishayan standing with three brand-new attendants in one of the small buildings which served as storerooms for the city, situated near the temple. This room had recently been re-plastered and now stood empty awaiting grain. It had become a temporary staging area for the wedding. She stopped, suddenly realizing that the small room was the same one Aya'tar had sneaked into with Imkanar nearly a harvest before, the night the babies were conceived. What a stain upon his memory that this man would now stand in that very room preparing himself to marry Aya'tar.

The lesser priestess felt a sense of righteous justice as she took a breath and stepped forward into the room. Before her stood the arrogant Ishayan with his three new men in attendance. She had heard a rumor that the last three had somehow died, and that did little to endear this man in her eyes. Well, the poisonous drink would take the edge out of his fight and correct that injustice. She sloshed the dish a few times as she approached to ensure that the powder was not noticed. With a forced smile, she stepped forward and made her presence known.

"Your bride believed that a drink would serve you well. On behalf of our city's best interests, please have this dish of the finest fermented

478

drink. It will make the evening more... relaxing," she said, holding out the cup and hoping desperately that he didn't see through her deception. Though she was mentally repulsed by the man, Isha'kau couldn't help but notice how dashing Ishayan looked. She focused on this now to help clear her mind and prevent him from seeing her real intent. His chest had been painted with a thick coating of red paint from just above the waist to just below the neck. A single black line followed his chin, down his neck, and just below his navel. This created a striking contrast. Below that, he wore an intricately braided leather corded belt with a beautiful multicolored flax loincloth that hung almost to the ground.

Around his neck, he wore many necklaces with many different beads, some of them even copper. Down the front of his handsome face, many black lines had been painted vertically. All in all, he was quite lovely, if not stunning. Regardless of his looks, Isha'kau was set upon deposing him as a husband. He could find some other woman somewhere else, and she was quite sure that another woman would be quite happy. What was most important was that Imkanar and Aya'tar became married.

"You look quite nice," she said with a playful giggle as she handed him the cup. She did her best to smile at the man and draw his attention from the drink. Isha'kau was not very good at manipulation, but she was at least capable of pulling off a simple flirtatious smile before leaving.

"Thank you, priestess," he said, accepting the dish and taking a lengthy sip of the brew. His attendants looked on as Isha'kau turned and slowly left the room. She had done all that she could, and it was up to the gods to do the rest. *I am your hand and your will, Isut,* she thought.

⊃ ⊃ ⊂

That morning, the sky was a deep rich blue, perhaps one of the most beautiful skies anyone had seen in a long time. Ember was excited because clear dark skies meant that she could sit beneath the stars later that night with Brig'dha and enjoy the view of the unknown dots of light. Even better, something so romantic as a wedding would likely provide the catalyst for a very romantic night. Ember's only worry was the possibility of something bad happening during the challenge. Luckily, she had been thinking of an emergency tactic to deal with just that possibility. Unfortunately, she had not mentioned it to anyone else yet. *They fear the plans I say aloud. If only they knew how many I kept to myself,* she mused.

"Romance is like a yawn. When you see two people walking by doing it, you want to do it too," Ember said to Brig'dha. Normally, the priestess would have probably flashed her a catty smile, but today she was far too worried about what was to come. The group walked toward the ceremonial dance grounds, where they would set up mats and wait for the event. No one was quite sure how things would turn out, but somehow everyone knew that this event would be memorable in one way or another.

The ceremonial dancing grounds were full of food, people, and every manner of festive accessory possible. Besides the typical clothing people wore, many had come wearing their best adornments and paints. Ember, Brig'dha, and Aethen sat on a small set of old and worn leather mats on the ground not far from the front of the festival, waiting for the wedding to begin. Beside them, what looked like an old person wrapped with leather skin sat huddled.

Imkanar was quite sure that he would die from the heat under his leather cover long before his lover stepped forward. He nervously handled the obsidian blade Ember had given him. It was not her personal blade but one she had traded for. Imkanar could not believe that she had handed him such an expensive item, but it seemed that when the fiery redhead decided upon a course of action, she went all the way and held nothing back. As a result, he now sat huddled in the disguise of an old man preparing to do something rather spontaneous. *I will either see the Sun set this evening with Aya'tar or lie dead on the ground,* he thought with a grimace.

Not far from his new friends and just below the temple roof stood Sar'Tawas impatiently waiting with Ianmu at his side. While Sar'Tawas had come with a flax net shawl to block the Sun from his shoulders and a short, linen wrap, Ianmu wore a short loincloth that would not impede her mobility and her entire body had been painted with an intricate pattern of black and white stripes. It was not uncommon for someone to completely cover themselves in paint for such a ceremonial event, but the main reason she had done this was to obscure her face from her brother. She did not want to be recognized, if possible. On her side, she carried a well-made flint dagger. *I am the hand of An'an. She is the wind I breathe; I am a bird in her sky...* she chanted mantras to herself over and over as the time for the challenge approached.

Isu'mamu, the elder in charge of the flax fields, stepped forward, aided by a younger man. She wore a very large woven reed sunshade while a younger cousin of hers stood beside her, constantly fanning the woman with a small fan made from bird feathers. She stood atop the temple, ready to begin the ritual. Marriage ceremonies were actually very short affairs. The majority of their purpose was merely to announce to everyone that two people were joined. The important part was the consummation of the marriage. Isut was a fertility goddess, and while everyone else danced, sang, and ate, the newlyweds were expected to retreat to a private location to consummate. In this case, the consummation would have to be delayed as Aya'tar had only recently given birth.

"People of Isut'na, be silent," she said, pausing for a few moments to catch her breath. Isu'mamu was very old, having seen 60 harvests, making her among the oldest people in the city. No matter what she said, people would give her respect simply by that virtue alone. The average age within the city was perhaps 20 to 25 harvests of age. The number of people who exceeded even 60 harvests could be counted on two hands.

"I remember so many harvests before when the young Yari'aya gave birth to Aya'tar from the great Utiakur. Now, that same priestess stands ready to wed with two babies of her own. I could not be prouder of her. Since she is the high priestess, it is now up to Isut'Sanup'ramu'man Isha'kau to perform the ceremony. Please, banish all unpleasant thoughts from your minds. We wish the gods to be with us," she concluded, slowly stepping back with the help of her assistant. Her words were taken with great respect, not only for her age but also for her wisdom.

Isha'kau stepped forward, painted from head to toe, completely white with clay and having small black rings around her arms and legs. Across her face was a series of black lines, and her hair was adorned with long black vulture feathers. Around her waist, she wore a long red died loincloth made of the finest linen. Around her neck, a leather cord was tied with a long dark vulture feather hanging between her breasts. It was the same vulture feather handed to her by Aethen, a reminder that the Goddess stood ready to intervene on behalf of Aya'tar.

The lesser priestess had never before performed a wedding, and to do so for the leader of the city and the son of the leader of another city was no small first step. She took two deep breaths and steadied herself with the entire city gathered behind her. She turned to face the city and all its inhabitants. She spread her arms wide, holding eagle feathers in each hand. This was the beginning of either a beautiful future or a tragic end. She began to sing the words that started the wedding ceremony.

Isut, the fertile soil,
Gunar, the seed of life.
For there to be new life, you must meet.
The bond between land and seed,

must be maintained until the Third World comes!
Come forth Isut'Sanup'ramu Aya'tar, the most fertile of the world.
Come forth Dunu'lekal'Ishayan, the most fertile seed.
You shall be joined as one under our watchful eyes and with a
strong hand.

Upon those ritualistic words, approached and came to stand before Isha'kau and the city. There were cheers from many, not only for her choice to become married but also for her beautiful attire. The lesser priestess couldn't help but feel slightly flattered as she had spent a significant period decorating Aya'tar herself. A moment later, the dashing Ishayan climbed the ladder from the side of the building, coming to stand upon its roof before Isha'kau and the city. There was a significant uproar and praise for the man throughout the crowd. Ishayan appeared as a great warrior, a man desired by nearly every woman in the city. He smiled as one woman after another in the crowd screamed her personal praise to him.

Seeing that Aya'tar was already becoming disturbed and obviously wanted this affair over as quickly as possible, Isha'kau quickly held her arms out once more to silence the crowd and get the ritual underway. There were only two more tasks to be completed, the joining of hands and the call for challengers. She could feel her heart pounding as she turned toward the two to be wed and gently compelled them to hold each other's hands. Isha'kau stood before Aya'tar and Ishayan, and swallowed hard. This was the moment everyone had been waiting for, the very last part of the ceremony to be completed before they could be formally declared married. Isha'kau turned to face the crowd, her pulse beating so rapidly that she worried she might faint.

"Do not worry, it will all be over soon, my bride," Ishayan whispered to Aya'tar as the crowd began to slowly calm. Aya'tar relaxed her hand to the point where Ishayan alone was grasping it. She was filled with despair, and his words did nothing to help.

"I do this for my children and for my city. I do not hate you, but I will never love you. I would give my life for my people and for my children, and that is what I am about to do," she whispered back. She would walk into a burning fire for her children, but she did not want this man to be under any misapprehension that her deeds now were born out of anything other than necessity. She wanted to be clear that there was no love involved.

"I know, and it doesn't bother me. I also do this… for Isut'na," he said with a smirk. Aya'tar turned toward the man. She always knew that there was a political and opportunistic component to his designs, but she never before heard him say it so plainly. *Goddess, I make this plea one more time. I would give my life or anything else but my own children or Imkanar for you to intervene. Please, Isut…* Aya'tar hoped her final plea would not go unanswered though she was moments away from tragedy. Isha'kau continued speaking to the crowd as they calmed, completing the final portion of the short ceremony.

"A bond must be clear of interruption. There cannot be any doubt, nor any further competition. When a man and woman are joined, it is until death! Does anyone now wish to make a claim against those to be joined? Speak your love now. This is the last opportunity you have, and to do so, afterward would be an offense to the Goddess!" she concluded. Most people sat back, waiting for this minor portion of the ceremony to conclude. It was extremely rare for anybody to stand up and say anything, as one of the only possible remedies to such a challenge was a fight to the death. On the rare occasions when it occurred, a man typically issued a challenge to the man to be wed. On even rarer occasions, a woman would come forward and challenge the bride. Isha'kau's heart raced faster than the winds of a storm as she waited for what she knew was to come.

Aya'tar felt dizzy as though she might faint, her heart seemingly stopping in her chest. Ishayan simply waited for the final words to pronounce the city his. With that announcement, he would achieve peacefully what his father otherwise intended to achieve with blood. He smiled with anticipation. Not far below, Sar'Tawas stood and took a deep breath, ready to issue his challenge. This was what he had waited for, the moment when he would challenge Ishayan and then suddenly swap himself for the deadly Ianmu. He took a deep breath, but right as he was about to speak, he was suddenly cut off!

"I challenge you, Ishayan!" came a scream from the crowd. Everyone looked, trying to find where the words had come from. Imkanar abruptly stood casting the leather cloak to the ground and began to walk toward the temple proudly and with no fear. At that moment, he was glorious, like a majestic eagle unfurling its wings and rising to the challenge. Aya'tar felt dizzy as she saw him approach. Tears welling in her eyes, she watched as her lover had suddenly arrived, and he now stood before the mighty Ishayan making an open challenge. Had the Goddess heard her pleas and answered her? Suddenly, fear began to rush through her as she remembered that the only way for him to win such a challenge was for Ishayan to back down or for him to defeat her groom-to-be in combat. Ishayan was not one to back down.

Brig'dha and Ember held one another tightly as they watched the romantic scene unfold. All around, people were immediately in an uproar. Some screamed that Imkanar was a usurper, a beast to be cast to the wilds, while others yelled support for the young man. Imkanar came to stand before the temple, looking up at everyone gathered above. Completely contrasting the eloquently decorated Ishayan, Imkanar stood wearing an old, tattered linen loincloth and a pair of dusty, worn sandals. Most surprisingly, he held a metalworker's stone hammer. He had left the beautiful and costly obsidian dagger back on the mat beside Ember, instead favoring the tool he had used most of his life, a last-minute decision.

"Isut'Sanup'ramu Aya'tar! You are the only woman I have ever loved and the mother of my children. I would rather choose death than a life without you. Many have tried to kill me over these last few moons, but with the help of friends and the Goddess, I have returned to take my rightful place at your side. Therefore, I challenge you, Ishayan, for the right to marry Aya'tar if she will have me!" he said. Aya'tar was breathing rapidly in short, shallow breaths, tears running from her eyes. Before her, Isha'kau was holding her hand to her chest to calm her heart.

Ishayan frowned at the approaching man. He had expected a challenge from the likes of Sar'Tawas but not from this man, a low-born worker by the look of him and the supposed father of his bride's children. Glancing at Aya'tar told him immediately the truth of the young man's claim. The woman was in a state of shock, a strange mixture of confusion and delight. The problem was that if he defeated this man in front of Aya'tar when it was evident that she still had feelings for him, it might taint their future relationship. His only hope was that Sar'Tawas would also challenge them both providing an opportunity for the low-born man to be killed by the older man and not him. It was a risk, but it was his only option, so he took it.

"I accept your challenge, low-born!" he yelled loudly for everyone to hear. Glancing once more at Aya'tar, he saw the fear in her eyes, just as he had expected. She only thought of him as the best option out of a group of very poor options. Regardless, he had hoped that one day the mighty priestess would come around. He did not dislike her and even hoped that she might one day, at least, respect him a little. Even as he thought this, Ishayan had no doubt in his mind that his bride-to-be would be rooting for the young man of low birth. It was at that moment that he noticed Sar'Tawas preparing to speak. He would easily kill this older man after Sar'Tawas first dispatched Aya'tar's true love. Ishayan need only let the two of them fight first.

"I challenge both of you for the right to marry Aya'tar. One of you is a foreigner. The other one of you is not worthy. I am from this city, highborn, and have what it takes to be the leader!" Sar'Tawas said, finally having his chance to yell out his challenge. Unlike the unexpected Imkanar, many people had expected Sar'Tawas to make his challenge. The older man stood proudly before the gathered people of the city. Once the chatter had died down, he once more addressed the crowd with the most important aspect of his challenge. Ember and Brig'dha sat with confused expressions, not having expected the sudden change of events.

"The rules of the city are clear. Anyone of older age, greater than 25 harvests, may call upon a champion to fight in their place," he said plainly. Most people said nothing, simply waiting to see who the champion would be while the elders muttered and nodded among themselves, unable to disagree with the truth of his claim. The average life span of a city dweller was between 25 and 35 harvests, though many Elders lived longer than this. Since elders might have to endure challenges from time to time, a rule was put in place so that they might call upon a younger champion to fight for them, and this was exactly the sort of scenario that had been in mind. Ember braced herself for the challenger to step forward. Her secret backup plan was now looking more and more like it would come to pass. She glanced at Brig'dha, realizing that the priestess was not going to like what she was about to do. She was already anxious enough around so many people, as it was.

"Who will be your champion, Sar'Tawas? What man will fight for you?" asked Kamar, the head of the city's defenses and hunters. Sar'Tawas smiled more deeply than he had before and stepped aside, allowing Ianmu to stand proudly before the city.

"I choose my concubine!" he said triumphantly. At her request, he did not use her name. While Ianmu was not the most uncommon of names, it would simply increase the likelihood of her brother recognizing her if he used it aloud. The sounds of shock, appreciation, and anticipation could be heard all around the venue. Most of the people in the city had seen the beautiful concubine before, and there had been rumors that she was quite skilled with a blade. Now, Sar'Tawas chose her over all the larger and stronger members of the Crafting Guild to fight for him. This was becoming more and more interesting to the average citizen of the city by the moment.

Brig'dha and Ember glanced at one another, worry on their faces. Imkanar facing Ishayan had been one thing, but now the young man had this extremely fearsome-looking woman to deal with. Ember could tell simply by looking at her and how she carried herself that the strikingly painted woman could likely fight well. If this concubine woman and Ishayan were to focus their attacks upon Imkanar, he would fall easily. Ember thought fast, needing to find a solution before her friend was killed. As hard as she thought, over and over, only one solution came to mind – the backup plan. It was drastic, and Brig'dha would not be pleased. She had originally intended to execute this backup plan in a slightly different way, but she could see no other alternative. Ember turned to face Brig'dha and placed her hand on the priestess' shoulder. Brig'dha looked back instantaneously, recognizing the stoic look upon Ember's face. She sighed, realizing that something horrible was about to happen. After all, this had all been an "Ember plan."

"Please trust me, there's no other way... and don't worry, I don't plan to marry Aya'tar..." Ember said with a smile and a wink. She stood up before Brig'dha had a chance to ask what that last bit meant. Before Brig'dha could stop her, Ember threw her arms out wide as she walked toward the main temple. She hoped that people would believe what she said and that it would sound convincing. Strangely, Ember's mind shifted back to a question she had been thinking of asking Brig'dha ever since they had become lovers. Perhaps if she survived this next event, she would ask. Ember wondered why she always waited for the worst possible time to consider asking important questions.

"Wait! Wait! Aya'tar, I can't live without you! We were meant for each other! I challenge all the other challengers for Aya'tar's hand in marriage!" she screamed as loudly as she could. All around her, there was stunned silence. Relationships between those of the same sex occurred, but not commonly marriage. Not only was this something that rarely happened, but more strangely, it was completely out of the blue. Even Aya'tar stared back in utter shock. All around, people muttered to themselves, asking the same question – who is this red-haired foreign woman? Sar'Tawas merely stared at the incensed redhead. Part of him was aggravated that she had stood to add a challenge to his claim, but another part of him was impressed that Aya'tar had kept a secret lover – an exotic and gorgeous one, too – on the side, and no one had noticed.

Ember stood her ground and looked as confident and serious as possible. She had no intentions of marrying Aya'tar, but perhaps she could help out Imkanar and then "accidentally" find herself defeated or simply have a change of heart at the end. Her decision was made in the moment and all too impulsively, as they usually were. Now, with the entire city staring at her, Ember swallowed hard, hoping that she hadn't done something more foolish than usual. Imkanar glared at Ember. At first, his anger surged as he thought that he had been betrayed, but then he realized that none of that made any sense. How could she have somehow developed a relationship with a woman from a distant land, a woman he had never even noticed? No, this had to be some sort of strange plan developed by Ember. He would play along with it, hoping that it would eventually make some form of sense. His pulse quickened, and adrenaline flowed as he realized what was about to happen.

Kamar stepped forward, looking quite annoyed by the events unfolding. He had hoped for a simple marriage that would end the problems Isut'na had faced for almost an entire harvest. Instead, everything had become suddenly so much more complicated. The rules of what was to come were well known, but he figured he would remind everyone once more as was the custom. Far off in the crowd, Brig'dha sat glaring in shock with her mouth wide open and fighting back a total meltdown.

She did it again... she... why doesn't she think first? she thought in horror.

"If there are no more challenges for the hand of Aya'tar," he paused for a moment and gave an irritated glare at the people gathered, "and if the high priestess will accept all of the challenges," he turned to the high priestess to see if she would accept her challengers. If the high priestess did not accept a challenger, that individual would be immediately rejected. Aya'tar looked back with a strange mix of fear and pleading in her eyes. She knew that there was no going back at this point. To reject anyone would force her into a political situation that would potentially damage the city. If she rejected Ishayan, there could be war with another city. If she rejected Sar'Tawas, there would be internal conflict and potentially an open revolt in the city. There was no way she would reject Imkanar, and she had the strangest feeling that the red-haired woman might be on the side of her lover. With no other choice, she nodded her approval to Kamar.

"Very well. Everyone knows the time-honored rules, but I will speak them again for those not born in the city. A single individual will completely walk around the city, returning to where they started. In that amount of time, the combatants will fight. Whoever is left standing at the end of this period is the winner. There are no combat rules, and let no family hold any other family accountable for the results. Each of these challengers is here because they chose to be... Well, most of them," he said, giving a wary glance to Ianmu. She simply stared back at him passively.

"Each of you, arm yourselves and stand before me when ready," Kamar said, indicating a place in the middle of the ceremonial grounds directly in front of the main temple. Ianmu pulled free her flint dagger and took her place before the temple without hesitation. She had spent the morning in deep prayer to An'an, and she was ready for whatever might come of this, even death. An'an did not punish those who gave all they could and failed, but she looked poorly on those who did not try or did not give their best effort. She simply stood before everyone, slowly taking deep breaths of the hot, humid air and readying her body for what was to come. She would either win control of the city for Sar'Tawas, thus propelling her own plans forward, or she would lie on the hot ground, dead.

Ishayan slowly stepped down the wooden ladder to the ground level pulling free an obsidian dagger even longer than Ember's. Like his sister, whom he still did not know he was about to fight, Ishayan was a fan of the blade. He had trained with it since he was a child; it was a family staple. Strangely, he felt slightly dizzy, and his heart beat faster than it should. Being a competent warrior, he wasn't particularly afraid, but his body was certainly out of sorts. Perhaps the drink he had consumed earlier had been stronger than he had thought.

As he approached the strikingly painted woman, he noticed something familiar about her, though he could not place it. She carried herself like a warrior and was definitely someone to watch out for. She kept her head down, not making eye contact with him. He could not decide if this was out of some fear or for some other unknown reason. Either way, if she survived this, he would have to learn more about this interesting woman.

Imkanar and Ember both approached the temple. Ember held her obsidian dagger, but she was surprised to see Imkanar holding a stone hammer and not the blade she had lent him. Curiously, it rather fitted the man. He had been a worker of metals, an extremely rare skill that required the use of a stone hammer. She suspected his weapon of choice might also have to do with how poorly he had performed with a dagger. They both glared at one another, Imkanar trying to figure out just what Ember had in mind. She flashed him a quick wink before turning to regard the other combatants.

Seeing the opportunity, Ianmu glanced at Ishayan to get his attention. She ever so slightly gestured towards Imkanar with her eyes, hinting that they should both attack him simultaneously and take him out of the fight early on. Ishayan ever so slightly nodded his head back, seemingly approving of the idea. He knew it was a dangerous alliance to make in a four-way battle when there could be only one victor, but if his deception proved successful, there would be only two adversaries to worry about. His goal would be the kill the most dangerous adversary first.

A young girl named Kitmu was selected to walk outside the city. It would not take her long to make her way around the buildings, but it would provide a means to time the event. During these events, people rarely died. Normally, they were simply rendered unconscious or too wounded to stand. Either way, Kamar glanced at the young girl and nodded, indicating that she should begin walking. It was time to begin.

"May the gods watch over you all... Begin!" he yelled. The moment he said it, Aya'tar's heart seemed to stop. Ishayan prepared to attack Imkanar at the same moment as the strikingly painted woman. Unfortunately for him, Ianmu had a separate agenda. She had already realized that her brother was the most deadly fighter in this quartet, other than perhaps herself. When she had suggested that they team up on Imkanar, she had done so simply to throw the man off guard.

Before anyone could do anything, Ishayan dashed forward with his dagger aiming straight for Imkanar's neck. He aborted his attack and twisted sideways as he caught sight of the concubine woman slashing at him with her dagger – betrayal. His movements came slower than he had expected they would, and he continued to feel a strange sensation tugging at his body as though sapping some of the strength. He ducked away from the betrayer's quick slash, but not before Imkanar seized the moment and brought the hammer flying down on his left shoulder. Ishayan rolled onto the ground in pain and temporarily out of the fight. Imkanar looked up from his victory just in time to catch sand in his face, kicked by the concubine as she turned to face Ember. With both men incapacitated, it was now between the women.

Ember watched the events happen in less time than it would take to count from one to three. The strikingly painted concubine was as fast as a forest mink and as deadly as a wolf. Then suddenly, the "mink-wolf" set her eyes upon a "fox." Ianmu burst forward, coming in high with her dagger in what was almost a leap. Ember knew this trick, for she had used it herself nearly three harvests before against the vile man who had enslaved her. She pretended as though she were going to block the high strike, but at the last moment, she dropped low and stepped sideways, leaving her foot planted on the ground directly in the path of the concubine.

Ianmu suddenly ducked and brought her dagger down to stab the redhead in the stomach, only to find that the woman had suddenly stepped to the side and out of her line of attack. Ianmu shifted her body weight and turned sideways to slash at the redhead or to block any attacks, but she tripped over Ember's foot which had been left in her path, and found herself falling hard onto the ground. She quickly rolled into a crouching position and scolded herself for choosing such a brazen initial attack. Such quick striking moves were fast and unexpected, but they provided the attacker with very little recourse if a victim were smart enough to evade the attack. She had hoped to win moments after it started, but the redhead didn't appear to be as easy of a mark as she had thought.

Ember quickly realized that she was up against a superior opponent. She had been fortunate enough to defeat the first attack from the concubine, but she knew that she wouldn't beat her in a conventional knife fight. As a child, she had often fought with the boys in the village, who were much larger and stronger than she was. Certain tricks could be used when dealing with a larger or stronger opponent, and she had just one in mind for the concubine. Ember held her dagger before her and approached Ianmu as though looking for an opportunity to strike.

Imkanar stood, blinking and trying to get the remainder of the sand from his eyes. It was not as bad as it could have been, but it didn't take too many granules in the eyes to make combat quite difficult. Worse, he could see the form of Ishayan standing and preparing to advance upon him. He grabbed the piece of skin between his nostrils and gave it a twist. The pain caused his eyes to water even more than they already had. It seemed to be working, but as he looked up, he saw a dagger slashing at his chest. Imkanar swung his hammer overhead, knowing that he wouldn't hit anything, but using the sudden shift in weight to pull his stomach backward just as the blade flew by. Only someone used to swinging a large, heavy stone hammer would have known that trick.

Unfazed by his evasion, Ishayan stepped forward to slash the young copper worker once more. Whatever was making him ill was making it harder and harder for him to press his attack, and this was providing an advantage to his younger and lesser experienced opponent. Turning the hammer upside down and using the hilt to block, Imkanar, again and again, stopped the slash of the dagger. Obsidian blades were extremely sharp but only useful for cutting, not thrusting. This was actually providing Imkanar with enough time to block each attack. His eyes were even becoming clear, but he could feel himself giving ground to the highborn, and he knew it was only a matter of time before he failed to block one of the slashes.

Ianmu was now on her feet and slowly circling the redhead, who was constantly looking for an opportunity to strike. She knew that her only real tactic at this point was to let the obviously less experienced redhead make an attack, then simply avoid it and slice her guts open. Ianmu lowered her blade as though she were contemplating doing something with it and purposefully opened herself to an overhead attack. She hoped that the redhead would take the bait.

Ember saw the opening and realized it was time for her most unconventional strategy. She came forward with the dagger, ready to slash the concubine across the face, but at the last moment, she tossed the dagger to the concubine.

"Here, catch!" she yelled, dropping to her knees right in front of the suddenly out of positioned concubine. She clenched her fist and punched up as hard as she could right between the concubine's legs. This had worked so many times before on boys teasing her when she was young, and she suspected it would have a similar effect on a woman. Luckily, Ianmu was wearing a simple loincloth, which made aiming for the most delicate parts all the easier. As Ember's fist made contact, driving Ianmu's soft bits against the woman's pubic bone with the strength of an archer's arms, Ianmu's world became a blur of pain.

She dropped her dagger and grabbed her loins, stepping backward and then falling to her knees, making the most horrible whimpering sound Ember had heard in a long time. For a brief moment, Ember actually felt sympathy for the woman as she stood over her. Ianmu slowly sank to the ground in too much pain to be a threat, at least for now. All around, there were screams from the crowd as many people audibly cringed at the thought of such a blow.

Ember turned to find Imkanar on the ground and on his back, holding Ishayan's dagger barely the length of a finger from his face as the highborn straddled him, pushing down as hard as he could. Their fight had degraded into rolling around on the ground. Forgetting to grab her own dagger, Ember rushed forward and kicked as hard as she could right into Ishayan's abdomen. He rolled off in pain, clutching the wound only to find Ember diving on top of him and punching him repeatedly in the face. Ever the brawler, Ember wasn't above simply beating any thoughts of marriage out of the man.

"Son of a jackal! Seed stealing bird! Degenerate creep!" she screamed as she pounded him over and over. Imkanar stood and rubbed the last of the sand from his eyes. Before him, he saw the concubine recovering from a grievous punch to her most precious regions while to his side, Ember straddled his previous foe, beating the man repeatedly in the face while yelling insults at him in her own language. He would take the opportunity to finish off the concubine, but as he looked again to the left, she was gone. He spun around looking for the woman who just moments before had been lying on the ground in pain. As he turned fully around, he saw her approaching.

Ianmu was still in intense pain, and she would be sure to kill the redhead in an equally painful manner as payment for such a wound, but right now, she was drawing upon her faith in An'an to overcome the pain she felt. In her agony, she had forgotten to look for her dagger, but she didn't need her dagger to kill this man. The strongest part of her body was her legs, and she would introduce the hammer-wielding man to true strength. She stepped forward and dove into a handstand, slamming both of her legs onto Imkanar's shoulders and wrapping them tightly. The move was so smooth and flowing that the young man had no time to react. Ianmu flexed her powerful abdominal muscles drawing her upper body above Imkanar's head. In effect, she was now sitting on his shoulders in front of him with her thighs wrapped around his neck. The crowd roared in excitement at having witnessed such an athletic feat.

Imkanar staggered backward, suddenly unable to support the weight of an entire woman connected to his neck. Losing his balance, he fell harshly to the ground, the woman attached to his neck making the fall even more painful. She simply lay back and squeezed as hard as she possibly could. Her legs constricted so tightly around his neck that within mere moments Imkanar could feel the blood being cut off. He had expected to spill his guts onto the sand or perhaps have his throat slit, but he never figured that he would be strangled to death by a woman. Ianmu hoped to finish the low-born quickly before the crazed redhead finished beating her brother to a pulp. Unfortunately, strangling someone to death took much longer than many realized. She would merely cause him to lose consciousness and then finish him with a dagger.

He flailed with his arms trying to grab hold of something, but he was nearly facedown and her legs were like a vice. Ianmu grabbed his hands and held them at bay. She was much weaker than him, but she had only to keep her legs wrapped around his neck for a few more moments, and it would all be over. She could feel his strength giving out. Under her breath, she chanted a continuous prayer to An'an for strength as she choked the man with her legs. Even now, he was beginning to stop struggling. It was just like how she had killed the priest to An'an.

Ishayan was in pretty rough shape with a bloody nose and lip. The strange effect sapping his strength for the entire fight had made it hard for him to stop the crazed redhead straddling his chest. Ember had initially beaten him several times with her fist until he had grabbed her by the neck with both hands, ready to squeeze the life out of the woman. She simply took a handful of sand from the ground and poured it right into his eyes, ending that attack. Now the man lay flat upon the ground bruised and bloodied, and for now, out of the fight. He wasn't quite sure why the redhead had not finished him off the moment he had been incapacitated by the sand, but he was too injured to consider that, at the moment.

Ember stood feeling slightly dizzy from the continuous exertion, only to find poor Imkanar being strangled to death by the concubine. With one great kick to the head, she ended Ishayan's struggle.

"Oh no, you don't!" she screamed, rushing over to try and pry the strikingly painted woman off Imkanar. He was only barely conscious and had all but stopped fighting. As a result, her hands were now free to repel Ember as she began trying to grab hold of the concubine's face and hair. Ianmu fought back with her hands, presenting a problem. In effect, the concubine was able to fight two battles simultaneously, and Imkanar was losing his fight. Ember knew exactly how to deal with this problem. *It worked a moment before... why not again,* she thought. She stood and began kicking the concubine in the head repeatedly with her foot. Each time her foot landed a blow, Ianmu saw strange colors and speckles appear in her vision. It only took a few good solid hits before she let go of Imkanar and passed into the blackness of unconsciousness. Ember was quite impressed at how effective a good kick could be. *By the gods, she has strong legs, but so do I,* she thought in grim amusement.

Ember grabbed the concubine by the hair and tugged her off Imkanar. She stood for a moment, realizing that if she did nothing more, she would have effectively won Aya'tar's hand in marriage. *You are as beautiful as a fire flower, but I already have a lover,* she mused. With everyone watching, she had to make the final victory of the young man as legitimate as possible. She jumped on top of Imkanar and began pretending to strangle the man as though she were attempting to finish what the concubine had started. He was only half-conscious with bloodshot eyes and a nearly purple face. At first, he didn't realize what Ember was doing to him, but after a moment, his mind began to focus, and he realized that she was rolling around in the dirt as though they were locked in some sort of struggle.

"You must fight! You have to defeat me!" she whispered loudly into his delirious face. It took him a few moments to realize what she said and pull himself together, but he knew what had to be done. Her hands were only barely wrapped around his throat, and he could breathe perfectly fine, though to anyone observing, it certainly looked as though she were out for his life. Smiling back at Ember, he gave her a wink. She wasn't going to like what he would do next, but it was the only way. His victory had to appear epic to prevent any possible future problems. He just hoped that Ember would play along with what he was about to do next, something he alone had the strength for.

Imkanar forced himself upright, grabbing Ember by the neck using the rest of his strength. She let go of him and grabbed hold of his hands as though trying to free herself. He slowly stood, seemingly lifting Ember by the neck. In reality, the grip she applied to his wrists, apparently attempting to free herself, was actually keeping most of the weight off her neck. She pretended to struggle as though she couldn't get away. All the while, Imkanar pretended to be exerting significant pressure upon her neck. He lifted her higher into the air, making a loud primal growl. The entire act was completely improvised, but they both hoped it would have the desired effect.

Imkanar looked straight into the sky as he held the redhead before him in a striking pose. Both Brig'dha and Aya'tar stood by, horrified at the sight, unable to determine if it were real or fake. Aethen began to stand, ready to rush to Ember's aid while Brig'dha grabbed hold of her knife, ready to rush forward and save her lover regardless of the consequences when suddenly he released her. The ruinous redhead dropped to her knees and then to the ground. She curled into the fetal position, pretending to barely breathe and certainly defeated. She hoped that their struggle had been believed.

"Isut… Gunar… I have defeated the enemies who kept me from the woman I love and our children. If I am not worthy of marrying Aya'tar, strike me down right now, and may my spirit be banished for all eternity!" he proclaimed, standing before his three fallen adversaries. Ianmu was slowly regaining consciousness, and Ember was curled up, gently waving her hand to signal that she no longer wanted a "relationship" with Aya'tar. Ishayan was still lying flat on his back, and it appeared that he would be doing so for quite some time. Brig'dha stood with her knife, unsure of what she should do. Aethen and Brig'dha exchanged confused glances.

Everyone waited, holding their breath, and expecting something to happen. Suddenly, little Kitmu strolled into the city's center, having completed her circuit around the outside. At that moment, it was over, and Imkanar stood victorious over all his opponents, both real and theatrical. All around, people broke their silence and began speaking among themselves. What would happen next? Brig'dha burst forth from the crowd shoving people out of the way to get to Ember, Aethen just behind her. She dropped to her knees before the ruined redhead and rolled her over to see how badly she had been injured. Ember looked up at her and smiled.

"Shhh... Just kneel there for a few moments and look horrified. We must keep up the act," Ember whispered to Brig'dha. The priestess looked down at her lover with a look of shock, happy surprise, but also some incredulous anger.

"Who says it's an act?" she replied. Aethen stood behind them, having just applied his hand rapidly to his face. *It's as though she doesn't think life is real... it's just a game to her,* he thought.

Imkanar climbed the small wooden ladder leading to the top of the temple. As he stepped upon the temple roof, Aya'tar slowly turned to face him. Her heart beat in her chest, and tears welled in her eyes. There was no way something like this could happen, no way that her misery could be suddenly changed... And yet her problems had been solved in just the time it took for a small girl to wander around the outside of the city. Isha'kau stood behind Aya'tar, tears streaking her face paint, fully overwhelmed by the romance of the moment. Imkanar ran forward and wrapped his arms firmly around Aya'tar, pulling her tightly against him. They had both longed for this embrace, and now it was finally upon them.

Isha'kau quickly stepped forward, ready to complete the marriage ceremony now that the drama had ended and before anything else could happen. Though her painted face prevented anyone from seeing her expression easily, deep down, she was deeply relieved that love had triumphed. She hoped to finish the ceremony before the challengers had a chance to stand, in the unlikely event that one of them might try to further impede the marriage. To that end, she decided to make things as quick as possible.

"Imkanar, Aya'tar, before all people gathered here and before the gods, do you agree to be bound unto death?" she asked, quickly. Both lovers answered at exactly the same time and without any hesitation.

"Yes!" With that, Imkanar led Aya'tar away from the ceremonial area and toward the ladder which descended into the temple, Isha'kau following closely behind. There would be no immediate consummation of the wedding, normally customary. Aya'tar had so recently birthed children that it was out of the question, but that wouldn't stop them from lying together and simply enjoying each other's company. It would not be long before the ceremony would be held to officially instate Imkanar as one of the two leaders of the city, along with his wife. After such a stunning battle before everyone, no one suspected that anyone would raise a protest. It was obviously the will of Isut.

Sar'Tawas holding a pot of wine

CHAPTER TWENTY SIX

THE TRADER IDMASA

The bright lights of our modern world have rendered the sky awash with light, drowning out the delicate points of light that comprise our galaxy. Yet, on an extremely dark night far from any city, it is possible to gain a glimpse of just how beautiful the night sky used to be in ancient times. Our ancestors likely gazed at the stars and planets above, wondering what they were and why they moved as they did. So important were celestial bodies to ancient peoples that their depictions can still be found on stone walls and carved into rock. Imkanar and young Ikanar are both named after their people's word for the planet Venus, likely believed to be a bright star by their people.

Ishayan entered the small room where he kept his possessions to gather them. He had awoken in the middle of the city's ceremonial grounds, bruised and beaten by the crazed redheaded woman and probably drugged by that snake, Isha'kau. He was now sure that she had slipped something in that drink she had offered him upon honeyed words. What else could explain his sudden weakness? Possession of the city had been stolen from him by a den of snakes living in this wretched city. But it was alright… It would be just fine.

If his counting of the days was correct, any time now, his father would be departing Nara'kit with as many as 800 warriors. He would have one and only one goal in mind – the conquest of Isut'na. He would just leave the city and journey until he met up with the main army. He would then return with the warriors and make his triumphant re-entrance of the city covered in blood. It soon would be his, and he would either take Aya'tar as his bride or leave her dead in a pool of her own blood. As he wiggled free one of his teeth made loose by the fight, he realized how much he didn't care whether she lived or died. He knew one thing for sure, he would watch that redhead screaming in agony as she died a horrible death impaled on a wooden.

ɔ ɔ ɔ
ɔ ɔ ɔ

That night, celebrations rang out all throughout the city. Naturally, the citizens enjoyed any opportunity to have a major celebration. The marriage of their leader, the climactic battle between lovers, and the victory of an underdog were all simply too romantic to not stir their delight and passions. Ember stood on the edge of the temple roof, looking down at nearly 2000 people singing, dancing, and eating, with torches lighting the night. Her neck was still a little sore, and she had several small wounds, but she was mostly in working order.

The Moon was waning as it slowly descended, low on the horizon, toward the Southwest. It was still greater than half illuminated, but it left the sky dark enough to see the never-ending expanse of stars filling the sky. A gentle wind blew across her hair, sending tingles over her bare skin. She still had some bruises and even a small cut on her side from the earlier battle, but all in all, she had come out of it quite well. Aya'tar had publicly declared her as a friend, their "relationship" having ended. Ember wasn't sure if everybody in the crowd completely understood or believed the strange short-lived relationship between Aya'tar and Ember, nor how the friendship had suddenly developed after her resounding defeat, but it had not seemed to have caused any problems for Imkanar. His epic defeat of Ember had been so theatrically intense that people even now continued speaking of it.

She had been a little embarrassed as people looked upon her after the defeat, but she had soon gotten over it. Her theatrics had saved two lovers from a horrible fate, a realization which tempered any negative feelings she had. As the night had fallen, Ember, Brig'dha, and Aethen had been invited into the temple to meet with Aya'tar and finally explain everything that had happened. The priestess and the initiate priestess both sat in awe as they listened to the entire story, not only of how the three friends had met Imkanar and helped him but also of how they had first come to the True South and their adventures beforehand. By the time they had finished, Aya'tar was completely convinced that Isut had played a role in the adventures of these strange northern people.

Brig'dha, Ember, Aethen, Imkanar, Aya'tar, and Isha'kau all sat on the temple's roof a short time later, enjoying a festive meal in celebration of the wedding. After a time, the newlyweds had again left the privacy of the temple, leaving Ember, Brig'dha, Isha'kau, and Aethen to enjoy the night, details of the events leading up to the wedding having been fully explained. In truth, Aya'tar was shocked by the amazing stories she had heard and simply wanted to lie in Imkanar's arms. She was tired of being in control and under constant threat and longed for a single night where she could lie in her lover's arms without any worry.

Ember felt a gentle hand touch her back and turned to find Brig'dha standing beside her. For a short time, they just stood looking at the Moon and wondering what might come next. Surely, there would be peace after all the strife. With Ishayan out of the picture and the two lovers now connected, Ember felt this might be the opportune time to ask Brig'dha something she had wanted to ask for a long time. In her own society, the relationship between two women would be awkward, though not technically forbidden. Luckily, the Southerners seemed relatively open to the idea. Having just witnessed the beautiful wedding ceremony between Aya'tar and Imkanar, however brief it may have been, Ember felt it was the time.

She turned to face Brig'dha and took a deep breath preparing to yet again ask an important question, perhaps even more important than the question she had asked on the harvest festival night under a similar sky. The priestess looked lost in thought as she gazed upon the stars. Strangely, it almost looked as though she were summoning the courage to say something herself, judging by her stance and breathing. Ember suspected that somehow the priestess was merely picking up on her own anticipation. Sometimes, two people who were close enough to one another were known to pick up on each other's moods, even when nothing was said. She felt that her bond to the priestess was at least that close or closer.

"Brig'dha... I have something important I wanted to ask you. I um..." But Brig'dha – quite uncharacteristically – interrupted her, placing her index finger across Ember's lips. Ember leaned back, slightly alarmed as Brig'dha looked back at her with a strange sort of fearful glance. Brig'dha's sudden shift from staring at the stars to looking as though she were about to ask the most important question she had ever asked took Ember completely off guard, derailing her. Of course, given the infrequency of Brig'dha bringing up an important topic in this manner, Ember simply shut up to listen to what her soft-spoken lover had to say.

"Before you ask me anything, I... I have something I need to ask you," she said, looking down for a moment and taking a deep breath, summoning the guts to move forward. Behind them, all conversation had ceased as Aethen, and Isha'kau sat watching. Ember noticed that everyone was suddenly paying attention, but before she could compute the purpose behind this pause, Brig'dha said it.

"Ember, we should never part. I guess what I'm trying to say is... Will you marry me?" Ember stared directly into Brig'dha's eyes for a short moment, unable to speak. Brig'dha had totally messed up her proposal.

"No!" she exclaimed, dumbfounded that Brig'dha had beaten her to it. Brig'dha's expression changed from one of hopeful anticipation to horror. Ember realized that she had misinterpreted, "No! You beat me to it," to mean. "No, I won't."

"Wait, that came out wrong. I meant, *no*, you beat me to it... Oh, whatever... YES! Yes, I will absolutely marry you without question!" Ember exclaimed, grabbing Brig'dha and pulling her into a tight embrace.

For a long time, both lovers simply held one another, unaware that their marriage proposals had been witnessed by most of the festival-goers below. It wasn't long before Brig'dha and Ember had a strange feeling that they were being stared at. The priestess slowly turned her head towards Isha'kau and the people on the roof, while Ember slowly turned towards the nearly 2000 guests below. Both were confronted by exactly the same sight. Everyone was watching them. *Oh no...* Brig'dha thought as her anxiety grew over the onlookers.

"Awkward..." Ember said, quickly leading Brig'dha away and down the stairs into the temple before the shy priestess had a full panic attack. Aethen turned to Isha'kau with a slightly worried expression. He had seen his fair share of taboos broken, and they often centered around religion. What worried him now was where Ember and Brig'dha had ventured. If they entered into one of their romantic escapades in the temple room, it might disturb the newlyweds or, worse, offend the local gods in some unknown way. One could never be too careful with gods and the way his two friends became when they were close could hardly be described as "careful."

"The goddess Isut is a fertility deity. No harm will come," the lesser priestess said with a smile, guessing what Aethen worried about.

"But two women cannot make a baby. Might that offend your gods?" Aethen asked.

"Neither can two old people, but that doesn't stop them from being lovers," she replied matter-of-factually.

"I'm not against it. I just worry that Isut..."

"Just leave it alone. Life is short, so let love be love," Isha'kau said with a smile.

Aethen calmed down, realizing that the woman sitting beside him reassuring him that everything would be alright was also a priestess of the very gods in question. He turned his attention to something of greater importance, the beautiful priestess sitting beside him with her legs dangling over the edge of the building playfully kicking them back and forth. Her deep brown eyes continued to captivate him, and he felt it was time to show her just how much he cared. His words failing him suddenly, he decided to try a gift instead. He had forgotten to give her the gifts he had brought the day before, the bird having made such a scene.

"This probably isn't the right time for this, but I wanted to also give you these," he said, digging in his leather pouch for the precious gifts. She looked back at him in confusion. He removed the shell bracelets, anklets, and a waist cord from his bag. Isha'kau's eyes lit at so much beautiful jewelry. Each string was a thin leather cord with many beautiful cowry shells laced through. No man would have traded so much to obtain such valuable items unless he were serious... very serious. To hand away such beautiful gifts, the sorts of gifts one might only be able to trade for once in a life was as good an indicator of commitment as anything else.

"I... I hope you like these," Aethen began to say as he fitted Isha'kau with each beautiful item. Her heart pounded with anticipation as she felt his gentle hands attaching each item much more delicately than he needed to be. She was still painted in her fertility priestess paint, she had officiated a wedding, and just watched a romantic proposal. If ever there was a night to fill her with the need to be romantic, this was it.

"Are you sure?" she asked as her blood pulsed with adrenaline.

"Yes," he replied, without hesitation. For a moment, she stared at him, unsure of what to say. She had fallen for the handsome northerner the moment she had met him, and it had taken all her willpower to merely tease and flirt with him until now. But learning that the Goddess had sent him had been too much. She would never find a better man, of that she was sure.

"Isha'kau... I know I have only known you a short time, but I feel like I... well, I love you," he said, just as sappy and shy as she could ever have hoped. As soon as he was done, the priestess pounced upon him, knocking the man flat on his back. She paused only a moment to ensure he was as ready as she to let go of the pretense of civility.

She didn't have words to express how romantic the night had become, but some actions could speak more than words. Within moments, they had rolled onto the leather and furs on the center of the roof where those below couldn't see, leaving their sparse clothing in a trail along the roof. Isha'kau nuzzled Aethen's face, still dazzled over his beautiful grey eyes and adorably confused look. How could a beautiful, handsome, innocent-minded, caring man – a man personally vouched for by her goddess – have fallen into her arms? As she straddled his waist, letting her slender fingers delicately explore his oh-so-toned abdomen, she whispered a prayer to Isut. A moment later, both of their long waits ended with mutual gasps. Isha'kau wondered if a second wedding would be needed before long.

ↄ ↄ ↄ

Isha'kau's bed turned out to be a stack of old fur with a soft blanket sewn from many old and worn furs. It had an oddly Isha'kau-like smell and likely needed to be left out in the sun for a day, but the bed was hardly on either of their minds as the women lay on their sides facing each other, their clothing tossed on the floor beside the bed. Brig'dha stretched her arms overhead, closing her hazel eyes and issuing a yawn, her entire body dancing with the giddy feeling of what had been said. Ember had said yes, and that mattered more than anything. That was when she felt the soft touch of her betrothed's hand against her cheek.

No other touch had ever felt right. Even the touch of people she had grown up around was a sensory disaster of discomfort and heightened awareness. But when Ember touched her, somehow, it was just soft. Why this was? She had no answer, but as the resplendent redhead softly cleared the hair from her face, she held back a tear at the rightness of it all. Intimacy was great, but nothing could compare to loving her best friend – truly, two women against the world, yet it seemed they had won.

When she opened her eyes, she found a pair of green eyes gazing back at her, though the dark room hid their true color from anyone who didn't already know. She had found someone who loved her, a strange and wonderous woman if that gender even properly described Ember. That was something else she had meant to ask… but now was not the time for words, as mouths had better use. Not one for staring, she closed her eyes and let Ember's soft hands begin to probe about as they so often did.

So hyper in normal life, Ember was almost delicate as she probed Brig'dha's soft skin. Each touch sent waves of arousal through the Moon Priestess, causing her to issue a breathy soprano, joining the sounds of the night's festivities just beyond the temple walls. A moment later, Brig'dha rolled onto her back and giggled as she felt so many soft kisses from her warrior. Ember's low, almost contralto voice accompanied the kisses, adding more tingles to Brig'dha's joy. All thoughts of what she had wanted to do evaporated as Ember took the lead. Instead, she lay back, letting the ever-descending kisses and playful hands fill her with joy as she softly prayed to her goddess, thanking her for such delights. Tonight, she would let Ember take the lead.

⊃ ⊃ ⊂

A soft glow appeared upon the horizon, and light gently filtered through the small window in the storeroom below the temple as Brig'dha opened her eyes. She and Ember had stumbled into the temple only to find Aya'tar and Imkanar lying together in each other's company. It seemed that everyone had the same idea in mind. Aya'tar had pointed towards the stairs leading down to the storeroom with a smile, and they had taken the hint. The lovers entered what appeared to be the room where Isha'kau generally lived. Seeing no one around, they had entered into a romantic embrace that had lasted much of the night. Strangely, as quick and impulsive as Ember was most of the time when the two were together, she could be the slowest and most methodical lover imaginable.

Brig'dha lay on her back, gently stroking her hand through her sleeping lover's hair as she contemplated what had just happened. Ember had meant to propose to her, but she had beaten the redhead to it and proposed first. She giggled, feeling slightly giddy, having beaten Ember to the punch. With luck, they would become married before long, and their lives would be permanently sealed in each other's arms, an ending Brig'dha wanted more than anything. There was something about being married that differed from simply being together. There was a feeling of depth and commitment that could not be matched by any other arrangement.

She rolled over to gently embrace the softly snoring redhead, happy to spend the rest of her life in that embrace. Likely, they would spend the following day hanging out by one of the marshy ponds or perhaps going for a walk near one of the forests to the West. They had attained such material wealth that neither woman needed to perform any work or task. In a way, they felt like the rulers of cities themselves, a city of two.

⊃ ⊃ ⊂

The day was warm, and the humidity had left Idmasa coated in sweat as he journeyed towards the city of Nara'kit. He had left Isut'na and journeyed to Nara'kit and then down south to trade with several of the most southern tribes before returning. With a large leather bag full of lead beads, Idmasa was looking forward to spending the rest of the harvest relaxing in Nara'kit. Unfortunately, they didn't have quite as much fermented drink as Isut'na, but he supposed that he could afford to trade for plenty.

As he cleared the top of a small hill, the city of Nara'kit came into view. It was a pleasant place similar in construction to the larger Du'ubria and Isut'na. Though the proto-city proper was smaller, several small settlements extended from the ancient tell, providing much of the workforce. Each settlement was surrounded by a palisade, reflecting the never-ending problem of raids in the area. Unfortunately, the raids had changed the peaceful and decentralized city of old into the almost jingoistic place Nara'kit had become. As if on cue, Idmasa noticed movement near the entry to the city. Before him and off in the distance marched a long string of what looked like warriors leaving the city and beginning their journey to the West, in the same direction as Isut'na.

For a moment, he merely watched, unable to accept what he was seeing – a raiding force so large that it outnumbered even a large village's entire population. He needed answers, and movement to his right provided a quick means to get them. A dozen women picked reeds and worked at basketry beside a small creek near the road. He walked towards the women briskly, drawing worried glances from them. One of the older women stood holding what looked like a fishing spear in her arms, just in case.

"Is there something we can help you with, good traveler?" the woman with the spear asked. This close to the city, it was unlikely that any man would seek violence, but it didn't seem like she was interested in taking chances. Unlike the lands outside of Isut'na, Nara'kit was much closer to many aggressive tribes. As a result, they had an army of warriors, and their people had learned to be more particular with whom they spoke.

"Pardon me, I mean you no harm. But that large group of warriors, are they marching on Isut'na?" he asked, pointing at the group of men leaving the city. The woman looked back at him, slightly suspicious of his question.

"You see, I'm a trader of many things, including magical paints which can protect a warrior in battle. If that is truly where they head, I will rush to meet up with them and see if I could trade some of my wares," he said with a smile, hoping that he would pass as more of an opportunistic trader than anything else. The woman appeared to visibly relax, realizing that the man was merely interested in trade.

"Yes, that's where our men march. My husband, Menamar, and his brother, Uritasa, are among them. If our warriors defeat the feeble city of Isut'na, our western borders will be much easier to defend. Then we can deal with those bastard raider tribes to the East. Go and see if you can sell some paints, and if you bump into my husband or his brother, give them my best," she said with a smile. Idmasa nodded his head and left toward the men. However, he intended to turn soon toward the West and make good time towards Isut'na.

Warning the people of Isut'na was the best choice for many reasons. Firstly, the people of Isut'na might reward him for the information, and then there was the excellent trade that would be lost if both cities were united under the same ruler. Much of his profit came from the differences between the two cities' economies. But what actually drove him more than anything was the memory of that strange woman he had escorted to Isut'na not so long before. He couldn't help it, but he had developed a strange sort of crush on her as he had escorted her. She had some form of proud nobility about her and inner strength. Perhaps it was some sort of conviction. In any respect, it attracted him, and the thought of her being killed in battle, or worse, was more than he could bear. *You're a silly old bastard, aren't you?* he said to himself with a chuckle as he turned toward the West.

ↄ ↄ ᴄ

The day was hot and humid like most of the warm season days in the True South. Ember and Brig'dha had spent the first half of the day down by one of the small marshy ponds situated near the city. Swimming in the water was enjoyable and a welcome respite to the warm air and hot sun. The waters were cool and offered a significant portion of mud and clay for the purposes of cleaning one's skin. There was a small island in the center of one of the ponds, just slightly big enough for a handful of people to lie upon. Conveniently, a swimmer could stand on the tiny island and easily dry off by merely basking in the Sun for just a few moments.

It had been a tenday since Aya'tar's wedding to Imkanar, and if their luck held out, their own wedding day would occur in just a few tendays time. The anticipation of such a long-awaited union had filled both lovers with a joy that had shaped each day since. Every little thing they did felt like it had more purpose than the before the pronouncement. Neither woman could think of anything that might stand between them and happiness as they remained in the True South. Instead of courting danger through adventure, the women spent their days relaxing in the ponds near the proto-city and enjoying a carefree lifestyle most people could not envision, made possible through the material wealth they had obtained from the crystal. In the end, it seemed that material wealth could buy a good measure of happiness if you spent it well.

Ember stood in the knee-deep water staring at the rustling rush as the wind danced across the delicate green reeds when suddenly she was attacked by splash after splash of cool water. Brig'dha playfully splashed the contents of the small pond across Ember's back, sending waves of chill through her body. Brig'dha was not one for swimming in deep water, but this pond was quite shallow, and the water was simply too inviting. There were several small lakes and ponds around the city, some used for water, some for retting the flax to make it easier to remove the fibers from the plant, and a couple where people tended to swim. This pond was of the latter sort.

"Have you seen Mew recently? I haven't seen him since yesterday morning," Brig'dha asked, having tired of splashing the redhead. Ember combed the hair out of her face with her fingers, enjoying the feel of the warm Sun against her skin. Her skin, already darker than most of her birth-people due to her father's forest people heritage, had darkened even more in the constant sun. She supposed it would darken even more as they had decided to stay in the city of Isut'na for at least another harvest. She was already enjoying that decision. Ember looked up at the blue sky, which was so clear that it was almost dark blue with nearly no clouds on the horizon in any direction. This truly was a day of days.

"He's probably worried that you are splashing people with water. You know how afraid he is to get wet," Ember said, relaxing in the Sun. The warrior bent down to pick up a rush woven hat she used to block the Sun from her head when Brig'dha noticed something moving off in the distance and pointed. Her cares lost in the beautiful sunlit water, Ember casually affixed the hat to her head before noticing. She just wasn't in the mood to do anything but relax.

"Hey, what's that? It looks like... maybe an old man running?" Ember glanced in the direction to see for herself. Sure enough, down the main road headed to the East, it did appear that a middle-aged man was half walking, half running frantically toward the city. Such scenes were never omens of anything good, and Ember sighed as she expected the worst. She glanced up at the beautiful blue sky and closed her eyes for a few moments savoring the beauty of the day. Somehow, she knew that when she spoke to the man, that beauty would change.

"Darn, and it was starting to be such a nice day, too," she mumbled. She stepped from the water and slung her hair back and forth a few times, letting the excess water come free. Ember fastened her loincloth around her waist and carried her sandals in one hand with her obsidian blade in the other. It was important to never let one's guard down, even so close to the city. Besides, not far ahead of her and approaching fast was a frantic-looking man that she was pretty sure she had never before met. She reluctantly stood and awaited his arrival.

ↄ ↄ ↄ

Idmasa had been walking ahead of the Nara'kit army for several days, but he was not young anymore, and they had been closing the gap. He had made sure to awaken early each morning and make quick time ahead of the army. Even now, he did not believe that the mighty army of Nara'kit had any idea that he was ahead of them. Though everything had been going well so far, early that morning, he had awoken to find the army clearly visible and not even a morning's walk behind him. He simply couldn't keep up this kind of pace for this many days, and he was glad that the city was finally before him.

As he approached Isut, he periodically ran a short distance in small spurts. Were he half his age, he would have already arrived. Idmasa had once been quite athletic. His only hope was that he could warn the people of Isut'na before it was too late. Not only would such a battle be bad for business, but Idmasa had never liked the idea of watching people die for any reason. Strangely enough, he kept thinking about the poor concubine woman he had left behind. Deep down, he wondered if she had been the main catalyst behind his decision to warn the city. He shook his head, surprised at his own motivations.

He approached one of the small lakes surrounding the city when the strangest woman stepped out to greet him. She had thick and shiny waist-length red hair, and her skin, though tanned and brown, was completely differently colored than anyone he knew. More strangely, she had bright green eyes, and her face was shaped differently from anyone he had seen. He slowed down as he approached her, suddenly enchanted by her strange and exotic beauty. Behind her stood another woman of similar beauty and equally exotic features, though much darker. Idmasa gazed at the women as he approached, catching his breath. Before he made a scene of gawking, he remembered the reason he had run so far.

"Woman, I am old and nearly out of breath from running. I've never seen you before, but do you live in Isut'na?" he asked, trying to catch his breath. The woman stepped forward, nodding her head to indicate that she did indeed live in the city. Ember bent down, fastening her sandals, annoyed at being called, "woman," but determining that this winded old man was not a threat. He wasn't sure if he should feel flattered or insulted. At least, he had found a young and healthy person who could run much faster than he and alert the city. Idmasa looked at the woman most seriously as his news was quite grave.

"Heed what I am about to tell you because if you do not, the city of Isut'na will fall to the forces of Nara'kit by the end of the day!" Ember glared at the man, her eyes rolling at his words. *Yep... and that's what I get for trying to have a good day,* she thought as she waited to hear what the old man had to say.

ↄ ↄ ↄ

Ember stood on top of a building facing out in the direction from where the army of Nara'kit would likely approach. The heroic act of a trader named Idmasa had sent her running all the way from the lake where she had been swimming to the city, passing the word at each field she passed. Idmasa himself had slowed down and calmly walked to the city with Brig'dha, once Ember had taken the role of harold from him. Now, everyone awaited the approach of the enemy. They had not had much time to prepare, but thanks to Idmasa, the trader, they had at least not been caught completely by surprise.

Kamar stood in the center of the ceremonial grounds wearing a thick leather hide piece strapped to his chest for protection along with a spear in one hand. His other hand assisted his mouth at barking out orders. This was a moment that he had hoped would never come, but now it was upon him. The thought of what lay ahead filled the old warrior with dread. Isut'na had perhaps two dozen warriors ready to help the city, but the rest would be drawn up from farmers and laborers. Isut'na was simply not as militaristic as Nara'kit, and if Idmasa, the trader, was to be believed, an army of perhaps 300 to 400 strong and able warriors with an equal number of armed farmers was just over the hill and approaching fast. He shook his head at the thought.

They had begun by sealing the few entrances into the city, narrow passageways between tall buildings, with huge rocks kept by those passages for just that purpose, as well as anything else that could be

508

jammed in the way. Ladders were pulled atop buildings to prevent them from being used by the enemy. Kamar's few warriors were passing out spears, clubs, large rocks, and even bows and arrows to anyone who could use them. Building an army of farmers was not easy, but it was all they had.

Most women and children had gathered in the upper-level buildings toward the center of the city, which were the most protected, leaving mostly men to fight the battle. Ember and Brig'dha would not be joining the families, instead opting to fight for the city in which they now lived. In general, combat was typically performed by the men, but there were no rules in Isut'na which prevented women, duemuas, or narmu from taking up arms in defense of the city. Several other women, perhaps 120, had elected to help in the fight. Most notably Ember, Brig'dha, and Zah'namu.

With their young child Kam'ir safely protected with the other children, Zah'namu stood with a long spear in hand, ready to help defend the city. Her logic was simple – if the city fell, what purpose would there be in her hiding? As an elder's wife, she and her husband's lives would be forfeit if the city fell. If that were to happen, the only hope for their child was that no one would give away the fact that he was their child. Unfortunately, this could be the precursor to a massacre and not simply an occupation for all she knew. She hoped that her child would survive to see the next morning, if nothing more.

She would like to see that morning with him, but there was no way that Zah'namu would leave the horror of the bloody battlefield for her husband to face alone when she was strong and could throw a spear. Looking at the faces of the other women who had elected to fight revealed similar motives. They were young and old, married in single. Some fought for the city, while others fought for their families. Zah'namu was most surprised when she saw the exotic travelers from the Northwest checking their weapons and standing with the other warriors. For some reason, this brought her a strange sense of hope.

Even Sar'Tawas had taken it upon himself to help with the city's defenses. While Kamar and nearly a third of the city's inhabitants climbed atop the buildings preparing to defend the walls, he took with him nearly 100 farmers and craftsmen. It was important to seal as many of the passageways into the city as possible and remove anything of value and carry it to the higher levels where it could be defended if the men fought their way into the city. Even if they defeated the forces from Nara'kit, losing the valuable grain and other foods that would normally carry them through the colder season could be just as devastating.

Sar'Tawas stood by one of the largest grain storage rooms watching as nearly a dozen flax field women labored back and forth carrying the sacks from the room. Not far away, twenty men slid a large rock into place to protect the entryway closest to the grain storage. His scheming to control the city would have to wait for now. Sar'Tawas truly cared about the inhabitants of Isut'na, and he would do everything in his power to make sure that no one was harmed and nothing was lost. *What use is a ruined city for me, anyway?* he thought with dry mirth.

Not far away atop one of the outer buildings sat the redheaded warrior preparing for what was to come. Ember could not wrap her mind around the idea of so many warriors advancing on the city in a single attack. How could they possibly defend against so many people? When raiders attacked a village, they usually did so in small bands, perhaps a dozen. Combat was not organized and typically involved groups of people rushing around in random directions trying to scare each other rather than actually kill. Idmasa, the trader, described a large and organized body of warriors purpose-driven to kill and controlled like ants. The idea simply made no sense to Ember.

She watched as the last of the fieldworkers finished gathering what they could and headed for the city. Most of the supplies and crops would have to be left behind, as there simply was not enough time to remove that much material from the fields. Ember thanked the gods once more that the strange trader man had given them any warning at all. If the vast army had crossed the top of the hill unannounced, they could have descended upon the fields slaughtering an overwhelming a good percentage of the city's labor force before anybody could have taken any action.

She still wore the same linen loincloth she had applied after leaving the water, while Brig'dha wore her string skirt. Brig'dha had taken a moment to apply ash across Ember's face and around her eyes, reducing the glare of the day. Next, she had quickly given Ember a series of black bands around her arms, legs, and body, the paint of a man. Ember had returned the favor applying black dots across Brig'dha's face under her eyes, and black swirls around her body. Both of their cultures believed strongly that any warrior who did battle did so at their own peril if not properly painted. Among both of their people, it was the wife's job to paint her husband for war, and the irony was not lost on either woman.

A moment later, everyone saw the dreaded flash of light from the top of the hill to the East. The flash immediately caught Ember's attention and filled her with anticipation and dread. A young man had been sent to that hill carrying with him a small, polished obsidian mirror, the kind people used to apply makeup. He was to flash the mirror as soon as he saw people coming and then return to the city as fast as possible. Frantically he flashed it catching the Sun before turning and running the long-distance back to the city.

As he approached the city wall a short while later, a rope was lowered for him to climb up. Only moments later, the first of the Nara'kit warriors broke the edge of the horizon. Ember stared at the large number of warriors coming over the hill. For the most part, those warriors who were clothed wore a loincloth of leather along with sandals, though there was some variation. Some of them wore thick leather pieces tied to various parts of their body to reduce the likelihood of an arrow finding their flesh. Unfortunately, any such protection would make fighting much hotter and reduce maneuverability. Their faces and bodies were painted strikingly with war paint, and their heads decorated with feathers.

At the front of the group were two men wearing much more colorful outfits than the rest of the warriors. These two would be the leaders, most likely the ruler of Nara'kit and his son, Ishayan. All around, Ember heard sounds of panic and distress as the sheer number of warriors began to sink in. Despite the city's small guard force and everyone who would fight holding a weapon, Isut'na had barely 900 defenders, almost half of the population. While this seemed like more than the warriors coming, most of these defenders had little if any experience in combat. Of its nearly 2500 citizens, the large majority were either too young or too old to fight.

Ember glanced over her left shoulder and saw a young man barely 17 harvests age clutching a hunting bow. Beside him was a woman of approximately the same age holding two small throwing spears. She thought the woman's name might be Kara'tar, but she had only heard the name the man had used to call her moments before. Each of them had a painted, red-tipped hawk feather in their hair. Their hands were coupled together as lovers, and they each wore similarly painted faces as well as similarly terrified expressions. This was more than a battle for land and wealth, this was a fight to continue their very lives, and they knew it. Both of them glanced at Ember, and she smiled back at them with as brave of an expression as she could muster. Yet, deep down, she was frightened too.

Nervously, Ember checked her quiver and found 24 arrows with standard stone arrowheads and a 25th arrow carrying the magical copper arrowhead she had obtained along with their jewelry. Making more arrows would not be that complicated, but this was all she would have for this battle. She hoped that the enemy would tire and leave after an exchange of arrow fire. Somehow she didn't expect that they would give up that easily. Brig'dha stood beside Ember, dagger in hand and ready to support the wounded. She carried a small reed basket full of ointment and salt for wounds in her other hand. Brig'dha knelt beside Ember and placed her hand gently on the "resurrected" redhead's shoulder, looking her lover deep in the eyes in rare and prolonged eye-contact.

"Don't die again," she whispered. At first, Ember found the comment slightly humorous, considering its reference. But the look of fear on Brig'dha's face quickly washed away any humor. She was quite serious. This was a fight for life or death, and it was very likely that in a short time, many would die. For a while, the two simply knelt before one another, looking deeply into each other's eyes. Life seemed to be one terrifying fight after the other, and there were no guarantees that either of them would live. They were each glad for the time that they had spent together and desperately hoped that there would be more to come.

"Try to keep your head down. I don't want you to die for the first time," she replied to the frightened priestess. Brig'dha was certainly upset, but Ember knew that she would stand her ground no matter how frightened she got. There was an inner strength to Brig'dha that didn't show on her otherwise worried-looking face. Many people on this day would live because of Brig'dha's care, and it brought strength to Ember to think of that.

"I have a potion I made earlier today," Brig'dha said, holding up a small clay dish with a strange white substance within. Ember examined the substance hoping to take their minds off what was to come.

"What is it, and what is it do?" Brig'dha smiled and looked down for a moment before speaking.

"It is a mixture of mother's milk and salt, and I believe it will help with wounds. The milk from a mother, as you know, carries the essence of life within it. So, I figured that if I..." Brig'dha continued her explanation of how her potion might work while Ember sat beside her, listening. For all they knew, this might be their last discussion.

Ↄ Ↄ Ↄ

An'sankup'Anteanar stood before his warriors just outside of the arrow range of Isut'na. He had brought 100 dedicated archers and another 300 trained warriors, along with almost 400 regular men of the city who armed themselves with farm tools and hunting weapons ready to scale the walls, perhaps the largest military force ever assembled. They had brought with them several wooden ladders as well as a multitude of stretched leather shields to protect against arrows while they attacked. Anteanar was not a fan of attacking towards the evening, but he was reasonably confident that the city of Isut'na would fall before the Sun reached the horizon. If he could merely get a handful of men inside of the city, their entire meager defense would likely fall apart.

He turned once more to look upon his vast army with pride. Other cities, such as Du'ubria, one day known as Catalhoyuk, had only a handful of warriors, while smaller tribes often had none. The reason that he had 400 dedicated warriors to bring to battle was because of the decisions he made as a ruler, decisions that would see him prevail while Isut'na fell. While Isut'na and Du'ubria were in relatively peaceful locations, Nara'kit was flanked by many hostile tribes who had long given them reason to maintain such an uncommon force.

Of course, he wished that it had not come to this and that his son had succeeded. The boy had left proclaiming that he would take control of the city peacefully by winning the heart of its ruler, a woman named Aya'tar. Instead, they had encountered him on his way back to the city, quite literally bruised and beaten. It had been humiliating, but in the end, it would prove a valuable lesson for his enthusiastic son. Once he took control of Isut'na, Anteanar was keen on leaving his son in charge of what was left of the city. It was simply too difficult for him to control two cities simultaneously.

"Everyone is ready, father. What is your command?" Ishayan asked as he stood beside Anteanar, holding a heavily decorated and ornate wooden war club. Both men wore ornate leather pieces covering large portions of their bodies to protect against arrows. The leather had been carved with symbols depicting the Sun and other sacred shapes. Their hair sported many eagle and vulture feathers, the holiest feathers worn. Even their loincloths were made of the finest flax and dyed red for the occasion. Ishayan was pleased that his father had seen fit to bring his battle gear along with him. It would not have been proper to attack the city wearing dirty sandals and without fresh clothing.

He wanted nothing more than to destroy the city and recover what was left of it as his own. He had been insulted and humiliated within these walls, and the chance to return the favor so quickly made his mouth water. He would plunge his dagger deep within the gut of the treacherous Aya'tar, her pathetic lover, that strange knife-wielding bitch, and the bizarre redhead. Their bodies would be placed on pikes in front of the temple for everyone to see. It was best that he got rid of that entire line of vipers. Besides, there would be many other women to choose from among the spoils from the city. Perhaps he might even find a sacred duemuas to take as a slave.

"These are not warriors. These are nothing but women with fishing spears. We brought plenty of extra arrows, and I intend to use them. Have the archers move within range and fire over their buildings. They will beg for surrender after we fill perhaps 100 or 200 of them with our arrows. But first, let us make a proper offering. May An'an bring us to victory!" the ruler said to his son, shaking him from his thoughts of vengeance.

Behind him stepped a man who had been shaven completely clean of any hair. The man's body was covered in black ornate magical shapes from top to bottom. Beside him stood a woman equally covered in magical shapes and wearing an elaborate plume of long black feathers attached to the back of her hair and emanating from her head like spokes of light toward the sky. They were the priest and priestess of the gods, An'an being chief among them. Anteanar and Ishayan both stood back to allow them to do their work. Only a fool would begin a battle without first properly imploring the gods.

CHAPTER TWENTY SEVEN

YOU BRAVE STUPID FOOL

Organized combat in the Neolithic period was limited at best, if it happened at all. The resources and weaponry required for extended combat and full-out total war would not be present until the dawn of the Bronze Age. This meant that military engagement would be limited to a few hundred combatants, and typically only a few dozen. Nature and precedent for battle were probably rooted more in resource conflicts, raids, and minor disputes, than major organized political conflict, as would be seen in later millennia. The weapons used were commonly hunting implements, such as bows and spears, and conventional tools, such as an ax or adze. While true armor did not exist, simple stretched hide shields may have been used for protection. Archaeologically speaking, it is important to consider that the battle about to take place was possible, but very unlikely.

Aethen knelt beside Ember and Brig'dha, looking over the edge of one of the buildings as a woman and a cleanly shaven, bald man stepped forward, letting their long linen capes fall to the ground. Their bodies were intricately painted with extremely complex magical shapes. The woman wore a very large, feathered headdress emanating feathers high above her head in each direction, like spokes. Everything about them screamed of a priest and priestess, from their paint to their very well-made linen loincloths.

They led forward a young cow with a flax cord around its neck. They held their arms up in the air for a short time, chanting invocations to various regional deities, including An'an. This was the ceremony before the battle. Beside Aethen, one of the flax farmers slowly lifted his bow, nocking an arrow. At first, Aethen didn't realize what the man was doing, then it suddenly became apparent. He began to draw the bowstring while taking aim.

"I bet I can put one right in that big shiny bald head, or maybe kill that woman," he said, just about ready to loose the arrow. Brig'dha reached out, grabbing the bow and knocking it sideways right as the man fired his arrow. The arrow flew through the air and landed an arm's length from the woman as she chanted. She was so involved with the ritual that she never opened her eyes or even realized how close she had come to death. That level of connection to the spirits was unnerving to the people of Isut'na. The farmer turned an enraged glare at Brig'dha, as she had just saved the life of an enemy.

"You fool! If you kill the priestess of their gods, you will further aid them! Their men will fight twice as hard, and their gods will help them even more!" Brig'dha said, scolding the man in an uncharacteristic outburst. Other people around him nodded their heads, confirming what the priestess said. One simply didn't shoot a priest or priestess, at least not until you could be sure that their gods had truly abandoned them. There was nothing so terrifying as the retribution of the gods.

The bald man held the cow tightly while the woman knelt before the animal, still chanting. Then, while beginning a ritual song, she brandished a large obsidian knife. Though many people gathered to defend Isut'na seemed unsure of what was about to happen, Brig'dha stared with anticipation, knowing exactly what was to come. For a short time, everybody watched as the woman sang her song of magic, when suddenly – in a single stroke – she slashed open the cow's neck, spilling its blood all over the ground and all over her. As the priest and three warriors from Nara'kit held the cow, preventing it from fleeing, the woman continued to sing as she knelt before the animal bathing in its warm flowing blood. It covered her hair, face, and her entire body while she held her arms out, continuing the magic. The animal staggered and slowly sank to the ground as the woman stood and continued to sing, letting everyone see the blood.

"She is likely channeling their gods directly. This does not bode well for us," Brig'dha said. As they watched, the woman walked down the line of warriors, wiping her hand across the blood that covered her body and then smearing it across each of their heads, a blessing from An'an. There was barely enough blood in total to touch every warrior, but somehow she managed to mark each one of them. With the ritual completed, the priest and the priestess stood back from the battle as their men prepared to step entirely within arrow range. It was about to start.

Ember pulled an arrow from her quiver and began to nock it to the bowstring when suddenly one of the two leaders – it looked like Ishayan – advanced forward, motioning with his arm to signal nearly one-fourth of the warriors to walk forward, toward the walls. She paused, suddenly more curious about what she saw than what she was doing. Beside her, a woman knelt, staring over the edge of the building equally curious. She had intricate scarification marks across her face, and Ember thought she recognized the woman from one of the trading areas though she could not remember which. Nearly 100 of the men came to stand in a long line just ever so slightly behind the arrow which had been fired at the priestess. They all came to a halt very purposefully at that point and began readying their bows.

"Do you think that they're trying to scare us into giving up our crops?" the woman asked anyone nearby her who might listen. Ember glanced at her, the two women making fearful eye contact.

"I don't think so… I believe they want more than your crops," Ember said solemnly. The woman glanced at her, fear in her eyes. Then, setting her spear down, she held out a flint knife for Ember to see.

"If they come to take me... I won't let them... Whatever it takes, they won't have me," she said with finality, swallowing hard. There were murmurs all around as people tried to decide what to do. There were calls from many for someone to come forward and make peace. An argument broke out over the best strategy to negotiate their way out of this problem. Fear was growing in the hearts of the defenders as the archers slowly advanced. Turning her attention from the woman back to the army, Ember stared at the men standing behind the single-fired arrow, trying to make sense of what she saw. As she watched, one of the men lifted grass and watched it fall before him, caught by the wind. Suddenly, she realized what they were doing...

"Get down! Everyone get down!" Ember yelled as loudly as she could. The wind was blowing towards the city, allowing the Nara'kit archers' arrows to fly farther than the arrow fired from Isut'na. The Nara'kit archers had used that same arrow to reveal how close they could stand without being hit. With that realization and her quick scream of warning, many defenders dropped flat on the roofs. Some also realized what Ember had, while many simply fell flat out of fear. At that moment, the Nara'kit archers drew back their 100 bows and loosed a small storm of death upon the city.

The arrows flew high into the air carried by the wind, raining down upon the people of Isut'na. The arrows made a loud sound as they all flew as a deadly wave. Many people had placed wood or stretched leather hide shields over their backs to protect them from arrows or spears raining down, but this did not save everyone. As Ember watched, a man not far to her right took an arrow in his lower back and began screaming and grasping at the blood-covered shaft. Behind her, she could hear many women shrieking as the arrows rained down from above.

As soon as the first volley of arrows had landed, the second volley of arrows was launched, and then a third. All the casualties so far were on the side of Isut'na. It seemed that Nara'kit's gods truly were on their side, judging by the wind. One man stood and pulled his bow back to its maximum draw in a vain effort to hit the warriors. He let loose an arrow, but the arrow fell short of its mark, and not before two buried themselves into his chest. All around, there were screams of the frightened, the wounded, and the dying. There were cries from people that the city should just surrender before it was too late, and that the gods had already abandoned them. The arrow storm had precisely the effect the attackers had wanted it to have.

Ember shook her head and took a deep breath to regain her focus. A quick glance to her left revealed that Brig'dha was on her knees helping a wounded man, but otherwise, she appeared okay. As long as Brig'dha survived, Ember would not give up hope. Unfortunately, it seemed that the rest of the city was quickly losing whatever hope they had. They desperately needed some action or deed to inspire the people before their morale was destroyed. Ember remembered frightening the wolves from poor Tes by her brash actions and loud screams. Sometimes one did not have to be stronger than an enemy, just more intimidating.

Seeing that his archers were not being attacked, the leader of the Nara'kit army ordered the rest of his soldiers to rush forwards and begin scaling the buildings which served as a wall. Ember peered over the edge of the wall and saw three large ladders carried by warriors as they approached the buildings. The men approached the walls and began lifting the ladders into place. They were having free run of the city's defenses and meeting almost no resistance. Their shower of arrows had delivered a terrible and frightening attack directly into the heart of the peoples' courage. Worse, people could be heard all around her, suggesting that the city should surrender. The sounds of the wounded and dying only adding to their fears. Beside her, the woman with the knife and spear awaited her chance to hurl the deadly weapon at the enemy.

ↄ ↄ ↄ

At the nearest entrance to the city, dozens of Nara'kit Warriors tugged at the large rocks and building materials that had been placed in their paths and began to tear them free. It would not be long before the warriors began entering the city. Kamar's small force of defenders rushed forward with clubs and spears to push back the intrusion. With most of the city cowering in fear and only a few barely brave enough to stand against the Nara'kit forces, it would not be much longer before the city fell.

Kamar's small group of men rushed towards the nearest entryway, where the men from Nara'kit could be seen pulling free the obstructions. The defenders stopped just before the last large rocks blocking the gateway into the city. They held their weapons at the ready, adrenaline flowing as they waited for the inevitable. The last large stones which blocked the entryway were pushed out of the way by the warriors of Nara'kit. Kamar's men stood their ground, sweat dripping down their faces in the heat. Moments later, his six warriors met nearly 20 Nara'kit warriors forcing their way through the narrow passageway into the city.

Men rushed forward, swinging club and ax at one another in a violent dance of blood and death. Kamar swung his war club, knocking the ax from an enemy's hand, then reversing his swing to catch the man square in the face. The warrior dropped to his knees, holding what was left of his face as another jumped over the top of him to take his place at the front. Beside him, a Nara'kit warrior swung his adze catching one of Kamar's men in the side of the head, ending his life in one quick and violent cleave. For a moment, it seemed as though the enemy was winning, but it was not long before his five remaining veteran defenders began to push the greater number, but less experienced, Nara'kit forces back. Within moments, many of the Nara'kit warriors began to retreat, realizing they were outmatched.

Kamar stood back from the fight and looked up toward the buildings to see how the defenders on the roofs were doing. He watched as one of the ladders was roughly placed against one of the buildings causing screams from those near. He began to worry as it seemed that the people of Isut'na were barely mounting a resistance, though the defenders technically outnumbered the attackers. The arrow showers had taken the resolve of all but the most veteran of warriors. Suddenly, one of the warriors broke free of his men and came rushing upon him with a war club in hand. Kamar turned and saw the man approaching, but not in time.

With his club held high, the warrior rushed at him, about to swing and end Kamar's life. Abruptly, the man screamed as a spear flew through the air and slammed right into his stomach so deeply that the tip burst through his lower back. The man staggered, running right into Kamar and then falling to the ground beside him in the fetal position, clutching the spear and wallowing in horrible agony. Behind him, Kamar turned to see his wife Zah'namu approaching with four farmer women armed with clubs and spears to reinforce the breach. She bent down and placed her foot against the man's chest, grabbing her spear. The warrior reached up, trying to remove her hands from the weapon, but she continued to twist and pull the spear, wrenching it free in a violent tug. A moment later, the man stopped struggling, apparently succumbing to the wound.

"Thank you!" he said, lost for words in the moment. He vowed that if both of them made it through this battle, he would find some way to repay the bravery of his wife. The problem was that his 900 defenders were mostly fleeing in panic. It only took a few moments for Kamar's group, along with Zah'namu's reinforcements, to plug up a hole in the wall, but he could not be sure that other avenues into the city had not been exploited. The significant danger of letting the enemy into the city, even a small number of them, was the havoc they could loose while running through the city, unchecked. Most of the citizens were on the second-floor buildings hidden away, but there were still plenty of people trying to secure the precious wheat and other materials, or, at least, hide them. If any of those vulnerable groups ran into marauding Nara'kit forces, they would certainly be killed. He had to hope that someone could rally the defenders on the buildings before all was lost.

ɔ ɔ ɔ

Not far North of where Ember knelt, Aethen and Isha'kau crouched low, doing their best to defend the city as well as stay alive. While Aethen clutched his bow, Isha'kau held a small basket full of rocks. Every few moments, the pair would rise up and into the line of fire, a great personal risk each time. Aethen would take aim and launch a deadly arrow at an attacker, while Isha'kau would hurl a rock at an oncoming warrior. Aethen was quite impressed to see how effective the rocks actually were. When thrown from a good height and with good aim, a fist-size rock hitting a warrior in the head would at the least incapacitate him, if not kill the man outright.

"I should be back in the temple praying to Isut and Gunar with Aya'tar instead of throwing rocks," Isha'kau said, lying on her back and fumbling with her next deadly rock missile. Aethen looked back at her with a smile, though he was quite glad that she had chosen to remain with him. Beside the pair were nearly a dozen farmers, mostly armed with spears and rocks and all hoping for the best.

"If it makes you feel better, I'm glad to have you by my side," he said, giving her a wink. Isha'kau was unable to contemplate how he could be so relaxed in the face of such an attack. Yet, Aethen seemed to be in control of his emotions, almost stoic. His confidence was infectious, filling the people around him with a sense of hope. At that moment, Isha'kau and Aethen nodded to one another and rolled over, standing up to take another shot. Aethen's arrow flew true but was blocked by a stretched leather shield held by a Nara'kit warrior. Just as the man lowered his shield, he caught a rock to the face ending his charge, courtesy of the lesser priestess. To her right, a farmer grabbed ahold of an arrow that had just appeared in his chest, screaming and falling forward to his death. Things were getting out of hand.

ɔ ɔ ᴄ

Ember turned to see that most Isut'na forces were hiding or fleeing. It had taken only a few volleys of arrows to send what little forces the city had into flight. On the buildings around her, she saw what looked to be perhaps 100 to 200 defenders ducking low and popping up only to fire an arrow or throw a spear. Beside her, the woman with the intricate facial scarification suddenly stood and hurled her light fishing spear at the approaching warriors. Luck was on her side as the small but agile fishing spear flew true, catching a Nara'kit warrior in the leg and effectively taking him out of the fight, even though he would likely live.

But when Ember looked to her right, she caught sight of the woman with the red-painted feather dropping her spear and staggering backward, an arrow in her arm as she caught a war club in the face. Kara'tar, if that was her name, stumbled and fell off the wall of buildings into the courtyard below. A moment later, the man who had killed her met a similar end. Unfortunately, too few good defenders fought on, and for every brave defender holding their ground, many more were wounded, dead, or fleeing. Around her were perhaps a dozen wounded people clutching arrow wounds, as well as many who could be heard on the ground beneath the buildings wailing in agony. Far from defending, they were quickly losing. Perhaps three lengths of a man from where she knelt, Brig'dha worked tirelessly assisting those wounded who might live.

They had started with enough people to repel the warriors climbing the ladders, but the majority had fled. Two ladders had already found their way to the sides of buildings, and a third was approaching. What Ember needed was to find a way to rally the hundreds of potential defenders who had lost heart in the arrow volleys. There was, unfortunately, only one way she could think to do this. Nearly everyone she had seen standing to get a good shot had paid for it with their lives. With their men now scaling the walls, the Nara'kit archers had stopped firing volleys making standing a little safer, but there were still arrows flying over the walls now and then. Adrenaline rushed through her body as she thought of what she was about to do. Ember whispered a prayer to the Goddess of the Moon.

"Goddess, please watch over me. If I die, please spare my love," she whispered. Ember slung her bow over her head, the string across her chest. The ladder about to be placed against the side of the wall near her would go up at a very shallow angle and then be pushed higher and higher into a safer angle if it went anything like the other two had. It was that same ladder she sought to use to reach the ground. Looking once more at the Nara'kit forces, she saw what looked like their leader barking orders at his men. That was the man she wished to kill. But what she was about to do was nearly suicidal. Unfortunately, sometimes only the brashest actions would succeed due to their unpredictability. Besides, how could this be worse than being chased by wolves or facing the large man who had enslaved her so long before? Ember took several deep breaths prepping herself. Then, she suddenly stood to her full height, turning her back upon the enemy as though they were not even there.

"Do not be afraid! We outnumber them two to one!" she screamed, all the while expecting to feel the piercing bite of an arrow in her back. She held her arms out for all to see that she was, apparently, unafraid of the enemy. She nearly screamed in fear as one arrow after another flew past her, all the while forcing her face to remain calm as she fought not to cower in her all-to-real terror. All around, people glanced in her direction, watching to see what would happen.

"I will show you! I will show you that we can win!" she cried and then turned to run toward the third ladder. This was a big gamble – if she were killed, it could demoralize the already fearful people. However, if she were successful, it might be just the sort of push Isut'na's people needed. Ember dashed across the building top right past Brig'dha, who looked up too late to say anything. Ember jumped down to the next building, landing and coming up in a roll. At that moment, the ladder slammed into the side of the building at a shallow angle. Ember pulled free her knife and slit both of her sandal straps, leaving the footwear behind. For what she was about to do, a sandal would only increase the risk of falling. Her feet were tough after a life often spent barefoot, and she was unaffected by the ground. Deep down, she was in near panic over what she was about to do, her vision threatening to tunnel in fear.

Ember ran straight for the ladder, literally jumping up on the top rung and then running down the ladder, which was merely a 45° angle. The four men at the bottom were so shocked as they saw her running down the ladder that they did not even oppose her when she jumped to the ground and took off running toward the leader of the Nara'kit forces. As she ran, people behind her screamed support as they began to hope against all hopes that she might be successful in whatever daring and reckless maneuver she was undertaking. It was only a few moments before she had run halfway between the city and the Nara'kit forces, and no one had even fired a single arrow at her yet. She had to assume that her actions were so sudden and reckless that many just did not know how to respond to them, instead just watching her.

Strangely, her activities had almost halted the entire attack as almost everyone turned to see the woman rushing towards nearly 800 heavily armed warriors. Ember slid to a stop and pulled free her bow and an arrow, quickly nocking it as she came to the halfway point. She could nock and fire arrows faster than anyone she knew, and she would put that skill to the test here and now. She aimed at the leader and let loose her first arrow. Far behind, Brig'dha stared over the edge of the building, her mouth nearly separating from her skull in abject horror.

ɔ ɔ ɔ

Everything had been going quite well when suddenly, Anteanar saw his men reacting to something strange, something abrupt. He turned, expecting to see some sort of strange counterattack but instead, what greeted his eyes was simply beyond anything he could have expected. A strange woman with painted skin and bright red hair like the embers of fire was literally running down a ladder, which had not been lifted up to a proper angle yet. As he watched, the woman ran with a bow across her chest and a wild look in her eyes. She ran straight toward his men as though she were going to take them all on herself. He merely watched, expecting at any moment an arrow to bury itself deep in the brazen woman, and yet, none did. It almost seemed like his men were waiting to see what happened when she made it to their lines. Suddenly, she came to a halt and brought her bow to bear directly in his path. His interest suddenly switched to alarm as she drew an arrow and took aim upon him faster than he thought anyone could.

Anteanar ducked sideways as the reckless redhead launched an arrow at him. Behind him, he heard the scream of one of his archers taking the missed arrow in the arm. The idea that a single woman, a strange one from a faraway land at that, would run down one of his own ladders and take a shot at him was ridiculous, to say the least. How she had not already been killed yet was itself some strange will of the gods, but he could remedy that. He waved his arm towards the woman, indicating that his archers should end her life, when to his surprise, she grabbed another arrow from her quiver and nocked it in a smooth, practiced motion. His eyes widened as she pulled the arrow back and let loose the deadly missile while at the same time turning and beginning to run.

The arrow seemed to come at him in slow-motion, curving ever so slightly and then slamming into his waist just above his hip bone. Strangely, as he looked down and saw the blood squirting from just above the cord which held his loincloth, it didn't seem to hurt. It certainly felt strange and tingly. He stepped backward, his breathing increasing as the blood started to flow quicker. He felt weaker, as though his strength had just left him. Behind him, one of his warriors grabbed his arms as he slowly sank to the ground. It was all so confusing, but that was how life-threatening injuries sometimes occurred.

"Did you kill her?" he sputtered. The man looked at him for a moment, seemingly confused by the question, though in reality, he was more confused that the man's interest lay in the redhead when he had been so grievously wounded.

"No, she flees even now!" he said.

"Everyone attack! Everyone! Ishayan, you are in charge," he screamed as shock began to set in. Suddenly, the wound began to hurt much more than it had.

☊ ☊ ☊

Ember ran as fast as she had ever run, weaving left and right with arrows flying over her. She expected at any moment to catch one in the back. Behind her, dozens of warriors rushed forward with clubs, each hoping to catch her and avenge their fallen leader – ironically, blocking most of the archers who might have had a clear shot at the retreating redhead. Suddenly Kamar appeared at the top of one of the buildings screaming to attack. Two dozen Isut'na archers fired back at the men pursuing Ember catching nearly half of them with deadly arrows. The same archers began to pelt the warriors approaching the ladders while women and older men tossed rocks down upon the heads of warriors trying to scale the ladders. The city was finally beginning to realize that it could defend itself. Seeing such a brave action by a single person had done more to restore confidence in the citizens than Ember had realized.

When Ember got to the same ladder she had run down, she found all the warriors lying around it, either dead from arrow wounds and rocks to the head. She dashed right up the ladder, which was still sitting at an angle too low for multiple men to climb. As soon as she got to the roof, she dropped to her knees and placed her hand over her chest breathing heavily. She had more adrenaline flowing through her body than she knew what to do with. She whispered her thanks to the Goddess and any spirits who had helped. She just could not believe that she had lived. In fact, she had benefited from the Nara'kit archers initially watching, expecting her to charge their lines in some heroic, but foolish effort, and then die. That had secured the first half of her trip, while indecision and a lot of weaving as she ran, and the mass of pursing warriors had saved her as she left.

Brig'dha rushed over and grabbed her in a deep embrace. Ember looked up at the priestess and smiled with a mixture of exhilaration and amazement that she had survived. Her smile ended when Brig'dha suddenly released her, then slapped her hard across the face. She looked at Ember for a moment, tears streaking her face paint, and then reached forward, grabbing Ember once more in a teary embrace. Ember had never been held so tightly by the priestess, for she could feel Brig'dha's fingernails starting to dig into her back, breaking the skin.

"You fool... you brave, stupid fool. This is why I love you..." she said, whimpering. As soon as she pulled herself free from Ember, she began carefully applying a mixture of yarrow and salt to the various wounds Ember had received, unknowingly. Three different arrows had nicked her arms and legs, each glancing her. This was likely a result of her erratic darting back and forth as she ran. She had learned as a child during snowball fights and rock wars never to run in a straight line. She knew Brig'dha was angry, and she knew that the priestess had a good reason to be.

Not far away, the woman with the scarification marks across her face lay holding a second fishing spear and having witnessed the entire brave event. She had nearly been struck by an arrow and had almost turned and fled. Having witnessed the strange redhead from the distant land so boldly assaulting the very leader of the enemy army had filled her with strength. She would make sure that her spear found the chest of the next enemy who came into range. They would not take her as a spoil because she would fight them with her last breath. Isut had not forsaken them, it seemed.

CHAPTER TWENTY EIGHT
THE BATTLE OF ISUT'NA

Neolithic warfare was an extremely dangerous affair in which nearly any significant wound would likely prove fatal within a short while. Besides simple herbal remedies and a few basic first-aid-style medical techniques, very little could be done for the wounded other than keeping them comfortable and waiting for them to recover or perish. Luckily, Ember didn't consider these horrors as she ran down the ladder and rushed straight at the enemy leader. Her actions might seem a bit far-fetched, but we have many examples of individuals standing before overwhelming odds and, somehow, escaping. Perhaps a good example of a similar event occurred during WWII when Audie Murphy climbed a burning tank to personally hold off hundreds of advancing German soldiers for over an hour.

While the battle raged on, Sar'Tawas had been helping secure the city's provisions in the most secure buildings towards the Western walls of the city. He kept Ianmu nearby with her deadly dagger, just in case. The woman seemed calmer with what was going on than he had expected. He was nervous and expected disaster at every turn. He knew that she was skilled with a blade, but why she wasn't panicking, he could not be entirely sure. His only hope was that after this battle, assuming that the Nara'kit forces did not win, he could convince the Elder Council this attack was evidence that the Goddess was not on their side. Perhaps if he did a good job of guarding the city's resources, he could even show them that he was a better choice. He might even have Ianmu at his side, as his wife.

He certainly was not under the delusion that she loved him, but deep down, he had grown quite attached to the woman. It was more than just some base need or physical attraction, though she was quite beautiful. His interest was really more in her cunning and skill. He was attracted to how in control she was, how strong she could be. He was still impressed that she had actually concealed her strongest traits from him for so long. He would never be able to think of her now as anything less than his comrade and equal. In fact, she was probably more than equal in many categories.

Perhaps, they could come to some understanding and maybe even more, given time.

All of that would have to happen after this battle. Right now, his primary goal was to save as many people and as much grain and provisions as possible. It was not just his duty as a member of the Elder Council which motivated him. Though he craved power, Sar'Tawas actually did care about the city's inhabitants. Without the precious grain and other materials they needed for day-to-day life, many would die if this harvest's cold season came early or was intense. To that end, he had emptied all but one last storehouse of grain and other important foodstuffs, hiding their contents in the safer second-level buildings. The sound of combat approached, but he figured there would be enough time to get just a little bit more, maybe even entirely saving the final storehouse's stock. He turned his attention to one of the farmer women setting down a large sack of wheat grain.

"You, Kir... Kirmua, right?" he asked the woman. She nodded back with a smile, seemingly impressed that such an important man even knew her name. He vaguely recalled that she worked in one of the wheat fields and sometimes in the flax fields. She had not yet taken a husband and had no children, likely the reason that she was down here with Sar'Tawas in harm's way. Most mothers had taken refuge with their children in the upper levels. He would start with her and see if he could find someone else to help grab the last of the wheat from the storehouse. At this rate, he might even have to start carrying bags himself.

"Run back to the east storeroom and see if there's anything left, and bring it," he said. It was risky to send her out for another trip to the storeroom, but the sounds of fighting didn't seem too close yet. He glanced down at her apron waist cord and saw a simple flint knife. If she did encounter any warriors, it wouldn't end well. He closed his eyes and turned, hoping he could find someone else to help her. Nervously, he felt his own waist cord, hoping that he had remembered to bring his dagger. If he could find one or two more people to help, he would go with them and do his best to make sure they returned alive. If he brought along Ianmu, he suspected that he had a fighting chance.

Ianmu watched as Sar'Tawas ushered three women hurriedly into a building, each carrying a large clay pot or basket full of grain. She was pleased that he was helping to protect the innocent, but she was worried about what would happen in the long run. Nara'kit's forces were much more dangerous than the weak Isut'na forces. Worse, her father and her brother were in charge. Neither of them had any weakness or compassion and would kill perhaps half of the city's populace merely to frighten the other half into submission. Despite all the people that she had killed to reach her goals, Ianmu did not wish death upon the innocent and only killed when it was absolutely needed.

She chuckled, sarcastically. She couldn't call herself necessarily good, but she wasn't quite ready to condemn her own actions, either. Exactly what made something good and what made something bad? People killed animals all the time simply to stay alive. How did that make her any different? She killed the terrible old priest who had no intention of ever letting her live the life she had worked so hard for. Her actions resulted in the death of a violent farmer who would probably have done something terrible to somebody else at some point. She did find some regret in the death of the priestess, but she wasn't there. She didn't see exactly what had transpired, so it made it difficult, or, at least, convenient depending on the point of view, for her to pass judgment upon herself.

It was all quite subjective as far as she could tell. The only objective component to it was the will of An'an. So long as she did what An'an asked, she was on the side of right, no matter how wrong the task was. She could still remember what the Goddess had said to her as she lay there begging for any sign. *You will change the fate of many people. You will be my messenger to the city of Isut'na. You will pluck the old plants from the ground and sow something new.*

Returning her focus to the present, Ianmu watched a worried farmer woman scurry by. Behind her, she could hear the screams of many people as they fought and died by one of the entrances to the city. It would not be long now before some warriors forced their way in. She heard another sound behind her and turned to see who had made it, her hand moving toward the place on her belt where a dagger was fastened. A moment later, the worried farmer woman returned carrying a large clay pot atop her head, likely full of seeds of wheat. Sweat ran down her face from the heat of the day and the exertion of carrying the wheat. She flashed a worried expression at Ianmu as she passed.

Suddenly, a Nara'kit warrior burst from around the corner with his wooden war club held high. The farmer woman came to a halt and made a strange whimpering sound of fear as she stood before the man with the club. With both hands holding the clay pot above her head and only her small knife at her side, she was completely defenseless before the warrior. Before Ianmu could react or the farmer could say anything, he swung the implement smashing the face of the defenseless woman. Her blood splattered in every direction along with the wheat seeds. Without a sound, her body slowly sank to the ground and twitched, blood pooling beneath her ruined face.

The warrior turned to regard Ianmu and began to smile. The man seemed overwhelmed by a lust for violence, quite caught up in the moment. While extreme violence was abhorrent to most people, some people seemed to enjoy it more than anything else. This man was obviously one such person. He approached, waving his club tauntingly at Ianmu while another Nara'kit warrior with a bow came around the other side of the building. Ianmu looked at the woman lying on the ground face-down, her body still twitching as her life evaporated. Beside her ruined face, the jar she had tried so hard to protect was smashed and slowly mixing with her blood. Her face had been bludgeoned for absolutely no reason. If he had threatened her with the club, she would probably have surrendered, and yet he had dispassionately killed her. *Why? Why would you do that? This is not the way of An'an!* she thought, suddenly enraged.

Sar'Tawas came around the corner at that very moment, having failed to find help and now coming to assist the woman. Before him was a violent scene he had not expected to find. His bodyguard concubine stood between two warriors from Nara'kit, one with a readied bow and the other holding a bloodied war club. Not far from the man with the club lay the body of the woman he had sent to gather wheat. For a moment, he stared in horror at the scene before him. For all his bluster and all his plotting, Sar'Tawas was disturbed more deeply by what he had just witnessed than he had expected he would be. He had sent the woman, and now she lay dead at his feet. Worse, it looked like the archer was preparing to fire at Ianmu.

The two warriors saw the older man stepping out from behind the building, but their focus was on the strange woman who stood before them brandishing a blade as though she knew how to use it. The warrior with the bow certainly had an interest in claiming a woman as his prize, but not one who would stand before him with a blade. Those types of women were too much trouble. They would quickly dispatch her and then capture the man. He looked like an Elder and might know where more people were hiding.

"An'an has made us invincible. We will destroy your city and kill your people, but you won't live to see that..." said the man with the war club, a smile on his face. Ianmu could plainly see the streak of cow blood across the man's chest, likely the magical protection he spoke of. He did not realize that he now stood before a priestess of An'an, chosen by the Goddess herself. She stepped forward, squeezing her fist around the hilt of her dagger. Everything about this man angered her, especially the dead woman at her feet.

"So, you follow An'an? I am Ianmu'kimun, daughter of An'sankup'Anteanar, chosen priestess of An'an, and I will gladly help introduce you to her!" she said, approaching the warrior. The man with the club hesitated at hearing the name of their leader. If he had heard her correctly, this woman had just introduced herself as the daughter of the ruler of Nara'kit. Confused by her actions, he swung with his club, hoping to simply kill the oddly behaving woman. She casually ducked as the club flew right over her head, missing widely. Springing forward, she jammed her dagger into his lower abdomen and began to saw back and forth as she raised it up his stomach, spilling his guts across the sand. He tried to step back, but she pushed forward, quickly eviscerating him as he stood in shock. She moved at a blinding speed and with delicate precision. The man screamed in horror, but before he could do anything, Ianmu kicked with her foot knocking him to the ground.

She was suddenly slammed sideways by something large and strong as she turned. Ianmu rolled across the ground and came up in a crouched fighting position, her dagger at the ready to strike back at whoever had attacked her. Strangely, standing in front of her was Sar'Tawas, and it appeared that he had just slammed into her forcing her to the ground. Was this treachery? Had her announcement of her formal title turned Sar'Tawas against her? She prepared to spring at the man when she realized that his face held the expression of sorrow, not anger or aggression. Behind him stood the Archer. The Archer's bow no longer held an arrow.

Sar'Tawas stumbled a moment later, an arrow protruding from his back and blood dripping to the ground. The archer had fired his arrow, and Sar'Tawas had forced Ianmu out of the way, saving her life at the cost of his own. The man whom she had thought was merely interested in her abilities and control of the city had just traded fates with her. He had laid down his life to save hers, and she could not even begin to understand why. He smiled at her as dark blood poured from the wound. A terrible rage overcame Ianmu as Sar'Tawas sank to his knees and the archer standing behind him came into view. He was quickly nocking another arrow, likely expecting to be attacked. On the ground near Ianmu lay his companion whimpering with his guts hanging from his abdomen and slowly dying an agonizing death, his own blood mixing with that of the woman he had mercilessly killed.

She stared at him for just a moment, but before she could allow her emotions to take hold, she clutched her dagger firmly and bolted from the ground with one and only one target in mind. The archer watched in terror as the extremely fast woman burst after him, amazingly dodging an arrow he fired at nearly point-blank range. Only a moment later, her dagger plunged through one of the man's eyes, causing him to shriek in agony and drop to the ground. He wouldn't likely die from the wound, but she would deal with him later. She let the weapon go and rushed back to find that Sar'Tawas was now lying face down on the ground with the arrow protruding from his back.

Ianmu rushed to his side and knelt before the man turning him over so that she could see his face. There had been many times when she had wanted nothing more than to slice the man's throat. Yet, as he lay before her dying, all she wanted was to stop him from leaving her. She wasn't sure that it was love, more of a deep friendship born out of necessity. Whatever it was, it hurt her more deeply than she had expected. It was a pain in her chest that felt like a dagger digging though her innards. Worse was the feeling of helplessness she felt. There was simply nothing she could do to save him, and panic filled her veins.

"Are you... are you really the daughter of that wretched son of a jackal, Anteanar?" he asked her, making a strange wheezing sound. When an arrow entered the back, as this arrow had, it disrupted the ability of the victim to breathe. Blood would fill in the lungs, and death would come quickly. She looked down at the man and could see that he was quickly losing his life. The vast amount of dark blood coming from the wound told her that something more important had also been struck, something vital. Dark blood was much worse than light-colored blood as it meant that most of his spirit was leaking and would soon leave his body.

"I am Ianmu'kimun, daughter of An'sankup'Anteanar. I am a secret priestess of An'an on a holy mission to do her will. I had nothing to do with this… this massacre. I chose you because you were the most powerful man I could find in the city. I will avenge you," she said as tears formed in her eyes. Ianmu was not one for crying, but for some reason, the anger and hate which had consumed her during the short skirmish were slowly transforming into a deep and painful sorrow. She had never felt a loss like this before, and it overwhelmed her. *Did the friends and family of the murdered priestess feel like this when she had died?* She quickly pushed the feelings from her mind as they stung like looking at the Sun. How such a thought had crept in made no sense... none of it made any sense. Her head hurt... her very spirit cried out with emotions she barely understood.

"I never got my wall... I told them we... needed a... wa..." he whispered. She sat there looking at the man. He smiled slightly and then slowly drifted off into the next world. In his side was an arrow that had been meant for her. Ianmu sat over his body softly crying, something she had never done for anyone. The most bizarre thing of all was that she didn't even know why. As she cried, she kept repeating in her mind her Goddess' words. *You will change the fate of many people. You will be my messenger to the city of Isut'na. You will pluck the old plants from the ground and sow something new.* Had she misunderstood the message? Had she misunderstood her purpose? She placed her hands on the sides of his head and tried desperately to hear anything from his spirit.

"Please, Sar'Tawas, An'an, anyone... Tell me what I'm supposed to do... Tell me what I'm doing wrong!" she screamed into the air. The only thing that she heard was the agonizing moans coming from the man she had stabbed in the eye. His sounds were making it hard for her to hear Sar'Tawas's spirit. She slowly stood and began to approach the man. She would be happy to aid him in that endeavor if he liked screaming so much. Afterward, she might better hear the spirit of Sar'Tawas as he passed to the next world.

ↄ ↄ ↄ

Isha'kau dropped flat upon her stomach as an arrow flew past, much closer than any previous. She had thrown over two dozen rocks and had wounded at least eight Nara'kit warriors, though only two of them were probably out of the fight. Each rock toss was dangerous, and every time she stood to throw a rock, she knew it might be her last, though she did her best to ignore the risks. She knew Isut was with her.

As she selected another rock, she again looked at the ladder not far to her right and the group of Isut'na farmers struggling with wooden poles and spears to push back the more deadly Nara'kit warriors. The enemy was climbing the ladder in a bold effort to take the side of the building and gain entry into the city. She rolled over into a crouch, preparing to stand and throw her next rock. Not far to her left, Aethen knelt with a fresh quiver of arrows preparing to do the same thing. Suddenly, she heard a loud scream behind her and to her right, causing her to look.

The Nara'kit warriors fighting their way to the top of the ladder had successfully killed two farmers trying to repel them, sending one of the men falling backward with a loud and bloodcurdling scream to his death upon the ground below. As three warriors came to stand on the side of the building, one turned and immediately began rushing for Isha'kau, attempting to kill some of the people who were causing the wall climbers the most trouble. Behind him, the other two men caught arrows, courtesy of Kamar and some of his men.

Isha'kau stood with a rock in hand, seeing the large man rushing toward her, a war club in his hand, his body covered in striking battle paint. Across his chest was a smear of sacred cow blood, and the look upon his face was that of one committed to a violent act. As he charged toward her, the lesser priestess was suddenly filled with terror, no longer separated from her enemies by distance. There was nowhere for her to run, and she was the first person he would meet with his war club. Terror filled her veins, but she stood her ground. Isha'kau knew when she had stood upon the building as a defender that it could mean her life. She loved life and feared death, as well as the pain of dying, but memories of Hullamu's sacrifice reminded her that some things were worth dying for.

She tossed the rock at the man, but it merely clipped his arm, doing very little to stop him. As he came upon her, he screamed a vicious battle cry raising his weapon high, meaning to cleave her head in half. In terror, Isha'kau stepped backward but slipped and dropped to her knees in nearly a split. The weapon swung just past her head, missing her by barely a fingers width. The man barely stopped his own momentum, trying to swing his weapon back and kill the woman. It wouldn't do to leave an enemy alive behind him, especially with several more Isut'na defenders ahead of him. Unfortunately, his momentum and rapid twisting momentarily left him extremely off-balance and standing on the edge of a building.

With adrenaline filling her veins and realizing that she wouldn't get another chance, Isha'kau, still in a split on the roof, simply pushed the man with both hands. Off-balance as he was, he tumbled – unable to stop himself – from the side of the building, landing on the ground in an awkward position. The priestess glanced over the edge of the building to see the fallen man; his face forever frozen in surprise. Isha'kau rolled back onto her knees safely away from arrow fire and took a few moments to breathe before rejoining the battle. To her left, Aethen turned to see what all the sound and yelling was about, but he saw that Isha'kau looked okay and so he gave her a wink and returned to what he was doing.

ↄ ↄ ↄ

Ishayan watched as his warriors were repelled from the nearest entryway to the city. The group he had sent to the other side of the city had failed to report back, and all three of the ladders were either destroyed or severely damaged. Worse, their arrow supplies were down to a quarter. He turned to see his father being tended to by the priest and priestess. All he wanted was to see those who had robbed him at his moment of triumph wiggling on pikes, but for right now, he would have to accept retreat. If he kept pressing the attack, there was a chance he might fully lose.

"Everyone, let's move back to the woods and prepare for tomorrow morning," he said begrudgingly. They had brought enough arrowheads and shafts to replenish most of their arrows by the morning, and they would also need some new ladders. Ishayan headed toward his wounded father to see how he was doing. All around him, the wounded were being dragged and carried toward the forest, not far to the North. He doubted there would be any swarm of warriors in some retaliatory attack. *The weaklings will be happy to be rid of us,* he sneered.

ɔ ɔ ɔ

Aethen wandered along the top of the wall of buildings that separated the inside of Isut'na and the outside. Not far ahead sat a woman with dark brown hair leaning against a small wall built around the edge of the building, her head buried in her knees. Most of the wounded were on the other side of the city, and Aethen had wandered over to the back side to get away from their screams. He was of no help with the dying, and he needed to clear his mind. He still felt guilty about leaving them to their fates, but he could do nothing more than endure their screams if he stayed.

As he approached the woman, he noted that she wore an apron with long tassels and sandals, her tanned skin decorated with black paint forming stripes and other interesting patterns. She had quite a lot of blood on her hands and a rather large knife, two observations that piqued his curiosity. Aethen was pretty sure that the blood was not hers as she seemed to be in decent health, other than being curled up and apparently upset. Strangely, he was certain that he had seen this woman before. She reminded him of the woman who had fought with Imkanar and Ember.

Aethen wandered over and sat beside her, curious to learn if she needed some company. His own love interest was busy helping with the wounded, and she had only enough time to flash him a forced smile, though Isha'kau looked quite haggard. He wondered if this woman had helped with the defense of the entryways. Perhaps she had battled some warriors. If she had defended an entryway, her current state might be the result. Not everyone could kill an enemy and just walk away as though it meant nothing. He could sympathize with this point. An uneasy feeling crossed his own mind as he remembered several of the men on ladders who probably still lay on the ground where his arrows had left them.

"Hey, are you all right?" he asked the woman in a gentle voice. She looked up with red, tear-streaked eyes, her war paint streaked with tears. She seemed to recognize him and stared slightly incredulously at Aethen. He vaguely recalled seeing the woman around the town with some distinguished looking man not long before. She stood out from the other women of the city due to her overly flashy clothing and her bright and full body covering body paint. Most women wore only minimal body paints and let them blend together over many days. As he continued to look at her, he became more and more convinced that this was the woman who fought Ember during the wedding. That woman had been extremely skilled with a blade. If this was her, she might have single-handedly defended an entire entryway.

"Is it all worth it?" she asked, hoarsely.

"I think it is," he said.

"What do you do when everything you believe in gets turned upside down?" She continued to look down at the ground below as she whispered. Aethen thought about her words for a few moments.

"I doubt many things, but I never doubt my friends. They are real, and when I fall, they can pick me up," he said. The woman thought about that for a little bit. It seemed to Aethen that some belief of hers had been thrown into doubt, something he suspected was common after such bloodshed. He certainly had a lot of images he would likely see for many harvests to come – things he'd like to forget.

"How do you make a difference? How do you change the fate of many people if you're not the leader? Are we all just powerless? Do we just run around waiting to die?" she spat, waving her hand for emphasis. Her questions were much deeper than Aethen had expected. Whatever the crisis this woman was dealing with, it wasn't simply the result of the battle, but something much deeper.

"I know how my friend Ember made a difference. During the battle, when many were cowering in fear, she stood in front of a hail of arrows and screamed that all was not lost," he said, hoping to inspire her with the story of what his incredibly idiotic and reckless friend had done not long before, though he gave the story a more heroic touch. The brown-eyed woman looked him deep in the face searching for the truth of his words.

"She ran down the ladder... They had not pushed the ladder all the ways up yet," he added, clarifying the point when the woman gave him a confused look.

"Anyway, she ran all the way across the battlefield and shot an arrow and struck the leader of Nara'kit!" As soon as he finished, he realized that the woman was now very alertly staring at him. She reached out and grabbed him by the hair, suddenly drawing forth her dagger and placing it at Aethen's neck. She had transformed from a tired and frightened looking woman into a deadly warrior in mere moments.

"Tell me what happened to Anteanar. If you lie, I will kill you," she said flatly, and he did not doubt any word of it.

"Um... if by Anteanar, you mean the leader?" She nodded. "Oh, well, I don't think he died. He took an arrow to the gut and was carried off. The other man, Ishayan, I think his name was, seemed to take charge," he said, pointing to his lower abdomen about where the arrow had struck the older man. The woman looked him over, carefully listening to every word he said. Her grip was strong, and she looked as though she knew exactly how to use the dagger. Aethen just waited, hoping she wouldn't slice.

The woman let him go suddenly and burst into hysterical laughter, which concluded in an almost whimpering sound. She stood and turned to look out over the horizon as the last pink colors from the Sun disappeared. Aethen crawled back a little and then stood. Though she had threatened his life, she had not otherwise harmed him. He decided that everybody had the right to be a little bit upset after what had happened today. Regardless, he made sure that he was out of her arm's reach.

"You say she stood before the entire army of Nara'kit, arrows flying by her body... she was unharmed?" she asked, never once turning to look at Aethen.

"Um... Yeah. She gets like that sometimes. It's like she's filled with a spirit or something..." he said, slowly turning and walking away. Aethen hoped he had helped the woman and not made things worse, but he didn't want to stay to find out how much more homicidal she might act. There was a limited number of death threats he could deal with on any given day.

Ianmu stood four buildings above the ground over the city's western side a short time later. To her left, the tiny sliver of the Moon rose in the East, while to her right, the fires from the Nara'kit army began to light as the men worked tirelessly in the woods preparing for the next day. She knew her own people, and she knew that once they had been whipped into a battle frenzy that was supported by the Goddess, or at least, so they thought, they would not be so easily defeated. All this talk about the woman named Ember standing before her own people's army filled her with rage. Ianmu hated her father, and his likely mortal wound did not bring her sorrow. Her entire family was loathsome and to be rid of them was not necessarily a bad thing, but how could it be that this one woman, this Ember, was causing all of this? Wasn't she the one who was supposed to be An'an's messenger, the woman to pluck the old and make it new? Wasn't she the one to cause the change?

Now she stood at the edge of the city – in fact, the very edge of the tallest building – with the only real friend she had lying dead in the street not that far away, dead from an arrow meant for her. Everything was just so confusing, and answers did not make themselves clear. She looked over the edge and saw a drop of nearly six lengths of a man. She began to contemplate quietly stepping forward and letting it all end. The Goddess could then tell her personally what she had done wrong. There was something almost relaxing about the idea that there was a possible end, and this realization brought the tiniest feeling of control. She nearly laughed, a bitter laugh, at how absurd her thoughts were. She had fought so hard to live, yet now, the feeling that she had an immediate control of her very death brought comfort to her acing spirit.

Ianmu sighed, a final tear streaking down her dirty, painted face. No, it would not be that simple. She had come so far and done so much for her goals… An'an's goals. Her thoughts and inner turmoil would take a long time to heal if they ever did. But right now, she would visit this Ember woman and deal with her directly. Her mind was a mix of emotions, and her thoughts darted erratically.

☾ ☾ ☾

Ember passed Isha'kau as she walked through the main ceremonial area. All around were dozens of wounded people moaning in pain. Isha'kau and Aya'tar worked tirelessly with nearly a hundred others to keep the wounded comfortable and treat their injuries as best as possible. It was likely that many of them would die from the injuries they sustained, many being pretty severe and typically caused by arrows and falls. It wasn't long before Ember found Brig'dha kneeling over a man with an arrow stuck in his arm. The man was biting down on a stick and screaming as loudly as he could through his clenched teeth while three other men held him down.

Ember leaned in to see what the priestess was doing and found to her horror that Brig'dha was cutting the flesh around the arrow wound to remove the barbed arrowhead. Ember waited while Brig'dha performed the operation, carefully cutting and pulling free the head. While many of the arrows used had been quickly made for the battle, this particular arrow was one of the more intricately designed hunting arrows whose heads detached. That made the cutting and removal much more complicated as every piece needed to be removed from the wound if the man wanted any chance of surviving. Pieces of a broken weapon left within the body carried with them the bad spirit energy of the person who had wished them harm. This could slowly consume a person and was one of the many causes of burning sweats.

The primary cause of death with many of these wounds was burning sweats. A red area would form around the wound, and pus would flow. Eventually, the wounded victim would begin to sweat, their skin growing hot to the touch. Most interestingly, the victim would usually complain that they were freezing. Red blotches would follow and a fever where the person would sometimes simply go unconscious or begin hallucinating. It was believed that the hallucinations were actually the gateway between the two realms of this world and the next opening. This was similar to those rare and gifted people who heard spirit voices in their heads, those lucky few who heard the words from the First and Third Worlds. The only way to prevent this from happening was to place the individual near a raging fire and keep them very warm. Unfortunately, even this technique only occasionally helped.

Behind them, a woman screamed as Isha'kau poured a mixture of boiled urine and salt onto her wounds. This, as well as salt and honey, would help reduce the blood flow and prevent evil spirits from seeping into the wounds. The screaming left Ember on edge every single time someone yelled. Brig'dha looked extremely exhausted, and the position of the Moon high in the Southeast told Ember that they better get some sleep before the morning. She was quite sure that the enemy would be back. Besides the wounded, Ember could hear the screams of those Nara'kit warriors who had been left behind. It sounded as though some of the warriors of Isut'na had crept outside of the city to attend to them... It didn't sound like they were using salt or honey.

Ɔ Ɔ Ɔ

Ishayan stood before a tree as it fell to the ground. All around him, large makeshift fires had been lit as his men worked tirelessly preparing new arrows, repairing weapons, and treating the wounded. His father had brought a priest and a priestess of An'an, along with nearly two dozen laborers who now worked feverishly to make new climbing ladders. Without the time or the supplies to make traditional ladders, trees were felled and limbed to make poles that could be easily climbed. The remaining limb stubs of branches made barely acceptable climbing tools. Unfortunately, his men would have to make do with what they had.

Many of the men were already uneasy about what the morrow might bring. They had expected a quick and easy conquest of the allegedly weak city of Isut'na. Instead, a single crazed redhead had mortally wounded their leader while groups of farmers and laborers had killed or wounded almost a fourth of their soldiers with simple hunting bows and crude spears. This was not the way it was supposed to be. Worse, rumors were starting to spread that the redhead had been a manifestation of Isut, or, at least, a champion of their local goddess. The only explanation people had for how she could charge their defenses without being killed. Having faced her in single combat, Ishayan knew that she was not chosen by a god but merely a simple woman. As he thought this, some of the wounds on his head began to hurt again.

Ishayan continued to pace back and forth while his men worked. Not far from him lay his wounded father attended to by the priestess of An'an. She worked feverishly to save the man, but Ishayan knew that it wouldn't be much longer before he was the ruler of Nara'kit. As he approached, he could see that the blood continued to seep from his father's wounds, though at a much slower rate than before. The redhead had hit him somewhere vital. He continued to stare at his wounded father, but Anteanar was not what was on his mind. He would find some method, divine some technique that would allow him to defeat Isut'na. He would have his revenge.

"I do not think that he will even make it through the night. Soon, his spirit will dance with An'an," the priestess said, looking up toward Ishayan. Her body was still covered head to toe in the dried cow blood from her earlier ritual, and she would not wash the blood from her body until the battle was over. He glanced at her momentarily, then turned and left, deep in thought. The priestess felt bad for the man, obviously in such a mourning over his father's wounds that he could not even find words. She turned back to the man and continued praying to the Goddess.

CHAPTER TWENTY NINE
WARRIOR PRIESTESS OF AN'AN

The fictitious fertility deities Isut and An'an are based upon the later goddesses Ishtar and Inanna. Though often described interchangeably, Inanna and Ishtar were not entirely the same. Instead, they were likely two or more similar deities who combined into one myth, a process known as syncretism. Inanna was worshipped at least as far back as 4500 BCE, a mere 1000 years after Ember's time, around the lands of the fertile crescent, while the later Ishtar was worshipped primarily by the Akkadians of the same general region. Much as Ishtar and Inanna are often considered aspects of the same deity, perhaps Isut and An'an might truly be different names for the same goddess. Like Inanna and Ishtar, their domains include sex, love, change, and war. Unlike Inanna and Ishtar, their portfolios also include a heavy focus on fertility, though this made sense in their time and place.

It is important to note that Isut and An'an are entirely fictitious, as are their implied connections to the later Ishtar and Inanna. Still, Inanna very possibly originated among late Neolithic or early Bronze Age peoples roughly 1400km to the East, Ishtar likely appearing much later. For interested readers, a good book about Inanna and Ishtar is the book, Ishtar, by Louise M. Pryke, 2017, Routledge Publishing.

The night was at its darkest point as Ianmu walked past the field of wounded looking for the woman who had taken upon herself Ianmu's role as the bringer of change. She did not wish any harm to the woman, even though she was likely responsible for wounding her father. A wound in the area of the body that the man she had described was almost certainly going to be fatal, if not painful. Her father's cruelty more than accounted for this, and she would not shed a tear. In fact, her only regret about the wound was that her brother had apparently also survived. She wished, and not for the first time that an arrow had found him. What she wanted now was to confront this woman. She wanted to see what this Ember person had that she lacked. She wanted answers.

She had asked several people along the way and had been told that she could find this Ember in one of the buildings where travelers stayed, along with some lover named Brig'dha. After a while, she found the very building Ember was supposed to be occupying. For some reason, she hesitated at the door, consumed by anxiety. She had entered into the battle less worried than she was now. Sometimes, the most frightening thing was to know the truth, and while she wanted to know, that knowledge terrified her. Brushing aside her hair, Ianmu lifted the leather door covering and entered.

Almost immediately, she encountered a small furry creature, some species of cat. She pulled free her dagger, expecting to be attacked by the fierce and wild creature, but instead, it simply wandered over to her legs and began to brush up against her, making a loud purring sound. If things weren't already strange enough, they were now quite bizarre. Animals like this were not domesticated, and to find one that would lovingly caress your leg was almost disturbing, though she had to admit it was oddly cute.

Before her lay an unexpected sight: two women sleeping together on a stone bench bed with furs as a married couple would. The brown-haired woman was lying face down and gently snoring while the other woman lay in a half-hearted attempt at spooning. Ianmu approached the two women and knelt by their bed. She reached to push the hair out of the face of the woman lying on her side. She assumed that one of these two women was Ember, though she did not know which one. The light was dim, but as she took the hair into her hands, she noticed how different it looked from the region's people. Suddenly, she began to recognize the woman. To make matters worse, Ember abruptly rolled onto her back, and her face came fully into view though she was still asleep. This was the one who had literally kicked her into unconsciousness. She could still remember being punched between her legs, and she winced at the thought.

Before her lay the woman who had beaten her senseless and stolen her easiest chance at victory. Ianmu lifted her dagger and placed it against Ember's stomach. The blade was as sharp as glass, and one slice would spill her guts all over the floor. She would live long enough to see that it was Ianmu who had killed her. Strangely, she hesitated. This woman had also killed her vile father and defeated her brother, providing him with an equal beating. If the account of that man she had spoken to was correct, and several of the people she had asked along the way had recounted the same basic story, this woman had stood arms wide open before the entire army of Nara'kit. Arrows passed her by without striking.

Had An'an sent her as a messenger, or perhaps as a wake-up call to Ianmu? Suddenly, Ember reached for the dagger and sloppily pushed it away from her stomach. She mumbled something playfully in a language Ianmu didn't recognize. Did she think that Ianmu was her lover, the woman on the other side of the bed? As she glared at the woman's face, Ianmu found it harder and harder to hate her. She had risked her life to save the high priestess Aya'tar from marrying a man she didn't love. While most people in the city probably thought the woman had some kind of interest in Aya'tar, Ianmu was not such a fool that she didn't obviously see what had actually happened. The anger of being beaten and the terrible headaches she had suffered the next day had faded in her memory enough that she did not feel compelled to kill this Ember.

Around the neck of her lover, Ianmu caught sight of an extremely beautiful necklace. She reached forward and took the pendant in her hands to observe it in what little light came through the small window. To her surprise, it was a large chunk of river-smoothed amber with what looked like a flower forever trapped within its honeyed form. She gazed at the beautiful and wondrous item, wondering how these women had come to possess such a thing. Strangely, she almost felt the energy coursing through the item. Whoever this woman was, she was indeed loved by some god. Suddenly, Ember reached forward, grabbed her hand holding the necklace, and pulled it against her chest. At first, Ianmu lifted her dagger, ready to strike, but she soon realized that Ember was either asleep and dreaming or only barely awake.

"Ehg, wennus'du… ne'ke… sewep," the redhead whispered in the heavily accented voice of her native tongue. Ianmu felt her warm skin and the beat of her heart, and though she did not know the words this Ember person had spoken, she believed she knew what they had meant. Ember held her hand under the mistaken belief that it was her lover Brig'dha's hand. She pulled her hand free from Ember's grasp and dropped to her knees. Her emotions were a wreck, and she was still completely lost. She no longer knew for certain that she was doing the right thing or even what the right thing might be. Something about the sleeping woman struck her as being divinely touched.

Ianmu stood and walked towards the door to leave. Along the way, she encountered the small fuzzy creature. She stopped and knelt before the little creature feeling an overwhelming urge to simply pet it. As she pet the creature, she began to recount everything that had happened to her since she had left her city. She remembered the people she had killed, the deceit she had sown, but most importantly, the only man who had ever been her friend. The knife fell to the floor as Ianmu found herself holding the small cat and quietly sobbing. Even she occasionally reached her limit. Mew nuzzled the assassin-priestess, pleased to know that no matter what, everyone eventually bent to his furry will.

ↄ ↄ ↄ

The Moon was in the Northwest and just below the horizon when the Nara'kit army left the forest heading back to Isut'na. They had replenished most of their arrows and now possessed six long tree poles, branches cut to stubs, providing a natural means of climbing. While not a traditional ladder, and certainly not as useful as the ladders they had left against the buildings of Isut'na when they had fled, there were more of them. Having so many additional climbing tools would allow his men to saturate the defenses of Isut'na in a way that his limited supply of ladders had not.

Ishayan walked before his soldiers, now numbering 624 in strength. In reality, barely three dozen had actually died, but the rest were wounded and unable to fight, many left behind and likely killed by the enemy where they lay. Battle typically left many more wounded than actually dead. The true horror was for those who were wounded. They could look forward to many days of agonizing pain as they either recovered from their wounds or succumb to them and the sweats. Given a choice, many of the wounded would seek to have their own lives taken swiftly rather than endure the pain. As soon as the battle was over, Ishayan would make sure to provide such services to the brave warriors who deserved it.

Anteanar had survived the night, but it wasn't long before it became apparent that he would soon pass. Blood had begun to flow from places where it shouldn't, and the pain he suffered had become immeasurable. The priest had gone so far as to give him herbs to induce sleep. Unfortunately, it was quite likely that Anteanar would never awake from that sleep. Either way, it was apparent to all that Ishayan would soon be the ruler of their city. His zealous sister had left, never to be seen again, and now his overbearing and violent father lay dying, or maybe even dead. Things were looking up for Ishayan.

He wasn't about to lose, and he had a special plan for victory, a secret trick he hoped the fools defending Isut'na might fall for. While everyone was paying attention to the large marching army with its visible climbing poles and archers, who would notice a small force wandering around the other side of the city with their own climbing pole? It was a special and untested deception Ishayan had come up with as they marched through the forest, but he suspected it would work.

This entire business would be over and done with soon, and his enemies would lie dead before him. He made a promise to himself that before the Sun set, the bodies of the annoying redhead and Aya'tar would be wriggling on wooden pikes. He would be the ruler of Isut'na and Nara'kit, perhaps the strongest man in the world. He laughed as he walked towards the city. The Goddess had looked well upon him, and now it would be finished. *I am the raging Brown River, I am the Spear of An'an, I am vengeance!* he thought, almost laughing.

ↄ ↄ ↄ

Isha'kau and Aethen stood atop the Western buildings dressed for battle. Isha'kau held a battle club blessed by Isut, its haft adored with many hawk feathers. She had painted her body white and black striped with clay paint and soot. She wore a red-dyed linen loincloth, while around her neck, she had donned the cowry shell necklace and the vulture feather Aethen had given her. Aethen stood by her side with his bow and quiver full of arrows. His long black hair now sported several hawk feathers, and he wore his own cowry shell necklace, leather loincloth, and boots. It was too hot for much else. If they made it through this, Aethen intended to ask Isha'kau to marry him. Life was apparently too short and too dangerous not to take the chance.

Isha'kau had decorated Aethen's face with symbols of protection using black paints. She had spent extra time and extra care to ensure that each symbol was applied while she chanted. She did not want to take any chances that the man she had recently found might die. Being a fertility priestess without a lover or a spouse was troublesome at best, and she doubted that she would find anyone quite as interesting as Aethen. Most importantly, she was frightened of losing someone else that she cared for. She really did love the man and hoped that they might live and perhaps become something more than just lovers.

Behind them, Brig'dha had just finished adding the last touches of magical face paint to Ember's face. She had blessed the paints that morning to ensure no arrows would find her lover. This was required as Ember seemed incapable of staying out of danger. Her face was now covered with intricate black circles and other swirl-like designs in the traditional fashion of Brig'dha's people. She had gone so far as to cover her entire body with the same general design leaving Ember quite striking. The feisty redhead stood proudly with her bow strapped across her chest and a quiver full of arrows. Around her neck and arms were gold and copper jewelry, and her hair sported a beautiful hawk feather. She

545

wore a short leather loincloth for clothing, linen feeling too loose and too easily torn for the action which was to come, and a pair of sandals.

Brig'dha stood beside her lover wearing thick black swirl body paints, though she had opted for a long and wide leather apron covering both the front and back of her waist, the traditional warm season garment of her people. She would not be likely deep in the fighting, instead taking care of the wounded as she had done in the previous battle. Ember made sure that the priestess had, at least, two daggers on her, as Brig'dha was unwilling to carry any weapon heavier. It wasn't that she would not fight but that she simply knew that she was no good with anything so heavy as a war club or a bow. Brig'dha had other methods for defeating her enemies, and, even now, she began to pray to the Goddess of the Moon for aid, the Amber of Life pendant in her hands.

Beside them, Aya'tar stood tall and proud as she watched the enemy army approaching. The high priestess wore a flax string skirt and leather sandals. Isha'kau had painted her entire body in black, white, and red stripes, each as thick as a hand. Her head was adorned with eagle and vulture feathers, and she wore a blessed war club at her waist, her children in her arms. To even look upon her was to be in awe. This would likely be the day everything was decided, the final battle. Though she was not keen on fighting in the front lines, she would certainly give a good fight to any Nara'kit warrior whom she encountered.

At her side stood Imkanar wielding a war club and wearing his simple leather loincloth and boots. He had smeared common wood ash across his face to make himself look more striking but refused anything more complex. Aya'tar was unsure if he was trying to make some sort of statement by wearing the clothing of an average person, but if that was what he wished, she would not stand in his way. As long as he stood by her side, her ever brave husband, that was all that truly mattered. She just hoped that he would still be at her side when the battle ended.

"With that fool Ishayan in charge and after the battle they had yesterday, I don't think they're going to hold back today," Isha'kau said. There were nods of agreement from everyone. Warriors who had recently tasted the sting of defeat but who were still willing to attack once more would likely come with everything they had. Unlike his father, Ishayan was not very skilled in battle and would likely have no other strategy. Isha'kau merely said aloud what everyone else had already suspected.

"Luckily, everyone now knows that they can be defeated. We just have to keep them off the walls. Kamar's men spent half of the night reinforcing each of the pathways into the city," she continued. Though many had been wounded, over 500 people now stood ready for the defense of the city. Many who had cowered the day before now stood ready to repel the invaders. The news of Ember's brazen assault on the leader of Nara'kit had spread like wildfire through the city. There had even been speculation among some that the redhead had been possessed by the goddess Isut, though people who knew her realized that it had just been an incredibly lucky act of bravery and absurd foolishness.

Not far from the city was the forest where the Nara'kit army had spent the night bivouacked. Not long after the Sun had risen, they began to emerge from the woods in three long rows of men, perhaps a little weaker in strength but now carrying five large poles. There were murmurs from people all around as various explanations for the poles were ventured. Ember knew exactly what they were. Her own people used poles with limbs removed, leaving about a hand's length of the limb as a stepping point. They were useful in climbing trees for honey and climbing onto roofs. These were simply a replacement for the ladders they lost the day before.

"They will try to scale the walls with those poles. We must keep them on the ground and outside of the city. Do you have any more rocks or anything that can be thrown down upon people as they climb, like before?" Ember asked Aya'tar. Without answering Ember directly, she turned to Kamar drawing the attention of most of the defenders. Everyone awaited the first orders to be handed down from Aya'tar.

"Kamar, have everyone bring as much stone, sand, and other objects that can be thrown, up top. If they want to climb, it's going to hurt!" Everyone did as the high priestess commanded. Standing atop the building painted from head to toe in battle paints and carrying her two children in her arms, the high priestess was an impressive figure. Ember hoped that the others would continue to be in awe of her presence. They could not afford to lose heart as many had done the day before. Unfortunately, she would retreat to the temple when the fighting started as the loss of the high priestess would likely be demoralizing enough to crush Isut'na.

Imkanar had also wished to remain at Aya'tar's side within the temple. Having just come to be at her side after so long, Imkanar could barely handle the notion of his lover locked away in some temple and out of his sight. What if some enemy warriors found a way into the temple when he was not there? It had taken a lot of coaxing, but she had finally convinced him to help lead the attack as her representative. He was in better physical shape, not being required to nurse two children. It would also help the people to know that the new co-ruler of their city stood with them while the priestess remained in the temple praying to the gods for success. Imkanar sighed reluctantly as Aya'tar prepared to leave for the temple. At least, she would be protected by Isha'kau.

As the two priestesses prepared to leave, Aethen turned once more to regard Isha'kau. She stood proudly beside the high priestess, both women painted in striking colors. He knew that she must leave to the temple to defend the altar of Isut as well as the high priestess and her children. He would much rather have her by his side, but everyone had their part to play. The lesser priestess could see the worry on his face, and it gave her pause. She opened her mouth, ready to explain why she had to go, but Aethen simply held his hand up and gave her a nod.

"You go do what you have to do. If they get past us, you are the last line of defense," he said with a smile. She felt much better knowing that he accepted why she must remain in the temple and that he trusted her. She was also flattered to know that she was the woman he wanted by his side during the battle, even if that could not be. Isha'kau suddenly stepped forwards, wrapping her arms around Aethen and pressing his face against hers, as the people of the True South did not actually kiss. Some of her battle paint smeared on his chest, a blessing from the Goddess, he figured. He would wear that mark with pride. Isha'kau released him but did not break her stare. There was something on her mind, something she had wanted to say.

"If we live through this... I mean, after this is all over," she began to say, but Aethen cut her off, unwilling to be deprived of the question he had always wanted to ask. He remembered how Brig'dha had beaten Ember to the question, and he wasn't going to go down that easily. This was earlier than he had wanted to ask, but there was no way to avoid it now. He placed his hands upon Isha'kau's arms and gazed deeply into her dark brown eyes. Before he could speak, she could see his tanned skin blushing, so strong was the reaction of what he was about to say. The lesser priestess breathed deeply, knowing full well that she would slap him across the face if the words that he next spoke were not a proposal.

"Isha'kau, will you be by my side forever? Will you marry me?" he asked. She stared back in shock, not just that he would ask the question but also that he had beaten her to the punch. She nodded her head yes and returned for a second embrace. Not far away, Aya'tar and Imkanar gazed on at the two.

"It's about time she found someone. How can she be a priestess to a goddess of fertility and yet never have a lover?" Aya'tar said matter-of-factly. Imkanar nodded his agreement. Off to the side, Brig'dha and Ember held each other's hands, completely enthralled in the moment. They couldn't help it. They were both hopeless romantics.

ᗞ ᗞ ᗞ

As the enemy approached the wall, everyone prepared for battle. Near Ember was a handful of women lying on their stomachs to avoid arrow fire with large piles of rocks and other objects they could throw on anyone foolish enough to try to climb the wall near where they lay waiting. Not far to her left crouched Aethen and a dozen men with bows. Everyone was pretty sure the attack would occur against the Western wall. As a result, most of the defenses had been placed at this point. Nevertheless, Ember couldn't help but consider the disaster if the enemy suddenly advanced on a different side of the city. It was a risk but a reasonably calculated one.

The majority of wounded, women and children, and the elderly had taken refuge once more in the second and third story buildings inside the city and away from the action. Of the defenders, approximately a third were women, while the remaining two-thirds were men. Almost none of them were full-time warriors, the majority being farmers. Ember was quite sure that everyone present would do their best. Brig'dha had already explained to her that if she went once more rushing off toward the enemy, she might as well not come back. The priestess would likely strangle her to death in some sort of violent rage. Ember chuckled under her breath at the thought, though she understood Brig'dha's fears deep down. She had lost her spouse once before, and she had nearly lost Ember a few times.

ᗞ ᗞ ᗞ

Ishayan stepped forward, coming to stand close to arrow range. Before him, the priestess and priest of An'an danced and sang quickly, preparing the warriors for battle. Even Ishayan, as impatient as he was, was not fool enough to challenge the priests on this point. If the gods were watching, he might very well receive the blessing he needed to win by the actions his priest and priestess now took. If she were not watching, his men certainly were, and they would be disheartened if they did not feel that the Goddess was on their side. Either way, he just waited for the short ritual to conclude.

When this was over, he would have to discover whether or not the priestess' husband lived through the battle. Her name was Kit'tanu, and he had an eye for her. She had taken the place of the high priestess after his wayward sister killed the old fool. He had ensured that her husband, a useless man named Uritasa, would be one of the first men to assault the city. He was beginning to develop an interest in the woman, and placing her husband on the front line was just one more move toward one of his many goals. If everything was going well, he might just have to make sure that he secured her as well. *Everything is within reach of those who have the strength to grasp it!* he mused as he watched the priestess dance.

Behind him, his archers stood ready to fire upon the tops of the buildings, while before him, nearly 500 warriors stood ready to slam their six wooden climbing poles against the sides of the buildings and take the city. Even if they succeeded, the losses would still likely be heavy, but they would be rewarded ten times over upon taking the second city. The fighting would be intense, but if he could get some men onto the roofs, he had a chance. The only way for him to lose now would be if Isut'na's forces could keep his men outside long enough. He had to keep the pace of battle going or risk defeat.

Unwilling to wait for victory, Ishayan waved his arms, signaling the advance of his men. The priest and priestess appeared to have mostly concluded, though the priest flashed an irritated glare at Ishayan. Likely, the man considered Ishayan's call for his men to move before the ritual had fully completed as a form of hubris, but he didn't care. He could taste the blood of war, and it called to him. Men rushed forward under arrow fire carrying six large wooden climbing poles. They were driven by a will to please their gods as well as the promise of the spoils of the city. Once the city was taken, material goods could be raided, and women could be captured.

ↄ ↄ ↄ

Below them, perhaps two hundred or more warriors rushed forwards with the climbing poles. Everyone stood, drawing arrows and firing at the oncoming warriors. Several Nara'kit warriors fell to the ground clutching grievous wounds. Suddenly, the enemy archers launched a barrage of retaliatory arrows catching many of Isut'na's defenders off guard. Ember watched to her left as one man caught an arrow in the leg, stumbling backward. She reached forward, trying to catch his arm, but the man tripped in agony and fell two lengths of a man to the ground, landing on his head. She looked away, trying to ignore what just happened as there was plenty more to come.

All around her, people screamed and launched arrows back and forth. The exchange of fire had initially started one-sided with Isut'na defenders launching arrow after arrow on the approaching army. Unfortunately, when the Nara'kit warriors fired back, many defenders began ducking, more interested in saving themselves than saving the city. Ember could not be angry with them as it took a significant amount of willpower to stand before arrows. This was something she had done twice before, and every single time was terrifying. It was easy to condemn people for being frightened until one faced the enemy.

Not far to her right, a group of men slammed one of the five poles on the side of the building, right beside the group of women she had earlier seen. A woman beside the pole grabbed ahold of it and started trying to push it sideways to force it to the ground. Suddenly, the woman took an arrow to the chest and slumped forward over the edge of the wall without even a scream, her heart pierced by flint. The other women recoiled from the sudden and gruesome event, unsure of what to do next. Below them, two men stood with bows, ready to kill the next foolish person to try and push their climbing pole away. Ember saw four more men rushing forward to climb the pole, clubs in hand.

"Throw the rocks at them!" Ember screamed at the women though two of them were sobbing over the dead woman and trying to pull her body back onto the roof. The others hastily lifted the rocks they had and began launching them over the side of the roof aimlessly at the men below. None of the rocks hit the men as the women were throwing them without aim, too nervous about standing before the enemy archers and suffering the same fate as the first woman had. The warriors were doing their best to dodge the rocks without paying attention to anything else. Ember popped her head up and shot an arrow catching one of the men in the neck. As the other men turned to regard Ember, one of the women saw their attention drawn and tossed a well-aimed rock catching one of them on the side of the head. The man staggered backward and fell to the ground, probably not dead but definitely not able to fight.

It wasn't long before others nearby noticed the pattern and began using the same technique of crisscrossing arrow fire and stones. The warriors from Nara'kit could not keep their eyes on so many different opponents from so many different directions, each waiting until a man was distracted by the other. They were losing their advantage as they approached the wall. One by one, Nara'kit's warriors were falling with only an occasional casualty on Isut'na's side. If they could keep this up, the forces of Nara'kit would soon retreat. Hope was beginning to grow in everyone's hearts as everything seemed to be going well.

"The other side! They come from the other side! By the gods, help me!" Suddenly, a horrific scream from inside the city and behind the defenders turned many heads. A middle-aged woman came rushing through the central ceremonial ground in the city's center, holding a baby in her arms with an arrow stuck deep in her shoulder. She barely made it to the buildings with the defenders before dropping to the ground in shock. Several people quickly ran to the woman's aid.

"By Gunar's horn, look!" screamed a farmer pointing his bow at the eastern buildings behind them. Everyone turned to see nearly two dozen warriors climbing over the buildings to their backs. It only took a moment to realize what had happened. A small group of warriors had taken one of the climbing poles around to the backside, probably late at night. The men were painted black with soot which had likely prevented anyone from seeing them as they approached. They had waited until the attack had distracted everyone and then climbed the walls of the buildings completely unseen. Though there were not many within the walls, even a few of them could cause tremendous damage and demoralize the defenders.

Kamar took nearly 30 people with him and rushed to the other side of the city to engage the enemy forces. Unfortunately, everyone's attention had turned to the attack at their rear, which had given several of the people climbing up the front a brief moment of pause, which they had used to their full advantage. A man not far to Ember's left got smashed in the face by a war club as a warrior climbed up a pole and onto the roof. A moment later, a woman standing beside him stabbed the Nara'kit man in the gut with a fishing spear while another man ran up and clubbed him with a war club. Together, the man and the woman pushed the first warrior from the building, but many more were coming up behind him.

Right beside Brig'dha, two men worked to push a climbing pole away from the building wall when arrows suddenly struck them both from a barrage sent against that very point. The men fell backward, grievously wounded and leaving the pole untouched. Brig'dha lifted her head from the wounded man she was helping and saw the head of a man rising before her, a flint dagger clutched in his teeth. Any moment, he would come over the wall, and she would have a lot more than just a few arrows to deal with.

She reached into her leather pouch and produced a handful of the smelly yellow powder she had traded for last cold season, the powder she used in fire magic. The man placed his hand on the wall and pulled the knife from his mouth, ready to finish hauling himself atop the building. Before him knelt a woman with no visible weapons in her hands. He was not sure whether or not he would take her for a prize or simply kill her, but it seemed that the Goddess smiled upon him. As he watched, the woman extended her hand toward him, slowly opening it to reveal an oddly colored powder. Brig'dha turned to face the man, opened her hand, and blew the yellow dust into his eyes in one quick motion.

He screamed, grabbing his eyes with both hands and sliding backward all of the ways down the pole catching many of its outstretched branch pieces in a very painful and likely permanent way. All the men below jumped out of the way as the man slid painfully down the pole, giving Brig'dha the opportunity she needed to push the pole sideways. It fell to the ground as two more defenders came to help. Brig'dha almost felt bad for the man whom she could see rolling around on the ground holding his stomach and groin, as well as his eyes. In all reality, he would likely live, though possibly blinded, with untold injuries twixed his legs. *That is what raiders get,* she thought with anger, though her compassion threatened her resolve, so she pushed thoughts of the man from her mind.

ꙩ ꙩ ꙩ

"Uritasa! Uritasa! An'an, don't let him be dead! Please!" screamed Kit'tanu, the priestess, as she ran as fast as she could, stepping over bodies both wounded and dead. Before her lay her fallen husband. A rock thrown by someone on top of one of the buildings had clipped the side of his head, causing him to stagger and fall. The priestess frantically dragged the dead man's body, who lay across her husband, to the side. The dead man had been killed by an arrow to the neck, a quick but grisly death. Her husband was covered in blood, as was she, though her blood had come from a sacrificial cow while his came from a wound on his head.

Kit'tanu dropped to her knees and placed her head against his chest. She was relieved to hear the sound of life within his body and immediately threw her arms out wide in prayer to An'an to spare his life. There she knelt in the middle of a raging battle praying before her wounded husband without hesitation as arrows flew past her, and yet strangely, nobody took aim at the blood-soaked priestess. She was obviously unarmed and covered from head to toe in sacrificial blood. Few would be foolish enough to incur the anger of her Goddess, and most would simply let her be, a tiny island of humanity in a sea of blood and death.

☽ ☽ ☽

Ianmu sat on a building to the North, watching the combat and juggling many feelings around in her mind. She had replayed what An'an had said in her mind so many times. *You will change the fate of many people. You will be my messenger to the city of Isut'na. You will pluck the old plants from the ground, and you will sow something new.* With her brother in charge of Nara'kit and her father dead or dying, how could she change the fate of many people? The only thing she seemed to be any good at now was hiding while others died on both sides. Part of her screamed to take up arms in defense of the city, while a smaller part of her felt that she had an obligation to aid her own people.

Her mind was awash, and in the center of it all was the face of the dead man Sar'Tawas. She still could not account for what strange effect he had upon her. It was more friendship than love, but it had become deep and had harmed her when he had been killed. Strangely, even the poor woman who had died needlessly carrying the wheat continued to dance in her mind. She had felt nothing when she had killed the priest, an evil man to begin with. Killing the men who had sought to take her life had also caused no major troubles with her sleep. The farmer woman had been a common woman just trying to survive; not a warrior, which might have explained why her death disturbed Ianmu. But Sar'Tawas had certainly not been an innocent man. She continued juggling such confusing thoughts when a movement to her right caught her attention.

Strangely, she saw men climbing up the eastern buildings and sneaking their way into the city. The men were painted black with soot and keeping their heads down as they sneaked onto the roofs. You crafty son of a jackal, she thought. Ishayan had obviously come up with a strategy to split Isut'na's weak forces. The city had more defenders, but most of them were inexperienced farmers. Nara'kit's men were used to conquering smaller villages and tribes nearby. It had looked as though Isut'na would win until this moment. If she were in charge of Nara'kit, she would end the battle. Unfortunately, with her father's passing, if it had happened yet, Ishayan would take control. He would certainly pluck the old weeds and replace them with something new...

Suddenly it hit her. What if she had misunderstood the Goddess? She was to be the messenger to the city of Isut'na, but that did not actually mean that she would take control of the city. Replacing something old with something new she had taken to mean killing off the leaders of Isut'na and forging a new leadership with her in control. But how had she come to that exact conclusion? The more she thought about it, the more she realized that she had merely assumed the proper course of action. If Ishayan and her father failed to live through the battle, she would be the eldest member of her family still alive, and by definition, the ruler of Nara'kit.

It seemed very likely that her father was either dead or would be soon, but Ishayan was a much different story. He was skilled with the blade and possessed a cunning mind. She was quite sure he was alive and leading the army against the city. If he died while taking the walls, so much the better. However, if he successfully invaded the city, perhaps she might take the opportunity to place a knife in his back. Ishayan and Anteanar represented the old ways of Nara'kit. This violent path threatened the lives of so many people in Isut'na. Perhaps she would pluck this old and violent way from the world with a simple slash to Ishayan's throat. In doing so, she would save many people and at the same time be the messenger of An'an to the people of Isut'na.

At that very moment, she turned to see a large vulture flying overhead, gracefully soaring beneath a gorgeous blue. A feeling of euphoria suddenly washed over her, causing her to genuflect, her knees coming to rest upon the building roof. Above her, the vulture circled, and she knew An'an had returned, just as she had promised, to view the climactic realization of her word. *I am a fool... I have done your will, and yet I have done so completely misunderstanding your words,* she thought. A tear streaked from her eye as she realized how close she had come to complete failure and how close she was to success, in An'an's name.

She stood almost weak with a mixture of elation and anger. How could she possibly have been so stupid as to not put this together before now? Gods tended to trick people with their words, and it was easy to confuse their intent, but this had been so clear. She would have time to scold herself and lament her mistakes when the blood had dried, but for now, she needed to find her brother while there was still a city to save. The big question was, where to find Ishayan? If he were successful, as it certainly looked as though he would be, she could guess where he would likely head. She pulled out her dagger and raised her arms in prayer. This would be it. She would wait for her brother exactly where she knew he would go and complete the will of An'an.

"I see now... I see! Why was I blind before? An'an, your message was simple, and yet I did not realize that the people I would save and the word I would carry would require the death of the old ways..." Soon, she would head for that final confrontation.

ↄ ↄ ↄ

"Everyone, the attack behind us has been stopped! We must repel these jackals before us! We must not be the weakest point!" Imkanar screamed, placing his foot on a Nara'kit warrior's back and tugging his war club free from the man's skull. The young man was covered in blood with many minor wounds, but his forces had successfully repelled the climbing poles in the Southwestern corner of the city. Imkanar could not help but feel the urge to join Aya'tar. He felt as though something bad was looming. Looking up, he watched as several vultures flew overhead, likely attracted by the battle and the possibility of a quick meal. The signs were present, and he would not ignore them and leave the priestess by herself. He had stood his ground and defended the walls of Isut'na with a handful of brave people, and now he felt as though his wife needed him.

"You, Ul'kanasa, you are in charge. I'll be joining the priestess at the temple," he said to a younger man who had proven himself several times that day. Before the man could say anything, Imkanar jumped off the side of the building, landing on the ground and dashing off toward the temple. Ul'kanasa, a wheat farmer who had never really been involved with anything so important in his life, stood on the wall having just been placed in charge of its defense. Wasting no time, he turned to begin barking orders to those around him to ensure that the walls held. He didn't know why he had been given such a responsibility, but he certainly wasn't going to let Imkanar down.

ↄ ↄ ↄ

What had seemed like a near victory was suddenly turning into possible defeat. While the Southwestern walls were firmly in control of Isut'na, the central Western walls were quickly being taken. From two poles, men from below had fought their way onto the rooftops and were now pouring onto the city's high ground, forcing the defenders back. Facing one of the groups was Aethen and a dozen defenders while

Brig'dha stood with perhaps ten defenders on her side against the other incursion. Unfortunately, Ember had taken at least fifty defenders with her to halt a group of warriors trying to climb the wall in a different location, leaving Brig'dha behind. Even Kamar was busy inside the walls hunting down those who had breached the Eastern walls.

Brig'dha stood just behind her small line of defenders holding back a large group of Nara'kit warriors. There were simply too many of them advancing on her small force. She dropped to her knees to implore her Goddess to intervene. In one hand, she held a feather high in the sky while she pressed against her heart with the other hand. Below her, she could feel the groan of the wooden planks caked in dried mud which held up the roofs to the buildings. As more warriors climbed the poles, the wood groaned more and more. Brig'dha tried to clear her mind of such distractions and concentrate solely on her prayers.

One by one, the Isut'na defenders backed away from the men piling on the roof. The enemy was gathering before they advanced, apparently tired of being picked off one by one. The defenders backed up and passed Brig'dha, leaving her between them and the Nara'kit warriors. A few moments later, Brig'dha knelt alone upon the roof, abandoned by the citizens who moments before had stood beside her, ready to defend that building roof. Nearly thirty Nara'kit warriors piled on top of the roof directly adjacent to the one on which Brig'dha knelt praying. Seeing the priestess deep in prayer and realizing that they could move in her direction nearly unopposed, the men rallied together and began climbing down to the roof Brig'dha knelt upon.

The men came to a halt before the priestess, many unwilling to attack her for fear of the spiritual powers she might unleash upon them. Many knew that killing a priest or priestess while they were in direct communication with their deity could easily cause offense to the deity, and very few of the men gathered before her were willing to take that sort of risk. Ember glanced behind her to see how Brig'dha was doing and was horrified to see nearly thirty warriors gathered before the priestess menacing her and yet seemingly unwilling to strike a blow. Brig'dha knelt before the men with her eyes closed and her arms stretched out wide, imploring her Goddess.

Seeing so many warriors approaching her, Ember left the side of the wall she defended and rushed toward her lover. She jumped from the roof upon which she had stood, landing right beside Brig'dha and standing with her dagger in hand before the thirty men who were slowly approaching across the roof. Had it been any other woman, they would have simply rushed her. Fortunately for Ember, many of these men had witnessed her daring act the day before and were more cautious as a result. Many believed her to be an aspect of Isut or her agent. This, and the priestess, held the men back. Ember stood before the men holding her arms out wide and in defiance.

"Thirty on one, you frightened little children..." she said, spitting onto the ground in disgust. Her determination in the face of so many warriors gave the men pause for only a moment. Suddenly, a cracking sound was heard, and the center poles holding up the roof broke. Half of the men fell straight through the boards and into the room below, with the other half sliding toward the center and trying to hold on. Ember stepped back to avoid falling in herself, her free hand grabbing Brig'dha's waist cord and pulling the befuddled brunette back.

"Say thanks to the Goddess for me!" Ember said to a bewildered Brig'dha as she rushed forward with her dagger to sink a few blows on the hands of any men holding on to their side of the hole. Brig'dha only stared at the hole, still kneeling, amazed that her Goddess had answered her in such a direct and sudden manner. All around, the remaining forces of Isut'na who had witnessed the event became emboldened, many of them turning around and returning to the fight. Wars were not won by sheer strength but often by perception and will. Even a superior enemy could be routed if they could be made fearful enough.

Ember fell onto her knees right at the edge of the collapsed roof and began stabbing with her obsidian dagger into the arms and hands of the men holding on, causing many of them grave injury as they slipped and fell into the building with deep wounds to their hands. She wasn't necessarily trying to kill any of them but cause them an injury that would take them out of combat. Ember was not against killing her enemy to save her friends, but she would always wound before taking life, if at all possible. There was enough death in the world as it was. She could still remember what Brig'dha asked her in broken trade language so long ago as the women drifted along in their small boat. Is it moral to kill your enemy? She took a deep breath as the last nearby man fell to the floor below with a thud. *Yeah, we are doing the right thing, but only when we show mercy. We are all just trying to get out of this alive.*

Ɔ Ɔ Ɔ

Aethen turned to see a large number of men threatening Ember and Brig'dha as many of Isut'na's forces turned and fled when suddenly the top of the building opened up and swallowed most of the Nara'kit warriors they faced. Moments later, Ember rushed forward, stabbing at them with her dagger. He shook his head. *May we all be so luck...* He had been holding the tops of three buildings along with a team of farmers who had been making excellent use of many of their farm tools.

Suddenly, he caught sight of a familiar-looking figure climbing one of the wooden poles which had been left undefended by fleeing defenders, along with a few men. It was none other than Ishayan himself. The man was covered in heavy leather pieces and stood triumphantly atop the building. Along with him were a group of what appeared to be veteran warriors covered in ritual blood and ready to kill. Before he could say or do anything, Ishayan and his warriors began to run in the direction of the temple. The first thing that went through his mind was the face of his beloved Isha'kau...

"Ember!" he yelled as loud as he could, trying to get the attention of the feisty redhead, but instead, Brig'dha turned to pay him heed.

"Temple!" he yelled, pointing in the direction of the temple. Brig'dha followed his point, then dove forward, grabbing ahold of Ember's foot and tugging it. Ember turned from her stabbing, and the two began to speak for just a moment. Then, a moment later, both women stood and dashed for the temple, leaving a large pile of Nara'kit warriors behind scrambling to get back onto the roof, many with grievous stab wounds to the hands and face.

CHAPTER THIRTY
LOVE KNOWS NO BOUNDS

Humanity is the product of billions of years of evolution upon a slowly cooling planet, orbiting a middle-aged star, nestled in a chaotic galaxy, and born of an entropic cosmos. We are made from the stars and bathe within their energy, a harmonious dance of what could be and what is. Love is a complex and emergent property of sentients, an application of empathy, and a necessity of any complex social species. Love is our most beautiful gift, causing our greatest joys and deepest sorrows, a vice which we crave and use to work our greatest glories.

Humanity's ability to inflict harm and impose its will through force of conflict and threat of violence is tamed by our capacity for love and compassion. No matter what we possess, where we venture, or what we do, perhaps the most important part of our lives are the people who we love and how those people shape who we are. It is that love, empathy, and compassion that makes the human race beautiful and provides hope for our future, should we choose to embrace it in all of its many forms.

Ishayan ran across roof after roof with ten of his finest warriors to his back. They had suffered vastly greater losses than he had expected. Perhaps half of his warriors were now dead or wounded, and the only reason his remaining men fought was that the promise of Isut'na lay so close to their grasp. The men he had sent up the backside of the city had been defeated, and the other major foothold into the city had fallen, quite literally, simply due to its own weight. Worse, it had done so before a praying priestess, and now the fool defenders of Isut'na would assume that their weak goddess had not abandoned them. There was still one final way to seal the city's fate, one final move he could make to save the day.

What Ishayan needed now was to cripple their morale by killing their leader. If the high priestess fell, disorder would spread throughout the city and its defenders. Many fearful citizens teetering on the edge of surrender would finally give in. Just a few rooftops ahead lay the temple to the goddess Isut, perhaps the most important building in the entire city. He knew it would be defended by several people, people most likely willing to die in its defense. Only moments before, he had caught sight of what looked like the dirty little low-born Imkanar rushing into the temple, adding to his troubles. Luckily, he had brought along his ten greatest warriors to ensure victory. Very soon, he would stand atop the temple tossing Aya'tar and Imkanar's heads, and those of their children, onto the ceremonial grounds for all to see how weak Isut really was. The people of Isut'na would fall before him in anguish.

Suddenly, an Isut'na defender came into view, standing atop the temple. He drew his bow and loosed an arrow directly into Ishayan. The arrow flew through the air faster than anyone could react, slamming right into the leather armor pieces Ishayan wore across his chest. The arrow broke apart as its tip failed to pierce the heavy, multi-layered rawhide armor that covered his chest, abdomen, legs, and even arms. Most of his warriors wore nothing more than sandals and a loincloth, perhaps a third being wholly nude, but Ishayan preferred the protection of the magical leather. It had been blessed by the priests of An'an, and that protection showed as the arrowhead exploded on impact. Stone just could not penetrate the hardened leather.

The archer stared in disbelief at his failed arrow when suddenly, one of Ishayan's elite warriors fired a similarly perfect shot back at him. Unfortunately for the archer, he wore no armor. He slumped to the ground holding the arrow deep in his chest and coughing as his lungs filled with blood, but his agony lasted only a short time as Ishayan rushed by him, slashing his war club and replacing his pain with infinite darkness.

ɔ ɔ ɔ

Ember and Brig'dha climbed down the side of the building and ran toward the temple to defend it. Up ahead, she could see what looked like Ishayan running across the rooftops headed for the temple with a group of warriors behind him. As they approached the temple, a man stepped forward with a bow and fired. For a brief moment, Ember hoped against all luck that the arrow would kill Ishayan and end this madness, but instead, it amazingly bounced off the leather he wore across his chest. What manner of magic could reflect arrows?

"He wears armor of magic! Only something magical can pierce it, most likely," Brig'dha announced, also witnessing the feat. Ember stopped running and dropped to her knees to rummage through her quiver. She only had three arrows left, but one of them was fitted with the magical copper arrowhead she had bought almost a harvest before. Finding the object, she pulled it from her quiver. She held the arrow before her and saw the sharp copper edge along with the magical symbols carefully etched into it. She could almost feel the tingle in her hand as she held the arrow, its magic was so strong. She knew it was a good decision to buy it – she just hadn't realized why at the time.

"Something magical, you say? I think I have a gift for Ishayan, something for him to remember us by as he journeys to oblivion," she said, handing the arrow to Brig'dha and grabbing an ordinary arrow from her quiver. Brig'dha looked at the arrow for a moment, unsure of exactly what Ember wanted from her.

"What do you expect me to do with this? I don't even have a bow! I…" But Ember placed a firm hand on the priestess' shoulder.

"Bless it! Bless it with all your strength and hand it to me when it's ready!" she said as the two began running toward the temple once more. Suddenly, three Nara'kit warriors emerged from the side of one of the buildings, each with linen and other goods in their arms, one of them even holding a terrified woman bound by a leather cord. They were surprised to see warriors already taking spoils, but perhaps these men thought that Isut'na would fall, and they might get an early start. The closest man turned to regard Ember. He held a war club and smiled in a less than pleasing sort of way. Ember held her arm out, warning Brig'dha back.

"You work on that arrow. Let me take care of these guys," she said. Above all, Ember hated raiders, and that's just what these men had become when they began to take spoils.

Ꙩ Ꙩ Ꙩ

Below the temple, Ianmu watched as her brother, along with ten warriors, ran above her. In front of her was a small doorway that apparently was used to access the temple, likely as a means to bring supplies in without interrupting temple activities. There might even be a small storehouse under the temple if these buildings worked the way they did in Nara'kit. She climbed through the doorway, dagger in hand, and discovered that there was indeed a small storehouse, as well as two small beds and even an oven. It looked as though somebody had been living down here, perhaps one of the priestesses. But most importantly, a small and very narrow staircase led up into the main temple above.

Ianmu dropped to her knees and held her hands up high with the dagger in them, praying to An'an for the help she would need. She didn't really care whether or not Aya'tar lived, though she had some respect for the woman. She had survived an assassination attempt and even took back the man she loved. Given her realization of An'an's true will, she no longer cared if Aya'tar possessed the city. If everything went the way she expected, she would kill her brother and take possession of Nara'kit in a very short moment or die trying. She shook her head, banishing thoughts of what had come to pass from her mind. She was still extremely angry with herself for having gone through so much under what was likely a misinterpretation of a simple message. She would have plenty of time to rage over that later. Right now, she would have her happy ending and would carve it out of somebody's chest if she had to.

☽ ☾ ☾

Aya'tar knelt before the altar of Isut, chanting continuously for the support of the Goddess. To her right, Isha'kau knelt before the horns of Gunar, equally pleading to the God for help and strength. Standing out of the way so that he would not interfere, or worse, be wounded by any stray magic, Imkanar waited with a war club in hand. The war club reminded him of the stone hammer he used when metalworking. He would defend Aya'tar with his life, but that would be much easier holding a weapon that felt more natural to him than a knife. He had been worried that she would be angry with him for having effectively come to check up on her with nothing more than a premonition that something bad would happen but no real evidence. Luckily, Aya'tar had been feeling a similar premonition and had welcomed him.

Two of Isut'na's few warriors were ready to defend the high priestess and the altars by the ladder leading down from the roof. The ladder, which allowed easy access from the roof, had been pulled down to make entry into the room slightly more challenging though the drop was still only about one and one-half times the height of a man. The simple jump had not bothered Imkanar, who had used the secret storeroom entrance, known to only a few. The fate of the entire city rested on those protecting the sacred altars and the priestesses. If they fell, the city would likely fall moments afterward.

The sounds of combat could be heard from the small doorway leading down from the ceiling, yet the sound of fighting close to the entryway made little sense. When Imkanar had left the buildings, the Nara'kit forces had been all but defeated, and there had been no warriors inside the temple. The two warriors grasped their clubs, ready for whatever might come their way. Imkanar glanced nervously at Aya'tar, squeezing the handle of his club tightly. He had received a premonition, and it looked like it might come true. Aya'tar began to chant louder and more pleadingly, hoping that Isut and Gunar might intercede on their behalf. Not far behind Imkanar and the altars was the small bed where both of their children lay quietly sleeping, the usual women who helped Aya'tar having fled to seek refuge in other parts of the city.

As they waited nervously, Imkanar thought he saw the light flickering above the temple entryway as though somebody had approached. He watched the doorway, waiting to see if somebody might look in. Perhaps a bird had merely flown across, blocking the Sun and momentarily creating a shadow... Suddenly, warriors began to drop into the room, one at a time. The first warrior who landed on the floor never got up, his head bludgeoned by a war club. The warrior who swung that blow was smashed to the floor as another Nara'kit warrior landed on top of him and then another as each of the elite warriors dropped from the opening in the ceiling, landing on the men below. The fight for the temple room had just begun.

Imkanar rushed forward, swinging his club high overhead. The warrior in front of him held out his own battle club to block the heavy war club, but Imkanar's aim was refined from metalworking, and he planted the stone head of his war club right onto the handle of the warrior's weapon, crushing the man's hand. The warrior stepped backward, screaming as he held his ruined hand, dozens of bones shattered from the impact of the stone. Another warrior stepped forward and swung his war club, narrowly missing Imkanar's head.

Isha'kau turned to see two warriors heading for the children. She grabbed her obsidian knife and rushed to block them. The lesser priestess dove in front of the two men slashing with her blade, causing both of them to back away momentarily. She had halted their initial assault, but it became quickly apparent that she was one woman with a small obsidian knife versus two large warriors brandishing heavy war clubs. The men each took different directions, slowly approaching her and forcing her to choose one to attack while leaving herself open to the other. Isha'kau stepped backward, knowing that at any moment, it would all be over.

Aya'tar was chanting at a feverish pace to the Goddess when she heard the commotion to her left, where her children slept. Her concentration was instantly broken, and she grabbed the ceremonial dagger from the altar and stood to help her children. Before she could move forward, a hand grasped her on the shoulder, and she turned to find a Nara'kit warrior swinging his war club down upon her. He never finished the swing is Imkanar ducked past the man attacking him and swung his war club into the back of the neck of the man assaulting his wife, killing him in one hit.

"Halt!" yelled Ishayan, bringing his men to a halt. On the ground lay dead both warriors charged with defending the temple. Around them were three more Nara'kit warriors, two dead and one in agony over his ruined hand. More warriors piled in from the ceiling entry above, filling the room, each an armed and seasoned veteran. The odds were now more than two to one in favor of Nara'kit as Imkanar, Aya'tar, and Isha'kau stood back, weapons drawn. They stood between the children and the Nara'kit warriors while Ishayan and his remaining seven men leered, menacingly. With combat briefly paused, Ishayan advanced, matching Aya'tar's glare with great severity.

"All is lost. Your city is overrun with my warriors, and the battle is over. Agree to be my first wife and abandon that pathetic excuse for a man you call a husband. Give me control of the city under oath before your gods, and I will stop the slaughter while some of your people still live. Isut'na is mine, and your children's lives are now in your hands," he said flatly. In reality, he planned to dispose of them and put someone else in charge of the city while he returned to take direct control of Nara'kit. But right now, the battle was far less one-sided than he made it out to be. He needed her to concede so that he could stop the forces of Isut'na before they actually did defeat what was left of his army.

Aya'tar stood at a crossroads of fate. Aside from some dramatic strategy or extreme bad luck, the only real explanation for Ishayan standing before her was that he was correct and her forces were scattered and defeated. The high priestess turned to see the look of determination and outrage on Imkanar's face, but then she saw the two babies lying on the sleeping mat behind Isha'kau. She was sure that regardless of her choice, Isha'kau would die before she let the children be harmed. She wondered how both babies could sleep through something like this? Yet, how could she choose between her children and Isha'kau, a sister in all but name, and her beloved husband and city? How could anyone make such a choice?

Aya'tar dropped to her knees and wept, for she knew there was only one possible answer to give, but for some reason, she couldn't bring herself to say it. If she refused him, she knew that Ishayan would simply kill Imkanar and then her children. She could see it all playing out in her mind as Isha'kau died defending the children, and she was killed moments later. The city would be entirely sacked, and hundreds would die. But how could she possibly bring herself to openly accept such terms?

"It's all right. If the cost is my life to save yours and our children, that's a fair trade... it always has been," Imkanar said slowly, lowering his weapon. Behind him, Isha'kau stared, mouth open in shock at what Imkanar had just said. Aya'tar wanted nothing more than to reject Imkanar's words, but she knew that Ishayan would take his battle club to her children's heads without a thought. She lifted her head towards Ishayan and slowly began to stand, mustering all the courage she had left in her body to be strong in the middle of such horror. She opened her mouth to say the words that must be said, to speak that which was unspeakable.

"I... In... the name of... Isut... I..." the high priestess started to say, tears running down her face, all the while, Ishayan glaring at her with a growing smile. This was his moment of glory... his absolute victory.

Ↄ Ↄ Ↄ

Ember ducked and rolled forward as a club swung overhead. As soon as she hit the ground, she rolled to her right as the second man slammed his club into the ground right where she had just been. Brig'dha stayed back from the fight holding the arrow and continuing to bless it as she watched Ember fighting two of the three men, the third standing behind them with the woman he had taken prisoner. Ember looked to see the two men slowly approaching her from two different sides, seemingly impressed that she had survived their first attacks. From a crouching position, Ember grabbed hold of some sand with her left hand and took note of the man approaching her on the left, all the while listening as the man approached on the right.

The sounds of the man's footsteps on the right abruptly changed in the way of someone shifting their body weight. Ember suddenly tossed the sand in her left-hand overhead, catching the man right in the face as he brought his war club up high, ready to come down on her head. At that moment, the man on the left rushed forward, swinging his large flint knife. She stood from her crouching position, throwing her arm up and catching the man's flint knife against the copper bracelet on her arm, shattering the stone blade against the unyielding metal, a portent of a distant future to come. In the same motion, she jammed her dagger straight through his chin and into his skull.

She pulled the dagger free in stepped back as the man dropped to his knees and then to the ground. The man she had cast the sand upon was frantically trying to open his eyes, knowing an enemy stood before him whom he could not see. Ember rushed forward, bringing her knee as hard as she could right into the man's gut. He dropped his war club and doubled over. She cut the achilles tendon connecting the man's calf muscle to his heel in one slash. He screamed, doubling over and holding the wound, no longer a threat to anyone. The man might never again walk, but Ember felt no pity for slavers. She turned her attention next to the man with the captured woman, a man slowly backing away. She smiled menacingly as she slowly approached him, wiping the blood from her dagger across her chest.

"Let the woman go, unharmed, and I will let you flee like the coward you are," she said. Seeing the crazed redhead standing before his two fallen companions and recognizing that this was the very same woman who had rushed down the ladder and fired an arrow directly at his leader the day before, the man suddenly felt less brave.

"You... you're some sort of spirit... An incarnation of Isut!" he said, pointing at her and stepping backward.

"That's right, I am the spirit of vengeance, and I give you this one chance to flee, or I will carry your spirit to oblivion," Ember said as maniacally as she could, hoping the man would believe her and flee. The Nara'kit warrior suddenly pushed his slave forward and then turned and ran as fast as he could toward whatever entry he had come through. Brig'dha paused her chanting to scold Ember over her hubris. She shook her head, still quite amazed that Ember could ask her to implore the gods to help them while at the same time taking their names in vain. The redhead shrugged, having no real excuse for her actions but a sly grin. She walked over to the poor woman and cut her bindings free. It was time for them to enter the temple and rescue Aya'tar before Ishayan had a chance to do her harm.

ꙅ ꙅ ꙅ

I... I surr..." the high priestess began but was cut off before she could finish her reluctant words by the sound of an outraged woman, a woman whose voice Ishayan knew quite well.

"Ishayan, you vicious little snake. I should have killed you before I left!" Suddenly, everyone in the room turned to the source of the words. Ianmu stepped from the small entryway to the storeroom upon the very stairs where Isha'kau and Hullamu used to hide and gossip. She came to stand equally distant between both groups. Ishayan turned to regard his younger sister. She stood tall, wearing a linen apron with tassels and a pair of sandals, and covered from head to toe with battle paint. She carried a sharp flint dagger in one hand and wore a necklace with a single feather around her neck.

"Well, what did I find here? If it isn't little Ianmu'kimun, my child sister and first daughter to the city of Nara'kit. The very woman who strangled to death the high priest of An'an before disappearing into the wilds," he said in disgust, mocking her younger age. For a moment, he glared at her with unbridled disgust. She was not someone he expected to find in the temple room of Isut'na. In reality, he was not even sure that she was even alive until that moment. She had been rejected as a priestess to An'an and had fled the city, but not before killing the former high priest. He could not deny that the high priest had deserved his fate and part of him respected her for that, but he had suspected that she had headed far from the likes of Nara'kit or Isut'na.

"Dunu'lekal'Ishayan, pathetic son of the savage excuse for a father, An'sankup'Anteanar, the former ruler of all Nara'kit. A bunch of violent fools with long names and short... tempers. So, you tried to marry the high priestess here, and you got beaten into a bloody mess by some random foreign woman. You are a pathetic little man-boy who can't achieve anything without an army behind you. I have all the army I need right here," she said with a smile, holding her knife for him to see. Ishayan threw his war club to the ground and pulled out a long obsidian blade. His sister's death was long overdue, and perhaps she could follow Anteanar into the next world.

"You can repeat all of that for father after I kill you," he said, squeezing the handle tightly, his muscles tensing. Ianmu took a deep breath, preparing to move. This battle would be quick but intense. Ishayan might be a coward, but he was still skilled with a blade.

"You are so pathetic. You couldn't even defeat the city on your own. You had to lie to them... to tell them that they were defeated. Even now, Nara'kit's forces are fleeing. You can't even win without a lie, and you know it," she said coldly. Behind her, Aya'tar perked up, hearing the news that perhaps all was not lost. While the news filled Aya'tar, Isha'kau, and Imkanar with hope, hearing it sent Ishayan into a sudden rage. His normally calm demeanor was thrown to the wind.

"Die, you snake!" Ishayan screamed as he and his warriors burst forward. Isha'kau held her ground before the children with the obsidian knife while Imkanar swung his weapon overhead and down upon one of the warriors. The man raised his own war club to block the club, but the impact from Imkanar's strong arm was so intense that the war club smashed him in the head, forcing his own weapon aside. He would hold nothing back and never let his priestess, lover, and wife be forced to make such a choice. Again and again, he swung the weapon, literally pounding the warriors before him into the floor. He felt the spirit of Gunar fill him as he worked them like raw metal, one swing after the next, forging their deaths.

One of the warriors rushed for Isha'kau, hoping to quickly take the smaller woman out of combat. He swung his war club sideways, trying to catch her body with the heavy stone head. Isha'kau threw her entire upper body backward in an arch, her head almost to the floor, with the club passing just over her stomach. Just as the club passed, she rotated her body in a full circle as she rose, slashing the man's gut open with the blade of her obsidian dagger and returning to a standing stance. An entire life spent dancing rituals had made Isha'kau extremely flexible, and the man had assumed that she would simply freeze up when he swung. He staggered backward and fell onto his side, his intestines spilling from his abdomen.

"No one will harm these children, as Isut as my witness!" she challenged, before gagging as she nearly vomited from adrenaline and fear. Almost immediately, another man came rushing at her in apparent outrage over her defeat of the first man. Seeing Isha'kau off-balance and rushed by a man twice her size, Aya'tar reached for the only thing that she knew would stop his advance, an eggshell oil lamp. She grabbed the hot lamp and tossed it right into the man's face. Oil squirted every direction, and the man screamed as his hair and face caught fire. The animal fat oil by itself would not catch fire easily, even with a flame touching it, but in combination with his hair, it became an immediate torch, his hair the wick. The man screamed, running around trying to stop his hair from burning, which only made it worse.

Ianmu ducked as the first warrior swung at her, but the second warrior's club came sideways and quicker than she could dodge. Instead, she grabbed hold of his swinging arm and rolled along it until she was facing the same direction as him, her knife held backward and buried deep in his abdomen. Ianmu pulled free the dagger, quickly pairing a slash from Ishayan. Her mischievous brother stood back from the main fight attempting to opportunistically slash whoever was weakest or close enough. Her disdain for him grew even greater when even the recently pregnant high priestess scored a greater victory than he, her combatant running away with his hair alight.

Ishayan realized almost immediately that there was no way he could defeat his sister one-on-one. She was just too fast. She had always been quicker with a knife than anyone else he knew, a natural. As his warriors fell one at a time, he began to panic. This was supposed to be an easy victory. Things were degrading around him fast, but if he could get out of the city, he would at least keep Nara'kit, and he could return another day to settle the score. Perhaps he could even send assassins to kill all the people who had wronged him, then return in a few harvests with another army. The problem would be getting out of the building alive, but that would be made much easier if he had the help of a hostage.

The man with the burning hair had put the flame out and was now savagely attacking Imkanar and Aya'tar in some sort of pain-fueled rage along with another unscathed warrior. The pair traded blows with Imkanar while Aya'tar repeatedly slashed with her ceremonial dagger keeping the two men from flanking her husband. Behind them, Ianmu was preoccupied with her own warrior, one of his best. So far, the warrior she now faced had survived longer than anyone she had faced in recent history, actively blocking many of her strikes. Off to the side, Isha'kau had her hands busy with the last warrior of the group. The Initiate priestess' battle ended quickly when the man attacking her stepped backward to avoid her dagger and slipped on the bloody entrails of one of his fellow warriors, hitting his head against the same stone bench Hullamu was buried beneath, breaking his neck. Isha'kau glared at the suddenly dead man, startled by how abruptly he had died. *Thank you, my friend,* she thought, knowing Hullamu's spirit had likely intervened from beyond this world.

The room was in disarray with people lying all over the floor and his enemies quickly killing all his warriors. Ishayan took the opportunity to rush at the priestess, Isha'kau, the poisoner, if he recalled. Behind her were the babies, the only hostages that were easy to carry and who might gain him his freedom. He dashed at the lesser priestess as fast as he could and simply rammed her against the bed. Being prepared for the impact, Ishayan received only a few minor bruises. He quickly stood and grabbed one of the children, turning to leave. Behind him, Isha'kau fought to get the wind back in her lungs after having been hit so hard. He would have preferred to have killed her right then, but escape was the only thing on his mind.

"Aya'tar! He... has... little Hullamu! He's... taken a baby!" Isha'kau screamed between gasps. She waved at everyone to go after Ishayan as she slowly stood holding her dagger to defend the remaining baby, little Ikanar. Everyone turned just in time to see Ishayan rush to the small opening from which Ianmu had entered. Imkanar slashed his war club, catching one of the warriors in the face and ending his struggle forever, but not before the man's war club clipped Imkanar's shoulder, causing it to go completely numb and dropping the man to his knees. Suddenly, the man with the burned face stepped before Aya'tar with nothing but vengeance in his eyes. Seeing one of her children being carried out of the temple and then finding this large man standing before her blocking rescue, Aya'tar was suddenly overcome with a mother's rage.

The man with the burned face and hair began to speak, probably to say some sort of lengthy threat. Aya'tar didn't even let him get his first word out. She rushed forward heedless of any danger and smashed into the man sending both of them to the floor. Fueled by fear and raw fury, she repeatedly stabbed with her ceremonial dagger, all the while looking at the door, almost in tears at her frustration and fear. The blade was as sharp as glass and cut the man deeply everywhere it hit. He savagely punched her twice, yet she kept cutting, her instinct to save her child overpowering all worry for herself.

Quickly, the man's body became a lacerated waste as the dagger chipped and broke apart under her wild fury. The moment the man stopped moving, she jumped off and rushed for the door after her stolen child, her body powered by adrenaline. Behind her, on the floor lay the twitching form of the burned man, multiple knife wounds penetrating his skull through his eyes and anywhere else the blade could find. He had made the mistake of standing between a mother and her child. *Monologue always gets you killed,* Isha'kau thought, in shock.

Though his left arm was completely numb from the impact, Imkanar grabbed his war club and rushed after Aya'tar. As he left, he passed Ianmu, who continued to battle the most senior of Nara'kit warriors. She parried strike after strike from the man's fierce war club, then suddenly dove forward, slashing at him. He stepped aside, slapping her in the back with his hand and forcing her forward and past him. As she came to a stop, she ducked and rolled forward just as the club flew overhead, catching the air right where she had just stood. This last warrior was much more dangerous than the others. Ianmu recognized him as Kurunar, one of the three leading warriors of the city.

Seeing only one enemy left standing, Isha'kau rushed with her dagger to aid the woman she had known up until recently as being the concubine of Sar'Tawas. She certainly didn't seem like a concubine, now. The man swung his club at Isha'kau, missing her, but Ianmu carved a long gash across his back in the opening provided. In a rage, he swung at Ianmu, who narrowly avoided the club by dropping to her knees at the last moment. The wild slashing rage allowed Isha'kau to step in and plunge her dagger deep into his armpit, causing a sudden loss of blood. The man staggered backward with the dagger still jammed under his arm. Ianmu rushed forward and slapped the war club sideways with her left arm, plunging her dagger with her right hand directly into the man's throat and twisting as the stone blade broke.

Isha'kau stepped back between the crazed woman and the remaining baby, reaching for a small flint dagger on the floor. She didn't know how the woman would react now that she had given up her true identity as a member of Nara'kit's ruling family. The woman fought like an aspect of the Goddess herself. Isha'kau was pretty sure that there would be no way she could stop the woman if she came for the child, but she wouldn't stand before the Goddess without having at least done everything she could to save the children. She wasn't the best warrior or even the best priestess, but she knew what was right, and nothing would stop her from doing the right thing, not even death itself. *Goddess, protect me... Gunar, give me strength...*

Ianmu slowly turned, blood-drenched down her arm, and leveled her gaze upon Isha'kau. The priestess found herself starting to involuntarily shake in fear as Ianmu approached. She had watched the woman's violent and nearly inhuman display of skill and was quite sure that she was about to die at the hands of what might very well be a living aspect of the enemy goddess, An'an. Isha'kau held out her knife to ward off the deadly woman, but when Ianmu came close enough, she simply snatched the knife from her hand as a mother took a toy from an unruly child. Unlike the warriors she had fought before, the initiate priestess knew that she had no chance of defeating this powerful woman. Ianmu regarded the brave, terrified priestess. The woman held her arms wide, blocking Ianmu from the remaining child, her eyes holding the look of a woman sure she was about to die, but unwilling to back down, no matter the cost.

"I understand now. An'an has chosen a different path for me than I originally thought. It has taken this city and its people to show me the way. People like you. Stay with the baby and protect it, priestess of Isut, Isha'kau," she said calmly, turning and walking toward the door.

Somewhere out there, her brother was trying to get out of the city using an innocent baby as a human shield. For her first act as the rightful leader of her people, Ianmu would take his life. Afterward, she would call off the rest of Nara'kit's forces and return to her rightful city to restore the ways of An'an. Isha'kau slowly sank to her knees with her eyes closed in thanks to the Goddess.

Ɔ Ɔ Ɔ

Ember and Brig'dha entered one of the buildings on the ground level and climbed the small ladder up to the second level. Before them was the temple entrance. Quite a period of time had passed since the group led by Ishayan had disappeared into the temple, and Ember was nearly in a panic over what could have transpired in that amount of time. The pair approached the entryway, hearing nothing but an ominous silence in the room below. Suddenly, from beneath them, Ishayan burst forth from the building. He didn't make it very far before an Isut'na defender approached with his spear drawn. Moments later, high priestess Aya'tar rushed through the doorway with a broken dagger in hand, screaming for him to stop, Imkanar right on her heels.

All three of them surrounded Ishayan with weapons ready. Ember and Brig'dha stood upon the temple roof, unsure of what to do next. Nobody advanced upon the man because he held before him a baby. Ember stared intently at the child, slightly turning her head in disbelief, mouth wide open. It couldn't be. Unless her eyes deceived her, that coward Ishayan held in his hands one of Aya'tar's own children, a hostage to ensure he made it out of the city.

"Stay back, or I'll kill the child! I swear I'll do it!" he screamed, holding the child tightly against his chest. One of his hands held the child's torso while the other was placed firmly around its neck, ready to twist at any moment. Filled with horror, Aya'tar dropped to her knees and began to plead for her child. Both Aya'tar and Imkanar begged him to take the place of the baby. But it didn't matter to Ishayan. He would not let the child go for any reason. All around him, his men were either fleeing or dead. He knew the battle was over. While he held the life of the small child in his hands, he was safe. His life and that of the child had just become linked. As soon as Aya'tar calmed down, he would walk from the city, and as soon as he got the chance, he would kill the child and run. If nothing more, he would use that as payment for her treachery.

"Your arrows cannot penetrate my magic armor, and if any of you try to grab me, I will break this child's neck! I will walk from your wretched city unharmed, or you will lose the child of your leader!" he screamed aloud, slowly turning so everyone could see the child.

"Aeeya! If only I could get a clear shot at him," Ember said, holding her bow and seeing no possible angle to shoot at the man without greatly endangering the child. All around, other defenders approached, some with bows. Brig'dha suddenly had an idea, a deception for the great deceiver himself. She took the arrow, which she had just finished blessing, and handed it to Ember. Ember could feel the spirit energy within the arrow causing her arm to tingle. The head was made of shiny copper with magic shapes carved into the metal, almost as sharp as her obsidian blade. The arrow was made with wider hawk feather fletchings to ensure it found its proper target. Ember had been told that it could penetrate anything. Now what she needed was a target on the man. Brig'dha flashed Ember a smile and then stood waving her arms and yelling loudly at Ishayan. *Now, who's doing something daring,* Ember thought with a chuckle at what was obviously a Brig'dha plan.

"I think it's fake! The baby doesn't look real!" Brig'dha yelled loudly with her heavy accent, drawing many onlookers.

"What are you doing? It's obviously a real baby," Ember said, confused, both by the plan and Brig'dha yelling... a rare occurrence.

"Yeah, but he might turn to show everyone or raise it up high," Brig'dha countered. Ember grunted approval. *That's actually a good plan,* she thought, realizing that Brig'dha plans sounded pretty good.

"That doesn't look like a real baby! You are fooling us! Show us it's real or we will shoot you where you stand!" Ember yelled. Aya'tar began to panic at the thought that somebody might fire an arrow at what was really a living, breathing child and began pleading for everyone within the sound of her voice not to fire. Ishayan knew that everyone around him could see that it was a child, but there were too many people with ranged weapons pointing at him from a distance who might not realize. With how intense the battle had been, Aya'tar's people might not heed her words, and he might end up with an arrow in his face, the only overly exposed place on him. He knew that his magic armor would protect his body, but holding the baby over his head would ensure that everyone saw it was real, and it would protect his only vulnerable point. Ishayan quickly lifted the child over his head, the infant beginning to cry aloud in fear.

"Do you see this? Do you see how real this child is? I will leave this place now, and none of you will stop me!" he screamed and began to slowly walk toward the main entranceway to the city. He kept a watchful eye, slowly turning and looking at each person he saw with a bow making sure that they saw the defenseless child in his arms. He would make it out of the city, no matter what.

"Goddess, guide my arrow..." Ember whispered as the baby suddenly lifted over the man's head, giving her a clear shot. At that moment, Ishayan caught sight of Ember, her red hair blowing in the wind. Though unnerving to have arrows pointed at him, he had already been shot several times that day, and his magical leather armor had reflected each of the stone projectile points. He stopped and turned to regard the redhead, the woman who had beaten him so severely not so long before. He had wanted nothing more than to kill her, and he would certainly get his revenge in good time, but for right now, he could, at least, remind her that she could not harm him. This time, he would be victorious on his own terms.

"You, the woman with the red hair! Do you not see this child in my arms? One day I will come for you, but today I will leave, or this child dies!" he said, holding little Hullamu high overhead. Ember was not paying attention to the child but instead watching grass and debris on the ground below as the wind gently blew. Abruptly, all the small objects that she had noted on the ground in between her and the target stopped moving as the wind died for a moment. Ember relaxed her finger's hold upon the bowstring and felt it roll free from her grasp, loosing her arrow. The deadly missile flew true and stuck with a thud.

Aya'tar screamed...

Ishayan stepped back, unable to believe that the reckless redhead had been foolish enough to fire an arrow. The damn thing had hit him in the rib cage, and he could feel a strange burning sensation where it had hit. Pain or no pain, there was no way it could have penetrated the armor. He looked down, ready to laugh, when he realized – to his shock – that the arrow had gone right through the leather and even through the rib cage piercing sideways between two ribs. Ishayan slowly stepped backward as blood began to drip out of his leather armor. All around him stood Isut'na defenders holding back only because of the child. He staggered, the world becoming slightly blurry and strange sparkly lights appearing here and there in his vision. As he staggered backward, he let the baby go, but a firm set of hands grabbed the child. He dropped to his knees... his life was ending, and for the first time, he was truly filled with fear.

Imkanar stepped back, holding the child in his hands and offering little Hullamu to her mother. The priestess held the child crying, though happy to see that no real harm had been done. From behind them stepped Ianmu from the doorway, holding a dagger in her blood-soaked hands. She slowly crossed the battlefield and came to a stop before her brother. She reached out and grabbed him by the hair. He looked up at her with fear in his eyes but unable to do much more than watch, as his lifeblood quickly pooled at her feet. He breathed words that might have been "help me," though she did not hear what they were and did not care to ask.

"You have brought shame to our family. Worse than that, you have displeased the Goddess. An'an is a goddess of strength and cunning, as well as war, but also love, passion, and fertility. She has no room in the next world for cowards and fools. To hold a child hostage to save yourself from death in battle... I can think of way to displease her more. I have changed the fate of many people. I am the messenger of An'an to the city of Isut'na. I have plucked the old plants from the ground and sown new..." she said cryptically. Ianmu dropped to her knees, facing her brother and continuing to hold him by the hair lest he fall from loss of blood. His breathing was shallow, and he was beginning to convulse.

"An'an, this war was started in your name, and it will end in your name. Old crops have been harvested, and the new have been planted. With this sacrifice, I declare peace between the people of Nara'kit and Isut'na in your name!" she said. Ianmu slashed Ishayan's throat open in one quick slice of her dagger, letting what was left of his blood spray across her body. He fell to the ground at her knees and stopped moving. The priestess of An'an slowly stood with her arms out, allowing the dagger to fall to the ground and showing everyone who bore witness the blood of the sacrifice.

"It is done! We are at peace..."

☽ ☽ ☽

Given the declaration of peace by Ianmu and its acceptance by Imkanar and Aya'tar, the wounded of Nara'kit had been allowed to leave the city, and all hostilities had ended abruptly. There had been widespread death on both sides. When the tally was finally taken, 102 citizens of Isut'na were dead, with another 235 wounded, while 254 Nara'kit warriors journeyed to the next world, leaving 276 wounded and 270 uninjured. A bloody conflict with this many casualties had never been recorded in the annals of song for either city. It was simply unprecedented.

As Brig'dha stood before all the wounded being treated, she wondered if armed conflict was beginning to enter into a new era, an era of larger armies and greater bloodshed. She closed her eyes, praying to the Goddess that this was not true. The feel of a soft fluffy creature brushing up against her leg brought a smile to her face and returned her to the world of the living. Little Mew gently brushed back and forth at her feet, begging to be held. Somehow, he had slept through most of the battle, barely interested in the odd sounds outside of their building. She realized that he wasn't quite so little anymore, though he, at least, remained a runt of a wildcat. She bent down and scooped up the cat. Due to the heat, he was very lethargic and would likely whine to be carried back to their short-term accommodation for water and rest.

Holding Mew, Brig'dha slowly walked through the field of wounded with tears in her eyes. They had been gathered into two basic categories, those who would likely live and those who would probably die. Salt, honey, and yarrow were used to treat their wounds for those who would live. Arrows were cut free from flesh, wounds seared shut, or honey poured over them. Isha'kau and Aya'tar worked tirelessly along with three devout Isut followers applying magical symbols to each person to heal their injuries. For the people too far gone to save, some were put out of their misery quickly with a knife after a ritual was performed to ensure their journey to the next world. Others were kept company by their families and often provided with portions of fermented fruit and honey drink to ease their passing. It would be at least a moon, perhaps four tendays, until the taint from this day was fully cleaned from the ritual ground.

Later that day, the concubine Ianmu, now revealed to everyone as the daughter of the late Anteanar, assumed her new role as leader of Nara'kit and with that her new title of An'an'sanup'ramu Ianmu. The title literally meant Priestess Vessel of the Goddess An'an, Ianmu, dropping the "kimun" portion of her title as it no longer validly described her, given her disowning of her deceased father. For her first act as the leader and self-assumed high priestess of An'an, Ianmu presented Aya'tar with a small An'an statuette asking that a small shrine to An'an be set up in the main temple. The logic was quite simple, if the people of Isut'na included An'an in worship, even in a small way, it would drastically reduce the urge of any of her people to ever wish war against Isut'na again. Though Aya'tar was less than pleased with the city of Nara'kit, she accepted the offer for the peace that it would bring. To Aya'tar, nothing was sweeter than peace.

Not far away, the priestess of An'an, Kit'tanu knelt beside her wounded husband, Uritasa. He had been among the first men to attack the wall that morning and had suffered a wound from a rock hurled from the walls. The wound had been to his head, and she had spent the entire day by his side praying for him to awaken, even as the battle raged on. All around her, people died though not one arrow or spear ever came her way. Why she had not been killed, she could not say. As he looked up at her, his head seemed to hurt a little less. She smiled down at him as tears flowed like the growing season rains... tears of relief.

"You are... still covered in cow blood," he said, feeling quite groggy. She nearly laughed with relief that he was alright. Why the now dead Ishayan had sent her husband, an archer, and not the sort of man to attack the wall, to the front lines was anyone's guess. She was simply glad this was over. She had not told him about her morning sickness yet, but she supposed it was time to let the man know that she carried their child. *An'an bless us all,* she thought.

ɔ ɔ ɔ

Three tendays had passed since the battle for Isut'na, and things were looking up. Many had recovered from their wounds or were, at least, looking much better. Many would remain wounded for many tendays to come, if not even multiple harvests. A snapped tendon or a severely broken bone might never fully heal. War was an incredibly dangerous business, and just surviving was no guarantee of a happy ending. Though many wounded would recover, there wasn't a single citizen who did not know of at least one person who had died or who lay wounded. Of the fallen, the highest-ranking casualty was the leader of the Crafting Guild, Sar'Tawas. His body had been recovered and buried beneath the trading area, hoping that his spirit might continue to bring fortune to Isut'na. Strangely, the former "concubine"-turned leader of Nara'kit did not stay for the burial, though she left a single black feather and a clay jar of fermented drink to be buried with the man.

While the living recovered, the dead had been buried or cremated, and ceremonies had been performed en masse for many of the fallen. The sacred ceremonial grounds had been ritualistically cleaned, as had most of the city with the aid of volunteer Isut devotees, those who honored the Goddess as mere lay worshipers but were blessed to perform minor rituals, a holdback from before Isut'na had an organized leadership or priest caste. Most importantly, the birth of a healthy duemuas child, not one tenday after the battle, signaled the gods' favor. Having male and female genitalia, a duemuas was considered a direct blessing from Gunar and Isut. Aya'tar could only hope the child would grow to become a priest, perhaps even a high priest. Both genders were represented, so the term priest was usually used as there was no gender-neutral title.

Aya'tar turned her attention back to the ritual at hand. She stood atop the temple roof before hundreds of gathered citizens preparing to join lovers. She wore a long red and green dyed linen skirt that ended at the ground, barely covering her bare feet. Her upper body was painted white with intricate black and red magical designs. Her head sported many long vulture and eagle feathers. Today was a special occasion, a magical moment when two sets of lovers became joined forever. Aya'tar turned to face the crowd gathered before the temple to witness such an important wedding. She took a deep breath with her eyes closed and spoke the ritual words before the wedding, reciting them from memory without effort.

> *Isut, the fertile soil,*
> *Gunar, the seed of life.*
> *For there to be a life you must meet.*
> *The bond between land and seed,*
> *must be maintained until the Third World comes!*
> *Come forth Brig'dha of the Blue River people,*
> *the most fertile of the world.*
> *Come forth Ember of the Great River people,*
> *the most fertile of the world.*
> *Come forth Isut'Sanup'ramu Isha'kau,*
> *the most fertile of the world.*
> *Come forth, Aethen of the Blue River people, the most fertile seed.*
> *You shall be joined as one under our watchful eyes and with a strong hand.*

Aya'tar turned to examine each couple and look for any signs that the Goddess or the God did not favor their marriages. As she stood before them, she could see nothing wrong with the couples. To her left stood Aethen of the Blue Sea People. He was decorated in a long red loincloth made from fine linen with black striped paint designs running from his feet all the way to his face. In his hair were two hawk feathers, and around his neck, he wore a necklace with a large, beautiful cowry shell. He smiled so deeply that Aya'tar wanted to rush to his side and give him a big hug, but she suspected that would not be proper. She had her own husband, but she couldn't help but find Aethen quite handsome, a proud and exotic Northerner.

With a smile, she turned to the woman standing beside him, the now full priestess Isut'Sanup'ramu Isha'kau. She was so excited that she seemed almost flustered by the occasion. She wore a beautiful headdress of songbird feathers and the customary reed skirt. Her body was painted from top to bottom with red and yellow decorations, and she stood barefoot, as was customary during weddings. Around her neck, wrists, waist, and ankles, she wore leather cords with beautiful cowry shells given to her by Aethen. It was truly a spectacle to wear such beautiful and rare jewelry, and Isha'kau enjoyed the attention.

Turning to her right, Aya'tar examined the other couple to be wed on this beautiful, if not overly hot, day. Ember of the Great River people stood before her with her waist-length red hair and bright green eyes. She wore a set of hawk feathers in her hair, courtesy of Brig'dha. There had been a debate between Brig'dha, Ember, and Aya'tar over what they should wear. Tradition stated that the woman wore a reed skirt while the man wore a loincloth. Ember and Brig'dha now found themselves in a situation where there was no male.

Given the uncommon joining Ember had opted to wear her linen loincloth, taking on the more masculine dress. Ember didn't mind as she never felt like her gender really fit the concept of "woman." Her skin had been painted from top to bottom in the designs of her people, black and red bands covering her body. Ember wore a copper and gold torc with copper bracelets. She smiled at Aya'tar so excited she could almost laugh aloud. Ember had always wondered if she would marry and to whom. She always suspected that she would end up with some strong warrior man, but things had turned out much differently than she had foreseen. She could think of no one she would rather spend the rest of her life with. *Ha! I'm the big tough warrior, now!* she thought, nearly laughing aloud.

Standing beside her and holding hands was priestess Brig'dha of the Blue Sea People. Brig'dha happily wore her string dress and matching torc, though her bracelets were gold. Her entire body was lightly stained black with soot and painted from top to bottom with white clay circles to resemble the stars of the sky. Her long brown hair was tied in many small braids, and she held a ritualistic feather in her free hand. Around her neck, she wore the Amber of Life necklace, a powerful magical item. Aya'tar was truly in awe over such a powerful and magical fertility item, being the high priestess of a fertility goddess herself. She found it hard to take her eyes off the flower entombed pendent, but she forced herself to do so.

Brig'dha stood breathing deeply in anticipation of what was to come, her marriage to the woman she loved. She remembered those horrible days following the death of her late husband Mohdan and how she had never suspected that she would ever feel happy again. *I would follow you into oblivion, my Kaelu,* she thought, tingles of pleasure dancing up and down her spine.

He had died from an unknown sickness, and she had been forced to labor among people who would later try to sacrifice her. Ember had saved her life and given her a purpose to live, a reason to love. Ember's own story had started as a young woman, barely an adult, who had left her tribe on a journey to the ends of the world. A quest given by the gods themselves. Together, they had traveled over most of the known world and seen more than most people would see in their entire lives. They had come to rely on one another and would give their own lives for each other if called upon to do so. There was really only one thing left for them to do about this.

"Do each of you agree to live for the rest of your lives in each other's care? Do you swear to be joined before the gods themselves?" Aya'tar asked, smiling at both couples. Isha'kau nodded yes, and Aethen spoke the same.

"There will be no other but you, Isha'kau, in this life or the next. This I swear!" he said. Ember and Brig'dha both looked at one another, no question in their minds as to their answer. At the exact same time, they both answered "Yes!" Aya'tar turned to the crowd and waited until all was silent.

"These bonds must be clear of interruption. There cannot be any doubt, nor any further competition. When a man and woman are joined," she paused for a moment, "or when any two people are joined, it is until death. Does anyone now wish to make a claim against any to be joined? Speak your love now as this will be the last opportunity you have. To do so afterward would be an offense to the Goddess herself!" Aya'tar concluded. For a short moment, everyone went silent, and breaths were held. Ember could hold her breath longer than anyone, and Brig'dha looked like she might pass out.

"Wait!" came a scream from the crowd, turning everyone's head toward the woman who yelled it. Isha'kau instantly glared at Aethen, who looked back confused. Ember slowly moved her hand towards her knife, and Brig'dha sighed, expecting some new drama. The woman jumped forward, grabbing her small child, who had broken free from her grasp and tried to run off. It only took a moment before everyone realized that this was merely an inopportune moment for the mother to scream. The woman looked up at everyone, turning red with embarrassment and trying to smile away what had happened. She waved her hands apologetically at Aya'tar, indicating that she was not challenging anyone.

All around, laughter broke out as the tense moment was suddenly calmed. Ember puffed out her long-held breath of air, relaxing her grip on the knife. Sometimes, she worried that she might be a little too cautious. The high priestess cleared her throat and turned to regard the four people awaiting her final pronouncement. Aya'tar didn't want anything else bad to happen. She was sick of dramatic events and prayed every day for monotony. She smiled at the couples but with an obviously exasperated expression, indicating her urge to move on before something else went wrong.

"All right, I now proclaim Aethen and Isha'kau bonded! May you have many beautiful children and live long and healthy lives!" she said, instantly causing Isha'kau to grasp Aethen in a deep passionate embrace. The crowd went wild with enthusiastic sounds. A moment later, Brig'dha shyly stepped forward, causing Aethen and Isha'kau to pause and turn to meet them.

"This is going to sound like a strange question to ask right now, but were you thinking of having children soon?" she asked. The pair nodded their heads in assent.

"Yes, actually. We hoped this very wedding night would be the night. There is no greater luck than to become pregnant the night of your bonding," Isha'kau said enthusiastically. Aethen was a little embarrassed as his people were much less open about such topics. Fertility, sex, and other such subjects were considered normal conversation in the True South. Brig'dha smiled, removing the Amber of Life necklace from around her neck, and gently placing it over Isha'kau's head. The amber piece hung between her breasts, catching the evening light and reflecting a brilliant orange glow for everyone to see.

"This is the Amber of Life, a powerful item. Its magic has brought life to many people, and if you wear it tonight, it will fill you with life, too!" Brig'dha said, embracing Isha'kau in a hug and then stepping back to hold hands once more with Ember. Isha'kau stood in awe of the item. Childbirth was a dangerous process, and the likelihood of becoming pregnant in only one night was at best one in three, usually much lower than that. To be handed such a precious item, such a powerful magical implement, would vastly increase the likelihood that she would have a healthy child and live to watch it grow. The priestess held the pendant, unable to thank Ember or Brig'dha. She was simply overcome with joy. Before it became awkward, Ember turned her attention back to Aya'tar, giving a nod that the high priestess should continue.

"Ember and Brig'dha, I have not forgotten you. Love knows no bounds and pleases the gods in any shape it takes. Before the entire city of Isut'na and before the Goddess herself, I proclaim you bonded for life. May you continue to inspire us all and live long and healthy lives!" At that moment, Ember and Brig'dha turned to face each other, and the world seemed to disappear. They melded into each other's arms like molden copper, a tight embrace and a bond even stronger than any they had before. The Sun was setting on the horizon, and soon the new Moon would rise in the East, a Moon so dark that the skies would be illuminated by only the stars themselves.

Aethen lifted Isha'kau and carried her to a private place in the city where the newly bonded lovers could be alone to explore their love. Ember watched them leave and then turned to look at Brig'dha once more. The priestess could see that Ember was calculating whether or not she could lift and carry her. Ember, though quite lithe, was reasonably strong from her travels and use of the bow. Brig'dha was also not particularly heavy, but neither woman was quite sure that they had the muscle mass to pull off the romantic exit Aethen had made.

"I love you, but I don't want to fall off the building to our deaths. Please don't try to pick me up," Brig'dha said with a smile, easily recognizing Ember's intentions. The reluctant redhead smiled, accepting defeat. Before she could come up with some other plan, Brig'dha interjected her own.

"Let's walk to that tiny island in the pond. Nothing will bother us there, and the world will be ours, at least for the night," Brig'dha said, drawing a slight frown from Ember, her plans to carry Brig'dha thwarted by the likes of common sense. "Aeeya."

ↄ ↄ ↄ

The stars filled the sky and stretched from horizon to horizon. If one looked to the Southeast, the Moon was ever so barely visible as a blackened disk, a new moon. Ember and Brig'dha lay on the small island in the middle of the pond under the vast sea of stars. Little Mew had followed them from the city and had spent a short time complaining that the water was preventing him from being handled before finally quieting and napping beside the water.

Above them, the skies themselves put on a show commemorating their union as streak after streak flew across the sky. It was well known to most that the sky would become filled with many falling stars on some occasions. This night was exceptionally dark, and the stars that fell lit the sky with their beautiful glow. Nothing that either woman could imagine was more peaceful and relaxing than to lie together hand-in-hand on the tiny island with nothing but the stars above. Such freedoms were rarer and sweeter than a hundred magical pendants or giant blue crystals.

Suddenly, a searing red light flew across the sky, much brighter and much lower than any of the others, leaving a tiny trail of speckles behind it for just a moment. Brig'dha gasped at the beauty of the falling star, but when she turned her head to see Ember, her lover was on her side gazing back, instead. As their eyes met, another bright flash of light flew overhead, but they didn't look up at the stars. Ember placed her hand upon Brig'dha's hip while the priestess softly pressed her fingers into Ember's hair.

"What will we do now?" Brig'dha playfully asked as she casually twisted Ember's hair around her fingers, longing to wrap herself in the long, red hair which hung past Ember's hips. She hated being touched, yet when she was in the right mood, Ember's touch didn't seem to bother her. In fact, Ember had been the only person she had ever enjoyed being held by, yet another way that she knew their love was blessed by the Moon Goddess.

"Perhaps we will stay here for a while and enjoy the warmth," Ember replied, not realizing the leading question for what it really was. Brig'dha almost squealed with a mixture of anticipation and joyful frustration at her lover's quirkiness but continued.

"Do you ever want to return to our people, or maybe again visit the people of Tornhemal?" she asked, tightening her grasp of Ember's hair and hoping the redhead got the hint.

"Maybe, but I think we could take a harvest to just live. Besides, I'm hoping to bully Aethen and Isha'kau into naming their first children after us," Ember said with a smile. Brig'dha lay on her back, gazing once more at the stars, unable to believe Ember's mind was, for once, not amorous. Then, suddenly, Ember rolled partly atop her and smiled down, playfully brushing the hair from Brig'dha's face.

"I bet you forgot..." Ember said slyly.

"Forgot what?" Brig'dha replied, now confused.

"You are a harvest older now. Your people judge age as the passing of each warm season, right?" the feisty redhead asked with a foxy smile.

"So do yours... So, we are both a harvest older," Brig'dha said, acknowledging the fact.

"Well then… happy birthday, Brig'dha!"

Slowly, they lifted their bodies until they knelt in the sand. Ember reached forward and pulled the knot causing Brig'dha's string skirt to spill to the ground. Brig'dha reached for the cord holding Ember's loincloth, only to frown as she found it triple knotted, as usual. Before the mood was impacted, Ember pulled her obsidian blade free and slit the cord, then casually tossed their garments and weapon aside. Before her knelt the beautiful Brig'dha, her soft, dark brown skin painted like the stars. Ember's eyes trailed down her generous curves and ample breasts before returning to her beautiful hazel eyes, framed in dark brown, wavy hair. She was the most wonderful person Ember had ever met, and now she would be part of Ember's life forever.

Brig'dha returned the measuring gaze as she looked down at the redhead, slowly returning her eyes to meet. The beautiful warrior's own body was lithe, her abdomen textured with each muscle visible beneath her lighter skin, ending with her smaller breasts and strong shoulders. Her arms were nearly as defined as a man's, owing to her use of the bow, and honestly hard for Brig'dha to look away from, yet she did. Those powerful arms would hold her soon, and be forever hers. A moment later, her eyes fell upon the playful, foxy smile of the emerald-eyed river woman, her visage nearly bringing tears to Brig'dha's eyes, so much did she love this woman.

"You can do more than look, my warrior wife… in the entire world, only you may touch me," the moon priestess purred, taking Ember's hands and placing them where she wanted them.

Ember was a graspy sort of person and quickly began experiencing Brig'dha by touch. As she did, Brig'dha took Ember's beautiful face in her hands and gently pressed their lips together, feeling the softness she desired. She pressed her tongue forward, closing her eyes and feeling Ember's strong yet gentle touch. She intended to take her time tonight. They were joined metaphorically and literally, and she wanted neither to end. She would be slow, purposeful, and as delicate as a feather in the wind.

"E'geneh, ehg wennus dhue… Meg'wennus…" Ember whispered as Brig'dha expressed her deepest love.

"Happy birthday, Kaelu…" she purred.

EPILOGUE

It was not long after the battle of Isut'na when Ianmu left to return to the city of Nara'kit to assume control as its leader. Strangely, within nearly half of a harvest of taking control of Nara'kit, a healthy baby boy was born, though she had no known husband or lover, and very few were bold enough to inquire about its source. Ianmu named the child Saranar after one of several male incarnations of An'an.

Sar'Tawas was not the most honorable man, nor a man deserving of her respect, and yet he had traded his life for hers in some strange split-second decision which he had not lived long enough to explain. For reasons which she could never fully quantify, Ianmu had come to appreciate him on some level. She knew the child was his, and she would repay his sacrifice by raising Saranar.

Barely half of a harvest after the birth of Saranar, Isha'kau, and Aethen celebrated the birth of a baby girl, born alive and healthy. Like her father, she had a tiny tuft of dark hair and strangely gray eyes. Though Ember tried mercilessly to convince them to name their child after her, much to Brig'dha's chagrin, they instead chose to name her Asatar, a variation of the word Assaetarsu, meaning love. Brig'dha was much happier with this name, not only because she found it beautiful but also because she suspected that there could only be one Ember in the world at a time.

The warm season slowly ended, followed by the harvest season and the cold season. Ember and Brig'dha remained within the city with little Mew, enjoying the peace they had fought so hard to earn. Life could be cruel, and death could come quickly, and so they spent each day living life to its fullest and trying their best to get along as wife and wife. Strangely, no matter how much they enjoyed the peace and the calm, it was not long before both women began to dream of what was over the horizon. Far to the East and to the South lay new undiscovered lands. It was only a matter of time before every bird took flight.

Ember with her fishing spear and a wels catfish

EMBER'S LANGUAGE

Neolithic languages are entirely unknown and will likely never be known. They were not recorded in any known way, leaving us to guess based on limited, often deeply hypothetical models. In the books, many cultures have languages the reader will encounter. This was done to provide realism, though it is important to understand that these languages are, at best, hypothetical, and mostly just educated guesses. Ember's language is entirely created by the author using a method of following root words from the oldest regional languages backward, examining how they changed, then extrapolating how they might have been. This method is called comparative reconstruction. Unfortunately, the level of unknown elements makes Ember's language so filled with unknown variables that it may be no better than a simple guess. Either way, the languages spoken in the series are internally consistent and follow strict structures and rules.

Ember's language follows a very loosely subject-verb-object word order. As an example, one might say, "Ember carries the rock," in which the parts of the sentence are: "Ember [subject] carries [verb] the [particle] rock [object]." In fact, the sentence can be used in other orders, such as, "The rock, Ember carries," and this may be done to emphasize the object or even the verb. Another interesting feature is the non-verbal aspects of the language. Often, head gestures indicate directions, while hand gestures indicate actions. This is often depicted in the book using brackets to describe the gestures: "The river [nods toward the East]" versus the modern, English equivalent of, "The river is to the East."

The use of the letter "h" in many words in the language indicates elongated vowels. While various markings are used in linguistics to indicate this, the author chose a direct, phonetic method to prevent the reader from needing to know this. For example, the word "Aneha," meaning 'blossom," would be pronounced, An-nay-ah, where the 'h' is used to elongate the e sound. Otherwise, the reader might accidentally pronounce the word as, Ann-ee-ah.

Adjective – Adjectives are often connected to a noun using a single quote. Example, "A big stick" would be, "A big'stick." When spoken, both words are pronounced as a single word with a brief pause at the single quote.

Adverb – Adverbs are often connected to a verb using a quote. Example, "He almost tripped" would be, "He almost'tripped." When spoken, both words are pronounced as a single word with a brief pause at the single quote.

Determiner – Determiners are usually not used, such as "a," "this," and "that." Example, "A tree is big" might be spoken as, "Tree is big". A head nod or non-verbal indicator may be included.

Exclamation – When a word is spoken with exclamation, the most prominent vowel is usually elongated. For example, sleep "sewep", would be exclaimed as, "seeewep!"

Conjunction – Conjunctions are often implicit, not using conditional words, like "if." Example, "If you eat this, you will be sorry!" would be spoken as, "You eat this, you will be sorry!"

Pluralization – Words are pluralized by adding a modifying sound. For words ending with an e or eh, an "a" sound is added. For all other words, an "e" sound is added. Example, the word for woman, "Geneh," would be pluralized as "Geneha, while the word for wolf, "vokas," would be pluralized as "vokase."

Preposition – Sometimes added before the word it affects using a single quote when the affect is significant or to be stressed. Example, "I saw her pass it to'them."

Pronouns – Female, male and gender-neutral pronouns exist, though most words are not gendered. Ember's language places very little emphasis on gender pronouns, often using a person's name or simply implying the subject.

Verbs – Verbs are often connected to a noun using a single quote. Example, "the cat ran" would be, "the cat'ran." When spoken, both words are pronounced as a single word with a brief pause at the single quote.

VOCABULARY

1	un	Close (near)	dhuak
2	dun	Dark	kar
3	tun	Daughter	daka
4	kuv	Dead	mordh
5	pun	Deer	vahen
6	ses	Drink/Eat	po'eh
7	sev	Do Not	maedhe
8	dukuv	Do	edhe
9	nen	Early	eu
10	des	Ember	kaelu
3rd Gender	wergene	Enjoy	turto
Agree	ya	Equal	sahm
Alive/life	giae	Far	kehl
Always	deleh	Father	patr
Am	kah	Fertility	aipe
Ash	kene	Festival/Ritual	kue
Ask	aes	Fertility Fest	aipku
Bad	duhs	Fear	deueh
Baby (Young)	kende	Feel	ten
Be/is/are	eshe	Fire	ehkne
Beautiful	wehnose	Fish	pehsk
Berry	marag	For/to	de
Big (Great)	meg	Forest	dahru
Bite	dek	From	aph
Bitter	deke	Fuck	aeeya
Biter	aeleh	Good	ehsu
Blade	akore	Hair	keris
Blood	esnee	Harm	derg
Blossom	aneha	Have	kehp
Blow	behs	Her/She	dehmoh
Boat	naulos	Hello	eleh
Bone	ohsdh	Help	kik
Bow	wehbueg	Hope	aeis
Buy (Trade)	kraeh	Hot	gehr
Cloth	keteh	I	ehg
Cold	ne'gehr	Is/be	eshe
Copper	aos	Join	ghed
City	meg'uek	Journey	deru
Char (from fire)	meg'kene	Kill	kerord

Know	ehuedh		Sit	sehde
Leather	lereh		South	sewh
Like (Similar)	ehig		Sorry	behunas
Little	pew		Star	sier
Look	spegh		Stupid	morehs
Love	wennus		Spirit	enesu
Make	kehr		Take	gheab
Man (Male)	wer		Textile (woven)	wheskeh
Marry	gheme		Thank you	ehshe
Might (Should)	dehmagh		That	en
Mother	matr		Third Gender	wergene
Moon	meneh		This	keh
My	ehg		Thief	meyus
My	e'(object)		To (for)	de
Me	eag		Thought	menh
Me (for/to)	(ki)eag		Touch	kreah
Name	nome		Tree	dehrue
Night	nehk		Try	dedhe
Neck	kopel		Until/till	dehe
Negation	ne'(object)		Us	es
Next	nes		Warrior	kor'ghe
New	neuh		Water	aka
Nothing	nehk		Wait	stehk
No	ne		We	es
Now	ke		Weave	whese
Obsidian	mehlek		Well	sueh
Of	apu		What	kehd
Our	wedh		Why	kehne
People	dau		Will	wit
Prepare	ekos		With	khu
Pottery	kort		With you	khum
Quiet	tas		Wolf	vokas
Question	pehkseh		Woman	geneh
Raven	aukrose		Word	aeg'lk
Ready	ekose		World	lenh
Red	errutas		Work	peh'os
River	denn		When	eome
Rock/Stone	ondah		Who	khas
Run	dremo		Year	ahden
Say	sehke		Yes	eya
Sharp	meg'ak		You	tuh (dhue)
Shut up	taseh		Vulture	veasehes
Sleep	sewep			

ABOUT THE AUTHOR

Ishtar Watson has an academic background in both computer science and archaeology. They live on the eastern coast of the United States with their super-smart spouse and a handful of cats. Ishtar has written several novels and LGBTQIA+ (pre)historic adventure-romance short stories and novellas. Their hobbies include archaeology, especially Neolithic clothing and adornment and prehistoric depictions in media and video games, astrophotography, model rocketry, weaving and spinning prehistoric textiles, nuclear physics (specifically gamma spectroscopy), mineralogy, archery, artificial intelligence, and writing.

Having Autism, ADHD, and Tourette Syndrome, along with many comorbid conditions, such as misophonia and dyslexia, Ishtar enjoys writing stories with neurodivergent characters. Their spouse is also neurodivergent having ADHD and Autism – this mix of conditions forming the basis for many of the characters' neurodivergence and positive representation in the series. Ishtar (they/she) and their spouse (they/she) are both non-binary and proponents of neurodivergent and LGBTQIA+ people.

They have lived in western Maine, the Navajo Nation in Arizona, along the coast of Virginia, and a half dozen other places. They have traveled from Japan to the UK and many places in between. Their eventual goal is to become a Doctor of Computer Science and work with archaeologists – interdisciplinary collaboration. And yes, they love swimming, eating fish, singing, and dancing… and they loathe bullies.

Thank you for purchasing an independently published literary work. Writing, editing, and publishing a novel entirely by oneself is quite a lot of work (especially when the author has dyslexia). I appreciate you as the reader – you are why I write. **Please consider leaving a review and rating,** as this is the most important thing you can do for <u>any</u> author. Words cannot express how much a review means to an author.

~Ishtar ♡

Author's Notes

Age of Marriage – A popular misbelief is that ancient people married and had children much earlier than today. In fact, the age of marriage and adulthood (often different) have varied significantly over time and culture. Typically, male ages for marriage are older than female, and higher-status people are wed earlier than commoners. Ancient people may have noticed that having a child in one's twenties resulted in significantly better outcomes than being younger or older. Most recently, a team of researchers at Indiana University determined the most frequent age of conception over the last 250,000 years was 23.3 ±, again undermining this strange misbelief.

Richard J. Wang, et al. Human generation times across the past 250,000 years. Sci. Adv. 9,1. (2023). DOI:10.1126/sciadv.abm7047.

Body Coloring – Many characters wear various paints and dyes throughout the book. There is some evidence for the use of such coloring, and this is certainly the practice of many historically recorded peoples. The exact coloring and designs were inspired by the anthropomorphic artwork of the period, pigments recovered from archaeological sites, and some imagination. Possible pigments include blackcurrant, raspberry, yarrow, ocher, and oil and ash, though a wide variety were likely used.

Body Weight – Our modern world tends to push unrealistic body images upon us. In fact, what is considered "beautiful" or "correct" in one culture may not be in another. A significant percentage of prehistoric anthropomorphic figurines depict women with large breasts and buttocks, their bodies heavyset. We don't know if they found this beautiful or perhaps this look merely represented their gods or spirits. Regardless, throughout the series, this look is often depicted as an ideal – a juxtaposition with the unrealistic standards we force on women, today. While Aya'tar, Ianmu, and Brig'dha meet this ideal, Ember does not, being quite muscular and "sporty." This is done to draw the reader's attention to the absurdity of contemporary unrealistic beauty standards.

Catalhoyuk – Anyone familiar with the Anatolian Neolithic will immediately recognize that I based my proto-cities on Catalhoyuk, a great proto-city in the Konya plain of Turkey. In fact, Catalhoyuk exists within the book as Du'ubria, a fictional name I invented as the original name, or names are entirely unknown. In fact, Catalhoyuk may have been abandoned by the dates when our story is set, specifically January 5598 BCE to October 5597 BCE. As the date of abandonment continues to slide further back, I note this several times in subsequent books and continue to write as though they had not (too late to change the story). Though Isut'na is based on Catalhoyuk, it is important to consider the many differences between Catalhoyuk and Isut'na and Nara'kit, which I discuss in many places within the books.

Clothing – Perhaps nothing is more critical to me than prehistoric fashion. Far too often, Neolithic illustrations and exhibits will feature Neolithic people wearing full-length tunics, often made from what appears to be almost modern materials and design. White and pastel colors are commonplace, as are design elements without evidentiary basis in archaeology. Worse, clothing with design characteristics not found until thousands of years later are often depicted in the media. I call these "white linen tunics" and similar inaccuracies the "white linen tunic" fallacy. Though it can be challenging to say if the cause of these depictions is some strange modesty-induced censorship or perhaps a wanton disregard for the evidence. Mostly, it's simply bad science.

Gold Torcs – Realistically, there is no significant evidence to support the adornments Ember obtains. In nearly 1000 years, such items will appear and of far greater quality than what Ember obtained, and the techniques to make such jewelry did exist, so it isn't beyond reason that some may have existed. Such items could have been made, and likely were between Ember's time and when the first significant find of such items, the Varna Necropolis. Still, it is important to consider this aspect of the book an unsupported guess.

LGBTQIA+ – Throughout the story, we are introduced to several LGBTQIA+ characters, though I chose to make some of them less obvious. Perhaps the most plainly visible character is Brig'dha, a cisgender lesbian woman. Visible, though less clearly defined, is Ember, who is a non-binary woman of sapphic orientation, though her thoughts sometimes sway toward pansexuality. If Ember lived today, her pronouns would be she/they, while Brig'dha would be she/her, both considering themselves lesbian.

Unlike many novels featuring non-binary characters, Ember does not use they/them pronouns, at least in the first two novels. Her language doesn't contain hard gendered pronouns, meaning this wasn't an issue until she arrived in Isut'na. However, you may note that directly calling her a woman irritates her. Of course, even from book one, Ember has never presented consistently as a typical woman of her culture, often wearing traditionally masculine clothing and dismissing the normative gender roles of her people. Among her people, a wergene (third gender) is usually reserved for males conforming to traditionally feminine roles, which is why she never takes on this identity. However, the gender spectrum of a narmu, the Isut'na equivalent of non-binary, is a much better fit. Perhaps she will consider this in the future (find out in book 3, Ember of Ashes).

Neurodivergence – Differences in human brains are common and should be celebrated, not pathologized. Throughout the series, many characters are depicted with different neural variations. For example, Ember experiences ADHD, while Brig'dha is autistic. I chose these variations as I experience them both, along with several others. Another major character in the series is neurodivergent, yet I have only left hints. This is a plot arc I will explore later in a positive and affirming way. There are many ways to experience reality, and each is valid.

Tokens – Representations of material goods using symbols have been well documented since the Bronze Age in ancient Sumer, Egypt, and potentially even as far back as the Neolithic. While there is evidence for possible token usage in the Neolithic, this is still a speculative area of research. What Ember did with the grain tokens would become commonplace in another millennium, though perhaps even beforehand.

Trauma and PTSD – As a person with CPTSD and PTSD, I wanted to include aspects of this. Both Ember and Brig'dha have experienced significant trauma events, but they respond to them differently. Ember tends to have dreams and occasional intrusive thoughts. Yet, her people's belief that killing an enemy is moral has reduced some of her trauma as she doesn't hold herself to blame for her enemies' deaths. Brig'dha masks her trauma just as she masks her autism. However, her fears over losing Ember and the depression her memories bring her are both symptoms of her experiences. Trauma changes our lives, yet it does not have to define us. We can live and enjoy life, though it is critical to get treatment if you have or suspect you may have experienced trauma. There is help ♡

- Cover Art, by Alexandra Filipek © 2022
- Kaelu with her bow, by Stiffler and K. © 2016, 2022
- Leather wrap skirt, by Alexandra Filipek © 2022
- Leather shirt with beadwork, by Alexandra Filipek © 2022
- Mew the Cat, by Alexandra Filipek © 2022
- Ember's loincloth and leggings, by Alexandra Filipek © 2022
- The Amber of Life pendant, by Alexandra Filipek © 2022
- Leather apron with beadwork, by Alexandra Filipek © 2022
- Isut'Sanup'ramu Aya'tar praying to Isut, by Stiffler and K. © 2016, 2022
- Flax string skirt, by Alexandra Filipek © 2022
- Gold and copper torc and matching bracelets, by Alexandra Filipek © 2022
- Ianmu the "concubine" or Ianmu'kimun of Nara'kit, by Alexandra Filipek © 2022
- Sar'Tawas holding a pot of wine, by Alexandra Filipek © 2022
- Ember with her fishing spear and a wels catfish, by Stiffler and K. © 2016, 2022

You can find more from these fine artists at their websites:

Stiffler and K. – FindChaos.com
Alexandra Filipek – Alexandra.Filipek.us

I cannot thank them enough for their efforts to bring my characters and story alive with their amazing illustrative talent.

~Ishtar

Suggested Reading

Below is a selection of books I have found of great use while writing the Ember series. I recommend these books, especially Dr. E. W. Barber's Women's work: The first 20,000 years. I hope this knowledge inspires you and brings you a sense of academic and scientific joy, as it has me.

~Ishtar

Amkreutz, L., & Vaart-Verschoof, S. van der (Eds.). (2022). *Doggerland. lost world under the North Sea*. Sidestone Press.

Barber, E. W. (1994). *Women's work: The first 20,000 years, women, cloth and society in early times, Elizabeth Wayland Barber*. W.W.Norton.

Barber, E. W. (2005). *Prehistoric textiles: The development of cloth in the Neolithic and bronze ages: With special reference to the Aegean*. Princeton University Press.

Baysal, E. L. (2019). *Personal ornaments in prehistory: An exploration of body augmentation from the Palaeolithic to the early bronze age*. Oxbow Books.

Conneller, C. (Ed.). (2022). *The Mesolithic in Britain: Landscape and society in Times of Change*. Routledge, Taylor et Francis Group.

Fowler, C., Harding, J., & Hofmann, D. (Eds.). (2015). *The Oxford Handbook of Neolithic Europe*. Oxford University Press.

Gilligan, I. (2019). *Climate, clothing, and agriculture in prehistory: Linking evidence, causes, and effects*. Cambridge University Press.

Gleba, M., & Mannering, U. (Eds.). (2019). *Textiles and textile production in Europe from prehistory to Ad 400*. Oxbow Books.

Greaney, S., Pollard, J., & Whittle, A. (Eds.). 2023. Ancient DNA and the European Neolithic. Relations and Descent. Oxbow Books, Oxford.

Heath, J. M. (2017). *Warfare in Neolithic Europe: An archaeological and anthropological analysis*. Pen & Sword Archaeology.

Insoll, T. (Ed.). (2017). *The Oxford Handbook of Prehistoric Figurines*. Oxford University Press.

Koch, J. K., & Kirleis, W. (Eds.). (2019). *Gender transformations in prehistoric and Archaic Societies*. Sidestone Press.

Lukes, A., & Zvelebil, M. (Eds.). (2004). *Lbk dialogues: Studies in the formation of the Linear Pottery culture*. BAR Publishing, Oxford, UK.

Nelson, S. M., & Rosen-Ayalon, M. (Eds.). (2002). *In pursuit of gender: Worldwide archaeological approaches*. Altamira Press.

Tringham, R. (1971). *Hunters, fishers and farmers of Eastern Europe, 6000-3000 B.C.* Hutchinson and Co.

Vasic, V. (2020). Personal adornment in the Neolithic Middle East: A case study of Çatalhöyük. Ex Oriente, Berlin.

Whittle, A., Pollard, J., & Greaney, S. (Eds.). (2022). *Ancient Dna and the European Neolithic: Relations and Descent*. Oxbow Books.

A SELECTED READING

**A selected reading from Ember of Ashes
book Three of the Ember series.**

Chapter 1: Pavari the Priest
(Warning – may contain very mild spoilers)

Pavari looked up from the fire they were tending upon hearing the indication of someone creeping up the rickety wooden ladder. The sound of the wood creaking echoed around the temple and brought a sudden shift to the monotony of a calm, lazy morning. It seemed a little early for a visitor, but perhaps a little company would help. Having someone stop by would also give them a reprieve from the loneliness of solitude. Living by themselves and nearly a day's walk north of the city was hardly the way to meet people, though Pavari preferred the quiet life away from the complex dealings of the proto-city.

Breakfast had been bland, a single raw egg, and now they might have an excuse to cook something more filling. Perhaps some salted meat could be heated with fragrant spices, or maybe even a fish if the visitor brought any. People visiting the temple often brought food and other donations. Of course, the best people brought fermented beverages, as far as Pavari was concerned.

The temple of Teva, god of the world, and Tesi, goddess of the sky, was situated high upon one of the few hills overlooking the great Nadhi River. Since time unknown, priests and priestesses had lived high upon this hill away from the central city of Naduru and the outlying villages adorning the Nadhi River. Like so many before them, Pavari spent each day maintaining the ritual camp and meditating towards becoming closer to the gods.

Painted in red ocher and black body paint, Pavari sat upon a leather mat wearing a loin covering made from local plants attached at their waist by a leather cord, and plain leather sandals, deep in meditation. The broad, cave-like alcove was filled with the scent of burning wood and fragrant herbs. The dim light and thick aromas gave the alcove, naturally cut into the hill, a slightly spiritual feel as it towered above the river and the landscape looking out towards the otherwise flatlands to the Southeast.

Pavari was neither regarded by the masculine nor feminine aspects, assuming a gender-neutral role. Though not the most common occurrence among their people, those who did not fit either gender or found themselves to be a gender different from the gender they had been assumed to be at birth would often assume their proper gender at a young age and be raised as such. This was the way of most people within the region, though Pavari had heard of travelers from the North and East where this custom was not practiced. For this reason, "they" served as a more appropriate pronoun than "he" or "she."

They continued to meditate as the sounds of two distinct individuals entering the alcove grew stronger. More people meant more chances for food or fermented drink, a blessed event, in their opinion. The footfalls were heavy, most likely indicating two men who were not concerned about being heard. One of the men approached the altar to the gods of the world while the other came to stand before Pavari. Finishing their meditation, the priest opened their eyes to see what fate befell them and hoped it was something to eat.

Before Pavari stood a man of average height wearing a coarse leather loincloth and a thick leather corded necklace with large, thick clay beads sparsely placed around his neck. Though he had a certain charisma about him, he still appeared disheveled. His hair was scruffy and not well kept, and he wore a grim look. Pavari decided that his disheveled look somehow added to his charisma, in perhaps a hard to quantify sort of way. Unfortunately, while his face appeared friendly enough, he had a strange gleam in his eye, which the priest found a little unsettling.

Turning toward the altar, Pavari observed the other man. He was of similar build, though nude, but his eyes tended to glare in an almost excited way as though expecting some intriguing result unknown to anyone else. The second man gave them a creepy feeling, though they could not quite decide why. Priest or not, anyone would get a bad omen about this pair, Pavari decided. Worse, they hadn't brought any food or drink, by the look of it – the worst omen of all.

"We have come for the Statuette of the Gods," Hatya said flatly and with a certain terminality in his tone. He hoped the priest would resist and provide him with even more amusement than the river priestess had. He waited for a moment expecting the priest to react, but they sat peacefully, and quite annoyingly, still. Hend, the scruffy man, remained quiet as well, waiting to see if the priest would react to his otherwise creepy companion. Seeing no reaction, Hatya, the nude man, taunted them more.

"In case you guessed, that means we are not leaving any witnesses. Since you are sacred and important, I will let you decide whether you want us to throw you off the ledge or thunk you over the head with a club. Your choice," he offered with a snicker. Hend wondered if the message could have been delivered a little more subtly, but his slightly more violent companion was quite correct. It would not do to leave witnesses to the crime of killing the senior priest and stealing the Statuette of the Gods.

Hatya stood before the statuette, seemingly unwilling to grasp such a holy item, likely for fear that he might be struck down by the magical energies which surely coursed through the mystical stone. Hend stood with a club in hand, expecting the priest to make a run for it. But, suddenly, Pavari began to laugh... A burst of hysterical laughter filled the alcove with echoes as though they intended for the whole world to hear. Hend stepped back from the priest, unsure of what to make of such unexpected behavior from someone who was supposed to die.

Pavari stopped laughing for a moment and reached behind them to get a leather cord from a nearby basket. They began pulling their hair back into a ponytail, as men commonly wore their hair. Both would-be assassins merely waited and watched as the most divine person from any of the local villages or the city knelt before them, casually putting their hair up while still softly chuckling as though their proclamations of death were amusing. Victims were supposed to be frightened, not amused, a realization unnerving to both men.

"You wish to steal the Statuette of the Gods and then strike dead their priest? You are going to do this in the sacred temple to the God of the World and the Goddess of the Sky, in full view of the Goddess of the River? What fools you must be... What absurd fools. And you didn't even bring me anything to drink. Well... I welcome you. Send me to see my gods so I might tell them of your absurdity, in person. I wonder what they will think of your actions? I suspect they will indeed consider your actions with great care, though I doubt either of you have deeply thought about them."